THE
ALEXANDRIA QUARTET

The
Alexandria Quartet

by

LAWRENCE DURRELL

JUSTINE

BALTHAZAR

MOUNTOLIVE

CLEA

FABER AND FABER

24 Russell Square

London

Justine first published in 1957
Balthazar first published in 1958
Mountolive first published in 1958
Clea first published in 1960
First published in this edition 1969
by Faber and Faber Limited
24 Russell Square London W.C.1
Printed in Great Britain by
C. Tinling & Co. Ltd., Liverpool, London and Prescot.
All rights reserved

SBN 571 05204 5

PREFACE

THIS group of four novels is intended to be read as a single work under the collective title of The Alexandria Quartet; a suitable descriptive subtitle might be 'a word continuum'. In trying to work out my form I adopted, as a rough analogy, the relativity proposition. The first three were related in an intercalary fashion, being 'siblings' of each other and not 'sequels'; only the last novel was intended to be a true sequel and to unleash the time dimension. The whole was intended as a challenge to the serial form of the conventional novel: the time-saturated novel of the day.

Among the workpoints at the end I have sketched in a number of possible ways of continuing to deploy these characters and situations in further instalments — but this is only to suggest that even if the group of books were extended indefinitely the result would never become *roman fleuve*; if, that is to say, the axis of the work has been properly laid down it should be possible to radiate from it in any direction without losing the strictness and congruity of its relation to 'a continuum'.

It has been possible, for this edition, to correct a number of small slips pointed out by readers and critics, and also to add some small passages which were cut out of the original volumes in the MS. stage. The changes are not very great. *Balthazar* and *Mountolive* both lose half a dozen lines of text. *Clea* gains a small section, and a new translation from C. P. Cavafy.

L.D.

France 1962

CONTENTS

JUSTINE

NOTE

The characters in this story, the first of a group, are all inventions together with the personality of the narrator, and bear no resemblance to living persons. Only the city is real.

I am accustoming myself to the idea of regarding every sexual act as a process in which four persons are involved. We shall have a lot to discuss about that.

S. FREUD: *Letters*

There are two positions available to us — either crime which renders us happy, or the noose, which prevents us from being unhappy. I ask whether there can be any hesitation, lovely Thérèse, and where will your little mind find an argument able to combat that one?

D. A. F. DE SADE: *Justine*

To
EVE
these memorials of her native city

PART I

The sea is high again today, with a thrilling flush of wind. In the midst of winter you can feel the inventions of spring. A sky of hot nude pearl until midday, crickets in sheltered places, and now the wind unpacking the great planes, ransacking the great planes. . . .

I have escaped to this island with a few books and the child — Melissa's child. I do not know why I use the word 'escape'. The villagers say jokingly that only a sick man would choose such a remote place to rebuild. Well, then, I have come here to heal myself, if you like to put it that way. . . .

At night when the wind roars and the child sleeps quietly in its wooden cot by the echoing chimney-piece I light a lamp and walk about, thinking of my friends — of Justine and Nessim, of Melissa and Balthazar. I return link by link along the iron chains of memory to the city which we inhabited so briefly together: the city which used us as its flora — precipitated in us conflicts which were hers and which we mistook for our own: beloved Alexandria!

I have had to come so far away from it in order to understand it all! Living on this bare promontory, snatched every night from darkness by Arcturus, far from the lime-laden dust of those summer afternoons, I see at last that none of us is properly to be judged for what happened in the past. It is the city which should be judged though we, its children, must pay the price.

*　*　*　*　*

Capitally, what is this city of ours? What is resumed in the word Alexandria? In a flash my mind's eye shows me a thousand dust-tormented streets. Flies and beggars own it today — and those who enjoy an intermediate existence between either.

Five races, five languages, a dozen creeds: five fleets turning through their greasy reflections behind the harbour bar. But there are more than five sexes and only demotic Greek seems to distinguish among them. The sexual provender which lies to hand is staggering in its variety and profusion. You would never

17

mistake it for a happy place. The symbolic lovers of the free Hellenic world are replaced here by something different, something subtly androgynous, inverted upon itself. The Orient cannot rejoice in the sweet anarchy of the body — for it has outstripped the body. I remember Nessim once saying — I think he was quoting — that Alexandria was the great winepress of love; those who emerged from it were the sick men, the solitaries, the prophets — I mean all who have been deeply wounded in their sex.

★ ★ ★ ★ ★

Notes for landscape-tones. . . . Long sequences of tempera. Light filtered through the essence of lemons. An air full of brick-dust — sweet-smelling brick-dust and the odour of hot pavements slaked with water. Light damp clouds, earth-bound yet seldom bringing rain. Upon this squirt dust-red, dust-green, chalk-mauve and watered crimson-lake. In summer the sea-damp lightly varnished the air. Everything lay under a coat of gum.

And then in autumn the dry, palpitant air, harsh with static electricity, inflaming the body through its light clothing. The flesh coming alive, trying the bars of its prison. A drunken whore walks in a dark street at night, shedding snatches of song like petals. Was it in this that Anthony heard the heart-numbing strains of the great music which persuaded him to surrender for ever to the city he loved?

The sulking bodies of the young begin to hunt for a fellow nakedness, and in those little cafés where Balthazar went so often with the old poet of the city,* the boys stir uneasily at their backgammon under the petrol-lamps: disturbed by this dry desert wind — so unromantic, so unconfiding — stir, and turn to watch every stranger. They struggle for breath and in every summer kiss they can detect the taste of quicklime. . . .

★ ★ ★ ★ ★

I had to come here in order completely to rebuild this city in my brain — melancholy provinces which the old man* saw as full of the 'black ruins' of his life. Clang of the trams shuddering in their metal veins as they pierce the iodine-coloured *meidan* of Mazarita. Gold, phosphorus, magnesium paper. Here we so often met. There was a little coloured stall in summer with slices of water-melon and the vivid water-ices she liked to eat. She would

18

come a few minutes late of course — fresh perhaps from some assignation in a darkened room, from which I avert my mind; but so fresh, so young, the open petal of the mouth that fell upon mine like an unslaked summer. The man she had left might still be going over and over the memory of her; she might be as if still dusted by the pollen of his kisses. Melissa! It mattered so little somehow, feeling the lithe weight of the creature as she leaned on one's arm smiling with the selfless candour of those who had given over with secrets. It was good to stand there, awkward and a little shy, breathing quickly because we knew what we wanted of each other. The messages passing beyond conscience, directly through the flesh-lips, eyes, water-ices, the coloured stall. To stand lightly there, our little fingers linked, drinking in the deep camphor-scented afternoon, a part of city. . . .

*   *   *   *   *

I have been looking through my papers tonight. Some have been converted to kitchen uses, some the child has destroyed. This form of censorship pleases me for it has the indifference of the natural world to the constructions of art — an indifference I am beginning to share. After all, what is the good of a fine metaphor for Melissa when she lies buried deep as any mummy in the shallow tepid sand of the black estuary?

But those papers I guard with care are the three volumes in which Justine kept her diary, as well as the folio which records Nessim's madness. Nessim noticed them when I was leaving and nodded as he said:

'Take these, yes, read them. There is much about us all in them. They should help you to support the idea of Justine without flinching, as I have had to do.' This was at the Summer Palace after Melissa's death, when he still believed Justine would return to him. I think often, and never without a certain fear, of Nessim's love for Justine. What could be more comprehensive, more surely founded in itself? It coloured his unhappiness with a kind of ecstasy, the joyful wounds which you'd think to meet in saints and not in mere lovers. Yet one touch of humour would have saved him from such dreadful comprehensive suffering. It is easy to criticize, I know. I know.

*   *   *   *   *

In the great quietness of these winter evenings there is one clock: the sea. Its dim momentum in the mind is the fugue upon which this writing is made. Empty cadences of sea-water licking its own wounds, sulking along the mouths of the delta, boiling upon those deserted beaches — empty, forever empty under the gulls: white scribble on the grey, munched by clouds. If there are ever sails here they die before the land shadows them. Wreckage washed up on the pediments of islands, the last crust, eroded by the weather, stuck in the blue maw of water . . . gone!

★　　★　　★　　★　　★

Apart from the wrinkled old peasant who comes from the village on her mule each day to clean the house, the child and I are quite alone. It is happy and active amid unfamiliar surroundings. I have not named it yet. Of course it will be Justine — who else?

As for me I am neither happy nor unhappy; I lie suspended like a hair or a feather in the cloudy mixtures of memory. I spoke of the uselessness of art but added nothing truthful about its consolations. The solace of such work as I do with brain and heart lies in this — that only *there*, in the silences of the painter or the writer can reality be reordered, reworked and made to show its significant side. Our common actions in reality are simply the sackcloth covering which hides the cloth-of-gold — the meaning of the pattern. For us artists there waits the joyous compromise through art with all that wounded or defeated us in daily life; in this way, not to evade destiny, as the ordinary people try to do, but to fulfil it in its true potential — the imagination. Otherwise why should we hurt one another? No, the remission I am seeking, and will be granted perhaps, is not one I shall ever see in the bright friendly eyes of Melissa or the sombre brow-dark gaze of Justine. We have all of us taken different paths now; but in this, the first great fragmentation of my maturity, I feel the confines of my art and my living deepened immeasurably by the memory of them. In thought I achieve them anew; as if only here — this wooden table over the sea under an olive tree, only here can I enrich them as they deserve. So that the taste of this writing should have taken something from its living subjects — their breath, skin, voices — weaving them into the supple tissues of human memory. I want them to live again to the point where pain becomes art. . . . Perhaps this is a useless attempt, I cannot say. But I must try.

JUSTINE

Today the child and I finished the hearth-stone of the house together, quietly talking as we worked. I talk to her as I would to myself if I were alone; she answers in an heroic language of her own invention. We buried the rings Cohen bought for Melissa in the ground under the hearth-stone, according to the custom of this island. This will ensure good luck to the inmates of the house.

* * * * *

At the time when I met Justine I was almost a happy man. A door had suddenly opened upon an intimacy with Melissa — an intimacy not the less marvellous for being unexpected and totally undeserved. Like all egoists I cannot bear to live alone; and truly the last year of bachelorhood had sickened me — my domestic inadequacy, my hopelessness over clothes and food and money, had all reduced me to despair. I had sickened too of the cockroach-haunted rooms where I then lived, looked after by one-eyed Hamid, the Berber servant.

Melissa had penetrated my shabby defences not by any of the qualities one might enumerate in a lover — charm, exceptional beauty, intelligence — no, but by the force of what I can only call her charity, in the Greek sense of the word. I used to see her, I remember, pale, rather on the slender side, dressed in a shabby sealskin coat, leading her small dog about the winter streets. Her blue-veined phthisic hands, etc. Her eyebrows artificially pointed upwards to enhance those fine dauntlessly candid eyes. I saw her daily for many months on end, but her sullen aniline beauty awoke no response in me. Day after day I passed her on my way to the Café Al Aktar where Balthazar waited for me in his black hat to give me 'instruction'. I did not dream that I should ever become her lover.

I knew that she had once been a model at the Atelier — an unenviable job — and was now a dancer; more, that she was the mistress of an elderly furrier, a gross and vulgar commercial of the city. I simply make these few notes to record a block of my life which has fallen into the sea. Melissa! Melissa!

* * * * *

I am thinking back to the time when for the four of us the known world hardly existed; days became simply the spaces between dreams, spaces between the shifting floors of time, of acting, of living out the topical. . . . A tide of meaningless affairs

21

nosing along the dead level of things, entering no climate, leading us nowhere, demanding of us nothing save the impossible — that we should be. Justine would say that we had been trapped in the projection of a will too powerful and too deliberate to be human — the gravitational field which Alexandria threw down about those it had chosen as its exemplars. . . .

*　　*　　*　　*　　*

Six o'clock. The shuffling of white-robed figures from the station yards. The shops filling and emptying like lungs in the Rue des Soeurs. The pale lengthening rays of the afternoon sun smear the long curves of the Esplanade, and the dazzled pigeons, like rings of scattered paper, climb above the minarets to take the last rays of the waning light on their wings. Ringing of silver on the money-changers' counters. The iron grille outside the bank still too hot to touch. Clip-clop of horse-drawn carriages carrying civil servants in red flowerpots towards the cafés on the sea-front. This is the hour least easy to bear, when from my balcony I catch an unexpected glimpse of her walking idly towards the town in her white sandals, still half asleep. Justine! The city unwrinkles like an old tortoise and peers about it. For a moment it relinquishes the torn rags of the flesh, while from some hidden alley by the slaughter-house, above the moans and screams of the cattle, comes the nasal chipping of a Damascus love-song; shrill quarter-tones, like a sinus being ground to powder.

Now tired men throw back the shutters of their balconies and step blinking into the pale hot light — etiolated flowers of after-noons spent in anguish, tossing upon ugly beds, bandaged by dreams. I have become one of these poor clerks of the conscience, a citizen of Alexandria. She passes below my window, smiling as if at some private satisfaction, softly fanning her cheeks with the little reed fan. It is a smile which I shall probably never see again for in company she only laughs, showing those magnificent white teeth. But this sad yet quick smile is full of a quality which one does not think she owns — the power of mischief. You would have said that she was of a more tragic cast of character and lacked common humour. Only the obstinate memory of this smile is to make me doubt it in the days to come.

*　　*　　*　　*　　*

I have had many such glimpses of Justine at different times, and of course I knew her well by sight long before we met: our city does not permit anonymity to any with incomes of over two hundred pounds a year. I see her sitting alone by the sea, reading a newspaper and eating an apple; or in the vestibule of the Cecil Hotel, among the dusty palms, dressed in a sheath of silver drops, holding her magnificent fur at her back as a peasant holds his coat — her long forefinger hooked through the tag. Nessim has stopped at the door of the ballroom which is flooded with light and music. He has missed her. Under the palms, in a deep alcove, sit a couple of old men playing chess. Justine has stopped to watch them. She knows nothing of the game, but the aura of stillness and concentration which brims the alcove fascinates her. She stands there between the deaf players and the world of music for a long time, as if uncertain into which to plunge. Finally Nessim comes softly to take her arm and they stand together for a while, she watching the players, he watching her. At last she goes softly, reluctantly, circumspectly into the lighted world with a little sigh.

Then in other circumstances, less creditable no doubt to herself, or to the rest of us: how touching, how pliantly feminine this most masculine and resourceful of women could be. She could not help but remind me of that race of terrific queens which left behind them the ammoniac smell of their incestuous loves to hover like a cloud over the Alexandrian subconscious. The giant man-eating cats like Arsinoe were her true siblings. Yet behind the acts of Justine lay something else, born of a later tragic philosophy in which morals must be weighed in the balance against rogue personality. She was the victim of truly heroic doubts. Nevertheless I can still see a direct connection between the picture of Justine bending over the dirty sink with the fœtus in it, and poor Sophia of Valentinus who died for a love as perfect as it was wrong-headed.

*   *   *   *   *

At that epoch, Georges-Gaston Pombal, a minor consular official, shares a small flat with me in the Rue Nebi Daniel. He is a rare figure among the diplomats in that he appears to possess a vertebral column. For him the tiresome treadmill of protocol and entertainment — so like a surrealist nightmare — is full of exotic charm. He sees diplomacy through the eyes of a Douanier Rousseau. He indulges himself with it but never allows it to engulf what remains of his intellect. I suppose the secret of his success is his tremendous idleness, which almost approaches the supernatural.

He sits at his desk in the Consulate-General covered by a perpetual confetti of pasteboard cards bearing the names of his colleagues. He is a pegamoid sloth of a man, a vast slow fellow given to prolonged afternoon siestas and Crebillon *fils*. His handkerchiefs smell wondrously of *Eau de Portugal*. His most favoured topic of conversation is women, and he must speak from experience for the succession of visitors to the little flat is endless, and rarely does one see the same face twice. 'To a Frenchman the love here is interesting. They act before they reflect. When the time comes to doubt, to suffer remorse, it is too hot, nobody has the energy. It lacks *finesse*, this animalism, but it suits me. I've worn out my heart and head with love, and want to be left alone—above all, *mon cher*, from this Judeo-Coptic mania for *dissection*, for analysing the subject. I want to return to my farmhouse in Normandy heart-whole.'

For long periods of the winter he is away on leave and I have the little dank flat to myself and sit up late, correcting exercise books, with only the snoring Hamid for company. In this last year I have reached a dead-end in myself. I lack the will-power to do anything with my life, to better my position by hard work, to write: even to make love. I do not know what has come over me. This is the first time I have experienced a real failure of the will to survive. Occasionally I turn over a bundle of manuscript or an old proof-copy of a novel or book of poems with disgusted inattention; with sadness, like someone studying an old passport.

From time to time one of Georges' numerous girls strays into my net by calling at the flat when he is not there, and the incident serves for a while to sharpen my *taedium vitae*. Georges is thoughtful and generous in these matters for, before going away (knowing how poor I am) he often pays one of the Syrians from Golfo's tavern in advance, and orders her to spend an occasional night in the flat *en disponibilité*, as he puts it. Her duty is to cheer me up, by no means an enviable task especially as on the surface there is nothing to indicate lack of cheerfulness on my part. Small talk has become a useful form of automatism which goes on long after one has lost the need to talk; if necessary I can even make love with relief, as one does not sleep very well here: but without passion, without attention.

Some of these encounters with poor exhausted creatures driven to extremity by physical want are interesting, even touching, but I have lost any interest in sorting my emotions so that they exist for me like dimensionless figures flashed on a screen. 'There are only three things to be done with a woman' said Clea once. 'You can love her, suffer for her, or turn her into literature.' I was experiencing a failure in all these domains of feeling.

I record this only to show the unpromising human material upon which Melissa elected to work, to blow some breath of life into my nostrils. It could not have been easy for her to bear the double burden to her own poor circumstances and illness. To add my burdens to hers demanded real courage. Perhaps it was born of desperation, for she too had reached the dead level of things, as I myself had. We were fellow-bankrupts.

For weeks her lover, the old furrier, followed me about the streets with a pistol sagging in the pocket of his overcoat. It was consoling to learn from one of Melissa's friends that it was unloaded, but it was nevertheless alarming to be haunted by this old man. Mentally we must have shot each other down at every street corner of the city. I for my part could not bear to look at that heavy pock-marked face with its bestial saturnine cluster of tormented features smeared on it — could not bear to think of his gross intimacies with her: those sweaty little hands covered as thickly as a porcupine with black hair. For a long time this went on and then after some months an extraordinary feeling of intimacy seemed to grow up between us. We nodded and smiled at each other when we met. Once, encountering him at a bar, I stood for nearly an hour beside him; we were on the point of talking to each other, yet somehow neither of us had the courage to begin it. There was no common subject of conversation save Melissa. As I was leaving I caught a glimpse of him in one of the long mirrors, his head bowed as he stared into the wineglass. Something about his attitude — the clumsy air of a trained seal grappling with human emotions — struck me, and I realized for the first time that he probably loved Melissa as much as I did. I pitied his ugliness, and the blank pained incomprehension with which he faced emotions so new to him as jealousy, the deprivation of a cherished mistress.

Afterwards when they were turning out his pockets I saw among the litter of odds and ends a small empty scent-bottle of the cheap kind that Melissa used; and I took it back to the flat where it stayed on the mantelpiece for some months before it was thrown away by Hamid in the course of a spring-clean. I never told Melissa of this; but often when I was alone at night while she was dancing, perhaps of necessity sleeping with her admirers, I studied this small bottle, sadly and passionately reflecting on this horrible old man's love and measuring it against my own; and tasting too, vicariously, the desperation which makes one clutch at some small discarded object which is still impregnated with the betrayer's memory.

I found Melissa, washed up like a half-drowned bird, on the dreary littorals of Alexandria, with her sex broken. . . .

$$* \quad * \quad * \quad * \quad *$$

Streets that run back from the docks with their tattered rotten supercargo of houses, breathing into each others' mouths, keeling over. Shuttered balconies swarming with rats, and old women whose hair is full of the blood of ticks. Peeling walls leaning drunkenly to east and west of their true centre of gravity. The black ribbon of flies attaching itself to the lips and eyes of the children — the moist beads of summer flies everywhere; the very weight of their bodies snapping off ancient flypapers hanging in the violet doors of booths and cafés. The smell of the sweat-lathered Berberinis, like that of some decomposing stair-carpet. And then the street noises: shriek and clang of the water-bearing Saidi, dashing his metal cups together as an advertisement, the unheeded shrieks which pierce the hubbub from time to time, as of some small delicately-organized animal being disembowelled. The sores like ponds — the incubation of a human misery of such proportions that one is aghast, and all one's feelings overflow into disgust and terror.

I wished I could imitate the self-confident directness with which Justine threaded her way through these streets towards the café where I waited for her: El Bab. The doorway by the shattered arch where in all innocence we sat and talked; but already our conversation had become impregnated by understandings which we took for the lucky omens of friendship merely. On that dun mud floor, feeling the quickly cooling cylinder of the earth dip towards the darkness, we were possessed only by a desire to communicate ideas and experiences which overstepped the range of thought normal to conversation among ordinary people. She talked like a man and I talked to her like a man. I can only remember the pattern and weight of these conversations, not their substance. And leaning there on a forgotten elbow, drinking the cheap *arak* and smiling at her, I inhaled the warm summer perfume of her dress and skin — a perfume which was called, I don't know why, *Jamais de la vie.*

* * * * *

These are the moments which possess the writer, not the lover, and which live on perpetually. One can return to them time and time again in memory, or use them as a fund upon which to build the part of one's life which is writing. One can debauch them with words, but one cannot spoil them. In this context too, I recover another such moment, lying beside a sleeping woman in a cheap room near the mosque. In that early spring dawn, with its dense dew, sketched upon the silence which engulfs a whole city before the birds awaken it, I caught the sweet voice of the blind *muezzin* from the mosque reciting the *Ebed* — a voice hanging like a hair in the palm-cooled upper airs of Alexandria. 'I praise the perfection of God, the Forever existing' (this repeated thrice, ever more slowly, in a high sweet register). 'The perfection of God, the Desired, the Existing, the Single, the Supreme: the perfection of God, the One, the Sole: the perfection of Him who taketh unto himself no male or female partner, nor any like Him, nor any that is disobedient, nor any deputy, equal or offspring. His perfection be extolled.'

The great prayer wound its way into my sleepy consciousness like a serpent, coil after shining coil of words — the voice of the *muezzin* sinking from register to register of gravity — until the whole morning seemed dense with its marvellous healing powers, the intimations of a grace undeserved and unexpected, impregnating that shabby room where Melissa lay, breathing as lightly as a gull, rocked upon the oceanic splendours of a language she would never know.

* * * * *

Of Justine who can pretend that she did not have her stupid side? The cult of pleasure, small vanities, concern for the good opinion of her inferiors, arrogance. She could be tiresomely exigent when she chose. Yes. Yes. But all these weeds are watered by money. I will say only that in many things she thought as a man, while in her actions she enjoyed some of the free vertical independence of the masculine outlook. Our intimacy was of a strange mental order. Quite early on I discovered that she could mind-read in an unerring fashion. Ideas came to us simultaneously.

I remember once being made aware that she was sharing in her mind a thought which had just presented itself to mine, namely: 'This intimacy *should go no further*, for we have already exhausted all its possibilities in our respective imaginations: and what we shall end by discovering, behind the darkly woven colours of sensuality, will be a friendship so profound that we shall become bondsmen forever.' It was, if you like, the flirtation of minds prematurely exhausted by experience which seemed so much more dangerous than a love founded in sexual attraction.

Knowing how much she loved Nessim and loving him so much myself, I could not contemplate this thought without terror. She lay beside me, breathing lightly, and staring at the cherub-haunted ceiling with her great eyes. I said: 'It can come to nothing, this love-affair between a poor schoolteacher and an Alexandrian society woman. How bitter it would be to have it all end in a conventional scandal which would leave us alone together and give you the task of deciding how to dispose of me.' Justine hated to hear the truth spoken. She turned upon one elbow and lowering those magnificent troubled eyes to mine she stared at me for a long moment. 'There is no choice in this matter' she said in that hoarse voice I had come to love so much. 'You talk as if there was a choice. We are not strong or evil enough to exercise choice. All this is part of an experiment arranged by something else, the city perhaps, or another part of ourselves. How do I know?'

I remember her sitting before the multiple mirrors at the dressmaker's, being fitted for a shark-skin costume, and saying: 'Look! five different pictures of the same subject. Now if I wrote I would try for a multi-dimensional effect in character, a sort of prism-sightedness. Why should not people show more than one profile at a time?'

Now she yawned and lit a cigarette; and sitting up in bed clasped her slim ankles with her hands; reciting slowly, wryly, those marvellous lines of the old Greek poet about a love-affair long since past — they are lost in English. And hearing her speak his lines, touching every syllable of the thoughtful ironic Greek with tenderness, I felt once more the strange equivocal power of the city — its flat alluvial landscape and exhausted airs — and knew her for a true child of Alexandria; which is neither Greek, Syrian nor Egyptian, but a hybrid: a joint.

And with what feeling she reached the passage where the old man throws aside the ancient love-letter which had so moved him and exclaims: 'I go sadly out on to the balcony; anything to change this train of thought, even if only to see some little movement in the city I love, in its streets and shops!' Herself pushing open the shutters to stand on the dark balcony above a city of coloured lights: feeling the evening wind stir from the confines of Asia: her body for an instant forgotten.

*　　*　　*　　*　　*

'Prince' Nessim is of course a joke; at any rate to the shop-keepers and black-coated *commerçants* who saw him drawn sound-lessly down the Canopic way in the great silver Rolls with the daffodil hub-caps. To begin with he was a Copt, not a Moslem. Yet somehow the nickname was truly chosen for Nessim was princely in his detachment from the common greed in which the decent instincts of the Alexandrians — even the very rich ones — foundered. Yet the factors which gave him a reputation for eccentricity were neither of them remarkable to those who had lived outside the Levant. He did not care for money, except to spend it — that was the first: the second was that he did not own a *garçonnière,* and appeared to be quite faithful to Justine — an unheard of state of affairs. As for money, being so inordinately rich he was possessed by a positive distaste for it, and would never carry it on his person. He spent in Arabian fashion and gave notes of hand to shopkeepers; night-clubs and restaurants accepted his signed cheques. Nevertheless his debts were punctually honoured, and every morning Selim his secretary was sent out with the car to trace the route of the previous day and to pay any debts ac-cumulated in the course of it.

This attitude was considered eccentric and high-handed in the extreme by the inhabitants of the city whose coarse and derived distinctions, menial preoccupations and faulty education gave them no clue to what style in the European sense was. But Nessim was born to this manner, not merely educated to it; in this little world of studied carnal moneymaking he could find no true province of operation for a spirit essentially gentle and contem-plative. The least assertive of men, he caused comment by acts which bore the true stamp of his own personality. People were inclined to attribute his manners to a foreign education, but in fact Germany and England had done little but confuse him and unfit him for the life of the city. The one had implanted a taste for metaphysical speculation in what was a natural Mediterranean mind, while Oxford had tried to make him donnish and had only succeeded in developing his philosophic bent to the point where he was incapable of practising the art he most loved, painting. He thought and suffered a good deal but he lacked the resolution to dare — the first requisite of a practitioner.

Nessim was at odds with the city, but since his enormous fortune brought him daily into touch with the business men of the place they eased their constraint by treating him with a humorous indulgence, a condescension such as one would bestow upon someone who was a little soft in the head. It was perhaps not surprising if you should walk in upon him at the office — that sarcophagus of tubular steel and lighted glass — and find him seated like an orphan at the great desk (covered in bells and pulleys and patent lights) — eating brown bread and butter and reading Vasari as he absently signed letters or vouchers. He looked up at you with that pale almond face, the expression shuttered, withdrawn, almost pleading. And yet somewhere through all this gentleness ran a steel cord, for his staff was perpetually surprised to find out that, inattentive as he appeared to be, there was no detail of the business which he did not know; while hardly a transaction he made did not turn out to be based on a stroke of judgement. He was something of an oracle to his own employees — and yet (they sighed and shrugged their shoulders) he seemed not to care! Not to care about gain, that is what Alexandria recognizes as madness.

I knew them by sight for many months before we actually met — as I knew everyone in the city. By sight and no less by repute: for their emphatic, authoritative and quite conventionless way of living had given them a certain notoriety among our provincial city-dwellers. She was reputed to have had many lovers, and Nessim was regarded as a *mari complaisant*. I had watched them dancing together several times, he slender and with a deep waist like a woman, and long arched beautiful hands; Justine's lovely head — the deep bevel of that Arabian nose and those translucent eyes, enlarged by belladonna. She gazed about her like a half-trained panther.

Then: once I had been persuaded to lecture upon the native poet of the city at the *Atelier des Beaux Arts* — a sort of club where gifted amateurs of the arts could meet, rent studios and so on. I had accepted because it meant a little money for Melissa's new coat, and autumn was on the way. But it was painful to me, feeling the old man all round me, so to speak, impregnating the gloomy streets around the lecture-room with the odour of those verses distilled from the shabby but rewarding loves he had experienced — loves perhaps bought with money, and lasting a few moments, yet living on now in his verse — so deliberately and tenderly had he captured the adventive minute and made all its colours fast. What an impertinence to lecture upon an ironist who so naturally, and with such fineness of instinct took his subject-matter from the streets and brothels of Alexandria! And to be talking, moreover, not to an audience of haberdashers' assistants and small clerks — his immortals — but to a dignified semi-circle of society ladies for whom the culture he represented was a sort of blood-bank: they had come along for a transfusion. Many had actually foregone a bridge-party to do so, though they knew that instead of being uplifted they would be stupefied.

I remember saying only that I was haunted by his face — the horrifyingly sad gentle face of the last photograph; and when the solid burghers' wives had dribbled down the stone staircase into the wet streets where their lighted cars awaited them, leaving the gaunt room echoing with their perfumes, I noticed that they had left behind them one solitary student of the passions and the arts. She sat in a thoughtful way at the back of the hall, her legs crossed in a mannish attitude, puffing a cigarette. She did not look at me but crudely at the ground under her feet. I was flattered to think that perhaps one person had appreciated my difficulties. I gathered up my damp brief case and ancient mackintosh and made my way down to where a thin penetrating drizzle swept the streets from the direction of the sea. I made for my lodgings where by now Melissa would be awake, and would have set out our evening meal on the newspaper-covered table, having first sent Hamid out to the baker's to fetch the roast — we had no oven of our own.

It was cold in the street and I crossed to the lighted blaze of shops in Rue Fuad. In a grocer's window I saw a small tin of olives with the name *Orvieto* on it, and overcome by a sudden longing to be on the right side of the Mediterranean, entered the shop: bought it: had it opened there and then: and sitting down at a marble table in that gruesome light I began to eat Italy, its dark scorched flesh, hand-modelled spring soil, dedicated vines. I felt that Melissa would never understand this. I should have to pretend I had lost the money.

I did not see at first the great car which she had abandoned in the street with its engine running. She came into the shop with swift and resolute suddenness and said, with the air of authority that Lesbians, or women with money, assume with the obviously indigent: 'What did you mean by your remark about the anti-nomian nature of irony?' — or some such sally which I have forgotten.

Unable to disentangle myself from Italy I looked up boorishly and saw her leaning down at me from the mirrors on three sides of the room, her dark thrilling face full of a troubled, arrogant reserve. I had of course forgotten what I had said about irony or anything else for that matter, and I told her so with an indifference that was not assumed. She heaved a short sigh, as if of natural relief, and sitting down opposite me lit a French *caporal* and with short decisive inspirations blew thin streamers of blue smoke up into the harsh light. She looked to me a trifle unbalanced, as she watched me with a candour I found embarrassing — it was as if she were trying to decide to what use I could be put. 'I liked' she said 'the way you quoted his lines about the city. Your Greek is good. Doubtless you are a writer.' I said: 'Doubtless.' Not to be known always wounds. There seemed no point in pursuing all this. I have always hated literary conversation. I offered her an olive which she ate swiftly, spitting the pit into her gloved hand like a cat where she held it absently, saying: 'I want to take you to Nessim, my husband. Will you come?'

A policeman had appeared in the doorway, obviously troubled about the abandoned car. That was the first time I saw the great house of Nessim with its statues and palm loggias, its Courbets and Bonnards — and so on. It was both beautiful and horrible. Justine hurried up the great staircase, pausing only to transfer her olive-pit from the pocket of her coat to a Chinese vase, calling all the time to Nessim. We went from room to room, fracturing the silences. He answered at last from the great studio on the roof and racing to him like a gun-dog she metaphorically dropped me at his feet and stood back, wagging her tail. She had achieved me.

Nessim was sitting on the top of a ladder reading, and he came slowly down to us, looking first at one and then at the other. His shyness could not get any purchase of my shabbiness, damp hair, tin of olives, and for my part I could offer no explanation of my presence, since I did not know for what purpose I had been brought here.

I took pity on him and offered him an olive; and sitting down together we finished the tin, while Justine foraged for drinks, talking, if I remember, of Orvieto where neither of us had been. It is such a solace to think back to that first meeting. Never have I been closer to them both — closer, I mean, to their marriage; they seemed to me then to be the magnificent two-headed animal a marriage could be. Watching the benign warmth of the light in his eye I realized, as I recalled all the scandalous rumours about Justine, that whatever she had done had been done in a sense *for him* — even what was evil or harmful in the eyes of the world. Her love was like a skin in which he lay sewn like the infant Heracles; and her efforts to achieve herself had led her always towards, and not away from him. The world has no use for this sort of paradox I know; but it seemed to me then that Nessim knew and accepted her in a way impossible to explain to someone for whom love is still entangled with the qualities of possessiveness. Once, much later, he told me: 'What was I to do? Justine was too strong for me in too many ways. I could only out-love her — that was my long suit. I went ahead of her — I anticipated every lapse; she found me already there, at every point where she fell down, ready to help her to her feet and show that it did not matter. After all she compromised the least part of me — my reputation.'

This was much later: before the unlucky complex of misfortunes had engulfed us we did not know each other well enough to talk as freely as this. I also remember him saying, once — this was at the summer villa near Bourg El Arab: 'It will puzzle you when I tell you that I thought Justine great, in a sort of way. There are forms of greatness, you know, which when not applied in art or religion make havoc of ordinary life. Her gift was misapplied in being directed towards love. Certainly she was bad in many ways, but they were all small ways. Nor can I say that she harmed nobody. But those she harmed most she made fruitful. She expelled people from their old selves. It was bound to hurt, and many mistook the nature of the pain she inflicted. Not I.' And smiling his well-known smile, in which sweetness was mixed with an inexpressible bitterness, he repeated softly under his breath the words: 'Not I.'

* * * * *

Capodistria . . . how does he fit in? He is more of a goblin than a man, you would think. The flat triangular head of the snake with the huge frontal lobes; the hair grows forward in a widow's peak.

A whitish flickering tongue is forever busy keeping his thin lips moist. He is ineffably rich and does not have to lift a finger for himself. He sits all day on the terrace of the Brokers' Club watching the women pass, with the restless eye of someone endlessly shuffling through an old soiled pack of cards. From time to time there is a flick, like a chameleon's tongue striking — a signal almost invisible to the inattentive. Then a figure slips from the terrace to trail the woman he had indicated. Sometimes his agents will quite openly stop and importune women on the street in his name, mentioning a sum of money. No one is offended by the mention of money in our city. Some girls simply laugh. Some consent at once. You never see vexation on their features. Virtue with us is never feigned. Nor vice. Both are natural.

Capodistria sits remote from it all, in his immaculate shark-skin coat with the coloured silk handkerchief lolling at his breast. His narrow shoes gleam. His friends call him *Da Capo* because of a sexual prowess reputed to be as great as his fortune — or his ugliness. He is obscurely related to Justine who says of him: 'I pity him. His heart has withered in him and he has been left with the five senses, like pieces of a broken wineglass.' However a life of such striking monotony does not seem to depress him. His family is noted for the number of suicides in it, and his psychological inheritance is an unlucky one with its history of mental disturbance and illness. He is unperturbed however and says, touching his temples with a long forefinger: 'All my ancestors went wrong here in the head. My father also. He was a great womanizer. When he was very old he had a model of the perfect woman built in rubber — life-size. She could be filled with hot water in the winter. She was strikingly beautiful. He called her Sabina after his mother, and took her everywhere. He had a passion for travelling on ocean liners and actually lived on one for the last two years of his life, travelling backwards and forwards to New York. Sabina had a wonderful wardrobe. It was a sight to see them come into the dining-saloon, dressed for dinner. He travelled with his keeper, a manservant called Kelly. Between them, held on either side like a beautiful drunkard, walked Sabina in her marvellous evening clothes. The night he died he said to Kelly: "Send Demetrius a telegram and tell him that Sabina died in my arms tonight without any pain." She was buried with him off Naples.' His laughter is the most natural and unfeigned of any I have ever heard.

34

Later when I was half mad with worry and heavily in Capodistria's debt, I found him less accommodating a companion; and
one night, there was Melissa sitting half drunk on the footstool
by the fire holding in those long reflective fingers the I.O.U. which
I had made out to him with the curt word '*discharged*' written
across it in green ink. . . . These memories wound. Melissa said:
'Justine would have paid your debt from her immense fortune. I
did not want to see her increase her hold over you. Besides, even
though you no longer care for me I still wanted to do something
for you — and this was the least of sacrifices. I did not think that it
would hurt you so much for me to sleep with him. Have you not
done the same for me—I mean did you not borrow the money from
Justine to send me away for the X-ray business? Though you lied
about it I knew. I won't lie, I never do. Here, take it and destroy it:
but don't gamble with him any more. He is not of your kind.' And
turning her head she made the Arab motion of spitting.

*   *   *   *   *

Of Nessim's outer life — those immense and boring receptions,
at first devoted to business colleagues but later to become devoted
to obscure political ends — I do not wish to write. As I slunk
through the great hall and up the stairs to the studio I would pause
to study the great leather shield on the mantelpiece with its plan
of the table — to see who had been placed on Justine's right and
left. For a short while they made a kindly attempt to include me
in these gatherings but I rapidly tired of them and pleaded illness,
though I was glad to have the run of the studio and the immense
library. And afterwards we would meet like conspirators and
Justine would throw off the gay, bored, petulant affectations which
she wore in her social life. They would kick off their shoes and
play piquet by candle-light. Later, going to bed, she would catch
sight of herself in the mirror on the first landing and say to her
reflection: 'Tiresome pretentious hysterical Jewess that you are!'

*   *   *   *   *

Mnemjian's Babylonian barber's shop was on the corner of
Fuad I and Nebi Daniel and here every morning Pombal lay down
beside me in the mirrors. We were lifted simultaneously and
swung smoothly down into the ground wrapped like dead Pharaohs,
only to reappear at the same instant on the ceiling, spread out like
specimens. White cloths had been spread over us by a small black

boy while in a great Victorian moustache-cup the barber thwacked up his dense and sweet-smelling lather before applying it in direct considered brush-strokes to our cheeks. The first covering complete, he surrendered his task to an assistant while he went to the great strop hanging among the flypapers on the end wall of the shop and began to sweeten the edge of an English razor.

Little Mnemjian is a dwarf with a violet eye that has never lost its childhood. He is the Memory man, the archives of the city. If you should wish to know the ancestry or income of the most casual passer-by you have only to ask him; he will recite the details in a sing-song voice as he strops his razor and tries it upon the coarse black hair of his forearm. What he does not know he can find out in a matter of moments. Moreover he is as well briefed in the living as in the dead; I mean this in the literal sense, for the Greek Hospital employs him to shave and lay out its victims before they are committed to the undertakers — a task which he performs with relish tinged by racial unction. His ancient trade embraces the two worlds, and some of his best observations begin with the phrase: 'As so-and-so said to me with *his last breath.*' He is rumoured to be fantastically attractive to women and he is said to have put away a small fortune earned for him by his admirers. But he also has several elderly Egyptian ladies, the wives and widows of pashas, as permanent clients upon whom he calls at regular intervals to set their hair. They have, as he says slyly, 'got beyond everything' — and reaching up over his back to touch the unsightly hump which crowns it he adds with pride: '*This* excites them.' Among other things, he has a gold cigarette case given to him by one of these admirers in which he keeps a stock of loose cigarette-paper. His Greek is defective but adventurous and vivid and Pombal refuses to permit him to talk French, which he does much better.

He does a little mild procuring for my friend, and I am always astonished by the sudden flights of poetry of which he is capable in describing his *protégées.* Leaning over Pombal's moon-like face he will say, for example, in a discreet undertone, as the razor begins to whisper: 'I have something for you — *something special.*' Pombal catches my eye in the mirror and looks hastily away lest we infect one another by a smile. He gives a cautious grunt. Mnemjian leans lightly on the balls of his feet, his eyes squinting slightly. The small wheedling voice puts a husk of double meaning round everything he says, and his speech is not the less remarkable for being punctuated by small world-weary sighs. For a while nothing more is said. I can see the top of Mnemjian's head in the mirror — that obscene outcrop of black hair which he had trained into a spitcurl at each temple, hoping no doubt to draw attention away from that crooked *papier-mâché* back of his. While he works with a razor his eyes dim out and his features become as expressionless as a bottle. His fingers travel as coolly upon our live faces as they do upon those of the fastidious and (yes, lucky) dead. 'This time' says Mnemjian 'you will be delighted from every point of view. She is young, cheap and clean. You will say to yourself, a young partridge, a honey-comb with all its honey sealed in it, a dove. She is in difficulties over money. She has recently come from the lunatic asylum in Helwan where her husband tried to get her locked up as mad. I have arranged for her to sit at the Rose Marie at the end table on the pavement. Go and see her at one o'clock; if you wish her to accompany you give her the card I will prepare for you. But remember, you will pay only me. As one gentleman to another it is the only condition I lay down.'

He says nothing more for the time. Pombal continues to stare at himself in the mirror, his natural curiosity doing battle with the forlorn apathy of the summer air. Later no doubt he will bustle into the flat with some exhausted, disoriented creature whose distorted smile can rouse no feelings in him save those of pity. I cannot say that my friend lacks kindness, for he is always trying to find work of some sort for these girls; indeed most of the consulates are staffed by ex-casuals desperately trying to look correct; whose jobs they owe to Georges' importunities among his colleagues of the career. Nevertheless there is no woman too humble, too battered, too old, to receive those outward attentions — those little gallantries and *sorties* of wit which I have come to associate with the Gallic temperament; the heady meretricious French charm which evaporates so easily into pride and mental indolence — like French thought which flows so quickly into sand-moulds, the original *esprit* hardening immediately into deadening concepts. The light play of sex which hovers over his thought and actions has, however, an air of disinterestedness which makes it qualitatively different from, say, the actions and thoughts of Capodistria, who often joins us for a morning shave. Capodistria has the purely involuntary knack of turning everything into a woman; under his eyes chairs become painfully conscious of their bare legs. He impregnates things. At table I have seen a water-melon become conscious under his gaze so that it felt the seeds inside it stirring with life! Women feel like birds confronted by a viper when they gaze into that narrow flat face with its tongue always moving across the thin lips. I think of Melissa once more: *hortus conclusus, soror mea sponsor.* . . .

★   ★   ★   ★   ★

'*Regard dérisoire*' says Justine. 'How is it you are so much one of us and yet . . . you are not?' She is combing that dark head in the mirror, her mouth and eyes drawn up about a cigarette. 'You are a mental refugee of course, being Irish, but you miss our *angoisse.*' What she is groping after is really the distinctive quality which emanates not from us but from the landscape — the metallic flavours of exhaustion which impregnate the airs of Mareotis.

As she speaks I am thinking of the founders of the city, of the soldier-God in his glass coffin, the youthful body lapped in silver, riding down the river towards his tomb. Or of that great square negro head reverberating with a concept of God conceived in the spirit of pure intellectual play — Plotinus. It is as if the preoccupations of this landscape were centred somewhere out of reach of the average inhabitant — in a region where the flesh, stripped by over-indulgence of its final reticences, must yield to a preoccupation vastly more comprehensive: or perish in the kind of exhaustion represented by the works of the Mouseion, the guileless playing of hermaphrodites in the green courtyards of art and science. Poetry as a clumsy attempt at the artificial insemination of the Muses; the burning stupid metaphor of Berenice's hair glittering in the night sky above Melissa's sleeping face. 'Ah!' said Justine once 'that there should be something free, something Polynesian about the licence in which we live.' Or even Mediterranean, she might have added, for the connotation of every kiss would be different in Italy or Spain; here our bodies were chafed by the harsh desiccated winds blowing up out of the deserts of Africa and for love we were forced to substitute a wiser but crueller mental tenderness which emphasized loneliness rather than expurgated it.

Now even the city had two centres of gravity — the true and magnetic north of its personality: and between them the temperament of its inhabitants sparked harshly like a leaky electric discharge. Its spiritual centre was the forgotten site of the Soma where once the confused young soldier's body lay in its borrowed

Godhead; its temporal site the Brokers' Club where like Caballi*
the cotton brokers sat to sip their coffee, puff rank cheroots and
watch Capodistria — as people upon a river-bank will watch the
progress of a fisherman or an artist. The one symbolized for me the
great conquests of man in the realms of matter, space and time —
which must inevitably yield their harsh knowledge of defeat to the
conqueror in his coffin; the other was no symbol but the living
limbo of free-will in which my beloved Justine wandered, searching with such frightening singleness of mind for the integrating
spark which might lift her into a new perspective of herself. In her,
as an Alexandrian, licence was in a curious way a form of self-
abnegation, a travesty of freedom; and if I saw her as an exemplar
of the city it was not of Alexandria, or Plotinus that I was forced
to think, but of the sad thirtieth child of Valentinus who fell, 'not
like Lucifer by rebelling against God, but by desiring too ardently
to be united to him'.* Anything pressed too far becomes a sin.

Broken from the divine harmony of herself she fell, says the
tragic philosopher, and became the manifestation of matter; and
the whole universe of her city, of the world, was formed out of her
agony and remorse. The tragic seed from which her thoughts and
actions grew was the seed of a pessimistic gnosticism.

That this identification was a true one I know — for much later
when, with so many misgivings, she invited me to join the little
circle which gathered every month about Balthazar, it was always
what he had to say about gnosticism which most interested her. I
remember her asking one night, so anxiously, so pleadingly if she
had interpreted his thinking rightly: 'I mean, that God neither
created us nor wished us to be created, but that we are the work
of an inferior deity, a Demiurge, who wrongly believed himself to
be God? Heavens, how probable it seems; and this overweening
hubris has been handed on down to our children.' And stopping
me as we walked by the expedient of standing in front of me and
catching hold of the lapels of my coat she gazed earnestly into my
eyes and said: 'What do you believe? You never say anything. At
the most you sometimes laugh.' I did not know how to reply for
all ideas seem equally good to me; the fact of their existence proves
that someone is creating. Does it matter whether they are objectively right or wrong? They could never remain so for long. 'But
it matters' she cried with a touching emphasis. 'It matters deeply
my darling, deeply.'

We are the children of our landscape; it dictates behaviour and

39

even thought in the measure to which we are responsive to it. I can think of no better identification. 'Your doubt, for example, which contains so much anxiety and such a thirst for an absolute truth, is so different from the scepticism of the Greek, from the mental play of the Mediterranean mind with its deliberate resort to sophistry as part of the *game* of thought; for you thought is a weapon, a theology.'

'But how else can action be judged?' 'It cannot be judged comprehensively until thought itself can be judged, for our thoughts themselves are acts. It is an attempt to make partial judgements upon either that leads to misgivings.'

I liked so much the way she would suddenly sit down on a wall, or a broken pillar in that shattered backyard to Pompey's Pillar, and be plunged in an inextinguishable sorrow at some idea whose impact had only just made itself felt in her mind. 'You really believe so?' she would say with such sorrow that one was touched and amused at the same time. 'And why do you smile? You always smile at the most serious things. Ah! surely you should be sad?' If she ever knew me at all she must later have discovered that for those of us who feel deeply and who are at all conscious of the inextricable tangle of human thought there is only one response to be made — ironic tenderness and silence.

In a night so brilliant with stars where the glow-worms in the shrill dry grass gave back their ghostly mauve lambence to the sky there was nothing else to do but sit by her side, stroking that dark head of beautiful hair and saying nothing. Underneath, like a dark river, the noble quotation which Balthazar had taken as a text and which he read in a voice that trembled partly with emotion and partly with the fatigue of so much abstract thought: 'The day of the *corpora* is the night for the *spiritus*. When the bodies cease their labour the spirits in man begin their work. The waking of the body is the sleep of the spirit and the spirit's sleep a waking for the body.' And later, like a thunderclap: '*Evil is good perverted.*'*

*   *   *   *   *

That Nessim had her watched I for a long time doubted; after all, she seemed as free as a bat to flit about the town at night, and never did I hear her called upon to give an account of her movements. It could not have been easy to spy upon someone so protean, in touch with the life of the town at so many points. Nevertheless it is possible that she was watched lest she should come to harm.

One night an incident brought this home to me, for I had been asked to dine at the old house. When they were alone we dined in a little pavilion at the end of the garden where the summer coolness could mingle with the whisper of water from the four lions' heads bordering the fountain. Justine was late on this particular occasion and Nessim sat alone, with the curtains drawn towards the west reflectively polishing a yellow jade from his collection in those long gentle fingers.

It was already forty minutes past the hour and he had already given the signal for dinner to begin when the little black telephone extension gave a small needle-like sound. He crossed to the table and picked it up with a sigh, and I heard him say, 'yes' impatiently; then he spoke for a while in a low voice, the language changing abruptly to Arabic, and for a moment I had the sudden intuitive feeling that it was Mnemjian talking to him over the wire. I do not know why I should feel this. He scribbled something rapidly on an envelope and putting down the receiver stood for a second memorizing what he had written. Then he turned to me, and it was all of a sudden a different Nessim who said: 'Justine may need our help. Will you come with me?' And without waiting for an answer he ran down the steps, past the lily-pond in the direction of the garage. I followed as well as I could and it could only have been a matter of minutes before he swung the little sports car through the heavy gates into Rue Fuad and began to weave his way down to the sea through the network of streets which slide down towards Ras El Tin. Though it was not late there were few people about and we raced away along the curving flanks of the Esplanade towards the Yacht Club grimly overtaking the few horse-drawn cabs ('carriages of love') which dawdled up and down by the sea.

At the fort we doubled back and entered the huddled slums which lie behind Tatwig Street, our blond headlights picking out the ant-hill cafés and crowded squares with an unaccustomed radiance; from somewhere behind the immediate skyline of smashed and unlimbered houses came the piercing shrieks and ululations of a burial procession, whose professional mourners made the night hideous with their plaints for the dead. We abandoned the car in a narrow street by the mosque and Nessim entered the shadowy doorway of some great tenement house, half of which consisted of shuttered and barred offices with blurred nameplates. A solitary *boab* (the *concierge* of Egypt) sat on his perch wrapped in clouts, for all the world like some discarded material object (an old motor tyre, say) — smoking a short-stemmed hubble-bubble. Nessim spoke to him sharply, and almost before the man could reply passed through the back of the building into a sort of dark backyard flanked by a series of dilapidated houses built of earth-brick and scaly plaster. He stopped only to light his cigarette-lighter, and by its feeble light we began to quest along the doors. At the fourth door he clicked the machine shut and knocked with his fist. Receiving no answer he pushed it open.

A dark corridor led to a small shadowy room lit by the feeble light of rush-lamps. This was apparently our destination.

The scene upon which we intruded was ferociously original, if for no other reason than that the light, pushing up from the mud floor, touched out the eyebrows and lips and cheek-bones of the participants while it left great patches of shadow on their faces — so that they looked as if they had been half-eaten by the rats which one could hear scrambling among the rafters of this wretched tenement. It was a house of child prostitutes, and there in the dimness, clad in ludicrous biblical night-shirts, with rouged lips, arch bead fringes and cheap rings, stood a dozen fuzzy-haired girls who could not have been much above ten years of age; the peculiar innocence of childhood which shone out from under the fancy-dress was in startling contrast to the barbaric adult figure of the French sailor who stood in the centre of the room on flexed calves, his ravaged and tormented face thrust out from the neck towards Justine who stood with her half-profile turned towards us. What he had just shouted had expired on the silence but the force with which the words had been uttered was still visible in the jut of the chin and the black corded muscles which held his head upon his shoulders. As for Justine, her face was lit by a sort of painful academic precision. She held a bottle raised in one hand, and it was clear that she had never thrown one before, for she held it the wrong way.

On a rotting sofa in one corner of the room, magnetically lit by the warm shadow reflected from the walls, lay one of the children horribly shrunk up in its nightshirt in an attitude which suggested death. The wall above the sofa was covered in the blue imprints of juvenile hands — the talisman which in this part of the world guards a house against the evil eye. It was the only decoration in the room; indeed the commonest decoration of the whole Arab quarter of the city.

We stood there, Nessim and I, for a good half-second, astonished by the scene which had a sort of horrifying beauty — like some hideous coloured engraving for a Victorian penny bible, say, whose subject matter had somehow become distorted and displaced. Justine was breathing harshly in a manner which suggested that she was on the point of tears.

We pounced on her, I suppose, and dragged her out into the street; at any rate I can only remember the three of us reached the sea and driving the whole length of the Corniche in clean bronze moonlight, Nessim's sad and silent face reflected in the driving-mirror, and the figure of his silent wife seated beside him, gazing out at the crashing silver waves and smoking the cigarette which she had burrowed from the pockets of his jacket. Later, in the garage, before we left the car, she kissed Nessim tenderly on the eyes.

*   *   *   *   *

All this I have come to regard as a sort of overture to that first real meeting face to face, when such understanding as we had enjoyed until then — a gaiety and friendship founded in tastes which were common to the three of us — disintegrated into something which was not love — how could it have been? — but into a sort of mental possession in which the bonds of a ravenous sexuality played the least part. How did we let it come about — matched as we were so well in experience, weathered and seasoned by the disappointments of love in other places?

In autumn the female bays turn to uneasy phosphorus and after the long chafing days of dust one feels the first palpitations of the autumn, like the wings of a butterfly fluttering to unwrap themselves. Mareotis turns lemon-mauve and its muddy flanks are starred by sheets of radiant anemones, growing through the quickened plaster-mud of the shore. One day while Nessim was away in Cairo I called at the house to borrow some books and to my surprise found Justine alone in the studio, darning an old pullover. She had taken the night train back to Alexandria, leaving Nessim to attend some business conference. We had tea together and then, on a sudden impulse took our bathing things and drove out through the rusty slag-heaps of Mex towards the sand-beaches off Bourg El Arab, glittering in the mauve-lemon light of the fast-fading afternoon. Here the open sea boomed upon the carpets of fresh sand the colour of oxidized mercury; its deep melodious percussion was the background to such conversation as we had. We walked ankle deep in the spurge of those shallow dimpled pools, choked here and there with sponges torn up by the roots and flung ashore. We passed no one on the road I remember save a gaunt Bedouin youth carrying on his head a wire crate full of wild birds caught with lime-twigs. Dazed quail.

We lay for a long time, side by side in our wet bathing costumes to take the last pale rays of the sun upon our skins in the delicious evening coolness. I lay with half-shut eyes while Justine (how clearly I see her!) was up on one elbow, shading her eyes with the palm of one hand and watching my face. Whenever I was talking she had the habit of gazing at my lips with a curious half-mocking, an almost impertinent intentness, as if she were waiting for me to mispronounce a word. If indeed it all began at this point I have forgotten the context, but I remember the hoarse troubled voice saying something like: 'And if it should happen to us — what would you say?' But before I could say anything she leaned down and kissed me — I should say derisively, antagonistically, on the mouth. This seemed so much out of character that I turned with some sort of half-formulated reproach on my lips — but from here on her kisses were like tremendous soft breathless stabs punctuating the savage laughter which seemed to well up in her — a jeering unstable laughter. It struck me then that she was like someone who had had a bad fright. If I said now: 'It must not happen to us' she must have replied: 'But let us *suppose*. What if it did?' Then — and this I remember clearly — the mania for self-justification seized her (we spoke French: language creates national character) and between those breathless half-seconds when I felt her strong mouth on my own and those worldly brown arms closing upon mine: 'I would not mistake it for gluttony or self-indulgence. We are too worldly for that: simply we have something to learn from each other. What is it?'

What was it? 'And is this the way?' I remember asking as I saw the tall toppling figure of Nessim upon the evening sky. 'I do not know' she said with a savage, obstinate desperate expression of humility upon her face, 'I do not know'; and she pressed herself upon me like someone pressing upon a bruise. It was as if she wished to expunge the very thought of me, and yet in the fragile quivering context of every kiss found a sort of painful surcease — like cold water on a sprain. How well I recognized her now as a child of the city, which decrees that its women shall be the voluptuaries not of pleasure but of pain, doomed to hunt for what they least dare to find!

She got up now and walked away down the long curving perspective of the beach, crossing the pools of lava slowly, her head bent; and I thought of Nessim's handsome face smiling at her from every mirror in the room. The whole of the scene which we had just enacted was invested in my mind with a dream-like improbability. It was curious in an objective sort of way to notice how my hands trembled as I lit a cigarette and rose to follow her.

But when I overtook her and halted her the face she turned to me was that of a sick demon. She was in a towering rage. 'You thought I simply wanted to make love? God! haven't we had enough of that? How is it that you do not *know* what I feel for once? How is it?' She stamped her foot in the wet sand. It was not merely that a geological fault had opened in the ground upon which we had been treading with such self-confidence. It was as if some long-disused mineshaft in my own character had suddenly fallen in. I recognized that this barren traffic in ideas and feelings had driven a path through towards the denser jungles of the heart; and that here we became bondsmen in the body, possessors of an enigmatic knowledge which could only be passed on — received, deciphered, understood — by those rare complementaries of ours in the world. (How few they were, how seldom one found them!) 'After all' I remember her saying, 'this has nothing to do with sex' which tempted me to laugh though I recognized in the phrase her desperate attempt to dissociate the flesh from the message it carried. I suppose this sort of thing always happens to bankrupts when they fall in love. I saw then what I should have seen long before: namely that our friendship had ripened to a point when we had already become in a way part-owners of each other.

I think we were both horrified by the thought; for exhausted as we were we could not help but quail before such a relationship. We did not say any more but walked back along the beach to where we had left our clothes, speechless and hand in hand. Justine looked utterly exhausted. We were both dying to get away from each other, in order to examine our own feelings. We did not speak to each other again. We drove into the city and she dropped me at the usual corner near my flat. I snapped the door of the car closed and she drove off without a word or a glance in my direction.

As I opened the door of my room I could still see the imprint of Justine's foot in the wet sand. Melissa was reading, and looking up at me she said with characteristic calm foreknowledge: 'Something has happened — what is it?' I could not tell her since I did not myself know. I took her face in my hands and examined it silently, with a care and attention, with a sadness and hunger I don't ever remember feeling before. She said: 'It is not me you are seeing, it is someone else.' But in truth I was seeing Melissa for the first time. In some paradoxical way it was Justine who was now permitting me to see Melissa as she really was — and to recognize my love for her. Melissa smilingly reached for a cigarette and said: 'You are falling in love with Justine' and I answered as sincerely, as honestly, as painfully as I could: 'No Melissa, it is worse than that' — though I could not for the life of me have explained how or why.

When I thought of Justine I thought of some great freehand composition, a cartoon of a woman representing someone released from bondage in the male. 'Where the carrion is' she once quoted proudly from Boehme, speaking of her native city, 'there the eagles will gather.' Truly she looked and seemed an eagle at this moment. But Melissa was a sad painting from a winter landscape contained by dark sky; a window-box with a few flowering geraniums lying forgotten on the windowsill of a cement-factory.

There is a passage in one of Justine's diaries which comes to mind here. I translate it here because though it must have referred to incidents long preceding those which I have recounted yet nevertheless it almost exactly expresses the curiously ingrown quality of a love which I have come to recognize as peculiar to the city rather than to ourselves. 'Idle' she writes 'to imagine falling in love as a correspondence of minds, of thoughts; it is a simultaneous firing of two spirits engaged in the autonomous act of growing up. And the sensation is of something having noiselessly exploded inside each of them. Around this event, dazed and preoccupied, the lover moves examining his or her own experience; her gratitude alone, stretching away towards a mistaken donor, creates the illusion that she communicates with her fellow, but this is false. The loved object is simply one that has shared an experience at the same moment of time, narcissistically; and the desire to be near the beloved object is at first not due to the idea of possessing it, but simply to let the two experiences compare themselves, like reflections in different mirrors. All this may precede the first look, kiss, or touch; precede ambition, pride or envy; precede the first declarations which mark the turning point — for from here love degenerates into habit, possession, and back to loneliness.' How characteristic and how humourless a delineation of the magical gift: and yet how true . . . of Justine!

'Every man' she writes elsewhere, and here I can hear the hoarse and sorrowful accents of her voice repeating the words as she writes them: 'Every man is made of clay and daimon, and no woman can nourish both.'

That afternoon she went home to find that Nessim had arrived by the afternoon plane. She complained of feeling feverish and went early to bed. When he came to sit by her side and take her temperature she said something which struck him as interesting enough to remember — for long afterwards he repeated it to me: 'This is nothing of medical interest — a small chill. Diseases are not interested in those who want to die.' And then with one of those characteristic swerves of association, like a swallow turning in mid-air she added, 'Oh! Nessim, I have always been so strong. Has it prevented me from being truly loved?'

*　　*　　*　　*　　*

It was through Nessim that I first began to move with any free-dom in the great cobweb of Alexandrian society; my own exiguous earnings did not even permit me to visit the night-club where Melissa danced. At first I was a trifle ashamed of being forever on the receiving end of Nessim's hospitality, but we were soon such fast friends that I went everywhere with them and never gave the matter a thought. Melissa unearthed an ancient dinner-jacket from one of my trunks and refurbished it. It was in their company that I first visited the club where she danced. It was strange to sit between Justine and Nessim and watch the flaky white light suddenly blaze down upon a Melissa I could no longer recognize under a layer of paint which gave her gentle face an air of gross and precocious unimaginativeness. I was horrified too at the banality of her dancing, which was bad beyond measure; yet watching her make those gentle and ineffectual movements of her slim hands and feet (the air of a gazelle harnessed to a water-wheel) I was filled with tenderness at her mediocrity, at the dazed and self-deprecating way she bowed to the lukewarm applause. Afterwards she was made to carry a tray round and take up a collection for the orchestra, and this she did with a hopeless timidity, coming to the table where I sat with lowered eyes under those ghastly false lashes, and with trembling hands. My friends did not know at that time of our relationship; but I noticed Justine's curious and mocking glance as I turned out my pockets and found a few notes to thrust into the tray with hands that shook not less than Melissa's — so keenly did I feel her embarrassment.

Afterwards when I got back to the flat a little tipsy and exhilarated from dancing with Justine I found her still awake, boiling a kettle of water over the electric ring: 'Oh, why' she said 'did you put all that money into the collecting tray? A whole week's wages: are you mad? What will we eat tomorrow?'

We were both hopelessly improvident in money matters, yet somehow we managed better together than apart. At night, walking back late from the night-club, she would pause in the alley outside the house and if she saw my light still burning give a low whistle and I, hearing the signal, would put down the book I was reading and creep quietly down the staircase, seeing in my mind's eye her lips pursed about that low liquid sound, as if to take the soft imprint of a brush. At the time of which I write she was still being followed about and importuned by the old man or his agents. Without exchanging a word we would join hands and hurry down the maze of alleys by the Polish Consulate, pausing from time to time in a dark doorway to see if there was anyone on our trail. At last, far down where the shops tailed away into the blue we would step out into the sea-gleaming milk-white Alexandrian midnight — our preoccupations sliding from us in that fine warm air; and we would walk towards the morning star which lay throbbing above the dark velvet breast of Montaza, touched by the wind and the waves.

In these days Melissa's absorbed and provoking gentleness had all the qualities of a rediscovered youth. Her long uncertain fingers — I used to feel them moving over my face when she thought I slept, as if to memorize the happiness we had shared. In her there was a pliancy, a resilience which was Oriental — a passion to serve. My shabby clothes — the way she picked up a dirty shirt seemed to engulf it with an overflowing solicitude; in the morning I found my razor beautifully cleaned and even the toothpaste laid upon the brush in readiness. Her care for me was a goad, provoking me to give my life some sort of shape and style that might match the simplicity of hers. Of her experiences in love she would never speak, turning from them with a weariness and distaste which suggested that they had been born of necessity rather than desire. She paid me the compliment of saying: 'For the first time I am not afraid to be light-headed or foolish with a man.'

Being poor was also a deep bond. For the most part our excursions were the simple excursions that all provincials make in a sea-side town. The little tin tram bore us with the clicking of its wheels to the sand-beaches of Sidi Bishr, or we spent Shem El Nessim in the gardens of Nouzha, camped on the grass under the oleanders among some dozens of humble Egyptian families. The inconvenience of crowds brought us both distraction and great intimacy. By the rotting canal watching the children dive for coins in the ooze, or eating a fragment of water-melon from a stall we wandered among the other idlers of the city, anonymously happy. The very names of the tram stops echoed the poetry of these journeys: Chatby, Camp de César, Laurens, Mazarita, Glymenopoulos, Sidi Bishr. . . .

Then there was the other side: coming back late at night to find her asleep with her red slippers kicked off and the little hashish-pipe beside her on the pillow . . . I would know that one of her depressions had set in. At such times there was nothing to be done with her; she would become pale, melancholy, exhausted-looking, and would be unable to rouse herself from her lethargy for days at a time. She talked much to herself, and would spend hours listening to the radio and yawning, or going negligently through a bundle of old film magazines. At such times when the *cafard* of the city seized her I was at my wits' end to devise a means of rousing her. She would lie with far-seeing eyes like a sibyl, stroking my face and repeating over and over again: 'If you knew how I have lived you would leave me. I am not the woman for you, for any man. I am exhausted. Your kindness is wasted.' If I protested that it was not kindness but love she might say with a grimace: 'If it were love you would poison me rather than let me go on like this.' Then she would begin to cough with her uncollapsed lung and, unable to bear the sound, I would go for a walk in the dark Arab-smudged street, or visit the British Council library to consult reference books: and here, where the general impression of British culture suggested parsimony, indigence, intellectual strap-hanging — here I would pass the evening alone, glad of the studious rustle and babble around me.

But there were other times too: those sun-tormented afternoons — 'honey-sweating,' as Pombal called them — when we lay together bemused by the silence, watching the yellow curtains breathing tenderly against the light — the quiet respirations of the wind off Mareotis which matched our own. Then she might rise and consult the clock after giving it a shake and listening to it intently: sit naked at the dressing-table to light a cigarette — looking so young and pretty, with her slender arm raised to show the cheap bracelet I had given her. ('Yes, I am looking at myself, but it helps me to think about you.') And turning aside from this fragile mirror-worship she would swiftly cross to the ugly scullery which was my only bath-room, and standing at the dirty iron sink would wash herself with deft swift movements, gasping at the coldness of the water, while I lay inhaling the warmth and sweetness of the pillow upon which her dark head had been resting: watching the long bereft Greek face, with its sane pointed nose and candid eyes, the satiny skin that is given only to the thymus-dominated, the mole upon her slender stalk of the neck. These are the moments which are not calculable, and cannot be assessed in words; they live on in the solution of memory, like wonderful creatures, unique of their kind, dredged up from the floors of some unexplored ocean.

*　　*　　*　　*　　*

Thinking of that summer when Pombal decided to let his flat to Pursewarden, much to my annoyance. I disliked this literary figure for the contrast he offered to his own work — poetry and prose of real grace. I did not know him well but he was financially successful as a novelist which made me envious, and through years of becoming social practice had developed a sort of *savoir faire* which I felt should never become part of my own equipment. He was clever, tallish and blond and gave the impression of a young man lying becalmed in his mother. I cannot say that he was not kind or good, for he was both — but the inconvenience of living in the flat with someone I did not like was galling. However it would have involved greater inconvenience to move so I accepted the box-room at the end of the corridor at a reduced rent, and did my washing in the grimy little scullery.

Pursewarden could afford to be convivial and about twice a week I was kept up by the noise of drinking and laughter from the flat. One night quite late there came a knock at the door. In the corridor stood Pursewarden, looking pale and rather perky — as if he had just been fired out of a gun into a net. Beside him stood a stout naval stoker of unprepossessing ugliness — looking like all naval stokers; as if he had been sold into slavery as a child. 'I say' said Pursewarden shrilly, 'Pombal told me you were a doctor; would you come and take a look at somebody who is ill?' I had once told Georges of the year I spent as a medical student with the result that for him I had become a fully-fledged doctor. He not only confided all his own indispositions to my care — which included frequent infestations of body-crabs — but he once went so far as to try and persuade me to perform an abortion for him on the dining-room table. I hastened to tell Pursewarden that I was certainly not a doctor, and advised him to telephone for one: but the phone was out of order, and the *boab* could not be roused from his sleep: so more in the spirit of disinterested curiosity than anything I put on a mackintosh over my pyjamas and made my way along the corridor. This was how we met!

Opening the door I was immediately blinded by the glare and smoke. The party did not seem to be of the usual kind, for the guests consisted of three or four maimed-looking naval cadets, and a prostitute from Golfo's tavern, smelling of briny paws and *taphia*.* Improbably enough, too, she was bending over a figure seated on the end of a couch — the figure which I now recognize as Melissa, but which then seemed like a catastrophic Greek comic mask. Melissa appeared to be raving, but soundlessly for her voice had gone — so that she looked like a film of herself without a sound-track. Her features were a cave. The older woman appeared to be panic-sticken, and was boxing her ears and pulling her hair; while one of the naval cadets was splashing water rather inexpertly upon her from a heavily decorated chamber-pot which was one of Pombal's dearest treasures and which bore the royal arms of France on its underside. Somewhere out of sight someone was being slowly, unctuously sick. Pursewarden stood beside me surveying the scene, looking rather ashamed of himself.

Melissa was pouring with sweat, and her hair was glued to her temples; as we broke the circle of her tormentors she sank back into an expressionless quivering silence, with this permanently engraved shriek on her face. It would have been wise to try and find out where she had been and what she had been eating and drinking, but a glance at the maudlin, jabbering group around me showed that it would be impossible to get any sense out of them. Nevertheless, seizing the boy nearest me I started to interrogate him when the hag from Golfo's, who was herself in a state of hysterics, and was only restrained by a naval stoker (who had her pinioned from behind), began to shout in a hoarse chewed voice. 'Spanish fly. He gave it to her.' And darting out of the arms of her captor like a rat she seized her handbag and fetched one of the sailors a resounding crack over the head. The bag must have been full of nails for he went down swimming and came up with fragments of shattered crockery in his hair.

She now began to sob in a voice which wore a beard and call for the police. Three sailors converged upon her with blunt fingers extended advising, exhorting, imploring her to desist. Nobody wanted a brush with the naval police. But neither did anyone relish a crack from that Promethean handbag, bulging with french letters and belladonna bottles. She retreated carefully step by step. (Meanwhile I took Melissa's pulse, and ripping off her blouse listened to her heart. I began to be alarmed for her, and indeed for Pursewarden who had taken up a strategic position behind an armchair and was making eloquent gestures at everyone.) By now the fun had started, for the sailors had the roaring girl cornered — but unfortunately against the decorative Sheraton cupboard which housed Pombal's cherished collection of pottery. Reaching behind her for support her hands encountered an almost inexhaustible supply of ammunition, and letting go her handbag with a hoarse cry of triumph she began to throw china with a single-mindedness and accuracy I have never seen equalled. The air was all at once full of Egyptian and Greek tear-bottles, Ushabti, and Sèvres. It could not be long now before there came the familiar and much-dreaded banging of hob-nailed boots against the door-lintels, as lights were beginning to go on all round us in the building. Pursewarden's alarm was very marked indeed; as a resident and moreover a famous one he could hardly afford the sort of scandal which the Egyptian press might make out of an affray like this. He was relieved when I motioned to him and started to wrap the by now almost insensible figure of Melissa in the soft Bukhara rug. Together we staggered with her down the corridor and into the blessed privacy of my box-room where, like Cleopatra, we unrolled her and placed her on the bed.

I had remembered the existence of an old doctor, a Greek, who lived down the street, and it was not long before I managed to fetch him up the dark staircase, stumbling and swearing in a transpontine demotic, dropping catheters and stethoscopes all the way. He pronounced Melissa very ill indeed but his diagnosis was ample and vague — in the tradition of the city. 'It is everything' he said,

'malnutrition, hysteria, alcohol, hashish, tuberculosis, Spanish fly
... help yourself' and he made the gesture of putting his hand in
his pocket and fetching it out full of imaginary diseases which he
offered us to choose from. But he was also practical, and proposed
to have a bed ready for her in the Greek Hospital next day. Meanwhile she was not to be moved.

I spent that night and the next on the couch at the foot of the
bed. While I was out at work she was confided to the care of one-
eyed Hamid, the gentlest of Berberines. For the first twelve hours
she was very ill indeed, delirious at times, and suffered agonizing
attacks of blindness — agonizing because they made her so afraid.
But by being gently rough with her we managed between us to
give her courage enough to surmount the worst, and by the afternoon of the second day she was well enough to talk in whispers.
The Greek doctor pronounced himself satisfied with her progress.
He asked her where she came from and a haunted expression came
into her face as she replied 'Smyrna'; nor would she give the name
and address of her parents, and when he pressed her she turned her
face to the wall and tears of exhaustion welled slowly out of her
eyes. The doctor took up her hand and examined the wedding-
finger. 'You see' he said to me with a clinical detachment, pointing
out the absence of a ring, 'that is why. Her family has disowned her
and turned her out of doors. It is so often these days . . .' and he
shook a shaggy commiserating head over her. Melissa said nothing.
but when the ambulance came and the stretcher was being prepared to take her away she thanked me warmly for my help, pressed
Hamid's hand to her cheek, and surprised me by a gallantry to
which my life had unaccustomed me: 'If you have no girl when I
come out, think of me. If you call me I will come to you.'* I do not
know how to reduce the gallant candour of the Greek to English.

So I had lost sight of her for a month or more; and indeed I did
not think of her, having many other preoccupations at this time.
Then, one hot blank afternoon, when I was sitting at my window
watching the city unwrinkle from sleep I saw a different Melissa
walk down the street and turn into the shadowy doorway of the
house. She tapped at my door and walked in with her arms full of
flowers, and all at once I found myself separated from that forgotten evening by centuries. She had in her something of the same
diffidence with which I later saw her take up a collection for the
orchestra in the night-club. She looked like a statue of pride hanging its head.

A nerve-racking politeness beset me. I offered her a chair and she sat upon the edge of it. The flowers were for me, yes, but she had not the courage to thrust the bouquet into my arms, and I could see her gazing distractedly around for a vase into which she might put them. There was only an enamel washbasin full of half-peeled potatoes. I began to wish she had not come. I would have liked to offer her some tea but my electric ring was broken and I had no money to take her out — at this time I was sliding ever more steeply into debt. Besides, I had sent Hamid out to have my only summer suit ironed and was clad in a torn dressing-gown. She for her part looked wonderfully, intimidatingly smart, with a new summer frock of a crisp vine-leaf pattern and a straw hat like a great gold bell. I began to pray passionately that Hamid would come back and create a diversion. I would have offered her a cigarette but my packet was empty and I was forced to accept one of her own from the little filigree cigarette-case she always carried. This I smoked with what I hoped was an air of composure and told her that I had accepted a new job near Sidi Gabr, which would mean a little extra money. She said she was going back to work; her contract had been renewed: but they were giving her less money. After a few minutes of this sort of thing she said that she must be leaving as she had a tea-appointment. I showed her out on the landing and asked her to come again whenever she wished. She thanked me, still clutching the flowers which she was too timid to thrust upon me and walked slowly downstairs. After she had gone I sat on the bed and uttered every foul swear-word I could re-member in four languages — though it was not clear to me whom I was addressing. By the time one-eyed Hamid came shuffling in I was still in a fury and turned my anger upon him. This startled him considerably: it was a long time since I had lost my temper with him, and he retired into the scullery muttering and shaking his head and invoking the spirits to help him.

After I had dressed and managed to borrow some money from Pursewarden — while I was on my way to post a letter — I saw Melissa again sitting in the corner of a coffee shop, alone, with her hands supporting her chin. Her hat and handbag lay beside her and she was staring into her cup with a wry reflective air of amusement. Impulsively I entered the place and sat down beside her. I had come, I said, to apologize for receiving her so badly, but . . . and I began to describe the circumstances which had preoccupied me, leaving nothing out. The broken electric-ring, the absence of

Hamid, my summer-suit. As I began to enumerate the evils by which I was beset they began to seem to me slightly funny, and altering my angle of approach I began to recount them with a lugubrious exasperation which coaxed from her one of the most delightful laughs I have ever heard. On the subject of my debts I frankly exaggerated, though it was certainly a fact that since the night of the affray Pursewarden was always ready to lend me small sums of money without hesitation. And then to cap it all, I said, she had appeared while I was still barely cured of a minor but irritating venereal infection — the fruit of Pombal's solicitude — contracted no doubt from one of the Syrians he had thoughtfully left behind him. This was a lie but I felt impelled to relate it in spite of myself. I had been horrified I said at the thought of having to make love again before I was quite well. At this she put out her hand and placed it on mine while she laughed, wrinkling up her nose: laughing with such candour, so lightly and effortlessly, that there and then I decided to love her.

We idled arm in arm by the sea that afternoon, our conversations full of the débris of lives lived without forethought, without architecture. We had not a taste in common. Our characters and predispositions were wholly different, and yet in the magical ease of this friendship we felt something promised us. I like, also, to remember that first kiss by the sea, the wind blowing up a flake of hair at each white temple — a kiss broken off by the laughter which beset her as she remembered my account of the trials I was enduring. It symbolized the passion we enjoyed, its humour and lack of intenseness: its charity.

*   *   *   *   *

Two subjects upon which it was fruitless to question Justine too closely: her age, her origins. Nobody — possibly not even, I believe, Nessim himself — knew all about her with any certainty. Even the city's oracle Mnemjian seemed for once at loss, though he was knowledgeable about her recent love affairs. Yet the violet eyes narrowed as he spoke of her and hesitantly he volunteered the information that she came from the dense Attarine Quarter, and had been born of a poor Jewish family which had since emigrated to Salonika. The diaries are not very helpful either since they lack clues — names, dates, places — and consist for the most part of wild flights of fancy punctuated by bitter little anecdotes and sharp line-drawings of people whose identity is masked by a letter of the alphabet. The French she writes in is not very correct, but spirited and highly-flavoured; and carries the matchless quality of that husky speaking-voice. Look: 'Clea speaking of her childhood: thinking of mine, passionately thinking. The childhood of my race, my time. . . . Blows first in the hovel behind the Stadium; the clock-mender's shop. I see myself now caught in the passionate concentration of watching a lover's sleeping face as I so often saw him bent over a broken timepiece with the harsh light pouring down noiselessly over him. Blows and curses, and printed everywhere on the red mud walls (like the blows struck by conscience) the imprint of blue hands, fingers outstretched, that guarded us against the evil eye. With these blows we grew up, aching heads, flinching eyes. A house with an earthen floor alive with rats, dim with wicks floating upon oil. The old money-lender drunk and snoring, drawing in with every breath the compost-odours, soil, excrement, the droppings of bats; gutters choked with leaves and breadcrumbs softened by piss; yellow wreaths of jasmine, heady, meretricious. And then add screams in the night behind other shutters in that crooked street: the *bey* beating his wives because he was impotent. The old herb-woman selling herself every night on the flat ground among the razed houses — a sulky mysterious whining. The soft *pelm* noise of bare black feet passing on the baked mud street, late at night. Our room bulging with darkness and pestilence, and we Europeans in such disharmony with the fearful animal health of the blacks around us. The copulations of boabs shaking the house like a palm-tree. Black tigers with gleaming teeth. And everywhere the veils, the screaming, the mad giggle under the pepper-trees, the insanity and the lepers. Such things as children see and store up to fortify or disorient their lives. A camel has collapsed from exhaustion in the street outside the house. It is too heavy to transport to the slaughter-house so a couple of men come with axes and cut it up there and then in the open street, alive. They hack through the white flesh — the poor creature looking ever more pained, more aristocratic, more puzzled as its legs are hacked off. Finally there is the head still alive, the eyes open, looking round. Not a scream of protest, not a struggle. The animal submits like a palm-tree. But for days afterwards the mud street is soaked in its blood and our bare feet are printed by the moisture.

'Money falling into the tin bowls of beggars. Fragments of every language — Armenian, Greek, Amharic, Moroccan Arabic; Jews from Asia Minor, Pontus, Georgia: mothers born in Greek settlements on the Black Sea; communities cut down like the branches of trees, lacking a parent body, dreaming of Eden. These are the poor quarters of the white city; they bear no resemblance to those lovely streets built and decorated by foreigners where the brokers sit and sip their morning papers. Even the harbour does not exist for us here. In the winter, sometimes, rarely, you can hear the thunder of a siren — but it is another country. Ah! the misery of harbours and the names they conjure when you are going nowhere. It is like a death — a death of the self uttered in every repetition of the word *Alexandria, Alexandria.*'

* * * * *

Rue Bab-el-Mandeb, Rue Abou-el-Dardar, Minet-el-Bassal (streets slippery with discarded fluff from the cotton marts) Nouzha (the rose-garden, some remembered kisses) or bus stops with haunted names like Saba Pacha, Mazloum, Zizinia Bacos, Schutz, Gianaclis. A city becomes a world when one loves one of its inhabitants.

* * * * *

One of the consequences of frequenting the great house was that I began to be noticed and to receive the attention of those who considered Nessim influential and presumed that if he spent his time with me I must also, in some undiscovered fashion, be either rich or distinguished. Pombal came to my room one afternoon while I was dozing and sat on my bed: 'Look here' he said, 'you are beginning to be noticed. Of course a *cicisbeo* is a normal enough figure in Alexandrian life, but things are going to become socially very boring for you if you go out with those two so much. Look!' And he handed me a large and florid piece of pasteboard with a printed invitation on it for cocktails at the French Consulate. I read it uncomprehendingly. Pombal said: 'This is very silly. My chief, the Consul-General, is impassionated by Justine. All attempts to meet her have failed so far. His spies tell him that you have an entrée into the family circle, indeed that you are . . . I know, I know. But he is hoping to displace you in her affections.' He laughed heavily. Nothing sounded more preposterous to me at this time. 'Tell the Consul-General' I said . . . and uttered a forcible remark or two which caused Pombal to click his tongue reprovingly and shake his head. 'I would love to' he said 'but, *mon cher*, there

57

is a Pecking Order among diplomats as there is among poultry. I depend upon him for my little cross.'

Heaving his bulk round he next produced from his pocket a battered little yellow-covered novelette and placed it on my knees. 'Here is something to interest you. Justine was married when she was very young to a French national, Albanian by descent, a writer. This little book is about her — a post-mortem on her; it is quite decently done.' I turned the novel over in my hands. It was entitled *Moeurs* and it was by a certain Jacob Arnauti. The flyleaf showed it to have enjoyed numerous reprintings in the early thirties. 'How do you know this?' I asked, and Georges winked a large, heavy-lidded reptilian eye as he replied. 'We have been making enquiries. The Consul can think of nothing but Justine, and the whole staff has been busy for weeks collecting information about her. *Vive la France!*'

When he had gone I started turning the pages of *Moeurs*, still half-dazed by sleep. It was very well written indeed, in the first person singular, and was a diary of Alexandrian life as seen by a foreigner in the early thirties. The author of the diary is engaged on research for a novel he proposes to do — and the day to day account of his life in Alexandria is accurate and penetrating; but what arrested me was the portrait of a young Jewess he meets and marries: takes to Europe: divorces. The foundering of this marriage on their return to Egypt is done with a savage insight that throws into relief the character of Claudia, his wife. And what astonished and interested me was to see in her a sketch of Justine I recognized without knowing: a younger, a more disoriented Justine, to be sure. But unmistakable. Indeed whenever I read the book, and this was often, I was in the habit of restoring her name to the text. It fitted with an appalling verisimilitude.

They met, where I had first seen her, in the gaunt vestibule of the Cecil, in a mirror. 'In the vestibule of this moribund hotel the palms splinter and refract their motionless fronds in the gilt-edged mirrors. Only the rich can afford to stay permanently — those who live on in the guilt-edged security of a pensionable old age. I am looking for cheaper lodgings. In the lobby tonight a small circle of Syrians, heavy in their dark suits, and yellow in their scarlet *tarbushes*, solemnly sit. Their hippopotamus-like womenfolk, lightly moustached, have jingled off to bed in their jewellery. The men's curious soft oval faces and effeminate voices are busy upon jewel-boxes — for each of these brokers carries his

choicest jewels with him in a casket; and after dinner the talk has
turned to male jewellery. It is all the Mediterranean world has left
to talk about; a self-interest, a narcissism which comes from sexual
exhaustion expressing itself in the possessive symbol: so that meeting a man you are at once informed what he is worth, and meeting
his wife you are told in the same breathless whisper what her
dowry was. They croon like eunuchs over the jewels, turning them
this way and that in the light to appraise them. They flash their
sweet white teeth in little feminine smiles. They sigh. A white-
robed waiter with a polished ebony face brings coffee. A silver
hinge flies open upon heavy white (like the thighs of Egyptian
women) cigarettes each with its few flecks of *hashish*. A few grains
of drunkenness before bedtime. I have been thinking about the
girl I met last night in the mirror: dark on marble-ivory white:
glossy black hair: deep suspiring eyes in which one's glances sink
because they are nervous, curious, turned to sexual curiosity. She
pretends to be a Greek, but she must be Jewish. It takes a Jew to
smell out a Jew; and neither of us has the courage to confess our
true race. I have told her I am French. Sooner or later we shall
find one another out.

'The women of the foreign communities here are more beautiful
than elsewhere. Fear, insecurity dominates them. They have the
illusion of foundering in the ocean of blackness all around. This
city has been built like a dyke to hold back the flood of African
darkness; but the soft-footed blacks have already started leaking
into the European quarters: a sort of racial osmosis is going on.
To be happy one would have to be a Moslem, an Egyptian woman
— absorbent, soft, lax, overblown; given to veneers; their waxen
skins turn citron-yellow or melon-green in the naphtha-flares.
Hard bodies like boxes. Breasts apple-green and hard — a reptilian coldness of the outer flesh with its bony outposts of toes and
fingers. Their feelings are buried in the pre-conscious. In love they
give out nothing of themselves, having no self to give, but enclose
themselves around you in an agonized reflection — an agony of
unexpressed yearning that is at the opposite pole from tenderness,
pleasure. For centuries now they have been shut in a stall with the
oxen, masked, circumcised. Fed in darkness on jams and scented
fats they have become tuns of pleasure, rolling on paper-white
blue-veined legs.

'Walking through the Egyptian quarter the smell of flesh
changes — ammoniac, sandal-wood, saltpetre, spice, fish. She

would not let me take her home — no doubt because she was ashamed of her house in these slums. Nevertheless she spoke wonderfully about her childhood. I have taken a few notes: returning home to find her father breaking walnuts with a little hammer on the table by the light of an oil-lamp. I can see him. He is no Greek but a Jew from Odessa in fur cap with greasy ringlets. Also the kiss of the Berberin, the enormous rigid penis like an obsidian of the ice age; leaning to take her underlip between beautiful unfiled teeth. We have left Europe behind here and are moving towards a new spiritual latitude. She gave herself to me with such contempt that I was for the first time in my life surprised at the quality of her anxiety; it was as if she were desperate, swollen with disaster. And yet these women belonging to these lost communities have a desperate bravery very different to ours. They have explored the flesh to a degree which makes them true foreigners to us. How am I to write about all this? Will she come, or has she disappeared forever? The Syrians are going to bed with little cries, like migrating birds.'

She comes. They talk. ('Under the apparent provincial sophistication and mental hardness I thought I detected an inexperience, not of the world to be sure but of society. I was interesting, I realized, as a foreigner with good manners — and she turned upon me now the shy-wise regard of an owl from those enormous brown eyes whose faintly bluish eyeballs and long lashes threw into relief the splendour of the pupils, glittering and candid.')

It may be imagined with what breathless, painful anxiety I first read this account of a love-affair with Justine; and truly after many re-readings the book, which I now know almost by heart, has always remained for me a document, full of personal pain and astonishment. 'Our love' he writes in another place 'was like a syllogism to which the true premises were missing: I mean regard. It was a sort of mental possession which trapped us both and set us to drift upon the shallow tepid waters of Mareotis like spawning frogs, a prey to instincts based in lassitude and heat. . . . No, that is not the way to put it. It is not very just. Let me try again with these infirm and unstable tools to sketch Claudia. Where shall we begin?

'Well, her talent for situations had served her well for twenty years of an erratic and unpunctual life. Of her origins I learned little, save that she had been very poor. She gave me the impression of someone engaged in giving a series of savage caricatures of herself — but this is common to most lonely people who feel that their true self can find no correspondence in another. The speed with which she moved from one milieu to another, from one man, place, date to another, was staggering. But her instability had a magnificence that was truly arresting. The more I knew her the less predictable she seemed; the only constant was the frantic struggle to break through the barrier of her autism. And every action ended in error, guilt, repentance. How often I remember — "Darling, this time it will be different, I promise you."

'Later, when we went abroad: at the Adlon, the pollen of the spotlights playing upon the Spanish dancers fuming in the smoke of a thousand cigarettes; by the dark waters of Buda, her tears dropping hotly among the quietly flowing dead leaves; riding on the gaunt Spanish plains, the silence pock-marked by the sound of our horses' hooves: by the Mediterranean lying on some forgotten reef. It was never her betrayals that upset me — for with Justine the question of male pride in possession became somehow secondary. I was bewitched by the illusion that I could really come to know her; but I see now that she was not really a woman but the incarnation of Woman admitting no ties in the society we inhabited. "I hunt everywhere for a life that is worth living. Perhaps if I could die or go mad it would provide a focus for all the feelings I have which find no proper outlet. The doctor I loved told me I was a nymphomaniac — but there is no gluttony or self-indulgence in my pleasure, Jacob. It is purely wasted from that point of view. The waste, my dear, the waste! You speak of taking pleasure sadly, like the puritans do. Even there you are unjust to me. I take it tragically, and if my medical friends want a compound word to describe the heartless creature I seem, why they will have to admit that what I lack of heart I make up in soul. That is where the trouble lies." These are not, you see, the sort of distinctions of which women are usually capable. It was as if somehow her world lacked a dimension, and love had become turned inwards into a kind of idolatry. At first I mistook this for a devastating and self-consuming egotism, for she seemed so ignorant of the little prescribed loyalties which constitute the foundations of affection between men and women. This sounds pompous, but never mind. But now, remembering the panics and exaltations which she endured, I wonder whether I was right. I am thinking of those tiresome dramas — scenes in furnished bedrooms, with Justine turning on the taps to drown the noise of her own crying. Walking up and down, hugging her arms in her armpits, muttering to herself, she seemed to smoulder like a tar-barrel on the point of explosion. My indifferent health and poor nerves — but above all my European sense of humour — seemed at such times to goad her beyond endurance. Suffering, let us say, from some imagined slight at a dinner-party she would patrol the strip of carpet at the foot of the bed like a panther. If I fell asleep she might become enraged and shake my by the shoulders, crying: "Get up, Jacob, I am suffering, can't you see?" When I declined to take part in this charade she would perhaps break something upon the dressing-table in order to have an excuse to ring the bell. How many fearful faces of night-maids have I not seen confronted by this wild figure saying with a terrifying politeness: "Oblige me by clearing up the dressing-table. I have clumsily broken something." Then she would sit smoking cigarette after cigarette. "I know exactly what this is" I told her once. "I expect that every time you are unfaithful to me and consumed by guilt you would like to provoke me to beat you up and give a sort of remission for your sins. My dear, I simply refuse to pander to your satisfactions. You must carry your own burdens. You are trying hard to get me to use a stockwhip on you. But I only pity you." This, I must confess, made her very thoughtful for a moment and involuntarily her hands strayed to touch the smooth surface of the legs she had so carefully shaved that afternoon. . . .

'Latterly, too, when I began to weary of her, I found this sort of abuse of the emotions so tiresome that I took to insulting her and laughing at her. One night I called her a tiresome hysterical Jewess. Bursting into those terrible hoarse sobs which I so often heard that even now in memory the thought of them (their richness, their melodious density) hurts me, she flung herself down on her own bed to lie, limbs loose and flaccid, played upon by the currents of her hysteria like jets from a hose.

'Did this sort of thing happen so often or is it that my memory has multiplied it? Perhaps it was only once, and the echoes have misled me. At any rate I seem to hear so often the noise she made unstopping the bottle of sleeping tablets, and the small sound of the tablets falling into the glass. Even when I was dozing I would count, to see that she did not take too many. All this was much later, of course; in the early days I would ask her to come into my bed and self-conscious, sullen, cold, she would obey me. I was foolish enough to think that I could thaw her out and give her the physical peace upon which — I thought — mental peace must depend. I was wrong. There was some unresolved inner knot which she wished to untie and which was quite beyond my skill as a lover or a friend. Of course. Of course. I knew as much as could be known of the psychopathology of hysteria at that time. But there was some other quality which I thought I could detect behind all this. In a way she was not looking for life but for some integrating revelation which would give it point.

'I have already described how we met — in the long mirror of the Cecil, before the open door of the ballroom, on a night of carnival. The first words we spoke were spoken, symbolically enough, in the mirror. She was there with a man who resembled a cuttle-fish and who waited while she examined her dark face attentively. I stopped to adjust an unfamiliar bow-tie. She had a hungry natural candour which seemed proof against any suggestion of forwardness as she smiled and said: "There is never enough light." To which I responded without thought: "For women perhaps. We men are less exigent." We smiled and I passed her on my way to the ballroom, ready to walk out of her mirror-life forever, without a thought. Later the hazards of one of those awful English dances, called the Paul Jones I believe, left me facing her for a waltz. We spoke a few disjointed words — I dance badly; and here I must confess that her beauty made no impression on me. It was only later when she began her trick of drawing hasty ill-defined designs round my character, throwing my critical faculties into disorder by her sharp penetrating stabs; ascribing to me qualities which she invented on the spur of the moment out of that remorseless desire to capture my attention. Women must attack writers — and from the moment she learned I was a writer she felt disposed to make herself interesting by dissecting me. All this would have been most flattering to my *amour-propre* had some of her observations been further from the mark. But she was acute, and I was too feeble to resist this sort of game — the mental ambuscades which constitute the opening gambits of a flirtation.

'From here I remember nothing more until that night — that marvellous summer night on the moon-drenched balcony above the sea with Justine pressing a warm hand on my mouth to stop me talking and saying something like: "Quick. *Engorge-moi*. From desire to revulsion — let's get it over." She had, it seemed, already exhausted me in her own imagination. But the words were spoken with such weariness and humility — who could forbear to love her?

'It is idle to go over all this in a medium as unstable as words. I remember the edges and corners of so many meetings, and I see a sort of composite Justine, concealing a ravenous hunger for information, for power through self-knowledge, under a pretence of feeling. Sadly I am driven to wonder whether I ever really moved her — or existed simply as a laboratory in which she could work. She learned much from me: to read and reflect. She had achieved neither before. I even persuaded her to keep a diary in order to clarify her far from commonplace thoughts. But perhaps what I took to be love was merely a gratitude. Among the thousand discarded people, impressions, subjects of study — somewhere I see myself drifting, floating, reaching out arms. Strangely enough it was never in the *lover* that I really met her but in the *writer*. Here we clasped hands — in that amoral world of suspended judgements where curiosity and wonder seem greater than order — the syllogistic order imposed by the mind. This is where one waits in silence, holding one's breath, lest the pane should cloud over. I watched over her like this. I was mad about her.

'She had of course many secrets being a true child of the Mouseion, and I had to guard myself desperately against jealousy or the desire to intrude upon the hidden side of her life. I was almost successful in this and if I spied upon her it was really from curiosity to know what she might be doing or thinking when she was not with me. There was, for example, a woman of the town whom she visited frequently, and whose influence on her was profound enough to make me suspect an illicit relationship; there was also a man to whom she wrote long letters, though as far as I could see he lived in the city. Perhaps he was bedridden? I made inquiries, but my spies always brought me back uninteresting information. The woman was a fortune-teller, elderly, a widow. The man to whom she wrote — her pen shrilling across the cheap notepaper — turned out to be a doctor who held a small part-time post on a local consulate. He was not bedridden; but he was a homosexual, and dabbled in hermetic philosophy which is now so much in vogue. Once she left a particularly clear impression on my blotting-pad and in the mirror (the mirror again!) I was able to read:—"my life there is a sort of Unhealed Place as you call it which I try to keep full of people, accidents, diseases, anything that comes to hand. You are right when you say it is an apology for better living, wiser living. But while I respect your disciplines and your knowledge I feel that if I am ever going to come to terms

with myself I must work *through* the dross in my own character
and burn it up. Anyone could solve my problem artificially by
placing it in the lap of a priest. We Alexandrians have more pride
than that — and more respect for religion. It would not be fair to
God, my dear sir, and whoever else I fail (I see you smile) I am
determined not to fail Him whoever He is."

'It seemed to me then that if this was part of a love-letter it was
the kind of love-letter one could only address to a saint; and again
I was struck, despite the clumsiness and incorrectness of the
writing, by the fluency with which she could dissociate between
ideas of different categories. I began to see her in an altered light;
as somebody who might well destroy herself in an excess of wrong-
headed courage and forfeit the happiness which she, in common
with all the rest of us, desired and lived only to achieve. These
thoughts had the effect of qualifying my love for her, and I found
myself filled sometimes by disgust for her. But what made me
afraid was that after quite a short time I found to my horror that I
could not live without her. I tried. I took short journeys away from
her. But without her I found life full of consuming boredom which
was quite insupportable. I had fallen *in love*. The very thought
filled me with an inexplicable despair and disgust. It was as if I
unconsciously realized that in her I had met my evil genius. To
come to Alexandria heart-whole and to discover an *amor fati* — it
was a stroke of ill-luck which neither my health nor my nerves
felt capable of supporting. Looking in the mirror I reminded myself that I had turned forty and already there was a white hair or
two at my temples! I thought once of trying to end this attachment,
but in every smile and kiss of Justine I felt my resolutions founder.
Yet with her one felt all around the companionship of shadows
which invaded life and filled it with a new resonance. Feeling so
rich in ambiguities could not be resolved by a sudden act of the
will. I had at times the impression of a woman whose every kiss
was a blow struck on the side of death. When I discovered, for
example (what I knew) that she had been repeatedly unfaithful to
me, and at times when I had felt myself to be closest to her, I felt
nothing very sharp in outline; rather a sinking numbness such as
one might feel on leaving a friend in hospital, to enter a lift and fall
six floors in silence, standing beside a uniformed automaton whose
breathing one could hear. The silence of my room deafened me.
And then, thinking about it, gathering my whole mind about the
fact I realized that what she had done bore no relation to myself: it

was an attempt to free herself for me: to give me what she knew belonged to me. I cannot say that this sounded any better to my ears than a sophistry. Nevertheless my heart seemed to know the truth of this and dictated a tactful silence to me to which she responded with a new warmth, a new ardour, of gratitude added to love. This again disgusted me somewhat.

'Ah! but if you had seen her then as I did in her humbler, gentler moments, remembering that she was only a child, you would not have reproached me for cowardice. In the early morning, sleeping in my arms, her hair blown across that smiling mouth, she looked like no other woman I could remember: indeed like no woman at all, but some marvellous creature caught in the Pleistocene stage of her development. And later again, thinking about her as I did and have done these past few years I was surprised to find that though I loved her wholly and knew that I should never love anyone else — yet I shrank from the thought that she might return. The two ideas co-existed in my mind without displacing one another. I thought to myself with relief "Good. I *have* really loved at last. That is something achieved"; and to this my alter ego added: "Spare me the pangs of love *requited* with Justine." This enigmatic polarity of feeling was something I found completely unexpected. If this was love then it was a variety of the plant which I have never seen before. ("Damn the word" said Justine once. "I would like to spell it backwards as you say the Elizabethans did God. Call it *evol* and make it a part of 'evolution' or 'revolt'. Never use the word to me.")'

*　　*　　*　　*　　*

These later extracts I have taken from the section of the diary which is called *Posthumous Life* and is an attempt the author makes to sum up and evaluate these episodes. Pombal finds much of this banal and even dull; but who, knowing Justine, could fail to be moved by it? Nor can it be said that the author's intentions are not full of interest. He maintains for example that real people can only exist in the imagination of an artist strong enough to contain them and give them form. 'Life, the raw material, is only lived *in potentia* until the artist deploys it in his work. Would that I could do this service of love for poor Justine.' (I mean, of course, 'Claudia'.) 'I dream of a book powerful enough to contain the elements of her — but it is not the sort of book to which we are accustomed these days. For example, on the first page a synopsis of the plot in a few lines. Thus we might dispense with the narrative articulation. What follows would be drama freed from the burden of form. *I would set my own book free to dream.*'

But of course one cannot escape so easily from the pattern which he regards as imposed but which in fact grows up organically within the work and appropriates it. What is missing in his work — but this is a criticism of all works which do not reach the front rank — is a sense of *play*. He bears down so hard upon his subject-matter; so hard that it infects his style with some of the unbalanced ferocity of Claudia herself. Then, too, everything which is a fund of emotion becomes of equal importance to him: a sign uttered by Claudia among the oleanders of Nouzha, the fireplace where she burnt the manuscript of his novel about her ('For days she looked at me as if she were trying to read my book in me'), the little room in the Rue Lepsius. . . . He says of his characters: 'All bound by time in a dimension which is not reality *as we would wish it to be* — but is created by the needs of the work. For all drama creates bondage, and the actor is only significant to the degree that he is bound.'

But setting these reservations aside, how graceful and accurate a portrait of Alexandria he manages to convey; Alexandria and its women. There are sketches here of Leonie, Gaby, Delphine — the pale rose-coloured one, the gold, the bitumen. Some one can identify quite easily from his pages. Clea, who still lives in that high studio, a swallow's nest made of cobwebs and old cloth — he has her unmistakably. But for the most part these Alexandrian girls are distinguished from women in other places only by a terrifying honesty and world-weariness. He is enough of a writer to have isolated these true qualities in the city of the Soma. One could not expect more from an intruder of gifts who almost by mistake pierced the hard banausic shell of Alexandria and discovered himself.

As for Justine herself, there are few if indeed any references to Arnauti in the heavily armoured pages of her diary. Here and there I have traced the letter A, but usually in passages abounding with the purest introspection. Here is one where the identification might seem plausible:

'What first attracted me in A was his room. There always seemed to me some sort of ferment going on there behind the heavy shutters. Books lay everywhere with their jackets turned inside out or covered in white drawing-paper — as if to hide their titles. A huge litter of newspapers with holes in them, as if a horde of mice had been feasting in them — A's cuttings from "real life" as he called it, the abstraction which he felt to be so remote from his own. He would sit down to his newspapers as if to a meal in a patched dressing-gown and velvet slippers, snipping away with a pair of blunt nail-scissors. He puzzled over "reality" in the world outside his work like a child; it was presumably a place where people could be happy, laugh, bear children.'

A few such sketches comprise the whole portrait of the author of *Moeurs*; it seems a meagre and disappointing reward for so much painstaking and loving observation; nor can I trace one word about their separation after this brief and fruitless marriage But it was interesting to see from his book how he had made the same judgements upon her character as we were later to make, Nessim and I. The compliance she extorted from us all was the astonishing thing about her. It was as if men knew at once that they were in the presence of someone who could not be judged according to the standards they had hitherto employed in thinking about women. Clea once said of her (and her judgements were seldom if ever charitable): 'The true whore is man's real darling — like Justine; she alone has the capacity to wound men. But of course our friend is only a shallow twentieth-century reproduction of the great *hetairae* of the past, the type to which she belongs without knowing it, Lais, Charis and the rest. . . . Justine's role has been taken from her and on her shoulders society has placed the burden of guilt to add to her troubles. It is a pity. For she is truly Alexandrian.'

For Clea too the little book of Arnauti upon Justine seemed shallow and infected by the desire to explain everything. 'It is our disease' she said 'to want to contain everything within the frame of reference of a psychology or a philosophy. After all Justine cannot be justified or excused. She simply and magnificently *is*; we have to put up with her, like original sin. But to call her a nympho-maniac or to try and Freudianise her, my dear, takes away all her mythical substance — the only thing she really is. Like all amoral people she verges on the Goddess. If our world were a world there would be temples to accommodate her where she would find the peace she was seeking. Temples where one could outgrow the sort of inheritance she has: not these damn monasteries full of pimply little Catholic youths who have made a bicycle saddle of their sexual organs.'

She was thinking of the chapters which Arnauti has entitled *The Check*, and in which he thinks he has found the clue to Justine's instability of heart. They may be, as Clea thinks, shallow, but since everything is susceptible of more than one explanation they are worth consideration. I myself do not feel that they explain Justine, but to a degree they do illuminate her actions — those immense journeys they undertook together across the length and breadth of Europe. 'In the very heart of passion' he writes, adding in parentheses '(passion which to her seemed the most facile of gifts) there was a check — some great impediment of feeling which I became aware of only after many months. It rose up between us like a shadow and I recognized, or thought I did, the true enemy of the happiness which we longed to share and from which we felt ourselves somehow excluded. What was it?

'She told me one night as we lay in that ugly great bed in a rented room — a gaunt rectangular room of a vaguely French-Levantine shape and flavour: a stucco ceiling covered with decomposing cherubs and posies of vine-leaves. She told me and left me raging with a jealousy I struggled to hide — but a jealousy of an entirely novel sort. Its object was a man who though still alive, *no longer existed.* It is perhaps what the Freudians would call a screen-memory of incidents in her earliest youth. She had (and there was no mistaking the force of this confession for it was accompanied by floods of tears, and I have never seen her weep like that before or since) — she had been raped by one of her relations. One cannot help smiling at the commonplaceness of the thought. It was impossible to judge at what age. Nevertheless — and here I thought I had penetrated to the heart of the Check: from this time forward she could obtain no satisfaction in love unless she mentally recreated these incidents and re-enacted them. For her we, her lovers, had become only mental substitutes for this first childish act — so that love, as a sort of masturbation, took on all the colours of neurasthenia; she was suffering from an imagination dying of anaemia, for she could possess no one thoroughly in the flesh. She could not appropriate to herself the love she felt she needed, for her satisfactions derived from the crepuscular corners of a life she was no longer living. This was passionately interesting. But what was even more amusing was that I felt this blow to my *amour propre* as a man exactly as if she had confessed to an act of deliberate unfaithfulness. What! Every time she lay in my arms she could find no satisfaction save through this memory? In a way,

c

then, I could not possess her: had never done so. I was merely a dummy. Even now as I write I cannot help smiling to remember the strangled voice in which I asked who the man was, and where he was. (What did I hope to do? Challenge him to a duel?) Nevertheless there he was, standing squarely between Justine and I; between Justine and the light of the sun.

'But here too I was sufficiently detached to observe how much love feeds upon jealousy, for as a woman out of my reach yet in my arms, she became ten times more desirable, more necessary. It was a heartbreaking predicament for a man who had no intention of falling in love, and for a woman who only wished to be delivered of an obsession and set free to love. From this something else followed: if I could break the Check I could possess her truly, as no man had possessed her. I could step into the place of the shadow and receive her kisses truly; now they fell upon a corpse. It seemed to me that I understood everything now.

'This explains the grand tour we took, hand in hand so to speak, in order to overcome this succubus together with help of science. Together we visited the book-lined cell of Czechnia, where the famous mandarin of psychology sat, gloating pallidly over his specimens. Basle, Zurich, Baden, Paris — the flickering of steel rails over the arterial systems of Europe's body: steel ganglia meeting and dividing away across mountains and valleys. Confronting one's face in the pimpled mirrors of the Orient Express. We carried her disease backwards and forwards over Europe like a baby in a cradle until I began to despair, and even to imagine that perhaps Justine did not wish to be cured of it. For to the involuntary check of the psyche she added another — of the will. Why this should be I cannot understand; but she would tell no one his name, the shadow's name. A name which by now could mean everything or nothing to her. After all, somewhere in the world he must be now, his hair thinning and greying from business worries or excesses, wearing a black patch over one eye as he did always after an attack of ophthalmia. (If I can describe him to you it is because once I actually saw him.) "Why should I tell people his name?" Justine used to cry. "He is nothing to me now — has never been. He has completely forgotten these incidents. Don't you see he is dead? When I see him. . . ." This was like being stung by a serpent. "So you do see him?" She immediately withdrew to a safer position. "Every few years, passing in the street. We just nod."

'So this creature, this pattern of ordinariness, was still breathing, still alive! How fantastic and ignoble jealousy is. But jealousy for a figment of a lover's imagination borders on the ludicrous.

'Then once, in the heart of Cairo, during a traffic jam, in the breathless heat of a midsummer night, a taxi drew up beside ours and something in Justine's expression drew my gaze in the direction of hers. In that palpitant moist heat, dense from the rising damp of the river and aching with the stink of rotten fruit, jasmine and sweating black bodies, I caught sight of the very ordinary man in the taxi next to us. Apart from the black patch over one eye there was nothing to distinguish him from the thousand other warped and seedy business men of this horrible city. His hair was thinning, his profile sharp, his eye beady: he was wearing a grey summer suit. Justine's expression of suspense and anguish was so marked however that involuntarily I cried: "What is it?"; and as the traffic block lifted and the cab moved off she replied with a queer flushed light in her eye, an air almost of drunken daring: "The man you have all been hunting for." But before the words were out of her mouth I had understood and as if in a bad dream stopped our own taxi and leaped out into the road. I saw the red tail light of his taxi turning into Sulieman Pacha, too far away for me even to be able to distinguish its colour or number. To give chase was impossible for the traffic behind us was dense once more. I got back into the taxi trembling and speechless. So this was the man for whose name Freud had hunted with all the great might of his loving detachment. For this innocent middle-aged man Justine had lain suspended, every nerve tense as if in the act of levitation, while the thin steely voice of Magnani had repeated over and over again: "Tell me his name; you must tell me his name"; while from the forgotten prospects where her memory lay confined her voice repeated like an oracle of the machine-age: "I cannot remember. I cannot remember."

'It seemed to me clear then that in some perverted way she did not wish to conquer the Check, and certainly all the power of the physicians could not persuade her. This was the bare case without orchestration, and here lay the so-called nymphomania with which these reverend gentlemen assured me that she was afflicted. At times I felt convinced that they were right; at others I doubted. Nevertheless it was tempting to see in her behaviour the excuse that every man held out for her the promise of a release in her passional self, release from this suffocating self-enclosure where sex could only be fed by the fat flames of fantasy.

'Perhaps we did wrong in speaking of it openly, of treating it as a problem, for this only invested her with a feeling of self-importance and moreover contributed a nervous hesitation to her which until then had been missing. In her passional life she was direct — like an axe falling. She took kisses like so many coats of paint. I am puzzled indeed to remember how long and how vainly I searched for excuses which might make her amorality if not palatable at least understandable. I realize now how much time I wasted in this way; instead of enjoying her and turning aside from these preoccupations with the thought: "She is as untrustworthy as she is beautiful. She takes love as plants do water, lightly, thoughtlessly." Then I could have walked arm in arm with her by the rotting canal, or sailed on sundrenched Mareotis, enjoying her as she was, taking her as she was. What a marvellous capacity for unhappiness we writers have! I only know that this long and painful examination of Justine succeeded not only in making her less sure of herself, but also more consciously dishonest; worst of all, she began to look upon me as an enemy who watched for the least misconstruction, the least word or gesture which might give her away. She was doubly on her guard, and indeed began to accuse me of an insupportable jealousy. Perhaps she was right. I remember her saying: "You live now among my imaginary intimacies. I was a fool to tell you everything, to be so honest. Look at the way you question me now. Several days running the same questions. And at the slightest discrepancy you are on me. You know I never tell a story the same way twice. Does that mean that I am lying?"

'I was not warned by this but redoubled my efforts to penetrate the curtain behind which I thought my adversary stood, a black patch over one eye. I was still in correspondence with Magnani and tried to collect as much evidence as possible which might help him elucidate the mystery, but in vain. In the thorny jungle of guilty impulses which constitute the human psyche who can find a way — even when the subject wishes to co-operate? The time we wasted upon futile researches into her likes and dislikes! If Justine had been blessed with a sense of humour what fun she could have had with us. I remember a whole correspondence based upon the confession that she could not read the words "Washington D.C." on a letter without a pang of disgust! It is a matter of deep regret to me now that I wasted this time when I should have been loving her as she deserved. Some of these doubts must also have afflicted old Magnani for I recall him writing: "and my dear boy we must never forget that this infant science we are working at, which seems so full of miracles and promises, is at best founded on much that is as shaky as astrology. After all, these important *names* we give to things! Nymphomania may be considered another form of virginity if you wish; and as for Justine, she may never have been in love. Perhaps one day she will meet a man before whom all these tiresome chimeras will fade into innocence again. You must not rule this thought out". He was not, of course, trying to hurt me — for this was a thought I did not care to admit to myself. But it penetrated me when I read it in this wise old man's letter.'

*   *   *   *   *

I had not read these pages of Arnauti before the afternoon at Bourg El Arab when the future of our relationship was compromised by the introduction of a new element — I do not dare to use the word love, for fear of hearing that harsh sweet laugh in my imagination: a laugh which would somewhere be echoed by the diarist. Indeed so fascinating did I find his analysis of his subject, and so closely did our relationship echo the relationship he had enjoyed with Justine that at times I too felt like some paper character out of *Moeurs*. Moreover, here I am, attempting to do the same sort of thing with her in words — though I lack his ability and have no pretensions to being an artist. I want to put things down simply and crudely, without style — the plaster and whitewash; for the portrait of Justine should be rough-cast, with the honest stonework of the predicament showing through.

After the episode of the beach we did not meet for some small time, both of us infected by a vertiginous uncertainty — or at least I was. Nessim was called away to Cairo on business but though Justine was, as far as I knew, at home alone, I could not bring myself to visit the studio. Once as I passed I heard the Blüthner and was tempted to ring the bell — so sharply defined was the image of her at the black piano. Then once passing the garden at night I saw someone — it must have been she — walking by the lily-pond, shading a candle in the palm of one hand. I stood for a moment uncertainly before the great doors wondering whether to ring or not. Melissa at this time also had taken the occasion to visit a friend in Upper Egypt. Summer was growing apace, and the town was sweltering. I bathed as often as my work permitted, travelling to the crowded beaches in the little tin tram.

Then one day while I was lying in bed with a temperature

brought on by an overdose of the sun Justine walked into the dank calm of the little flat, dressed in a white frock and shoes, and carrying a rolled towel under one arm with her handbag. The magnificence of her dark skin and hair glowed out of all this whiteness with an arresting quickness. When she spoke her voice was harsh and unsteady, and it sounded for a moment as if she had been drinking — perhaps she had. She put one hand out and leaned upon the mantelshelf as she said: 'I want to put an end to all this as soon as possible. I feel as if we've gone too far to go back.' As for me I was consumed by a terrible sort of desirelessness, a luxurious anguish of body and mind which prevented me from saying anything, thinking anything. I could not visualize the act of love with her, for somehow the emotional web we had woven about each other stood between us; an invisible cobweb of loyalties, ideas, hesitations which I had not the courage to brush aside. As she took a step forward I said feebly: 'This bed is so awful and smelly. I have been drinking. I tried to make love to myself but it was no good — I kept thinking about you.' I felt myself turning pale as I lay silent upon my pillows, all at once conscious of the silence of the little flat which was torn in one corner by the dripping of a leaky tap. A taxi brayed once in the distance, and from the harbour, like the stifled roar of a minotaur, came a single dark whiff of sound from a siren. Now it seemed we were completely alone together.

The whole room belonged to Melissa — the pitiful dressing-table full of empty powder-boxes and photos: the graceful curtain breathing softly in that breathless afternoon air like the sail of a ship. How often had we not lain in one another's arms watching the slow intake and recoil of that transparent piece of bright linen? Across all this, the image of someone dearly loved, held in the magnification of a gigantic tear moved the brown harsh body of Justine naked. It would have been blind of me not to notice how deeply her resolution was mixed with sadness. We lay eye to eye for a long time, our bodies touching, hardly communicating more than the animal lassitude of that vanishing afternoon. I could not help thinking then as I held her tightly in the crook of an arm how little we own our bodies. I thought of the words of Arnauti when he says: 'It dawned on me then that in some fearful way this girl had shorn me of all my *force morale*. I felt as if I had had my head shaved.' But the French, I thought, with their endless gravitation between *bonheur* and *chagrin* must inevitably suffer when they come up against something which does not admit of *préjugés*; born for tactics and virtuosity, not for staying-power, they lack the little touch of crassness which armours the Anglo-Saxon mind. And I thought: 'Good. Let her lead me where she will. She will find me a match for her. And there'll be no talk of *chagrin* at the end.' Then I thought of Nessim, who was watching us (though I did not know) as if through the wrong end of an enormous telescope: seeing our small figures away on the skyline of his own hopes and plans. I was anxious that he should not be hurt.

But she had closed her eyes — so soft and lustrous now, as if polished by the silence which lay so densely all around us. Her trembling fingers had become steady and at ease upon my shoulder. We turned to each other, closing like the two leaves of a door upon the past, shutting out everything, and I felt her happy spontaneous kisses begin to compose the darkness around us like successive washes of a colour. When we had made love and lay once more awake she said: 'I am always so bad the first time, why is it?'

'Nerves perhaps. So am I.'

'You are a little afraid of me.'

Then rising on an elbow as if I had suddenly woken up I said: 'But Justine, what on earth are we going to make of all this? If this is to be — ' But she became absolutely terrified now and put her hand over my mouth, saying: 'For God's sake, no justifications! Then I shall know we are wrong! For nothing can justify it, nothing. And yet it has got to be like this.' And getting out of bed she walked over to the dressing-table with its row of photos and powder-boxes and with a single blow like that of a leopard's paw swept it clean. '*That*' she said 'is what I am doing to Nessim and you to Melissa! It would be ignoble to try and pretend otherwise.' This was more in the tradition that Arnauti had led me to expect and I said nothing. She turned now and started kissing me with such a hungry agony that my burnt shoulders began to throb until tears came into my eyes. 'Ah!' she said softly and sadly. 'You are crying. I wish I could. I have lost the knack.'

I remember thinking to myself as I held her, tasting the warmth and sweetness of her body, salt from the sea — her earlobes tasted of salt — I remember thinking: 'Every kiss will take her near Nessim, but separate me further from Melissa.' But strangely enough I experienced no sense of despondency or anguish; and for her part she must have been thinking along the same lines for she suddenly said: 'Balthazar says that the natural traitors — like you and I — are really Caballi. He says we are dead and live this life as a sort of limbo. Yet the living can't do without us. We infect them with a desire to experience more, to grow.'

I tried to tell myself how stupid all this was — a banal story of an adultery which was among the cheapest commonplaces of the city: and how it did not deserve romantic or literary trappings. And yet somewhere else, at a deeper level, I seemed to recognize that the experience upon which I had embarked would have the deathless finality of a lesson learned. 'You are too serious' I said, with a certain resentment, for I was vain and did not like the sensation of being carried out of my depth. Justine turned her great eyes on me. 'Oh no!' she said softly, as if to herself 'It would be silly to spread so much harm as I have done and not to realize that it is my role. Only in this way, by knowing what I am doing, can I ever outgrow myself. It isn't easy to be me. I *so much* want to be responsible for myself. Please never doubt that.'

We slept, and I was only woken by the dry click of Hamid's key turning in the lock and by his usual evening performance. For a pious man, whose little prayer mat lay rolled and ready to hand on the kitchen balcony, he was extraordinarily superstitious. He was as Pombal said, 'djinn-ridden', and there seemed to be a djinn in every corner of the flat. How tired I had become of hearing his muttered '*Destoor, destoor*', as he poured slops down the kitchen sink — for here dwelt a powerful djinn and its pardon had to be invoked. The bathroom too was haunted by them, and I could always tell when Hamid used the outside lavatory (which he had been forbidden to do) because whenever he sat on the water-closet a hoarse involuntary invocation escaped his lips ('Permission O ye blessed ones!') which neutralized the djinn which might otherwise have dragged him down into the sewage system. Now I heard him shuffling round the kitchen in his old felt slippers like a boa-constrictor muttering softly.

I woke Justine from a troubled doze and explored her mouth and eyes and fine hair with the anguished curiosity which for me has always been the largest part of sensuality. 'We must be going' I said. 'Pombal will be coming back from the Consulate in a little while.'

I recall the furtive languor with which we dressed and silent as accomplices made our way down the gloomy staircase into the street. We did not dare to link arms, but our hands kept meeting involuntarily as we walked, as if they had not shaken off the spell of the afternoon and could not bear to be separated. We parted speechlessly too, in the little square with its dying trees burnt to the colour of coffee by the sun; parted with only one look — as if we wished to take up emplacements in each other's mind forever.

It was as if the whole city had crashed about my ears; I walked about in it aimlessly as survivors must walk about the streets of their native city after an earthquake, amazed to find how much that had been familiar was changed. I felt in some curious way deafened and remember nothing more except that much later I ran into Pursewarden and Pombal in a bar, and that the former recited some lines from the old poet's famous 'The City' which struck me with a new force — as if the poetry had been newly minted: though I knew them well. And when Pombal said: 'You are abstracted this evening. What is the matter?' I felt like answering him in the words of the dying Amr:* 'I feel as if heaven lay close upon the earth and I between them both, breathing through the eye of a needle.'

PART II

To have written so much and to have said nothing about Balthazar is indeed an omission — for in a sense he is one of the keys to the City. The key: Yes, I took him very much as he was in those days and now in my memory I feel that he is in need of a new evaluation. There was much that I did not understand then, much that I have since learned. I remember chiefly those interminable evenings spent at the Café Al Aktar playing backgammon while he smoked his favourite Lakadif in a pipe with a long stem. If Mnemjian is the archives of the City, Balthazar is its Platonic *daimon* — the mediator between its Gods and its men. It sounds far-fetched, I know.

I see a tall man in a black hat with a narrow brim. Pombal christened him 'the botanical goat'. He is thin, stoops slightly, and has a deep croaking voice of great beauty, particularly when he quotes or recites. In speaking to you he never looks at you directly — a trait which I have noticed in many homosexuals. But in him this does not signify inversion, of which he is not only not ashamed, but to which he is actually indifferent; his yellow goat-eyes are those of a hypnotist. In not looking at you he is sparing you from a regard so pitiless that it would discountenance you for an evening. It is a mystery how he can have, suspended from his trunk, hands of such monstrous ugliness. I would long since have cut them off and thrown them into the sea. Under his chin he has one dark spur of hair growing, such as one sometimes sees upon the hoof of a sculptured Pan.

Several times in the course of those long walks we took together, beside the sad velvet broth of the canal, I found myself wondering what was the quality in him which arrested me. This was before I knew anything about the Cabal. Though he reads widely Balthazar's conversation is not heavily loaded with the kind of material that might make one think him bookish: like Pursewarden. He loves poetry, parable, science and sophistry — but there is a lightness of touch and a judgement behind his thinking. Yet underneath the lightness there is something else — a resonance which gives his thinking density. His vein is aphoristic, and it sometimes gives him the touch of a minor oracle. I see now that he was one of those rare people who had found a philosophy for himself and whose life was occupied in trying to live it. I think this is the unanalysed quality which gives his talk cutting-edge.

As a doctor he spends much of his working-time in the government clinic for venereal disease. (He once said dryly: 'I live at the centre of the city's life — its genito-urinary system: it is a sobering sort of place.') Then, too, he is the only man whose paederasty is somehow no qualification of his innate masculinity of mind. He is neither a puritan nor its opposite. Often I have entered his little room in the Rue Lepsius — the one with the creaking cane chair — and found him asleep in bed with a sailor. He has neither excused himself at such a time nor even alluded to his bedfellow. While dressing he will sometimes turn and tenderly tuck the sheet round his partner's sleeping form. I take this naturalness as a compliment.

He is a strange mixture; at times I have heard his voice tremble with emotion as he alludes to some aspect of the Cabal which he has been trying to make comprehensible to the study-group. Yet once when I spoke enthusiastically of some remarks he had made he sighed and said, with that perfect Alexandrian scepticism which somehow underlay an unquestionable belief in and devotion to the Gnosis: 'We are all hunting for rational reasons for believing in the absurd.' At another time after a long and tiresome argument with Justine about heredity and environment he said: 'Ah! my dear, after all the work of the philosophers on his soul and the doctors on his body, what can we say we really know about man? That he is, when all is said and done, just a passage for liquids and solids, a pipe of flesh.'

He had been a fellow-student and close friend of the old poet, and of him he spoke with such warmth and penetration that what he had to say always moved me. 'I sometimes think that I learned more from studying him than I did from studying philosophy. His exquisite balance of irony and tenderness would have put him among the saints had he been a religious man. He was by divine choice only a poet and often unhappy but with him one had the feeling that he was catching every minute as it flew and turning it upside down to expose its happy side. He was really using himself up, his inner self, in living. Most people lie and let life play upon them like the tepid discharges of a douche-bag. To the Cartesian proposition: "I think, therefore I am", he opposed his own, which must have gone something like this: "I imagine, therefore I belong and am free".'

Of himself Balthazar once said wryly: 'I am a Jew, with all the Jew's bloodthirsty interest in the ratiocinative faculty. It is the clue to many of the weaknesses in my thinking, and which I am learning to balance up with the rest of me — through the Cabal chiefly.'

★   ★   ★   ★   ★

I remember meeting him, too, one bleak winter evening, walking along the rain-swept Corniche, dodging the sudden gushes of salt water from the conduits which lined it. Under the black hat a skull ringing with Smyrna, and the Sporades where his childhood lay. Under the black hat too the haunting illumination of a truth which he afterwards tried to convey to me in an English not the less faultless for having been learned. We had met before, it is true, but glancingly: and would have perhaps passed each other with a nod had not his agitation made him stop me and take my arm. 'Ah! you can help me!' he cried, taking me by the arm. 'Please help me.' His pale face with its gleaming goat-eyes lowered itself towards mine in the approaching dusk.

The first blank lamps had begun to stiffen the damp paper background of Alexandria. The sea-wall with its lines of cafés swallowed in the spray glowed with a smudged and trembling phosphorescence. The wind blew dead south. Mareotis crouched among the reeds, stiff as a crouching sphinx. He was looking, he said, for the key to his watch — the beautiful gold pocket-watch which had been made in Munich. I thought afterwards that behind the urgency of his expression he masked the symbolic meaning that this watch had for him: signifying the unbound time which flowed through his body and mine, marked off for so many years now by this historic timepiece. Munich, Zagreb, the Carpathians. . . . The watch had belonged to his father. A tall Jew, dressed in furs, riding in a sledge. He had crossed into Poland lying in his mother's arms, knowing only that the jewels she wore in that snowlit landscape were icy cold to the touch. The watch had ticked softly against his father's body as well as his own — like time fermenting in them. It was wound by a small key in the shape of an *ankh* which he kept attached to a strip of black ribbon on his key-ring. 'Today is Saturday' he said hoarsely 'in Alexandria.' He spoke as if a different sort of time obtained here, and he was not wrong. 'If I don't find the key it will stop.' In the last gleams of the wet dusk he tenderly drew the watch from its silk-lined waist-coat pocket. 'I have until Monday evening. It will stop.' Without the key it was useless to open the delicate golden leaf and expose the palpitating viscera of time itself stirring. 'I have been over the ground three times. I must have dropped it between the café and the hospital.' I would gladly have helped him, but night was falling fast; and after we had walked a short distance examining the interstices of the stones we were forced to give up the search. 'Surely' I said 'you can have another key cut for it?' He answered impatiently; 'Yes. Of course. But you don't understand. It belonged to this watch. It was part of it.'

We went, I remember, to a café on the sea-front and sat despondently before a black coffee while he croaked on about this historic watch. It was during this conversation that he said: 'I think you know Justine. She has spoken to me warmly of you. She will bring you to the Cabal.' 'What is that?' I asked. 'We study the Cabbala' he said almost shyly; 'we are a sort of small lodge. She said you knew something about it and would be interested.' This astonished me for I had never, as far as I knew, mentioned to Justine any line of study which I was pursuing — in between long bouts of lethargy and self-disgust. And as far as I knew the little suitcase containing the Hermetica and other books of the kind had always been kept under my bed locked. I said nothing however. He spoke now of Nessim, saying: 'Of all of us he is the most happy in a way because he has no preconceived idea of what he wants in return for his love. And to love in such an unpremeditated way is something that most people have to re-learn after fifty. Children have it. So has he. I am serious.'

'Did you know the writer Arnauti?'

'Yes. The author of *Moeurs*.'

'Tell me about him.'

'He intruded on us, but he did not see the spiritual city underlying the temporal one. Gifted, sensitive, but very French. He found Justine too young to be more than hurt by her. It was ill luck. Had he found another a little older — all our women are Justines, you know, in different styles — he might have — I will not say written better, for his book is well written: but he might have found in it a sort of resolution which would have made it more truly a work of art.'

He paused and took a long pull at his pipe before adding slowly:

'You see in his book he avoided dealing with a number of things which he knew to be true of Justine, but which he ignored for purely artistic purposes — like the incident of her child. I suppose he thought it smacked of melodrama.'

'What child was this?'

'Justine had a child, by whom I do not know. It was kidnapped and disappeared one day. About six years old. A girl. These things do happen quite frequently in Egypt as you know. Later she heard that it had been seen or recognized and began a frantic hunt for it through the Arab quarter of every town, through every house of ill-fame, since you know what happens to parentless children in Egypt. Arnauti never mentioned this, though he often helped her follow up clues, and he must have seen how much this loss contributed to her unhappiness.'

'Who did Justine love before Arnauti?'

'I cannot remember. You know many of Justine's lovers remained her friends; but more often I think you could say that her truest friends were never lovers. The town is always ready to gossip.'

But I was thinking of a passage in *Moeurs* where Justine comes to meet him with a man who is her lover. Arnauti writes: 'She embraced this man, her lover, so warmly in front of me, kissing him on the mouth and eyes, his cheeks, even his hands, that I was puzzled. Then it shot through me with a thrill that it was really *me* she was kissing in her imagination.'

Balthazar said quietly: 'Thank God I have been spared an undue interest in love. At least the invert escapes this fearful struggle to give oneself to another. Lying with one's own kind, enjoying an experience, one can still keep free the part of one's mind which dwells in Plato, or gardening, or the differential calculus. Sex has left the body and entered the imagination now; that is why Arnauti suffered so much with Justine, because she preyed upon all that he might have kept separate — his artist-hood if you like. He is when all is said and done a sort of minor Antony, and she a Cleo. You can read all about it in Shakespeare. And then, as far as Alexandria is concerned, you can understand why this is really a city of incest — I mean that here the cult of Serapis was founded. For this etiolation of the heart and reins in love-making must make one turn inwards upon one's sister. The lover mirrors himself like Narcissus in his own family: there is no exit from the predicament.'

All this was not very comprehensible to me, yet vaguely I felt a sort of correspondence between the associations he employed; and certainly much of what he said seemed to — not explain, but to offer a frame to the picture of Justine — the dark, vehement creature in whose direct and energetic handwriting I had first read this quotation from Laforgue: 'Je n'ai pas une jeune fille qui saurait me goûter. Ah! oui, une garde-malade! Une garde-malade pour l'amour de l'art, ne donnant ses baisers qu'à des mourants, des gens *in extremis.* . . .' Under this she wrote: 'Often quoted by A and at last discovered by accident in Laforgue.'

'Have you fallen out of love with Melissa?' said Balthazar suddenly. 'I do not know her. I have only seen her. Forgive me. I have hurt you.'

It was at this time that I was becoming aware of how much Melissa was suffering. But not a word of reproach ever escaped her lips, nor did she ever speak of Justine. But she had taken on a lacklustre, unloved colour — her very flesh; and paradoxically enough though I could hardly make love to her without an effort, yet I felt myself at this time to be more deeply in love with her than ever. I was gnawed by a confusion of feelings and a sense of frustration which I had never experienced before; it made me sometimes angry with her.

It was so different from Justine, who was experiencing much the same confusion as myself between her ideas and her intentions, when she said: 'Who invented the human heart, I wonder? Tell me, and then show me the place where he was hanged.'

*   *   *   *   *

Of the Cabal itself, what is there to be said? Alexandria is a town of sects and gospels. And for every ascetic she has always thrown up one religious libertine — Carpocrates, Anthony — who was prepared to founder in the senses as deeply and truly as any desert father in the mind. 'You speak slightingly of syncretism' said Balthazar once, 'but you must understand that to work here at all — and I am speaking now as a religious maniac not a philosopher — one must try to reconcile two extremes of habit and behaviour which are not due to the intellectual disposition of the inhabitants, but to their soil, air, landscape. I mean extreme sensuality and intellectual asceticism. Historians always present syncretism as something which grew out of a mixture of warring intellectual principles; that hardly states the problem. It is not even a question of mixed races and tongues. It is the national peculiarity of the Alexandrians to seek a reconciliation between the two deepest psychological traits of which they are conscious. That is why we are hysterics and extremists. That is why we are the incomparable lovers we are.'

This is not the place to try and write what I know of the Cabbala, even if I were disposed to try and define 'The unpredicated ground of that Gnosis'; no aspiring hermetic could — for these fragments of revelation have their roots in the Mysteries. It is not that they are not to be revealed. They are raw experiences which only initiates can share.

I have dabbled in these matters before in Paris, conscious that in them I might find a pathway which could lead me to a deeper understanding of myself — the self which seemed to be only a huge, disorganized and shapeless society of lusts and impulses. I regarded this whole field of study as productive for my inner man, though a native and inborn scepticism kept me free from the toils of any denominational religion. For almost a year I had studied under Mustapha, a Sufi, sitting on the rickety wooden terrace of his house every evening listening to him talk in that soft cobweb voice. I had drunk sherbet with a wise Turkish Moslem. So it was with a sense of familiarity that I walked beside Justine through the twisted warren of streets which crown the fort of Kom El Dick, trying with one half of my mind to visualize how it must have looked when it was a Park sacred to Pan, the whole brown soft hillock carved into a pine-cone. Here the narrowness of the streets produced a sort of sense of intimacy, though they were lined only by verminous warrens and benighted little cafés lit by flickering rush-lamps. A strange sense of repose invested this little corner of the city giving it some of the atmosphere of a delta village. Below on the amorphous brown-violet *meidan* by the railway station, forlorn in the fading dusk, little crowds of Arabs gathered about groups of sportsmen playing at single-stick, their shrill cries muffled in the fading dusk. Southward gleamed the tarnished platter of Mareotis. Justine walked with her customary swiftness, and in silence, impatient of my tendency to lag behind and peer into the doorways on those scenes of domestic life which (lighted like toy theatres) seemed filled with a tremendous dramatic significance.

The Cabal met at this time in what resembled a disused curator's wooden hut, built against the red earth walls of an embankment, very near to Pompey's Pillar. I suppose the morbid sensitivity of the Egyptian police to political meetings dictated the choice of such a *venue*. One crossed the wilderness of trenches and parapets thrown up by the archaeologist and followed a muddy path through the stone gate; then turning sharply at right angles one entered this large inelegant shack, one of whose walls was the earth side of an embankment and whose floor was of tamped earth. The interior was strongly lit by two petrol lamps and furnished with chairs of wicker.

The gathering consisted of about twenty people drawn from various parts of the city. I noticed with some surprise the lean bored figure of Capodistria in one corner. Nessim was there, of course, but there were very few representatives of the richer or more educated sections of the city. There was, for example, an elderly clock-maker I knew well by sight — a graceful silver-haired man whose austere features had always seemed to me to demand a violin under them in order to set them off. A few nondescript elderly ladies. A chemist. Balthazar sat before them in a low chair with his ugly hands lying in his lap. I recognized him at once as if in an entirely new context as the habitué of the Café Al Aktar with whom I had once played backgammon. A few desultory minutes passed in gossip while the Cabal waited upon its later members; then the old clock-maker stood up and suggested that Balthazar should open proceedings, and my friend settled back in his chair, closed his eyes and in that harsh croaking voice which gradually gathered an extraordinary sweetness began to talk. He spoke, I remember, of the *fons signatus* of the psyche and of its ability to perceive an inherent order in the universe which underlay the apparent formlessness and arbitrariness of phenomena. Disciplines of mind could enable people to penetrate behind the veil of reality and to discover harmonies in space and time which corresponded to the inner structure of their own psyches. But the study of the Cabbala was both a science and a religion. All this was of course familiar enough. But throughout Balthazar's expositions extraordinary fragments of thought would emerge in the form of pregnant aphorisms which teased the mind long after one had left his presence. I remember him saying, for example, 'None of the great religions has done more than exclude, throw out a long range of prohibitions. But prohibitions create the desire they are intended to cure. We of this Cabal say: *indulge but refine*. We are enlisting everything in order to make man's wholeness match the wholeness of the universe — even pleasure, the destructive granulation of the mind in pleasure.'

The constitution of the Cabal consisted of an inner circle of initiates (Balthazar would have winced at the word but I do not know how else to express it) and an outer circle of students to which Nessim and Justine belonged. The inner circle consisted of twelve members who were widely scattered over the Mediterranean — in Beirut, Jaffa, Tunis and so on. In each place there was a small academy of students who were learning to use the strange mental-emotional calculus which the Cabbala has erected about the idea of God. The members of the inner Cabal corresponded frequently with one another, using the curious old form of writing, known as the *boustrophedon*; that is to say a writing which is read from right to left and from left to right in alternate lines. But the letters used in their alphabet were ideograms for mental or spiritual states. I have said enough.

On that first evening Justine sat there between us, her arms linked lightly in ours, listening with a humility and concentration that were touching. At times the speaker's eye rested on her for a moment with a glance of affectionate familiarity. Did I know then — or was it afterwards I discovered — that Balthazar was perhaps her only friend and certainly the only confidant she had in the city? I do not remember. ('Balthazar is the only man to whom I can tell everything. He only laughs. But somehow he helps me to dispel the hollowness I feel in everything I do.') And it was to Balthazar that she would always write those long self-tortured letters which interested the curious mind of Arnauti. In the diaries she recorded how one moonlight night they gained access to the Museum and sat for an hour among the statues 'sightless as nightmares' listening to him talk. He said many things which struck her then but later when she came to try and write them down they had vanished. Yet she did remember him saying in a quiet reflective voice something about 'those of us who are bound to submit our bodies to the ogres,' and the thought penetrated her marrow as a reference to the sort of life she was leading. As for Nessim, I remember him telling me that once, when he was in a great agony of mind about Justine, Balthazar remarked dryly to him: '*Omnis ardentior amator propriae uxoris adulter est.*' Adding as he did so: 'I speak now as a member of the Cabal, not as a private person. Passionate love even for a man's own wife is also adultery.'

* * * * *

Alexandria Main Station: midnight. A deathly heavy dew. The noise of wheels cracking the slime-slithering pavements. Yellow pools of phosphorous light, and corridors of darkness like tears in the dull brick façade of a stage set. Policemen in the shadows. Standing against an insanitary brick wall to kiss her goodbye. She is going for a week, but in the panic, half-asleep I can see that she may never come back. The soft resolute kiss and the bright eyes fill me with emptiness. From the dark platform comes the crunch of rifle-butts and the clicking of Bengali. A detail of Indian troops on some routine transfer to Cairo. It is only as the train begins to move, and as the figure at the window, dark against the darkness, lets go of my hand, that I feel Melissa is really leaving; feel everything that is inexorably denied — the long pull of the train into the silver light reminds me of the sudden long pull of the vertebrae of her white back turning in bed. 'Melissa' I call out, but the giant sniffing of the engine blots out all sound. She begins to tilt, to curve and slide; and quick as a scene-shifter the station packs away advertisement after advertisement, stacking them in the darkness. I stand as if marooned on an iceberg. Beside me a tall Sikh shoulders the rifle he has stopped with a rose. The shadowy figure is sliding away down the steel rails into the darkness; a final lurch and the train pours away down a tunnel, as if turned to liquid.

I walk about Moharrem-Bey that night, watching the moon cloud over, preyed upon by an inexpressible anxiety.

Intense light behind cloud; by four o'clock a thin pure drizzle like needles. The poinsettias in the Consulate garden stark with silver drops standing on their stamens. No birds singing in the dawn. A light wind making the palm trees sway their necks with a faint dry formal clicking. The wonderful hushing of rain on Mareotis.

Five o'clock. Walking about in her room, studying inanimate objects with intense concentration. The empty powder-boxes. The depilatories from Sardis. The smell of satin and leather. The horrible feeling of some great impending scandal. . . .

I write these lines in very different circumstances and many months have elapsed since that night; here, under this olive-tree, in the pool of light thrown by an oil lamp, I write and relive that night which has taken its place in the enormous fund of the city's memories. Somewhere else, in a great study hung with tawny curtains Justine was copying into her diary the terrible aphorisms of Herakleitos. The book lies beside me now. On one page she has written: 'It is hard to fight with one's heart's desire; whatever it wishes to get, it purchases at the cost of soul.' And lower down in the margins: 'Night-walkers, Magians, Bakchoi, Lenai and the *initiated. . . .'*

* * * * *

Was it about this time that Mnemjian startled me by breathing into my ear the words: 'Cohen is dying, you know?' The old furrier had drifted out of sight for some months past. Melissa had heard that he was in hospital suffering from uraemia. But the orbit we once described about the girl had changed; the kaleidoscope had tilted once more and he had sunk out of sight like a vanished chip of coloured glass. Now he was dying? I said nothing as I sat exploring the memories of those early days — the encounters at street-corners and bars. In the long silence that ensued Mnemjian scraped my hairline clean with a razor and began to spray my head with bay-rum. He gave a little sigh and said: 'He has been asking for your Melissa. All night, all day.'

'I will tell her' I said, and the little memory man nodded with a mossy conspiratorial look in his eyes. 'What a horrible disease' he said under his breath, 'he smells so. They scrape his tongue with a spatula. Pfui!' And he turned the spray upwards towards the roof as if to disinfect the memory: as if the smell had invaded the shop.

Melissa was lying on the sofa in her dressing-gown with her face turned to the wall. I thought at first she was asleep, but as I came in she turned and sat up. I told her Mnemjian's news. 'I know' she said. 'They sent me word from the hospital. But what can I do? I cannot go and see him. He is nothing to me, never was, never will be.' Then getting up and walking the length of the room she added in a rage which hovered on the edge of tears. 'He has a wife and children. What are they doing?' I sat down and once more confronted the memory of that tame seal staring sadly into a human wineglass. Melissa took my silence for criticism I suppose for she came to me and shook me gently by the shoulders, rousing me from my thoughts. 'But if he is dying?' I said. The question was addressed as much to myself as to her. She cried out suddenly and kneeling down placed her head on my knees. 'Oh, it is so disgusting! Please do not make me go.'

'Of course not.'

'But if you think I should I will have to.'

I said nothing. Cohen was in a sense already dead and buried. He had lost his place in our history, and an expenditure of emotional energy on him seemed to me useless. It had no relation to the real man who lay among the migrating fragments of his old body in a whitewashed ward. For us he had become merely an historic figure. And yet here he was, obstinately trying to insist on his identity, trying to walk back into our lives at another point in the circumference. What could Melissa give him now? What could she deny him?

'Would you like me to go?' I said. The sudden irrational thought had come into my mind that here, in the death of Cohen, I could study my own love and its death. That someone *in extremis*, calling for help to an old lover, could only elicit a cry of disgust — this terrified me. It was too late for the old man to awake compassion or even interest in my lover, who was already steeped in new misfortunes against the backcloth of which the old had faded, rotted. And in a little time perhaps, if she should call on me or I on her? Would we turn from each other with a cry of emptiness and disgust? I realized then the truth about all love: that it is an absolute which takes all or forfeits all. The other feelings, compassion, tenderness and so on, exist only on the periphery and belong to the constructions of society and habit. But she herself — austere and merciless Aphrodite — is a pagan. It is not our brains or instincts which she picks — but our very bones. It terrified me to think that this old man, at such a point in his life, had been unable to conjure up an instant's tenderness by the memory of anything he had said or done: tenderness from one who was at heart the most tender and gentle of mortals.

To be forgotten in this way was to die the death of a dog 'I shall go and see him for you' I said, though my heart quailed in disgust at the prospect; but Melissa had already fallen asleep with her dark head upon my knees. Whenever she was upset about anything she took refuge in the guileless world of sleep, slipping into it as smoothly and easily as a deer or a child. I put my hands inside the faded kimono and gently rubbed her shallow ribs and flanks. She stirred half-awake and murmured something inaudible as she allowed me to lift her and carry her gently back to the sofa. I watched her sleeping for a long time.

It was already dark and the city was drifting like a bed of seaweed towards the lighted cafés of the upper town. I went to Pastroudi and ordered a double whisky which I drank slowly and thoughtfully. Then I took a taxi to the Hospital.

I followed a duty-nurse down the long anonymous green corridors whose oil-painted walls exuded an atmosphere of damp.

The white phosphorescent bulbs which punctuated our progress wallowed in the gloom like swollen glow-worms.

They had put him in the little ward with the single curtained bed which was, as I afterwards learned from Mnemjian, reserved for critical cases whose expectation of life was short. He did not see me at first, for he was watching with an air of shocked exhaustion while a nurse disposed his pillows for him. I was amazed at the masterful, thoughtful reserve of the face which stared up from the mattress, for he had become so thin as almost to be unrecognizable. The flesh had sunk down upon his cheek-bones exposing the long slightly curved nose to its very roots and throwing into relief the carved nostrils. This gave the whole mouth and jaw a buoyancy, a spirit which must have characterized his face in earliest youth. His eyes looked bruised with fever and a dark stubble shaded his neck and throat, but under this the exposed lines of the face were as clean as those of the face of a man of thirty. The images of him which I had so long held in my memory — a sweaty porcupine, a tame seal — were immediately dissolved and replaced by this new face, this new man who looked like — one of the beasts of the Apocalypse. I stood for a long minute in astonishment watching an unknown personage accepting the ministration of the nurses with a dazed and regal exhaustion. The duty-nurse was whispering in my ear: 'It is good you have come. Nobody will come and see him. He is delirious at times. Then he wakes and asks for people. You are a relation?'

'A business associate' I said.

'It will do him good to see a face he knows.'

But would he recognize me, I wondered? If I had changed only half as much as he had we would be complete strangers to one another. He was lying back now, the breath whistling harshly through that long vulpine nose which lay resting against his face like the proud figurehead of an abandoned ship. Our whispers had disturbed him, for he turned upon me a vague but nevertheless pure and thoughtful eye which seemed to belong to some great bird of prey. Recognition did not come until I moved forward a few paces to the side of the bed. Then all at once his eyes were flooded with light — a strange mixture of humility, hurt pride, and innocent fear. He turned his face to the wall. I blurted out the whole of my message in one sentence. Melissa was away, I said, and I had telegraphed her to come as quickly as possible; meanwhile I had come to see if I could help him in any way. His shoulders shook, and I thought that an involuntary groan was about to burst from his lips; but presently in its place came the mockery of a laugh, harsh, mindless and unmusical. As if directed at the dead carcass of a joke so rotten and threadbare that it could compel nothing beyond this ghastly *rictus* gouged out in his taut cheeks.

'I know she is here' he said, and one of his hands came running over the counterpane like a frightened rat to grope for mine. 'Thank you for your kindness.' And with this he suddenly seemed to grow calm, though he kept his face turned away from me. 'I wanted' he said slowly, as if he were collecting himself in order to give the phrase its exactest meaning, 'I wanted to close my account honourably with her. I treated her badly, very badly. She did not notice, of course; she is too simple-minded, but good, such a good girl.' It sounded strange to hear the phrase *'bonne copine'* on the lips of an Alexandrian, and moreover pronounced in the chipped trailing sing-song accent common to those educated here. Then he added, with considerable effort, and struggling against a formidable inner resistance. 'I cheated her over her coat. It was really sealskin. Also the moths had been at it. I had it relined. Why should I do such a thing? When she was ill I would not pay for her to see the doctor. Small things, but they weigh heavy.' Tears crowded up into his eyes and his throat tightened as if choked by the enormity of such thoughts. He swallowed harshly and said: 'They were not really in my character. Ask any business man who knows me. Ask any one.'

But now confusion began to set in, and holding me gently by the hand he led me into the dense jungle of his illusions, walking among them with such surefootedness and acknowledging them so calmly that I almost found myself keeping company with them too. Unknown fronds of trees arched over him, brushing his face, while cobbles punctuated the rubber wheels of some dark ambulance full of metal and other dark bodies, whose talk was of limbo — a repulsive yelping streaked with Arabic objurgations. The pain, too, had begun to reach up at his reason and lift down fantasies. The hard white edges of the bed turned to boxes of coloured bricks, the white temperature chart to a boatman's white face.

They were drifting, Melissa and he, across the shallow blood-red water of Mareotis, in each other's arms, towards the rabble of mud-huts where once Rhakotis stood. He reproduced their conversations so perfectly that though my lover's share was inaudible I could nevertheless hear her cool voice, could deduce her questions from the answers he gave her. She was desperately trying to persuade him to marry her and he was temporizing, unwilling to lose the beauty of her person and equally unwilling to commit himself. What interested me was the extraordinary fidelity with which he reproduced this whole conversation which obviously in his memory ranked as one of the great experiences of his life. He did not know then how much he loved her; it had remained for me to teach him the lesson. And conversely how was it that Melissa had never spoken to me of marriage, had never betrayed to me the depth of her weakness and exhaustion as she had to him? This was deeply wounding. My vanity was gnawed by the thought that she had shown him a side of her nature which she had kept hidden from me.

Now the scene changed again and he fell into a more lucid vein. It was as if in the vast jungle of unreason we came upon clearings of sanity where he was emptied of his poetic illusions. Here he spoke of Melissa with feeling but coolly, like a husband or a king. It was as if now that the flesh was dying the whole funds of his inner self, so long dammed up behind the falsities of a life wrongly lived, burst through the dykes and flooded the foreground of his consciousness. It was not only Melissa either, for he spoke of his wife — and at times confused their names. There was also a third name, Rebecca, which he pronounced with a deeper reserve, a more passionate sorrow than either of the others. I took this to be his little daughter, for it is the children who deliver the final *coup de grâce* in all these terrible transactions of the heart.

Sitting there at his side, feeling our pulses ticking in unison and listening to him as he talked of my lover with a new magistral calm I could not help but see how much there was in the man which Melissa might have found to love. By what strange chance had she missed the real person? For far from being an object of contempt (as I had always taken him to be) he seemed to be now a dangerous rival whose powers I had been unaware of; and I was visited by a thought so ignoble that I am ashamed to write it down. I felt glad that Melissa had not come to see him die lest seeing him, as I saw him now, she might at a blow rediscover him. And by one of those paradoxes in which love delights I found myself more jealous of him in his dying than I had ever been during his life. These were horrible thoughts for one who had been so long a patient and attentive student of love, but I recognized once more in them the austere mindless primitive face of Aphrodite.

In a sense I recognized in him, in the very resonance of his voice when he spoke her name, a maturity which I lacked; for he had surmounted his love for her without damaging or hurting it, and allowed it to mature as all love should into a consuming and de-personalized friendship. So far from fearing to die, and importuning her for comfort, he wished only to offer her, from the inexhaustible treasury of his dying, a last gift.

The magnificent sable lay across a chair at the end of the bed wrapped in tissue paper; I could see at a glance that it was not the sort of gift for Melissa, for it would throw her scant and shabby wardrobe into confusion, outshining everything. 'I was always worried about money' he said felicitously 'while I was alive. But when you are dying you suddenly find yourself in funds.' He was able for the first time in his life to be almost light-hearted. Only the sickness was there like some patient and cruel monitor.

He passed from time to time into a short confused sleep and the darkness hummed about my tired ears like a hive of bees. It was getting late and yet I could not bring myself to leave him. A duty-nurse brought me a cup of coffee and we talked in whispers. It was restful to hear her talk, for to her illness was simply a profession which she had mastered and her attitude to it was that of a journeyman. In her cold voice she said: 'He deserted his wife and child for *une femme quelconque*. Now neither the wife nor the woman who is his mistress wants to see him. Well!' She shrugged her shoulders. These tangled loyalties evoked no feeling of compassion in her, for she saw them simply as despicable weaknesses. 'Why doesn't the child come? Has he not asked for her?' She picked a front tooth with the nail of her little finger and said: 'Yes. But he does not want to frighten her by letting her see him sick. It is, you understand, not pleasant for a child.' She picked up an atomizer and languidly squirted some disinfectant into the air above us, reminding me sharply of Mnemjian. 'It is late' she added; 'are you going to stay the night?'

I was about to make a move, but the sleeper awoke and clutched at my hand once more. 'Don't go' he said in a deep fragmented but sane voice, as if he had overheard the last few phrases of our conversation. 'Stay a little while. There is something else I have been thinking over and which I must reveal to you.' Turning to the nurse he said quietly but distinctly, 'Go!' She smoothed the bed and left us alone once more. He gave a great sigh which, if one had not been watching his face, might have seemed a sigh of plenitude, happiness. 'In the cupboard' he said 'you will find my clothes.'

93

There were two dark suits hanging up, and under his direction I detached a waistcoat from one of them, in the pockets of which I burrowed until my fingers came upon two rings. 'I had decided to offer to marry Melissa *now* if she wished. That is why I sent for her. After all what use am I? My name?' He smiled vaguely at the ceiling. 'And the rings — ' he held them lightly, reverently in his fingers like a communion wafer. 'These are rings she chose for herself long ago. So now she must have them. Perhaps. . . .' He looked at me for a long moment with pained, searching eyes. 'But no' he said, 'you will not marry her. Why should you? Never mind. Take them for her, and the coat.'

I put the rings into the shallow breast-pocket of my coat and said nothing. He sighed once more and then to my surprise, in a small gnome's tenor muffled almost to inaudibility sang a few bars of a popular song which had once been the rage of Alexandria, *Jamais de la vie*, and to which Melissa still danced at the cabaret. 'Listen to the music!' he said, and I thought suddenly of the dying Antony in the poem of Cavafy — a poem he had never read, would never read. Sirens whooped suddenly from the harbour like planets in pain. Then once more I heard this gnome singing softly of *chagrin* and *bonheur*, and he was singing not to Melissa but to Rebecca. How different from the great heart-sundering choir that Antony heard — the rich poignance of strings and voices which in the dark street welled up — Alexandria's last bequest to those who are her exemplars. Each man goes out to his own music, I thought, and remembered with shame and pain the clumsy movements that Melissa made when she danced.

He had drifted now to the very borders of sleep and I judged that it was time to leave him. I took the coat and put it in the bottom drawer of the cupboard before tip-toeing out and summoning the duty-nurse. 'It is very late' she said.

'I will come in the morning' I said. I meant to.

Walking slowly home through the dark avenue of trees, tasting the brackish harbour wind, I remembered Justine saying harshly as she lay in bed: 'We use each other like axes to cut down the ones we really love.'

       ★   ★   ★   ★   ★

We have been told so often that history is indifferent, but we always take its parsimony or plenty as somehow planned; we never really listen. . . .

JUSTINE

Now on this tenebrous peninsula shaped like a plane-leaf, fingers outstretched (where the winter rain crackles like straw among the rocks), I walk stiffly sheathed in wind by a sealine choked with groaning sponges hunting for the meaning to the pattern.

As a poet of the historic consciousness I suppose I am bound to see landscape as a field dominated by the human wish — tortured into farms and hamlets, ploughed into cities. A landscape scribbled with the signatures of men and epochs. Now, however, I am beginning to believe that the wish is inherited from the site; that man depends for the furniture of the will upon his location in place, tenant of fruitful acres or a perverted wood. It is not the impact of his freewill upon nature which I see (as I thought) but the irresistible growth, through him, of nature's own blind unspecified doctrines of variation and torment. She has chosen this poor forked thing as an exemplar. Then how idle it seems for any man to say, as I once heard Balthazar say: 'The mission of the Cabal, if it has one, is so to ennoble function that even eating and excreting will be raised to the rank of arts.' You will see in all this the flower of a perfect scepticism which undermines the will to survive. Only love can sustain one a little longer.

I think, too, that something of this sort must have been in Arnauti's mind when he wrote: 'For the writer people as psychologies are finished. The contemporary psyche has exploded like a soap-bubble under the investigations of the mystagogues. What now remains to the writer?'

Perhaps it was the realization of this which made me select this empty place to live for the next few years — this sunburnt headland in the Cyclades. Surrounded by history on all sides, this empty island alone is free from every reference. It has never been mentioned in the annals of the race which owns it. Its historic past is refunded, not into time, but into place — no temples, groves, amphitheatres, to corrupt ideas with their false comparisons. A shelf of coloured boats, a harbour over the hills, and a little town denuded by neglect. That is all. Once a month a steamer touches on its way to Smyrna.

These winter evenings the sea-tempests climb the cliffs and invade the grove of giant untended planes where I walk, talking a sudden wild slang, slopping and tilting the schooner trees.

I walk here with those coveted intimations of a past which none can share with me; but which time itself cannot deprive me of. My hair is clenched back to my scalp and one hand guards the

95

burning dottle of my pipe from the force of the wind. Above, the sky is set in a brilliant comb of stars. Antares guttering up there, buried in spray. . . . To have cheerfully laid down obedient books and friends, lighted rooms, fireplaces built for conversation — the whole parish of the civilized mind — is not something I regret but merely wonder at.

In this choice too I see something fortuitous, born of impulses which I am forced to regard as outside the range of my own nature. And yet, strangely enough, it is only here that I am at last able to re-enter, reinhabit the unburied city with my friends; to frame them in the heavy steel webs of metaphors which will last half as long as the city itself — or so I hope. Here at least I am able to see their history and the city's as one and the same phenomenon.

But strangest of all: I owe this release to Pursewarden — the last person I should ever have considered a possible benefactor. That last meeting, for example, in the ugly and expensive hotel bedroom to which he always moved on Pombal's return from leave . . . I did not recognize the heavy musty odour of the room as the odour of his impending suicide — how should I? I knew he was unhappy; even had he not been he would have felt obliged to simulate unhappiness. All artists today are expected to cultivate a little fashionable unhappiness. And being Anglo-Saxon there was a touch of maudlin self-pity and weakness which made him drink a bit. That evening he was savage, silly and witty by turns; and listening to him I remember thinking suddenly: 'Here is someone who in farming his talent has neglected his sensibility, not by accident, but deliberately, for its self-expression might have brought him into conflict with the world, or his loneliness threatened his reason. He could not bear to be refused admittance, while he lived, to the halls of fame and recognition. Underneath it all he has been steadily putting up with an almost insupportable consciousness of his own mental poltroonery. And now his career has reached an interesting stage: I mean beautiful women, whom he always felt to be out of reach as a timid provincial would, are now glad to be seen out with him. In his presence they wear the air of faintly distracted Muses suffering from constipation. In public they are flattered if he holds a gloved hand for an instant longer than form permits. At first all this must have been balm to a lonely man's vanity; but finally it has only furthered his sense of insecurity. His freedom, gained through a modest financial success, has begun to bore him. He has begun to feel more and more wanting in true greatness while his name has been daily swelling in size like some disgusting poster. He has realized that people are walking the street with a Reputation now and not a man. They see him no longer — and all his work was done in order to draw attention to the lonely, suffering figure he felt himself to be. His name has covered him like a tombstone. And now comes the terrifying thought perhaps there *is* no one left to see? Who, after all, is he?'

I am not proud of these thoughts, for they betray the envy that every failure feels for every success; but spite may often see as clearly as charity. And indeed, running as it were upon a parallel track in my mind went the words which Clea once used about him and which, for some reason, I remembered and reflected upon: 'He is unlovely somewhere. Part of the secret is his physical ungainliness. Being wizened his talent has a germ of shyness in it. Shyness has laws: you can only give yourself, tragically, to those who least understand. For to understand one would be to admit pity for one's frailty. Hence the women he loves, the letters he writes to the women he loves, stand as ciphers in his mind for the women he thinks he wants, or at any rate deserves — *cher ami.*' Clea's sentences always broke in half and ended in that magical smile of tenderness — 'am I my brother's keeper?' . . .

(What I most need to do is to record experiences, not in the order in which they took place — for that is history — but in the order in which they first became significant for me.)

What, then, could have been his motive in leaving me five hundred pounds with the sole stipulation that I should spend them with Melissa? I thought perhaps that he may have loved her himself but after deep reflection I have come to the conclusion that he loved, not her, but my love for her. Of all my qualities he envied me only my capacity to respond warmly to endearments whose value he recognized, perhaps even desired, but from which he would be forever barred by self-disgust. Indeed this itself was a blow to my pride for I would have liked him to admire — if not the work I have done — at least the promise it shows of what I have yet to do. How stupid, how limited we are — mere vanities on legs!

We had not met for weeks, for we did not habitually frequent each other, and when we did it was in the little tin *pissotière* in the main square by the tram-station. It was after dark and we would never have recognized each other had not the head-lights of a car occasionally drenched the foetid cubicle in white light like spray.

'Ah!' he said in recognition: unsteadily, thoughtfully, for he was drunk. (Some time, weeks before, he had left me five hundred pounds; in a sense he had summed me up, judged me — though that judgement was only to reach me from the other side of the grave.)

The rain cropped at the tin roof above us. I longed to go home, for I had had a very tiring day, but I feebly lingered, obstructed by the apologetic politeness I always feel with people I do not really like. The slightly wavering figure outlined itself upon the darkness before me. 'Let me' he said in a maudlin tone 'confide in you the secret of my novelist's trade. I am a success, you a failure. The answer, old man, is sex and plenty of it.' He raised his voice and his chin as he said, or rather declaimed, the word 'sex': tilting his scraggy neck like a chicken drinking and biting off the word with a half-yelp like a drill-serjeant. 'Lashings of sex' he repeated more normally, 'but remember' and he allowed his voice to sink to a confidential mumble, '*stay buttoned up tight*. Eternal grandma strong to save. You must stay buttoned up and suffering. Try and look as if you had a stricture, a book society choice. What is not permissible is rude health, ordure, the natural and the funny. That was all right for Chaucer and the Elizabethans but it won't make the grade today — buttoned up tightly with stout Presbyterian buttons.' And in the very act of shaking himself off he turned to me a face composed to resemble a fly-button — tight, narrow and grotesque. I thanked him but he waved aside the thanks in a royal manner. 'It's all free' he said, and leading me by the hand he piloted me out into the dark street. We walked towards the lighted centre of the town like bondsmen, fellow writers, heavy with a sense of different failures. He talked confidentially to himself of matters which interested him in a mumble which I could not interpret. Once as we turned into the Rue des Soeurs he stopped before the lighted door of a house of ill-fame and pronounced: 'Baudelaire says that copulation is the lyric of the mob. Not any more, alas! For sex is dying. In another century we shall lie with our tongues in each other's mouths, silent and passionless as sea-fruit. Oh yes! Indubitably so.' And he quoted the Arabic proverb which he uses as an epigraph to his trilogy: 'The world is like a cucumber — today it's in your hand, tomorrow up your arse.' We then resumed our stitching, crab-like advance in the direction of his hotel, he repeating the word 'indubitably' with obvious pleasure at the soft plosive sound of it.

He was unshaven and haggard, but in comparatively good spirits after the walk and we resorted to a bottle of gin which he kept in the commode by his bed. I commented on the two bulging suit-cases which stood by the dressing-table ready packed; over a chair lay his raincoat stuffed with newspapers, pyjamas, toothpaste, and so on. He was catching the night train for Gaza, he said. He wanted to slack off and pay a visit to Petra. The galley-proofs of his latest novel had already been corrected, wrapped up and addressed. They lay dead upon the marble top of the dressing-table. I recognized in his sour and dejected attitude the exhaustion which pursues the artist after he has brought a piece of work to completion. These are the low moments when the long flirtation with suicide begins afresh.

Unfortunately, though I have searched my mind, I can recall little of our actual conversation, though I have often tried to do so. The fact that this was our last meeting has invested it, in retrospect, with a significance which surely it cannot have possessed. Nor, for the purposes of this writing, has he ceased to exist; he has simply stepped into the quicksilver of a mirror as we all must — to leave our illnesses, or evil acts, the hornets' nest of our desires, still operative for good or evil in the real world — which is the memory of our friends. Yet the presence of death always refreshes experience thus — that is its function to help us deliberate on the novelty of time. Yet at that moment we were both situated at points equidistant from death — or so I think. Perhaps some quiet pre-meditation blossomed in him even then — no matter. I cannot tell. It is not mysterious that any artist should desire to end a life which he has exhausted — (a character in the last volume exclaims: 'For years one has to put up with the feeling that people do not care, really care, about one; then one day with growing alarm, one realizes that it is God who does not care: and not merely that he does not *care*, he does not care *one way or the other*').

But this aside reminds me of one small fragment of that drunken conversation. He spoke derisively of Balthazar, of his preoccupa-tion with religion, of the Cabal (of which he had only heard). I listened without interrupting him and gradually his voice ran down like a time-piece overcome by the weight of seconds. He stood up to pour himself a drink and said: 'One needs a tremendous ignorance to approach God. I have always known too much, I suppose.'

These are the sort of fragments which tease the waking mind

on evenings like these, walking about in the wintry darkness; until at last I turn back to the crackling fire of olive-wood in the old-fashioned arched hearth where Justine lies asleep in her cot of sweet-smelling pine.

How much of him can I claim to know? I realize that each person can only claim one aspect of our character as part of his knowledge. To every one we turn a different face of the prism. Over and over again I have found myself surprised by observations which brought this home to me. As for example when Justine said of Pombal, 'one of the great primates of sex.' To me my friend had never seemed predatory; only self-indulgent to a ludicrous degree. I saw him as touching and amusing, faintly to be cherished for an inherent ridiculousness. But she must have seen in him the great soft-footed cat he was (to her).

And as for Pursewarden, I remember, too, that in the very act of speaking thus about religious ignorance he straightened himself and caught sight of his pale reflection in the mirror. The glass was raised to his lips, and now, turning his head he squirted out upon his own glittering reflection a mouthful of the drink. That remains clearly in my mind; a reflection liquefying in the mirror of that shabby, expensive room which seems now so appropriate a place for the scene which must have followed later that night.

★　　★　　★　　★　　★

Place Zagloul — silverware and caged doves. A vaulted cave lined with black barrels and choking with the smoke from frying whitebait and the smell of *retzinnato*. A message scribbled on the edge of a newspaper. Here I spilt wine on her cloak, and while attempting to help her repair the damage, accidentally touched her breasts. No word was spoken. While Pursewarden spoke so brilliantly of Alexandria and the burning library. In the room above a poor wretch screaming with meningitis. . . .

★　　★　　★　　★　　★

Today, unexpectedly, comes a squinting spring shower, stiffening the dust and pollen of the city, flailing the glass roof of the studio where Nessim sits over his *croquis* for his wife's portrait. He has captured her sitting before the fire with a guitar in her hands, her throat snatched up by a spotted scarf, her singing head bent. The noise of her voice is jumbled in the back of his brain like the sound-track of an earthquake run backwards. Prodigious archery

100

over the parks where the palm-trees have been dragged back taut; a mythology of yellow-maned waves attacking the Pharos. At night the city is full of new sounds, the pulls and stresses of the wind, until you feel it has become a ship, its old timbers groaning and creaking with every assault of the weather.

This is the weather Scobie loves. Lying in bed will he fondle his telescope lovingly, turning a wistful eye on the blank wall of rotting mud-brick which shuts off his view of the sea.

Scobie is getting on for seventy and still afraid to die; his one fear is that he will awake one morning and find himself lying dead — Lieutenant-Commander Scobie. Consequently it gives him a severe shock every morning when the water-carriers shriek under his window before dawn, waking him up. For a moment, he says, he dare not open his eyes. Keeping them fast shut (for fear that they might open on the heavenly host or the cherubims hymning) he gropes along the cake-stand beside his bed and grabs his pipe. It is always loaded from the night before and an open matchbox stands beside it. The first whiff of seaman's plug restores both his composure and his eyesight. He breathes deeply, grateful for the reassurance. He smiles. He gloats. Drawing the heavy sheepskin which serves him as a bedcover up to his ears he sings his little triumphal paean to the morning, his voice crackling like tinfoil. '*Taisez-vous, petit babouin: laissez parler votre mère.*'

His pendulous trumpeter's cheeks become rosy with the effort. Taking stock of himself he discovers that he has the inevitable headache. His tongue is raw from last night's brandy. But against these trifling discomforts the prospect of another day in life weighs heavily. '*Taisez-vous, petit babouin*', and so on, pausing to slip in his false teeth. He places his wrinkled fingers to his chest and is comforted by the sound of his heart at work, maintaining a tremulous circulation in that venous system whose deficiencies (real or imaginary I do not know) are only offset by brandy in daily and all-but lethal doses. He is rather proud of his heart. If you ever visit him when he is in bed he is almost sure to grasp your hand in a horny mandible and ask you to feel it: 'Strong as a bullock, what? Ticking over nicely', is the way he puts it, in spite of the brandy. Swallowing a little you shove your hand inside his cheap night-jacket to experience those sad, blunt, far-away little bumps of life — like a foetal heart in the seventh month. He buttons up his pyjamas with a touching pride and gives his imitation roar of animal health. 'Bounding from my bed like a lion' — that is another of his phrases. You have not experienced the full charm of the man until you have actually seen him, bent double with rheumatism, crawling out from between his coarse cotton sheets like a derelict. Only in the warmest months of the year do his bones thaw out sufficiently to enable him to stand fully erect. In the summer afternoons he walks the Park, his little cranium glowing like a minor sun, his briar canted to heaven, his jaw set in a violent grimace of lewd health.

No mythology of the city would be complete without its Scobie, and Alexandria will be the poorer for it when his sun-cured body wrapped in a Union Jack is finally lowered into the shallow grave which awaits him at the Roman Catholic cemetery by the tramline.

His exiguous nautical pension is hardly enough to pay for the one cockroach-infested room which he inhabits in the slum-area behind Tatwig Street; he ekes it out with an equally exiguous salary from the Egyptian Government which carries with it the proud title of Bimbashi in the Police Force. Clea has painted a wonderful portrait of him in his police uniform with the scarlet tarbush on his head, and the great fly-whisk, as thick as a horse's tail, laid gracefully across his bony knees.

It is Clea who supplies him with tobacco and I with admiration, company, and weather permitting, brandy. We take it in turns to applaud his health, and to pick him up when he has struck himself too hard on the chest in enthusiastic demonstration of it. Origins he has none — his past proliferates through a dozen continents like a true subject of myth. And his presence is so rich with imaginary health that he needs nothing more — except perhaps an occasional trip to Cairo during Ramadan when his office is closed and when presumably all crime comes to a standstill because of the fast.

Youth is beardless, so is second childhood. Scobie tugs tenderly at the remains of a once handsome and bushy torpedo-beard — but very gently, caressingly, for fear of pulling it out altogether and leaving himself quite naked. He clings to life like a limpet, each year bringing its hardly visible sea-change. It is as if his body were being reduced, shrunk, by the passing of the winters; his cranium will soon be the size of a baby's. A year or two more and we will be able to squeeze it into a bottle and pickle it forever. The wrinkles become ever more heavily indented. Without his teeth his face is the face of an ancient ape; above the meagre beard his two cherry-red cheeks known affectionately as 'port' and 'starboard', glow warm in all weathers.

Physically he has drawn heavily on the replacement department; in nineteen-ten a fall from the mizzen threw his jaw two points west by south-west, and smashed the frontal sinus. When he speaks his denture behaves like a moving staircase, travelling upwards and round inside his skull in a jerky spiral. His smile is capricious; it might appear from anywhere, like that of the Cheshire Cat. In ninety-eight he made eyes at another man's wife (so he says) and lost one of them. No one except Clea is supposed to know about this, but the replacement in this case was rather a crude one. In repose it is not very noticeable, but the minute he becomes animated a disparity between his two eyes becomes obvious. There is also a small technical problem — his own eye is almost permanently bloodshot. On the very first occasion when he treated me to a reedy rendering of 'Watchman, What of the Night?', while he stood in the corner of the room with an ancient chamber-pot in his hand, I noticed that his right eye moved a trifle slower than his left. It seemed then to be a larger imitation of the stuffed eagle's eye which lours so glumly from a niche in the public library. In winter, however, it is the false eye and not the true which throbs unbearably making him morose and foul-mouthed until he has applied a little brandy to his stomach.

Scobie is a sort of protozoic profile in fog and rain, for he carries with him a sort of English weather, and he is never happier than when he can sit over a microscopic wood-fire in winter and talk. One by one his memories leak through the faulty machinery of his mind until he no longer knows them for his own. Behind him I see the long grey rollers of the Atlantic at work, curling up over his memories, smothering them in spray, blinding him. When he speaks of the past it is in a series of short dim telegrams — as if already communications were poor, the weather inimical to transmission. In Dawson City the ten who went up the river were frozen to death. Winter came down like a hammer, beating them senseless: whisky, gold, murder — it was like a new crusade northward into the timberlands. At this time his brother fell over the falls in Uganda; in his dream he saw the tiny figure, like a fly, fall and at once get smoothed out by the yellow claw of water. No: that was later when he was already staring along the sights of a carbine into the very brain-box of a Boer. He tries to remember exactly *when* it must have been, dropping his polished head into his hands; but the grey rollers intervene, the long effortless tides patrol the barrier between himself and his memory. That is why the phrase came to me: a *sea-change* for the old pirate: his skull looks palped and sucked down until only the thinnest integument separates his smile from the smile of the hidden skeleton. Observe the brain-case with its heavy indentations: the twigs of bone inside his wax fingers, the rods of tallow which support his quivering shins. . . . Really, as Clea has remarked, old Scobie is like some little old experimental engine left over from the last century, something as pathetic and friendly as Stephenson's first Rocket.

He lives in his little sloping attic like an anchorite. 'An ancho-rite!' that is another favourite phrase; he will pop his cheek vul-garly with his finger as he utters it, allowing his rolling eye to insinuate all the feminine indulgences he permits himself in secret. This is for Clea's benefit, however; in the presence of 'a perfect lady' he feels obliged to assume a protective colouring which he sheds the moment she leaves. The truth is somewhat sadder. 'I've done quite a bit of scout-mastering' he admits to me *sotto voce* 'with the Hackney Troop. That was after I was invalided out. But I had to keep out of England, old boy. The strain was too much for me. Every week I expected to see a headline in the *News of the World*, "Another youthful victim of scoutmaster's dirty wish." Down in Hackney things didn't matter so much. My kids were experts in woodcraft. Proper young Etonians I used to call them. The scoutmaster before me got twenty years. It's enough to make one have Doubts. These things made you think. Somehow I couldn't settle down in Hackney. Mind you, I'm a bit past every-thing now but I do like to have my peace of mind—just in case. And somehow in England one doesn't feel free any more. Look at the way they are pulling up clergymen, respected churchmen and so on. I used to lie awake worrying. Finally I came abroad as a private tooter—Tony Mannering, his father was an M.P., wanted an excuse to travel. They said he had to have a tooter. He wanted to go into the Navy. That's how I fetched up here. I saw at once it was nice and free-and-easy here. Got a job right off with the Vice Squad under Nimrod Pasha. And here I am, dear boy. And no complaints do you see? Looking from east to west over this fertile Delta what do I see? Mile upon mile of angelic little black bottoms.'

The Egyptian Government, with the typical generous quixotry the Levant lavishes on any foreigner who shows a little warmth and friendliness, had offered him a means to live on in Alexandria. It is said that after his appointment to the Vice Squad vice assumed such alarming proportions that it was found necessary to up-grade and transfer him; but he himself always maintained that his transfer to the routine C.I.D. branch of the police had been a deserved promotion — and I for my part have never had the courage to tease him on the subject. His work is not onerous. For a couple of hours every morning he works in a ramshackle office in the upper quarter of the town, with the fleas jumping out of the rotten woodwork of his old-fashioned desk. He lunches modestly at the Lutetia and, funds permitting, buys himself an apple and a bottle of brandy for his evening meal there. The long fierce summer afternoons are spent in sleep, in turning over the newspapers which he borrows from a friendly Greek newsvendor. (As he reads the pulse in the top of his skull beats softly.) Ripeness is all.

The furnishing of his little room suggests a highly eclectic spirit; the few objects which adorn the anchorite's life have a severely personal flavour, as if together they composed the personality of their owner. That is why Clea's portrait gives such a feeling of completeness, for she has worked into the background the whole sum of the old man's possessions. The shabby little crucifix on the wall behind the bed, for example; it is some years since Scobie accepted the consolations of the Holy Roman Church against old age and those defects of character which had by this time become second nature. Nearby hangs a small print of the Mona Lisa whose enigmatic smile has always reminded Scobie of his mother. (For my part the famous smile has always seemed to me to be the smile of a woman who has just dined off her husband.) However this too has somehow incorporated itself into the existence of Scobie, established a special and private relationship. It is as if his Mona Lisa were like no other; it is a deserter from Leonardo.

Then, of course, there is the ancient cake-stand which serves as his commode, bookcase and escritoire in one. Clea has accorded it the ungrudging treatment it deserves, painting it with a microscopic fidelity. It has four tiers, each fringed with a narrow but elegant level. It cost him ninepence farthing in the Euston Road in 1911, and it has travelled twice round the world with him. He will help you admire it without a trace of humour or self-consciousness. 'Fetching little thing, what?' he will say jauntily, as he takes a cloth and dusts it. The top tier, he will explain carefully, was designed for buttered toast: the middle for shortbreads: the bottom tier is for 'two kinds of cake'. At the moment, however, it is fulfilling another purpose. On the top shelf lie his telescope, compass and Bible; on the middle tier lies his correspondence which consists only of his pension envelope; on the bottom tier, with tremendous gravity, lies a chamber-pot which is always referred to as 'the heirloom', and to which is attached a mysterious story which he will one day confide to me.

The room is lit by one weak electric-light bulb and a cluster of rush lights standing in a niche which also houses an earthenware jar full of cool drinking water. The one uncurtained window looks blindly out upon a sad peeling wall of mud. Lying in bed with the smoky feeble glare of the night-lights glinting in the glass of his compass — lying in bed after midnight with the brandy throbbing in his skull he reminds me of some ancient wedding-cake, waiting only for someone to lean forward and blow out the candles!

His last remark at night, when one has seen him safely to bed and tucked him in — apart from the vulgar 'Kiss Me Hardy' which is always accompanied by a leer and a popped cheek — is more serious. 'Tell me honestly' he says. 'Do I look my age?'

Frankly Scobie looks anybody's age; older than the birth of tragedy, younger than the Athenian death. Spawned in the Ark by a chance meeting and mating of the bear and the ostrich; delivered before term by the sickening grunt of the keel on Ararat. Scobie came forth from the womb in a wheel chair with rubber tyres, dressed in a deer-stalker and a red flannel binder. On his prehensile toes the glossiest pair of elastic-sided boots. In his hand a ravaged family Bible whose fly-leaf bore the words 'Joshua Samuel Scobie 1870. Honour thy father and thy mother'. To these possessions were added eyes like dead moons, a distinct curvature of the pirate's spinal column, and a taste for quinqueremes. It was not blood which flowed in Scobie's veins but green salt water, deep-sea stuff. His walk is the slow rolling grinding trudge of a saint walking on Galilee. His talk is a green-water jargon swept up in five oceans — an antique shop of polite fable bristling with sextants, astrolabes, porpentines and isobars. When he sings, which he so often does, it is in the very accents of the Old Man of the Sea. Like a patron saint he has left little pieces of his flesh all over the world, in Zanzibar, Colombo, Togoland, Wu Fu: the little deciduous morsels which he has been shedding for so long now, old antlers, cuff-links, teeth, hair. . . . Now the retreating tide has left him high and dry above the speeding currents of time, Joshua the insolvent weather-man, the islander, the anchorite.

*   *   *   *   *

Clea, the gentle, lovable, unknowable Clea is Scobie's greatest friend, and spends much of her time with the old pirate; she deserts her cobweb studio to make him tea and to enjoy those interminable monologues about a life which has long since receded, lost its vital momentum, only to live on vicariously in the labyrinths of memory.

As for Clea herself: is it only my imagination which makes it seem so difficult to sketch her portrait? I think of her so much — and yet I see how in all this writing I have been shrinking from dealing directly with her. Perhaps the difficulty lies here: that there does not seem to be an easy correspondence between her habits and her true disposition. If I should describe the outward structures of her life — so disarmingly simple, graceful, self-contained — there is a real danger that she might seem either a nun for whom the whole range of human passions had given place to an absorbing search for her subliminal self or a disappointed and ingrown virgin who had deprived herself of the world because of some psychic instability, or some insurmountable early wound.

Everything about her person is honey-gold and warm in tone; the fair, crisply-trimmed hair which she wears rather long at the back, knotting it simply at the downy nape of her neck. This focuses the candid face of a minor muse with its smiling grey-green eyes. The calmly disposed hands have a deftness and shapeliness which one only notices when one sees them at work, holding a paint-brush perhaps or setting the broken leg of a sparrow in splints made from match-ends.

I should say something like this: that she had been poured, while still warm, into the body of a young grace: that is to say, into a body born without instincts or desires.

To have great beauty; to have enough money to construct an independent life; to have a skill — these are the factors which persuade the envious, the dispirited to regard her as undeservedly lucky. But why, ask her critics and observers, has she denied herself marriage?

She lives in modest though not miserly style, inhabiting a comfortable attic-studio furnished with little beyond an iron bed and a few ragged beach chairs which in the summer are transferred bodily to her little bathing cabin at Sidi Bishr. Her only luxury is a glittering tiled bathroom in the corner of which she has installed a minute stove to cope with whatever cooking she feels inclined to do for herself; and a bookcase whose crowded shelves indicate that she denies it nothing.

She lives without lovers or family ties, without malices or pets, concentrating with single-mindedness upon her painting which she takes seriously, but not too seriously. In her work, too, she is lucky; for these bold yet elegant canvases radiate clemency and humour. They are full of a sense of play — like children much-beloved.

But I see that I have foolishly spoken of her as 'denying herself marriage'. How this would anger her: for I remember her once saying: 'If we are to be friends you must not think or speak about me as someone who is denying herself something in life. My solitude does not deprive me of anything, nor am I fitted to be other than I am. I want you to see how successful I am and not imagine me full of inner failings. As for love itself — *cher ami* — I told you already that love interested me only very briefly — and men more briefly still; the few, indeed the one, experience which marked me was an experience with a woman. I am still living in the happiness of that perfectly *achieved* relationship: any physical substitute would seem today horribly vulgar and hollow. But do not imagine me as suffering from any fashionable form of broken heart. No. In a funny sort of way I feel that our love has really gained by the passing of the love-object; it is as if the physical body somehow stood in the way of love's true growth, its self-realization. Does that sound calamitous?' She laughed.

We were walking, I remember, along the rainswept Corniche in autumn, under a darkening crescent of clouded sky; and as she spoke she put her arm affectionately through mine and smiled at me with such tenderness that a passer-by might have been forgiven for imagining that we ourselves were lovers.

'And then' she went on 'there is another thing which perhaps you will discover for yourself. There is something about love — I will not say defective for the defect lies in ourselves: but something we have mistaken about its nature. For example, the love you now feel for Justine is not a different love for a different object but the same love you feel for Melissa trying to work itself out through the medium of Justine. Love is horribly stable, and each of us is only allotted a certain portion of it, a ration. It is capable of appearing in an infinity of forms and attaching itself to an infinity of people. But it is limited in quantity, can be used up, become shopworn and faded before it reaches its true object. For its destination lies somewhere in the deepest regions of the psyche where it will come to recognize itself as self-love, the ground upon which we build the sort of health of the psyche. I do not mean egoism or narcissism.'

It was conversations like these: conversations lasting sometimes far into the night, which first brought me close to Clea, taught me that I could rely upon the strength which she had quarried out of self-knowledge and reflection. In our friendship we were able to share our private thoughts and ideas, to test them upon one another, in a way that would have been impossible had we been linked more closely by ties which, paradoxically enough, separate more profoundly than they join, though human illusion forbids us to believe this. 'It is true' I remember her saying once, when I had mentioned this strange fact, 'that in some sense I am closer to you than either Melissa or Justine. You see, Melissa's love is too confiding: it blinds her. While Justine's cowardly monomania sees one through an invented picture of one, and this forbids you to do anything except to be a demoniac like her. Do not look hurt. There is no malice in what I say.'

But apart from Clea's own painting, I should not forget to mention the work she does for Balthazar. She is the clinic painter. For some reason or other my friend is not content with the normal slipshod method of recording medical anomalies by photographs. He is pursuing some private theory which makes him attach importance to the pigmentation of the skin in certain stages of his pet diseases. The ravages of syphilis, for example, in every degree of anomaly, Clea has recorded for him in large coloured drawings of terrifying lucidity and tenderness. In a sense these are truly works of art; the purely utilitarian object has freed the painter from any compulsion towards self-expression; she has set herself to record; and these tortured and benighted human members which Balthazar picks out daily from the long sad queue in the outpatients' ward (like a man picking rotten apples from a barrel) have all the values of depicted human faces — abdomens blown like fuses, skin surfaces shrunken and peeling like plaster, carcinomata bursting through the rubber membranes which retain them. . . . I remember the first time I saw her at work; I had called on Balthazar at the clinic to collect a certificate for some routine matter in connection with the school at which I worked. Through the glass doors of the surgery I caught a glimpse of Clea, whom I did not then know, sitting under the withered pear-tree in the shabby garden. She was dressed in a white medical smock, and her colours were laid out methodically beside her on a slab of fallen marble. Before her, seated half-crouching upon a wicker chair, was a big-breasted sphinx-faced *fellah* girl, with her skirt drawn up above her waist to expose some choice object of my friend's study. It was a brilliant spring day, and in the distance one could hear the scampering of the sea. Clea's capable and innocent fingers moved back and forth upon the white surface of the paper, surely, deftly, with wise premeditation. Her face showed the rapt and concentrated pleasure of a specialist touching in the colours of some rare tulip.

When Melissa was dying it was for Clea that she asked; and it was Clea who spent whole nights at her bedside telling her stories and tending her. As for Scobie — I do not dare to say that their inversion constituted a hidden bond — sunk like a submarine cable linking two continents — for that might do an injustice to both. Certainly the old man is unaware of any such matter; and she for her part is restrained by her perfect tact from showing him how hollow are his boasts of love-making. They are perfectly matched, and perfectly happy in their relationship, like a father and daughter. On the only occasion when I heard him rally her upon not being married Clea's lovely face became round and smooth as that of a schoolgirl, and from the depths of an assumed seriousness which completely disguised the twinkle of the imp in her grey eyes, she replied that she was waiting for the right man to come along: at which Scobie nodded profoundly, and agreed that this was the right line of conduct.

It was from a litter of dusty canvases in one corner of her studio that I unearthed a head of Justine one day — a half profile, touched in impressionistically and obviously not finished. Clea caught her breath and gazed at it with all the compassion a mother might show for a child which she recognized as ugly, but which was none the less beautiful for her. 'It is ages old' she said; and after much reflection gave it to me for my birthday. It stands now on the old arched mantelshelf to remind me of the breathless, incisive beauty of that dark and beloved head. She has just taken a cigarette from between her lips, and she is about to say something which her

mind has already formulated but which has so far only reached the
eyes. The lips are parted, ready to utter it in words.

*　　*　　*　　*　　*

A mania for self-justification is common both to those whose
consciences are uneasy and to those who seek a philosophic ration-
ale for their actions: but in either case it leads to strange forms of
thinking. The idea is not spontaneous, but *voulue*. In the case of
Justine this mania led to a perpetual flow of ideas, speculations on
past and present actions, which pressed upon her mind with the
weight of a massive current pressing upon the walls of a dam. And
for all the wretched expenditure of energy in this direction, for all
the passionate contrivance in her self-examination, one could not
help distrusting her conclusions, since they were always changing,
were never at rest. She shed theories about herself like so many
petals. 'Do you not believe that love consists wholly of paradoxes?'
she once asked Arnauti. I remember her asking me much the same
question in that turbid voice of hers which somehow gave the
question tenderness as well as a sort of menace. 'Supposing I were
to tell you that I only allowed myself to approach you to save myself from the danger and ignominy of falling deeply in love with
you? I felt I was saving Nessim with every kiss I gave you.' How
could this, for example, have constituted the true motive for that
extraordinary scene on the beach? No rest from doubt, no rest
from doubt. On another occasion she dealt with the problem from
another angle, not perhaps less truthfully: 'The moral is — what
is the moral? We were not simply gluttons, were we? And how
completely this love-affair has repaid all the promises it held out
for us — at least for me. We met and the worst befell us, but the
best part of us, our lovers. Oh! please do not laugh at me.'

For my part I remained always stupefied and mumchance at all
the avenues opened up by these thoughts; and afraid, so strange
did it seem to talk about what we were actually experiencing in such
obituary terms. At times I was almost provoked like Arnauti, on a
similar occasion, to shout: 'For the love of God, stop this mania
for unhappiness or it will bring us to disaster. You are exhausting
our lives before we have a chance to live them.' I knew of course the
uselessness of such an exhortation. There are some characters in
this world who are marked down for self-destruction, and to these
no amount of rational argument can appeal. For my part Justine
always reminded me of a somnambulist discovered treading the

perilous leads of a high tower; any attempt to wake her with a shout might lead to disaster. One could only follow her silently in the hope of guiding her gradually away from the great shadowy drops which loomed up on every side.

But by some curious paradox it was these very defects of character — these vulgarities of the psyche — which constituted for me the greatest attraction of this weird kinetic personage. I suppose in some way they corresponded to weaknesses in my own character which I was lucky to be able to master more thoroughly than she could. I know that for us love-making was only a small part of the total picture projected by a mental intimacy which proliferated and ramified daily around us. How we talked! Night after night in shabby sea-front cafés (trying ineffectually to conceal from Nessim and other common friends an attachment for which we felt guilty). As we talked we insensibly drew nearer and nearer to each other until we were holding hands, or all but in each other's arms: not from the customary sensuality which afflicts lovers but as if the physical contact could ease the pain of self-exploration.

Of course this is the unhappiest love-relationship of which a human being is capable — weighed down by something as heart-breaking as the post-coital sadness which clings to every endearment, which lingers like a sediment in the clear waters of a kiss. 'It is easy to write of kisses' says Arnauti, 'but where passion should have been full of clues and keys it served only to slake our thoughts. It did not convey information as it usually does. There was so much else going on.' And indeed in making love to her I too began to understand fully what he meant in describing the Check as 'the parching sense of lying with some lovely statue which was unable to return the kisses of the common flesh which it touches. There was something exhausting and perverting about loving so well and yet loving so little.'

The bedroom for example with its bronze phosphorous light, the pastels burning in the green Tibetan urn diffusing a smell of roses to the whole room. By the bed the rich poignant scent of her powder hanging heavy in the bed-curtains. A dressing-table with its stoppered cream and salves. Over the bed the Universe of Ptolemy! She has had it drawn upon parchment and handsomely framed. It will hang forever over her bed, over the ikons in their leather cases, over the martial array of philosophers. Kant in his nightcap feeling his way upstairs. Jupiter Tonans. There is some-how a heavy futility in this array of great ones — among whom she has permitted Pursewarden an appearance. Four of his novels are to be seen though whether she has put them there specially for the occasion (we are all dining together) I cannot say. Justine surrounded by her philosophers is like an invalid surrounded by medicines — empty capsules, bottles and syringes. 'Kiss her' says Arnauti 'and you are aware that her eyes do not close but open more widely, with an increasing doubt and madness. The mind is so awake that it makes any gift of the body partial — a panic which will respond to nothing less than a *curette*. At night you can hear her brain ticking like a cheap alarm-clock.'

On the far wall there is an idol the eyes of which are lit from within by electricity, and it is to this graven mentor that Justine acts her private role. Imagine a torch thrust through the throat of a skeleton to light up the vault of the skull from which the eyeless sockets ponder. Shadows thrown on the arch of the cranium flap there in imprisonment. When the electricity is out of order a stump of candle is soldered to the bracket: Justine then, standing naked on tip-toes to push a lighted match into the eyeball of the God. Immediately the furrows of the jaw spring into relief, the shaven frontal bone, the straight rod of the nose. She has never been tranquil unless this visitant from distant mythology is watching over her nightmares. Under it lie a few small inexpensive toys, a celluloid doll, a sailor, about which I have never had the courage to question her. It is to this idol that her most marvellous dialogues are composed. It is possible, she says, to talk in her sleep and be overheard by the wise and sympathetic mask which has come to represent what she calls her Noble Self — adding sadly, with a smile of misgiving, 'It does exist you know.'

The pages of Arnauti run through my mind as I watch her and talk to her. 'A face famished by the inward light of her terrors. In the darkness long after I am asleep she wakes to ponder on something I have said about our relationship. I am always waking to find her busy with something, preoccupied; sitting before the mirror naked, smoking a cigarette, and tapping with her bare foot on the expensive carpet.' It is strange that I should always see Justine in the context of this bedroom which she could never have known before Nessim gave it to her. It is always here that I see her undergoing those dreadful intimacies of which he writes. 'There is no pain compared to that of loving a woman who makes her body accessible to one and yet who is incapable of delivering her true self — because she does not know where to find it.' How often, lying beside her, I have debated these observations which, to the ordinary reader, might pass unnoticed in the general flux and reflux of ideas in *Moeurs*.

She does not slide from kisses into sleep — a door into a private garden — as Melissa does. In the warm bronze light her pale skin looks paler — the red eatable flowers growing in the cheeks where the light sinks and is held fast. She will throw back her dress to un-roll her stocking and show you the dark cicatrice above the knee, lodged between the twin dimples of the suspender. It is indescrib-able the feeling I have when I see this wound — like a character out of the book — and recall its singular origin. In the mirror the dark head, younger and more graceful now than the original it has outlived, gives back a vestigial image of a young Justine — like the calcimined imprint of a fern in chalk: the youth she believes she has lost.

I cannot believe that she existed so thoroughly in some other room; that the idol hung elsewhere, in another setting. Somehow I always see her walking up the long staircase, crossing the gallery with its *putti* and ferns, and then entering the low doorway into this most private of rooms. Fatma, the black Ethiopian maid, follows her. Invariably Justine sinks on to the bed and holds out her ringed fingers as with an air of mild hallucination the negress draws them off the long fingers and places them in a small casket on the dressing-table. The night on which Pursewarden and I dined alone with her we were invited back to the great house, and after examining the great cold reception rooms Justine suddenly turned and led the way upstairs, in search of an ambience which might persuade my friend whom she greatly admired and feared, to relax.

Pursewarden had been surly all evening, as he often was, and had busied himself with the drinks to the exclusion of anything else. The little ritual with Fatma seemed to free Justine from con-straint; she was free to be natural, to move about with 'that insolent unbalanced air, cursing her frock for catching in the cupboard door', or pausing to apostrophize herself in the great spade-shaped mirror. She told us of the mask, adding sadly: 'It sounds cheap and rather theatrical, I know. I turn my face to the wall and talk to it. I forgive myself my trespasses as I forgive those who trespass against me. Sometimes I rave a little and beat on the wall when I remember the follies which must seem insignificant to others or to God — if there is a God. I speak to the person I always imagine inhabiting a green and quiet place like the 23rd Psalm.' Then coming to rest her head upon my shoulder and put her arms round me, 'That is why so often I ask you to be a little tender with me. The edifice feels as if it had cracked up here. I need little strokes and endearments like you give Melissa; I know it is she you love. Who could love me?'

Pursewarden was not, I think, proof against the naturalness and charm of the tones in which she said this, for he went to the corner of the room and gazed at her bookshelf. The sight of his own books made him first pale and then red, though whether with shame or anger I could not tell. Turning back he seemed at first about to say something, but changed his mind. He turned back once more with an air of guilty chagrin to confront that tremendous shelf. Justine said: 'If you wouldn't consider it an impertinence I should so like you to autograph one for me' but he did not reply. He stayed quite still, staring at the shelf, with his glass in his hand. Then he wheeled about and all of a sudden he appeared to have become completely drunk; he said in a fierce ringing tone: 'The modern novel! The *grumus merdae* left behind by criminals upon the scene of their misdeeds.' And quietly falling sideways, but taking care to place his glass upright on the floor he passed immediately into a profound sleep.

The whole of the long colloquy which ensued took place over this prostrate body. I took him to be asleep, but in fact he must have been awake for he subsequently reproduced much of Justine's conversation in a cruel satirical short story, which for some reason amused Justine though it caused me great pain. He described her black eyes shining with unshed tears as she said (sitting at the mirror, the comb travelling through her hair, crackling and sputtering like her voice). 'When I first met Nessim and knew that I was falling in love with him I tried to save us both. I deliberately took a lover — a dull brute of a Swede, hoping to wound him and force him to detach himself from his feeling for me. The Swede's wife had left him and I said (anything to stop him snivelling): "Tell me how she behaves and I will imitate her. In the dark we are all meat and treacherous however our hair kinks or skin smells. Tell me, and I will give you the wedding-smile and fall into your arms like a mountain of silk." And all the time I was thinking over and over again: "Nessim. Nessim." '

I remember in this context, too, a remark of Pursewarden's which summed up his attitude to our friends. 'Alexandria!' he said (it was on one of those long moonlit walks). 'Jews with their cafeteria mysticism! How could one deal with it in words? Place and people?' Perhaps then he was meditating this cruel short story and casting about for ways and means to deal with us. 'Justine and her city are alike in that they both have a strong flavour without having any real character.'

I am recalling now how during that last spring (forever) we walked together at full moon, overcome by the soft dazed air of the city, the quiet ablutions of water and moonlight that polished it like a great casket. An aerial lunacy among the deserted trees of the dark squares, and the long dusty roads reaching away from midnight to midnight, bluer than oxygen. The passing faces had become gem-like, tranced — the baker at his machine making the staff of tomorrow's life, the lover hurrying back to his lodging, nailed into a silver helmet of panic, the six-foot cinema posters borrowing a ghastly magnificence from the moon which seemed laid across the nerves like a bow.

We turn a corner and the world becomes a pattern of arteries, splashed with silver and deckle-edged with shadow. At this far end of Kom El Dick not a soul abroad save an occasional obsessive policeman, lurking like a guilty wish in the city's mind. Our footsteps run punctually as metronomes along the deserted pavements: two men, in their own time and city, remote from the world, walking as if they were treading one of the lugubrious canals of the moon. Pursewarden is speaking of the book which he has always wanted to write, and of the difficulty which besets a city-man when he faces a work or art.

'If you think of yourself as a sleeping city for example . . . what? You can sit quiet and hear the processes going on, going about their business; volition, desire, will, cognition, passion, conation. I mean like the million legs of a centipede carrying on with the body powerless to do anything about it. One gets exhausted trying to circumnavigate these huge fields of experience. We are never free, we writers. I could explain it much more clearly if it was dawn. I long to be musical in body and mind. I want style, consort. Not the little mental squirts as if through the ticker-tape of the mind. It is the age's disease, is it not? It explains the huge waves of occultism lapping round us. The Cabal, now, and Balthazar. He will never understand that it is with God we must be the most careful; for He makes such a powerful appeal to what is *lowest* in human nature — our feeling of insufficiency, fear of the unknown, personal failings; above all our monstrous egotism which sees in the martyr's crown an athletic prize which is really hard to attain. God's real and subtle nature must be clear of distinctions: a glass of spring-water, tasteless, odourless, merely refreshing: and surely its appeal would be to the few, the very few, real contemplatives?

'As for the many it is already included in the part of their nature which they least wish to admit or examine. I do not believe that there is any system which can do more than pervert the essential idea. And then, all these attempts to circumscribe God in words or ideas. . . . No one thing can explain everything: though everything can illuminate something. God, I must be still drunk. If God were anything he would be an art. Sculpture or medicine. But the immense extension of knowledge in this our age, the growth of new sciences, makes it almost impossible for us to digest the available flavours and put them to use.

'Holding a candle in your hand, I mean, you can throw the shadow of the retinal blood-vessels on the wall. It isn't silent enough. It's never dead still in there: never quiet enough for the trismegistus to be fed. All night long you can hear the rush of blood in the cerebral arteries. The loins of thinking. It starts you going back along the cogs of historical action, cause and effect. You can't rest ever, you can't give over and begin to scry. You climb through the physical body, softly parting the muscle-schemes to admit you — muscle striped and unstriped; you examine the coil ignition of the guts in the abdomen, the sweetbreads, the liver choked with refuse like a sink-filter, the bag of urine, the red unbuckled belt of the intestines, the soft horny corridor of the oesophagus, the glottis with its mucilage softer than the pouch of a kangaroo. What do I mean? You are searching for a co-ordinating scheme, the syntax of a Will which might stabilize everything and take the tragedy out of it. The sweat breaks out on your face, a cold panic as you feel the soft contraction and expansion of the viscera busy about their job, regardless of the man watching them who is yourself. A whole city of processes, a factory for the production of excrement, my goodness, a daily sacrifice. An offering to the toilet for every one you make to the altar. Where do they meet? Where is the correspondence? Outside in the darkness by the railway bridge the lover of this man waits for him with the same indescribable maggotry going on in her body and blood; wine swilling the conduits, the pylorus disgorging like a sucker, the incommensurable bacteriological world multiplying in every drop of semen, spittle, sputum, musk. He takes a spinal column in his arms, the ducts flooded with ammonia, the meninges exuding their pollen, the cornea glowing in its little crucible. . . .'

He begins now that shocking boyish laughter, throwing back his head until the moonlight plays upon his perfect white teeth under the trimmed moustache.

It was on such a night that our footsteps led us to Balthazar's door, and seeing his light on, we knocked. The same night, on the old horn gramophone (with an emotion so deep that it was almost horror) I heard some amateur's recording of the old poet reciting the lines which begin:

> *Ideal voices and much beloved*
> *Of those who died, of those who are*
> *Now lost for us like the very dead;*
> *Sometimes within a dream they speak*
> *Or in the ticking brain a thought revives them. . . .*

These fugitive memories explain nothing, illuminate nothing: yet they return again and again when I think of my friends as if the very circumstances of our habits had become impregnated with what we then felt, the parts we then acted. The slither of tyres across the waves of the desert under a sky blue and frost-bound in winter; or in summer a fearful lunar bombardment which turned the sea to phosphorus — bodies shining like tin, crushed in electric bubbles; or walking to the last spit of sand near Montaza, sneaking through the dense green darkness of the King's gardens, past the drowsy sentry, to where the force of the sea was suddenly crippled and the waves hobbled over the sand-bar. Or walking arm-in-arm down the long gallery, already gloomy with an unusual yellow winter fog. Her hand is cold so she has slipped it in my pocket. Today because she has no emotion whatsoever she tells me that she is in love with me — something she has always refused to do. At the long windows the rain hisses down suddenly. The dark eyes are cool and amused. A centre of blackness in things which trembles and changes shape. 'I am afraid of Nessim these days. He has changed.' We are standing before the Chinese paintings from the Louvre. 'The meaning of space' she says with disgust. There is no form, no pigment, no lens any more — simply a gaping hole into which the infinite drains slowly into the room: a blue gulf where the tiger's body was, emptying itself into the preoccupied atmosphere of the studios. Afterwards we walk up the dark staircase to the top floor to see Sveva, to put on the gramophone and dance. The little model pretends that she is heartbroken because Pombal has cast her off after a 'whirlwind romance' lasting nearly a month.

My friend himself is a little surprised at the force of an attachment which could make him think of one woman for so long a time. He has cut himself while shaving and his face looks grotesque with a moustache of surgical tape stuck to it. 'It is a city of aberrations' he repeats angrily. 'I very nearly married her. It is infuriating. Thank God that the veil lifted when it did. It was seeing her naked in front of the mirror. All of a sudden I was disgusted — though I mentally admitted a sort of Renaissance dignity in the fallen breasts, the waxy skin, the sunken belly and the little peasant paws. All of a sudden I sat up in bed and said to myself "My God! She is an elephant in need of a coat of whitewash!"'

Now Sveva is quietly sniffing into her handkerchief as she recounts the extravagant promises which Pombal has made her, and which will never be fulfilled. 'It was a curious and dangerous attachment for an easy-going man' (hear Pombal's voice explaining). 'It felt as if her cool murderous charity had eaten away my locomotive centres, paralysed my nervous system. Thank God I am free to concentrate on my work once more.'

He is troubled about his work. Rumours of his habits and general outlook have begun to get back to the Consulate. Lying in bed he plans a campaign which will get him crucified and promoted to a post with more scope. 'I have decided that I simply must get my cross. I am going to give several skilfully graded parties. I shall count on you: I shall need a few shabby people at first in order to give my boss the feeling that he can patronize me socially. He is a complete *parvenu* of course and rose on his wife's fortune and judicious smarming of powerful people. Worst of all he has a distinct inferiority complex about my own birth and family background. He has still not quite decided whether to do me down or not; but he has been taking soundings at the Quai D'Orsay to see how well padded I am there. Since my uncle died, of course, and my godfather the bishop was involved in that huge scandal over the brothel in Reims, I find myself rather less steady on my feet. I shall have to make the brute feel protective, feel that I need encouraging and bringing out. Pouagh! First a rather shabby party with one celebrity only. Oh, why did I join the service? Why have I not a small fortune of my own?'

Hearing all this in Sveva's artificial tears and then walking down the draughty staircase again arm in arm thinking not of Sveva, not of Pombal, but of the passage in Arnauti where he says of Justine: 'Like women who think by biological precept and without the help of reason. To such women how fatal an error it is to give oneself; there is simply a small chewing noise, as when the cat reaches the backbone of the mouse.'

The wet pavements are slick underfoot from the rain, and the air has become dense with the moisture so ardently longed for by the trees in the public gardens, the statues and other visitants. Justine is away upon another tack, walking slowly in her glorious silk frock with the dark lined cape, head hanging. She stops in front of a lighted shop-window and takes my arms so that I face her, looking into my eyes: 'I am thinking about going away' she says in a quiet puzzled voice. 'Something is happening to Nessim and I don't know what it is as yet.' Then suddenly the tears come into her eyes and she says: 'For the first time I am afraid, and I don't know why.'

PART III

That second spring the khamseen was worse than I have ever known it before or since. Before sunrise the skies of the desert turned brown as buckram, and then slowly darkened, swelling like a bruise and at last releasing the outlines of cloud, giant octaves of ochre which massed up from the Delta like the drift of ashes under a volcano. The city has shuttered itself tightly, as if against a gale. A few gusts of air and a thin sour rain are the forerunners of the darkness which blots out the light of the sky. And now unseen in the darkness of shuttered rooms the sand is invading everything, appearing as if by magic in clothes long locked away, books, pictures and teaspoons. In the locks of doors, beneath fingernails. The harsh sobbing air dries the membranes of throats and noses, and makes eyes raw with the configurations of conjunctivitis. Clouds of dried blood walk the streets like prophecies; the sand is settling into the sea like powder into the curls of a stale wig. Choked fountain-pens, dry lips — and along the slats of the Venetian shutters thin white drifts as of young snow. The ghostly feluccas passing along the canal are crewed by ghouls with wrapped heads. From time to time a cracked wind arrives from directly above and stirs the whole city round and round so that one has the illusion that everything — trees, minarets, monuments and people have been caught in the final eddy of some great whirlpool and will pour softly back at last into the desert from which they rose, reverting once more to the anonymous wave-sculptured floor of dunes. . . .

I cannot deny that by this time we had both been seized by an exhaustion of spirit which had made us desperate, reckless, impatient of discovery. Guilt always hurries towards its complement, punishment: only there does its satisfaction lie. A hidden desire for some sort of expiation dictated Justine's folly which was greater than mine; or perhaps we both dimly sensed that, bound as we were hand and foot to each other, only an upheaval of some sort could restore each to his vulgar right mind. These days were full of omens and warnings upon which our anxiety fed.

One-eyed Hamid told me one day of a mysterious caller who

had told him that he must keep careful watch on his master as he was in great danger from some highly-placed personage. His description of the man might have been that of Selim, Nessim's secretary: but it also might have been any of the 150,000 inhabitants of the province. Meanwhile Nessim's own attitude to me had changed, or rather deepened into a solicitous and cloying sweetness. He shed his former reserve. When he spoke to me he used unfamiliar endearments and took me affectionately by the sleeve. At times as we spoke he would flush suddenly: or tears would come into his eyes and he would turn aside his head to hide them. Justine watched this with a concern which was painful to observe. But the very humiliation and self-reproach we felt at wounding him only drove us closer together as accomplices. At times she spoke of going away: at times I did the same. But neither of us could move. We were forced to await the outcome with a fatality and exhaustion that was truly fearful to experience.

Nor were our follies diminished by these warnings; rather did they multiply. A dreadful inadvertency reigned over our actions, an appalling thoughtlessness marked our behaviour. Nor did we (and here I realized that I had lost myself completely) even hope to avert whatever fate might be in store for us. We were only foolishly concerned lest we might not be able to share it — lest it might separate us! In this plain courting of martyrdom I realized that we showed our love at its hollowest, its most defective. 'How disgusting I must seem to you' said Justine once 'with my obscene jumble of conflicting ideas: all this sickly preoccupation with God and a total inability to obey the smallest moral injunction from my inner nature like being faithful to a man one adores. I tremble for myself, my dear one, I tremble. If only I could escape from the tiresome classical Jewess of neurology. . . . If only I could peel it off.'

During this period, while Melissa was away in Palestine on a cure (I had borrowed the money from Justine in order for her to go) we had several narrow escapes. For example, one day we were talking, Justine and I, in the great bedroom of the house. We had come in from bathing and had taken cold showers to get the salt off our skins. Justine sat on the bed naked under the bathroom towel which she had draped round her like a chiton. Nessim was away in Cairo where he was supposed to make a radio broadcast on behalf of some charity or other. Outside the window the trees nodded their dusty fronds in the damp summer air, while the faint huddle of traffic on Rue Fuad could be heard.

Nessim's quiet voice came to us from the little black radio by the bed, converted by the microphone into the voice of a man prematurely aged. The mentally empty phrases lived on in the silence they invaded until the air seemed packed with commonplaces. But the voice was beautiful, the voice of someone who had elaborately isolated himself from feeling. Behind Justine's back the door into the bathroom was open. Beyond it, a pane of clinical whiteness, lay another door leading to an iron fire-escape — for the house had been designed round a central well so that its bathrooms and kitchens could be connected by a cobweb of iron staircases such as span the engine-room of a ship. Suddenly, while the voice was still talking and while we listened to it, there came the light youthful patter of footsteps on the iron staircase outside the bathroom: a step unmistakably that of Nessim — or of any of the 150,000 inhabitants of the province. Looking over Justine's shoulder I saw developing on the glass panel of the frosted door, the head and shoulders of a tall slim man, with a soft felt hat pulled down over his eyes. He developed like a print in a photographer's developing-bowl. The figure paused with outstretched hand upon the knob of the door. Justine, seeing the direction of my glance, turned her head. She put one naked arm round my shoulders as both of us, with a feeling of complete calm whose core, like a heart beating, was a feverish impotent sexual excitement watched the dark figure standing there between two worlds, depicted as if on an X-ray screen. He would have found us absurdly posed, as if for a photograph, with an expression, not of fear but of guiltless relief upon our faces.

For a long time the figure stood there, as if in deep thought, perhaps listening. Then it shook its head once, slowly, and after a moment turned away with an air of perplexity to dissolve slowly on the glass. As it turned it seemed to slip something into the right-hand pocket of its coat. We heard the steps slowly diminishing — a dull descending scale of notes — on the iron ladder in the well. We neither of us spoke, but turned as if with deepened concentration to the little black radio from which the voice of Nessim still flowed with uninterrupted urbanity and gentleness. It seemed impossible that he could be in two places at once. It was only when the announcer informed us that the speech had been recorded that we understood. Why did he not open the door?

I suppose the truth is that he had been seized by the vertiginous uncertainty which, in a peaceable nature, follows upon a decision to act. Something had been building itself up inside him all this time, grain by grain, until the weight of it had become insupportable. He was aware of a profound interior change in his nature which had at last shaken off the long paralysis of impotent love which had hitherto ruled his actions. The thought of some sudden concise action, some determining factor for good or evil, presented itself to him as an intoxicating novelty. He felt (or so I divined it) like a gambler about to stake the meagre remains of a lost fortune upon one desperate throw. But the nature of his action had not yet been decided upon. What form should it take? A mass of uneasy fantasies burst in.

Let us suppose that two major currents had reached their confluence in this desire to act; on the one hand the dossier which his agents had collected upon Justine had reached such proportions that it could not be ignored; on the other he was haunted by a new and fearful thought which for some reason had not struck him before — namely that Justine was really falling in love at last. The whole temper of her personality seemed to be changing; for the first time she had become reflective, thoughtful, and full of the echoes of a sweetness which a woman can always afford to spend upon the man she does not love. You see, he too had been dogging her steps through the pages of Arnauti.

'Originally I believed that she must be allowed to struggle towards me through the jungle of the Check. Whenever the wounding thought of her infidelity came upon me I reminded myself that she was not a pleasure-seeker, but a hunter of pain in search of herself — and me. I thought that if one man could release her from herself she would then become accessible to all men, and so to me who had most claim upon her. But when I began to see her melting like a summer ice-cap, a horrible thought came to me: namely that he who broke the Check must keep her forever, since the peace he gave her was precisely that for which she was hunting so frantically through our bodies and fortunes. For the first time my jealousy, helped forward by my fear, mastered me.' He might have explained it thus.

Yet it has always seemed fantastic to me that even now he was jealous of everyone except the true author of Justine's present concern — myself. Despite the overwhelming mass of evidence he hardly dared to allow himself to suspect me. It was not love that is blind, but jealousy. It was a long time before he could bring himself to trust the mass of documentation his agents had piled up around us, around our meetings, our behaviour. But by now the facts had obtruded themselves so clearly that there was no possibility of error. The problem was how to dispose of me — I do not mean in the flesh so much. For I'd become merely an image standing in his light. He saw me perhaps dying, perhaps going away. He did not know. The very uncertainty was exciting to the pitch of drunkenness. Of course I am only supposing this.

But side by side with these preoccupations were others — the posthumous problems which Arnauti had been unable to solve and which Nessim had been following up with true Oriental curiosity over a period of years. He was now near to the man with the black patch over one eye — nearer than any of us had ever been. Here was another piece of knowledge which as yet he could not decide how best to use. If Justine was really ridding herself of him, however, what good would there be in revenging himself upon the true person of the mysterious being? On the other hand if I was about to step into the place vacated by the image? . . .

I asked Selim point-blank whether he had ever visited my flat to warn one-eyed Hamid. He did not reply but lowered his head and said under his breath, 'My master is not himself these days.'

Meanwhile my own fortunes had taken an absurd and unexpected turn. One night there came a banging on the door and I opened it to admit the dapper figure of an Egyptian Army officer clad in resplendent boots and tarbush, carrying under his arm a giant fly-whisk with an ebony handle. Yussouf Bey spoke nearly perfect English, allowing it to fall negligently from his lips, word by well-chosen word, out of an earnest coal-black face fitted with a dazzle of small perfect teeth like seed-pearls. He had some of the endearing solemnity of a talking water-melon just down from Cambridge. Hamid brought him habitual coffee and a sticky liqueur, and over it he told me that a great friend of mine in a high position very much wished to see me. My thoughts at once turned to Nessim; but this friend, the water-melon asserted, was an Englishman, an official. More he could not say. His mission was confidential. Would I go with him and visit my friend?

I was full of misgivings. Alexandria, outwardly so peaceful, was not really a safe place for Christians. Only last week Pombal had come home with a story of the Swedish vice-consul whose car had broken down on the Matrugh road. He had left his wife alone in it while he walked to the nearest telephone-point in order to ring up the consulate and ask them to send out another car. He had arrived back to find her body sitting normally on the back seat — without a head. Police were summoned and the whole district was combed. Some Bedouin encamped nearby were among those interrogated. While they were busy denying any knowledge of the accident, out of the apron of one of the women rolled the missing head. They had been trying to extract the gold teeth which had been such an unpleasant feature of her party-smile. This sort of incident was not sufficiently uncommon to give one courage in visiting strange quarters of the town after dark, so it was with no feeling of jauntiness that I followed the soldier into the back of a staff-car behind a uniformed driver and saw myself being whirled towards the seedier quarters of the town. Yussouf Bey stroked his neat little brush-stroke moustache with the anticipatory air of a musician tuning an instrument. It was useless to question him further: I did not wish to betray any of the anxiety I felt. So I made a sort of inner surrender to the situation, lit a cigarette, and watched the long dissolving strip of the Corniche flow past us.

Presently the car dropped us and the soldier led me on foot through a straggle of small streets and alleys near the Rue Des Soeurs. If the object here was to make me lose myself it succeeded almost immediately. He walked with a light self-confident step, humming under his breath. Finally we debouched into a suburban street full of merchants' stores and stopped before a great carved door which he pushed open after having first rung a bell. A court-yard with a stunted palm-tree; the path which crossed it was punctuated by a couple of feeble lanterns standing on the gravel. We crossed it and ascended some stairs to where a frosted electric light bulb gleamed harshly above a tall white door. He knocked, entered and saluted in one movement. I followed him into a large, rather elegant and warmly-lighted room with neat polished floors enhanced by fine Arab carpets. In one corner seated at a high inlaid desk with the air of a man riding a penny-farthing sat Scobie, with a scowl of self-importance overlapping the smile of welcome with which he greeted me. 'My God' I said. The old pirate gave a Drury Lane chuckle and said: 'At last, old man, at last.' He did not rise however but sat on in his uncomfortable high-backed chair, tarbush on head, whisk on knee, with a vaguely impressive air. I noticed an extra pip on his shoulder, betokening heaven knows what increase of rank and power. 'Sit down, old man' he said with an awkward sawing movement of the hand which bore a faint resemblance to a Second Empire gesture. The soldier was dismissed and departed grinning. It seemed to me that Scobie did not look very much at ease in these opulent surroundings. He had a slightly defensive air. 'I asked them to get hold of you' he said, sinking his voice to a theatrical whisper 'for a very special reason.' There were a number of green files on his desk and a curiously disembodied-looking tea-cosy. I sat down.

He now rose quickly and opened the door. There was nobody outside. He opened the window. There was no one standing on the sill. He placed the tea-cosy over the desk telephone and re-seated himself. Then, leaning forward and speaking carefully, he rolled his glass eye at me as with a conspiratorial solemnity he said: 'Not a word to anyone, old man. Swear you won't say a word'. I swore. '*They've made me head of the Secret Service.*' The words fairly whistled in his dentures. I nodded in amazement. He drew a deep sucking breath as if he had been delivered of a weight and went on. 'Old boy, there's going to be a war. Inside information.' He pointed a long finger at his own temple. 'There's going to be a war. The enemy is working night and day, old boy, right here among us.' I could not dispute this. I could only marvel at the new Scobie who confronted me like a bad magazine illustration. 'You can help us scupper them, old man' he went on with a devastating air of authority. 'We want to take you on our strength.' This sounded most agreeable. I waited for details. 'The most dangerous gang of all is right here, in Alexandria' the old man creaked and boomed, 'and you are in the centre of it. All friends of yours.'

I saw through the knotted eyebrows and the rolling excited eye the sudden picture of Nessim, a brief flash, as of intuition, sitting at his huge desk in the cold steel-tube offices watching a telephone ring while the beads of sweat stood out on his forehead. He was expecting a message about Justine — one more twist of the knife. Scobie shook his head. 'Not him so much' he said. 'He's in it, of course. The leader is a man called Balthazar. Look what the censorship have been picking up.'

He extracted a card from a file and passed it to me. Balthazar writes an exquisite hand and the writing was obviously his; but I could not help smiling when I saw that the reverse of the postcard contained only the little chessboard diagram of the *boustrophedon*. Greek letters filled up the little squares. 'He's got so much damn cheek he sends them through the open post.' I studied the diagram and tried to remember the little I had learned from my friend of the calculus. 'It's a nine-power system. I can't read this one' I said. Scobie added breathlessly: 'They have regular meetings, old man, to pool information. We know this for a fact.' I held the postcard lightly in my fingers and seemed to hear the voice of Balthazar saying: 'The thinker's job is to be suggestive: that of the saint to be silent about his discovery.'

Scobie was leaning back in his chair now with unconcealed self-satisfaction. He had puffed himself out like a pouter-pigeon. He took his tarbush off his head, looked at it with an air of complaisant patronage, and placed it on the tea-cosy. Then he scratched his fissured skull with bony fingers and went on — 'We simply can't break the code' he said. 'We've got dozens of them' — he indicated a file full of photostatic reproductions of similar postcards. 'They've been round the code-rooms: even to the Senior Wranglers in the Universities. No good, old man.' This did not surprise me. I laid the postcard on the pile of photostats and returned to the contemplation of Scobie. 'That is where you come in' he said with a grimace, 'if you will come in, old man. We want you to break the code however long it takes you. We'll put you on a damn good screw, too. What do you say?'

What could I say? The idea was too delightful to be allowed to melt. Besides during the last months my schoolwork had fallen off so much that I was sure my contract was not going to be renewed at the end of the present term. I was always arriving late from some meeting with Justine. I hardly bothered to correct papers any more. I had become irritable and surly with my colleagues and directors. Here was a chance to become my own man. I heard Justine's voice in my head saying: 'Our love has become like some fearful misquotation in a popular saying' as I leaned forward once more and nodded my head. Scobie expelled a breath of relieved pleasure and relaxed once more into the pirate. He confided his office to an anonymous Mustapha who apparently dwelt somewhere in the black telephone — Scobie always looked into the mouthpiece as he spoke, as if into a human eye. We left the building together and allowed a staff car to take us down towards the sea. Further details of my employment could be discussed over the little bottle of brandy in the bottom of the cake-stand by his bed.

We allowed ourselves to be dropped on the Corniche and walked together the rest of the way by a brilliant bullying moonlight, watching the old city dissolve and reassemble in the graphs of evening mist, heavy with the inertia of its surrounding desert, of

the green alluvial Delta which soaked into its very bones, informing its values. Scobie talked inconsequently of this and that. I
remember him bemoaning the fact that he had been left an orphan
at an early age. His parents had been killed together under dramatic circumstances which gave him much food for reflection. 'My
father was an early pioneer of motoring, old man. Early road races,
flat out at twenty miles an hour — all that sort of thing. He had his
own landau. I can see him now sitting behind the wheel with a big
moustache. Colonel Scobie, M.C. A Lancer he was. My mother
sat beside him, old man. Never left his side, not even for road
races. She used to act as his mechanic. The newspapers always
had pictures of them at the start, sitting up there in bee-keeper's
veils — God knows why the pioneers always wore those huge veils.
Dust, I suppose.'

The veils had proved their undoing. Rounding a hairpin in the
old London–Brighton road-race his father's veil had been sucked
into the front axle of the car they were driving. He had been
dragged into the road, while his companion had careered on to
smash headlong into a tree. 'The only consolation is that that is
just how he would have liked to go out. They were leading by
quarter of a mile.'

I have always been very fond of ludicrous deaths and had great
difficulty in containing my laughter as Scobie described this mis-
adventure to me with portentous rotations of his glass eye. Yet as
he talked and I listened to this, half my thoughts were running
upon a parallel track, busy about the new job I was to undertake,
assessing it in terms of the freedom it offered me. Later that night
Justine was to meet me near Montaza — the great car purring like
a moth in the palm-cooled dusk of the road. What would she say
to it? She would be delighted of course to see me freed from the
shackles of my present work. But a part of her would groan inwardly at the thought that this relief would only create for us
further chances to consort, to drive home our untruth, to reveal
ourselves more fully than ever to our judges. Here was another
paradox of love; that the very thing which brought us closer together — the *boustrophedon* — would, had we mastered the virtues
which it illustrated, have separated us forever — I mean in the
selves which preyed upon each other's infatuated images.

'Meanwhile' as Nessim was to say in those gentle tones so full
of the shadowy sobriety which comes into the voice of those who
have loved truly and failed to be loved in return, 'meanwhile I was

dwelling in the midst of a vertiginous excitement for which there was no relief except through an action the nature of which I could not discern. Tremendous bursts of self-confidence were succeeded by depressions so deep that it seemed I would never recover from them. With a vague feeling that I was preparing myself for a contest — as an athlete does — I began to take fencing lessons and learned to shoot with a pocket automatic. I studied the composition and effects of poisons from a manual of toxicology which I borrowed from Dr Fuad Bey.' (I am inventing only the words.)

He had begun to harbour feelings which would not yield to analysis. The periods of intoxication were followed by others in which he felt, as if for the first time, the full weight of his loneliness: an inner agony of spirit for which, as yet, he could find no outward expression, either in paint or in action. He mused now incessantly upon his early years, full of a haunting sense of richness: his mother's shadowy house among the palms and poinsettias of Aboukir: the waters pulling and slithering among the old fort's emplacements, compiling the days of his early childhood in single condensed emotions born from visual memory. He clutched at these memories with a terror and clarity he had never experienced before. And all the time, behind the screen of nervous depression — for the incomplete action which he meditated lay within him like a *coitus interruptus* — there lived the germ of a wilful and uncontrolled exaltation. It was as if he were being egged on, to approach nearer and nearer . . . to what exactly? He could not tell; but here his ancient terror of madness stepped in and took possession of him, disturbing his physical balance, so that he suffered at times from attacks of vertigo which forced him to grope around himself like a blind man for something upon which to sit down — a chair or sofa. He would sit down, panting slightly and feeling the sweat beginning to start out on his forehead; but with relief that nothing of his interior struggle was visible to the casual onlooker. Now too he noticed that he involuntarily repeated phrases aloud to which his conscious mind refused to listen. 'Good' she heard him tell one of his mirrors, 'so you are falling into a neurasthenia!' And later as he was stepping out into the brilliant starlit air, dressed in his well-cut evening clothes Selim, at the wheel of the car, heard him add: 'I think this Jewish fox has eaten my life.'

At times, too, he was sufficiently alarmed to seek, if not the help, at least the surcease of contact with other human beings: a doctor who left him with a phosphorous tonic and a regimen he did not follow. The sight of a column of marching Carmelites, tonsured like mandrils, crossing Nebi Daniel drove him to renew his lapsed friendship with Father Paul who in the past had seemed so profoundly happy a man, folded into his religion like a razor into its case. But now the kind of verbal consolations offered him by this lucky, happy, unimaginative brute only filled him with nausea.

One night he knelt down beside his bed — a thing he had not done since his twelfth year — and deliberately set himself to pray. He stayed there a long time, mentally spellbound, tongue-tied, with no words or thoughts shaping themselves in his mind. He was filled by some ghastly inhibition like a mental stroke. He stayed like this until he could stand it no longer — until he felt that he was on the point of suffocating. Then he jumped into bed and drew the sheets over his head murmuring broken fragments of oaths and involuntary pleadings which he did not recognize as emanating from any part of himself.

Outwardly however there were no signs of these struggles to be seen; his speech remained dry and measured despite the fever of the thoughts behind it. His doctor complimented him on his excellent reflexes and assured him that his urine was free from excess albumen. An occasional headache only proved him to be a victim of *petit mal* — or some other such customary disease of the rich and idle.

For his own part he was prepared to suffer thus as long as the suffering remained within the control of his consciousness. What terrified him only was the sensation of utter loneliness — a reality which he would never, he realized, be able to communicate either to his friends or to the doctors who might be called in to pronounce upon anomalies of behaviour which they would regard only as symptoms of disorder.

He tried feverishly to take up his painting again, but without result. Self-consciousness like a poison seemed to eat into the very paint, making it sluggish and dead. It was hard even to manipulate the brush with an invisible hand pulling at one's sleeve the whole time, hindering, whispering, displacing all freedom and fluidity of movement.

Surrounded as he was by this menacing twilight of the feelings he turned once more, in a vain effort to restore his balance and composure, to the completion of the Summer Palace — as it was jokingly called; the little group of Arab huts and stables at Abousir.

Long ago, in the course of a ride to Benghazi along the lonely shoreline, he had come upon a fold in the desert, less than a mile from the sea, where a fresh spring suddenly burst through the thick sand pelt and hobbled a little way down towards the desolate beaches before it was overtaken and smothered by the dunes. Here the Bedouin, overtaken by the involuntary hunger for greenness which lies at the heart of all desert-lovers, had planted a palm and a fig whose roots had taken a firm subterranean grip upon the sandstone from which the pure water ran. Resting with the horses in the shade of these young trees, Nessim's eye had dwelt with wonder upon the distant view of the old Arab fort, and the long-drawn white scar of the empty beach where the waves pounded night and day. The dunes had folded themselves hereabouts into a long shapely valley which his imagination had already begun to people with clicking palm-trees and the green figs which, as always near running water, offer a shade so deep as to be like a wet cloth pressed to the skull. For a year he had allowed the spot to mature in his imagination, riding out frequently to study it in every kind of weather, until he had mastered its properties. He had not spoken of it to anyone, but in the back of his mind had lurked the idea of building a summer pleasure house for Justine — a miniature oasis where she could stable her three Arab thoroughbreds and pass the hottest season of the year in her favourite amusements, bathing and riding.

The spring had been dug out, channelled and gathered into the marble cistern which formed the centre-piece to the little court-yard, paved with rough sandstone, around which the house and stables were to stand. As the water grew so the green grew with it; shade created the prongy abstract shapes of cactus and the bushy exuberance of Indian corn. In time even a melon-bed was achieved — like some rare exile from Persia. A single severe stable in the Arab style turned its back upon the winter sea-wind, while in the form of an L grew up a cluster of storerooms and small living-rooms with grilled windows and shutters of black iron.

Two or three small bedrooms, no larger than the cells of medieval monks, gave directly into a pleasant oblong central room with a low ceiling, which was both living and dining-room; at one end a fireplace grew up massive and white, and with decorated lintels suggested by the designs of Arab ceramics. At the other end stood a stone table and stone benches reminiscent of some priory refectory used by desert fathers perhaps. The severity of the room was discountenanced by rich Persian rugs and some tremendous carved chests with gilt ornamentation writhing over their hooked clasps and leather-polished sides. It was all of a controlled simplicity which is the best sort of magnificence. On the severe white-washed walls, whose few grilled windows offered sudden magnificent slotted views of beach and desert, hung a few old trophies of hunting or meditation, like: an Arab lance-pennon, a Buddhist *mandala*, a few assegais in exile, a longbow still used for hunting of hares, a yacht-burgee. There were no books save an old Koran with ivory covers and tarnished metal clasps, but several packs of cards lay about on the sills, including the Grand Tarot for amateur divination and a set of Happy Families. In one corner, too, there stood an old samovar to do justice to the one addiction from which they both suffered — tea-drinking.

The work went forward slowly and hesitantly, but when at last, unable to contain his secret any longer, he had taken Justine out to see it, she had been unable to contain her tears as she walked about it, from window to window of the graceful rooms, to snatch now a picture of the emerald sea rolling on the sand, now a sudden whorled picture of the dunes sliding eastward into the sky. Then she sat down abruptly before the thorn fire in her habit and listened to the soft clear drumming of the sea upon the long beaches mingled with the cough and stamp of the horses in their new stalls beyond the courtyard. It was late autumn, then, and in the moist gathering darkness the fireflies had begun to snatch fitfully, filling them both with pleasure to think that already their oasis had begun to support other life than their own.

What Nessim had begun was now Justine's to complete. The small terrace under the palm-tree was extended towards the east and walled in to hold back the steady sand-drift which, after a winter of wind, would move forward and cover the stones of the courtyard in six inches of sand. A windbreak of junipers contributed a dull copper humus of leaf-mould which in time would become firm soil nourishing first bushes and later other and taller trees.

She was careful, too, to repay her husband's thoughtfulness by paying a tribute to what was then his ruling passion — astronomy. At one corner of the L-shaped block of buildings she laid down a small observatory which housed a telescope of thirty magnifications. Here Nessim would sit night after night in the winter, dressed in his old rust-coloured *abba*, staring gravely at Betelgeuse, or hovering over books of calculations for all the world like some medieval soothsayer. Here too their friends could look at the moon or by altering the angle of the barrel catch sudden smoky glimpses of the clouds of pearl which the city always seemed to exhale from afar.

All this, of course began to stand in need of a guardian, and it came as no surprise to them when Panayotis arrived and took up his residence in a tiny room near the stables. This old man with his spade beard and gimlet-eyes had been for twenty years a secondary school teacher at Damanhur. He had taken orders and spent nine years at the monastery of St Catherine in Sinai. What brought him to the oasis it was impossible to tell for at some stage in his apparently unadventurous life he had had his tongue cut out of his head. From the signs he made in response to questions it might seem that he had been making a pilgrimage on foot to the little shrine of St Menas situated to the west when he had stumbled upon the oasis. At any rate there seemed nothing fortuitous about his decision to adopt it. He fitted it to perfection, and for a small salary stayed there all the year round as watchman and gardener. He was an able-bodied little old man, active as a spider, and fearfully jealous of the green things which owed their life to his industry and care. It was he who coaxed the melon-bed into life and at last persuaded a vine to start climbing beside the lintel of the central doorway. His laughter was an inarticulate clucking, and he had a shy habit of hiding his face in the tattered sleeve of his old beadle's soutane. His Greek loquacity, dammed up behind his disability, had overflowed into his eyes where it sparkled and danced at the slightest remark or question. What more could anyone ask of life, he seemed to say, than this oasis by the sea?

What more indeed? It was the question that Nessim asked himself repeatedly as the car whimpered towards the desert with hawk-featured Selim motionless at the wheel. Some miles before the Arab fort the road fetches away inland from the coast and to reach the oasis one must swerve aside off the tarmac along an outcrop of stiff flaky dune — like beaten white of egg, glittering and mica-shafted. Here and there where the swaying car threatens to sink its driving-wheels in the dune they always find purchase again on the bed of friable sandstone which forms the backbone to the whole promontory. It was exhilarating to feather this sea of white crispness like a cutter travelling before a following wind.

It had been in Nessim's mind for some time past — the suggestion had originally been Pursewarden's — to repay the devotion of old Panayotis with the only kind of gift the old man would understand and find acceptable: and he carried now in his polished brief-case a dispensation from the Patriarch of Alexandria permitting him to build and endow a small chapel to St Arsenius in his house. The choice of saint had been, as it always should be, fortuitous. Clea had found an eighteenth-century ikon of him, in pleasing taste, lying among the lumber of a Muski stall in Cairo. She had given it to Justine as a birthday present.

These then were the treasures they unpacked before the restless bargaining eye of the old man. It took them some time to make him understand for he followed Arabic indifferently and Nessim knew no Greek. But looking up at last from the written dispensation he clasped both hands and threw up his chin with a smile; he seemed about to founder under the emotions which beset him. Everything was understood. Now he knew why Nessim had spent such hours considering the empty end-stable and sketching on paper. He shook his hands warmly and made inarticulate clucking-noises. Nessim's heart went out to him with a kind of malicious envy to see how wholehearted his pleasure was at this act of thoughtfulness. From deep inside the *camera obscura* of the thoughts which filled his mind he studied the old beadle carefully, as if by intense scrutiny to surprise the single-heartedness which brought the old man happiness, peace of mind.

Here at least, thought Nessim, building something with my own hands will keep me stable and unreflective — and he studied the horny old hands of the Greek with admiring envy as he thought of the time they had killed for him, of the thinking they had saved him. He read into them years of healthy bodily activity which imprisoned thought, neutralized reflection. And yet . . . who could say? Those long years of school-teaching: the years in the monastery: and now the long winter solitude which closed in around the oasis, when only the boom and slither of the sea and the whacking of palm-fronds were there to accompany one's thoughts. . . . There is always time for spiritual crises, he thought, as he doggedly mixed cement and dry sand in a wooden mortar.

But even here he was not to be left alone for Justine, with that maddening guilty solicitude which she had come to feel for the man whom she loved, and yet was trying to destroy, appeared with her trio of Arabs and took up her summer quarters at the oasis. A restless, moody, alert familiar. And then I, impelled by the fearful pangs her absence created in me, smuggled a note to her telling her either that she must return to the city or persuade Nessim to invite me out to the Summer Palace. Selim duly arrived with the car and motored me out in a sympathetic silence into which he did not dare to inject the slightest trace of contempt.

For his part Nessim received me with a studied tenderness; in fact, he was glad to see us again at close quarters, to detach us from the fictitious framework of his agents' reports and to judge for himself if we were . . . what am I to say? 'In love?' The word implies a totality which was missing in my mistress, who resembled one of those ancient goddesses in that her attributes proliferated through her life and were not condensed about a single quality of heart which one could love or unlove. 'Possession' is on the other hand too strong: we were human beings not Brontë cartoons. But English lacks the distinctions which might give us (as Modern Greek does) a word for passion-love.

Apart from all this, not knowing the content and direction of Nessim's thoughts I could in no way set his inmost fears at rest: by telling him that Justine was merely working out with me the same obsessive pattern she had followed out in the pages of Arnauti. She was creating a desire of the will which, since it fed secretly on itself, must be exhausted like a lamp — or blown out. I knew this with only a part of my mind: but there I detected the true lack in this union. It was not based on any repose of the will. And yet how magically she seemed to live — a mistress so full of wit and incantation that one wondered how one had ever managed to love before and be content in the quality of the loving.

At the same time I was astonished to realize that the side of me which clave to Melissa was living its own autonomous existence, quietly and surely belonging to her yet not wishing her back. The letters she wrote me were gay and full and unmarred by any shadow of reproof or self-pity; I found in all she wrote an enlargement of her self-confidence. She described the little sanatorium where she was lodged with humour and a nimble eye, describing the doctors and the other patients as a holidaymaker might. On paper she seemed to have grown, to have become another woman. I answered her as well as I was able but it was hard to disguise the shiftless confusion which reigned in my life; it was equally impossible to allude to my obsession with Justine — we were moving through a different world of flowers and books and ideas, a world quite foreign to Melissa. Environment had closed the gates to her, not lack of sensibility. 'Poverty is a great cutter-off' said Justine once, 'and riches a great shutter-off.' But she had gained admittance to both worlds, the world of want and the world of plenty, and was consequently free to live naturally.

But here at least in the oasis one had the illusion of a beatitude which eluded one in town life. We rose early and worked on the chapel until the heat of the day began, when Nessim retired to his business papers in the little observatory and Justine and I rode down the feathery dunes to the sea to spend our time in swimming and talking. About a mile from the oasis the sea had pushed up a great coarse roundel of sand which formed a shallow-water lagoon beside which, tucked into the pectoral curve of a dune, stood a reed hut roofed with leaves, which offered the bather shade and a changing-place. Here we spent most of the day together. The news of Pursewarden's death was still fresh, I remember, and we discussed him with a warmth and awe, as if for the first time we were seriously trying to evaluate a character whose qualities had masked its real nature. It was as if in dying he had cast off from his earthly character, and taken on some of the grandiose proportions of his own writings, which swam more and more into view as the memory of the man itself faded. Death provided a new critical referent, and a new mental stature to the tiresome, brilliant, ineffectual and often tedious man with whom we had had to cope. He was only to be seen now through the distorting mirror of anecdote or the dusty spectrum of memory. Later I was to hear people ask whether Pursewarden had been tall or short, whether he had worn a moustache or not: and these simple memories were the hardest to recover and to be sure of. Some who had known him well said his eyes had been green, others that they had been brown. . . . It was amazing how quickly the human image was dissolving into the mythical image he had created of himself in his trilogy *God is a Humorist*.

Here, in these days of blinding sunlight, we talked of him like people anxious to capture and fix the human memory before it quite shaded into the growing myth; we talked of him, confirming and denying and comparing, like secret agents rehearsing a cover story, for after all the fallible human being had belonged to *us*, the myth belonged to the world. It was now too that I learned of him saying, one night to Justine, as they watched Melissa dance: 'If I thought there were any hope of success I would propose marriage to her tomorrow. But she is so ignorant and her mind is so deformed by poverty and bad luck that she would refuse out of incredulity.'

But step by step behind us Nessim followed with his fears. One day I found the word 'Beware' ($\Pi\rho o\sigma o\chi\hat{\eta}$) written in the sand with a stick at the bathing-place. The Greek word suggested the hand of Panayotis but Selim also knew Greek well.

This further warning was given point for me by an incident which occurred very shortly afterwards when, in search of a sheet of notepaper on which to write to Melissa, I strayed into Nessim's little observatory and rummaged about on his desk for what I needed. I happened to notice that the telescope barrel had been canted downwards so that it no longer pointed at the sky but across the dunes towards where the city slumbered in its misty reaches of pearl cloud. This was not unusual, for trying to catch glimpses of the highest minarets as the airs condensed and shifted was a favourite pastime. I sat on the three-legged stool and placed my eye to the eye-piece, to allow the faintly trembling and vibrating image of the landscape to assemble for me. Despite the firm stone base on which the tripod stood the high magnification of the lens and the heat haze between them contributed a feathery vibration to the image which gave the landscape the appearance of breathing softly and irregularly. I was astonished to see — quivering and jumping, yet pin-point clear — the little reed hut where not an hour since Justine and I had been lying in each other's arms, talking of Pursewarden. A brilliant yellow patch on the dune showed up the cover of a pocket *King Lear* which I had taken out with me and forgotten to bring back; had the image not trembled so I do not doubt but that I should have been able to read the title on the cover. I stared at this image breathlessly for a long moment and became afraid. It was as if, all of a sudden, in a dark but familiar room one believed was empty a hand had suddenly reached out and placed itself on one's shoulder. I tip-toed from the observatory with the writing pad and pencil and sat in the arm-chair looking out at the sea, wondering what I could say to Melissa.

*   *   *   *   *

That autumn, when we struck camp and returned to the city for its winter season, nothing had been decided; the feeling of crisis had even diminished. We were all held there, so to speak, in the misty solution of everyday life out of which futurity was to crystallize whatever drama lay ahead. I was called upon to begin my new job for Scobie and addressed myself helplessly to the wretched *boustrophedon* upon which Balthazar continued to instruct me, in between bouts of chess. I admit that I tried to allay my pangs of conscience in the matter by trying at first to tell Scobie's office the truth — namely that the Cabal was a harmless sect devoted to Hermetic philosophy and that its activities bore no reference to espionage. In answer to this I was curtly told that I must not believe their obvious cover-story but must try to break the code. Detailed reports of the meetings were called for and these I duly supplied, typing out Balthazar's discourses on Ammon and Hermes Trismegistus with a certain peevish pleasure, imagining as I did so the jaded government servants who have to wade through the stuff in damp basements a thousand miles away. But I was paid and paid well; for the first time I was able to send Melissa a little money and to make some attempt to pay Justine what I owed her.

It was interesting, too, to discover which of my acquaintances were really part of the espionage grape-vine. Mnemjian, for example, was one; his shop was a clearing-post for general intelligence concerning the city, and was admirably chosen. He performed his duties with tremendous care and discretion, and insisted on shaving me free of charge; it was disheartening to learn much later on that he patiently copied out his intelligence summaries in triplicate and sold copies to various other intelligence services.

Another interesting aspect of the work was that one had the power to order raids to be made on the house of one's friends. I enjoyed very much having Pombal's apartment raided. The poor fellow had a calamitous habit of bringing official files home to work on in the evening. We captured a whole set of papers which delighted Scobie for they contained detailed memoranda upon French influence in Syria, and a list of French agents in the city. I noticed on one of these lists the name of the old furrier, Cohen.

Pombal was badly shaken by this raid and went about looking over his shoulder for nearly a month afterwards, convinced that he was being shadowed. He also developed the delusion that one-eyed Hamid had been paid to poison him and would only eat food cooked at home after I had first tasted it. He was still waiting for his cross and his transfer and was very much afraid that the loss of the files would prejudice both, but as we had thoughtfully left him the classification-covers he was able to return them to their series with a minute to say that they had been burnt 'according to instructions'.

He had been having no small success lately with his carefully graduated cocktail-parties — into which he occasionally introduced guests from the humbler spheres of life like prostitution or the arts. But the expense and boredom were excruciating and I remember him explaining to me once, in tones of misery, the origin of these functions. 'The cocktail-party — as the name itself indicates — was originally invented by dogs. They are simply bottom-sniffings raised to the rank of formal ceremonies.' Nevertheless he persevered in them and was rewarded by the favours of his Consul-General whom, despite his contempt, he still regarded with a certain childish awe. He even persuaded Justine, after much humorous pleading, to put in an appearance at one of these functions in order to further his plans for crucifixion. This gave us a chance to study Pordre and the small diplomatic circle of Alexandria — for the most part people who gave the impression of being painted with an air-brush, so etiolated and diffused did their official personalities seem to me.

Pordre himself was a whim rather than a man. He was born to be a cartoonist's butt. He had a long pale spoiled face, set off by a splendid head of silver hair which he used to affect. But it was a lackey's countenance. The falseness of his gestures (his exaggerated solicitude and friendship for the merest acquaintances) grated disagreeably and enabled me to understand both the motto my friend had composed for the French Foreign Office and also the epitaph which he once told me should be placed on the tomb of his Chief. ('His mediocrity was his salvation.') Indeed, his character was as thin as a single skin of gold leaf — the veneer of culture which diplomats are in a better position to acquire than most men.

The party went off to perfection, and a dinner invitation from Nessim threw the old diplomat into a transport of pleasure which was not feigned. It was well known that the King was a frequent guest at Nessim's table and the old man was already writing a despatch in his mind which began with the words: 'Dining with the King last week I brought the conversation round to the question of .... He said ... I replied. ...' His lips began to move, his eyes to unfocus themselves, as he retired into one of those public trances for which he was famous, and from which he would awake with a start to astonish his interlocutors with a silly cod's smile of apology.

For my part I found it strange to revisit the little tank-like flat where I had passed nearly two years of my life; to recall that it was here, in this very room, that I haa first encountered Melissa. It had undergone a great transformation at the hands of Pombal's latest mistress. She had insisted upon its being panelled and painted off-white with a maroon skirting-board. The old arm-chairs whose stuffing used to leak slowly out of the rents in their sides had been re-upholstered in some heavy damask material with a pattern of *fleur-de-lis* while the three ancient sofas had been banished completely to make floor-space. No doubt they had been sold or broken up. 'Somewhere' I thought in quotation from a poem by the old poet, 'somewhere those wretched old things must still be knocking about.' How grudging memory is, and how bitterly she clutches the raw material of her daily work.

Pombal's gaunt bedroom had become vaguely *fin de siécle* and was as clean as a new pin. Oscar Wilde might have admitted it as a set for the first act of a play. My own room had reverted once more to a box-room, but the bed was still there standing against the wall by the iron sink. The yellow curtain had of course disappeared and had been replaced by a drab piece of white cloth. I put my hand to the rusted frame of the old bed and was stabbed to the heart by the memory of Melissa turning her candid eyes upon me in the dusky half-light of the little room. I was ashamed and surprised by my grief. And when Justine came into the room behind me I kicked the door shut and immediately began to kiss her lips and hair and forehead, squeezing her almost breathless in my arms lest she should surprise the tears in my eyes. But she knew at once, and returning my kisses with that wonderful ardour that only friendship can give to our actions, she murmured: 'I know. I know.'

Then softly disengaging herself she led me out of the room and closed the door behind us. 'I must tell you about Nessim' she said in a low voice. 'Listen to me. On Wednesday, the day before we left the Summer Palace, I went for a ride alone by the sea. There was a big flight of herring-gulls over the shoreline and all of a sudden I saw the car in the distance rolling and scrambling down the dunes towards the sea with Selim at the wheel. I couldn't make out what they were doing. Nessim was in the back. I thought she would surely get stuck, but no: they raced down to the water's edge where the sand was firm and began to speed along the shore towards me. I was not on the beach but in a hollow about fifty yards from the sea. As they came racing level with me and the gulls rose I saw that Nessim had the old repeating-gun in his hands. He raised it and fired again and again into the cloud of gulls, until the magazine was exhausted. Three or four fell fluttering into the sea, but the car did not stop. They were past me in a flash. There must have been a way back from the long beach to the sandstone and so back on to the main road because when I rode in half an hour later the car was back. Nessim was in his observatory. The door was locked and he said he was busy. I asked Selim the meaning of this scene and he simply shrugged his shoulders and pointed at Nessim's door. "He gave me the orders" was all he said. But, my dear, if you had seen Nessim's face as he raised the gun. . . .' And thinking of it she involuntarily raised her long fingers to her own cheeks as if to adjust the expression on her own face. 'He looked mad.'

In the other room they were talking politely of world politics and the situation in Germany. Nessim had perched himself gracefully on Pordre's chair. Pombal was swallowing yawns which kept returning distressingly enough in the form of belches. My mind was still full of Melissa. I had sent her some money that afternoon and the thought of her buying herself some fine clothes — or even spending it in some foolish way — warmed me. 'Money' Pombal was saying playfully to an elderly woman who had the appearance of a contrite camel. 'One should always make sure of a supply. For only with money can one make more money. Madame certainly knows the Arabic proverb which says: "Riches can buy riches, but poverty will scarcely buy one a leper's kiss." '

'We must go' said Justine, and staring into her warm dark eyes as I said good-bye I knew that she divined how full of Melissa my mind was at the moment; it gave her handshake an added warmth and sympathy.

I suppose it was that night, while she was dressing for dinner that Nessim came into her room and addressed her reflection in the spade-shaped mirror. 'Justine' he said firmly, 'I must ask you not to think that I am going mad or anything like that but — has Balthazar ever been more than a friend to you?' Justine was placing a cigale made of gold on the lobe of her left ear; she looked up at him for a long second before answering in the same level, equable tone: 'No, my dear.'

'Thank you.'

Nessim stared at his own reflection for a long time, boldly, comprehensively. Then he sighed once and took from the waistcoat-pocket of his dress-clothes a little gold key, in the form of an ankh. 'I simply cannot think how this came into my possession' he said, blushing deeply and holding it up for her to see. It was the little watch-key whose loss had caused Balthazar so much concern. Justine stared at it and then at her husband with a somewhat startled air. 'Where was it?' she said.

'In my stud-box.'

Justine went on with her toilette at a slower pace, looking curiously at her husband who for his part went on studying his own features with the same deliberate rational scrutiny. 'I must find a way of returning it to him. Perhaps he dropped it at a meeting. But the strange thing is. . . .' He sighed again. 'I don't remember.' It was clear to them both that he had stolen it. Nessim turned on his heel and said: 'I shall wait for you downstairs.' As the door closed softly behind him Justine examined the little key with curiosity.

★   ★   ★   ★   ★

At this time he had already begun to experience that great cycle of historical dreams which now replaced the dreams of his childhood in his mind, and into which the City now threw itself — as if at last it had found a responsive subject through which to express the collective desires, the collective wishes, which informed its culture. He would wake to see the towers and minarets printed on the exhausted, dust-powdered sky, and see as if *en montage* on them the giant footprints of the historical memory which lies behind the recollections of individual personality, its mentor and guide: indeed its inventor, since man is only an extension of the spirit of place.

These disturbed him for they were not at all the dreams of the night-hours. They overlapped reality and interrupted his waking mind as if the membrane of his consciousness had been suddenly torn in places to admit them.

Side by side with these giant constructions — Palladian galleries of images drawn from his reading and meditation on his own past and the city's — there came sharper and sharper attacks of unreasoning hatred against the very Justine he had so seldom known, the comforting friend and devoted lover. They were of brief duration but of such fierceness that, rightly regarding them as the obverse of the love he felt for her, he began to fear not for her safety but for his own. He became afraid of shaving in the sterile white bathroom every morning. Often the little barber noticed tears in the eyes of his subject as he noiselessly spread the white apron over him.

But while the gallery of historical dreams held the foreground of his mind the figures of his friends and acquaintances, palpable and real, walked backwards and forwards among them, among the ruins of classical Alexandria, inhabiting an amazing historical space-time as living personages. Laboriously, like an actuary's clerk he recorded all he saw and felt in his diaries, ordering the impassive Selim to type them out.

He saw the Mouseion, for example, with its sulky, heavily-sub-sidized artists working to a mental fashion-plate of its founders: and later among the solitaries and wise men the philosopher, patiently wishing the world into a special private state useless to anyone but himself — for at each stage of development each man resumes the whole universe and makes it suitable to his own inner nature: while each thinker, each thought fecundates the whole universe anew.

The inscriptions on the marbles of the Museum murmured to him as he passed like moving lips. Balthazar and Justine were there waiting for him. He had come to meet them, dazzled by the moon-light and drenching shadow of the colonnades. He could hear their voices in the darkness and thought, as he gave the low whistle which Justine would always recognize as his: 'It is mentally vulgar to spend one's time being so certain of first principles as Balthazar is.' He heard the elder man saying: 'And morality is nothing if it is merely a form of good behaviour.'

He walked slowly down through the arches towards them. The marble stones were barred with moonlight and shadow like a zebra. They were sitting on a marble sarcophagus-lid while somewhere in the remorseless darkness of the outer court someone was walking up and down on the springy turf lazily whistling a phrase from an aria of Donizetti. The gold cigales at Justine's ears transformed her at once into a projection from one of his dreams and indeed he saw them both dressed vaguely in robes carved heavily of moon-light. Balthazar in a voice tortured by the paradox which lies at the heart of all religion was saying: 'Of course in one sense even to preach the gospel is evil. This is one of the absurdities of human logic. At least it is not the gospel but the preaching which involves us with the powers of darkness. That is why the Cabal is so good for us; it posits nothing beyond a science of Right Attention.'

They had made room for him on their marble perch but here again, before he could reach them the fulcrum of his vision was disturbed and other scenes gravely intervened, disregarding congruence and period, disregarding historic time and common probability.

He saw so clearly the shrine the infantry built to Aphrodite of the Pigeons on that desolate alluvial coast. They were hungry. The march had driven them all to extremities, sharpening the vision of death which inhabits the soldier's soul until it shone before them with an unbearable exactness and magnificence. Baggage-animals dying for lack of fodder and men for lack of water. They dared not pause at the poisoned spring and wells. The wild asses, loitering so exasperatingly just out of bowshot, maddened them with the promise of meat they would never secure as the column evolved across the sparse vegetation of that thorny coast. They were supposed to be marching upon the city despite the omens. The infantry marched in undress though they knew it to be madness. Their weapons followed them in carts which were always lagging. The column left behind it the sour smell of unwashed bodies — sweat and the stale of oxen: Macedonian slingers-of-the-line farting like goats.

Their enemies were of a breath-taking elegance — cavalry in white armour which formed and dissolved across the route of their march like clouds. At close range one saw they were men in purple cloaks, embroidered tunics and narrow silk trousers. They wore gold chains round their intricate dark necks and bracelets on their javelin-arms. They were as desirable as a flock of women. Their voices were high and fresh. What a contrast they offered to the slingers, case-hardened veterans of the line, conscious only of winters which froze their sandals to their feet or summers whose sweat dried the leather underfoot until it became as hard as dry marble. A gold bounty and not passion had entrained them in this adventure which they bore with the stoicism of all wage-earners. Life had become a sexless strap sinking deeper and ever deeper into the flesh. The sun had parched and cured them and the dust had rendered them voiceless. The brave plumed helmets with which they had been issued were too hot to wear at midday. Africa, which they had somehow visualized as an extension of Europe — an extension of terms, of references to a definitive past — had already asserted itself as something different: a forbidding darkness where the croaking ravens matched the dry exclamations of spiritless men, and rationed laughter fashioned from breath simply the chittering of baboons.

Sometimes they captured someone — a solitary frightened man out hunting hares — and were amazed to see that he was human like themselves. They stripped his rags and stared at human genitals with an elaborate uncomprehending interest. Sometimes they despoiled a township or a rich man's estate in the foothills, to dine on pickled dolphin in jars (drunken soldiers feasting in a barn among the oxen, unsteadily wearing garlands of wild nettles and drinking from captured cups of gold or horn). All this was before they even reached the desert. . . .

Where the paths had crossed they had sacrificed to Heracles (and in the same breath murdered the two guides, just to be on the safe side); but from that moment everything had begun to go wrong. Secretly they knew they would never reach the city and invest it. And God! Never let that winter bivouac in the hills be repeated. The fingers and noses lost by frostbite! The raids! In his memory's memory he could still hear the squeaking munching noise of the sentry's footsteps all winter in the snow. In this territory the enemy wore fox-skins on their heads in a ravenous peak and long hide tunics which covered their legs. They were silent, belonging uniquely as the vegetation did to these sharp ravines and breath-stopping paths of the great watershed.

With a column on the march memory becomes an industry, manufacturing dreams which common ills unite in a community of ideas based on privation. He knew that the quiet man there was thinking of the rose found in her bed on the day of the Games. Another could not forget the man with the torn ear. The wry scholar pressed into service felt as dulled by battle as a chamberpot at a symposium. And the very fat man who retained the curious personal odour of a baby: the joker, whose sallies kept the vanguard in a roar? He was thinking of a new depilatory from Egypt, of a bed trade-marked Heracles for softness, of white doves with clipped wings fluttering round a banqueting table. All his life he had been greeted at the brothel door by shouts of laughter and a hail of slippers. There were others who dreamed of less common pleasures — hair dusty with white lead, or else schoolboys in naked ranks marching two abreast at dawn to the school of the Harpmaster, through falling snow as thick as meal. At vulgar country Dionysia they carried amid roars the giant leather phallus, but once initiated took the proffered salt and the phallus in trembling silence. Their dreams proliferated in him, and hearing them he opened memory to his consciousness royally, prodigally, as one might open a major artery.

It was strange to move to Justine's side in that brindled autumn moonlight across such an unwholesome tide of memories: he felt his physical body displacing them by its sheer weight and density. Balthazar had moved to give him room and he was continuing to talk to his wife in low tones. (They drank the wine solemnly and sprinkled the lees on their garments. The generals had just told them they would never get through, never find the city.) And he remembered so vividly how Justine, after making love, would sit cross-legged on the bed and begin to lay out the little pack of Tarot cards which were always kept on the shelf among the books — as if to compute the degree of good fortune left them after this latest plunge into the icy underground river of passion which she could neither subdue nor slake. ('Minds dismembered by their sexual part' Balthazar had said once 'never find peace until old age and failing powers persuade them that silence and quietness are not hostile.')

Was all the discordance of their lives a measure of the anxiety which they had inherited from the city or the age? 'Oh my God' he almost said. 'Why don't we leave this city, Justine, and seek an atmosphere less impregnated with the sense of deracination and failure?' The words of the old poet came into his mind, pressed down like the pedal of a piano, to boil and reverberate around the frail hope which the thought had raised from its dark sleep.*

'My problem' he said to himself quietly, feeling his forehead to see if he had a fever 'is that the woman I loved brought me a faultless satisfaction which never touched her own happiness': and he thought over all the delusions which were now confirming themselves in physical signs. I mean: he had beaten Justine, beaten her until his arm ached and the stick broke in his hands. All this was a dream of course. Nevertheless on waking he had found his whole arm aching and swollen. What could one believe when reality mocked the imagination by its performance?

At the same time, of course, he fully recognized that suffering, indeed all illness, was itself an acute form of self-importance, and all the teachings of the Cabal came like a following wind to swell his self-contempt. He could hear, like the distant reverberations of the city's memory, the voice of Plotinus speaking, not of flight away from intolerable temporal conditions but towards a new light, a new city of Light. 'This is no journey for the feet, however. Look into yourself, withdraw into yourself and look.' But this was the one act of which he now knew himself for ever incapable.

It is astonishing for me, in recording these passages, to recall how little of all this interior change was visible on the surface of his life — even to those who knew him intimately. There was little to put one's finger on — only a sense of hollowness in the familiar — as of a well-known air played slightly out of key. It is true that at this period he had already begun to entertain with a prodigality hitherto unknown to the city, even among the richest families. The great house was never empty now. The great kitchen-quarters where we so often boiled ourselves an egg or a glass of milk after a concert or a play — dusty and deserted then — were now held by a permanent garrison of cooks, surgical and histrionic, capped in floury steeples. The upper rooms, tall staircase, galleries and salons echoing to the mournful twining of clocks were patrolled now by black slaves who moved as regally as swans about important tasks. Their white linen, smelling of the goose-iron, was spotless — robes divided by scarlet sashes punctuated at the waist by clasps of gold fashioned into turtles' heads: the rebus Nessim had chosen for himself. Their soft porpoise eyes were topped by the conventional scarlet flower-pots, their gorilla hands were cased in white gloves. They were as soundless as death itself.

If he had not so far outdone the great figures of Egyptian society in lavishness he might have been thought to be competing with them for advancement. The house was perpetually alive to the cool fern-like patterns of a quartet, or to the foundering plunge of saxophones crying to the night like cuckolds.

The long beautiful reception-rooms had been pierced with alcoves and unexpected corners to increase their already great seating-capacity and sometimes as many as two or three hundred guests sat down to elaborate and meaningless dinners — observing their host lost in the contemplation of a rose lying upon an empty plate before him. Yet his was not a remarkable distraction for he could offer to the nonentities of common conversation a smile — surprising as one who removes an upturned glass to show, hidden by it, some rare entomological creature whose scientific name he had not learned.

What else is there to add? The small extravagances of his dress were hardly noticeable in one whose fortune had always seemed oddly matched against a taste for old flannel trousers and tweed coats. Now in his ice-smooth sharkskin with the scarlet cummerbund he seemed only what he should always have been — the richest and most handsome of the city's bankers: those true foundlings of the gut. People felt that at last he had come into his own. This was how someone of his place and fortune should live. Only the diplomatic corps smelt in this new prodigality a run of hidden motives, a plot perhaps to capture the King, and began to haunt his drawing-room with their studied politenesses. Under the slothful or foppish faces one was conscious of curiosity stirring, a desire to study Nessim's motives and designs, for nowadays the King was a frequent visitor to the great house.

Meanwhile all this advanced the central situation not at all. It was as if the action which Nessim had been contemplating grew with such infinite slowness, like a stalactite, that there was time for all this to fill the interval — the rockets ploughing their furrows of sparks across the velvet sky, piercing deeper and ever deeper into the night where Justine and I lay, locked in each other's arms and minds. In the still water of the fountains one saw the splash of human faces, ignited by these gold and scarlet stars as they rose hissing into heaven like thirsty swans. In the darkness, the warm hand on my arm, I could watch the autumn sky thrown into convulsions of coloured light with the calm of someone for whom the whole unmerited pain of the human world had receded and diffused itself — as pain does when it goes on too long, spreading from a specific member to flood a whole area of the body or the mind. The lovely grooves of the rockets upon the dark sky filled us only with the sense of a breath-taking congruence to the whole nature of the world of love which was soon to relinquish us.

This particular night was full of a rare summer lightning: and hardly had the display ended when from the desert to the east a thin crust of thunder formed like a scab upon the melodious silence. A light rain fell, youthful and refreshing, and all at once the darkness was full of figures hurrying back into the shelter of the lamplit houses, dresses held ankle-high and voices raised in shrill pleasure. The lamps printed for a second their bare bodies against the transparent materials which sheathed them. For our part we turned wordlessly into the alcove behind the sweet-smelling box-hedges and lay down upon the stone bench carved in the shape of a swan. The laughing chattering crowd poured across the entrance of the alcove towards the light; we lay in the cradle of darkness feeling the gentle prickle of the rain upon our faces. The last fuses were being defiantly lit by men in dinner-jackets and through her hair I saw the last pale comets gliding up into the darkness. I tasted, with the glowing pleasure of the colour in my brain, the warm guiltless pressure of her tongue upon mine, her arms upon mine. The magnitude of this happiness — we could not speak but gazed abundantly at each other with eyes full of unshed tears.

From the house came the dry snap of champagne-corks and the laughter of human beings. 'Never an evening alone now.'

'What is happening to Nessim?'

'I no longer know. When there is something to hide one becomes an actor. It forces all the people round one to act as well.'

The same man, it was true, walked about on the surface of their common life — the same considerate, gentle punctual man: but in a horrifying sense everything had changed, he was no longer there. 'We've abandoned each other' she said in a small expiring whisper and drawing herself closer pressed to the very hilt of sense and sound the kisses which were like summaries of all we had shared, held precariously for a moment in our hands, before they should overflow into the surrounding darkness and forsake us. And yet it was as if in every embrace she were saying to herself: 'Perhaps through this very thing, which hurts so much and which I do not want ever to end — maybe through this I shall find my way back to Nessim.' I was filled suddenly by an intolerable depression.

Later, walking about in the strident native quarter with its jabbing lights and flesh-wearing smells, I wondered as I had always wondered, where time was leading us. And as if to test the validity of the very emotions upon which so much love and anxiety could base themselves I turned into a lighted booth decorated by a strip of cinema poster — the huge half-face of a screen-lover, meaningless as the belly of a whale turned upwards in death — and sat down upon the customer's stool, as one might in a barber's shop, to wait my turn. A dirty curtain was drawn across the inner door and from behind it came faint sounds, as of the congress of creatures unknown to science, not specially revolting — indeed interesting as the natural sciences are for those who have abandoned any claims of cultivating a sensibility. I was of course drunk by this time and exhausted — drunk as much on Justine as upon the thin-paper-bodied *Pol Roget*.

There was a tarbush lying upon the chair beside me and absently

I put it on my head. It was faintly warm and sticky inside and the thick leather lining clung to my forehead. 'I want to know what it really means' I told myself in a mirror whose cracks had been pasted over with the trimmings of postage stamps. I meant of course the whole portentous scrimmage of sex itself, the act of penetration which could lead a man to despair for the sake of a creature with two breasts and *le croissant* as the picturesque Levant slang has it. The sound within had increased to a sly groaning and squeaking — a combustible human voice adding itself to the jostling of an ancient wooden-slatted bed. This was presumably the identical undifferentiated act which Justine and I shared with the common world to which we belonged. How did it differ? How far had our feelings carried us from the truth of the simple, devoid beast-like act itself? To what extent was the treacherous mind — with its interminable *catalogue raisonné* of the heart — responsible? I wished to answer an unanswerable question; but I was so desperate for certainty that it seemed to me that if I surprised the act in its natural state, motivated by scientific money and not love, as yet undamaged by the idea, I might surprise the truth of my own feelings and desires. Impatient to deliver myself from the question I lifted the curtain and stepped softly into the cubicle which was fitfully lighted by a buzzing staggering paraffin lamp turned down low.

The bed was inhabited by an indistinct mass of flesh moving in many places at once, vaguely stirring like an ant-heap. It took me some moments to define the pale and hairy limbs of an elderly man from those of his partner — the greenish-hued whiteness of convex woman with a boa constrictor's head — a head crowned with spokes of toiling black hair which trailed over the edges of the filthy mattress. My sudden appearance must have suggested a police raid for it was followed by a gasp and complete silence. It was as if the ant-hill had suddenly become deserted. The man gave a groan and a startled half-glance in my direction and then as if to escape detection buried his head between the immense breasts of the woman. It was impossible to explain to them that I was investigating nothing more particular than the act upon which they were engaged. I advanced to the bed firmly, apologetically, and with what must have seemed a vaguely scientific air of detachment I took the rusty bed-rail in my hands and stared down, not upon them for I was hardly conscious of their existence, but upon myself and Melissa, myself and Justine. The woman turned a pair of large gauche charcoal eyes upon me and said something in Arabic.

They lay there like the victims of some terrible accident, clumsily engaged, as if in some incoherent experimental fashion they were the first partners in the history of the human race to think out this peculiar means of communication. Their posture, so ludicrous and ill-planned, seemed the result of some early trial which might, after centuries of experiment, evolve into a disposition of bodies as breathlessly congruent as a ballet-position. But nevertheless I recognized that this had been fixed immutably, for all time — this eternally tragic and ludicrous position of engagement. From this sprang all those aspects of love which the wit of poets and madmen had used to elaborate their philosophy of polite distinctions. From this point the sick, the insane started growing; and from here too the disgusted and dispirited faces of the long-married, tied to each other back to back, so to speak, like dogs unable to disengage after coupling.

The peal of soft cracked laughter I uttered surprised me, but it reassured my specimens. The man raised his face a few inches and listened attentively as if to assure himself that no policeman could have uttered such a laugh. The woman re-explained me to herself and smiled. 'Wait one moment' she cried, waving a white blotched hand in the direction of the curtain, 'I will not be long.' And the man, as if reprimanded by her tone, made a few convulsive movements, like a paralytic attempting to walk — impelled not by the demands of pleasure but by the purest courtesy. His expression betrayed an access of politeness — as of someone rising in a crowded tram to surrender his place to a *mutilé de la guerre*. The woman grunted and her fingers curled up at the edges.

Leaving them there, fitted so clumsily together, I stepped laughing out into the street once more to make a circuit of the quarter which still hummed with the derisive, concrete life of men and women. The rain had stopped and the damp ground exhaled the tormentingly lovely scent of clay, bodies and stale jasmine. I began to walk slowly, deeply bemused, and to describe to myself in words this whole quarter of Alexandria for I knew that soon it would be forgotten and revisited only by those whose memories had been appropriated by the fevered city, clinging to the minds of old men like traces of perfume upon a sleeve: Alexandria, the capital of Memory.

The narrow street was of baked and scented terra cotta, soft now from rain but not wet. Its whole length was lined with the coloured booths of prostitutes whose thrilling marble bodies were posed modestly each before her doll's house, as before a shrine. They sat on three-legged stools like oracles wearing coloured slippers, out in the open street. The originality of the lighting gave the whole scene the colours of deathless romance, for instead of being lit from above by electric light the whole street was lit by a series of stabbing carbide-lamps standing upon the ground: throwing thirsty, ravishing violet shadows upwards into the nooks and gables of the dolls' houses, into the nostrils and eyes of its inhabitants, into the unresisting softness of that furry darkness. I walked slowly among these extraordinary human blooms, reflecting that a city like a human being collects its predispositions, appetites and fears. It grows to maturity, utters its prophets, and declines into hebetude, old age or the loneliness which is worse than either. Unaware that their mother city was dying, the living still sat there in the open street, like caryatids supporting the darkness, the pains of futurity upon their very eyelids; sleeplessly watching, the immortality-hunters, throughout the whole fatidic length of time.

Here was a painted booth entirely decorated by *fleur-de-lis* carefully and correctly drawn upon a peach-coloured ground in royal blue. At its door sat a giant bluish child of a negress, perhaps eighteen years of age, clad in a red flannel nightgown of a vaguely mission-house *allure*. She wore a crown of dazzling narcissus on her black woollen head. Her hands were gathered humbly in her lap — an apron full of chopped fingers. She resembled a heavenly black bunny sitting at the entrance of a burrow. Next door a woman fragile as a leaf, and next her one like a chemical formula rinsed out by anaemia and cigarette smoke. Everywhere on these brown flapping walls I saw the basic talisman of the country — imprint of a palm with outspread fingers, seeking to ward off the terrors which thronged the darkness outside the lighted town. As I walked past them now they uttered, not human monetary cries, but the soft cooing propositions of doves, their quiet voices filling the street with a cloistral calm. It was not sex they offered in their monotonous seclusion among the yellow flares, but like the true inhabitants of Alexandria, the deep forgetfulness of parturition, compounded of physical pleasures taken without aversion.

The dolls' houses shivered and reeled for a second as the wind of the sea intruded, pressing upon loose fragments of cloth, unfastened partitions. One house lacked any backcloth whatever and staring through the door one caught a glimpse of a courtyard with a stunted palm-tree. By the light thrown out from a bucket of burning shavings three girls sat on stools, dressed in torn kimonos, talking in low tones and extending the tips of their fingers to the elf-light. They seemed as rapt, as remote as if they had been sitting around a camp fire on the steppes.

(In the back of my mind I could see the great banks of ice — snowdrifts in which Nessim's champagne-bottles lay, gleaming bluish-green like aged carp in a familiar pond. And as if to restore my memory I smelt my sleeves for traces of Justine's perfume.)

I turned at last into an empty café where I drank coffee served by a Saidi whose grotesque squint seemed to double every object he gazed upon. In the far corner, curled up on a trunk and so still that she was invisible at first sat a very old lady smoking a *narguileh* which from time to time uttered a soft air-bubble of sound like the voice of a dove. Here I thought the whole story through from beginning to end, starting in the days before I ever knew Melissa and ending somewhere soon in an idle pragmatic death in a city to which I did not belong; I say that I thought it through, but strangely enough I thought of it not as a personal history with an individual accent so much as part of the historical fabric of the place. I described it to myself as part and parcel of the city's behaviour, completely in keeping with everything that had gone before, and everything that would follow it. It was as if my imagination had become subtly drugged by the ambience of the place and could not respond to personal, individual assessments. I had lost the capacity to feel even the thrill of danger. My sharpest regret, characteristically enough, was for the jumble of manuscript notes which might be left behind. I had always hated the incomplete, the fragmentary. I decided that they at least must be destroyed before I went a step further. I rose to my feet — only to be struck by a sudden realization that the man I had seen in the little booth had been Mnemjian. How was it possible to mistake that misformed back? This thought occupied me as I recrossed the quarter, moving towards the larger thoroughfares in the direction of the sea. I walked across this mirage of narrow intersecting alleys as one might walk across a battlefield which had swallowed up all the friends of one's youth; yet I could not help in delighting at every scent and sound — a survivor's delight. Here at one corner stood a flame-swallower with his face turned up to the sky, spouting a column of flame from his mouth which turned black with flapping fumes at the edges and bit a hole in the sky. From time to time he took a swig at a bottle of petrol before throwing back his head once more and gushing flames six feet high. At every corner the violet shadows fell and foundered, striped with human experience — at once savage and tenderly lyrical. I took it as a measure of my maturity that I was filled no longer with despairing self-pity but with a desire to be claimed by the city, enrolled among its trivial or tragic memories — if it so wished.

It was equally characteristic that by the time I reached the little flat and disinterred the grey exercise books in which my notes had been scribbled I thought no longer of destroying them. Indeed I sat there in the lamp-light and added to them while Pombal discoursed on life from the other easy chair.

'Returning to my room I sit silent, listening to the heavy tone of her scent: a smell perhaps composed of flesh, faeces and herbs, all worked into the dense brocade of her being. This is a peculiar type of love for I do not feel that I possess her — nor indeed would wish to do so. It is as if we joined each other only in self-possession, became partners in a common stage of growth. In fact we outrage love, for we have proved the bonds of friendship stronger. These notes, however they may be read, are intended only as a painstaking affectionate commentary on a world into which I have been born to share my most solitary moments — those of coitus — with Justine. I can get no nearer to the truth.

'Recently, when it had been difficult to see her for one reason or another, I found myself longing so much for her that I went all the way down to Pietrantoni to try and buy a bottle of her perfume. In vain. The good-tempered girl-assistant dabbed my hands with every mark she had in stock and once or twice I thought that I had discovered it. But no. Something was always missing — I suppose the flesh which the perfume merely costumed. The undertow of the body itself was the missing factor. It was only when in desperation I mentioned Justine's name that the girl turned immediately to the first perfume we had tried. "Why did you not say so at first?" she asked with an air of professional hurt; everyone, her tone implied, knew the perfume Justine used except myself. It was unrecognizable. Nevertheless I was surprised to discover that *Jamais de la vie* was not among the most expensive or exotic of perfumes.'

(When I took home the little bottle they found in Cohen's waistcoat-pocket the wraith of Melissa was still there, imprisoned. She could still be detected.)

Pombal was reading aloud the long terrible passage from *Moeurs* which is called 'The Dummy Speaks'. 'In all these fortuitous collisions with the male animal I had never known release, no matter what experience I had submitted my body to. I always see in the mirror the image of an ageing fury crying: "*J'ai raté mon propre amour — mon amour à moi. Mon amour-propre, mon propre amour. Je l'ai raté. Je n'ai jamais souffert, jamais eu de joie simple et candide.*"'

He paused only to say: 'If this is true you are only taking advantage of an illness in loving her,' and the remark struck me like the edge of an axe wielded by someone of enormous and unconscious strength.

★ ★ ★ ★ ★

When the time for the great yearly shoot on Lake Mareotis came round Nessim began to experience a magical sense of relief. He recognized at last that what had to be decided would be decided at this time and at no other. He had the air of a man who has fought a long illness successfully. Had his judgement indeed been so faulty even though it had not been conscious? During the years of his marriage he had repeated on every day the words, 'I am so happy' — fatal as the striking of a grandfather-clock upon which silence is forever encroaching. Now he could say so no longer. Their common life was like some cable buried in the sand which, in some inexplicable way, at a point impossible to discover, had snapped, plunging them both into an unaccustomed and impenetrable darkness.

The madness itself, of course, took no account of circumstances. It appeared to superimpose itself not upon personalities tortured beyond the bounds of endurance but purely upon a given situation. In a real sense we all shared it, though only Nessim acted it out, exemplified it in the flesh, as a person. The short period which preceded the great shoot on Mareotis lasted for perhaps a month — certainly for very little more. Here again to those who did not know him nothing was obvious. Yet the delusions multiplied themselves at such a rate that in his own records they give one the illusion of watching bacteria under a microscope — the pullulation of healthy cells, as in cancer, which have gone off their heads, renounced their power to repress themselves.

The mysterious series of code messages transmitted by the street names he encountered showed definite irrefutable signs of a supernatural agency at work full of the threat of unseen punishment — though whether for himself or for others he could not tell. Balthazar's treatise lying withering in the window of a bookshop and the *same day* coming upon his father's grave in the Jewish cemetery — with those distinguishing names engraved upon the stone which echoed all the melancholy of European Jewry in exile.

Then the question of noises in the room next door: a sort of heavy breathing and the sudden simultaneous playing of three pianos. These, he knew, were not delusions but links in an occult chain, logical and persuasive only to the mind which had passed beyond the frame of causality. It was becoming harder and harder to pretend to be sane by the standards of ordinary behaviour. He was going through the *Devastatio* described by Swedenborg.

The coal fires had taken to burning into extraordinary shapes. This could be proved by relighting them over and over again to verify his findings — terrifying landscapes and faces. The mole on Justine's wrist was also troubling. At meal times he fought against his desire to touch it so feverishly that he turned pale and almost fainted.

One afternoon a crumpled sheet began breathing and continued for a space of about half an hour, assuming the shape of the body it covered. One night he woke to the soughing of great wings and saw a bat-like creature with the head of a violin resting upon the bedrail.

Then the counter-agency of the powers of good — a message brought by a ladybird which settled on the notebook in which he was writing; the music of Weber's *Pan* played *every day* between three and four on a piano in an adjoining house. He felt that his mind had become a battle-ground for the forces of good and evil and that his task was to strain every nerve to recognize them, but it was not easy. The phenomenal world had begun to play tricks on him so that his senses were beginning to accuse reality itself of inconsistency. He was in peril of a mental overthrow.

Once his waistcoat started ticking as it hung on the back of a chair, as if inhabited by a colony of foreign heartbeats. But when investigated it stopped and refused to continue for the benefit of Selim whom he had called into the room. The same day he saw his initials in gold upon a cloud reflected in a shop-window in the Rue St Saba. *Everything seemed proved by this.*

That same week a stranger was seated in the corner always reserved for Balthazar in the Café Al Aktar sipping an *arak* — the *arak* he had intended to order. The figure bore a strong yet distorted resemblance to himself as he turned in the mirror, unfolding his lips from white teeth in a smile. He did not wait but hurried to the door.

As he walked the length of the Rue Fuad he felt the entire pavement turn to sponge beneath his feet; he was foundering waist-deep in it before the illusion vanished. At two-thirty that afternoon he rose from a feverish sleep, dressed and set off to confirm an overpowering intuition that both Pastroudi and the Café Dordali were empty. They were, and the fact filled him with triumphant relief; but it was short-lived, for on returning to his room he felt all of a sudden as if his heart were being expelled from his body by the short mechanical movements of an air-pump. He had come to hate and fear this room of his. He would stand for a long time listening until the noise came again — the slither of wires being uncoiled upon the floor and the noise of some small animal, its shrieks being stifled, as it was bundled into a bag. Then distinctly the noise of suitcase-hasps being fastened with a snap and the breathing of someone who stood against the wall next door, listening for the least sound. Nessim removed his shoes and tip-toed to the bay-window in an attempt to see into the room next door. His assailant, it seemed to him, was an elderly man, gaunt and sharp-featured, with the sunk reddish eyes of a bear. He was unable to confirm this. Then, waking early on the very morning upon which the invitations for the great shoot must be issued he saw with horror from the bedroom window two suspicious-looking men in Arab dress tying a rope to a sort of windlass on the roof. They pointed to him and spoke together in low tones. Then they began to lower something heavy, wrapped in a fur coat, into the open street below. His hands trembled as he filled in the large white squares of pasteboard with that flowing script, selecting his names from the huge typewritten list which Selim had left on his desk. Nevertheless he smiled as well when he recalled how large a space was devoted in the local press each year to this memorable event — the great shoot on Mareotis. With so much to occupy him he felt that nothing should be left to chance and though the solicitous Selim hovered near, he pursed his lips and insisted on attending to all the invitations himself. My own, charged with every presage of disaster, stared at me now from the mantelpiece. I gazed at it, my attention scattered by nicotine and wine, recognizing that here, in some indefinable way, was the solution towards which we all had moved. ('Where science leaves off nerves begin.' *Moeurs*.)

'Of course you will refuse. You will not go?' Justine spoke so sharply that I understood that her gaze followed mine. She stood over me in the misty early morning light, and between sentences cocked an ear towards the heavily-breathing wraith of Hamid behind the door. 'You are not to tempt providence. Will you? Answer me.' And as if to make persuasion certain she slipped off her skirt and shoes and fell softly into bed beside me — warm hair and mouth, and the treacherous nervous movements of a body which folded against one as if hurt, as if tender from unhealed wounds. It seemed to me then — and the compulsion had nothing of bravado in it — it seemed to me then that I could no longer deprive Nessim of the satisfaction he sought of me, or indeed the situation of its issue. There was, too, underneath it all a vein of relief which made me fell almost gay until I saw the grave sad expression of my companion-in-arms. She lay, staring out of those wonderfully expressive dark eyes, as if from a high window in her own memory. She was looking, I knew, into the eyes of Melissa — into the troubled candid eyes of one who, with every day of increasing danger, moved nearer and nearer to us. After all, the one most to be wounded by the issue Nessim might be contemplating was Melissa — who else? I thought back along the iron chain of kisses which Justine had forged, steadily back into memory, hand over fist, like a mariner going down an anchor-chain into the darkest depths of some great stagnant harbour, memory.

From among many sorts of failure each selects the one which least compromises his self-respect: which lets him down the lightest. Mine had been in art, in religion, and in people. In art I had failed (it suddenly occurred to me at this moment) because I did not believe in the discrete human personality. ('Are people' writes Pursewarden 'continuously themselves, or simply over and over again so fast that they give the illusion of continuous features — the temporal flicker of old silent film?') I lacked a belief in the true authenticity of people in order to successfully portray them. In religion? Well, I found no religion worth while which contained the faintest grain of propitiation — and which can escape the charge? *Pace* Balthazar it seemed to me that all churches, all sects, were at the best mere academies of self-instruction against fear. But the last, the worst failure (I buried my lips in the dark living hair of Justine), the failure with people: it had been brought about by a gradually increasing detachment of spirit which, while it freed me to sympathize, forbade me possession. I was gradually, inexplicably, becoming more and more deficient in love, yet better and better at self-giving — the best part of loving. This, I realized with horror, was the hold I now had over Justine. As a woman, a natural possessive, she was doomed to try and capture the part of myself which was forever beyond reach, the last painful place of refuge which was for me laughter and friendship. This sort of loving had made her, in a way, desperate for I did not depend on her; and the desire to possess can, if starved, render one absolutely possessed in the spirit oneself. How difficult it is to analyse these relationships which lie under the mere skin of our actions; for loving is only a sort of skin-language, sex a terminology merely.

And further to render down this sad relationship which had caused me so much pain — I saw that pain itself was the only food of memory: for pleasure ends in itself — all they had bequeathed me was a fund of permanent health — life-giving detachment. I was like a dry-cell battery. Uncommitted, I was free to circulate in the world of men and women like a guardian of the true rights of love — which is not passion, nor habit (they only qualify it) but which is the divine trespass of an immortal among mortals — Aphrodite-in-arms. Beleaguered thus, I was nevertheless defined and realized in myself by the very quality which (of course) hurt me most: selflessness. *This* is what Justine loved in me — not my personality. Women are sexual robbers, and it was this treasure of detachment she hoped to steal from me — the jewel growing in the toad's head. It was the signature of this detachment she saw written across my life with all its haphazardness, discordance, disorderliness. My value was not in anything I achieved or anything I owned. Justine loved me because I presented to her something which was indestructible — a person already formed who could not be broken. She was haunted by the feeling that even while I was loving her I was wishing at the same time only to die! This she found unendurable.

And Melissa? She lacked of course the insight of Justine into my case. She only knew that my strength supported her where she was at her weakest — in her dealings with the world. She treasured every sign of my human weakness — disorderly habits, incapacity over money affairs, and so on. She loved my weaknesses because there she felt of use to me; Justine brushed all this aside as unworthy of her interest. She had detected another kind of strength. I interested her only in this one particular which I could not offer her as a gift nor she steal from me. This is what is meant by possession — to be passionately at war for the qualities in one another to contend for the treasures of each other's personalities. But how can such a war be anything but destructive and hopeless?

And yet, so entangled are human motives: it would be Melissa herself who had driven Nessim from his refuge in the world of fantasy towards an action which he knew we would all bitterly regret — our death. For it was she who, overmastered by the impulse of her unhappiness one night, approached the table at which he sat, before an empty champagne-glass, watching the cabaret with a pensive air: and blushing and trembling in her false eyelashes, blurted out eight words, '*Your wife is no longer faithful to you*' — a phrase which stood quivering in his mind from then on, like a thrown knife. It is true that for a long time now his dossiers had been swollen with reports of this dreaded fact but these reports were like newspaper-accounts of a catastrophe which had occurred a long way off, in a country which one had not visited. Now he was suddenly face to face with an eye-witness, a victim, a survivor.... The resonance of this one phrase refecundated his powers of feeling. The whole dead tract of paper suddenly rose up and screeched at him.

Melissa's dressing-room was an evil-smelling cubicle full of the coiled pipes which emptied the lavatories. She had a single poignant strip of cracked mirror and a little shelf dressed with the kind of white paper upon which wedding-cakes are built. Here she always set out the jumble of powders and crayons which she misused so fearfully.

In this mirror the image of Selim blistered and flickered in the dancing gas-jets like a spectre from the underworld. He spoke with an incisive finish which was a copy of his master's; in this copied voice she could feel some of the anxiety the secretary felt for the only human being he truly worshipped, and to whose anxieties he reacted like a planchette.

Melissa was afraid now, for she knew that offence given to the great could, by the terms of the city, be punished swiftly and dreadfully. She was aghast at what she had done and fought back a desire to cry as she picked off her eyelashes with trembling hands. There was no way of refusing the invitation. She dressed in her shabby best and carrying her fatigue like a heavy pack followed Selim to the great car which stood in deep shadow. She was helped in beside Nessim. They moved off slowly into the dense crepuscular evening of an Alexandria which, in her panic, she no longer recognized. They scouted a sea turned to sapphire and turned inland, folding up the slums, towards Mareotis and the bituminous slag-heaps of Mex where the pressure of the headlights now peeled off layer after layer of the darkness, bringing up small intimate scenes of Egyptian life — a drunkard singing, a biblical figure on a mule with two children escaping from Herod, a porter sorting sacks — swiftly, like someone dealing cards. She followed these familiar sights with emotion, for behind lay the desert, its emptiness echoing like a seashell. All this time her companion had not spoken, and she had not dared to risk so much as a glance in his direction.

Now when the pure steely lines of the dunes came up under the late moon Nessim drew the car to a standstill. Groping in his pocket for his cheque-book he said in a trembling voice, his eyes full of tears: 'What is the price of your silence?' She turned to him and, seeing for the first time the gentleness and sorrow of that dark face, found her fear replaced by an overwhelming shame. She recognized in his expression the weakness for the good which could never render him an enemy of her kind. She put a timid hand on his arm and said: 'I am so ashamed. Please forgive me. I did not know what I was saying.' And her fatigue overcame her so that her emotion which threatened her with tears turned to a yawn. Now they stared at one another with a new understanding, recognizing each other as innocents. For a minute it was almost as if they had fallen in love with each other from sheer relief.

The car gathered momentum again like their silence — and soon they were racing across the desert towards the steely glitter of stars, and a horizon stained black with the thunder of surf. Nessim, with this strange sleepy creature at his side, found himself thinking over and over again: 'Thank God I am not a genius — for a genius has nobody in whom he can confide.'

The glances he snatched at her enabled him to study her, and to study me in her. Her loveliness must have disarmed and disturbed him as it had me. It was a beauty which filled one with the terrible premonition that it had been born to be a target for the forces of destruction. Perhaps he remembered an anecdote of Pursewarden's in which she figured, for the latter had found her as Nessim himself had done, in the same stale cabaret; only on this particular evening she had been sitting in a row of dance-hostesses selling dance-tickets. Pursewarden, who was gravely drunk, took her to the floor and, after a moment's silence, addressed her in his sad yet masterful way: '*Comment vous défendez-vous contre la solitude?*' he asked her. Melissa turned upon him an eye replete with all the candour of experience and replied softly: '*Monsieur, je suis devenue la solitude même.*' Pursewarden was sufficiently struck to remember and repeat this passage later to his friends, adding: 'I suddenly thought to myself that here was a woman one might very well love.' Yet he did not, as far as I know, take the risk of revisiting her, for the book was going well, and he recognized in the kindling of this sympathy a trick being played on him by the least intent part of his nature. He was writing about love at the time and did not wish to disturb the ideas he had formed on the subject. ('I cannot fall in love' he made a character exclaim 'for I belong to that ancient secret society — the Jokers!'; and elsewhere speaking about his marriage he wrote: 'I found that as well as displeasing another I also displeased myself; now, alone, I have only myself to displease. Joy!')

Justine was still standing over me, watching my face as I composed these scorching scenes in my mind. 'You will make some excuse' she repeated hoarsely. 'You will not go.' It seemed to me impossible to find a way out of this predicament. 'How *can* I refuse?' I said. 'How can you?'

They had driven across that warm, tideless desert night, Nessim and Melissa, consumed by a sudden sympathy for each other, yet speechless. On the last scarp before Bourg El Arab he switched off the engine and let the car roll off the road. 'Come' he said. 'I want to show you Justine's Summer Palace.'

Hand in hand they took the road to the little house. The caretaker was asleep but he had the key. The rooms smelt damp and uninhabited, but were full of light reflected from the white dunes. It was not long before he had kindled a fire of thorns in the great fireplace, and taking his old *abba* from the cupboard he clothed himself in it and sat down before it saying: 'Tell me now, Melissa, who sent you to persecute me?' He meant it as a joke but forgot to smile, and Melissa turned crimson with shame and bit her lip. They sat there for a long time enjoying the firelight and the sensation of sharing something — their common hopelessness.

(Justine stubbed out her cigarette and got slowly out of bed. She began to walk slowly up and down the carpet. Fear had overcome her and I could see that it was only with an effort that she overcame the need for a characteristic outburst. 'I have done so many things in my life' she said to the mirror. 'Evil things, perhaps. But never inattentively, never wastefully. I've always thought of acts as messages, wishes from the past to the future, which invited self-discovery. Was I wrong? Was I wrong?' It was not to me she addressed the question now but to Nessim. It is so much easier to address questions intended for one's husband to one's lover. 'As for the dead' she went on after a moment, 'I have always thought that the dead think of us as dead. They have rejoined the living after this trifling excursion into quasi-life.' Hamid was stirring now and she turned to her clothes in a panic. 'So you must go' she said sadly, 'and so must I. You are right. We must go.' And then turning to the mirror to complete her toilet she added: 'Another grey hair' studying that wicked fashionable face.

Watching her thus, trapped for a moment by a rare sunbeam on the dirty window-pane, I could not help reflecting once more that in her there was nothing to control or modify the intuition which she had developed out of a nature gorged upon introspection: no education, no resources of intellection to battle against the imperatives of a violent heart. Her gift was the gift one finds occasionally in ignorant fortune-tellers. Whatever passed for thought in her was borrowed — even the remark about the dead which occurs in *Moeurs*; she had picked out what was significant in books not by reading them but by listening to the matchless discourses of Balthazar, Arnauti, Pursewarden, upon them. She was a walking abstract of the writers and thinkers whom she had loved or admired — but what clever woman is more?)

Nessim now took Melissa's hands between his own (they lay there effortless, cool, like wafers) and began to question her about me with an avidity which might have easily suggested that his passion was not Justine, but myself. One always falls in love with the love-choice of the person one loves. What would I not give to learn all that she told him, striking ever more deeply into his sympathies with her candours, her unexpected reserves? All I know is that she concluded stupidly, 'Even now they are not happy: they quarrel dreadfully: Hamid told me so when last I met him.' Surely she was experienced enough to recognize in these reported quarrels the very subject-matter of our love? I think she saw only the selfishness of Justine — that almost deafening lack of interest in other people which characterized my tyrant. She utterly lacked the charity of mind upon which Melissa's good opinion alone could be grounded. She was not really human — nobody wholly dedicated to the ego is. What on earth could I see in her? —

I asked this question of myself for the thousandth time. Yet Nessim, in beginning to explore and love Melissa as an extension of Justine, delineated perfectly the human situation. Melissa would hunt in him for the qualities which she imagined I must have found in his wife. The four of us were unrecognized complementaries of one another, inextricably bound together. ('We who have travelled much and loved much: we who have — I will not say suffered for we have always recognized through suffering our own self-sufficiency — only we appreciate the complexities of tenderness, and understand how narrowly love and friendship are related.' *Moeurs*.)

They talked now as a doomed brother and sister might, renewing in each other the sense of relief which comes to those who find someone to share the burden of unconfessed preoccupations. In all this sympathy an unexpected shadow of desire stirred within them, a wraith merely, the stepchild of confession and release. It foreshadowed, in a way, their own love-making, which was to come, and which was so much less ugly than ours — mine and Justine's. Loving is so much truer when sympathy and not desire makes the match; for it leaves no wounds. It was already dawn when they rose from their conversation, stiff and cramped, the fire long since out, and marched across the damp sand to the car, scouting the pale lavender light of dawn. Melissa had found a friend and patron; as for Nessim, he was transfigured. The sensation of a new sympathy had enabled him, magically, to become his own man again — that is to say, a man who could act (could murder his wife's lover if he so wished)!

Driving along that pure and natal coastline they watched the first tendrils of sunlight uncoil from horizon to horizon across the dark self-sufficient Mediterranean sea whose edges were at one and the same moment touching lost hallowed Carthage and Salamis in Cyprus.

Presently, where the road dips down among the dunes to the seashore Nessim once more slowed down and involuntarily suggested a swim. Changed as he was he felt a sudden desire that Melissa should see him naked, should approve the beauty which for so long had lain, like a suit of well-cut clothes in an attic cupboard, forgotten.

Naked and laughing, they waded out hand in hand, into the icy water feeling the tame sunlight glowing on their backs as they did so. It was like the first morning since the creation of the world.

Melissa, too, had shed with her clothes the last residual encumbrance of the flesh, and had become the dancer she truly was; for nakedness always gave her fulness and balance: the craft she lacked in the cabaret.

They lay together for a long time in perfect silence, seeking through the darkness of their feelings for the way forward. He realized that he had won an instant compliance from her — that she was now his mistress in everything.

They set off together for the city, feeling at the same time happy and ill-at-ease — for both felt a kind of hollowness at the heart of their happiness. Yet since they were reluctant to surrender each other to the life which awaited them they lagged, the car lagged, their silence lagged between endearments.

At last Nessim remembered a tumbledown café in Mex where one could find a boiled egg and coffee. Early though it was the sleepy Greek proprietor was awake and set chairs for them under a barren fig-tree in a backyard full of hens and their meagre droppings. All around them towered corrugated iron wharves and factories. The sea was present only as a dank and resonant smell of hot iron and tar.

He set her down at last on the street-corner she named and said good-bye in a 'wooden perfunctory' sort of way — afraid perhaps that some of his own office employees might oversee him. (This last is my own conjecture as the words 'wooden' and 'perfunctory', which smell of literature, seem somehow out of place.) The inhuman bustle of the city intervened once more, committing them to past feelings and preoccupations. For her part, yawning, sleepy and utterly natural as she was, she left him only to turn into the little Greek church and set a candle to the saint. She crossed herself from left to right as the orthodox custom is and brushed back a lock of hair with one hand as she stooped to the ikon, tasting in its brassy kiss all the consolation of a forgotten childhood habit. Then wearily she turned to find Nessim standing before her. He was deathly white and staring at her with a sweet burning curiosity. She at once understood everything. They embraced with a sort of anguish, not kissing, but simply pressing their bodies together, and he all at once began to tremble with fatigue. His teeth began to chatter. She drew him to a choir stall where he sat for some abstracted moments, struggling to speak, and drawing his hand across his forehead like someone who is recovering from drowning. It was not that he had anything to say to her, but this speechlessness made him fear that he was experiencing a stroke. He croaked: 'It is terribly late, nearly half past six.' Pressing her hand to his stubbled cheek he rose and like a very old man groped his way back through the great doors into the sunlight, leaving her sitting there gazing after him.

Never had the early dawn-light seemed so good to Nessim. The city looked to him as brilliant as a precious stone. The shrill telephones whose voices filled the great stone buildings in which the financiers really lived, sounded to him like the voices of great fruitful mechanical birds. They glittered with a pharaonic youthfulness. The trees in the park had been rinsed down by an unaccustomed dawn rain. They were covered in brilliants and looked like great contented cats at their toilet.

Sailing upwards to the fifth floor in the lift, making awkward attempts to appear presentable (feeling the dark stubble on his chin, retying his tie) Nessim questioned his reflection in the cheap mirror, puzzled by the whole new range of feelings and beliefs these brief scenes had given him. Under everything, however, aching like a poisoned tooth or finger, lay the quivering meaning of those eight words which Melissa had lodged in him. In a dazed sort of way he recognized that Justine was dead to him — from a mental picture she had become an engraving, a locket which one might wear over one's heart for ever. It is always bitter to leave the old life for the new — and every woman is a new life, compact and self-contained and *sui generis*. As a person she had suddenly faded. He did not wish to possess her any longer but to free himself from her. From a woman she had become a situation.

He rang for Selim and when the secretary appeared he dictated to him a few of the duller business letters with a calm so surprising that the boy's hand trembled as he took them down in his meticulous crowsfoot shorthand. Perhaps Nessim had never been more terrifying to Selim than he appeared at this moment, sitting at his great polished desk with the gleaming battery of telephones ranged before him.

Nessim did not meet Melissa for some time after this episode but he wrote her long letters, all of which he destroyed in the lavatory. It seemed necessary to him, for some fantastic reason, to explain and justify Justine to her and each of these letters began with a long painful exegesis of Justine's past and his own. Without this preamble, he felt, it would be impossible ever to speak of the way in which Melissa had moved and captivated him. He was

defending his wife, of course, not against Melissa, who had uttered
no criticism of her (apart from the one phrase) but against all the
new doubts about her which emerged precisely from his experience
with Melissa. Just as my own experience of Justine had illuminated
and re-evaluated Melissa for me so he looking into Melissa's grey
eyes saw a new and unsuspected Justine born therein. You see, he
was now alarmed at the extent to which it might become possible
to hate her. He recognized now that hate is only unachieved love.
He felt envious when he remembered the single-mindedness of
Pursewarden who on the flyleaf of the last book he gave Balthazar
had scribbled the mocking words:

Pursewarden on Life
N.B. Food is for eating
Art is for arting
Women for————
Finish
RIP

And when next they met, under very different circumstances
. . . But I have not the courage to continue. I have explored Melissa
deeply enough through my own mind and heart and cannot bear
to recall what Nessim found in her — pages covered with erasures
and emendations. Pages which I have torn from my diaries and
destroyed. Sexual jealousy is the most curious of animals and can
take up a lodgement anywhere, even in memory. I avert my face
from the thought of Nessim's shy kisses, of Melissa's kisses which
selected in Nessim only the nearest mouth to mine. . . .

From a crisp packet I selected a strip of pasteboard on which,
after so many shame-faced importunities, I had persuaded a local
jobbing printer to place my name and address, and taking up my
pen wrote:

mr ———— accepts with pleasure the
kind invitation of mr ———— to a duck
shoot on Lake Mareotis.

It seemed to me that now one might learn some important
truths about human behaviour.

*   *   *   *   *

Autumn has settled at last into the clear winterset. High seas
flogging the blank panels of stone along the Corniche. The
migrants multiplying on the shallow reaches of Mareotis. Waters
moving from gold to grey, the pigmentation of winter.

The parties assemble at Nessim's house towards twilight — a prodigious collection of cars and shooting-brakes. Here begins the long packing and unpacking of wicker baskets and gun-bags, conducted to the accompaniment of cocktails and sandwiches. Costumes burgeon. Comparison of guns and cartridges, conversation inseparable from a shooter's life, begin now, rambling, inconsequent, wise. The yellowish moonless dusk settles: the angle of the sunlight turns slowly upwards into the vitreous lilac of the evening sky. It is brisk weather, clear as waterglass.

Justine and I are moving through the spiderweb of our preoccupations like people already parted. She wears the familiar velveteen costume — the coat with its deeply cut and slanted pockets: and the soft velours hat pulled down over her brows — a schoolgirl's hat: leather jack-boots. We do not look directly at each other any more, but talk with a hollow impersonality. I have a splitting headache. She has urged upon me her own spare gun — a beautiful stout twelve by Purdey, ideal for such an unpractised hand and eye as mine.

There is laughter and clapping as lots are drawn for the makeup of the various parties. We will have to take up widely dispersed positions around the lake, and those who draw the western butts will have to make a long detour by road through Mex and the desert fringes. The leaders of each party draw paper strips in turn from a hat, each with a guest's name written upon it. Nessim has already drawn Capodistria who is clad in a natty leather jerkin with velvet cuffs, khaki gaberdine plus-fours and check socks. He wears an old tweed hat with a cock-pheasant's feather in it, and is festooned with bandoliers full of cartridges. Next comes Ralli the old Greek general, with ash-coloured bags under his eyes and darned riding-breeches; Pallis the French Charge d'Affaires in a sheepskin coat; lastly myself.

Justine and Pombal are joining Lord Errol's party. It is clear now that we are to be separated. All of a sudden, for the first time, I feel real fear as I watch the expressionless glitter of Nessim's eyes. We take our various places in the shooting-brakes. Selim is doing up the straps of a heavy pigskin gun-case. His hands tremble. With all the dispositions made the cars start up with a roar of engines, and at this signal a flock of servants scamper out of the great house with glasses of champagne to offer us a stirrup-cup. This diversion enables Justine to come across to our car and under the pretext of handing me a packet of smokeless cartridges to press my arm once, warmly, and to fix me for a half-second with those expressive black eyes shining now with an expression I might almost mistake for relief. I try to form a smile with my lips.

We move off steadily with Nessim at the wheel and catch the last rays of the sunset as we clear the town to run along the shallow dunelands towards Aboukir. Everyone is in excellent spirits, Ralli talking nineteen to the dozen and Capodistria keeping us entertained with anecdotes of his fabulous mad father. ('His first act on going mad was to file a suit against his two sons accusing them of wilful and persistent illegitimacy.') From time to time he raises a finger to touch the cotton compress which is held in position over his left eye by the black patch. Pallis has produced an old deerstalker with large ear-flaps which make him look like a speculative Gallic rabbit. From time to time in the driving mirror I catch Nessim's eye and he smiles.

The dusk has settled as we come to the shores of the lake. The old hydroplane whimpers and roars as it waits for us. It is piled high with decoys. Nessim assembles a couple of tall duck-guns and tripods before joining us in the shallow punt to set off across the reed-fringed wilderness of the lake to the desolate lodge where we are to spend the night. All horizons have been abruptly cut off now as we skirt the darkening channels in our noisy craft, disturbing the visitants of the lake with the roar of our engines; the reeds tower over us, and everywhere the sedge hassocks of islands rise out of the water with their promise of cover. Once or twice a long vista of water opens before us and we catch sight of the flurry of birds rising — mallard trailing their webs across the still surface. Nearer at hand the hither-and-thithering cormorants keep a curiosity-shop with their long slave-to-appetite beaks choked with sedge. All round us now, out of sight the teeming colonies of the lake are settling down for the night. When the engines of the hydroplane are turned off the silence is suddenly filled with groaning and gnatting of duck.

A faint green wind springs up and ruffles the water round the little wooden hut on the balcony of which sit the loaders waiting for us. Darkness has suddenly fallen, and the voices of the boatmen sound hard, sparkling, gay. The loaders are a wild crew; they scamper from island to island with shrill cries, their *galabeahs* tucked up round their waists, impervious to the cold. They seem black and huge, as if carved from the darkness. They pull us up to the balcony one by one and then set off in shallow punts to lay their armfuls of decoys while we turn to the inner room where paraffin lamps have already been lit. From the little kitchen comes the encouraging smell of food which we sniff appreciatively as we divest ourselves of our guns and bandoliers, and kick off our boots. Now the sportsmen fall to backgammon or tric-trac and bag-and-shot talk, the most delightful and absorbing masculine conversation in the world. Ralli is rubbing pigsfat into his old much-darned boots. The stew is excellent and the red wine has put everyone in a good humour.

By nine however most of us are ready to turn in; Nessim is busy in the darkness outside giving his last instructions to the loaders and setting the rusty old alarm clock for three. Capodistria alone shows no disposition to sleep. He sits, as if plunged in reflection, sipping his wine and smoking a cheroot. We speak for a while about trivialities; and then all of a sudden he launches into a critique of Pursewarden's third volume which has just appeared in the bookshops. 'What is astonishing' he says 'is that he presents a series of spiritual problems as if they were commonplaces and illustrates them with his characters. I have been thinking over the character of Parr the sensualist. He resembles me so closely. His apology for a voluptuary's life is fantastically good — as in the passage where he says that people only see in us the contemptible skirt-fever which rules our actions but completely miss the beauty-hunger underlying it. To be so struck by a face sometimes that one wants to devour it feature by feature. Even making love to the body beneath it gives no surcease, no rest. What is to be done with people like us?' He sighs and abruptly begins to talk about Alexandria in the old days. He speaks with a new resignation and gentleness about those far-off days across which he sees himself moving so serenely, so effortlessly as a youth and a young man. 'I have never got to the bottom of my father. His view of things was mordant, and yet it is possible this his ironies concealed a wounded spirit. One is not an ordinary man if one can say things so pointed that they engage the attention and memory of others. As once in speaking of marriage he said "In marriage they legitimized despair," and "Every kiss is the conquest of a repulsion." He struck me as having a coherent view of life but madness intervened and all I have to go on is the memory of a few incidents and sayings. I wish I could leave behind as much.'

I lie awake in the narrow wooden bunk for a while thinking over what he has been saying: all is darkness now and silence save for the low rapid voice of Nessim on the balcony outside talking to the loaders. I cannot catch the words. Capodistria sits for a while in the darkness to finish his cheroot before climbing heavily into the bunk under the window. The others are already asleep to judge by the heavy snoring of Ralli. My fear has given place to resignation once more; now at the borders of sleep I think of Justine again for a moment before letting the memory of her slide into the limbo which is peopled now only with far-away sleepy voices and the rushing sighing waters of the great lake.

It is pitch-dark when I awake at the touch of Nessim's gentle hand shaking my shoulder. The alarm clock has failed us. But the room is full of stretching yawning figures climbing from their bunks. The loaders have been curled up asleep like sheep-dogs on the balcony outside. They busy themselves in lighting the paraffin lamps whose unearthly glare is to light our desultory breakfast of coffee and sandwiches. I go down the landing stage and wash my face in the icy lake water. Utter blackness all around. Everyone speaks in low voices, as if weighed down by the weight of the darkness. Snatches of wind make the little lodge tremble, built as it is on frail wooden stilts over the water.

We are each allotted a punt and a gun-bearer. 'You'll take Faraj' says Nessim. 'He's the most experienced and reliable of them.' I thank him. A black barbaric face under a soiled white turban, un-smiling, spiritless. He takes my equipment and turns silently to the dark punt. With a whispered farewell I climb in and seat my-self. With a lithe swing of the pole Faraj drives us out into the channel and suddenly we are scoring across the heart of a black diamond. The water is full of stars, Orion down, Capella tossing out its brilliant sparks. For a long while now we crawl upon this diamond-pointed star-floor in silence save for the suck and lisp of the pole in the mud. Then we turn abruptly into a wider channel to hear a string of wavelets pattering against our prow while draughts of wind fetch up from the invisible sea-line tasting of salt.

Premonitions of the dawn are already in the air as we cross the darkness of this lost world. Now the approaches to the empty water ahead are shivered by the faintest etching of islands, sprouts of beard, reeds and sedge. And on all sides now comes the rich plural chuckle of duck and the shrill pinched note of the gulls to the sea-board. Faraj grunts and turns the punt towards a nearby island. Reaching out upon the darkness my hands grasp the icy rim of the nearest barrel into which I laboriously climb. The butts consist merely of a couple of dry wood-slatted barrels tied together and festooned with tall reeds to make them invisible. The loader holds the punt steady while I disembarrass him of my gear. There is nothing to do now but to sit and wait for the dawn which is rising slowly somewhere, to be born from this black expressionless darkness.

It is bitterly cold now and even my heavy greatcoat seems to offer inadequate protection. I have told Faraj that I will do my own loading as I do not want him handling my spare gun and cartridges in the next barrel. I must confess to a feeling of shame as I do so, but it sets my nerves at rest. He nods with an expressionless face and stands off with the punt in the next cluster of reeds, camouflaged like a scarecrow. We wait now with our faces turned towards the distant reaches of the lake — it seems for centuries.

Suddenly at the end of the great couloir my vision is sharpened by a pale disjunctive shudder as a bar of buttercup-yellow thickening gradually to a ray falls slowly through the dark masses of cloud to the east. The ripple and flurry of the invisible colonies of birds around us increases. Slowly, painfully, like a half-open door the dawn is upon us, forcing back the darkness. A minute more and a stairway of soft kingcups slides smoothly down out of heaven to touch in our horizons, to give eye and mind an orientation in space which it has been lacking. Faraj yawns heavily and scratches himself. Now rose-madder and warm burnt gold. Clouds move to green and yellow. The lake has begun to shake off its sleep. I see the black silhouette of teal cross my vision eastward. 'It is time' murmurs Faraj; but the minute hand of my wrist watch shows that we still have five minutes to go. My bones feel as if they have been soaked in the darkness. I feel suspense and inertia struggling for possession of my sleepy mind. By agreement there is to be no shooting before four-thirty. I load slowly and dispose my bandolier across the butt next me within easy reach. 'It is time' says Faraj more urgently. Nearby there is a plop and a scamper of some hidden birds. Out of sight a couple of coot squat in the middle of the lake pondering. I am about to say something when the first chapter of guns opens from the south — like the distant click of cricket-balls.

Now solitaries begin to pass, one, two, three. The light grows and waxes, turning now from red to green. The clouds themselves are moving to reveal enormous cavities of sky. They peel the morning like a fruit. Four separate arrowheads of duck rise and form two hundred yards away. They cross me trimly at an angle and I open up with a tentative right barrel for distance. As usual they are faster and higher than they seem. The minutes are ticking away in the heart. Guns open up nearer to hand, and by now the lake is in a general state of alert. The duck are coming fairly frequently now in groups, three, five, nine: very low and fast. Their wings purr, as they feather the sky, their necks reach. Higher again in mid-heaven there travel the clear formations of mallard, grouped like aircraft against the light, ploughing a soft slow flight. The guns squash the air and harry them as they pass, moving with a slow curling bias towards the open sea. Even higher and quite out of reach come chains of wild geese, their plaintive honking sounding clearly across the now sunny waters of Mareotis.

There is hardly time to think now: for teal and wigeon like flung darts whistle over me and I begin to shoot slowly and methodically. Targets are so plentiful that it is often difficult to choose one in the split second during which it presents itself to the gun. Once or twice I catch myself taking a snap shot into a formation. If hit squarely a bird staggers and spins, pauses for a moment, and then sinks gracefully like a handkerchief from a lady's hand. Reeds close over the brown bodies, but now the tireless Faraj is out poling about like mad to retrieve the birds. At times he leaps into the water with his *galabeah* tucked up to his midriff. His features blaze with excitement. From time to time he gives a shrill whoop.

They are coming in from everywhere now, at every conceivable angle and every speed. The guns bark and jumble in one's ears as they drive the birds backwards and forwards across the lake. Some of the flights though nimble are obviously war-weary after heavy losses; other solitaries seem quite out of their minds with panic. One young and silly duck settles for a moment by the punt, almost within reach of Faraj's hands, before it suddenly sees danger and spurts off in a slither of foam. In a modest way I am not doing too badly though in all the excitement it is hard to control oneself and to shoot deliberately. The sun is fairly up now and the damps of the night have been dispersed. In an hour I shall be sweating again in these heavy clothes. The sun shines on the ruffled waters of Mareotis where the birds still fly. The punts by now will be full of the sodden bodies of the victims, red blood running from the shattered beaks on to the floor-boards, marvellous feathers dulled by death.

I eke out my remaining ammunition as best I can but already by quarter past eight I have fired the last cartridge; Faraj is still at work painstakingly tracking down stragglers among the reeds with the single-mindedness of a retriever. I light a cigarette, and for the first time feel free from the shadow of omens and premonitions — free to breathe, to compose my mind once more. It is extraordinary how the prospect of death closes down upon the free play of the mind, like a steel shutter, cutting off the future which alone is nourished by hopes and wishes. I feel the stubble on my unshaven chin and think longingly of a hot bath and a warm breakfast. Faraj is still tirelessly scouting the islands of sedge. The guns have slackened, and in some quarters of the lake are already silent. I think with a dull ache of Justine, somewhere out there across the sunny water. I have no great fear for her safety for she has taken as her own gun-bearer my faithful servant Hamid.

I feel all at once gay and light-hearted as I shout to Faraj to cease his explorations and bring back the punt. He does so reluctantly and at last we set off across the lake, back through the channels and corridors of reed towards the lodge.

'Eight brace no good' says Faraj, thinking of the large professional bags we will have to face when Ralli and Capodistria return. 'For me it is very good' I say. 'I am a rotten shot. Never done as well.' We enter the thickly sown channels of water which border the lake like miniature canals.

At the end, against the light, I catch sight of another punt moving towards us which gradually defines itself into the familiar figure of Nessim. He is wearing his old moleskin cap with the ear-flaps up and tied over the top. I wave but he does not respond. He sits abstractedly in the prow of the punt with his hands clasped about his knees. 'Nessim' I shout. 'How did you do? I got eight brace and one lost.' The boats are nearly abreast now, for we are heading towards the mouth of the last canal which leads to the lodge. Nessim waits until we are within a few yards of each other before he says with a curious serenity, 'Did you hear? There's been an accident. Capodistria . . .' and all of a sudden my heart contracts in my body. 'Capodistria?' I stammer. Nessim still has the curious impish serenity of someone resting after a great expenditure of energy. 'He's dead' he says, and I hear the sudden roar of the hydroplane engines starting up behind the wall of reeds. He nods towards the sound and adds in the same still voice: 'They are taking him back to Alexandria.'

A thousand conventional commonplaces, a thousand conventional questions spring to my mind, but for a long time I can say nothing.

On the balcony the others have assembled uneasily, almost shamefacedly; they are like a group of thoughtless schoolboys for whom some silly prank has ended in the death of one of their fellows. The furry cone of noise from the hydroplane still coats the air. In the middle distance one can hear shouts and the noise of car-engines starting up. The piled bodies of the duck, which would normally be subject matter for gloating commentaries, lie about the lodge with anachronistic absurdity. It appears that death is a relative question. We had only been prepared to accept a certain share of it when we entered the dark lake with our weapons. The death of Capodistria hangs in the still air like a bad smell, like a bad joke.

Ralli had been sent to get him and had found the body lying face down in the shallow waters of the lake with the black eye-patch floating near him. It was clearly an accident. Capodistria's loader was an elderly man, thin as a cormorant, who sits now hunched over a mess of beans on the balcony. He cannot give a coherent account of the business. He is from Upper Egypt and has the weary half-crazed expression of a desert father.

Ralli is extremely nervous and is drinking copious draughts of brandy. He retells his story for the seventh time, simply because he must talk in order to quieten his nerves. The body could not have been long in the water, yet the skin was like the skin of a washerwoman's hands. When they lifted it to get it into the hydroplane the false teeth slipped out of the mouth and crashed on to the floor-boards frightening them all. This incident seems to have made a great impression on him. I suddenly feel overcome with fatigue and my knees start to tremble. I take a mug of hot coffee and, kicking off my boots, crawl into the nearest bunk with it. Ralli is still talking with deafening persistence, his free hand coaxing the air into expressive shapes. The others watch him with a vague and dispirited curiosity, each plunged in his own reflections. Capodistria's loader is still eating noisily like a famished animal, blinking in the sunlight. Presently a punt comes into view with three policemen perched precariously in it. Nessim watches their antics with an imperturbability flavoured ever so slightly with satisfaction; it is as if he were smiling to himself. The clatter of boots and musket-butts on the wooden steps, and up they come to take down our depositions in their note-books. They bring with them a grave air of suspicion which hovers over us all. One of them carefully manacles Capodistria's loader before helping him into the punt. The servant puts out his wrists for the iron cuffs with a bland uncomprehending air such as one sees on the faces of old apes when called upon to perform a human action which they have learned but not understood.

It is nearly one o'clock before the police have finished their business. The parties will all have ebbed back from the lake by now to the city where the news of Capodistria's death will be waiting for them. But this is not to be all.

One by one we straggle ashore with our gear. The cars are waiting for us, and now begins a long chaffering session with the loaders and boatmen who must be paid off; guns are broken up and the bag distributed; in all this incoherence I see my servant Hamid advancing timidly through the crowd with his good eye screwed up against the sunlight. I think he must be looking for me but no: he goes up to Nessim and hands him a small blue envelope. I want to describe this exactly. Nessim takes it absently with his left hand while his right is reaching into the car to place a box of cartridges in the glove-box. He examines the superscription once thoughtlessly and then once more with marked attention. Then keeping his eyes on Hamid's face he takes a deep breath and opens the envelope to read whatever is written on the half sheet of note-paper. For a minute he studies it and then replaces the letter in the envelope. He looks about him with a sudden change of expression, as if he suddenly felt sick and was looking about for a place where he might be so. He makes his way through the crowd and putting his head against a corner of mud wall utters a short panting sob, as of a runner out of breath. Then he turns back to the car, completely controlled and dry-eyed, to complete his packing. This brief incident goes completely unremarked by the rest of his guests.

Clouds of dust rise now as the cars begin to draw away towards the city; the wild gang of boatmen shout and wave and treat us to carved water-melon smiles studded with gold and ivory. Hamid opens the car door and climbs in like a monkey. 'What is it?' I say, and folding his small hands apologetically towards me in an attitude of supplication which means 'Blame not the bearer of ill tidings' he says in a small conciliatory voice: 'Master, the lady has gone. There is a letter for you in the house.'

It is as if the whole city had crashed about my ears: I walk slowly to the flat, aimlessly as survivors must walk about the streets of their native city after an earthquake, surprised to find how much that had been familiar has changed, Rue Piroua, Rue de France, the Terbana Mosque (cupboard smelling of apples), Rue Sidi Abou El Abbas (water-ices and coffee), Anfouchi, Ras El Tin (Cape of Figs), Ikingi Mariut (gathering wild flowers together, convinced she cannot love me), equestrian statue of Mohammed Ali in the square. . . . General Earle's comical little bust, killed Sudan 1885. . . . An evening multitudinous with swallows . . . the tombs at Kom El Shugafa, darkness and damp soil, both terrified by the darkness. . . . Rue Fuad as the old Canopic Way, once Rue Rosette. . . . Hutchinson disturbed the whole water-disposition of the city by cutting the dykes. . . . The scene in *Moeurs* where he tries to read her the book he is writing about her. 'She sits in the wicker chair with her hands in her lap, as if posing for a portrait, but with a look of ever-growing horror on her face. At last I can stand it no longer, and I throw down the manuscript in the fireplace, crying out: "What are they worth, since you understand nothing, these pages written from a heart pierced to the quick?" ' In my mind's eye I can see Nessim racing up the great staircase to her room to find a distraught Selim contemplating the empty cupboards and a dressing table swept clean as if by a blow from a leopard's paw.

In the harbour of Alexandria the sirens whoop and wail. The screws of ships crush and crunch the green oil-coated waters of the inner bar. Idly bending and inclining, effortlessly breathing as if in the rhythm of the earth's own systole and diastole, the yachts turn their spars against the sky. Somewhere in the heart of experience there is an order and a coherence which we might surprise if we were attentive enough, loving enough, or patient enough. Will there be time?

PART IV

The disappearance of Justine was something new to be borne. It changed the whole pattern of our relationship. It was as if she had removed the keystone to an arch: Nessim and I left among the ruins, so to speak were faced with the task of repairing a relationship which she herself had invented and which her absence now rendered hollow, echoing with a guilt which would, I thought, henceforward always overshadow affection.

His suffering was apparent to everyone. That expressive face took on a flayed unhealthy look — the pallor of a church martyr. In seeing him thus I was vividly reminded of my own feelings during the last meeting with Melissa before she left for the clinic in Jerusalem. The candour and gentleness with which she said: 'The whole thing is gone. . . . It may never come back. . . . At least this separation.' Her voice grew furry and moist, blurring the edges of the words. At this time she was quite ill. The lesions had opened again. 'Time to reconsider ourselves. . . . If only I were Justine. . . . I know you thought of her when you made love to me. . . . Don't deny it. . . . I know my darling. . . . I'm even jealous of your imagination. . . . Horrible to have self-reproach heaped on top of the other miseries. . . . Never mind.' She blew her nose shakily and managed a smile. 'I need rest so badly. . . . And now Nessim has fallen in love with me.' I put my hand over her sad mouth. The taxi throbbed on remorselessly, like someone living on his nerves. All round us walked the wives of the Alexandrians, smartly turned out, with the air of well-lubricated phantoms. The driver watched us in the mirror like a spy. The emotions of white people, he perhaps was thinking, are odd and excite prurience. He watched as one might watch cats making love.

'I shall never forget you.'

'Nor I. Write to me.'

'I shall always come back if you want.'

'Never doubt it. Get well, Melissa, you must get well. I'll wait for you. A new cycle will begin. It is all there inside me, intact. I feel it.'

The words that lovers use at such times are charged with distorting emotions. Only their silences have the cruel precision which aligns them to truth. We were silent, holding hands. She embraced me and signalled to the driver to set off.

'With her going the city took on an unnerving strangeness for him' writes Arnauti. 'Wherever his memory of her turned a familiar corner she recreated herself swiftly, vividly, and superimposed those haunted eyes and hands on the streets and squares. Old conversations leaped up and hit him among the polished table-tops of cafés where once they had sat, gazing like drunkards into each other's eyes. Sometimes she appeared walking a few paces ahead of him in the dark street. She would stop to adjust the strap of a sandal and he would overtake her with beating heart — only to find it was someone else. Particular doors seemed just about to admit her. He would sit and watch them doggedly. At other times he was suddenly seized by the irresistible conviction that she was about to arrive on a particular train, and he hurried to the station and breasted the crowd of passengers like a man fording a river. Or he might sit in the stuffy waiting-room of the airport after midnight watching the departures and arrivals, in case she were coming back to surprise him. In this way she controlled his imagination and taught him how feeble reason was; and he carried the consciousness of her going heavily about with him — like a dead baby from which one could not bring oneself to part.'

The night after Justine went away there was a freak thunderstorm of tremendous intensity. I had been wandering about in the rain for hours, a prey not only to feelings which I could not control but also to remorse for what I imagined Nessim must be feeling. Frankly, I hardly dared to go back to the empty flat, lest I should be tempted along the path Pursewarden had already taken so easily, with so little premeditation. Passing Rue Fuad for the seventh time, coatless and hatless in that blinding downpour, I happened to catch sight of the light in Clea's high window and on an impulse rang the bell. The front door opened with a whine and I stepped into the silence of the building from the dark street with its booming of rain in gutters and the splash of overflowing manholes.

She opened the door to me and at a glance took in my condition. I was made to enter, peel off my sodden clothes and put on the blue dressing-gown. The little electric fire was a blessing, and Clea set about making me hot coffee.

She was already in pyjamas, her gold hair combed out for the night. A copy of *A Rebours* lay face down on the floor beside the ash-tray with the smouldering cigarette in it. Lightning kept flashing fitfully at the window, lighting up her grave face with its magnesium flashes. Thunder rolled and writhed in the dark heavens outside the window. In this calm it was possible partly to exorcise my terrors by speaking of Justine. It appeared she knew all — nothing can be hidden from the curiosity of the Alexandrians. She knew all about Justine, that is to say.

'You will have guessed' said Clea in the middle of all this 'that Justine was the woman I told you once I loved so much.'

This cost her a good deal to say. She was standing with a coffee cup in one hand, clad in her blue-striped pyjamas by the door. She closed her eyes as she spoke, as if she were expecting a blow to fall upon the crown of her head. Out of the closed eyes came two tears which ran slowly down on each side of her nose. She looked like a young stag with a broken ankle. 'Ah! let us not speak of her any more' she said at last in a whisper. 'She will never come back.'

Later I made some attempt to leave but the storm was still at its height and my clothes still impossibly sodden. 'You can stay here' said Clea 'with me'; and she added with a gentleness which brought a lump into my throat, 'But please — I don't know how to say this — please don't make love to me.'

We lay together in that narrow bed talking of Justine while the storm blew itself out, scourging the window-panes of the flat with driven rain from the seafront. She was calm now with a sort of resignation which had a moving eloquence about it. She told me many things about Justine's past which only she knew; and she spoke of her with a wonder and tenderness such as people might use in talking of a beloved yet infuriating queen. Speaking of Arnauti's ventures into psycho-analysis she said with amusement: 'She was not really clever, you know, but she had the cunning of a wild animal at bay. I'm not sure she really understood the object of these investigations. Yet though she was evasive with the doctors she was perfectly frank with her friends. All that correspondence about the words "Washington D.C.", for example, which they worked so hard on — remember? One night while we were lying here together I asked her to give me her free associations from the phrase. Of course she trusted my discretion absolutely. She replied unerringly (it was clear she had already worked it out though she would not tell Arnauti): 'There is a town near Washington called Alexandria. My father always talked of going to visit some distant relations there. They had a daughter called Justine who was exactly my age. She went mad and was put away. She had been raped by a man.' I then asked her about D.C. and she said, "Da Capo. Capodistria".'

I do not know how long this conversation lasted or how soon it melted into sleep, but we awoke next morning in each other's arms to find that the storm had ceased. The city had been sponged clean. We took a hasty breakfast and I made my way towards Mnemjian's shop for a shave through streets whose native colours had been washed clean by the rain so that they glowed with warmth and beauty in that soft air. I still had Justine's letter in my pocket but I did not dare to read it again lest I destroy the peace of mind which Clea had given me. Only the opening phrase continued to echo in my mind with an obstinate throbbing persistence: 'If you should come back alive from the lake you will find this letter waiting for you.'

On the mantelpiece in the drawing-room of the flat there is another letter offering me a two-year contract as a teacher in a Catholic school in Upper Egypt. I sit down at once without thinking and draft my acceptance. This will change everything once more and free me from the streets of the city which have begun to haunt me of late so that I dream that I am walking endlessly up and down, hunting for Melissa among the dying flares of the Arab quarter.

With the posting of this letter of acceptance a new period will be initiated, for it marks my separation from the city in which so much has happened to me, so much of momentous importance: so much that has aged me. For a little while, however, life will carry its momentum forward by hours and days. The same streets and squares will burn in my imagination as the Pharos burns in history. Particular rooms in which I have made love, particular café tables where the pressure of fingers upon a wrist held me spellbound, feeling through the hot pavements the rhythms of Alexandria transmitted upwards into bodies which could only interpret them as famished kisses, or endearments uttered in voices hoarse with wonder. To the student of love these separations are a school, bitter yet necessary to one's growth. They help one to strip oneself mentally of everything save the hunger for more life.

Now, too, the actual framework of things is undergoing a subtle transformation, for other partings are also beginning. Nessim is going to Kenya for a holiday. Pombal has achieved crucifixion and a posting to the Chancery in Rome where I have no doubt he

will be happier. A series of leisurely farewell parties have begun
to serve the purposes of all of us; but they are heavy with the
absence of the one person whom nobody ever mentions any
more — Justine. It is clear too that a world war is slowly creeping
upon us across the couloirs of history — doubling our claims upon
each other and upon life. The sweet sickly smell of blood hangs
in the darkening air and contributes a sense of excitement, of
fondness and frivolity. This note has been absent until now.

The chandeliers in the great house whose ugliness I have come
to hate, blaze over the gatherings which have been convened to say
farewell to my friend. They are all there, the faces and histories I
have come to know so well, Sveva in black, Clea in gold, Gaston,
Claire, Gaby. Nessim's hair I notice has during the last few weeks
begun to be faintly touched with grey. Ptolemeo and Fuad are
quarrelling with all the animation of old lovers. All round me the
typical Alexandrian animation swells and subsides in conversations
as brittle and frivolous as spun glass. The women of Alexandria in
all their stylish wickedness are here to say good-bye to someone
who has captivated them by allowing them to befriend him. As for
Pombal himself, he has grown fatter, more assured since his eleva-
tion in rank. His profile now has a certain Neronian cast. He is
professing himself worried about me in *sotto voce*; for some weeks
we have not met properly, and he has only heard about my school-
mastering project tonight. 'You should get out' he repeats, 'back to
Europe. This city will undermine your will. And what has Upper
Egypt to offer? Blazing heat, dust, flies, a menial occupation. . . .
After all, you are not Rimbaud.'

The faces surging round us sipping toasts prevent my answering
him, and I am glad of it for I have nothing to say. I gaze at him
with a portentous numbness, nodding my head. Clea catches my
wrist and draws me aside to whisper: 'A card from Justine. She is
working in a Jewish *kibbutz* in Palestine. Shall I tell Nessim?'

'Yes. No. I don't know.'

'She asks me not to.'

'Then don't.'

I am too proud to ask if there is any message for me. The company has started to sing the old song 'For He's a Jolly Good
Fellow' in a variety of times and accents. Pombal has turned pink
with pleasure. I gently shake off Clea's hand in order to join in
the singing. The little consul-general is fawning and gesticulating
over Pombal; his relief at my friend's departure is so great that he

has worked himself up into a paroxysm of friendship and regret. The English consular group has the disconsolate air of a family of moulting turkeys. Madame de Venuta is beating time with an elegant gloved hand. The black servants in their long white gloves move swiftly from group to group of the guests like eclipses of the moon. If one were to go away, I catch myself thinking, to Italy perhaps or to France: to start a new sort of life: not a city life this time, perhaps an island in the Bay of Naples. . . . But I realise that what remains unresolved in my life is not the problem of Justine but the problem of Melissa. In some curious way the future, if there is one, has always been vested in her. Yet I feel powerless to influence it by decisions or even hopes. I feel that I must wait patiently until the shallow sequences of our history match again, until we can fall into step once more. This may take years — perhaps we will both be grey when the tide suddenly turns. Or perhaps the hope will die stillborn, broken up like wreckage by the tides of events. I have so little faith in myself. The money Pursewarden left is still in the bank — I have not touched a penny of it. For such a sum we might live for several years in some cheap spot in the sun.

Melissa still writes the spirited nonchalant letters which I have such difficulty in answering save by whining retorts about my circumstances or my improvidence. Once I leave the city it will be easier. A new road will open. I will write to her with absolute frankness, telling her all I feel — even those things which I believe her forever incapable of understanding properly. 'I shall return in the spring' Nessim is saying to the Baron Thibault 'and take up my summer quarters at Abousir. I am determined to slack off for about two years. I've been working too hard at business and it isn't worth it.' Despite the haunted pallor of his face one cannot help seeing in him a new repose, a relaxation of the will; the heart may be distracted, but the nerves are at last at rest. He is weak, as a convalescent is weak; but he is no longer ill. We talk and joke quietly for a while; it is clear that our friendship will repair itself sooner or later — for we now have a common fund of unhappiness upon which to draw. 'Justine' I say, and he draws in his breath slightly, as if one had run a small thorn under his fingernail, 'writes from Palestine.' He nods quickly and motions me with a small gesture. 'I know. We have traced her. There is no need to . . . I'm writing to her. She can stay away as long as she wishes. Come back in her own good time.' It would be foolish to deprive him of the hope and the consolation it must give him, but I know now that she will never return on the old terms. Every phrase of her letter to me made this clear. It is not us she had abandoned so much but a way of life which threatened her reason — the city, love, the sum of all that we had shared. What had she written to him, I wondered, as I recalled the short sobbing breath he had drawn as he leaned against the whitewashed wall?

*   *   *   *   *

On these spring mornings while the island slowly uncurls from the sea in the light of an early sun I walk about on the deserted beaches, trying to recover my memories of the time spent in Upper Egypt. It is strange when everything about Alexandria is so vivid that I can recover so little of that lost period. Or perhaps it is not so strange — for compared to the city life I had lived my new life was dull and uneventful. I remember the back-breaking sweat of school work: walks in the flat rich fields with their bumper crops feeding upon dead men's bones: the black silt-fed Nile moving corpulently through the Delta to the sea: the bilharzia-ridden peasantry whose patience and nobility shone through their rags like patents of dispossessed royalty: village patriarchs inton-ing: the blind cattle turning the slow globe of their waterwheels, blind-folded against monotony — how small can a world become? Throughout this period I read nothing, thought nothing, was nothing. The fathers of the school were kindly and left me alone in my spare time, sensing perhaps my distaste for the cloth, for the apparatus of the Holy Office. The children of course were a tor-ment — but then what teacher of sensibility does not echo in his heart the terrible words of Tolstoy: 'Whenever I enter a school and see a multitude of children, ragged thin and dirty but with their clear eyes and sometimes angelic expressions, I am seized with restlessness and terror, as though I saw people drowning'?

Unreal as all correspondence seemed, I kept up a desultory contact with Melissa whose letters arrived punctually. Clea wrote once or twice, and surprisingly enough old Scobie who appeared to be rather annoyed that he should miss me as much as he obviously did. His letters were full of fantastic animadversion against Jews (who were always referred to jeeringly as 'snipcocks') and, surprisingly enough, to passive pederasts (whom he labelled 'Herms', i.e. Hermaphrodites). I was not surprised to learn that the Secret Service had gravelled him, and he was now able to spend most of the day in bed with what he called a 'bottle of wallop' at his elbow. But he was lonely, hence his correspondence.

These letters were useful to me. My feeling of unreality had grown to such a pitch that at times I distrusted my own memory, finding it hard to believe that there had ever been such a town as Alexandria. Letters were a lifeline attaching me to an existence in which the greater part of myself was no longer engaged.

As soon as my work was finished I locked myself in my room and crawled into bed; beside it lay the green jade box full of hashish-loaded cigarettes. If my way of life was noticed or commented upon at least I left no loophole for criticism in my work. It would be hard to grudge me simply an inordinate taste for solitude. Father Racine, it is true, made one or two attempts to rouse me. He was the most sensitive and intelligent of them all and perhaps felt that my friendship might temper his own intellectual loneliness. I was sorry for him and regretted in a way not being able to respond to these overtures. But I was afflicted by a gradually increasing numbness, a mental apathy which made me shrink from contact. Once or twice I accompanied him for a walk along the river (he was a botanist) and heard him talk lightly and brilliantly on his own subject. But my taste for the landscape, its flatness, its unresponsiveness to the seasons had gone stale. The sun seemed to have scorched up my appetite for everything — food, company and even speech. I preferred to lie in bed staring at the ceiling and listening to the noises around me in the teachers' block: Father Gaudier sneezing, opening and shutting drawers; Father Racine playing a few phrases over and over again on his flute; the ruminations of the organ mouldering away among its harmonies in the dark chapel. The heavy cigarettes soothed the mind, emptying it of every preoccupation.

One day Gaudier called to me as I was crossing the close and said that someone wished to speak to me on the telephone. I could hardly comprehend, hardly believe my ears. After so long a silence who would telephone? Nessim perhaps?

The telephone was in the Head's study, a forbidding room full of elephantine furniture and fine bindings. The receiver, crepitating slightly, lay on the blotter before him. He squinted slightly and said with distaste 'It is a woman from Alexandria.' I thought it must be Melissa but to my surprise Clea's voice suddenly swam up out of the incoherence of memory: 'I am speaking from the Greek hospital. Melissa is here, very ill indeed. Perhaps even dying.'

Undeniably my surprise and confusion emerged as anger. 'But she would not let me tell you before. She didn't want you to see her ill — so thin. But I simply must now. Can you come quickly? She will see you now.'

In my mind's eye I could see the jogging night train with its interminable stoppings and startings in dust-blown towns and villages — the dirt and the heat. It would take all night. I turned to Gaudier and asked his permission to absent myself for the whole week-end. 'In exceptional cases we do grant permission' he said thoughtfully. 'If you were going to be married, for example, or if someone was seriously ill.' I swear that the idea of marrying Melissa had not entered my head until he spoke the words.

There was another memory, too, which visited me now as I packed my cheap suitcase. The rings, Cohen's rings, were still in my stud-box wrapped in brown paper. I stood for a while looking at them and wondering if inanimate objects also had a destiny as human beings have. These wretched rings, I thought — why, it was as if they had been anxiously waiting here all the time like human beings; waiting for some shabby fulfilment on the finger of someone trapped into a *mariage de convenance*. I put the poor things in my pocket.

Far off events, transformed by memory, acquire a burnished brilliance because they are seen in isolation, divorced from the details of before and after, the fibres and wrappings of time. The actors, too, suffer a transformation; they sink slowly deeper and deeper into the ocean of memory like weighted bodies, finding at every level a new assessment, a new evaluation in the human heart.

It was not anguish I felt so much at Melissa's defection, it was rage, a purposeless fury based, I imagine, in contrition. The enormous vistas of the future which in all my vagueness I had nevertheless peopled with images of her had gone by default now; and it was only now that I realized to what an extent I had been nourishing myself on them. It had all been there like a huge trust fund, an account upon which I would one day draw. Now I was suddenly bankrupt.

Balthazar was waiting for me at the station in his little car. He pressed my hand with rough and ready sympathy as he said, in a matter-of-fact voice: 'She died last night poor girl. I gave her morphia to help her away. Well.' He sighed and glanced sideways at me. 'A pity you are not in the habit of shedding tears. *Ça aurait été un soulagement.*'

'*Soulagement grotesque.*'

'*Approfondir les émotions . . . les purger.*'

'*Tais-toi*, Balthazar, shut up.'

'She loved you, I suppose.'

'*Je le sais.*'

'*Elle parlait de vous sans cesse. Cléa a été avec elle toute la semaine.*'

'*Assez.*'

Never had the city looked so entrancing in that soft morning air. I took the light wind from the harbour on my stubbled cheek like the kiss of an old friend. Mareotis glinted here and there between the palm-tops, between the mud huts and the factories. The shops along Rue Fuad seemed to have all the glitter and novelty of Paris. I had, I realized, become a complete provincial in Upper Egypt. Alexandria seemed a capital city. In the trim garden nurses were rolling their prams and children their hoops. The trams squashed and clicked and rattled. 'There is something else' Balthazar was saying as we raced along. 'Melissa's child, Nessim's child. But I suppose you know all about it. It is out at the summer villa. A little girl.'

I could not take all this in, so drunk was I on the beauty of the city which I had almost forgotten. Outside the Municipality the professional scribes sat at their stools, inkhorns, pens and stamped paper beside them. They scratched themselves, chattering amiably. We climbed the low bluff on which the hospital stood after threading the long bony spine of the Canopic Way. Balthazar was still talking as we left the lift and started to negotiate the long white corridors of the second floor.

'A coolness has sprung up between Nessim and myself. When Melissa came back he refused to see her out of a sort of disgust which I found inhuman, hard to comprehend. I don't know. . . . As for the child he is trying to get it adopted. He has come almost to hate it, I suppose. He thinks Justine will never come back to him so long as he has Melissa's child. For my part' he added more slowly 'I look at it this way: by one of those fearful displacements of which only love seems capable the child Justine lost was given back by Nessim not to her but to Melissa. Do you see?'

The sense of ghostly familiarity which was growing upon me now was due to the fact that we were approaching the little room in which I had visited Cohen when he was dying. Of course Melissa must be lying in the same narrow iron bed in the corner by the wall. It would be just like real life to imitate art at this point.

There were some nurses in the room busy whispering round the bed, arranging screens; but at a word from Balthazar they scattered and disappeared. We stood arm in arm in the doorway for a moment looking in. Melissa looked pale and somehow wizened. They had bound up her jaw with tape and closed the eyes so that she looked as if she had fallen asleep during a beauty treatment. I was glad her eyes were closed; I had been dreading their glance.

I was left alone with her for a while in the huge silence of that whitewashed ward and all of a sudden I found myself suffering from acute embarrassment. It is hard to know how to behave with the dead; their enormous deafness and rigidity is so studied. One becomes awkward as if in the presence of royalty. I coughed behind my hand and walked up and down the ward stealing little glances at her out of the corner of my eye, remembering the confusion which had once beset me when she called upon me with a gift of flowers. I would have liked to slip Cohen's rings on her fingers but they had already swathed her body in bandages and her arms were bound stiffly to her sides. In this climate bodies decompose so quickly that they have to be almost unceremoniously rushed to the grave. I said 'Melissa' twice in an uncertain whisper bending my lips to her ear. Then I lit a cigarette and sat down beside her on a chair to make a long study of her face, comparing it to all the other faces of Melissa which thronged my memory and had established their identity there. She bore no resemblance to any of them — and yet she set them off, concluded them. This white little face was the last term of a series. Beyond this point there was a locked door.

At such times one gropes about for a gesture which will match the terrible marble repose of the will which one reads on the faces of the dead. There is nothing in the whole ragbag of human emotions. 'Terrible are the four faces of love,' wrote Arnauti in another context. I mentally told the figure on the bed that I would take the child if Nessim would part with her, and this silent agreement made I kissed the high pale forehead once and left her to the ministrations of those who would parcel her up for the grave. I was glad to leave the room, to leave a silence so elaborate and forbidding. I suppose we writers are cruel people. The dead do not care. It is the living who might be spared if we could quarry the message which lies buried in the heart of all human experience.

('In the old days the sailing ships in need of ballast would collect tortoises from the mainland and fill great barrels with them, alive. Those that survived the terrible journey might be sold as pets for children. The putrefying bodies of the rest were emptied into the East India Docks. There were plenty more where they came from.')

I walked lightly effortlessly about the town like an escaped prisoner. Mnemjian had violet tears in his violet eyes as he embraced me warmly. He settled down to shave me himself, his every gesture expressing an emollient sympathy and tenderness. Outside on the pavements drenched with sunlight walked the citizens of Alexandria each locked into a world of personal relationships and fears, yet each seeming to my eyes infinitely remote from those upon which my own thoughts and feelings were busy. The city was smiling with a heartbreaking indifference, a *cocotte* refreshed by the darkness.

There remained only one thing to do now, to see Nessim. I was relieved to learn that he was due to come into town that evening. Here again time had another surprise in store for me for the Nessim who lived in my memories had changed.

He had aged like a woman — his lips and face had both broadened. He walked now with his weight distributed comfortably on the flat of his feet as if his body had already submitted to a dozen pregnancies. The queer litheness of his step had gone. Moreover he radiated now a flabby charm mixed with concern which made him at first all but unrecognizable. A foolish authoritativeness had replaced the delightful old diffidence. He was just back from Kenya.

I had hardly time to capture and examine these new impressions when he suggested that we should visit the Etoile together — the night-club where Melissa used to dance. It had changed hands, he added, as if this somehow excused our visiting it on the very day of her funeral. Shocked and surprised as I was I agreed without hesitation, prompted both by curiosity as to his own feelings and a desire to discuss the transaction which concerned the child — this mythical child.

When we walked down the narrow airless stairway into the white light of the place a cry went up and the girls came running to him from every corner like cockroaches. It appeared that he was well known now as an habitué. He opened his arms to them with a shout of laughter, turning to me for approval as he did so. Then taking their hands one after another he pressed them voluptuously to the breast pocket of his coat so that they might feel the outlines of the thick wallet he now carried, stuffed with banknotes. This gesture at once reminded me of how, when I was accosted one night in the dark streets of the city by a pregnant woman and trying to make my escape, she took my hand, as if to give me an idea of the pleasure she was offering (or perhaps to emphasize her need) and pressed it upon her swollen abdomen. Now, watching Nessim, I suddenly recalled the tremulous beat of the foetal heart in the eighth month.

It is difficult to describe how unspeakably strange I found it to sit beside this vulgar double of the Nessim I had once known. I studied him keenly but he avoided my eye and confined his conversation to laboured commonplaces which he punctuated by yawns that were one by one tapped away behind ringed fingers. Here and there, however, behind this new façade stirred a hint of the old diffidence, but buried — as a fine physique may be buried in a mountain of fat. In the washroom Zoltan the waiter confided in me: 'He has become truly himself since his wife went away. All Alexandria says so.' The truth was that he had become like all Alexandria.

Late that night the whim seized him to drive me to Montaza in the late moonlight; we sat in the car for a long time in silence, smoking, gazing out at the moonlit waves hobbling across the sand bar. It was during this silence that I apprehended the truth about him. He had not really changed inside. He had merely adopted a new mask.

*　*　*　*　*

In the early summer I received a long letter from Clea with which this brief introductory memorial to Alexandria may well be brought to a close.

'You may perhaps be interested in my account of a brief meeting with Justine a few weeks ago. We had, as you know, been exchanging occasional cards from our respective countries for some time past, and hearing that I was due to pass through Palestine into Syria she herself suggested a brief meeting. She would come, she said, to the border station where the Haifa train waits for half an hour. The settlement in which she works is somewhere near at hand, she could get a lift. We might talk for a while on the platform. To this I agreed.

'At first I had some difficulty in recognizing her. She has gone a good deal fatter in the face and has chopped off her hair carelessly at the back so that it sticks out in rats' tails. I gather that for the most part she wears it done up in a cloth. No trace remains of the old elegance or *chic*. Her features seem to have broadened, become more classically Jewish, lip and nose inclining more towards each other. I was shocked at first by the glittering eyes and the quick incisive way of breathing and talking — as if she were feverish. As you can imagine we were both mortally shy of each other.

'We walked out of the station along the road and sat down on the edge of a dry ravine, a wadi, with a few terrified-looking spring flowers about our feet. She gave the impression of already having chosen this place for our interview: perhaps as suitably austere. I don't know. She did not mention Nessim or you at first but spoke only about her new life. She had achieved, she claimed, a new and perfect happiness through "community-service"; the air with which she said this suggested some sort of religious conversion. Do not smile. It is hard, I know, to be patient with the weak. In all the back-breaking sweat of the Communist settlement she claimed to have achieved a "new humility". (Humility! The *last trap* that awaits the ego in search of absolute truth. I felt disgusted but said nothing.) She described the work of the settlement coarsely, unimaginatively, as a peasant might. I noticed that those once finely-tended hands were calloused and rough. I suppose people have a right to dispose of their bodies as they think fit, I said to myself, feeling ashamed because I must be radiating cleanliness and leisure, good food and baths. By the way, she is not a Marxist as yet — simply a work-mystic after the manner of Panayotis at Abousir. Watching her now and remembering the touching and tormenting person she had once been for us all I found it hard to comprehend the change into this tubby little peasant with the hard paws.

'I suppose events are simply a sort of annotation of our feelings — the one might be deduced from the other. Time carries us (boldly imagining that we are discrete egos modelling our own personal futures) — time carries us forward by the momentum of those feelings inside us of which we ourselves are least conscious. Too abstract for you? Then I have expressed the idea badly. I mean, in Justine's case, having become cured of the mental aberrations brought about by her dreams, her fears, she has been deflated like a bag. For so long the fantasy occupied the foreground of her life that now she is dispossessed of her entire stock-in-trade. It is not only that the death of Capodistria has removed the chief actor in this shadow-play, her chief gaoler. The illness itself had kept her on the move, and when it died it left in its place total exhaustion. She has, so to speak, extinguished with her sexuality her very claims on life, almost her reason. People driven like this to the very boundaries of freewill are forced to turn somewhere for help, to make absolute decisions. If she had not been an Alexandrian (i.e. sceptic) this would have taken the form of religious conversion. How is one to say these things? It is not a question of growing to be happy or unhappy. A whole block of one's life suddenly falls into the sea, as perhaps yours did with Melissa. But (this is how it works in life, the retributive law which brings good for evil and evil for good) her own release also released Nessim from the inhibitions governing his passional life. I think he always felt that so long as Justine lived he would never be able to endure the slightest human relationship with anyone else. Melissa proved him wrong, or at least so he thought; but with Justine's departure the old heartsickness cropped up and he was filled with overwhelming disgust for what he had done to her — to Melissa.

'Lovers are never equally matched — do you think? One always overshadows the other and stunts his or her growth so that the overshadowed one must always be tormented by a desire to escape, to be free to grow. Surely this is the only tragic thing about love?

'So that if from another point of view Nessim did plan Capodistria's death (as has been widely rumoured and believed) he could not have chosen a more calamitous path. It would indeed have been wiser to kill you. Perhaps he hoped in releasing Justine from the succubus (as Arnauti before him) he would free her for himself. (He said so once — you told me.) But quite the opposite has happened. He has granted her a sort of absolution, or poor Capodistria unwittingly did — with the result that she thinks of him now not as a lover but as a sort of arch-priest. She speaks of him with a *reverence* which would horrify him to hear. She will never go back, how could she? And if she did he would know at once that he had lost her forever — for those who stand in a confessional relationship to ourselves can never love us, never truly love us.

'(Of you Justine said simply, with a slight shrug: "I had to put him out of my mind".)

'Well, these are some of the thoughts that passed through my mind as the train carried me down through the orange groves to the coast; they were thrown into sharp relief by the book I had chosen to read on the journey, the penultimate volume of *God is a*

Humorist. How greatly Pursewarden has gained in stature since his death! It was before as if he stood between his own books and our understanding of them. I see now that what we found enigmatic about the man was due to a fault in ourselves. An artist does not live a personal life as we do, he hides it, forcing us to go to his books if we wish to touch the true source of his feelings. Underneath all his preoccupations with sex, society, religion, etc. (all the staple abstractions which allow the forebrain to chatter) there is, quite simply, a man *tortured beyond endurance by the lack of tenderness in the world*.

'And all this brings me back to myself, for I too have been changing in some curious way. The old self-sufficient life has transformed itself into something a little hollow, a little empty. It no longer answers my deepest needs. Somewhere deep inside a tide seems to have turned in my nature. I do not know why but it is towards you, my dear friend, that my thoughts have turned more and more of late. Can one be frank? Is there a friendship possible this side of love which could be sought and found? I speak no more of love — the word and its conventions have become odious to me. But is there a friendship possible to attain which is deeper, even limitlessly deep, and yet wordless, idealess? It seems somehow necessary to find a human being to whom one can be faithful, not in the body (I leave that to the priests) but in the culprit mind? But perhaps this is not the sort of problem which will interest you much these days. Once or twice I have felt the absurd desire to come to you and offer my services in looking after the child perhaps. But it seems clear now that you do not really need anybody any more, and that you value your solitude above all things. . . .'

There are a few more lines and then the affectionate superscription.

* * * * *

The cicadas are throbbing in the great planes, and the summer Mediterranean lies before me in all its magnetic blueness. Somewhere out there, beyond the mauve throbbing line of the horizon lies Africa, lies Alexandria, maintaining its tenuous grasp on one's affections through memories which are already refunding themselves slowly into forgetfulness; memory of friends, of incidents long past. The slow unreality of time begins to grip them, blurring the outlines — so that sometimes I wonder whether these pages record the actions of real human beings; or whether this is not simply the story of a few inanimate objects which precipitated drama around them — I mean a black patch, a watch-key and a couple of dispossessed wedding-rings. . . .

Soon it will be evening and the clear night sky will be dusted thickly with summer stars. I shall be here, as always, smoking by the water. I have decided to leave Clea's last letter unanswered. I no longer wish to coerce anyone, to make promises, to think of life in terms of compacts, resolutions, covenants. It will be up to Clea to interpret my silence according to her own needs and desires, to come to me if she has need or not, as the case may be. Does not everything* depend on our interpretation of the silence around us? So that. . . .

WORKPOINTS

Landscape-tones: steep skylines, low cloud, pearl ground with shadows in oyster and violet. Accidie. On the lake gunmetal and lemon. Summer: sand lilac sky. Autumn: swollen bruise greys. Winter: freezing white sand, clear skies, magnificent starscapes.

* * *

CHARACTER-SQUEEZES

Sveva Magnani: pertness, malcontent.
Gaston Pombal: honey-bear, fleshly opiates.
Teresa di Petromonti: farded Berenice.
Ptolomeo Dandolo: astronomer, astrologer, Zen.
Fuad El Said: black moon-pearl.
Josh Scobie: piracy.
Justine Hosnani: arrow in darkness.
Clea Montis: still waters of pain.
Gaston Phipps: nose like a sock, black hat.
Ahmed Zananiri: pole-star criminal.
Nessim Hosnani: smooth gloves, face frosted glass.
Melissa Artemis: patron of sorrow.
S. Balthazar: fables, work, unknowing.

* * *

Pombal asleep in full evening dress. Beside him on the bed a chamberpot full of banknotes he had won at the Casino.

* * *

Da Capo: 'To bake in sensuality like an apple in its jacket.'

* * *

Spoken impromptu by Gaston Phipps:
  'The lover like a cat with fish
  Longs to be off and will not share his dish.'

* * *

Accident or attempted murder? Justine racing along the desert road to Cairo in the Rolls when suddenly the lights give out. Sightless, the great car swarms off the road and whistling like an arrow buries itself in a sand-dune. It looked as if the wires had been filed down to a thread. Nessim reached her within half an hour. They embrace in tears.

*   *   *

Balthazar on Justine: 'You will find that her formidable manner is constructed on a shaky edifice of childish timidities.'

*   *   *

Clea always has a horoscope cast before any decision reached.

*   *   *

Clea's account of the horrible party; driving with Justine they had seen a brown cardboard box by the road. They were late so they put it in the back and did not open it until they reached the garage. Inside was dead baby wrapped in newspaper. What to do with this wizened homunculus? Perfectly formed organs. Guests were due to arrive, they had to rush. Justine slipped it into drawer of the hall desk. Party a great success.

*   *   *

Pursewarden on the 'n-dimensional novel' trilogy: 'The narrative momentum forward is counter-sprung by references backwards in time, giving the impression of a book which is not travelling from a to b but standing above time and turning slowly on its own axis to comprehend the whole pattern. Things do not all lead forward to other things: some lead backwards to things which have passed. A marriage of past and present with the flying multiplicity of the future racing towards one. Anyway, that was my idea.' . . .

*   *   *

'Then how long will it last, this love?' (in jest).
'I don't know.'
'Three weeks, three years, three decades. . .?'
'You are like all the others . . . trying to shorten eternity with numbers,' spoken quietly, but with intense feeling.

*   *   *

Conundrum: a peacock's eye. Kisses so amateurish they resembled an early form of printing.

*   *   *

JUSTINE

Of poems: 'I like the soft thudding of Alexandrines.' (Nessim).

* * *

Clea and her old father whom she worships. White haired, erect, with a sort of haunted pity in his eyes for the young unmarried goddess he has fathered. Once a year on New Year's Eve they dance at the Cecil, stately, urbanely. He waltzes like a clockwork man.

* * *

Pombal's love for Sveva: based on one gay message which took his fancy. When he awoke she'd gone, but she had neatly tied his dress tie to his John Thomas, a perfect bow. This message so captivated him that he at once dressed and went round to propose marriage to her because of her sense of humour.

* * *

Pombal was at his most touching with his little car which he loved devotedly. I remember him washing it by moonlight very patiently.

* * *

Justine: 'Always astonished by the force of my own emotions — tearing the heart out of a book with my fingers like a fresh loaf.'

* * *

Places: street with arcade: awnings: silverware and doves for .sale. Pursewarden fell over a basket and filled the street with apples.

* * *

Message on the corner of a newspaper. Afterwards the closed cab, warm bodies, night, volume of jasmine.

* * *

A basket of quail burst open in the bazaar. They did not try to escape but spread out slowly like spilt honey. Easily recaptured.

* * *

Postcard from Balthazar: 'Scobie's death was the greatest fun. How he must have enjoyed it. His pockets were full of love-letters to his aide Hassan, and the whole vice squad turned out to sob at his grave. All these black gorillas crying like babies. A very Alexandrian demonstration of affection. Of course the grave was too small for the coffin. The grave-diggers had knocked off for lunch, so a scratch team of policemen was brought into action. Usual muddle. The coffin fell over on its side and the old man nearly rolled out. Shrieks. The padre was furious. The British Consul nearly died of shame. But all Alexandria was there and a good time was had by all.'

*   *   *

Pombal walking in stately fashion down Rue Fuad, dead drunk at ten in the morning, clad in full evening dress, cloak and opera hat — but bearing on his shirt-front, written in lipstick, the words 'Torche-cul des républicains.'

*   *   *

(Museum)
Alexander wearing the horns of Ammon (Nessim's madness). He identified himself with A because of the horns?

*   *   *

Justine reflecting sadly on the statue of Berenice mourning her little daughter whom the Priests deified: 'Did that assuage her grief I wonder? Or did it make it more permanent?'

*   *   *

Tombstone of Apollodorus giving his child a toy. 'Could bring tears to one's eyes.' (Pursewarden) 'They are all dead. Nothing to show for it.'

*   *   *

Aurelia beseeching Petesouchos the crocodile god . . Narouz.

*   *   *

Lioness Holding a Golden flower. . .

*   *   *

Ushabti . . . little serving figures which are supposed to work for the mummy in the underworld.

*   *   *

Somehow even Scobie's death did not disturb our picture of him. I had already seen him long before in Paradise — the soft

conklin-coloured yams like the haunches of newly cooked babies:
the night falling with its deep-breathing blue slur over Tobago,
softer than parrot-plumage. Paper flamingoes touched with gold-
leaf, rising and falling on the sky, touched by the keening of the
bruise-dark water-bamboos. His little hut of reeds with the cane
bed, beside which still stands the honoured cake-stand of his earthly
life. Clea once asked him: 'Do you not miss the sea, Scobie?' and
the old man replied simply, without hesitation, 'Every night I put
to sea in my dreams.'

* * * * *

I copied out and gave her the two translations from Cavafy
which had pleased her though they were by no means literal. By
now the Cavafy canon has been established by the fine thoughtful
translations of Mavrogordato and in a sense the poet has been freed
for other poets to experiment with; I have tried to transplant
rather than translate — with what success I cannot say.

THE CITY

You tell yourself: I'll be gone
To some other land, some other sea,
To a city lovelier far than this
Could ever have been or hoped to be —
Where every step now tightens the noose:
A heart in a body buried and out of use:
How long, how long must I be here
Confined among these dreary purlieus
Of the common mind? Wherever now I look
Black ruins of my life rise into view.
So many years have I been here
Spending and squandering, and nothing gained.
There's no new land, my friend, no
New sea; for the city will follow you,
In the same streets you'll wander endlessly,
The same mental suburbs slip from youth to age,
In the same house go white at last —
The city is a cage.
No other places, always this
Your earthly landfall, and no ship exists
To take you from yourself. Ah! don't you see
Just as you've ruined your life in this

THE ALEXANDRIA QUARTET

One plot of ground you've ruined its worth
Everywhere now — over the whole earth?

THE GOD ABANDONS ANTONY

When suddenly at darkest midnight heard,
The invisible company passing, the clear voices,
Ravishing music of invisible choirs —
Your fortunes having failed you now,
Hopes gone aground, a lifetime of desires
Turned into smoke. Ah! do not agonize
At what is past deceiving
But like a man long since prepared
With courage say your last good-byes
To Alexandria as she is leaving.
Do not be tricked and never say
It was a dream or that your ears misled,
Leave cowards their entreaties and complaints,
Let all such useless hopes as these be shed,
And like a man long since prepared,
Deliberately, with pride, with resignation
Befitting you and worthy of such a city
Turn to the open window and look down
To drink past all deceiving
Your last dark rapture from the mystical throng
And say farewell, farewell to Alexandria leaving.

NOTES IN THE TEXT

Page 18. 'The Poet of the city.' C. P. Cavafy.

Page 18. 'The old man.' C. P. Cavafy.

Page 39. Caballi. The astral bodies of men who died a premature death 'They imagine to perform bodily actions while in fact they have no physical bodies but act in their thoughts.' *Paracelsus*.

Page 39. 'Held the Gnostic doctrine that creation is a mistake. . . . He imagines a primal God, the centre of a divine harmony, who sent out manifestations of himself in pairs of male and female. Each pair was inferior to its predecessor and Sophia ("wisdom") the female of the thirtieth pair, least perfect of all. She showed her imperfection not, like Lucifer, by rebelling from God, but by desiring too ardently to be united to him. She fell through love.' E. M. Forster, *Alexandria*.

Page 40. Quotation from Paracelsus.

Page 51. Taphia, Egyptian 'Red Biddy.'

Page 53. Greek text. ˋΟταν θά βγῶ, ἄν δέν ἔχῃς φιλενάδα, φώναξέ με.

Page 77. Amr, Conqueror of Alexandria, was a poet and soldier. Of the Arab invasion E. M. Forster writes: 'Though they had no intention of destroying her, they destroyed her, as a child might a watch. She never functioned again properly for over 1,000 years.'

Page 147. A translation of 'The City' is among the 'Workpoints.'

Page 195. See page 196.

BALTHAZAR

To
MY MOTHER
these memorials of an unforgotten city

The mirror sees the man as beautiful, the mirror loves the man; another mirror sees the man as frightful and hates him; and it is always the same being who produces the impressions.

D. A. F. DE SADE: Justine

Yes, we insist upon those details, you veil them with a decency which removes all their edge of horror; there remains only what is useful to whoever wishes to become familiar with man; you have no conception how helpful these tableaux are to the development of the human spirit; perhaps we are still so benighted with respect to this branch of learning only because of the stupid restraint of those who wish to write upon such matters. Inhabited by absurd fears, they only discuss the puerilities with which every fool is familiar and dare not, by turning a bold hand to the human heart, offer its gigantic idiosyncrasies to our view.

D. A. F. DE SADE: Justine

PART I

I

Landscape-tones: brown to bronze, steep skyline, low cloud, pearl ground with shadowed oyster and violet reflections. The lion-dust of desert: prophets' tombs turned to zinc and copper at sunset on the ancient lake. Its huge sand-faults like watermarks from the air; green and citron giving to gunmetal, to a single plum-dark sail, moist, palpitant: sticky-winged nymph. Taposiris is dead among its tumbling columns and seamarks, vanished the Harpoon Men . . . Mareotis under a sky of hot lilac.

> *summer*: *buff sand, hot marble sky.*
> *autumn*: *swollen bruise-greys.*
> *winter*: *freezing snow, cool sand.*
> *clear sky panels, glittering with mica.*
> *washed delta greens.*
> *magnificent starscapes.*

And spring? Ah! there is no spring in the Delta, no sense of refreshment and renewal in things. One is plunged out of winter into: wax effigy of a summer too hot to breathe. But here, at least, in Alexandria, the sea-breaths save us from the tideless weight of summer nothingness, creeping over the bar among the warships, to flutter the striped awnings of the cafés upon the Grande Corniche. I would never have . . .

*   *   *   *   *

The city, half-imagined (yet wholly real), begins and ends in us, roots lodged in our memory. Why must I return to it night after night, writing here by the fire of carob-wood while the Aegean wind clutches at this island house, clutching and releasing it, bending back the cypresses like bows? Have I not said enough about Alexandria? Am I to be reinfected once more by the dream of it and the memory of its inhabitants? Dreams I had thought safely locked up on paper, confided to the strong-rooms of memory! You will think I am indulging myself. It is not so. A single chance factor has altered everything, has turned me back upon my tracks. A memory which catches sight of itself in a mirror.

Justine, Melissa, Clea. . . . There were so few of us really — you would have thought them easily disposed of in a single book, would you not? So would I, so *did* I. Dispersed now by time and circumstance, the circuit broken forever. . . .

I had set myself the task of trying to recover them in words, reinstate them in memory, allot to each his and her position in my time. Selfishly. And with that writing complete, I felt that I had turned a key upon the doll's house of our actions. Indeed, I saw my lovers and friends no longer as living people but as coloured transfers of the mind; inhabiting my papers now, no longer the city, like tapestry figures. It was difficult to concede to them any more common reality than to the words I had used about them. What has recalled me to myself?

But in order to go on, it is necessary to go back: not that anything I wrote about them is untrue, far from it. Yet when I wrote, the full facts were not at my disposal. The picture I drew was a provisional one — like the picture of a lost civilization deduced from a few fragmented vases, an inscribed tablet, an amulet, some human bones, a gold smiling death-mask.

*   *   *   *   *

'We live' writes Pursewarden somewhere 'lives based upon selected fictions. Our view of reality is conditioned by our position in space and time — not by our personalities as we like to think. Thus every interpretation of reality is based upon a unique position. Two paces east or west and the whole picture is changed.' Something of this order. . . .

And as for human characters, whether real or invented, there are no such animals. Each psyche is really an ant-hill of opposing predispositions. Personality as something with fixed attributes is an illusion — but a necessary illusion *if we are to love!*

As for the something that remains constant . . . the shy kiss of Melissa is predictable, for example (amateurish as an early form of printing), or the frowns of Justine, which cast a shadow over those blazing dark eyes — orbits of the Sphinx at noon. 'In the end' says Pursewarden 'everything will be found to be true of everybody. Saint and Villain are co-sharers.' He is right.

I am making every attempt to be matter-of-fact. . . .

*   *   *   *   *

In the last letter which reached me from Balthazar he wrote: 'I think of you often and not without a certain grim humour. You have retired to your island, with, as you think, all the data about us and our lives. No doubt you are bringing us to judgement on paper in the manner of writers. I wish I could see the result. It must fall very far short of *truth*: I mean such truths as I could tell you about us all — even perhaps about yourself. Or the truths Clea could tell you (she is in Paris on a visit and has stopped writing to me recently). I picture you, wise one, poring over *Moeurs*, the diaries of Justine, Nessim, etc., imagining that the truth is to be found in them. Wrong! Wrong! A diary is the last place to go if you wish to seek the truth about a person. Nobody dares to make the final confession to themselves on paper: or at least, not about love. Do you know whom Justine really loved? You believed it was yourself, did you not? Confess!'

My only answer was to send him the huge bundle of paper which had grown up so stiffly under my slow pen and to which I had loosely given her name as a title — though *Cahiers* would have done just as well. Months passed after this — a blessed silence indeed, for it suggested that my critic had been satisfied, silenced.

I cannot say that I forgot the city, but I let the memory of it sleep. Yet of course, it was always there, as it always will be, hanging in the mind like the mirage which travellers so often see. Pursewarden has described the phenomenon in the following words:

'We were still almost a couple of hours' steaming distance before land could possibly come into sight when suddenly my companion shouted and pointed at the horizon. We saw, inverted in the sky, a full-scale mirage of the city, luminous and trembling, as if painted on dusty silk: yet in the nicest detail. From memory I could clearly make out its features, Ras El Tin Palace, the Nebi Daniel Mosque and so forth. The whole representation was as breath-taking as a masterpiece painted in fresh dew. It hung there in the sky for a considerable time, perhaps twenty-five minutes, before melting slowly into the horizon mist. An hour later, the *real* city appeared, swelling from a smudge to the size of its mirage.'

*   *   *   *   *

The two or three winters we have spent in this island have been lonely ones — dour and windswept winters and hot summers. Luckily, the child is too young to feel as I do the need for books, for conversation. She is happy and active.

Now in the spring come the long calms, the tideless, scentless days of premonition. The sea tames itself and becomes attentive. Soon the cicadas will bring in their crackling music, background to the shepherd's dry flute among the rocks. The scrambling tortoise and the lizard are our only companions.

I should explain that our only regular visitor from the outside world is the Smyrna packet which once a week crosses the headland to the south, always at the same hour, at the same speed, just after dusk. In winter, the high seas and winds make it invisible, but now — I sit and wait for it. You hear at first only the faint drumming of engines. Then the creature slides round the cape, cutting its line of silk froth in the sea, brightly lit up in the moth-soft darkness of the Aegean night — condensed, but without outlines, like a cloud of fireflies moving. It travels fast, and disappears all too soon round the next headland, leaving behind it perhaps only the half-uttered fragment of a popular song, or the skin of a tangerine which I will find next day, washed up on the long pebbled beach where I bathe with the child.

The little arbour of oleanders under the planes — this is my writing-room. After the child has gone to bed, I sit here at the old sea-stained table, waiting for the visitant, unwilling to light the paraffin lamp before it has passed. It is the only day of the week I know by name here — Thursday. It sounds silly, but in an island so empty of variety, I look forward to the weekly visit like a child to a school treat. I know the boat brings letters for which I shall have to wait perhaps twenty-four hours. But I never see the little ship vanish without regret. And when it has passed, I light the lamp with a sigh and return to my papers. I write so slowly, with such pain. Pursewarden once, speaking about writing, told me that the pain that accompanied composition was entirely due, in artists, to the fear of madness; 'force it a bit and tell yourself that you don't give a damn if you *do* go mad, and you'll find it comes quicker, you'll break the barrier.' (I don't know how true this all is. But the money he left me in his will has served me well, and I still have a few pounds between me and the devils of debt and work.)

I describe this weekly diversion in some detail because it was into this picture that Balthazar intruded one June evening with a suddenness that surprised me — I was going to write 'deafened' — there is no one to talk to here — but 'surprised me'. This evening something like a miracle happened. The little steamer, instead of disappearing as usual, turned abruptly through an arc of 150 degrees and entered the lagoon, there to lie in a furry cocoon of its own light: and to drop into the centre of the golden puddle it had created the long slow anchor-chain whose symbol itself is like a search for truth. It was a moving sight to one who, like myself, had been landlocked in spirit as all writers are — indeed, become like a ship in a bottle, sailing nowhere — and I watched as an Indian must perhaps have watched the first white man's craft touch the shores of the New World.

The darkness, the silence, were broken now by the uneven lap-lap of oars; and then, after an age, by the chink of city-shod feet upon shingle. A hoarse voice gave a direction. Then silence. As I lit the lamp to set the wick in trim and so deliver myself from the spell of this departure from the norm, the grave dark face of my friend, like some goat-like apparition from the Underworld, materialized among the thick branches of myrtle. We drew a breath and stood smiling at each other in the yellow light: the dark Assyrian ringlets, the beard of Pan. 'No — I am real!' said Balthazar with a laugh and we embraced furiously. Balthazar!

The Mediterranean is an absurdly small sea; the length and greatness of its history makes us dream it larger than it is. Alexandria indeed — the true no less than the imagined — lay only some hundreds of sea-miles to the south.

'I am on my way to Smyrna' said Balthazar, 'from where I was going to post you this.' He laid upon the scarred old table the immense bundle of manuscript I had sent him — papers now seared and starred by a massive interlinear of sentences, paragraphs and question-marks. Seating himself opposite with his Mephisthophelean air, he said in a lower, more hesitant tone:

'I have debated in myself very long about telling you some of the things I have put down here. At times it seemed a folly and an impertinence. After all, your concern — was it with *us* as *real* people or as "characters"? I didn't know. I still don't. These pages may lose me your friendship without adding anything to the sum of your knowledge. You have been painting the city, touch by touch, upon a curved surface — was your object poetry or fact? If the latter, then there are things which you have a right to know.'

He still had not explained his amazing appearance before me, so anxious was he about the central meaning of the visitation. He did so now, noticing my bewilderment at the cloud of fire-flies in the normally deserted bay. He smiled.

'The ship is delayed for a few hours with engine trouble. It is one of Nessim's. The captain is Hasim Kohly, an old friend:

perhaps you remember him? No. Well, I guessed from your description roughly where you must be living; but to be landed on your doorstep like this, I confess!' His laughter was wonderful to hear once more.

But I hardly listened, for his words had plunged me into a ferment, a desire to study his interlinear, to revise — not my book (that has never been of the slightest importance to me for it will never even be published), but my view of the city and its inhabitants. For my own personal Alexandria had become, in all this loneliness, as dear as a philosophy of introspection, almost a monomania. I was so filled with emotion I did not know what to say to him. 'Stay with us, Balthazar — ' I said, 'stay awhile. . . . '

'We leave in two hours' he said, and patting the papers before him: 'This may give you visions and fevers' he added doubtfully.

'Good' I said — 'I ask for nothing better.'

'We are all still real people' he said, 'whatever *you* try and do to us — those of us who are still alive. Melissa, Pursewarden — they can't answer back because they are dead. At least, so one thinks.'

'So one thinks. The best retorts always come from beyond the grave.'

We sat and began to talk about the past, rather stiffly to be sure. He had already dined on board and there was nothing I could offer him beyond a glass of the good island wine which he sipped slowly. Later he asked to see Melissa's child, and I led him back through the clustering oleanders to a place from which we could both look into the great firelit room where she lay looking beautiful and grave, asleep there with her thumb in her mouth. Balthazar's dark cruel eye softened as he watched her, lightly breathing. 'One day' he said in a low voice 'Nessim will want to see her. Quite soon, mark. He has begun to talk about her, be curious. With old age coming on, he will feel he needs her support, mark my words.' And he quoted in Greek: 'First the young, like vines, climb up the dull supports of their elders who feel their fingers on them, soft and tender; then the old climb down the lovely supporting bodies of the young into their proper deaths.' I said nothing. It was the room itself which was breathing now — not our bodies.

'You have been lonely here' said Balthazar.

'But splendidly, desirably lonely.'

'Yes, I envy you. But truthfully.'

And then his eye caught the unfinished portrait of Justine which Clea in another life had given me.

'That portrait' he said 'which was interrupted by a kiss. How good to see that again — how good!' He smiled. 'It is like hearing a loved and familiar statement in music which leads one towards an emotion always recapturable, never-failing.' I did not say anything. I did not dare.

He turned to me. 'And Clea?' he said at last, in the voice of someone interrogating an echo. I said: 'I have heard nothing from her for ages. Time doesn't count here. I expect she has married, has gone away to another country, has children, a reputation as a painter . . . everything one would wish her.'

He looked at me curiously and shook his head. 'No' he said; but that was all.

It was long after midnight when the seamen called him from the dark olive groves. I walked to the beach with him, sad to see him leave so soon. A rowboat waited at the water's edge with a sailor standing to his oars in it. He said something in Arabic.

The spring sea was enticingly warm after a day's sunshine and as Balthazar entered the boat the whim seized me to swim out with him to the vessel which lay not two hundred yards away from the shore. This I did and hovered to watch him climb the rail, and to watch the boat drawn up. 'Don't get caught in the screw' he called, and 'Go back before the engines start' — 'I will' — 'But wait — before you go —' He ducked back into a stateroom to reappear and drop something into the water beside me. It fell with a soft splash. 'A rose from Alexandria' he said, 'from the city which has everything but happiness to offer its lovers.' He chuckled. 'Give it to the child.'

'Balthazar, good-bye!'

'Write to me — if you dare!'

Caught like a spider between the cross mesh of lights, and turning towards those yellow pools which still lay between the dark shore and myself, I waved and he waved back.

I put the precious rose between my teeth and dog-paddled back to my clothes on the pebble beach, talking to myself.

And there, lying upon the table in the yellow lamplight, lay the great interlinear to *Justine* — as I had called it. It was cross-hatched, crabbed, starred with questions and answers in different-coloured inks, in typescript. It seemed to me then to be somehow symbolic of the very reality we had shared — a palimpsest upon which each of us had left his or her individual traces, layer by layer.

Must I now learn to see it all with new eyes, to accustom myself to the truths which Balthazar has added? It is impossible to describe with what emotion I read his words — sometimes so detailed and sometimes so briefly curt — as for example in the list he had headed 'Some Fallacies and Misapprehensions' where he said coldly: 'Number 4. That Justine "loved" you. She "loved", if anyone, Pursewarden. "What does that mean"? She was forced to use you as a decoy in order to protect him from the jealousy of Nessim whom she had married. Pursewarden himself did not care for her at all — supreme logic of love!'

In my mind's eye the city rose once more against the flat mirror of the green lake and the broken loins of sandstone which marked the desert's edge. The politics of love, the intrigues of desire, good and evil, virtue and caprice, love and murder, moved obscurely in the dark corners of Alexandria's streets and squares, brothels and drawing-rooms — moved like a great congress of eels in the slime of plot and counter-plot.

It was almost dawn before I surrendered the fascinating mound of paper with its comments upon my own real (inner) life and like a drunkard stumbled to my bed, my head aching, echoing with the city, the only city left where every extreme of race and habit can meet and marry, where inner destinies intersect. I could hear the dry voice of my friend repeating as I fell asleep: 'How much do you *care* to know. . . how much more do you *care* to know?' — 'I must know *everything* in order to be at last delivered from the city' I replied in my dream.

* * * * *

'When you pluck a flower, the branch springs back into place. This is not true of the heart's affections' is what Clea once said to Balthazar.

* * * * *

And so, slowly, reluctantly, I have been driven back to my starting-point, like a man who at the end of a tremendous journey is told that he has been sleepwalking. 'Truth' said Balthazar to me once, blowing his nose in an old tennis sock, 'Truth is what most contradicts itself in time.'

And Pursewarden on another occasion, but not less memorably: 'If things were always what they seemed, how impoverished would be the imagination of man!'

How will I ever deliver myself from this whore among cities — sea, desert, minaret, sand, sea?

No. I must set it all down in cold black and white, until such time as the memory and impulse of it is spent. I know that the key I am trying to turn is in myself.

II

Le cénacle Capodistria used to call us in those days when we gathered for an early morning shave in the Ptolemaic parlour of Mnemjian, with its mirrors and palms, its bead curtains and the delicious mimicry of clear warm water and white linen: a laying out and anointing of corpses. The violet-eyed hunchback himself officiated, for we were valued customers all (dead Pharaohs at the natron baths, guts and brains to be removed, renovated and replaced). He himself, the barber, was often unshaven having just hurried down from the hospital after shaving a corpse. Briefly we met here in the padded chairs, in the mirrors, before separating to go about our various tasks — Da Capo to see his brokers, Pombal to totter to the French consulate (mouth full of charred moths, hangover, sensation of having walked about all night on his eyeballs), I to teach, Scobie to the Police Bureau, and so on. . . .

I have somewhere a faded flashlight photograph of this morning ritual, taken by poor John Keats, the Global Agency correspondent. It is strange to look at it now. The smell of the gravecloth is on it. It is a speaking likeness of an Alexandrian spring morning: quiet rubbing of coffee pestles, curdling crying of fat pigeons. I recognize my friends by the very sounds they make: Capodistria's characteristic '*Quatsch*' and '*Pouagh*' at some political remark, followed by that dry cachinnation — the retching of a metal stomach; Scobie's tobacco cough '*Teuch, Teuch*': Pombal's soft '*Tiens*', like someone striking a triangle. '*Tiens*'.

And in one corner there I am, in my shabby raincoat — the perfected image of a schoolteacher. In the other corner sits poor little Toto de Brunel. Keats's photograph traps him as he is raising a ringed finger to his temple — the fatal temple.

Toto! He is an *original*, a *numéro*. His withered witch's features and small boy's brown eyes, widow's peak, queer *art nouveau* smile. He was the darling of old society women too proud to pay for gigolos. '*Toto, mon chou, c'est toi!*' (Madame Umbada), '*Comme il est charmant, ce Toto!*' (Athena Trasha). He lives on these dry crusts of approbation, an old woman's man, with the dimples

218

sinking daily deeper into the wrinkled skin of an ageless face, quite happy, I suppose. Yes.

'*Toto — comment vas-tu?*' — '*Si heureux de vous voir, Madame Martinengo!*'

He was what Pombal scornfully called 'a Gentleman of the Second Declension.' His smile dug one's grave, his kindness was anaesthetic. Though his fortune was small, his excesses trivial, yet he was right in the social swim. There was, I suppose, nothing to be done with him for he was a woman: yet had he been born one he would long since have cried himself into a decline. Lacking charm, his pederasty gave him a kind of illicit importance. '*Homme serviable, homme gracieux*' (Count Banubula, General Cervoni — what more does one want?).

Though without humour, he found one day that he could split sides. He spoke indifferent English and French, but whenever at loss for a word he would put in one whose meaning he did not know and the grotesque substitution was often delightful. This became his standard mannerism. In it, he almost reached poetry — as when he said 'Some flies have come off my typewriter' or 'The car is trepanned today' or 'I ran so fast I got dandruff.' He could do this in three languages. It excused him from learning them. He spoke a Toto-tongue of his own.

Invisible behind the lens itself that morning stood Keats — the world's sort of Good Fellow, empty of ill intentions. He smelt lightly of perspiration. *C'est le métier qui exige.* Once he had wanted to be a writer but took the wrong turning, and now his profession had so trained him to stay on the superficies of real life (acts and facts about acts) that he had developed the typical journalist's neurosis (they drink to still it): namely that Something has happened, or is about to happen, in the next street, and that they will not know about it until it is too late to 'send'. This haunting fear of missing a fragment of reality which one knows in advance will be trivial, even meaningless, had given our friend the conventional tic one sees in children who want to go to the lavatory — shifting about in a chair, crossing and uncrossing of legs. After a few moments of conversation he would nervously rise and say 'I've just forgotten something — I won't be a minute.' In the street he would expel his breath in a swish of relief. He never went far but simply walked around the block to still the unease. Everything always seemed normal enough, to be sure. He would wonder whether to phone Mahmoud Pasha about the defence estimates or wait till tomorrow.... He had a pocketful of peanuts which he cracked in his teeth and spat out, feeling restless, unnerved, he did not know why. After a walk he would come trotting back into the café, or barber's shop, beaming shyly, apologetically: an 'Agency Man' — our best-integrated modern type. There was nothing wrong with John except the level on which he had chosen to live his life — but you could say the same about his famous namesake, could you not?

I owe this faded photograph to him. The mania to perpetuate, to record, to photograph everything! I suppose this must come from the feeling that you don't enjoy anything fully, indeed are taking the bloom off it with every breath you draw. His 'files' were enormous, bulging with signed menus, bands off memorial cigars, postage stamps, picture postcards. . . . Later this proved useful, for somehow he had captured some of Pursewarden's *obiter dicta*.

Farther to the east sits good old big-bellied Pombal, under each eye a veritable diplomatic bag. Now here is someone on whom one can really lavish a bit of affection. His only preoccupation is with losing his job or being *impuissant*: the national worry of every Frenchman since Jean-Jacques. We quarrel a good deal, though amicably, for we share his little flat which is always full of un-considered trifles and trifles more considered: *les femmes*. But he is a good friend, a tender-hearted man, and really loves women. When I have insomnia or am ill: '*Dis donc, tu vas bien?*' Roughly, in the manner of a *bon copain*. '*Ecoute — tu veux une aspirine?*' or else '*Ou bien — j'ai une jaune amie dans ma chambre si tu veux. . . .*' (Not a misprint: Pombal called all *poules* '*jaunes femmes*'.) '*Hein? Elle n'est pas mal — et c'est tout payé, mon cher. Mais ce matin, moi je me sens un tout petit peu antiféministe— j'en ai marre, hein!*' Satiety fell upon him at such times. '*Je deviens de plus en plus anthropophage*' he would say, rolling that comical eye. Also, his job worried him; his reputation was pretty bad, people were beginning to talk, especially after what he calls '*l'affaire Sveva*'; and yesterday the Consul-General walked in on him while he was cleaning his shoes on the Chancery curtains. . . . '*Monsieur Pombal! Je suis obligé de vous faire quelques observations sur votre comportement officiel!*' Ouf! A reproof of the first grade. . . .

It explains why Pombal now sits heavily in the photograph, debating all this with a downcast expression. Lately we have become rather estranged because of Melissa. He is angry that I have fallen in love with her, for she is only a dancer in a night-club, and as such unworthy of serious attention. There is also a question of snobbery, for she is virtually living at the flat now and he feels this to be demeaning: perhaps even diplomatically unwise.

'Love' says Toto 'is a liquid fossil' — a felicitous epigram in all conscience. Now to fall in love with a banker's wife, that would be forgivable, though ridiculous. . . . Or would it? In Alexandria, it is only intrigue *per se* which is wholeheartedly admired; but to fall in love renders one ridiculous in society. (Pombal is a provincial at heart.) I think of the tremendous repose and dignity of Melissa in death, the slender body bandaged and swaddled as if after some consuming and irreparable accident. Well.

And Justine? On the day this picture was taken, Clea's painting was interrupted by a kiss, as Balthazar says. How am I to make this comprehensible when I can only visualize these scenes with such difficulty? I must, it seems, try to see a new Justine, a new Pursewarden, a new Clea. . . . I mean that I must try and strip the opaque membrane which stands between me and the reality of their actions — and which I suppose is composed of my own limitations of vision and temperament. My envy of Pursewarden, my passion for Justine, my pity for Melissa. Distorting mirrors, all of them. . . . The way is through fact. I must record what more I know and attempt to render it comprehensible or plausible to myself, if necessary, by an act of the imagination. Or can facts be left to themselves? Can you say 'he fell in love' or 'she fell in love' without trying to divine its meaning, to set it in a context of plausibilities? 'That bitch' Pombal said once of Justine. '*Elle a l'air d'être bien chambrée!* 'And of Melissa '*Une pauvre petite poule quelconque* . . .' He was right, perhaps, yet the true meaning of them resides elsewhere. Here, I hope, on this scribbled paper which I have woven, spider-like, from my inner life.

And Scobie? Well, he at least has the comprehensibility of a diagram — plain as a national anthem. He looks particularly pleased this morning for he has recently achieved apotheosis. After years as a Bimbashi in the Egyptian Police, in what he calls 'the evening of his life' he has just been appointed to . . . I hardly dare to write the words for I can see his shudder of secrecy, can see his glass eye rolling portentously round in its socket . . . the Secret Service. He is not alive any more, thank God, to read the words and tremble. Yes, the Ancient Mariner, the secret pirate of Tatwig Street, the man himself. How much the city misses him. (His use of the word 'uncanny'!). . . .

Elsewhere I have recounted how I answered a mysterious summons to find myself in a room of splendid proportions with my erstwhile pirate friend facing me across a desk, whistling through his ill-fitting dentures. I think his new assignment was as much a puzzle to him as it was to me, his only confidant. It is true of course that he had been long in Egypt and knew Arabic well; but his career had been comparatively obscure. What could an intelligence agency hope to get out of him? More than this — what did he hope to get out of me? I had already explained in detail that the little circle which met every month to hear Balthazar expound the principles of the Cabbala had no connection with espionage; it was simply a group of hermetic students drawn by their interest in the matter of the lectures. Alexandria is a city of sects — and the shallowest inquiry would have revealed to him the existence of other groups akin to the one concerned with the hermetic philosophy which Balthazar addressed: Steinerites, Christian Scientists, Ouspenskyists, Adventists. . . . What was it that riveted attention particularly on Nessim, Justine, Balthazar, Capodistria, etc.? I could not tell, nor could he tell me.

'They're up to something' he repeated weakly. 'Cairo says so.' Apparently, he did not even know who his own masters were. His work was invisibly dictated by a scrambler telephone, as far as I could understand. But whatever 'Cairo' was it paid him well: and if he had money to throw about on nonsensical investigations who was I to prevent him throwing it to me? I thought that my first few reports on Balthazar's Cabal would successfully damp all interest in it — but no. They wanted more and again more.

And this very morning, the old sailor in the photograph was celebrating his new post and the increase of salary it carried by having a haircut in the upper town, at the most expensive of shops— Mnemjian's.

I must not forget that this photograph also records a 'Secret Rendezvous'; no wonder Scobie looks distraught. For he is surrounded by the very spies into whose activities it is necessary to inquire — not to mention a French diplomat who is widely rumoured to be head of the French *Deuxième*. . . .

Normally Scobie would have found this too expensive an establishment to patronize, living as he did upon a tiny nautical pension and his exiguous Police salary. But now he is a great man.

He did not dare even to wink at me in the mirror as the

hunchback, tactful as a diplomat, elaborated a full-scale haircut out of mere air — for Scobie's glittering dome was very lightly fringed by the kind of fluff one sees on a duckling's bottom, and he had of late years sacrificed the torpedo beard of a wintry sparseness.

'I must say' he is about to say throatily (in the presence of so many suspicious people we 'spies' must speak 'normally'), 'I must say, old man, you get a spiffing treatment here, Mnemjian really does understand.' Clearing his throat, 'The whole art.' His voice became portentous in the presence of technical terms. 'It's all a question of Graduation — I had a close friend who told me, a barber in Bond Street. You simply got to graduate.' Mnemjian thanked him in his pinched ventriloquist's voice. 'Not at all' said the old man largely. 'I know the wrinkles.' *Now* he could wink at me. I winked back. We both looked away.

Released, he stood up, his bones creaking, and set his piratical jaw in a look of full-blooded health. He examined his reflection in the mirror with complacence. 'Yes' he said, giving a short authoritative nod, 'it'll do.'

'Electric friction for scalp, sir?'

Scobie shook his head masterfully as he placed his red flower-pot *tarbush* on his skull. 'It brings me out in goose pimples' he said, and then, with a smirk, 'I'll nourish what's left with *arak*.' Mnemjian saluted this stroke of wit with a little gesture. We were free.

But he was really not elated at all. He drooped as we walked slowly down Chérif Pacha together towards the Grande Corniche. He struck moodily at his knee with the horsehair fly-swatter, puffing moodily at his much-mended briar. Thought. All he said with sudden petulance was 'I can't stand that Toto fellow. He's an open nancy-boy. In my time we would have. . . .' He grumbled away into his skin for a long time and then petered into silence again.

'What is it, Scobie?' I said.

'I'm troubled' he admitted. 'Really troubled.'

When he was in the upper town his walk and general bearing had an artificial swagger — it suggested a White Man at large, brooding upon problems peculiar to White Men — their Burden as they call it. To judge by Scobie, it hung heavy. His least gesture had a resounding artificiality, tapping his knees, sucking his lip, falling into brooding attitudes before shop windows. He gazed at the people around him as if from stilts. These gestures reminded me in a feeble way of the heroes of domestic English fiction who stand before a Tudor fireplace, impressively whacking their riding-boots with a bull's pizzle.

By the time we had reached the outskirts of the Arab quarter, however, he had all but shed these mannerisms. He relaxed, tipped his *tarbush* up to mop his brow, and gazed around him with the affection of long familiarity. Here he belonged by adoption, here he was truly at home. He would defiantly take a drink from the leaden spout sticking out of a wall near the Goharri mosque (a public drinking fountain) though the White Man in him must have been aware that the water was far from safe to drink. He would pick a stick of sugar-cane off a stall as he passed, to gnaw it in the open street: or a sweet locust-bean. Here, everywhere, the cries of the open street greeted him and he responded radiantly.

'*Y'alla, effendi, Skob*'

'*Naharak said, ya Skob*'

'*Allah salimak.*'

He would sigh and say 'Dear people'; and 'How I love the place you have no idea!' dodging a liquid-eyed camel as it humped down the narrow street threatening to knock us down with its bulging sumpters of *bercim*, the wild clover which is used as fodder.

'May your prosperity increase'

'By your leave, my mother'

'May your day be blessed'

'Favour me, O sheik.'

Scobie walked here with the ease of a man who has come into his own estate, slowly, sumptuously, like an Arab.

Today we sat together for a while in the shade of the ancient mosque listening to the clicking of the palms and the hooting of sea-going liners in the invisible basin below.

'I've just seen a directive' said Scobie at last, in a sad withered little voice 'about what they call a Peddyrast. It's rather shaken me, old man. I don't mind admitting it — I didn't know the word. I had to look it up. At all costs, it says, we must exclude them. They are dangerous to the security of the net.' I gave a laugh and for a moment the old man showed signs of wanting to respond with a weak giggle, but his depression overtook the impulse, to leave it buried, a small hollowness in those cherry-red cheeks. He puffed furiously at his pipe. 'Peddyrast' he repeated with scorn, and groped for his matchbox.

'I don't think they quite understand at Home' he said sadly. 'Now the Egyptians, they don't give a damn about a man if he has

Tendencies — provided he's the Soul of Honour, like me.' He meant it. 'But now, old man, if I am to work for the . . . You Know What . . . I ought to tell them — what do you say?'

'Don't be a fool, Scobie.'

'Well, I don't know' he said sadly. 'I want to be honest with them. It isn't that I cause any harm. I suppose one shouldn't have Tendencies — any more than warts or a big nose. But what can I do?'

'Surely at your age very little?'

'Below the belt' said the pirate with a flash of his old form. 'Dirty. Cruel. Narky.' He looked archly at me round his pipe and suddenly cheered up. He began one of those delightful rambling monologues — another chapter in the saga he had composed around his oldest friend, the by now mythical Toby Mannering. 'Toby was once Driven Medical by his excesses — I think I told you. No? Well, he was. Driven Medical.' He was obviously quoting and with relish. 'Lord how he used to go it as a young man. Stretched the limit in beating the bounds. Finally he found himself under the Doctor, had to wear an Appliance.' His voice rose by nearly an octave. 'He went about in a leopard-skin muff when he had shore leave until the Merchant Navy rose in a body. He was put away for six months. Into a Home. They said "You'll have to have Traction" — whatever that is. You could hear him scream all over Tewkesbury, so Toby says. They say they cure you but they don't. They didn't him at any rate. After a bit, they sent him back. Couldn't do anything with him. He was afflicted with Dumb Insolence, they said. Poor Toby!'

He had fallen effortlessly asleep now, leaning back against the wall of the Mosque. ('A cat-nap' he used to say, 'but always woken by the ninth wave.' For how much longer, I wondered?) After a moment the ninth wave brought him back through the surf of his dreams to the beach. He gave a start and sat up. 'What was I saying? Yes, about Toby. His father was an M.P. Very High Placed. Rich man's son. Toby tried to go into the Church first. Said he felt The Call. I think it was just the costume, myself — he was a great amateur theatrical, was Toby. Then he lost his faith and slipped up and had a tragedy. Got run in. He said the Devil prompted him. "See he doesn't do it again" says the Beak. "Not on Tooting Common, anyway." They wanted to put him in chokey — they said he had a rare disease — cornucopia I think they called it. But luckily his father went to the Prime Minister and had the whole thing hushed up. It was lucky, old man, that at that time the whole Cabinet had Tendencies too. It was uncanny. The Prime Minister, even the Archbishop of Canterbury. They sympathized with poor Toby. It was lucky for him. After that, he got his master's ticket and put to sea.'

Scobie was asleep once more; only to wake again after a few seconds with a histrionic start. 'It was old Toby' he went on, without a pause, though now crossing himself devoutly and gulping 'who put me on to the Faith. One night when we were on watch together on the *Meredith* (fine old ship) he says to me: "Scurvy, there's something you should know. Ever heard of the Virgin Mary?" I had of course, vaguely. I didn't know what her duties were, so to speak. . . .'

Once more he fell asleep and this time there issued from between his lips a small croaking snore. I carefully took his pipe from between his fingers and lit myself a cigarette. This appearance and disappearance into the simulacrum of death was somehow touching. These little visits paid to an eternity which he would soon be inhabiting, complete with the comfortable forms of Toby and Budgie, and a Virgin Mary with specified duties. . . . And to be obsessed by such problems at an age when, as far as I could judge, there was little beyond verbal boasting to make him a nuisance. (I was wrong — Scobie was indomitable.)

After a while he woke again from this deeper sleep, shook himself and rose, knuckling his eyes. We made our way together to the sordid purlieus of the town where he lived, in Tatwig Street, in a couple of tumbledown rooms. 'And yet' he said once more, carrying his chain of thought perfectly, 'it's all very well for you to say I shouldn't tell them. But I wonder.' (Here he paused to inhale the draught of cooking Arab bread from the doorway of a shop and the old man exclaimed 'It smells like mother's lap!') His ambling walk kept pace with his deliberations. 'You see the Egyptians are marvellous, old man. Kindly. They know me well. From some points of view, they might look like felons, old man, but felons in a state of grace, that's what I always say. They make allowances for each other. Why, Nimrod Pasha himself said to me the other day "Peddyrasty is one thing — *hashish* quite another." He's serious, you see. Now I never smoke *hashish* when I'm on duty — that would be bad. Of course, from another point of view, the British couldn't do anything to a man with an official position like me. But if the Gyppos once thought they were — well, critical about me — old man, I might lose both jobs, and both salaries. That's what troubles me.'

We mounted the fly-blown staircase with its ragged rat-holes. 'It smells a bit' he agreed, 'but you get quite used to it. It's the mice. No, I'm not going to move. I've lived in this quarter for years now — years! Everybody knows me and likes me. And besides, old Abdul is only round the corner.'

He chuckled and stopped for breath on the first landing, taking off his flowerpot the better to mop his brow. Then he hung downwards, sagging as he always did when he was thinking seriously as if the very weight of the thought itself bore down upon him. He sighed. 'The thing' he said slowly, and with the air of a man who wishes at all costs to be explicit, to formulate an idea as clearly as lies within his power, 'the thing is about Tendencies — you only realize it when you're not a hot-blooded young sprig any more.' He sighed again. 'It's the lack of *tenderness*, old man. It all depends on cunning somehow, you get lonely. Now Abdul is a true friend.' He chuckled and cheered up once more. 'I call him the Bul Bul Emir. I set him up in his business, just out of friendly affection. Bought him everything: his shop, his little wife. Never laid a finger on him nor ever could, because I love the man. I'm glad I did now, because though I'm getting on, I still have a true friend. I pop in every day to see them. It's uncanny how happy it makes me. I really do enjoy their happiness, old man. They are like son and daughter to me, the poor perishing coons. I can't hardly bear to hear them quarrel. It makes me anxious about their kids. I think Abdul is jealous of her, and not without cause, mark you. She looks flirty to me. But then, sex is so powerful in this heat — a spoonful goes a long way as we used to say about rum in the Merchant Navy. You lie and dream about it like ice-cream, sex, not rum. And these Moslem girls — old boy — they circumcise them. It's cruel. Really cruel. It only makes them harp on the subject. I tried to get her to learn knitting or crewel-work, but she's so stupid she didn't understand. They made a joke of it. Not that I mind. I was only trying to help. Two hundred pounds it took me to set Abdul up — all my savings. But he's doing well now — yes, very well.'

The monologue had had the effect of allowing him to muster his energies for the final assault. We addressed the last ten stairs at a comfortable pace and Scobie unlocked the door of his rooms. Originally he had only been able to rent one — but with his new salary he had rented the whole shabby floor.

The largest was the old Arab room which served as a bedroom and reception-room in one. It was furnished by an uncomfortable looking truckle bed and an old-fashioned cake-stand. A few joss-sticks, a police calendar, and Clea's as yet unfinished portrait of the pirate stood upon the crumbling mantelpiece. Scobie switched on a single dusty electric light bulb — a recent innovation of which he was extremely proud ('Paraffin gets in the food') — and looked round him with unaffected pleasure. Then he tiptoed to the far corner. In the gloom I had at first overlooked the room's other occupant: a brilliant green Amazonian parrot in a brass cage. It was at present shrouded in a dark cloth, and this the old man now removed with a faintly defensive air.

'I was telling you about Toby' he said 'because last week he came through Alex on the Yokohama run. I got this from him — he had to sell — the damn bird caused such a riot. It's a brilliant conversationalist, aren't you Ron, eh? Crisp as a fart, aren't you?' The parrot gave a low whistle and ducked. 'That's the boy' said Scobie with approval and turning to me added 'I got Ron for a very keen price, yes, a very keen price. Shall I tell you why?'

Suddenly, inexplicably, he doubled up with laughter, nearly joining nose to knee and whizzing soundlessly like a small human top, to emerge at last with an equally soundless slap on his own thigh — a sudden paroxysm. 'You'd never imagine the row Ron caused' he said. 'Toby brought the bird ashore. He knew it could talk, but not Arabic. By God. We were sitting at a café yarning (I haven't seen Toby for five whole years) when Ron suddenly started. In Arabic. You know, he recited the Kalima, a very sacred, not to mention holy, text from the Koran. The Kalima. And at every other word, he gives a fart, didn't you Ron?' The parrot agreed with another whistle. 'It's so sacred, the Kalima' explained Scobie gravely, 'that the next thing was a raging crowd round us. It was lucky I knew what was going on. I knew that if a non-Moslem was caught reciting this particular text he was liable to Instant Circumcision!' His eye flashed. 'It was a pretty poor outlook for Toby to be circumcised like that while one was taking shore leave and I was worried. (I'm circumcised already.) However, my presence of mind didn't desert me. He wanted to punch a few heads, but I restrained him. I was in police uniform you see, and that made it easier. I made a little speech to the crowd saying that I was going to take the infidel and this perishing bird into chokey to hand them over to the Parquet. That satisfied them. But there was no way of silencing Ron, even under his little veil, was there Ron? The little bastard recited the Kalima all the way back here. We had to run for it. My word, what an experience!'

He was changing out of his police rig as he talked, placing his *tarbush* on the rusty iron nail above his bed, above the crucifix in the little alcove where a stone jar of drinking-water also stood. He put on a frayed old blazer with tin buttons, and still mopping his head went on: 'I must say — it was wonderful to see old Toby again after so long. He had to sell the bird, of course, after such a riot. Didn't dare go through the dock area again with it. But now I'm doubtful, for I daren't take it out of the room hardly for fear of what more it knows.' He sighed. 'Another good thing' he went on 'was the recipe Toby brought for Mock Whisky — ever heard of it? Nor had I. Better than Scotch and dirt cheap, old man. From now on I'm going to brew all my own drinks, thanks to Toby. Here. Look at this.' He indicated a grubby bottle full of some fiery-looking liquid. 'It's home-made beer' he said, 'and jolly good too. I made three, but the other two exploded. I'm going to call it Plaza beer.'

'Why?' I asked. 'Are you going to sell it?'

'Good Lord, no!' said Scobie. 'Just for home use.' He rubbed his stomach reflectively and licked his lips. 'Try a glass' he said.

'No thanks.'

The old man now consulted a huge watch and pursed his lips. 'In a little while I must say an Ave Maria. I'll have to push you out, old man. But just let's have a look and see how the Mock Whisky is getting on for a moment, shall we?'

I was most curious to see how he was conducting these new experiments and willingly followed him out on to the landing again and into the shabby alcove which now housed a gaunt galvanized iron bath which he must have bought specially for these illicit purposes. It stood under a grimy closet window, and the shelves around it were crowded with the impedimenta of the new trade — a dozen empty beer bottles, two broken, and the huge chamberpot which Scobie always called 'the Heirloom'; not to mention a tattered beach umbrella and a pair of goloshes. 'What part do these play?' I could not help asking, indicating the latter. 'Do you tread the grapes or potatoes in them?'

Scobie took on an old-maidish, squinting-down-the-nose expression which always meant that levity on the topic under discussion was out of place. He listened keenly for a moment, as if to sounds of fermentation. Then he got down on one shaky knee and regarded the contents of the bath with a doubtful but intense eye. His glass eye gave him a more than mechanical expression as it stared into the rather tired-looking mixture with which the bath was brimming. He sniffed dispassionately and tutted once before rising again with creaking joints. 'It doesn't look as good as I hoped' he admitted. 'But give it time, it has to be given time.' He tried some on his finger and rolled his glass eye. 'It seems to have gone a bit turpid' he admitted. 'As if someone had peed in it.' As Abdul and himself shared the only key to this illicit still I was able to look innocent.

'Do you want to try it?' he asked doubtfully.

'Thank you, Scobie — no.'

'Ah well' he said philosophically, 'maybe the copper sulphate wasn't fresh. I had to order the rhubarb from Blighty. Forty pounds. *That* looked pretty tired when it got here, I don't mind telling you. But I know the proportions are right because I went into it all thoroughly with young Toby before he left. It needs time, that's what it needs.'

And made buoyant once more by the hope, he led the way back into the bedroom, whistling under his breath a few staves of the famous song which he only sang aloud when he was drunk on brandy. It went something like this:

> '*I want*
>   *Someone to match my fancy*
> *I want*
>   *Someone to match my style*
> *I've been good for an awful long while*
> *Now I'll take her in my arms*
> *Tum ti Tum Tum ti charms. . . .'*

Somewhere here the melody fell down a cliff and was lost to sight, though Scobie hummed out the stave and beat time with his finger.

He was sitting down on the bed now and staring at his shabby shoes.

Abruptly, without apparent premeditation (though he closed his eyes fast as if to shut the subject away out of sight forever) Scobie lay back on the bed, hands behind his head, and said:

'Before you go, there's a small confession I'd like to make to you, old man. Right?'

I sat down on the uncomfortable chair and nodded. 'Right' he said emphatically and drew a breath. 'Well then: sometimes at the full moon, *I'm Took*. I come under *An Influence*.'

This was on the face of it a somewhat puzzling departure from accepted form, for the old man looked quite disturbed by his own revelation. He gobbled for a moment and then went on in a small humbled voice devoid of his customary swagger. 'I don't know what comes over me.' I did not quite understand all this. 'Do you mean you walk in your sleep, or what?' He shook his head and gulped again. 'Do you turn into a werewolf, Scobie?' Once more he shook his head like a child upon the point of tears. 'I slip on female duds and my Dolly Varden' he said, and opened his eyes fully to stare pathetically at me.

'You *what*?' I said.

To my intense surprise he rose now and walked stiffly to a cupboard which he unlocked. Inside, hanging up, moth-eaten and unbrushed, was a suit of female clothes of ancient cut, and on a nail beside it a greasy old cloche hat which I took to be the so-called 'Dolly Varden'. A pair of antediluvian court shoes with very high heels and long pointed toes completed this staggering outfit. He did not know how quite to respond to the laugh which I was now compelled to utter. He gave a weak giggle. 'It's silly, isn't it?' he said, still hovering somewhere on the edge of tears despite his smiling face, and still by his tone inviting sympathy in misfortune. 'I don't know what comes over me. And yet, you know, it's always the old thrill. . . .'

A sudden and characteristic change of mood came over him at the words: his disharmony, his discomfiture gave place to a new jauntiness. His look became arch now, not wistful, and crossing to the mirror before my astonished eyes, he placed the hat upon his bald head. In a second he replaced his own image with that of a little old tart, button-eyed and razor-nosed — a tart of the Waterloo Bridge epoch, a veritable Tuppeny Upright. Laughter and astonishment packed themselves into a huge parcel inside me, neither finding expression. 'For God's sake!' I said at last. 'You don't go around like that, do you, Scobie?'

'Only' said Scobie, sitting helplessly down on the bed again and relapsing into a gloom which gave his funny little face an even more comical expression (he still wore the Dolly Varden), 'only when the Influence comes over me. When I'm not fully Answerable, old man.'

He sat there looking crushed. I gave a low whistle of surprise which the parrot immediately copied. This was indeed serious. I understood now why the deliberations which had consumed him all morning had been so full of heart-searching. Obviously if one went around in a rig like that in the Arab quarter. . . . He must have been following my train of thought, for he said 'It's only sometimes when the Fleet's in.' Then he went on with a touch of self-righteousness: 'Of course, if there was ever any trouble, I'd say I was in disguise. I am a policeman when you come to think of it. After all, even Lawrence of Arabia wore a nightshirt, didn't he?' I nodded. 'But not a Dolly Varden' I said. 'You must admit, Scobie, it's most original . . .' and here the laughter overtook me.

Scobie watched me laugh, still sitting on the bed in that fantastic headpiece. 'Take if off!' I implored. He looked serious and pre-occupied now, but made no motion. 'Now you know all' he said. 'The best and the worst in the old skipper. Now what I was going to ── '

At this moment there came a knock at the landing door. With surprising presence of mind Scobie leaped spryly into the cup-board, locking himself noisily in. I went to the door. On the landing stood a servant with a pitcher full of some liquid which he said was for the Effendi Skob. I took it from him and got rid of him, before returning to the room and shouting to the old man who emerged once more ── now completely himself, bareheaded and blazered.

'That was a near shave' he breathed. 'What was it?' I indicated the pitcher. 'Oh, that ── it's for the Mock Whisky. Every three hours.'

'Well,' I said at last, still struggling with these new and indiges-tible revelations of temperament, 'I must be going.' I was still hovering explosively between amazement and laughter at the thought of Scobie's second life at full moon ── how had he managed to avoid a scandal all these years? ── when he said: 'Just a minute, old man. I only told you all this because I want you to do me a favour.' His false eye rolled around earnestly now under the pressure of thought. He sagged again. 'A thing like that could do me Untold Harm' he said. 'Untold Harm, old man.'

'I should think it could.'

'Old man,' said Scobie, 'I want you to confiscate my duds. It's the only way of controlling the Influence.'

'Confiscate them?'

'Take them away. Lock them up. It'll save me, old man. I know it will. The whim is too strong for me otherwise, when it comes.'

'All right' I said.

'God bless you, son.'

Together we wrapped his full-moon regalia in some newspapers and tied the bundle up with string. His relief was tempered with doubt. 'You won't lose them?' he said anxiously.

'Give them to me' I said firmly and he handed me the parcel meekly. As I went down the stairs he called after me to express relief and gratitude, adding the words: 'I'll say a little prayer for you, son.' I walked back slowly through the dock-area with the parcel under my arm, wondering whether I would ever dare to confide this wonderful story to someone worth sharing it with.

The warships turned in their inky reflections — the forest of masts and rigging in the Commercial Port swayed softly among the mirror-images of the water: somewhere a ship's radio was blaring out the latest jazz-hit to reach Alexandria:

> *Old Tiresias*
> *No-one half so breezy as,*
> *Half so free and easy as*
> *Old Tiresias.*

* * * * *

III

Somehow, then, the problem is just how to introject this new and disturbing material into (under?) the skin of the old without changing or irremediably damaging the contours of my subjects or the solution in which I see them move. The golden fish circling so languidly in their great bowl of light — they are hardly aware that their world, the field of their journeys, is a curved one. . . .

The sinking sun which had emptied the harbour roads of all but the black silhouettes of the foreign warships had nevertheless left a flickering greyness — the play of light without colour or resonance upon the surface of a sea still dappled with sails. Dinghies racing for home moved about the floor of the inner harbour, scuttling in and out among the ships like mice among the great boots of primitive cottagers. The sprouting tier of guns on the *Jean Bart* moved slowly — tilted — and then settled back into brooding stillness, aimed at the rosy heart of the city whose highest minarets still gleamed gold in the last rays of the sunset. The flocks of spring pigeons glittered like confetti as they turned their wings to the light. (Fine writing!)

But the great panels of the brass-framed windows in the Yacht Club blazed like diamonds, throwing a brilliant light upon the snowy tables with their food, setting fire to the glasses and jewellery and eyes in a last uneasy conflagration before the heavy curtains would be drawn and the faces which had gathered to greet Mountolive took on the warm pallors of candle-light.

The triumphs of polity, the resources of tact, the warmth, the patience. . . . Profligacy and sentimentality . . . killing love by taking things easy . . . sleeping out a chagrin. . . . This was Alexandria, the unconsciously poetical mother-city exemplified in the names and faces which made up her history. Listen.

Tony Umbada, Baldassaro Trivizani, Claude Amaril, Paul Capodistria, Dmitri Randidi, Onouphrios Papas, Count Banubula, Jacques de Guéry, Athena Trasha, Djamboulat Bey, Delphine de Francueil, General Cervoni, Ahmed Hassan Pacha, Pozzo di Borgo, Pierre Balbz, Gaston Phipps, Haddad Fahmy Amin,

Mehmet Adm, Wilmot Pierrefeu, Toto de Brunel, Colonel Neguib, Dante Borromeo, Benedict Dangeau, Pia dei Tolomei, Gilda Ambron. . . . The poetry and history of commerce, the rhyme-schemes of the Levant which had swallowed Venice and Genoa. (Names which the passer-by may one day read upon the tombs in the cemetery.)

The conversation rose in a steamy cloud to envelop Mountolive whose personal triumph it was and who stood talking to Nessim, his host, with the gentle-mannered expression on his face which, like a lens, betrayed all the stylized diffidence of his perfect breeding. The two men indeed were much alike; only Nessim's darkness was smooth, cleanly surfaced, and his eyes and hands restless. Despite a difference of age they were well matched — even to the tastes they shared, which the years had done nothing to diminish though they had hardly corresponded directly all the time Mountolive had been away from Egypt. It had always been to Leila that he wrote, not to her sons. Nevertheless, once he had returned, they were much together and found they had as much to discuss as ever in the past. You would hear the sharp pang of their tennis racquets every spring afternoon on the Legation court at an hour when everyone normally slept. They rode in the desert together or sat for hours side by side, studying the stars, at the telescope which Justine had had installed in the Summer Palace. They painted and shot in company. Indeed, since Mountolive's return they had become once more almost inseparables. Tonight the soft light touched them both with an equal distinction, yet softly enough to disguise the white hairs at Mountolive's temples and the crow's-feet around those thoughtful arbitrator's eyes. By candle-light the two men seemed exactly of an age if indeed not of the same family.

A thousand faces whose reverberating expressions I do not understand ('We are all racing under sealed handicaps' says a character in Pursewarden's book), and out of them all there is one only I am burning to see, the black stern face of Justine. I must learn to see even myself in a new context, after reading those cold cruel words of Balthazar. How does a man look when he is 'in love'? (The words in English should be uttered in a low bleating tone.) *Peccavi!* Imbecile! There I stand in my only decent suit, whose kneecaps are bagged and shiny with age, gazing fondly and short-sightedly around me for a glimpse of the woman who. . . . What does it matter? I do not need a Keats to photograph me. I do not suppose I am uglier than anyone else or less pleasant; and certainly my vanity is of a very general order — for how have I never stopped to ask myself for a second why Justine should turn aside to bestow her favours on me?

What could I give her that she could not get elsewhere? Does she want my bookish talk and amateurish love-making — she with the whole bargain-basement of male Alexandria in her grasp? 'A decoy!' I find this very wounding to understand, to swallow, yet it has all the authority of curt fact. Moreover, it explains several things which have been for me up to now inexplicable — such as the legacy Pursewarden left me. It was his guilt, I think, for what he knew Justine was doing to Melissa: in 'loving' me. While she, for her part, was simply protecting him against the possible power of Nessim (how gentle and calm he looks in the candle-light). He once said with a small sigh 'Nothing is easier to arrange in our city than a death or a disappearance.'

A thousand conversations, seeking out for each other like the tap-roots of trees for moisture — the hidden meaning of lives disguised in brilliant smiles, in hands pressed upon the eyes, in malice, in fevers and contents. (Justine now breakfasted silently surrounded by tall black footmen, and dined by candle-light in brilliant company. She had started from nothing — from the open street — and was now married to the city's handsomest banker. How had all this come about? You would never be able to tell by watching that dark, graceful form with its untamed glances, the smile of the magnificent white teeth. . . .). Yet one trite conversation can contain the germ of a whole life. Balthazar, for example, meeting Clea against a red brocade curtain, holding a glass of Pernod, could say: 'Clea, I have something to tell you'; taking in as he spoke the warm gold of her hair and a skin honeyed almost to the tone of burnt sugar by sea-bathing in the warm spring sunshine. 'What?' Her candid eyes were as blue as corn-flowers and set in her head like precision-made objects of beauty — the life-work of a jeweller. 'Speak, my dear.' Black head of hair (he dyed it), lowered voice set in its customary sardonic croak, Balthazar said: 'Your father came to see me. He is worried about an illicit relationship you are supposed to have formed with another woman. Wait — don't speak, and don't look hurt.' For Clea looked now as if he were pressing upon a bruise, the sad grave mouth set in a childish expression, imploring no further penetration. 'He says you are an innocent, a goose, and that Alexandria does not permit innocent people to. . . .'

'Please, Balthazar.'

'I would not have spoken had I not been impressed by his genuine anguish — not about scandal: who cares for gossip? But he was worried lest you should be hurt.'

In a small compressed voice, like some packaged thought squeezed to a hundredth of its size by machinery, Clea said:

'I have not been alone with Justine for months now. Do you understand? It ended when the painting ended. If you wish us to be friends you will never refer to this subject again' smiling a little tremulously, for in the same breath Justine came sailing down upon them, smiling warmly, radiantly. (It is quite possible to love those whom you most wound.) She passed, turning in the candle-light of the room like some great sea-bird, and came at last to where I was standing. 'I cannot come tonight' she whispered. 'Nessim wants me to stay at home.' I can feel still the uncomprehending weight of my disappointment at the words. 'You must' I muttered. Should I have known that not ten minutes before she had said to Nessim, knowing he hated bridge: 'Darling, can I go and play bridge with the Cervonis — do you need the car?' It must have been one of those rare evenings when Pursewarden consented to meet her out in the desert — meetings to which she went unerringly, like a sleep-walker. Why? *Why?*

Balthazar at this moment is saying: 'Your father said: "I cannot bear to watch it, and I do not know what to do. It is like watching a small child skipping near a powerful piece of unprotected machinery."' Tears came into Clea's eyes and slowly vanished again as she sipped her drink. 'It is over' she said, turning her back upon the subject and upon Balthazar in one and the same motion. She turned her sullen mouth now to the discussion of meaningless matters with Count Banubula, who bowed and swung as gallantly as Scobie's green parrot ducking on its perch. She was pleased to see that her beauty had a direct, clearly discernible effect upon him, like a shower of golden arrows. Presently, Justine herself passed again, and in passing caught Clea's wrist. 'How is it?' said Clea, in the manner of one who asks after a sick child. Justine gave the shadow of a grimace and whispered dramatically: 'Oh, Clea — it is very bad. What a terrible mistake. Nessim is wonderful — I should never have done it. *I am followed everywhere.*' They stared at each other sympathetically for a long moment. It was their first encounter for some time. (That afternoon, Pursewarden had written: 'A few hasty and not entirely unloving words from my sickbed about this evening.' He was not in bed but sitting at a cafe on the sea-front, smiling as he wrote.) Messages spoken and unspoken, crossing and interlacing, carrying the currents of our lives, the fears, dissimulations, the griefs. Justine was speaking now about her marriage which still exhibited to the outer world a clearness of shape and context — the plaster cast of a perfection which I myself had envied when first I met them both. 'The marriage of true minds' I thought; but where is the 'magnificent two-headed animal' to be found? When she first became aware of the terrible jealousy of Nessim, the jealousy of the spiritually impotent man, she had been appalled and terrified. She had fallen by mistake into a trap. (All this, like the fever-chart of a striken patient, Clea watched, purely out of friendship, with no desire to renew the love she felt for this dispersed unself-comprehending Jewess.)

Justine put the matter to herself another way, a much more primitive way, by thinking: up to now she had always judged her men by their smell. This was the first time ever that she had neglected to consult the sense. And Nessim had the odourless purity of the desert airs, the desert in summer, unconfiding and dry. Pure. How she hated purity! Afterwards? Yes, she was revolted by the little gold cross which nestled in the hair on his chest. He was a Copt — a Christian. This is the way women work in the privacy of their own minds. Yet out of shame at such thoughts she became doubly passionate and attentive to her husband, though even between kisses, in the depths of her mind, she longed only for the calm and peace of widowhood! Am I imagining this? I do not think so.

How had all this come about? To understand it is necessary to work backwards, through the great Interlinear which Balthazar has constructed around my manuscript, towards that point in time where the portrait which Clea was painting was interrupted by a kiss. It is strange to look at it now, the portrait, standing unfinished on the old-fashioned mantelpiece of the island house. 'An idea had just come into her mind, but had not yet reached the lips.' And then, softly, her lips fell where the painter's wet brush should have fallen. Kisses and brush-strokes — I should be writing of poor Melissa!

How distasteful all this subject-matter is — what Pursewarden has called 'the insipid kiss of familiars'; and how innocent! The black gloves she wore in the portrait left a small open space when they were buttoned up — the shape of a heart. And that innocent,

ridiculous kiss only spoke admiration and pity for the things
Justine was telling her about the loss of her child — the daughter
which had been stolen from her while it was playing on the river-
bank. 'Her wrists, her small wrists. If you could have seen how
beautiful and tame she was, a squirrel.' In the hoarseness of the
tone, in the sad eyes and the down-pointed mouth with a comma
in each cheek. And holding out a hand with finger and thumb
joined to describe the circuit of those small wrists. Clea took and
kissed the heart in the black glove. She was really kissing the child,
the mother. Out of this terrible sympathy her innocence projected
the consuming shape of a sterile love. But I am going too fast. Moreover, how am I to make comprehensible scenes which I myself see
only with such difficulty — these two women, the blonde and the
bronze in a darkening studio at Saint Saba, among the rags and
the paintpots and the warm gallery of portraits which lined the
walls, Balthazar, Da Capo, even Nessim himself, Clea's dearest
friend? It is hard to compose them in a stable colour so that the
outlines are not blurred.

Justine at this time . . . coming from nowhere, she had performed one trick regarded as clever by the provincials of Alexandria. She had married Arnauti, a foreigner, only to earn the contempt of society by letting him in the end divorce and abandon her.
Of the fate of the child, few people knew or cared. She was not 'in
society' as the saying goes. . . . For a time poverty forced her to do
a little modelling at so many piastres an hour for the art-students
of the Atelier. Clea, who knew her only by hearsay, passed through
the long gallery one day when she was posing and, struck by the
dark Alexandrian beauty of her face, engaged her for a portrait.
That was how those long conversations grew up in the silences of
the painter; for Clea liked her subjects to talk freely, provided they
stayed still. It gave a submarine life to their features, and filled
their looks with unconscious interpretations of thought — the true
beauty in otherwise dead flesh.

Clea's generous innocence — it needed something like that to
see the emptiness in which Justine lived with her particular sorrows — factual illustrations merely of a mind at odds with itself:
for we create our own misfortunes and they bear our own fingerprints. The gesture itself was simply a clumsy attempt to appropriate the mystery of true experience, true suffering — as by
touching a holy man the supplicant hopes for a transference of the
grace he lacks. The kiss did not for a moment expect itself to be

answered by another — to copy itself like the reflections of a moth in a looking-glass. That would have been too expensive a gesture had it been premeditated. So it proved! Clea's own body simply struggled to disengage itself from the wrappings of its innocence as a baby or a statue struggles for life under the fingers or forceps of its author. Her bankruptcy was one of extreme youth, Justine's ageless; her innocence was as defenceless as memory itself. Seeking and admiring only the composure of Justine's sorrow she found herself left with all the bitter lye of an uninvited love.

She was 'white of heart', in the expressive Arabic phrase, and painting the darkness of Justine's head and shoulders she suddenly felt as if, stroke by stroke, the brush itself had begun to imitate caresses she had neither foreseen nor even thought to permit. As she listened to that strong deep voice recounting these misfortunes, so desirable in that they belonged to the active living world of experience, she caught her breath between her teeth, trying now to think only of the unconscious signs of good breeding in her subject: hands still in the lap, voice low, the reserve which delineates true power. Yet even she, from her inexperience, could do little but pity Justine when she said things like 'I am not much good, you know. I can only inflict sadness, Arnauti used to say. He brought me to my senses and taught me that nothing matters except pleasure — which is the opposite of happiness, its tragic part, I expect.' Clea was touched by this because it seemed clear to her that Justine had never really experienced pleasure — one has to be generous for that. Egotism is a fortress in which the *conscience de soi-même*, like a corrosive, eats away everything. True pleasure is in giving, surely.

'As for Arnauti, he nearly drove me mad with his inquisitions. What I lost as a wife I gained as a patient — his interest in what he called "my case" outweighed any love he might have had for me. And then losing the child made me hate him where before I had only seen a rather sensitive and kindly man. You have probably read his book *Moeurs*. Much of it is invented — mostly to satisfy his own vanity and get his own back on me for the way I wounded his pride in refusing to be "cured" — so-called. You can't put a soul into splints. If you say to a Frenchman "I can't make love to you unless I imagine a palm-tree," he will go out and cut down the nearest palm-tree.'

Clea was too noble to love otherwise than passionately; and yet at the same time quite capable of loving someone to whom she spoke only once a year. The deep still river of her heart hoarded its images, ever reflecting them in the racing current, letting them sink deeper into memory than most of us can. Real innocence can do nothing that is trivial, and when it is allied to generosity of heart, the combination makes it the most vulnerable of qualities under heaven.

In this sudden self-consuming experience, comparable in its tension and ardour to those ridiculous passions which schoolgirls have so often for their mistresses — yet touched in by the fierce mature lines of nature (the demonic line-drawings of an expert love which Justine could always oppose as a response to those who faced her) — she felt really the growing-pains of old age: her flesh and spirit quailing before demands which it knows it cannot meet, which will tear it to rags. Inside herself she had the first stirrings of a sensation new to her: the sensation of a yolk inside her separating from the egg. These are the strange ways in which people grow up.

Poor dear, she was to go through the same ridiculous contortions as the rest of us — feeling her body like a bed of quick-lime clumsily slaked to burn away the corpse of the criminal it covered. The world of secret meetings, of impulses that brand one like an iron, of doubts — this suddenly descended upon her. So great was her confusion of mind that she would sit and stare at the metamorphosed Justine and try to remember what she really looked like on the other side of the transforming membrane, the cataract with which Aphrodite seals up the sick eyes of lovers, the thick, opaque form of a sacred sightlessness.

She would be in a fever all day until the appointed moment when her model met her. At four she stood before the closed door of the studio, seeing clearly through it to the corner where Justine already sat, turning over the pages of a *Vogue* and smoking as she waited, legs crossed. The idea crossed her mind. 'I pray to God she has not come, is ill, has gone away. How eagerly I would welcome indifference!' Surprised too, for these disgusts came from precisely the same quarters as the desire to hear once more that hoarse noble voice — they too arose only from the expectation of seeing her beloved once more. These polarities of feeling bewildered and frightened her by their suddenness.

Then sometimes she wished to go away simply in order to belong more fully to her familiar! Poor fool, she was not spared anything in the long catalogue of self-deceptions which constitute a love affair. She tried to fall back on other pleasures, to find that none existed. She knew that the heart wearies of monotony, that habit and despair are the bedfellows of love, and she waited patiently, as a very old woman might, for the flesh to outgrow its promptings, to deliver itself from an attachment which she now recognized was not of her seeking. Waited in vain. Each day she plunged deeper. Yet all this, at any rate, performed one valuable service for her, proving that relationships like these did not answer the needs of her nature. Just as a man knows inside himself from the first hour that he has married the wrong woman but that there is nothing to be done about it. She knew she was a woman at last and belonged to men — and this gave her misery a fugitive relief.

But the distortions of reality were deeply interesting to someone who recognized that for the artist in herself some confusions of sensibility were valuable. 'Walking towards the studio she would suddenly feel herself becoming breathlessly insubstantial, as if she were a figure painted on canvas. Her breathing became painful. Then after a moment she was overtaken by a feeling of happiness and well-being so intense that she seemed to have become weight-less. Only the weight of her shoes, it seemed, held her to the ground. At any moment she might fly off the earth's surface, breaking through the membrane of gravity, unable to stop. This feeling was so piercing that she had to stop and hold on to the nearest wall and then to walk along it bent double like someone on the deck of a liner in a hurricane. This was itself succeeded by other disagreeable sensations — as of a hot clamp round her skull, pressing it, of the beating of wings in her ears. Half-dreaming in bed, suddenly horns rammed downwards into her brain, impaling her mind; in a brazen red glare she saw the bloodshot eyes of the mithraic animal. It was a cool night with soft pockets of chemical light in the Arab town. The Ginks were abroad with their long oiled plaits and tinselled clothes; the faces of black angels; the men-women of the suburbs.' (I copy these words from the case history of a female mental patient who came under Balthazar's professional care — a nervous breakdown due to 'love' — requited or unrequited who can say? Does it matter? The aetiology of love and madness are identical except in degree, and this passage could serve not only for Clea but indeed for all of us.)

But it was not only of the past that Justine spoke but of a present which was weighing upon her full of decisions which must be taken. In a sense, everything that Clea felt was at this time mean-ingless to her. As a prostitute may be unaware that her client is a poet who will immortalize her in a sonnet she will never read, so Justine in pursuing these deeper sexual pleasures was unaware that they would mark Clea: enfeeble her in her power of giving undivided love — what she was most designed to give by temperament. Her youth, you see. And yet the wretched creature meant no harm. She was simply a victim of that Oriental desire to please, to make this golden friend of hers free of treasures which her own experience had gathered and which, in sum, were as yet meaningless to her. She gave everything, knowing the value of nothing, a true *parvenue* of the soul. To love (from any quarter) she could respond, but only with the worn felicities of friendship. Her body really meant nothing to her. It was a dupe. Her modesty was supreme. This sort of giving is really shocking because it is as simple as an Arab, without precociousness, unrefined as a drinking habit among peasants. It was born long before the idea of love was formed in the fragmented psyche of European man — the knowledge (or invention) of which was to make him the most vulnerable of creatures in the scale of being, subject to hungers which could only be killed by satiety, but never satisfied; which nourished a literature of affectation whose subject-matter would otherwise have belonged to religion — its true sphere of operation. How does one say these things?

Nor, in another scale of reference, is it of the slightest importance — that a woman disoriented by the vagaries of her feelings, tormented, inundated by frightening aspects of her own unrecognized selves, should like a soldier afraid of death, throw herself into the heart of the *mêlée* to wound those whom truly she most loved and most admired — Clea, myself, lastly Nessim. Some people are born to bring good and evil in greater measure than the rest of us — the unconscious carriers of diseases they cannot cure. I think perhaps we must study them, for it is possible that they promote creation in the very degree of the apparent corruption and confusion they spread or seek. I dare not say even now that she was stupid or unfeeling; only that she could not recognize what passed within herself ('the camera obscura of the heart'), could not put a precise frame around the frightening image of her own meaninglessness in the world of ordinary action. The sort of abyss which seemed to lie around her was composed of one quality — a failure of value, a failure to attach meaning which kills joy — which is itself only the internal morality of a soul which has discovered the royal road to happiness, whose nakedness does not shame itself.

It is easy for me to criticize now that I see a little further into the truth of her predicament and my own. She must, I know, have been bitterly ashamed of the trick she was playing on me and the danger into which she put me. Once at the Café El Bab where we were sitting over an *arak*, talking, she burst into tears and kissed my hands, saying: 'You are a good man, really a good man. And I am so sorry.' For what? For her tears? I had been speaking about Goethe. Fool! Imbecile! I thought I had perhaps moved her by the sensibility with which I expressed myself. I gave her presents. So had Clea, so did Clea now: and the strange thing was that for the first time her taste in choosing objects of *vertu* deserted this most gifted and sensitive of painters. Ear-rings and brooches of a commonness which was truly Alexandrian! I am at a loss to understand this phenomenon, unless to love is to become besotted. . . . Yes.

But then I don't know; I am reminded of Balthazar's dry marginal comment on the matter. 'One is apt' he writes 'to take a high moral tone about these things — but in fact, who will criticize himself for reaching up to pluck an apple lying ripe upon a sunwarmed wall? Most women of Justine's temperament and background would not have the courage to imitate her even if they were free to do so. Is it more or less expensive to the spirit to endure dreams and *petit mal* so that the physician will always find a hot forehead and a guilty air? I don't know. It is hard to isolate a moral quality in the free act. And then again, all love-making to one less instructed than oneself has the added delicious thrill which comes from the consciousness of perverting, of pulling them down into the mud from which passions rise — together with poems and theories of God. It is wiser perhaps not to make a judgement.'

But outside all this, in the sphere of daily life, there were problems about which Justine herself needed reassurance. 'I am astonished and a little horrified that Nessim whom I hardly know, has asked to marry me. Am I to laugh, dearest Clea, or be ashamed, or both?' Clea in her innocence was delighted at the news for Nessim was her dearest friend and the thought of him bringing his dignity and gentleness to bear on the very real unhappiness of Justine's life seemed suddenly illuminating — a solution to everything. When one invites rescue by the mess one creates around oneself, what better than that a knight should be riding by? Justine put her hands over her eyes and said with difficulty 'For a moment my heart leapt up and I was about to shout "yes"; ah, Clea my

dear, you will guess why. I need his riches to trace the child —
really, somewhere in the length and breadth of Egypt it must be,
suffering terribly, alone, perhaps ill-treated.' She began to cry
and then stopped abruptly, angrily. 'In order to safeguard us both
from what would be a disaster I said to Nessim "I could never
love a man like you: I could never give you an instant's happiness.
Thank you and good-bye." '

'But are you sure?'

'To use a man for his fortune, by God I'll never.'

'Justine, what do you want?'

'First the child. Then to escape from the eyes of the world into
some quiet corner where I can possess myself. There are whole
parts of my character I do not understand. I need time. Today
again Nessim has written to me. What can he want? He knows all
about me.'

The thought crossed Clea's mind: 'The most dangerous thing
in the world is a love founded on pity.' But she dismissed it and
allowed herself to see once more the image of this gentle, wise,
undissimulating man breasting the torrent of Justine's misfortunes
and damming them up. Am I unjust in crediting her with another
desire which such a solution would satisfy? (Namely, to be rid of
Justine, free from the demands she made upon her heart and mind.
She had stopped painting altogether.) The kindness of Nessim —
the tall dark figure which drifted unresponsively around the corridors of society — needed some such task; how could a knight of
the order born acquit himself if there were no castles and no des-
ponding maidens weaving in them? Their preoccupations matched
in everything — save the demand for love.

'But the money is nothing' she said; and here indeed she was
speaking of what she knew to be precisely true of Nessim. He himself did not really care about the immense fortune which was his.
But here one should add that he had already made a gesture which
had touched and overwhelmed Justine. They met more than once,
formally, like business partners, in the lounge of the Cecil Hotel
to discuss the matter of this marriage with the detachment of
Alexandrian brokers planning a cotton merger. This is the way of
the city. We are mental people, and wordly, and have always made
a clear distinction between the passional life and the life of the
family. These distinctions are part of the whole complex of Mediterranean life, ancient and touchingly prosaic.

'And lest an inequality of fortune should make your decision difficult' said Nessim, flushing and lowering his head, 'I propose to make you a birthday present which will enable you to think of yourself as a wholly independent person — simply as a woman, Justine. This hateful stuff which creeps into everyone's thoughts in the city, poisoning everything! Let us be free of it before deciding anything.' He passed across the table a slim green cheque with the words 'Three Thousand Pounds' written on it. She stared at it for a long time with surprise but did not touch it. 'It has not offended you' he said hastily at last, stammering in his anxiety. 'No' she said. 'It is like everything you do. Only what can I do about not loving you?'

'You must, of course, never try to.'

'Then what sort of life could we make?'

Nessim looked at her with hot shy eyes and then lowered his glance to the table, as if under a cruel rebuke. 'Tell me' she said after a silence. 'Please tell me. I cannot use your fortune and your position and give you nothing in exchange, Nessim.'

'If you would care to try' he said gently, 'we need not delude each other. Life isn't very long. One owes it to oneself to try and find a means to happiness.'

'Is it that you want to sleep with me?' asked Justine suddenly: disgusted yet touched beyond measure by his tone. 'You may. Yes. Oh! I would do anything for you, Nessim — anything.'

But he flinched and said: 'I am speaking about an understanding in which friendship and knowledge can take the place of love until and if it comes as I hope. Of course I shall sleep with you — myself a lover, and you a friend. Who knows? In a year perhaps. All Alexandrian marriages are business ventures after all. My God, Justine, what a fool you are. Can't you see that we might possibly need each other without ever fully realizing it? It's worth trying. Everything may stand in the way. But I can't get over the thought that in the whole city the woman I most *need* is you. There are any number a man may want, but to want is not to need. I may want others — you I need! I do not dare to say the same for you. How cruel life is, and how absurd.' Nobody had said anything like that to her before — had offered her a partnership as coolly designed, as wholly pure in intention. It must be admired from this point of view. 'You are not the sort of man to stake everything on a single throw at *rouge et noir*' she said slowly. 'Our bankers who are so brilliant with money are notoriously weak in the head when it comes to women.' She put her hand upon his wrist.

'You should have your doctor examine you, my dear. To take on a woman who has said that she can never love you — what sort of temerity is that? Ah, no!'

He did not say anything at all, recognizing that her words were really not addressed to him: they were part of a long internal argument with herself. How beautiful her disaffected face looked — chloroformed by its own simplicity: she simply could not believe that someone might value her for herself — if she had a self. He was indeed, he thought, like a gambler putting everything on the turn of a wheel. She was standing now upon the very edge of a decision, like a sleepwalker on a cliff: should she awake before she jumped, or let the dream continue? Being a woman, she still felt it necessary to pose conditions; to withdraw herself further into secrecy as this man encroached upon it with his steady beguiling gentleness. 'Nessim' she said, 'wake up.' And she shook him gently.

'I am awake' he said quietly.

Outside in the square with its palms nibbled by the sea-wind, a light rain was falling. It was the tenth Zu-el-Higga, the first day of Courban Bairam, and fragments of the great procession were assembling in their coloured robes, holding the great silk banners and censers, insignia of the religion they honoured, and chanting passages from the litany: litany of the forgotten Nubian race which every year makes its great resurrection at the Mosque of Nebi Daniel. The crowd was brilliant, spotted with primary colours. The air rippled with tambourines, while here and there in the lags of silence which fell over the shouts and chanting, there came the sudden jabbering of the long drums as their hide was slowly stiffened at the hissing braziers. Horses moaned and the gonfalons bellied like sails in the rain-starred afternoon. A cart filled with the prostitutes of the Arab town in coloured robes went by with shrill screams and shouts, and the singing of painted young men to the gnash of cymbals and scribbling of mandolines: the whole as gorgeous as a tropical animal.

'Nessim' she said foolishly. 'On one sole condition — that we sleep together absolutely tonight.' His features drew tight against his skull and he set his teeth tightly as he said angrily: 'You should have some intelligence to go with your lack of breeding — where is it?'

'I'm sorry' seeing how deeply and suddenly she had annoyed him. 'I felt in need of reassurance.' He had become quite pale.

'I proposed something so different' he said, replacing the cheque in his wallet. 'I am rather staggered by your lack of understanding. Of course we can sleep together if you wish to make it a condition. Let us take a room at the hotel here, now, this minute.' He looked really splendid when he was wounded like this, and suddenly there stirred inside her the realization that his quietness was not weakness, and than an uncommon sort of sensibility underlay these confusing thoughts and deliberate words, perhaps not altogether good, either. 'What could we prove to each other' he went on more gently 'by it or by its opposite: never making love?' She saw now how hopelessly out of context her words had been. 'I'm bitterly ashamed of my vulgarity.' She said this without really meaning the words, as a concession to his world as much as to himself — a world which dealt in the refinements of manners she was as yet too coarse to enjoy, which could afford to cultivate emotions *posées* by taste. A world which could only be knocked off its feet when you were skin to skin with it, so to speak! No, she did not mean the words, for vulgar as the idea sounded, she knew that she was right by the terms of her intuition since the thing she proposed is really, for women, the vital touchstone to a man's being; the knowledge, not of his qualities which can be analysed or inferred, but of the very flavour of his personality. Nothing except the act of physical love tells us this truth about one another. She bitterly regretted his unwisdom in denying her a concrete chance to see for herself what underlay his beauty and persuasion. Yet how could one insist?

'Good' he said, 'for our marriage will be a delicate affair, and very much a question of manners, until——'

'I'm sorry' she said. 'I really did not know how to treat honourably with you and avoid disappointing you.'

He kissed her lightly on the mouth as he stood up. 'I must go first and get the permission of my mother, and tell my brother. I am terribly happy, even though now I am furious with you.'

They went out to the car together and Justine suddenly felt very weak, as if she had been carried far out of her depth and abandoned in mid-ocean. 'I don't know what more to say.'

'Nothing. You must start living' he said as the car began to draw away, and she felt as if she had received a smack across the mouth. She went into the nearest coffee-shop and ordered a cup of hot chocolate which she drank with trembling hands. Then she combed her hair and made up her face. She knew her beauty was only an advertisement and kept it fresh with disdain. No, somewhere she was truly a woman.

Nessim took the lift up to his office, and sitting down at his desk wrote upon a card the following words: 'My dearest Clea, Justine has agreed to marry me. I could never do this if I thought it would qualify or interfere in any way with either her love for you or mine. . . .'

Then, appalled by the thought that whatever he might write to Clea might sound mawkish, he tore the note up and folded his arms. After a long moment of thought he picked up the polished telephone and dialled Capodistria's number. 'Da Capo' he said quietly. 'You remember my plans for marrying Justine? All is well.' He replaced the receiver slowly, as if it weighed a ton, and sat staring at his own reflection in the polished desk.

*　　*　　*　　*　　*

IV

It was now, having achieved the major task of persuasion, that his self-assurance fled and left him face to face with a sensation entirely new to him, namely an acute shyness, an acute unwillingness to face his mother directly, to confront her with his intentions. He himself was puzzled by it, for they had always been close together, their confidences linked by an affection too deep to need the interpretation of words. If he had ever been shy or awkward it was with his awkward brother, never with her. And now? It was not as if he even feared her disfavour — he knew she would fall in with his wishes as soon as they were spoken. What then inhibited him? He could not tell. Yet he flushed as he thought of her now, and passed the whole of that morning in restless automatic acts, picking up a novel only to lay it down, mixing a drink only to abandon it, starting to sketch and then abruptly dropping the charcoal to walk out into the garden of the great house, ill at ease. He had telephoned his office to say that he was indisposed and then, as always when he had told a lie, began to suffer in truth with an attack of indigestion.

Then he started to ask for the number of the old country house where Leila and Narouz lived, but changed his mind and asked the operator instead for the number of his garage. The car would be back, they told him, cleaned and greased by noon. He lay down and covered his face with his hands. Then he rang up Selim, his secretary, and told him to telephone to his brother and say that he was coming to Karm Abu Girg for the week-end. Heavens! what could be more normal? 'You go on like a chambermaid who has got engaged' he told himself hotly. Then for a moment he thought of taking someone with him to ease the strain of the meeting — Justine? Impossible. He picked up a novel of Pursewarden's and came upon the phrase: 'Love is like trench warfare — you cannot see the enemy, but you know he is there and that it is wiser to keep your head down.'

The doorbell rang. Selim brought him some letters to sign and then went silently upstairs to pack his bag and briefcase. There were papers he must take for Narouz to see — papers about the lift machinery needed to drain and reclaim the desert which fringed the plantations. Business matters were a welcome drug.

The Hosnani fortunes were deployed in two directions, separated into two spheres of responsibility, and each brother had his own. Nessim controlled the banking house and its ancillaries all over the Mediterranean, while Narouz lived the life of a Coptic squire, never stirring from Karm Abu Girg where the Hosnani lands marched with the fringe of the desert, gradually eating into it, expropriating it year by year, spreading their squares of cultivation — carob and melon and corn — and pumping out the salt which poisoned it.

'The car is here' said the hawk-faced secretary as he returned. 'Am I to drive you, sir?' Nessim shook his head and dismissed him quietly, before crossing the garden once more, chin in hand. He paused by the lily pond to study the fish — those expensive toys of the ancient Japanese Emperors, survivals from an age of luxury, which he had imported at such cost, only to find them gradually dying off of some unknown illness — homesickness, perhaps? Pursewarden spent hours watching them. He said that they helped him to think about art!

The great silver car stood at the door with the ignition key in the dashboard. He got in thoughtfully and drove slowly across the town, examining its parks and squares and buildings with a serene eye, but deliberately dawdling, irresolutely, emptying his mind by an act of will every time the thought of his destination came upon him. When he reached the sea he turned at last down the shining Corniche in the sunlight to watch the smooth sea and cloudless air for a moment, the car almost at a standstill. Then suddenly he changed gear and began to travel along the sea-shore at a more resolute pace. He was going home.

Soon he turned inland, leaving the town with its palms crackling in the spring wind and turning towards the barren network of faults and dried-out lake-beds where the metalled road gave place to the brown earth tracks along embankments lined with black swamps and fringed by barbed reeds and a cross-hatching of sweet-corn plantations. The dust came up between his wheels and filled the air of the saloon, coating everything in a fine-grained pollen. The windscreen became gradually snowed-up and he switched on the wipers to keep it clear.

Following little winding lanes which he knew by heart he came, after more than an hour, to the edge of a spit flanked by bluer water and left the car in the shadow of a tumbledown house, the remains perhaps of some ancient customs-shed built in the days when river traffic plied between Damietta and the Gulf: now drying up day by day, withering and cracking under the brazen Egyptian sky, forgotten by its keepers.

He locked the car carefully and followed a narrow path across a holding of poverty-stricken beanrows and dusty melons, fringed with ragged and noisy Indian corn, to come out upon a landing-stage where an aged ferryman awaited him in a ramshackle boat. At once he saw the horses waiting upon the other side, and the foreshortened figure of Narouz beside them. He threw up an excited arm in an awkward gesture of pleasure as he saw Nessim. Nessim stepped into the boat with beating heart.

'Narouz!' The two brothers, so unlike in physique and looks, embraced with feeling which was qualified in Nessim by the silent agony of a shyness new to him.

The younger brother, shorter and more squarely built than Nessim, wore a blue French peasant's blouse open at the throat and with the sleeves rolled back, exposing arms and hands of great power covered by curly dark hair. An old Italian cartridge bandolier hung down upon his haunches. The ends of his baggy Turkish trousers with an old-fashioned drawstring, were stuffed into crumpled old jackboots of soft leather. He ducked, excitedly, awkwardly, into his brother's arms and out again, like a boxer from a clinch. But when he raised his head to look at him, you saw at once what it was that had ruled Narouz' life like a dark star. His upper lip was split literally from the spur of the nose — as if by some terrific punch: it was a hare-lip which had not been caught up and basted in time. It exposed the ends of a white tooth and ended in two little pink tongues of flesh in the centre of his upper lip which were always wet. His dark hair grew down low and curly, like a heifer's, on to his brow. His eyes were splendid: of a blueness and innocence that made them almost like Clea's: indeed his whole ugliness took splendour from them. He had grown a ragged and uneven moustache over his upper lip, as someone will train ivy over an ugly wall — but the scar showed through wherever the hair was thin: and his short, unsatisfactory beard too was a poor disguise: looked simply as if he had remained unshaven for a week. It had no shape of its own and confused the outlines of his taurine neck and high cheekbones. He had a curious hissing shy laugh which he always pointed downward into the ground to hide his lip. The whole sum of his movements was ungainly — arms and legs somewhat curved and hairy as a spider — but they gave off a sensation of over-whelming strength held rigidly under control. His voice was deep and thrilling and held something of the magic of a woman's contralto.

Whenever possible they tried to have servants or friends with them when they met — to temper their shyness; and so today Narouz had brought Ali, his factor, with the horses to meet the ferry. The old servant with the cropped ears took a pinch of dust from the ground before Nessim's feet and pressed it to his fore-head before extending his hand for a handshake, and then diffi-dently partook of the embrace Nessim offered him — as someone he had loved from his childhood onwards. Narouz was charmed by his brother's easy, comradely but feeling gesture — and he laughed downwards into the ground with pleasure.

'And Leila?' said Nessim, in a low voice, raising his fingers to his temple for a moment as he did so.

'Is well' said Narouz in the tone that springs from a freshly rosined bow. 'This past two months. Praise God.'

Their mother sometimes went through periods of mental in-stability lasting for weeks, always to recover again. It was a quiet surrender of the real world that surprised no one any longer, for she herself now knew when such an attack was coming on and would make preparations for it. At such times, she spent all day in the little hut at the end of the rose-garden, reading and writing, mostly the long letters which Mountolive read with such tender-ness in Japan or Finland or Peru. With only the cobra for company, she waited until the influence of the *afreet* or spirit was spent. This habit had lasted for many years now, since the death of their father and her illness, and neither son took any account of these depar-tures from the normal life of the great house. 'Leila is well in her mind!' said Narouz again in that thrilling voice. 'So happy too that Mountolive is posted back. She looks years younger.'

'I understand.'

The two brothers now mounted their horses and started slowly along the network of embankments and causeways which led them over the lake with its panels of cultivation. Nessim always loved this ride for it evoked his real childhood — so much richer in variety than those few years spent in the house at Aboukir where Leila had moved for a while after their father's death. 'All your new lift pumps should be here next month' he shouted, and

Narouz chuckled with pleasure; but with another part of his mind he allowed the soft black earthworks of the river with its precarious tracks separating the squares of cultivated soil to lead him steadily back to the remembered treasures of his childhood here. For this was really Egypt — a Copt's Egypt — while the white city, as if in some dusty spectrum, was filled with the troubling and alien images of lands foreign to it — the intimations of Greece, Syria, Tunis.

It was a fine day and shallow draught boats were coursing among the beanfields towards the river tributaries, with their long curved spines of mast, lateen rigs bent like bows in the freshets. Somewhere a boatman sang and kept time on a finger-drum, his voice mixing with the sighing of *sakkias* and the distant village bangings of wheelwrights and carpenters manufacturing disc-wheels for wagons or the shallow-bladed ploughs which worked the alluvial riverside holdings.

Brilliant kingfishers hunted the shallows like thunderbolts, their wings slurring, while here and there the small brown owls, having forgotten the night habits of their kind, flew between the banks, or nestled together in songless couples among the trees.

The fields had begun to spread away on either side of the little cavalcade now, green and scented with their rich crops of *bercim* and beanrows, though the road still obstinately followed along the banks of the river so that their reflections rode with them. Here and there were hamlets whose houses of unbaked mud wore flat roofs made brilliant now by stacks of Indian corn which yellowed them. They passed an occasional line of camels moving down towards a ferry, or a herd of great black *gamoose* — Egyptian buffalo — dipping their shiny noses in the rich ooze and filth of some backwater, flicking the flies from their papery skins with lead tails. Their great curved horns belonged to forgotten frescoes.

It was strange now how slowly life moved here, he reflected with pleasure as he moved towards the Hosnani property — women churning butter in goatskins suspended from bamboo tripods or walking in single file down to the river with their pots. Men in robes of blue cotton at the waterwheels, singing, matrons swathed from crown to ankle in the light dusty black robes which custom demanded, blue-beaded against the evil eye. And then all the primeval courtesies of the road exchanged between passers-by to which Narouz responded in his plangent voice, sounding as if it belonged to the language as much as to the place. '*Naharak Said!*'

he cried cheerfully, or '*Said Embarak!*' as the wayfarers smiled and greeted them. 'May your day be blessed' thought Nessim in remembered translation as he smiled and nodded, overcome at the splendour of these old-fashioned greetings one never heard except in the Arab quarter of the city; 'may today be as blessed as yesterday.'

He turned and said 'Narouz' and his brother rode up beside him tenderly, saying 'Have you seen my whip?' Laughing downwards again, his tooth showing through the rent in his lip. He carried a splendid hippopotamus-hide whip, loosely coiled at his saddle-bow. 'I found the perfect one — after three years. Sheik Bedawi sent it down from Assuan. Do you know?' He turned those brilliant blue eyes upwards for a moment to stare into the dark eyes of his brother with intense joy. 'It is better than a pistol, at any rate a .99' he said, thrilled as a child. 'I've been practising hard with it — do you want to see?'

Without waiting for an answer he tucked his head down and rode forward at a trot to where some dozen chickens were scratching at the bare ground near a herdsman's cot. A frightened rooster running faster than the others took off under his horse's hooves: Nessim reined back to watch. Narouz' arm shot up, the long lash uncurled slowly on the air and then went rigid with a sudden dull welt of sound, a sullen thwack, and laughing, the rider dismounted to pick up the mutilated creature, still warm and palpitating, its wings half-severed from its body, its head smashed. He brought it back to Nessim in triumph, wiping his hand casually on his baggy trousers. 'What do you think?' Nessim gripped and admired the great whip while his brother threw the dead fowl to his factor, still laughing himself, and so slowly remounted. They rode side by side now, as if the spell upon their communication were broken, and Nessim talked of the new machinery which had been ordered and heard of Narouz' battle against drought and sand-drift. In such neutral subjects they could lose themselves and become natural. United most closely by such topics, they were like two blind people in love who can only express themselves through touch: the subject of their hands.

The holdings became richer now, planted out with tamarisk and carob, though here and there they passed the remains of properties abandoned by owners too poor or too lazy to contend with the deserts, which encircled the fertile strip on three sides. Old houses, fallen now into desuetude, abandoned and overgrown, stared out across the water with unframed windows and shattered doors. Their gates, half-smothered in bougainvillaea, opened rustily into gardens of wild and unkempt beauty where marble fountains and rotted statuary still testified to a glory since departed. On either side of them one could glimpse the well-wooded lands which formed the edge, the outer perimeter of the family estates — palm, acacia and sycamore which still offered the precarious purchase to life which without shade and water perished, reverted to the desert. Indeed, one was conscious of the desert here although one could not see it — melodramatically tasteless as a communion wafer.

Here an old island with a ruined palace; there tortuous paths and channels of running water where the slim bird-forms of river-craft moved about their task of loading *tibbin* (corn); they were nearing the village now. A bridge rose high upon mudbanks, crowned by a magnificent grove of palms, with a row of coloured boats waiting for the boom to lift. Here on the rise one glimpsed for a moment the blue magnetic haze of a desert horizon lying beyond this hoarded strip of plenty, of green plantations and water.

Round a corner they came upon a knot of villagers waiting for them who set up cries of 'What honour to the village!' and 'You bring blessings!' walking beside them as they rode smiling onwards. Some advanced on them, the notables, catching a hand to kiss, and some even kissing Nessim's stirrup-irons. So they passed through the village against its patch of emerald water and dominated by the graceful fig-shaped minaret, and the cluster of dazzling beehive domes which distinguished the Coptic church of their forefathers. From here, the road turned back again across the fields to the great house within its weather-stained outer walls, ruined and crumbling with damp in many places, and in others covered by such *graffiti* as the superstitious leave to charm the *afreet* — black talismanic handprints, or the legend '*B'ism'illah ma'sha'llah*' (may God avert evil). It was for these pious villagers that its tenants had raised on the corners of the wall tiny wooden windmills in the shape of men with revolving arms, to scare the *afreet* away. This was the manor-house of Karm Abu Girg which belonged to them.

Emin, the chief steward, was waiting at the outer gate with the usual gruff greetings which custom demanded, surrounded by a group of shy boys to hold the horses and help their riders dismount.

The great folding doors of the courtyard with their pistol bolts and inscribed panels were set back so that they could walk directly into the courtyard against which the house itself was built, tilted upon two levels — the ceremonial first floor looking down sideways along the vaulted arches below — a courtyard with its granaries and reception-rooms, storehouses and stables. Nessim did not cross the threshold before examining once more the faded but still visible cartoons which decorated the wall at the right-hand side of it — and which depicted in a series of almost hieroglyphic signs the sacred journey he had made to bathe in the Jordan: a horse, a motorcar, a ship, an aeroplane, all crudely represented. He muttered a pious text, and the little group of servants smiled with satisfaction, understanding by this that his long residence in the city had not made him forget country ways. He never forgot to do this. It was like a man showing his passport. And Narouz too was grateful for the tact such a gesture showed — which not only endeared his brother to the dependants of the house, but also strengthened his own position with them as the ruling master of it.

On the other side of the lintel, a similar set of pictures showed that he also, the younger brother, had made the pious pilgrimage which is incumbent upon every Copt of religious principles.

The main gateway was flanked on each side by a pigeon-tower — those clumsy columns built of earthen pitchers pasted together anyhow with mud-cement: which are characteristic of country houses in Egypt and which supplied the choicest dish for the country squire's table. A cloud of its inhabitants fluttered and crooned all day over the barrel-vaulted court. Here all was activity: the negro night-watchman, the *ghaffirs*, factors, stewards came forth one by one to salute the eldest brother, the heir. He was given a bowl of wine and a nosegay of flowers while Narouz stood by proudly smiling.

Then they went at ceremonial pace through the gallery with its windows of many-coloured glass which for a brief moment transformed them into harlequins, and then out into the rose garden with its ragged and unkempt arbour and winding paths towards the little summer-house where Leila sat reading, unveiled. Narouz called her name once to warn her as they neared the house, adding 'Guess who has come!' The woman quickly replaced her veil and turned her wise dark eyes towards the sunlit door saying: 'The boy did not bring the milk again. I wish you would tell him, Narouz.

His mind is salt. The snake must be fed regularly or it becomes ill-tempered.' And then the voice, swerving like a bird in mid-air, foundered and fell to a rich melodious near-sob on the name 'Nessim'. And this she repeated twice as they embraced with such trembling tenderness that Narouz laughed, swallowing, and tasted both the joy of his brother's love for Leila and his own bitterness in realizing that he, Nessim, was her favourite — the beautiful son. He was not jealous of Nessim; only heartsick at the melody in his mother's voice — the tone she had never used in speaking to him. It had always been so.

'I will speak to the boy' he said, and looked about him for signs of the snake. Egyptians regard the snake as too lucky a visitant to a house to kill and so tempt ill-luck, and Leila's long self-communing in the little summer-house would not have been complete without this indolent cobra which had learned to drink milk from a saucer like a cat.

Still holding hands they sat down together and Nessim started to speak of political matters with those dark, clever, youthful eyes looking steadily into his. From time to time, Leila nodded vigorously, with a determined air, while the younger son watched them both hungrily, with a heavy admiration at the concise way Nessim abbreviated and expressed his ideas — the fruit of a long public life. Narouz felt these abstract words fall dully upon his ear, fraught with meanings he only half-guessed, and though he knew that they concerned him as much as anyone, they seemed to him to belong to some rarer world inhabited by sophists or mathematicians — creatures who would forge and give utterance to the vague longings and incoherent desires he felt forming inside him whenever Egypt was mentioned or the family estates. He sucked the knuckle of his forefinger, and sat beside them, listening, looking first at his mother and then back to Nessim.

'And now Mountolive is coming back' concluded Nessim, 'and for the first time what we are trying to do will be understood. Surely he will help us, if it is possible? He understands.'

The name of Mountolive struck two ways. The woman lowered her eyes to her own white hands which lay before her upon a half-finished letter — eyes so brilliantly made up with kohl and antimony that to discern tears in them would have been difficult. Yet there were none. They sparkled only with affection. Was she thinking of those long letters which she had so faithfully written during the whole period of their separation? But Narouz felt a sudden stirring of jealousy in his brain at the mention of the name, under which, interred as if under a tombstone, he had hidden memories of a different epoch — of the young secretary of the High Commission whom his mother had — (mentally he never used the word 'loved' but left a blank space in his thoughts where it should stand); moreover of the sick husband in the wheelchair who had watched so uncomplainingly. Narouz' soul vibrated with his father's passion when Mountolive's name, like a note of music, was struck. He swallowed and stirred uneasily now as he watched his mother tremblingly fold a letter and slide it into an envelope. 'Can we trust him?' she asked Nessim. She would have struck him over the mouth if he had answered 'No.' She simply wanted to hear him pronounce the name again. Her question was a prompting, nothing more. He kissed her hand, and Narouz greedily admired his courtier's smiling air as he replied 'If we cannot, who can we trust?'

As a girl, Leila had been both beautiful and rich. The daughter of a blue-stocking, convent-bred and very much in society, she had been among the first Coptic women to abandon the veil and to start to take up the study of medicine against her parents' will. But an early marriage to a man very much older than herself had put an end to these excursions into the world of scope where her abilities might have given her a foot-hold. The temper of Egyptian life too was hostile to the freedom of women, and she had resigned a career in favour of a husband she very much admired and the uneventful round of country life. Yet somehow, under it all, the fire had burned on. She had kept friends and interests, had visited Europe every few years, had subscribed to periodicals in four languages. Her mind had been formed by solitude, enriched by books which she could only discuss in letters to friends in remote places, could only read in the privacy of the *harim*. Then came the advent of Mountolive and the death of her husband. She stood free and breathing upon the brink of a new world with no charge upon her but two growing sons. For a year she had hesitated between Paris and London as a capital of residence, and while she hesitated, all was lost. Her beauty, of which until then she had taken no particular account, as is the way with the beautiful, had been suddenly ravaged by a confluent smallpox which melted down those lovely features and left her only the magnificent eyes of an Egyptian sibyl. The black hideous veil which so long had seemed to her a symbol of servitude became now a refuge in which she could hide the ruins of a beauty which had been considered so outstanding in her youth. She had not the heart now to parade this new melted face through the capitals of Europe, to brave the silent condolences of friends who might remember her as she had once been. Turned back upon her tracks so summarily, she had decided to stay on and end her life in the family estates in such seclusion as might be permitted to her. Her only outlet now would be in letter-writing and in reading — her only care her sons. All the unsteadiness of her passions was canalized into this narrow field. A whole world of relations had to be mastered and she turned her resolution to it like a man. Ill-health, loneliness, boredom — she faced them one by one and overcame them — living here in retirement like a dethroned Empress, feeding her snake and writing her interminable letters which were full of the liveliness and sparkle of a life which now the veil masked and which could escape only through those still youthful dark eyes.

She was now never seen in society and had become something of a legend amongst those who remembered her in the past, and who indeed had once nicknamed her the 'dark swallow'. Now she sat all day at a rough deal table, writing in that tall thoughtful handwriting, dipping her quill into a golden inkpot. Her letters had become her very life, and in the writing of them she had begun to suffer fromt hat curious sense of distorted reality which writers have when they are dealing with real people; in the years of writing to Mountolive, for example, she had so to speak re-invented him so successfully that he existed for her now not so much as a real human being but as a character out of her own imagination. She had even almost forgotten what he looked like, what to expect of his physical presence, and when his telegram came to say that he expected to be in Egypt again within a few months, she felt at first nothing but irritation that he should intrude, bodily as it were, upon the picture projected by her imagination. 'I shall not see him' she muttered at first, angrily; and only then did she start to tremble and cover her ravaged face with her hands.

'Mountolive will want to see you' said Nessim, at last, as the conversation veered round in his direction again. 'When may I bring him? The Legation is moving up to summer quarters soon, so he will be in Alexandria all the time.'

'He must wait until I am ready' she said, once more feeling the anger stir in her at the intrusion of this beloved figment. 'After all these years.' And then she asked with a pathetic lustful eagerness, 'Is he old now — is he grey? Is his leg all right? Can he walk? That ski-ing fall in Austria. . . .'

To all this Narouz listened with cocked head and sullen heavy heart: he could follow the feeling in her voice as one follows a line of music.

'He is younger than ever' said Nessim, 'hasn't aged by a day': and to his surprise she took his hand, and putting it to her cheek she said brokenly 'Oh — you are horrible, both of you. Go. Leave me alone now. I have letters to write.'

She permitted no mirrors in the *harim* since the illness which had deprived her of her self-esteem; but privately in a gold-backed pocket-mirror, she touched and pencilled her eyes in secret — her remaining treasure — practising different make-ups on them, practising different glances and matching them to different remarks — trying to give what was left of her looks a vocabulary as large as her lively mind. She was like a man struck suddenly blind learning to spell, with the only member left him, his hands.

Now the two men walked back into the old house, with its cool but dusty rooms whose walls were hung with ancient carpets and embroidered mats, and crowded with gigantic carcasses of furniture long since outmoded — a sort of Ottoman Buhl such as one sees in the old houses of Egypt. Nessim's heartstrings were tugged by the memory of its ugliness, its old-fashioned Second Empire pieces and its jealously guarded routines. The steward, according to custom, had stopped all the clocks. This, in the language of Narouz, said 'Your stay with us is so brief, let us not be reminded of the flight of the hours. God made eternity. Let us escape from the despotism of time altogether.' These ancient and hereditary politenesses filled Nessim with emotion. Even the primitive sanitary arrangements — there were no bathrooms — seemed to him somehow in keeping with the character of things, though he loved hot water. Narouz himself slept naked winter and summer. He washed in the courtyard — a servant threw water over him from a pitcher. Indoors, he usually wore an old blue cloak and Turkish slippers. He smoked tobacco too in a narguileh the length of a musket.

While the elder brother unpacked his clothes, Narouz sat on the end of the bed studying the papers which filled the briefcase, musing with a quiet intentness, for they related to the machinery with the help of which he proposed to keep up and extend his attack on the dead sand. In the back of his mind he could see an army of trees and shrubs marching steadily forward into the emptiness —

carob and olive, vine and jujube, pistachio, peach and apricot, spreading around them the green colours of quickness in those tenantless areas of dust choked with sea-salt. He looked almost lustfully upon the pictures of equipment in the shiny brochures Nessim had brought him, lovingly touching them with his finger, hearing in his imagination the suck and swell of sweet water through pumps gradually expressing the dead salts from the ground and quickening it to nourish the sipping roots of his trees. Gebel Maryut, Abusir — his mind winged away like a swallow across the dunes into the Nitrian desert itself — mentally conquering it.

'The desert' said Narouz. 'By the way, will you ride out with me to the tents of Abu Kar tomorrow? I have been promised an Arab and I want to break it myself. It would make a pleasant excursion.' Nessim was at once delighted at the prospect. 'Yes' he said. 'But early' said Narouz, 'and we can pass the olive plantation for you to see what progress we're making. Will you? Please do!' He squeezed his arm. 'Since we started with the Tunisian *chimlali* we haven't had a single casualty. Oh, Nessim! I wish you stayed here. Your place is here.'

Nessim as always was beginning to wish the same. That night they dined in the old-fashioned way — so different from the impertinent luxury of Alexandrian forms — each taking his napkin from the table and proceeding to the yard for the elaborate hand-washing ceremony which preceded a meal in the country. Two servants poured for them as they stood side by side, washing their fingers with yellow soap, and rinsed them off with orange-water. Then to the table where their only cutlery was a wooden spoon each for dealing with soup — otherwise they broke the flat thin cakes of the country to dip into the dishes of cooked meats. Leila had always dined alone in the women's quarters, and retired to bed early so that the two brothers were left alone to their repast. They ate in leisurely fashion, with long pauses between the courses, and Narouz acted host, placing choice morsels upon Nessim's plate and breaking up the fowl and the turkey with his strong fingers the better to serve his guest. At last, when sweetmeats and fruit had been served, they returned once more to where the waiting servants stood and washed their hands again.

In the interval, the table had been cleared of dishes and set back to make room for the old-fashioned divans to pass through the room and out on to the balcony. Smoking materials had been set out — the long-barrelled *narguilehs* with Narouz' favourite tobacco and a silver dish of sweets. Here they sat together for a while in silence to drink their coffee. Nessim had kicked off his slippers and drawn his legs up under him: he sat with his chin in his hand wondering how he could impart his news, the marriage which nibbled at the edge of his mind: and whether he should be frank about his motives in choosing for a wife a woman who was of a different faith from his own. The night was hot and still, and the scent of magnolia blossom came up to the balcony in little drifts and eddies of air which made the candles flutter and dance; he was gnawed by irresolution.

In such a mood every promise of distraction offered relief, and he was pleased when Narouz suggested that the village singer should be called to play for them, a custom which they had so often enjoyed as youths. There is nothing more appropriate to the heavy silence of the Egyptian night than the childish poignance of the *kemengeh's* note. Narouz clapped his hands and despatched a message and presently the old man came from the servant's quarters where he dined each night on the charity of the house, walking with the slow and submissive step of extreme old age and approaching blindness. The sounding-board of his small viol was made from half a coconut. Narouz sprang up and settled him upon a cushion at the end of the balcony. There came footsteps in the courtyard and a familiar voice, that of the old schoolmaster Mohammed Shebab, who climbed the stairs, smiling and wrinkled, to clasp Narouz' hand. He had the bright hairy face of a monkey and wore, as usual, an immaculate dark suit with a rose in his button-hole. He was something of a dandy and an epicure and these visits to the great house were his only distraction, living as he did for the greater part of the year buried in the depths of the delta; he had brought the old treasured *narguileh* mouthpiece which he had owned for a quarter of a century. He was delighted to hear some music and listened with emotion to the wild *quasidas* that the old man sang — songs of the Arab canon full of the wild heart-sickness of the desert. The old voice, crumpled here and there like a fragile leaf, rose and fell upon the night; tracing the quavering melodic line of the songs as if it were following the ancient highways of half-obliterated thoughts and feelings. The little viol scribbled its complaints upon the text reaching back into their childhood. And now suddenly the singer burst into the passionate pilgrim song which expresses so marvellously the Moslem's longing for Mecca and his adoration of the Prophet — and the melody fluttered inside the brothers' hearts, imprisoned like a bird with beating wings. Narouz, though a Copt, was repeating 'All-*ah*, All-*ah!*' in a rapture of praise.

'Enough, enough' cried Nessim at last. 'If we are to be up early, we should sleep early, don't you think?'

Narouz sprang up too, and still acting the host, called for lights and water and walked before him to the guest-room. Here he waited until Nessim had washed and undressed and climbed into the creaking old-fashioned bed before bidding him good night. As he stood in the doorway, Nessim said impulsively: 'Narouz — I've something to tell you.' And then, overcome once more with shyness, added: 'But it will keep until tomorrow. We shall be alone, shan't we?' Narouz nodded and smiled. 'The desert is such torture for them that I always send them back at the fringe, the servants.'

'Yes.' Nessim well knew that Egyptians believe the desert to be an emptiness populated entirely by the spirits of demons and other grotesque visitants from Eblis, the Moslem Satan.

Nessim slept and awoke to find his brother, fully dressed, standing beside his bed with coffee and cigarettes. 'It's time' he said. 'I suppose in Alexandria you sleep late. . . .'

'No' said Nessim, 'strangely enough I am usually at my office by eight.'

'Eight! Oh! my poor brother' said Narouz mockingly, and helped him to dress. The horses were waiting and together they rode out upon a dawn with a thick bluish mist rising from the lake. Crisp air, inclining to frost — but already the sun was beginning to soak into the upper air and dry up the dew upon the minaret of the mosque.

Narouz led now, down winding ways, along the tortuous bridle paths, and across embankments, quite unerringly, for the whole land existed in his mind like the most detailed map by a master cartographer. He carried it always in his head like a battle-plan, knowing the age of every tree, the poundage of every well's water, the drift of sand to an inch. He was possessed by it.

Slowly they made a circuit of the great plantation, soberly assessing progress and discussing plans for the next offensive when the new machinery should be installed. And then, presently when they had come to a lonely spot by the river, screened on all sides by reeds, Narouz said 'Wait a second. . . .' and dismounted, taking as he did so the old leather game-bag from his shoulders. 'Something to hide' he said, smiling downwards shyly. Nessim watched him idly as he turned the bag over to tip its contents into the dank waters of the river. But he was not prepared to see a shrunken human head, lips drawn back over yellow teeth, eyes squinting inwards upon each other, roll out of the bag and sink slowly out of sight into the green depths beneath. 'What the devil's that?' he asked, and Narouz gave his little hissing titter at the ground and replied 'Abdel-Kader — head of.' He knelt down and started washing the bag out in the water, moving it vigorously to and fro, and then with a gesture turned it inside out as one might turn a sleeve and returned to his horse. Nessim was thinking deeply. 'So you had to do it at last' he said. 'I was afraid you might.'

Narouz turned his brilliant eyes upon his brother for a moment and said seriously: 'More troubles with Bedouin labour could have cost us a thousand trees next year. It was too much of a risk to take. Besides, he was going to poison me.'

He said no more and they rode on in silence until they reached the thinning edges of cultivation — the front line so to speak where the battle was actually being joined at present — a long ragged territory like the edges of a wound. Along the whole length of it infiltration from the arable land on the one side and the desert drainage on the other, both charged with the rotten salts, had poisoned the ground and made it the image of desolation.

Here only giant reeds and bulrushes grew or an occasional thorn bush. No fish could live in the brackish water. Birds shunned it. It lay in the stagnant belt of its own foul air, weird, obsessive and utterly silent — the point at which the desert and the sown met in a death-embrace. They rode now among towering rushes whose stems were bleached and salt-encrusted, glittering in the sun. The horses gasped and scrambled through the dead water which splashed upon them, crystallizing into spots of salt wherever it fell; pools of slime were covered with a crust of salt through which their plunging hooves broke, releasing horrible odours from the black mud beneath and sudden swarms of small stinging flies and mosquitoes. But Narouz looked about him with interest even here, his eyes alight, for he had already mentally planted this waste with carobs and green shrubs — conquered it. But they both held their breath and did not speak as they traversed this last mephitic barrier and the long patches of wrinkled mummy-like soil to which it gave place. Then at last they were on the edge of the desert and they paused in shadow while Narouz fished in his clothes for the little stick of blue billiard-marker's chalk. They rubbed a little chalk under each of their eyelids with a finger against the glare — as they had always done, even as children; and each tied a cloth around his head in Bedouin fashion.

And then: the first pure draughts of desert air, and the nakedness of space, pure as a theorem, stretching away into the sky drenched in all its own silence and majesty, untenanted except by such figures as the imagination of man has invented to people landscapes which are inimical to his passions and whose purity flays the mind.

Narouz gave a shout and the horses, suddenly awoken and filled with a sense of new freedom and space around them, started their peculiar tearing plunging gallop across the dunes, manes and tassels tossing, saddles creaking. They raced like this for many minutes, Nessim giggling with excitement and joy. It was so long since he had ridden at this wild gallop.

But they held it, completing a slow arc eastwards across scrubby land where wild flowers bloomed and butterflies tippled amongst the waste of dunes and the dingy tenacious specimens of plant-life. Their hooves rattled across shingle floors, through stone valleys with great sandstone needles and chines of rosy shale filling in the known horizons. Nessim was busy with his memories of those youthful nights camped out here under a sky hoary with stars, in a booming tent (whose frosted guy-ropes glittered like brilliants) pitched under Vega, the whole desert spread around them like an empty room. How did one come to forget the greatest of one's experiences? It was all lying there like a piano that one could play but which one had somehow forgotten to touch for years. He was irradiated by the visions of his inner eye and followed Narouz blindly. He saw them in all that immensity — two spots like pigeons flying in an empty sky.

They halted for a short rest in the shadow of a great rock — a purple oasis of darkness — panting and happy. 'If we put up a desert wolf' said Narouz 'I'll run it down with my *kurbash*,' and he caressed the great whip lovingly, running it through his fingers.

When they set off again, Narouz started a slow tacking path, questing about for the ancient caravan route — the *masrab* which would take them to the Quasur el Atash (Castles of the Thirsty) where the Sheik's men were due to meet them before noon. Once Nessim too had known these highways by heart — the smugglers' roads which had been used for centuries by the caravans which plied between Algiers and Mecca — the 'bountiful highways' which steered the fortunes of men through the wilderness of the desert, taking spices and stuffs from one part of Africa to another or affording to the pious their only means of reaching the Holy City. He was suddenly jealous of his brother's familiarity with the desert they had once equally owned. He copied him eagerly.

Presently Narouz gave a hoarse shout and pointed and in a little while they came upon the *masrab* — a highway of camel-tracks, deeply worn in some places into solid rock, but running in a wavy series, parallel from horizon to horizon. And here once more the younger brother set the pace. His blue shirt was now stained violet at the armpits. 'Nearly there' he cried, and out of the trembling pearly edges of the sky there swam slowly a high cluster of reddish basalt blocks, carved into the vague semblance (like a face in the fire) of a sphinx tortured by thirst; and there, gibbering in the dark shade of a rock, the little party waited to conduct them to the Sheik's tents — four tall lean men, made of brown paper, whose voices cracked at the edges of meaning with thirst, and whose laughter was like fury unleashed. To them they rode — into the embrace of arms like dry sticks and the thorny clicking of an unfamiliar Arabic in which Narouz did all the talking and explaining.

Nessim waited, feeling suddenly like a European, city-bred, a visitor: for the little party carried with them all the feeling of the tight inbred Arab world — its formal courtesies and feuds — its primitiveness. He surprised himself by seeking in his own mind the memory of a painting by Bonnard or a poem by Blake — as a thirsty man might grope at a spring for water. In such a way might a traveller present himself to some rude mountain clan, admiring their bunioned feet and coarse hairy legs, but grateful too that the sum of European culture was not expressed by their life-hating, unpleasure-loving strength. Here he suddenly lost his brother, parted company with him, for Narouz had plunged into the life of these Arabian herdsmen with the same intensity as he plunged into the life of his land, his trees. The great corded muscles in his hairy body were tense with pride, for he, a city-bred Alexandrian — almost a despised *Nasrany* — could out-shoot, out-talk and out-gallop any of them. On him whose mettle they knew they kept a speculative aboriginal eye; the gentle Nessim they had seen in many guises before, his well-kept hands betrayed a city gentleman. But they were polite.

A knowledge of forms only was necessary now, not insight, for these delightful desert folk were automata; thinking of Mountolive

Nessim smiled suddenly and wondered where the British had found the substance of their myths about the desert Arab. The fierce banality of their lives was so narrow, so regulated. If they stirred one at all it was as the bagpipe can, without expressing anything above the level of the primitive. He watched his brother handle them, simply from a knowledge of their forms of behaviour, as a showman handles dancing fleas. Poor souls! He felt the power and resource of his city-bred intelligence stir in him.

They all rode now in a compact group to the Sheik's tents, down long ribbed inclines of sand, through mirages of pastures which only the rain clouds imagined, until they came there, to the little circle of tents, manhood's skies of hide, invented by men whose childish memories were so fearful they had had perforce to invent a narrower heaven in which to contain the germ of the race; in this little cone of hide the first child was born, the first privacy of the human kiss invented. . . . Nessim wished bitterly that he could paint as well as Clea. Absurd thoughts, and out of place.

But the Sheik's tents were extensive, covering nearly two thousand square feet with a tent-cloth woven of goat-hair in broad stitches of black, green, maroon and white. Long tassels hung down from the seams, playing in the wind.

The Sheik and his sons, like a gallery of playing cards, awaited them with the conventional greetings to which Narouz at least knew every response. The Sheik himself conducted them to a tent saying 'This house is your house; do as you please. We are your servants.' And behind him pressed the water-carriers to bathe their hands and feet and faces — the latter now somewhat dry and blistered by the journey. They rested for at least an hour, for the heat of the day was at full, in that brown darkness. Narouz lay snoring upon the cushions with arms and legs outspread while Nessim dozed fitfully, awakening from time to time to watch him — the effortless progress of sleep which physical surrender to action always brings. He brooded upon his brother's ugliness — the magnificent set of white teeth showing through the pink rent in his upper lip. From time to time, too, as they rested, the headmen of the tribe called noiselessly, taking off their shoes at the entrance of the tent, to enter and kiss Nessim's hand. Each uttered the single word of welcome '*Mahubbah*' in a whisper.

It was late in the afternoon when Narouz woke and calling for water doused his body down, asking at the same time for a change of clothes which were at once brought to him by the Sheik's eldest son. He strode out into the heat of the sand saying: 'Now for the colt. It may take a couple of hours? You won't mind? We'll be back a bit late, eh?' Cushions had been set for them in the shade and here Nessim was glad to recline and watch his brother moving quickly across the dazzle of sand towards a group of colts which had been driven up for him to examine.

They played gracefully and innocently, the tossing of their heads and manes seeming to him 'like the surf of the June sea' as the proverb has it. Narouz stopped keenly as he neared them, watching. Then he shouted something and a man raced out to him with a bridle and bit. 'The white one' he cried hoarsely and the Sheik's sons shouted a response which Nessim did not catch. Narouz turned again, and softly with a queer ducking discretion, slipped in among the young creatures and almost before one could think was astride a white colt after having bridled it with a single almost invisible gesture.

The mythical creature stood quite still, its eyes wide and lustrous as if fully to comprehend this tremendous new intelligence of a rider upon its back, then a slow shudder rippled through its flesh — the tides of the panic which always greets such a collision of human and animal worlds. Horse and rider stood as if posing for a statue, buried in thought.

Now the animal suddenly gave a low whistling cry of fear, shook itself and completed a dozen curious arching jumps, stiffly as a mechanical toy, coming down savagely on its forelegs each time with the downthrust. This did not dislodge Narouz who only leaned forward and growled something in its ear that drove it frantic for it now set off at a ragged plunging tossing canter, turning and curvetting and ducking. They made a slow irregular circle round the tents until at last they came back to where the crowd of Arabs stood at the doorway of the main tent, watching silently. And now the poor creature, as if aware that some great portion of its real life — its childhood perhaps — was irrevocably over, gave another low whistling groan and broke suddenly into the long tireless flying gallop of its breed, aimed like a shooting-star to pierce the very sky, and whirled away across the dunes with its rider secured to it by the powerful scissors of his legs — firm as a figure held by ringbolts — diminishing rapidly in size until both were lost to sight. A great cry of approval went up from the tents and Nessim accepted, besides the curd cheese and coffee, the compliments which were his brother's due.

Two hours later Narouz brought her back, glistening with sweat, dejected, staggering, with only enough fight in her to blow dejectedly and stamp, conquered. But he himself was deliriously exhausted, dazed as if he had ridden through an oven, while his bloodshot eyes and drawn twitching face testified to the severity of the fight. The endearments he uttered to the horse came from between parched and cracked lips. But he was happy underneath it all — indeed radiant — as he croaked for water and begged leave of half an hour's rest before they should set out once more on the homeward journey. Nothing could finally tire that powerful body — not even the orgasm he had experienced in long savage battle. But closing his eyes now as he felt the water pouring over his head, he saw again the dark bleeding sun which shimmered behind their lids, image of fatigue, and felt the desert glare parching and cracking the water on his very skin. His mind was a jumble of sharp stabbing colours and apprehensions — as if the whole sensory apparatus had melted in the heat like a colour-box, fusing thought and wish and desire. He was light-headed with joy and felt as unsubstantial as a rainbow. Yet in less than half an hour he was ready for the journey back.

They set off with a different escort this time across the inclining rays of sunlight which threw their rose and purple shadows into the sockets of the dunes. They made good time to the Quasur el Atash. Narouz had made arrangements for the white colt to be delivered him later in the week by the Chief's sons, and he rode at ease now, occasionally singing a stave or two of a song. Darkness fell as they reached the Castles of the Thirsty and having said good-bye to their hosts set off once more across the desert.

They rode slowly at ease, watching the brindled waning moon come up on a silence broken only by the sudden stammer of their horses' hooves on a shingle bed, or the far-away ululations of jackals, and now, quite suddenly, Nessim found the barrier lifted and was able to say: 'Narouz, I am going to be married. I want you to tell Leila for me. I don't know why but I feel shy about it.'

For a minute Narouz felt himself turned to ice — a figure in a coat of mail; he seemed to sway in his saddle as with a delight so forced and hollow that it made his voice snap off short he crabbed out the words: 'To Clea, Nessim? To Clea?' feeling the blood come rushing back to his ticking nerves when his brother shook his head and stared curiously at him. 'No. Why? To Arnauti's ex-wife' replied Nessim with a controlled, a classical precision of utterance. They rode on with creaking saddles and Narouz, who was now grinning to himself with relief, cried 'I am so happy, Nessim! At last! You will be happy and have children.'

But here Nessim's mortal shyness overcame him again and he told Narouz all that he had learned about Justine and about the loss of her child, adding: 'She does not love me now, and does not pretend to: but who knows? If I can get her child back and give her some peace of mind and security, anything is possible.' He added after a moment 'Don't you think?' not because he wished for an opinion on the matter but simply to bridge the silence which poured in between them like a drifting dune. 'As for the child, it is difficult. The Parquet have investigated as best they could — and what little evidence they have points to *Magzub* (the Inspired One); there was a festival in the town that evening and he was there. He has been several times accused of kidnapping children but the case has always been dropped for lack of evidence.' Narouz pricked up his ears and bristled like a wolf. 'You mean the hypnotist?' Nessim said thoughtfully: 'I have sent to offer him a large sum of money — very large indeed — for what I want to know. Do you see?' Narouz shook his head doubtfully and picked at his short beard. 'He is the one who is mad' he said. 'He used to come to St Damiana every year. But strange-mad. *Zein-el-Abdin*. He is holy too.'

'That is the one' said Nessim; and as if struck by an afterthought Narouz reined both horses and embraced him, uttering the conventional congratulations in the family tongue. Nessim smiled and said: 'You will tell Leila? Please, my brother.'

'Of course.'

'After I have gone?'

'Of course.'

With the release of this tension and Narouz' ready compliance Nessim suddenly felt a load lifted from his mind. And correspondingly he suddenly felt very tired and on the point of sleep. They travelled briskly but without haste and it was towards midnight when they came once more within sight of the desert's edge. Here the horses put up a startled hare and Narouz made an attempt to ride it down with his whip but he missed it in the half-darkness.

'It is very good news' he cried on returning to Nessim's side, as if the little gallop across the moonlit dunes had given him all the time and detachment he needed to come to a considered opinion. 'Will you bring her to us next week — to Leila? I think I must have met her but cannot remember. Very dark? "A firefly's light in

darkness for such eyes" as the song goes?' He laughed his downward laugh.

Nessim yawned sleepily. 'Ach! my bones ache. That is what I
get for living in Alexandria. Narouz, before I fall asleep there was
one other thing I meant to ask you. I have not seen Pursewarden.
The meetings?'

Narouz drew a hissing inward breath and turned his bright eyes
to his brother, saying 'Yes. Very well. The next one is to be at the
mulid of St Damiana, in the desert.' He flexed the great muscles of
his shoulders. 'The whole ten families are coming — can you
believe it?'

'You will be careful' said his brother 'to see that everything is
done privately and there are no leaks.'

'Of course!' he cried.

'I mean' said Nessim 'that in the early stages this should not have
a political character. It must grow slowly with the understanding
of the matter. Eh? I do not think, for example, it is necessary for
you to actually speak to them, but rather to discuss. We can't risk.
You see, it is not only the British.'

Narouz jaunted a leg impatiently and picked his teeth. He
thought of Mountolive and sighed.

'It is also the French — and they are at cross-purposes. If we
are to use them both. . . .'

'I know, I know' said Narouz impatiently. Nessim looked at him
keenly. 'Attend' he said sharply, 'for much depends on your understanding just how far we can go at this stage.'

His reproof crushed Narouz. He flushed and joined his hands
together as he looked at his brother. 'I do' he said in a low hoarse
voice. Nessim at once felt ashamed of himself and took his arm. He
went on in his low confiding tone.

'You see, there are mysterious leaks from time to time. Old
Cohen, for example, the furrier who died last month. He was working for the French in Syria. On his return, the Egyptians knew all
about his mission. How? Nobody knows. Among our friends we
certainly have enemies — in Alexandria itself. Do you see?'

'I see.'

The next morning it was time for Nessim to return and the two
brothers rode out across the fields at a leisurely pace to the point
of rendezvous at the ferry. 'Why do you never come into the town?'
said Nessim. 'Come with me today. There's a ball at the Randidis'.
You'd enjoy it as a change.' Narouz as always wore a hang-dog

expression when anyone suggested an excursion into the city. 'I shall come at Carnival' he said slowly, looking at the ground, and his brother laughed and touched his arm. 'I knew you'd say that! Always, once a year at Carnival. I wonder why!'

But he knew; Narouz' mortal shyness about his hare-lip had driven him into a seclusion almost as unbroken as that of his mother. Only the black domino of the carnival balls permitted him to disguise the face he had come to loathe so much that he could no longer bear to see it even in a shaving-mirror. At the carnival ball he felt free. And yet there was another and indeed unexpected reason — a passion for Clea which had lasted for years now; for a Clea to whom he had never spoken, and indeed only twice seen when she came down with Nessim to ride on the estate. This was a secret which could not have been dragged out of him under torture, but to every carnival dance he came and drifted about in the crowd hoping vaguely that he might by accident meet this young woman whose name he had never uttered aloud to anyone until that day.

(He did not know that Clea loathed the carnival season and spent the time quietly drawing and reading in her studio.)

They parted now with a warm embrace and Nessim's car scribbled its pennants of dust across the warm air of the fields, eager to regain the coast road once more. A battleship in the basin was firing a twenty-one gun salute, in honour perhaps of some Egyptian dignitary, and the explosions appeared to make the clouds of pearl which always overhung the harbour in spring, tremble and change colour. The sea was high today, and four fishing-boats tacked furiously towards the town harbour with their catch. Nessim stopped only once, to buy himself a carnation for his buttonhole from the flower-vendor on the corner of Saad Zagloul. Then he went to his office, pausing to have his shoe-shine on the way up. The city had never seemed more beautiful to him. Sitting at his desk he thought of Leila and then of Justine. What would his mother have to say about his decision?

Narouz walked out to the summer-house that morning to discharge his mission; but first he picked a mass of blooms from the red and yellow roses with which to refill the two great vases which stood on either side of his father's portrait. His mother was asleep at her desk but the noise he made lifting the latch woke her at once. The snake hissed drowsily and then lowered its head to the ground once more.

'Bless you, Narouz' she said as she saw the flowers and rose at once to empty her vases. As they started to trim and arrange the new blooms, Narouz broke the news of his brother's marriage. His mother stood quite still for a long time, undisturbed but serious as if she were consulting her own inmost thoughts and emotions. At last she said, more to herself than anyone, 'Why not?' repeating the phrase once or twice as if testing its pitch.

Then she bit her thumb and turning to her younger son said 'But if she is an adventuress, after his money, I won't have it. I shall take steps to have her done away with. He needs my permission anyhow.'

Narouz found this overwhelmingly funny and gave an appreciative laugh. She took his hairy arm between her fingers. 'I will' she said.

'Please.'

'I swear it.'

He laughed now until he showed the pink roof of his mouth. But she remained abstracted, still listening to an inner monologue. Absently she patted his arm as he laughed and whispered 'Hush'; and then after a long pause she said, as if surprised by her own thoughts. 'The strange thing is, I mean it.'

'And you can't count on me, eh?' he said, still laughing but with the germ of seriousness in his words. 'You can't trust me to watch over my own brother's honour.' He was still swollen up toad-like by the laughter, though his expression had now become serious. 'My God' she thought, 'how ugly he is.' And her fingers went to the black veil, pressing through it to the rough cicatrices in her own complexion, touching them fiercely as if to smooth them out.

'My good Narouz' she said, almost tearfully, and ran her fingers through his hair; the wonderful poetry of the Arabic stirred and soothed him in one. 'My honeycomb, my dove, my good Narouz. Tell him yes, with my embrace. Tell him yes.'

He stood still, trembling like a colt, and drinking in the music of her voice and the rare caresses of that warm and capable hand.

'But tell him he must bring her here to us.'

'I will.'

'Tell him today.'

And he walked with his queer jerky sawing stride to the telephone in the old house. His mother sat at her dusty table and repeated twice in a low puzzled tone: 'Why should Nessim choose a Jewess?'

V

So much have I reconstructed from the labyrinth of notes which Balthazar has left me. 'To imagine is not necessarily to invent' he says elsewhere, 'nor dares one make a claim for omniscience in interpreting people's actions. One assumes that they have grown out of their feelings as leaves grow out of a branch. But can one work backwards, deducing the one form from the other? Perhaps a writer could if he were sufficiently brave to cement these apparent gaps in our actions with interpretations of his own to bind them together? What was going on in Nessim's mind? This is really a question for you to put to yourself.

'Or in Justine's for that matter? One really doesn't know; all I can say is that their esteem for each other grew in inverse ratio to their regard — for there never by common consent was any love between them as I have shown you. Perhaps it is as well. But in all the long discussions I had with them separately, I could not find the key to a relationship which failed signally — one could see it daily sinking as land sinks, as the level of a lake might sink, and not know why. The surface colouring was brilliantly executed and so perfect as to deceive most observers like yourself, for example. Nor do I share Leila's view — who never liked Justine. I sat beside her at the presentation which Narouz organized at the great *mulid* of Abu Girg which falls towards Easter every year. Justine had by then renounced Judaism to become a Copt in obedience to Nessim's wish, and as he could only marry her privately since she had already once been married, Narouz had to be content with a party which would present her to the great house and its dependants whose lives he was always anxious to cement into the family pattern.

'For four days then a huge encampment of tents and marquees grew up around the house — carpets and chandeliers and brilliant decorations. Alexandria was stripped bare of hothouse flowers and not less of its great social figures who made the somewhat mocking journey down to Abu Girg (nothing excites so much mocking amusement in the city as a fashionable wedding) to pay their respects and congratulate Leila. Local mudirs and sheiks, peasants

275

innumerable, dignitaries from near and far had flocked in to be entertained — while the Bedouin, whose tribal grounds fringed the estate, gave magnificent displays of horsemanship, galloping round and round the house firing their guns — for all the world as if Justine were a young bride — a virgin. Imagine the smiles of Athena Trasha, of the Cervonis! And old Abu Kar himself rode up the steps of the house on his white Arab and into the very reception-rooms with a bowl of flowers.

'As for Leila, she never for one moment took those clever eyes off Justine. She followed her with care like someone studying a historical figure. "Is she not lovely?" I asked as I followed her glance and she turned a quick bird-like glance in my direction before turning back to the subject of her absorbed study. "We are old friends, Balthazar, and I can talk to you. I was telling myself that she looked something like I did once, and that she is an adventuress; like a small dark snake coiled up at the centre of Nessim's life." I protested in a formal manner at this; she stared into my eyes for a long moment and then gave a slow chuckle. I was surprised by what she said next. "Yes, she is just like me — merciless in the pursuit of pleasure and yet arid — all her milk has turned into power-love. Yet she is also like me in that she is tender and kindly and a real man's woman. I hate her because she is like me, do you understand? And I fear her because she can read my mind." She began to laugh. "My darling" she called out to Justine, "come over here and sit by me." And she thrust upon her the one sort of confectionery she herself most loathed — crystallized violets — which I saw Justine accept with reserve — for she loathed them too. And so the two of them sat there, the veiled sphinx and the unveiled, eating sugar violets which neither could bear. I was delighted to be able to see women at their most primitive like this. Nor can I tell you very much about the validity of such judgements. We all make them about each other.

'The curious thing was, that despite this antipathy between the two women — the antipathy of affinity, you might say — there sprang up side by side with it a strange sympathy, a sense of identification with each other. For example when Leila at last dared to meet Mountolive it was done secretly and arranged by Justine. It was Justine who brought them together, both masked, during the carnival ball. Or so I heard.

'As for Nessim, I would, at the risk of over-simplification, say something like this: he was so innocent that he had not realized that you cannot live with a woman without in some degree falling in love with her — that possession is nine points of the jealousy? He was dismayed and terrified by the extent of his own jealousy for Justine and was honestly trying to practise something new for him — indifference. True or false? I don't know.

'And then, turning the coin round, I would say that what irked Justine herself unexpectedly was to find that the contract of wife undertaken so rationally, and at the level of a financial bargain, was somehow more binding than a wedding ring. One does not, as a woman (if passion seems to sanction it) think twice about being unfaithful to a husband; but to be unfaithful to Nessim seemed like stealing money from the till. What would you say?'

My own feeling (*pace* Balthazar) is that Justine became slowly aware of something hidden in the character of this solitary endearing long-suffering man; namely a jealousy all the more terrible and indeed dangerous for never allowing itself any outlet. Sometimes ... but here I am in danger of revealing confidences which Justine made to me during the period of the so-called love affair which so much wounded me and in which, as I learn now, she was only using me as a cover for other activities. I have described the progress of it all elsewhere; but if I were now to reveal all she told me of Nessim in her own words I should be in danger, primo, of setting down material perhaps distasteful to the reader and indeed unfair to Nessim himself. Secundo: I am not sure any more of its relative truth since it might have been part of the whole grand design of deception! In my own mind even those feelings ('important lessons learned' etc.) are all coloured by the central doubt which the Interlinear has raised in my mind. 'Truth is what most contradicts itself...'! What a farce it all is!

But what he says of the jealousy of Nessim must be true, however, for I lived for a while in its shadow, and there is no doubt about the effect it had on Justine. Almost from the beginning she had found herself followed, kept under surveillance, and very naturally this gave her a feeling of uncertainty: uncertainty made terrible by the fact that Nessim never openly spoke of it. It rested, an invisible weight of suspicion dogging and discolouring her commonest remarks, the most innocent of after-dinner walks. He would sit between the tall candles gently smiling at her while a whole silent inquisition unrolled reverberating in his mind. So at least she said.

The simplest and most sincere actions — a visit to a public

library, a shopping list, a message on a place-card — became baffling to the eye of a jealousy founded in emotional impotence. Nessim was torn to rags by her demands; she was torn to rags by the doubts she saw reflected in his eyes — by the very tenderness with which he put a wrap around her shoulders. It felt as if he were slipping a noose over her neck. In a queer sort of way this relationship echoed the psycho-analytic relationship described in *Moeurs* by her first husband — where Justine became for them all a Case rather than a person, chased almost out of her right mind by the tiresome inquisitions of those who never know when to leave ill alone. Yes, she had fallen into a trap, there is no doubt. The thought echoed in her mind like mad laughter. I hear it echo still.

So they went on side by side, like runners perfectly matched, offering to Alexandria what seemed the perfect pattern of a relationship all envied and none could copy. Nessim the indulgent, the uxorious, Justine the lovely and contented wife.

'In his own way' notes Balthazar 'I suppose he was only hunting for the truth. Isn't this becoming rather a ridiculous remark? We should drop it by common consent! It is after all such an odd business. Shall I give you yet another example from another quarter? Your account of Capodistria's death on the lake is the version which we all of us accepted at the time as likely to be true: in our minds, of course.

'But in the Police depositions, everyone concerned mentioned one particular thing — namely that when they raised his body from the lake in which it was floating, with the black patch beside it in the water, his false teeth fell into the boat with a clatter, and startled them all. Now listen to this: three months later I was having dinner with Pierre Balbz who was his dentist. He assured me that Da Capo had an almost perfect set of teeth and certainly no false teeth which could possibly have fallen out. Who then was it? I don't know. And if Da Capo simply disappeared and arranged for some decoy to take his place, he had every reason: leaving behind him debts of over two million. Do you see what I mean?

'Fact is unstable by its very nature. Narouz once said to me that he loved the desert because there "the wind blew out one's footsteps like candle-flames". So it seems to me does reality. How then can we hunt for the truth?'

* * * * *

Pombal was hovering between diplomatic tact and the low cunning of a provincial public prosecutor; the conflicting emotions played upon his fat face as he sat in his gout-chair with his fingers joined. He had the air of a man in complete agreement with himself. 'They say' he said, watching me keenly 'that you are now in the British *Deuxième*. Eh? Don't tell me, I know you can't speak. Nor can I if you ask me about myself. You *think* you know that I am in the French — but I deny the whole thing most strenuously. What I am asking is whether I should have you living in the flat. It seems somehow . . . how do you say? . . . Box and Cox. No? I mean, why don't we sell each other ideas, eh? I know you won't. Neither will I. Our sense of honour . . . I mean only *if* we are in the . . . ahem. But of course, you deny it and I deny it. So we are not. But you are not too proud to share my women, eh? *Autre chose.* Have a drink eh? The gin bottle is over there. I hid it from Hamid. Of course. I know that something is going on. I don't despair of finding out. Something . . . I wish I knew . . . Nessim, Capodistria . . . Well!'

'What have you done to your face?' I say to change the subject. He has recently started to grow a moustache. He holds on to it defensively as if my question constituted a threat to shave it off forcibly. 'My moustache, ah that! Well, recently I have had so many reproofs about work, not attending to it, that I analysed myself deeply, *au fond*. Do you know how many man-hours I am losing through women? You will never guess. I thought a moustache (isn't it hideous?) would put them off a bit, but no. It is just the same. It is a tribute, dear boy, not to my charm but to the low standards here. They seem to love me because there is nothing better. They love a well-hung diplomat — how do you say, *faisandé*? Why do you laugh? You are losing a lot of woman-hours too. But then you have the British Government behind you — the pound, eh? That girl was here again today. *Mon Dieu*, so thin and so uncared for! I offered her some lunch but she would not stay. And the mess in your room! She takes hashish, doesn't she? Well, when I go to Syria on leave you can have the whole place. Provided you respect my firescreen — isn't it good as for art, *hein?*'

He has had an immense and vivid firescreen made for the flat which bears the legend 'LEGERETE, FATALITE, MATERNITE' in poker-work.

'Ah well' he continues, 'so much for art in Alexandria. But as for that Justine, that is a better barbarian for you, no? I bet she — eh? Don't tell. Why are you not happier about it? You Englishmen, always gloomy and full of politics. *Pas de remords, mon cher.* Two women in tandem — who would want better? And one Left-Handed — as Da Capo calls Lesbians. You know Justine's reputation? Well, for my part, I am renouncing the whole——'

So Pombal flows in great good humour over the shallow river bed of his experience and standing on the balcony I watch the sky darkening over the harbour and hear the sullen hooting of ships' sirens, emphasizing our loneliness here, our isolation from the warm Gulf Stream of European feelings and ideas. All the currents slide away towards Mecca or to the incomprehensible desert and the only foothold in this side of the Mediterranean is the city we have come to inhabit and hate, to infect with our own self-contempts.

And then I see Melissa walk down the street and my heart contracts with pity and joy as I turn to open the flat door.

*   *   *   *   *

These quiet bemused island days are a fitting commentary to the thoughts and feelings of one walking alone on deserted beaches, or doing the simple duties of a household which lacks a mother. But I carry now the great Interlinear in my hand wherever I go, whether cooking or teaching the child to swim, or cutting wood for the fireplace. But these fictions all live on as a projection of the white city itself whose pearly skies are broken in spring only by the white stalks of the minarets and the flocks of pigeons turning in clouds of silver and amethyst; whose veridian and black marble harbour-water reflects the snouts of foreign men-of-war turning through their slow arcs, depicting the prevailing wind; or swallowing their own inky reflections, touching and overlapping like the very tongues and sects and races over which they keep their uneasy patrol: symbolizing the western consciousness whose power is exemplified in steel — those sullen preaching guns against the yellow metal of the lake and the town which breaks open at sunset like a rose.

*   *   *   *   *

PART II

VI

'Pursewarden!' writes Balthazar.

'I won't say that you have been less than just to him — only that he does not seem to resurrect on paper into a recognizable image of the man I knew. He seems to be a sort of enigma to you. (It is not enough, perhaps, to respect a man's genius — one must love him a little, no?) It may have been the envy you speak of which blinded you to his qualities, but somehow I doubt it; it seems to me to be very hard to envy someone who was so single-minded and moreover such a simpleton in so many ways, as to make him a real original (for example: money terrified him). I admit that I regarded him as a great man, a real original, and I knew him well — even though I have never, to this day, read a single book of his, not even the last trilogy which made such a noise in the world, though I pretend to have done so in company. I have dipped here and there. I feel I don't need to read more.

'I put down a few notes upon him here then, not to contradict you, wise one, but simply to let you compare two dissimilar images. But if you are wrong about him, you are not less wrong than Pombal who always credited him with an *humour noir* so dear to the French heart. But there was no spleen in the man and his apparent world-weariness was not feigned; while his cruelties of tongue were due to his complete simplicity and a not always delightful sense of mischief. Pombal never recovered I think from being nicknamed "*Le Prépuce Barbu*"; and if you will forgive me neither did you from Pursewarden's criticism of your own novels. Remember? "These books have a curious and rather forbidding streak of cruelty — a lack of humanity which puzzled me at first. But it is simply the way a sentimentalist would disguise his weakness. Cruelty here is the obverse of sentimentality. He wounds because he is afraid of going all squashy." Of course, you are right in saying that he was contemptous of your love of Melissa — and the nickname he gave you must have wounded also, suiting as it did your initials (Lineaments of Gratified Desire). "There goes old Lineaments in his dirty mackintosh." A poor joke, I know. But all this is not very real.

'I am turning out a drawer full of old mementoes and notes to-day in order to think about him a bit on paper; it is a holiday and the clinic is closed. It is risky work, I know, but perhaps I can answer a question which you must have put to yourself when you read the opening pages of the Interlinear: "How could Purse-warden and Justine . . . ?" I know.

'He had been in Alexandria before twice, before he met us all, and had once spent a winter at Mazarita working on a book: but this time he came back to do a short course of lectures at the Atelier, and as Nessim and I and Clea were on the committee, he could not avoid the side of Alexandrian life which most delighted and depressed him.

'Physical features, as best I remember them. He was fair, a good average height and strongly built though not stout. Brown hair and moustache — very small this. Extremely well-kept hands. A good smile though when not smiling his face wore a somewhat quizzical almost impertinent air. His eyes were hazel and the best feature of him — they looked into other eyes, into other ideas, with a real candour, rather a terrifying sort of lucidity. He was some-what untidy in dress but always spotlessly clean of person and abhorred dirty nails and collars. Yes, but his clothes were some-times stained with spots of the red ink in which he wrote. There!

'Really, I think his sense of humour had separated him from the world, into a privacy of his own, or else he had discovered for him-self the uselessness of having opinions and in consequence made a habit of usually saying the opposite of what he thought in a joking way. He was an ironist, hence he appeared often to violate good sense: hence too his equivocal air, the apparent frivolity with which he addressed himself to large subjects. This sort of serious clown-ing leaves footmarks in conversation of a peculiar kind. His little sayings stayed like the pawmarks of a cat in a pat of butter. To stupidities he would respond only with the word "*kwatz*".

'He believed, I think, that success was inherent in greatness. His own lack of financial success (he made very little money from his work, contrary to what you thought, and it all went to his wife and two children who lived in England) was inclined to make him doubt his powers. Perhaps he should have been born an American? I don't know.

'I remember going down to the dock to meet his boat with the panting Keats — who proposed to interview him. We were late and only caught up with him as he was filling in an immigration form. Against the column marked "religion" he had written *"Protestant — purely in the sense that I protest."*

'We took him for a drink so that Keats could interview him at leisure. The poor boy was absolutely nonplussed. Pursewarden had a particular smile for the Press. I still have the picture Keats took that morning. The sort of smile which might have hardened on the face of a dead baby. Later I got to know this smile and learned that it meant he was about to commit an outrage on accepted good sense with an irony. He was trying to amuse no-one but himself, mind you. Keats panted and puffed, looked "sincere" and probed, but all in vain. Later I asked him for a carbon copy of his interview which he typed out and gave me with his puzzled air, explaining that there was no "news" in the man. Pursewarden had said things like "It is the duty of every patriot to hate his country creatively" and "England cries out for brothels"; this last somewhat shocked poor Keats who asked him if he felt that "unbridled licence" would be a good thing in England. Did Pursewarden want to undermine religion?

'I can see as I write the wicked air with which my friend replied in shocked tones: "Good Lord, no! I would simply like to put an end to the cruelty to children which is such a distressing feature of English life — as well as the slavish devotion to pets which borders on the obscene." Keats must have gulped his way through all this, dotting and dashing in his shorthand book with rolling eye, while Pursewarden studied the further horizon. But if the journalist found this sort of exchange enigmatic, he was doubly puzzled by some of the answers to his political questions. For example, when he asked Pursewarden what he thought of the Conference of the Arab Committee which was due to start in Cairo that day, he replied: "When the English feel they are in the wrong, their only recourse is to cant." "Am I to understand that you are criticizing British policy?" "Of course not. Our statesmanship is impeccable." Keats fanned himself all the harder and abandoned politics forthwith. In answer to the question "Are you planning to write a novel while you are here?" Pursewarden said: "If I am denied every other means of self-gratification."

'Later Keats, poor fellow, still fanning that pink brow, said "He's a thorny bastard, isn't he?" But the odd thing was that he wasn't at all. Where can a man who really thinks take refuge in the so-called real world without defending himself against stupidity by the constant exercise of equivocation? Tell me that. Particularly a poet. He once said: "Poets are not really serious about ideas or people. They regard them much as a Pasha regards the members of an extensive *harim*. They are pretty, yes. They are for use. But there is no question of them being true or false, or having souls. In this way the poet preserves his freshness of vision, and finds everything miraculous. And this is what Napoleon meant when he described poetry as a *science creuse*. He was quite right from his own point of view."

'This robust mind was far from splenetic though its judgements were harsh. I have seen him so moved in describing Joyce's encroaching blindness and D. H. Lawrence's illness that his hand shook and he turned pale. He showed me once a letter from the latter in which Lawrence had written: "*In you I feel a sort of profanity — almost a hate for the tender growing quick in things, the dark Gods. . . .*" He chuckled. He deeply loved Lawrence but had no hesitation in replying on a post-card: "*My dear DHL. This side idolatry — I am simply trying not to copy your habit of building a Taj Mahal around anything as simple as a good f———k.*"

'He said to Pombal once: "*On fait l'amour pour mieux refouler et pour décourager les autres.*" And added: "I worry a great deal about my golf handicap." It always took Pombal a few moments to work out these non-sequiturs. "*Quel malin, ce type-là!*" he would mutter under his breath. Then and only then would Pursewarden permit himself a chuckle — having scored his personal victory. They were a splendid pair and used to drink together a great deal.

'Pombal was terribly affected by his death — really overcome, he retired to bed for a fortnight. Could not speak of him without tears coming into his eyes; this used to infuriate Pombal himself. "I never knew how much I loved the blasted man" he would say. . . . I hear Pursewarden's wicked chuckle in all this. No, you are wrong about him. His favourite adjective was "uffish!" or so he told me.

'His public lectures were disappointing, as you may remember. Afterwards, I discovered why. He read them out of a book. They were someone else's lectures! But once when I took him up to the Jewish school and asked him to talk to the children of the literary group, he was delightful. He began by showing them some card tricks and then congratulated the winner of the Literary Prize, making him read the prize essay aloud. Then he asked the children to write down three things in their notebooks which might help them some day if they didn't forget them. Here they are:

1. Each of our five senses contains an art.
2. In questions of art great secrecy must be observed.
3. The artist must catch every scrap of wind.

'Then he produced from his mackintosh pocket a huge packet of sweets upon which they all fell, he no less, and completed the most successful literary hour ever held at the school.

'He had some babyish habits, picked his nose, and enjoyed taking his shoes off under the table in a restaurant. I remember hundreds of meetings which were made easy and fruitful by his naturalness and humour but he spared no-one and made enemies. He wrote once to his beloved DHL: "*Maître, Maître, watch your step. No-one can go on being a rebel too long without turning into an autocrat.*"

'When he wished to discuss a bad work of art he would say in tones of warm approbation "Most effective." This was a feint. He was not interested enough in art to want to argue about it with others ("dogs snuffing over a bitch too small to mount") so he said "Most effective." Once when he was drunk he added: "The effective in art is what rapes the emotion of your audience without nourishing its values."

'Do you see? Do you see?

'All this was brought to bear on Justine like a great charge of swan-shot, scattering her senses and bringing her for the first time something she had despaired of ever encountering: namely laughter. Imagine what one touch of ridicule can do to a Higher Emotion! "As for Justine" said Pursewarden to me when he was drunk once, "I regard her as a tiresome old sexual turnstile through which presumably we must all pass — a somewhat vulpine Alexandrian Venus. By God, what a woman she would be if she were really natural and felt no guilt! Her behaviour would commend her to the Pantheon — but one cannot send her up there with a mere recommendation from the Rabbinate — a bundle of Old Testament ravings. What would old Zeus say?" He saw my reproachful glance at these cruelties and said, somewhat shamefacedly. "I'm sorry, Balthazar. I simply dare not take her seriously. One day I will tell you why."

'Justine herself wished very much to take him seriously but he absolutely refused to command sympathy or share the solitude from which he drew so much of his composure and self-possession.

'Justine herself, you know, could not bear to be alone.

'He was due, I remember, to lecture in Cairo to several societies affiliated to our own Arts Society, and Nessim, who was busy, asked Justine to take him down by car. That was how they came to find themselves together on a journey which threw up a sort of ludicrous shadow-image of a love-relationship, like a clever magic-lantern picture of a landscape, created by, strangely — not Justine at all — but a worse mischief-maker — the novelist himself. "It was Punch and Judy, all right!" said Pursewarden ruefully afterwards.

'He was at that time deeply immersed in the novel he was writing, and as always he found that his ordinary life, in a distorted sort of way, was beginning to follow the curvature of his book. He explained this by saying that any concentration of the will displaces life (Archimedes' bath-water) and gives it bias in motion. Reality, he believed, was always trying to copy the imagination of man, from which it derived. You will see from this that he was a serious fellow underneath much of his clowning and had quite comprehensive beliefs and ideas. But also, he had been drinking rather heavily that day as he always did when he was working. Between books he never touched a drop. Riding beside her in the great car, someone beautiful, dark and painted with great eyes like the prow of some Aegean ship, he had the sensation that his book was being rapidly passed underneath his life, as if under a sheet of paper containing the iron filings of temporal events, as a magnet is in that commonplace experiment one does at school: and somehow setting up a copying magnetic field.

'He never flirted, mind you; and if he started to approach Justine it was simply to try out a few speeches and attitudes, to verify certain conclusions he had reached in the book before actually sending it to the printer, so to speak! Afterwards, of course, he bitterly repented of this piece of self-indulgence. He was at that moment trying to escape from the absurd dictates of narrative form in prose: "He said" "She said" "He cocked an eye, shot a cuff, lifted a lazy head, etc." Was it possible, had he succeeded in "realizing" character without the help of such props? He was asking himself this as he sat there in the sand. ("Her eyelashes brushed his cheek." *Merde alors!* Had he written that?) Justine's thick black eyelashes were like . . . what? So it was that his kisses were really warm and wholehearted in an absent-minded way because they were in no way meant for her. (One of the great paradoxes of love. Concentration on the love-object and possession are the poisons.) And he discovered to her the fact that she was ridiculous, with a series of disarming and touching pleasantries at which she found herself laughing with a relief that seemed almost sinful. As for her: it was not only that his skin and hair were fresh and that his love-making was full of a lazy, unblushing enterprise; he was wholly himself in a curious way. It aroused in her an unfamiliar passionate curiosity. And then, the things he said! "Of course I've read *Moeurs* and had you pointed out a hundred times as the tragic central character. It's all right, written by a born *lettré*, of course, and smells fashionably of armpits and *eau de javel*. But surely you are making yourself a little self-important about it all? You have the impertinence to foist yourself on us as a problem — perhaps because you have nothing else to offer? It is foolish. Or perhaps it is that the Jew loves punishment and always comes back for more?" And suddenly, but completely, to take her firmly by the nape of the neck and force her down into the hot sand before she could find time to measure the extent of the insult or form a response in her mind. And then, while he was still kissing, to say something so ludicrous that the laughter and tears in her mind became one and the same sort of things, a mixture of qualities hard to endure.

' "For God's sake!" she said, having decided to behave as if outraged. He had been too quick for her. He had surprised her while she was half-asleep in her mind, so to speak.

' "Didn't you want to make love? My mistake!"

'She looked at him, a little disarmed by the mock-repentance of his expression. "No, of course not. Yes." Something inside her repeated "Yes, yes." An attachment without fingerprints — something as easy as sailing a boat or driving into deep water: "Fool!" she cried, and to her own surprise started laughing. A conquest by impudence? I don't know. I am only putting down my own views.

'She explained this to herself later by saying that for him sex was the nearest thing to laughter — quite free of particularity, neither sacred nor profane. Pursewarden himself has written that he thought it comic and sinister and divine in one. But she could not grasp and define the thing as she wished, for when she said to him "You are hopelessly promiscuous, like I am" he was really angry, really outraged. "Imbecile" he replied, "you have the soul of a clerk. For those who love poetry there is no such thing as *vers libre*." She did not understand this.

' "Oh, stop behaving like a pious old sin-cushion into which we all have to stick rusty pins of our admiration" he snapped. In his diary he added drily: "Moths are attracted by the flame of personality. So are vampires. Artists should take note and beware." And in the mirror he cursed himself roundly for this lapse, a self-indulgence which had brought him what most bored him — an intimate relationship. But in the sleeping face he too saw the childish inhabitant of Justine, the "calcimined imprint of a fern in chalk". He saw how she must have looked on the first night of love — hair torn and trailing over the pillow like a ruffled black dove, fingers like tendrils, warm mouth inhaling the airs of sleep; warm as a figure of pastry fresh from the oven. "Oh damn!" he cried aloud.

'Then in bed with her in a hotel crowded with Alexandrian acquaintances who might easily observe their rashness and carry their gossip back to the city they had left together that morning, he swore again. Pursewarden had much to hide, you know. He was not all he seemed. And at this time he did not dare to prejudice his relations with Nessim. The Bloody woman! I hear his voice.

' "*Ecoute. . . .*"

' "*Rien — silence.*"

' "*Mais chéri, nous sommes seuls.*" She was still sleepy. Cast an eye to a bolted door. She felt a momentary disgust at this bourgeois fear of his; afraid of intruders, spies, a husband?

' "*Qu'est-ce que c'est?*"

' "*Je m'écoute moi-même.*" Yellow eyes without a trace of discernible divinity in them; he was like a slender rock-god, with ruffled moustache. Past lives? "*Le coeur qui bat.*" Derisively he quoted a popular song.

' "*Tu n'es pas une femme pour moi — pas dans mon genre.*"

'This made her feel like a whipped dog specially as a moment ago he had been kissing her, breaking her down into successive images of pain and pleasure with an importunity which belonged, she now knew, only to his passion and not to himself.

' "What do you want?" she said, and struck him across the face to feel at once the stinging retort on her own cheek — like spray dashing over her. And now he began to fool again until she could not prevent herself from laughing.

'This weird translation of feelings into gestures which belied words and words which belied gestures, confused and disoriented her. She needed someone to tell her whether to laugh or to cry.

'As for Pursewarden, he believed with Rilke that no woman adds anything to the sum of Woman, and from satiety he had now taken refuge in the plenty of the imagination — the true field of merit for the artist. This is perhaps what made him seem to her somehow cold and unfeeling. "Somewhere inside you there is a nasty little Anglican clergyman" she told him and he considered the remark gravely on its merits. "Perhaps" he said, and added after a pause "But your humourlessness has made you an enemy of pleasure. *The* enemy. You have a premeditated approach to experience. I am a truer pagan." And he began to laugh. Great honesty can be crueller than anything else.

'He was sick, I think too, of all the "mud thrown up by the wheels of life" — so he writes. He had done his best to scrape off as much as he could, to tidy himself up. Was he now to be saddled with the inquisitions and ardours of a Justine — the marshy end of a personality which in a funny sort of way he had himself transcended? "By God, no!" he told himself. Can you see what a fool he was?

'His life had been a various and full one, and he had held a number of contract posts for some political branch of the Foreign Office, largely, I gather, connected with cultural relations. This work had taken him to several countries and he spoke at least three languages well. He was married and had two children although he was separated from his wife — and indeed never spoke about her without stammering — though I gather they corresponded affectionately and he was always most scrupulous in sending her money. What else? Yes, his real name was Percy and he was somewhat sensitive about it because of the alliteration, I suppose; hence his choice of Ludwig as a signature to his books. He was always delighted when his reviewers took him to be of German extraction.

'I think what frightened and delighted Justine about him most, however, was his somewhat contemptuous repudiation of Arnauti and his book *Moeurs*. Mind you, this too was overdone — he actually admired the book very much. But he used it as a stick to belabour Justine, describing her ex-husband as a "tiresome psychoanalytical turnkey with a belt full of rusty complexes". I must say, this delighted her. You see, here was someone who set no store by jargon and refused to regard her as a Case. Of course Pursewarden, the silly fool, was simply trying to get rid of her and this was not a very good way. Yet as a doctor I can testify to the therapeutic effects of insults in cases where medicine is at a loss to make any headway! Indeed, had Justine succeeded in making herself really interesting to him, she might have learned a lot of valuable lessons. Odd, isn't it? He really *was* the right man for her in a sort of way; but then as you must know, it is a law of love that the so-called "right" person always comes too soon or too late. As for Pursewarden, he withdrew his favours so abruptly that there was hardly time for her to measure the full force of his personality.

'But at the time of which I am writing he was busy insulting her in his somewhat precise idiosyncratic English or French (he had a few pet neologisms which he used with pleasure — one was the noun "bogue" which he had coined from "bogus"; *c'est de la grande bogue ça* or "what bloody bogue") — he insulted her, if one can use the expression, simply to discourage her. I must say I can hardly repress a laugh when I think of it: you could as easily discourage Justine as an equinox, and she was not disposed to abandon this experiment before she had learned as much as possible about herself from it. Predatory Judaic characteristic! Pursewarden was like Doctor Foster in the nursery rhyme.

'For her, his easy detachment gave him freshness of heart. Justine had never had anyone who *didn't* want or who could do without her before! All kinds of new resonances sprang out of making love to such a person. (Am I inventing this? No. I knew them both well and discussed each with the other.) Then, he could make her laugh — quite the most dangerous thing to do to a woman for they prize laughter most after passion. Fatal! No, he was not wrong when he told himself in the mirror: "Ludwig, thou art an imbecile."

'Worse, the mockery of his cruelty hurt her, and after making love, say, made her think something like this: "What he does is simple as a domestic impulse become habit — cleaning his shoes on a mat." Then unexpectedly would come some terrible mocking phrase like "We are all looking for someone lovely to be unfaithful to — did you think you were original?" Or else "The human race! If you can't do the trick with the one you've got, why — shut your eyes and imagine the one you can't get. Who knows? It's perfectly legal and secret. It's the marriage of true minds!" He was standing at the washbasin cleaning his teeth in white wine. She could have murdered him for looking so gay and self-possessed.

'Coming back from Cairo they had several rows. "As for your so-called illness — have you ever thought it might be just due to an inflamed self-pity?" She became so furious that she nearly drove the car off the road into a tree. "Miserable Anglo-Saxon!" she cried, on the point of tears — "Bully!"

'And he thought to himself: "Great Heavens! Here we are quarrelling like a couple of newly-weds. Soon we shall marry and live in filthy compatibility, feasting on each other's blackheads. Ugh! Dreadful isogamy of the Perfect Match. Perce, you gone and done it again." I can reconstruct this because he always spoke to himself in cockney when he was drunk as well as when he was alone.

' "If you try to hit me" he said happily "we shall have a crash." And the thought of a bitter little short story into which he might insert her. "What we need to establish for sex in art" he muttered "is a revulsion coefficient." She was still angry. "What are you muttering about?" — "Praying."

'For her, the moiety which remained after love-making then was not disgust or despair as it usually was, but laughter; and though furious with him she nevertheless found herself smiling at some absurdity of his even as she realized with a pang that he could never be achieved, attained as a man, nor would he even become a friend, except on his own terms. He offered an uncompanionate compassionless ardour which in a funny sort of way made his kisses thrilling. They were as healthy as the bite of a hungry child into a cooking-apple. And regretting this, with another part of her mind (there was an honest woman somewhere deep down) she found herself hoping he would never abandon this entrenched position, or retreat from it. Like all women, Justine hated anyone she could be certain of; and you must remember she had never had anyone as yet whom she could wholly admire — though that may sound strange to you. Here at last was someone she could not punish by her infidelities — an intolerable but delightful novelty. Women are very stupid as well as very profound.

'As for Justine, she was surprised by the new emotions he seemed capable of provoking. Quite simple things — for example she found her love extending itself to inanimate objects concerned with him, like his old meerschaum pipe with the much basted stem. Or his old hat, so battered and weather-stained — it hung behind the door like a water-colour of the man himself. She found herself cherishing objects he had touched or thrown aside. It seemed to her an infuriating sort of mental captivity to find herself stroking one of his old notebooks as if she were caressing his body, or tracing with her finger the words he had written on the shaving-mirror with his brush (from Stendhal): "You must boldly face a little anatomy if you want to discover an unknown principle" and "Great souls require nourishment."

'Once, when she discovered an Arab prostitute in his bed (while he himself was shaving in the other room and whistling an air from Donizetti) she was surprised to find that she was not jealous but curious. She sat on the bed and pinning the arms of the unfortunate girl to the pillow set about questioning her closely about what she had felt while making love to him. Of course, this scared the prostitute very much. "I am not angry" Justine repeated to the wailing creature, "I am puzzled. Tell me what I ask of you."

'Pursewarden had to come in and release his visitant and they all three sat on the bed together, Justine feeding her with crystallized fruit to calm her fears.

'Shall I go on? This analysis may give you pain — but if you are a real writer you will want to follow things to their conclusion, no? All this shows you how hard it was for Melissa. . . .

'If he succeeded in infuriating her it was because he could feel concern about her without any real affection. He did not always clown, or stay beyond her reach; that is what I mean by his honesty. He gave intellectual value for money — in fact he told her the real secret which lay hidden under the enigma of his behaviour. You will find it in one of his books. I know this because Clea quoted it to me as his most profound statement on human relationships. He said to her one night: "You see, Justine, I believe that Gods are men and men Gods; they intrude on each other's lives, trying to express themselves through each other — hence such apparent confusion in our human states of mind, our intimations of powers within or beyond us. . . . And then (listen) I think that very few people realize that sex is a psychic and not a physical act. The clumsy coupling of human beings is simply a biological paraphrase of this truth — a primitive method of introducing minds to each other, engaging them. But most people are stuck in the physical aspect, unaware of the poetic *rapport* which it so clumsily tries to teach. That is why all your dull repetitions of the same mistake are simply like a boring great multiplication table, and will remain so until you get your head out of the paper bag and start to think responsibly."

'It is impossible to describe the effect these words had on her: they threw her life and actions into relief in an entirely new way. She saw him all of a sudden in a new light, as a man whom one could "really love". Alas, he had already withdrawn his favours. . .

'When he next went to Cairo he elected to go alone and, made restless by his absence, she made the mistake of writing him a long passionate letter in which she clumsily tried to thank him for a friendship of whose real value to her he was *completely unaware* — that is true of all love again. He regarded this simply as another attempt to intrude upon him and sent her a telegram. (They corresponded through me. I have it still.)

"First nobody can own an artist so be warned. Second what good is a faithful body when the mind is by its very nature unfaithful? Third stop whining like an Arab, you know better. Fourth neurosis is no excuse. Health must be won and earned by a battle. Lastly it is honourable if you can't win to hang yourself."

'Once she happened upon him when he was very drunk at the Café Al Aktar; I gather that you and I had just left. You remember the evening? He had been rather insulting. It was the evening when I tried to show you how the nine-point proposition of the Cabal worked. I did not know then that you would type it all out and send it to the Secret Service! What a marvellous jest! But I love to feel events overlapping each other, crawling over one another like wet crabs in a basket. No sooner had we left than Justine entered. It was she who helped him back to his hotel and pushed him safely on to his bed. "Oh, you are the most despairing man!" she cried at that recumbent figure, at which he raised his arms and responded "I know it, I know it! I am just a refugee from the long slow toothache of English life. It is terrible to love life so much you can hardly breathe!" And he began to laugh — a laughter which was overtaken by nausea. She left him being sick in the washbasin.

'The next morning she went round early with some French reviews in one of which there was an article about his work. He was wearing nothing but a pyjama jacket and a pair of spectacles. On his mirror he had written with a wet shaving-stick, some words from Tolstoy: "I do not cease to reflect upon art and upon every form of temptation which obscures the spirit."

'He took the books from her without a word and made as if to shut the door in her face. "No" she said, "I'm coming in." He cleared his throat and said: "This is for the last time. I'm sick of being visited as one might visit the grave of a dead kitten." But she took him by the arms and he said, more gently, "A definite and complete stop, see?"

'She sat down on the end of the bed and lit a cigarette, considering him, as one might a specimen. "I am curious, after all your talk about self-possession and responsibility, to see just how Anglo-Saxon you are — unable to finish anything you start. Why do you look furtive?" This was a splendid line of attack. He smiled. "I'm going to work today."

' "Then I'll come tomorrow."

' "I shall have 'flu."

' "The day after."

' "I shall be going to the Zoo."

' "I shall come too."

'Pursewarden was now extremely rude; she knew she had scored a victory and was delighted. She listened to his honeyed insults as she tapped the carpet with her foot. "Very well" she said at last, "we shall see." (I am afraid you will have to make room in this for the essential comedy of human relations. You give it so little place.) The next day he put her out of his hotel-room by the neck, like a pet cat. The following day he woke and found the great car parked once more outside the hotel. "*Merde*" he cried and just to spite her dressed and went to the Zoo. She followed him. He spent the morning looking at the monkeys with the greatest attention. She was not blind to the insult. She followed him to a bench where he sat, eating the peanuts which he had originally bought to feed the monkeys. She always looked splendid when she was angry, with her nostrils quivering, and clad in that spotless shark-skin suit with a flower at her lapel.

' "Pursewarden" she said, sitting down.

' "You won't believe me" he said, "you bloody tiresome obsessive society figure. From now on you are going to leave me alone. Your money won't help you."

'It is a measure of his stupidity that he could use such language. She was delighted at making him so alarmed. You, of course, know how determined she is. But there was a reason — and underneath the insults she detected a genuine concern — something that did not bear at all on their relationship such as it was. Something else. What?

'You have already noted that she was an unerring mind-reader; and sitting beside him, watching his face, she said like someone reading a badly-written manuscript — "Nessim. Something to do with Nessim. You are afraid . . . not of him." And then in a flash the intuitive contact was made and she blurted out: "There is something regarding Nessim which you cannot afford to compromise: I understand." And she heaved a great sigh. "O Fool, why did you not tell me? Am I to forfeit your friendship because of this? Of course not. I don't care whether you want to sleep with me or not. But you — that is different. Thank God I've discovered what it was."

'He was too astonished to say anything. This mind-reading performance surprised him more than anything about her. He simply stared at her and said nothing, for a long time. "Oh, I am glad" she went on, "for that is so easily arranged. And it will not prevent us from meeting. We need never sleep together again if you don't wish it. But at least I shall be able to see you." Another category of the "love-beast", one which I am unable to define. She would have gone through fire for him by now.

'The silences of Nessim had already assumed huge proportions in her mind. They stretched away on every side like the desert itself — unnerving her. And since her own conscience was by its nature and even without reason, a guilty one, she had already begun to build up a defensive circle of friends whose harmless presences might obviate suspicion of her — the little court of homosexuals like Toto and Amar, whose activities and predispositions were sufficiently well-known to everybody to offer no cause for heart-burnings. She moved now like some sulky planet in the social life of the town, accepting the attentions of these neuters purely as a defence. In this way a general will utilize the features of a town he wishes to defend by building up ring within ring of earthworks. She did not know, for example, that the silences of Nessim betokened only despair and not suspense — for he never broke them.

'In your manuscripts, you hardly mention the question of the child — I told you once before that I thought Arnauti neglected that aspect of affairs in *Moeurs* because it seemed to him melodramatic. "To the childless all things are without resonance" says Pursewarden somewhere. But now the question of the child had become as important to Nessim as to Justine herself — it was his sole means of enlisting the love he desired from her — or so he thought. He fell upon the central problem like a fury, thinking that this would be the one means of penetrating the affective armour of his beautiful tacit wife; the wife he had married and hung up in a cobwebbed corner of his life, by the wrists, like a marionette on strings! Thank God I have never "loved", wise one, and never will! Thank God!

'Pursewarden writes somewhere (again from Clea): "English

has two great forgotten words, namely "helpmeet" which is much greater than "lover" and "loving-kindness" which is so much greater than "love" or even "passion".'

'Now Justine one day overheard part of a telephone conversation which led her to believe that Nessim had either located the missing child or knew something about it which he did not wish to reveal to her. As she passed through the hall he was putting down the telephone after having said: "Well then, I count on your discretion. She must never know." Never know what? Who was the "she"? One can be forgiven for jumping to conclusions. As he did not speak of the conversation for several days she taxed him with it. He now made the fatal mistake of saying that it had never taken place, that she had misheard a conversation with his secretary. Had he said that it related to something quite different, he would have been all right, but to accuse her of not hearing the words which had been ringing in her ears for several days like an alarm bell, this was fatal.

'At one blow she lost confidence in him and began to imagine all sorts of things. Why should he wish to keep from her any knowledge he might have gained about her child? After all, his original promise had been to do what he could to discover its fate. Was it then too horrible to speak of? Surely Nessim would tell her anything if indeed he knew anything? Why should he hold back a hypothetical knowledge of its fate? She simply could not guess but inside herself she felt that in some way the information was being held as a hostage is held — against something — what? Good behaviour?

'But Nessim, who had destroyed by this last clumsiness the last vestiges of regard she had for him, was grappling with a new set of factors. He himself had set great store by the recovery of the child as a means to the recovery of Justine herself; he simply did not dare to tell her — or indeed himself, so painful was it — that one day, after he had exhausted all his resources in an attempt to find out the truth, Narouz telephoned to say: "I saw the Magzub by chance last night and forced the truth out of him. The child is dead."

'This now rose between them like a great wall of China, shutting them off from any further ·contact, and making her afraid that he might even intend her harm. And this is where you come in.'

*   *   *   *   *

Yes, this alas is where I come in again, for it must have been approximately now that Justine came to my lecture on Cavafy and thence carried me off to meet the gentle Nessim; simple 'as an axe falling' — cleaving my life in two! It is inexpressibly bitter today to realize that she was putting me to a considered purpose of her own, the monster, trailing me before Nessim as a bullfighter trails a cloak, and simply to screen her meetings with a man with whom she herself did not even wish to sleep! But I have already described it all, so painfully, and in such great detail — trying to omit no flavour or crumb which would give the picture the coherence I felt it should possess. And yet, even now I can hardly bring myself to feel regret for the strange ennobling relationship into which she plunged me — presumably herself feeling nothing of its power — and from which I myself was to learn so much. Yes, truly it enriched me, but only to destroy Melissa. We must look these things in the face. I wonder why only *now* I have been told all this? My friends must all have known all along. Yet nobody breathed a word. But of course, the truth is that nobody ever does breathe a word, nobody interferes, nobody whispers while the acrobat is on the tight-rope; they just sit and watch the spectacle, waiting only to be wise after the event. But then, from another point of view, how would I, blindly and passionately in love with Justine, have received such unwelcome truths at the time? Would they have deflected me from my purpose? I doubt it.

I suppose that in all this Justine had surrendered to me only one of the many selves she possessed and inhabited — to this timid and scholarly lover with chalk on his sleeve!

Where must one look for justifications? Only I think to the facts themselves; for they might enable me to see now a little further into the central truth of this enigma called 'love'. I see the image of it receding and curling away from me in an infinite series like the waves of the sea; or, colder than a dead moon, rising up over the dreams and illusions I fabricated from it — but like the real moon, always keeping one side of the truth hidden from me, the nether side of a beautiful dead star. My 'love' for her, Melissa's 'love' for me, Nessim's 'love' for her, her 'love' for Pursewarden — there should be a whole vocabulary of adjectives with which to qualify the noun — for no two contained the same properties; yet all contained the one indefinable quality, one common unknown in treachery. Each of us, like the moon, had a dark side — could turn the lying face of 'unlove' towards the person who most loved and needed us. And just as Justine used my love, so Nessim used

Melissa's. . . . One upon the back of the other, crawling about 'like crabs in a basket'.

It is strange that there is not a biology of this monster which lives always among the odd numbers, though by all the romances we have built around it it should inhabit the evens: the perfect numbers the hermetics use to describe marriage!

'What protects animals, enables them to continue living? A certain attribute of organic matter. As soon as one finds life one finds it, it is inherent in life. Like most natural phenomena it is polarized — there is always a negative and a positive pole. The negative pole is pain, the positive pole sex. . . . In the ape and man we find the first animals, excluding tame animals, in which sex can be roused without an external stimulus. . . . The result is that the greatest of all natural laws, periodicity, is lost in the human race. The periodic organic condition which should rouse the sexual sense has become an absolutely useless, degenerate, pathological manifestation.'* (Pursewarden brooding over the monkey-house at the Zoo! Capodistria in his tremendous library of pornographic books, superbly bound! Balthazar at his occultism! Nessim facing rows and rows of figures and percentages!)

And Melissa? Of course, she was ill, indeed seriously ill, so that in a sense it is melodramatic in me to say that I killed her, or that Justine killed her. Nevertheless, nobody can measure the weight of the pain and neglect which I directly caused her. I remember now one day that Amaril came to see me, sentimental as a great dog. Balthazar had sent Melissa to him for X-rays and treatment.

Amaril was an original man in his way and a bit of a dandy withal. The silver duelling-pistols, the engraved visiting-cards in their superb case, clothes cut in all the elegance of the latest fashions. His house was full of candles and he wrote for preference on black paper with white ink. For him the most splendid thing in the world was to possess a fashionable woman, a prize grey-hound, or a pair of invincible fighting-cocks. But he was an agreeable man and not without sensibility as a doctor, despite these romantic foibles.

His devotion to women was the most obvious thing about him; he dressed for them. Yet it was accompanied by a delicacy, almost a pudicity, in his dealings with them — at least in a city where a woman was, as provender, regarded as something like a plateful of mutton; a city where women cry out to be abused.

But he idealized them, built up romances in his mind about

them, dreamed always of a complete love, a perfect understanding with one of the tribe. Yet all this was in vain. Ruefully he would explain to Pombal or to myself: 'I cannot understand it. Before my love has a chance to crystallize, it turns into a deep, a devouring *friendship*. These devotions are not for you womanizers, you wouldn't understand. But once this happens, passion flies out of the window. Friendship consumes us, paralyses us. Another sort of love begins. What is it? I don't know. A tenderness, a *tendresse*, something melting. *Fondante*.' Tears come into his eyes. 'I am really a woman's man and women love me. But — ' shaking his handsome head and blowing the smoke from his cigarette upwards to the ceiling he adds smiling, but without self-pity, 'I alone among men can say that while all women love me no one woman ever has. Not properly. I am as innocent of love (not sexual love, of course) as a virgin. Poor Amaril!'

It is all true. It was his very devotion to women which dictated his choice in medicine — gynaecology. And women gravitate to him as flowers do to the sunlight. He teaches them what to wear and how to walk; chooses their scents for them, dictates the colour of their lipsticks. Moreover, there is not a woman in Alexandria who is not proud to be seen out on his arm; there is not one who *if asked* (but he never asks) would not be glad to betray her husband or her lover for him. And yet . . . and yet. . . . A connecting thread has been broken somewhere, a link snapped. Such desires as he knows, the stifling summer desires of the body in the city of sensuality, are stifled among shop-girls, among his inferiors. Clea used to say 'One feels a special sort of fate in store for Amaril. Dear Amaril!'

Yes. Yes. But what? What sort of fate lies in store for such a romantic — such a devoted, loving, patient student of women? These are the questions I ask myself as I see him, elegantly gloved and hatted, driving with Balthazar to the hospital for an operation. . . .

He described to me Melissa's condition adding only: 'It would help her very much if she could be loved a bit.' A remark which filled me with shame. It was that very night that I had borrowed the money from Justine to send her to a clinic in Palestine much against her own will.

We walked together to the flat after having spent a few minutes in the public gardens discussing her case. The palms looked brilliant in the moonlight and the sea glittered under the spring winds. It seemed so out of place — serious illness — in this scheme of things. Amaril took my arms as we climbed the stairs and squeezed them gently. 'Life is hard' he said. And when we entered the bedroom once more to find her lying there in a trance with her pallid little face turned to the ceiling and the *hashish* pipe beside her on the table, he added, taking up his hat: 'It is always ... don't think I blame you ... no, I envy you Justine ... yet it is always *in extremis* that we doctors make the last desperate prescription for a woman patient — when all the resources of science have failed. Then we say "If only she could be loved!" He sighed and shook his handsome head.

There are always a hundred ways of justifying oneself but the sophistries of paper logic cannot alter the fact that after this kind of information in the Interlinear, the memory of those days haunts me afresh, torments me with guilts which I might never have been aware of before! I walk now beside the child which Melissa had by Nessim during that brief love-affair (was it 'love' again, or was he trying to use her to find out all he could about his wife? Perhaps one day I shall discover): I walk beside the child I say on these deserted beaches like a criminal, going over and over these fragments of the white city's life with regrets too deep to alter the tone of voice in which I talk to her. Where does one hunt for the key to such a pattern?

But it is clear that I was not alone in feeling such guilt: Pursewarden himself must have been feeling guilty — how else can I explain the money he left me in his will with the express request that it should be spent with Melissa? That at least is one problem solved.

Clea too, I know, felt the guilt of the wound we were all of us causing Melissa — though she felt it, so to speak, on behalf of Justine. She took it, so to speak, upon herself — appalled at the mischief which her lover was causing to us both for so little cause. It was she who now became Melissa's friend, champion and counsellor and who remained her closest confidante until she died. The selfless and innocent Clea, another fool! It does not pay to be honest in love! She said of Melissa: 'It is terrible to depend so utterly on powers that do not wish you well. To see someone always in your thoughts, like a stain upon reality. . . .' I think she was also thinking, perhaps, of Justine, up there in the big house among the tall candles and the oil-paintings by forgotten masters.

Melissa also said to her of me: 'With his departure *everything in nature* disappeared.' This was when she was dying. But nobody has the right to occupy such a place in another's life, nobody! You can see now upon what raw material I work in these long and passionate self-communings over a winter sea. 'She loved you' said Clea again 'because of your weakness — this is what she found endearing in you. Had you been strong you would have frightened away so timid a love.' And then lastly, before I bang the pages of my manuscript shut with anger and resentment, one last remark of Clea's which burns like a hot iron: 'Melissa said: "You have been my friend, Clea, and I want you to love him after I am gone. Do it with him, will you, and think of me? Never mind all this beastly love business. Cannot a friend make love on another's behalf? I ask you to sleep with him as I would ask the Panaghia to come down and bless him while he sleeps — like in the old ikons." ' How purely Melissa, how Greek!

On Sundays we would walk down together to visit Scobie, I remember; Melissa in her bright cotton frock and straw hat, smiling and eager at the thought of a full holiday from the dusty cabaret. Along the Grande Corniche with the waves dancing and winking across the bar, and the old horse-drawn cabs with their black jarveys in red flowerpots driving their dilapidated and creaking 'taxis-of-love'; and as we walked past they would call 'Love-taxi sir, madam. Only ten piastres an hour. I know a quiet place. . . .' And Melissa would giggle and turn away as we walked to watch the minarets glisten like pearls upon the morning light and the bright children's kites take the harbour wind.

Scobie usually spent Sundays in bed, and in winter nearly always contrived to have a cold. He would lie between the coarse linen sheets after having made Abdul give him what he called 'a cinnamon rub' (I never discovered what this was); with some formality, too, he would have a brick heated and placed at his feet to keep them warm. He had a small knitted cap on his head. As he read very little, he carried, like an ancient tribe, all his literature in his head and would, when alone, recite to himself for hours. He had quite an extensive repertoire of ballads which he thundered out with great energy, marking the beat with his hand. 'The Arab's Farewell to his Steed' brought real tears to his good eye, as did 'The harp that once through Tara's Halls'; while among the lesser-known pieces was an astonishing poem the metre of which by its galloping quality virtually enabled him to throw himself out of bed and half-way across the room if recited at full gale force. I once made him write it out for me in order to study its construction closely:

> *'By O'Neil close beleaguered, the spirits might droop*
> *Of the Saxon three hundred shut up in their coop*
> *Till Bagnal drew forth his Toledo and swore*
> *On the sword of a soldier to succour Portmore.*
>
> *His veteran troops in the foreign wars tried,*
> *Their features how bronzed and how haughty their stride,*
> *Step't steadily on; Ah! 'twas thrilling to see*
> *That thunder-cloud brooding o'er Beal-an-atha-Buidh!*
>
> *Land of Owen Aboo! and the Irish rushed on.*
> *The foe fired one volley — their gunners are gone.*
> *Before the bare bosoms the steel coats have fled,*
> *Or despite casque and corslet, lie dying or dead.*
>
> *And the Irish got clothing, coin, colours, great store,*
> *Arms, forage, and provender — plunder go leor.*
> *They munched the white manchets, they champed the brown chine,*
> *Fuliluah! for that day how the natives did dine!'*

Disappointingly, he could tell me nothing about it; it had lain there in his memory for half a century like a valuable piece of old silver which is only brought out on ceremonial occasions and put on view. Among the few other such treasures which I recognized was the passage (which he always declaimed with ardour) which ends:

> *'Come the four corners of the world in arms,*
> *We'll shock 'em.*
> *Trust Joshua Scobie to shock 'em!'*

Melissa was devoted to him and found him extraordinarily quaint in his sayings and mannerisms. He for his part was fond of her — I think chiefly because she always gave him his full rank and title — Bimbashi Scobie — which pleased him and made him feel of consequence to her as a 'high official'.

But I remember one day when we found him almost in tears. I thought perhaps he had moved himself by a recital of one of his more powerful poems ('We Are Seven' was another favourite); but no. 'I've had a quarrel with Abdul — for the first time' he admitted with a ludicrous blink. 'You know what, old man, he wants to take up circumcision.'

It was not hard to understand: to become a barber-surgeon rather than a mere cutter and shaver was a normal enough step for someone like Abdul to want to take; it was like getting one's Ph.D. But of course, I knew too Scobie's aversion to circumcision. 'He's gone and bought a filthy great pot of leeches' the old man went on indignantly. '*Leeches!* Started opening veins, he has. I said to him I said "If you think, my boy, that I set you up in business so as you could spend your time hyphenating young children for a piastre a time you're wrong," I said to him I said.' He paused for breath, obviously deeply affected by this development. 'But Skipper' I protested, 'it seems very natural for him to want to become a barber-surgeon. After all, circumcision is practised everywhere, even in England now.' Ritual circumcision was such a common part of the Egyptian scene that I could not understand why he should be so obviously upset by the thought. He pouted, tucked his head down, and ground his false teeth noisily. 'No' he said obstinately. 'I won't have it.' Then he suddenly looked up and said 'D'you know what? He's actually going to study under Mahmoud Enayet Allah — that old butcher!'

I could not understand his concern; at every festival or *mulid* the circumcision booth was a regular part of the festivities. Huge coloured pictures, heavily beflagged with the national colours, depicting barber-surgeons with pen-knives at work upon wretched youths spread out in dentists' chairs were a normal if bizarre feature of the side-shows. The doyen of the guild was Mahmoud himself, a large oval man, with a long oiled moustache, always dressed in full fig and apart from his red tarbush conveying the vague impression of some French country practitioner on French leave. He always made a resounding speech in classical Arabic offering circumcision free to the faithful who were too poor to meet the cost of it. Then, when a few candidates were forthcoming, pushed forward by eager parents, his two negro clowns with painted faces and grotesque clothes used to gambol out to amuse and distract the boys, inveigling them by this means into the fatal chair where they were, in Scobie's picturesque phrase, 'hyphenated', their screams being drowned by the noise of the crowd, almost before they knew what was happening.

I could not see what was amiss in Abdul's wanting to learn all he could from this don, so to speak, of hyphenation. Then I suddenly understood as Scobie said 'It's not the boy — they can do him for all I care. It's the girl, old man. I can't bear to think of that little creature being mutilated. I'm an Englishman, old man, you'll understand my feelings. I WON'T HAVE IT.' Exhausted by the force of his own voice, he sank back upon his pillow and went on. 'And what's more, I told Abdul so in no uncertain terms. "Lay a finger on the girl" I said "and I'll get you run in — see if I don't." But of course, it's heart-breaking, old man, 'cause they've been such friends, and the poor coon doesn't understand. He thinks I'm mad!' He sighed heavily twice. 'Their friendship was the best I ever had with anyone except Budgie, and I'm not exaggerating, old man. It really was. And now they're puzzled. They don't understand an Englishman's feelings. And I hate using the Influence of My Position.' I wondered what this exactly meant. He went on. 'Only last month we ran Abdel Latif in and got him closed down, with six months in chokey for unclean razors. He was spreading syphilis, old man. I had to do it, even though he was a friend. My duty. I warned him countless times to dip his razor. No, he wouldn't do it. They've got a very poor sense of disinfection here, old man. You know, they use styptic — shaving styptic for the circumcisions. It's considered more modern than the old mixture of black gunpowder and lemon-juice. Ugh! No sense of disinfection. I don't know how they don't all die of things, really I don't. But they were quite scared when we ran Abdel Latif in and Abdul has taken it to heart. I could see him watching me while I was telling him off. Measuring my words, like.'

But the influence of company always cheered the old man up and banished his phantoms, and it was not long before he was talking in his splendid discursive vein about the life history of Toby Mannering. 'It was he who put me on to Holy Writ, old man, and I was looking at The Book yesterday when I found a lot about circumcision in it. You know? The Amalekites used to collect foreskins like we collect stamps. Funny, isn't it?' He gave a sudden snort of a chuckle like a bull-frog. 'I must say they were ones! I suppose they had dealers, assorted packets, a regular trade, eh? Paid more for perforations!' He made a straight face for Melissa who came into the room at this moment. 'Ah well' he said, still shaking visibly at his own jest. 'I must write to Budgie tonight and tell him all the news.' Budgie was his oldest friend. 'Lives in Horsham, old man, makes earth-closets. He's collected a regular packet from them, has old Budgie. He's an FRZS, I don't quite know what it means, but he had it on his notepaper. Charles Donahue Budgeon FRZS. I write to him every week. Punctual. Always have done, always will do. Staunch, that's me. Never give up a friend.'

It was to Budgie, I think, the unfinished letter which was found in his rooms after his death and which read as follows:

'*Dear old pal, The whole world seems to have turned against me since I last wrote. I should have*'

Scobie and Melissa! In the golden light of those Sundays they live on, bright still with the colours that memory gives to those who enrich our lives by tears or by laughter — unaware themselves that they have given us anything. The really horrible thing is that the compulsive passion which Justine lit in me was quite as valuable as it would have been had it been 'real'; Melissa's gift was no less an enigma — what could she have offered me, in truth, this pale waif of the Alexandrian littoral? Was Clea enriched or beggared by her relations with Justine? Enriched — immeasurably enriched, I should say. Are we then nourished only by fictions, by lies? I recall the words Balthazar wrote down somewhere in his tall grammarian's handwriting: 'We live by selected fictions' and also: 'Everything is true of everybody. . . .' Were these words of Pursewarden's quarried from his own experience of men and women, or simply from a careful observation of us, our behaviours and their result? I don't know. A passage comes to mind from a novel in which Pursewarden speaks about the role of the artist in life. He says something like this: 'Aware of every discord, of every calamity in the nature of man himself, he can do nothing to warn his friends, to point, to cry out in time and to try to save them. It would be useless. For they are the deliberate factors of their own unhappiness. All the artist can say as an imperative is: "Reflect and weep." '

Was it consciousness of tragedy irremediable contained — not in the external world which we all blame — but in ourselves, in the human conditions, which finally dictated his unexpected suicide in that musty hotel-room? I like to think it was, but perhaps I am in danger of putting too much emphasis on the artist at the expense of the man. Balthazar writes: 'Of all things his suicide has remained for me an extraordinary and quite inexplicable freak. Whatever stresses and strains he may have been subjected to I cannot quite bring myself to believe it. But then I suppose we live in the shallows of one another's personalities and cannot really see into the depths beneath. Yet I should have said this was surprisingly out of character. You see, he was really at rest about his work which most torments the artists, I suppose, and really had begun to regard it as "divinely unimportant" — a characteristic phrase. I know this for certain because he once wrote me out on the back of an envelope an answer to the question "What is the object of writing?" His answer was this: "The object of writing is to grow a personality which in the end enables man to transcend art."

'He had odd ideas about the constitution of the psyche. For example, he said "I regard it as completely unsubstantial as a rainbow — it only coheres into identifiable states and attributes when attention is focused on it. The truest form of right attention is of course love. Thus 'people' are as much of an illusion to the mystic as 'matter' to the physicist when he is regarding it as a form of energy."

'He never failed to speak most slightingly of my own interests in the occult, and indeed in the work of the Cabal whose meetings you attended yourself. He said of this "Truth is a matter of direct apprehension — you can't climb a ladder of mental concepts to it."

'I can't get away from the feeling that he was at his most serious when he was most impudent. I heard him maintaining to Keats that the best lines of English poetry ever written were by Coventry Patmore. They were:

> *The truth is great and will prevail*
> *When none care whether it prevail or not.*

'And then, having said this, he added: "And their true beauty resides in the fact that Patmore when he wrote them did not know what he meant. *Sich lassen!*" You can imagine how this would annoy Keats. He also quoted with approval a mysterious phrase of Stendhal, namely: "The smile appears on the skin outside."

'Are we to assume from all this the existence of a serious person underneath the banter? I leave the question to you — your concern is a direct one.

'At the time when we knew him he was reading hardly anything but science. This for some reason annoyed Justine who took him to task for wasting his time in these studies. He defended himself by saying that the Relativity proposition was directly responsible for abstract painting, atonal music, and formless (or at any rate cyclic forms in) literature. Once it was grasped they were understood, too. He added: "In the Space and Time marriage we have the greatest Boy meets Girl story of the age. To our great-grandchildren this will be as poetical a union as the ancient Greek marriage of Cupid and Psyche seems to us. You see, Cupid and Psyche were facts to the Greeks, not concepts. Analogical as against analytical thinking! But the true poetry of the age and its most fruitful poem is the mystery which begins and ends with an *n*."

' "Are you serious about all this?"

' "Not a bit."

'Justine protested: "The beast is up to all sorts of tricks, even in his books." She was thinking of the famous page with the asterisk in the first volume which refers one to a page in the text which is mysteriously blank. Many people take this for a printer's error. But Pursewarden himself assured me that it was deliberate. "I refer the reader to a blank page in order to throw him back upon his own resources — which is where every reader ultimately belongs."

'You speak about the plausibility of our actions — and this does us an injustice, for we are all living people and have the right as such to take refuge in the suspended judgement of God if not the reader. So, while I think of it, let me tell you the story of Justine's laughter! You will admit that you yourself never heard it, not once, I mean in a way that was not mordant, not wounded. But Pursewarden did — at the tombs in Saqarra! By moonlight, two days after Sham el Nessim. They were there among a large party of sightseers, a crowd under cover of which they had managed to talk a little, like the conspirators they were: already at this time Pursewarden had put an end to her private visitations to his hotel-room. So it gave them a forbidden pleasure, this exchange of a few hoarded secret words; and at last this evening they came by chance to be alone, standing together in one of those overbearing and overwhelming mementoes to a specialized sense of death: the tombs.

'Justine had laddered her stockings and filled her shoes with sand. She was emptying them, he was lighting matches and gazing about him, and sniffing. She whispered she had been terribly worried of late by a new suspicion that Nessim had discovered something about her lost child which he would not tell her. Pursewarden was absently listening when suddenly he snapped his fingers which he had burnt on a match and said: "Listen, Justine — you know what? I re-read *Moeurs* again last week for fun and I had an idea; I mean if all the song and dance about Freud and your so-called childhood rape and so on are true — are they? I don't know. You could easily make it all up. But since you knew who the man in the wretched eyepiece was and refused to reveal his name to the wretched army of amateur psychologists headed by Arnauti, you must have had a good reason for it. What was it? It puzzles me. I won't tell anyone, I promise. Or is it all a lie?" She shook her head, "No."

'They walked out in a clear milk-white moonlight while Justine thought quietly. Then she said slowly: "It wasn't just shyness or an unwillingness to be cured as they called it — as he called it in the book. The thing was, he was a friend of ours, of yours, of all of us." Pursewarden looked at her curiously. "The man in the black patch?" he said. She nodded. They lit cigarettes and sat down on the sand to wait for the others. Feeling that everything she confided in him was absolutely secure she said quietly: "Da Capo." There was a long silence. "Well, stap me! The old Porn himself!" (He had coined this nickname from the word "pornographer".) And then very quietly and tentatively, Pursewarden went on: "I suddenly had the idea on re-reading all that stuff, you know, that if I had been in your shoes and the whole damn thing wasn't just a lie to make yourself more interesting to the psychopomps — I'd . . . well, I'd bloody well try and sleep with him again and try to lay the image that way. The idea suddenly came to me."

'This betrays, of course, his total ignorance of psychology. Indeed, it was a fatal step to suggest. But here, to his own surprise, she began to laugh — the first effortless, musical laugh he had ever heard her give. "I did" she said, now laughing almost too much for speech, "I did. You'll never guess what an effort it cost me, hanging about in the dark road outside his house, trying to pluck up courage to ring the bell. Yes, it occurred to me too. I was desperate. What would he say? We had been friends for years — with never of course a reference to this event. He had never referred to *Moeurs* and, you know, I don't believe he has read it ever. Perhaps he preferred, I always thought, to disregard the whole thing — to bury it tactfully."

'Laughter again overtook her, shaking her body so much that Pursewarden took her arm anxiously, not to let her interrupt the recital. She borrowed his handkerchief to mop her eyes and continued: "I went in at last. He was there in his famous library! I was shaking like a leaf. You see, I didn't know what note to strike, something dramatic, something pathetic? It was like going to the dentist. Really, it was funny, Pursewarden. I said at last 'Dear Da Capo, old friend, you have been my demon for so long that I have come to ask you to exorcise me once and for all. To take away the memory of a horrible childhood event. You must sleep with me!' You should have seen Da Capo's face. He was terribly thrown off guard and stammered: '*Mais voyons, Justine, je suis un ami de Nessim!*' and so on. He gave me a whisky and offered me an aspirin — sure that I had gone out of my mind. 'Sit down' he said, putting out a chair for me with shaking hands and sitting nervously down opposite me with a comical air of alarm — like a small boy accused of stealing apples." Her side was hurting and she pressed her hand to it, laughing with such merriment that it infected him and involuntarily he began to laugh too. "Poor Da Capo" she said, "he was so terribly shocked and alarmed to be told he had raped me when I was a street arab, a child. I have never seen a man more taken aback. He had completely forgotten, it is clear, and completely denied the whole thing from start to finish. In fact, he was outraged and began to protest. I wish you could have seen his face! Do you know what slipped out in the course of his self-justifications? A marvellous phrase '*Il y a quinze ans que je n'ai pas fait ça!*' " She threw herself now face downward on to Pursewarden's lap and stayed a moment, still shaking with laughter; and then she raised her head once more to wipe her eyes. She said "I finished my whisky at last and left, much to his relief; as I was at the door he called after me 'Remember you are both dining with me on Wednesday. Eight for eight-fifteen, white tie', as he had done these past few years. I went back home in a daze and drank half a bottle of gin. And you know, I had a strange thought that night in bed — perhaps you will find it shockingly out of place; a thought about Da Capo forgetting so completely an act which had cost me so many years of anxiety and indeed mental illness and had made me harm so many people. I said to myself 'This is perhaps the very way God himself forgets the wrongs he does to us in abandoning us to the mercies of the world.' " She threw back her smiling head and stood up.

'She saw now that Pursewarden was looking at her with tears of admiration in his eyes. Suddenly he embraced her warmly, kissing her more passionately perhaps than he had ever done. When she was telling me all this, with a pride unusual in her, she added: "And you know, Balthazar, that was better than any lover's kiss, it was a real reward, an accolade. I saw then that if things had been different I had it in me to make him love me — perhaps for the very defects in my character which are so obvious to everyone."

'Then the rest of the party came chattering up among the tombs and . . . I don't know what. I suppose they all drove back to the Nile and ended up at a night-club. What the devil am I doing scribbling all these facts down for you? Lunacy! You will only hate me for telling you things you would prefer not to know as a man and prefer perhaps to ignore as an artist. . . . These obstinate little dispossessed facts, the changelings of our human existence which one can insert like a key into a lock — or a knife into an oyster: will there be a pearl inside? Who can say? But somewhere they must exist in their own right, these grains of a truth which *"just slipped out"*. Truth is not what is uttered in full consciousness. It is always what "just slips out" — the typing error which gives the whole show away. Do you understand me, wise one? But I have not done. I shall never have the courage to give you these papers, I can see. I shall finish the story for myself alone.

'So from all this you will be able to measure the despair of Justine when that wretched fellow Pursewarden went and killed himself. In the act of being annoyed with him I find myself smiling, so little do I believe in his death as yet. She found this act as completely mysterious, as completely unforeseen as I myself did; but she poor creature had organized her whole careful deception around the idea of his living on! There was nobody except myself in whom to confide now; and you whom, if she did not love, God knows she did not hate, were in great danger. It was too late to do anything except make plans to go away. She was left with the "decoy"! Does one learn anything from these bitter truths? Throw all this paper into the sea, my dear boy, and read no more of the Interlinear. But I forget. I am not going to let you see it, am I? I shall leave you content with the fabrications of an art which "re-works reality to show its significant side." What significant side could she turn, for example, to Nessim, who at that time had become a prey to those very preoccupations which made him appear to everyone — himself included — mentally unstable? Of his more serious preoccupations at this time I could write a fair amount, for I have in the interval learned a good deal about his affairs and his political concerns. They will explain his sudden changeover into a great entertainer — the crowded house which you describe so well, the banquets and balls. But here . . . the question of censorship troubles me, for if I were to send you this and if you were, as you might, to throw this whole disreputable jumble of paper into the water, the sea might float it back to Alexandria perhaps directly into the arms of the Police. Better not. I will tell you only what seems politic. Perhaps later on I shall tell you the rest.

'Pursewarden's face in death reminded me very much of Melissa's;

they both had the air of just having enjoyed a satisfying private joke and of having fallen off to sleep before the smile had fully faded from the corners of the mouth. Some time before he had said to Justine: "I am ashamed of one thing only: because I have disregarded the first imperative of the artist, namely, create and starve. I have never starved, you know. Kept afloat doing little jobs of one sort or another: caused as much harm as you and more."

'That night, Nessim was already there in the hotel-room sitting with the body when I arrived, looking extraordinarily composed and calm but as if deafened by an explosion. Perhaps the impact of reality had dazed him? He was at this time going through that period of horrible dreams of which he had a transcript made, some of which you reproduce in your MS. They are strangely like echoes of Leila's dreams of fifteen years ago — she had a bad period after her husband died and I attended her at Nessim's request. Here again in judging him you trust too much to what your subjects say about themselves — the accounts they give of their own actions and their meaning. You would never make a good doctor. Patients have to be found out — for they *always* lie. Not that they can help it, it is part of the defence-mechanism of the illness — just as your MS. betrays the defence-mechanism of the dream which does not wish to be invaded by reality! Perhaps I am wrong? I do not wish to judge anyone unjustly or intrude upon your private territory. Will all these notes of mine cost me your friendship? I hope not, but I fear it.

'What was I saying? Yes, Pursewarden's face in death! It had the same old air of impudent contrivance. One felt he was playacting — indeed, I still do, so alive does he seem to me.

'It was Justine first who alerted me. Nessim sent her to me with the car and a note which I did not let her read. It was clear that Nessim had either learned of the intention or the fact before any of us — I suspect a telephone call by Pursewarden himself. At any rate, my familiarity with suicide cases — I have handled any number for Nimrod's night-patrol — made me cautious. Suspecting perhaps barbiturates or some other slow compound, I took the precaution of carrying my little stomach-pump with me among my antidotes. I confess that I thought with pleasure of my friend's expression when he woke up in hospital. But it seems I misjudged both his pride and his thoroughness for he was thoroughly and conclusively dead when we arrived.

'Justine raced ahead of me up the staircases of the gaunt hotel which he had loved so much (indeed, he had christened it Mount Vulture Hotel — I presume from the swarm of whores who fluttered about in the street outside it, like vultures).

'Nessim had locked himself into the room — we had to knock and he let us in with a certain annoyance, or so it seemed to me. The place was in the greatest disorder you can imagine. Drawers turned out, clothes and manuscripts and paintings everywhere; Pursewarden was lying on the bed in the corner with his nose pointing aloofly at the ceiling. I paused to unpack my big-intestine kit — method is everything in moments of stress — while Justine went unerringly across to the bottle of gin on the corner by the bed and took a long swig. I knew that this might contain the poison but said nothing — at such times there is little to say. The minute you get hysterical you have to take this kind of chance. I simply unpacked and unwound my aged stomach-pump which has saved more useless lives (lives impossible to live, shed like ill-fitting garments) than any such other instrument in Alexandria. Slowly, as befits a third-rate doctor, I unwound it, and with method, which is all a third-rate doctor has left to face the world with. . . .

'Meanwhile Justine turned to the bed and leaning down said audibly: "Pursewarden, wake up." Then she put her palms to the top of her head and let out a long pure wail like an Arab woman — a sound abruptly shut off, confiscated by the night in that hot airless little room. Then she began to urinate in little squirts all over the carpet. I caught her and pushed her into the bathroom. It gave me the respite I needed to have a go at his heart. It was silent as the Great Pyramid. I felt angry about it, because it was clear he had resorted to some beastly cyanide preparation — favoured, by the way, by your famous Secret Service. I was so exasperated that I clipped him over the ear — a blow he had long merited!

'All this time I had been aware that Nessim was suddenly active, but now I recovered, so to speak, and could turn my attention to him. He was turning out drawers and desks and cupboards like a maniac, examining manuscripts and papers, tossing things aside and picking things up with a complete lack of his usual phlegm. "What the hell are you doing?" I said angrily, to which he replied "There must be nothing for the Egyptian Police to find." And then he stopped as if he had said too much. Every mirror bore a soap-inscription. Nessim had partly obliterated one. I could only make out the letters OHEN . . . PALESTINE. . . .

'It was not long before there came the familiar knocking at the

door and the faces and tumult inseparable from such scenes everywhere in the world. Men with notebooks, and journalists, and
priests — Father Paul of all people turned up. At this, I half-
expected the corpse to rise up and throw something . . . but no;
Pursewarden remained with his nose cocked to the ceiling, in his
amused privacy.

'We stumbled out together, the three of us, and drove back to
the studio where the great failed paintings soothed us, and where
whisky gave us new courage to continue living. Justine said not a
word. Not a mortal word.'

★   ★   ★   ★   ★

VII

I turn now to another part of the Interlinear, the passage which Balthazar marked: 'So Narouz decided to *act*,' underlining the last word twice. Shall I reconstruct it — the scene I see so clearly, and which his few crabbed words in green ink have detonated in my imagination? Yes, it will enable me to dream for a moment about an unfrequented quarter of Alexandria which I loved.

The city, inhabited by these memories of mine, moves not only backwards into our history, studded by the great names which mark every station of recorded time, but also back and forth in the living present, so to speak — among its contemporary faiths and races: the hundred little spheres which religion or lore creates and which cohere softly together like cells to form the great sprawling jellyfish which is Alexandria today. Joined in this fortuitous way by the city's own act of will, isolated on a slate promontory over the sea, backed only by the moonstone mirror of Mareotis, the salt lake, and its further forevers of ragged desert (now dusted softly by the spring winds into satin dunes, patternless and beautiful as cloudscapes), the communities still live and communicate — Turks with Jews, Arabs and Copts and Syrians with Armenians and Italians and Greeks. The shudders of monetary transactions ripple through them like wind in a wheatfield; ceremonies, marriages and pacts join and divide them. Even the place-names on the old tram-routes with their sandy grooves of rail echo the unforgotten names of their founders — and the names of the dead captains who first landed here, from Alexander to Amr; founders of this anarchy of flesh and fever, of money-love and mysticism. Where else on earth will you find such a mixture?

And when night falls and the white city lights up the thousand candelabra of its parks and buildings, tunes in to the soft unearthly drum-music of Morocco or Caucasus, it looks like some great crystal liner asleep there, anchored to the horn of Africa — her diamond and fire-opal reflections twisting downwards like polished bars into the oily harbour among the battleships.

At dusk it can become like a mauve jungle, anomalous, stained with colours as if from a shattered prism; and rising into the pearly sky of the sunset falter up the steeples and minarets like stalks of giant fennel in a swamp rising up over the long pale lines of the sea-shore and the barbaric cafés where the negroes dance to the pop and drub of a finger-drum or to the mincing of clarinets.

'There are only as many realities as you care to imagine' writes Pursewarden.

Narouz always shunned Alexandria while he loved it passionately, with an exile's love; his hare-lip had made him timid to visit the centre, to encounter those he might know. He always hovered about its outskirts, not daring to go directly into the great lighted heart of it where his brother lived a life of devoted enterprise and *mondanité*. He came into it always humbly, on horseback, dressed as he was always dressed, to fulfil the transactions which concerned the property. It took a great effort to persuade him to put on a suit and visit it by car, though when absolutely necessary he had been known to do this also, but reluctantly. For the most part he preferred to do his work through Nessim; and of course the telephone guarded him from many such unwelcome journeys. Yet when his brother rang up one day and said that his agents had been unable to make the Magzub tell them what he knew about Justine's child, Narouz felt suddenly elated — as if fired by the consciousness that this task had now devolved on him. 'Nessim' he said, 'what is the month? Yes, Misra. Quite soon there will come the feast of Sitna Mariam, eh? I shall see if he is there and try to make him tell us something.' Nessim pondered this offer for so long that Narouz thought the line had been cut and cried sharply 'Hallo — hallo!' Nessim answered at once. 'Yes, yes. I am here. I am just thinking: you will be careful, won't you?' Narouz chuckled hoarsely and promised that he would. But he was always stirred by the thought that perhaps he might be able to help his brother. Curiously, he thought not at all about Justine herself, or what such information might mean to her; she was simply an acquisition of Nessim's whom he liked, admired, loved deeply, indeed automatically, because of Nessim. It was his duty to do whatever was necessary to help Nessim help her. No more. No less.

So it was that with soft stride, the awkward jaunty step (rising and falling on his toes, swinging his arms), he walked across the brown dusk-beshadowed *meidan* outside the main railway station of Alexandria on the second day of Sitna Mariam. He had stabled his horse in the yard of a friend, a carpenter, not far from the place where the festivities of the saint were held. It was a hot rank summer night.

With the dusk that vast and threadbare expanse of empty ground always turned first gold and then brown — to brown cracked cardboard — and then lastly to violet as the lights began to prick the on-coming darkness, as the backcloth of the European city itself began to light up window by window, street by street, until the whole looked like a cobweb in which the frost has set a million glittering brilliants.

Camels somewhere snorted and gnarred, and the music and odour of human beings came across the night towards him, rich with the memories of the fairs he had visited with his parents as a child. In his red tarbush and work-stained clothes he knew he would not be singled out by the crowd as one different from themselves. It was characteristic too that, though the festival of Sitna Mariam celebrated a Christian Coptic saint, it was attended and enjoyed by all, not least the Moslem inhabitants of the town, for Alexandria is after all still Egypt: all the colours run together.

A whole encampment of booths, theatres, brothels and shops — a complete township — had sprung up in the darkness, fitfully lit by oil and paraffin stoves, by pressure lamps and braziers, by candle-light and strings of dazzling coloured electric bulbs. He walked lightly into the press of human beings, his nostrils drinking in the scent of aromatic foods and sweetmeats, of stale jasmine and sweat, and his ears the hum of voices which provided a background to those common sounds which always followed the great processions through the town, lingering on the way at every church for a recital of sacred texts, and coming gradually to the site of the festival.

To him all this scattered novelty — the riches of bear-dancers and acrobats, the fire-swallowers blowing six-foot plumes of flame from up-cast mouths: the dancers in rags and parti-coloured caps: indeed everything that to the stranger would have been a delight was so to him only because it was so utterly commonplace — so much a belonging part of his own life. Like the small child he once had been he walked in the brilliance of the light, stopping here and there with smiling eyes to stare at some familiar feature of the fair. A conjurer dressed in tinsel drew from his sleeve endless many-coloured handkerchiefs, and from his mouth twenty small live chicks, crying all the time in the voice of the seabird: '*Galli-Galli-Galli-Galli Houp!*'; Manouli the monkey in a paper hat brilliantly rode round and round his stall on the back of a goat. Towering on either side of the thoroughfare rose the great booths with their sugar figurines brilliant with tinsel, depicting the loves and adventures of the creatures inhabiting the folk-lore of the Delta — heroes like Abu Zeid and Antar, lovers like Yuna and Aziz. He walked slowly, with an unpremeditated carelessness, stopping for a while to hear the storytellers, or to buy a lucky talisman from the famous blind preacher Hussein who stood like an oak tree, magnificent in the elf-light, reciting the ninety-nine holy names.

From the outer perimeter of darkness came the crisp click of sportsmen at singlestick, dimly sounding against the hoarse rumble of the approaching procession with its sudden bursts of wild music — kettle-drums and timbrels like volleys of musketry — and the long belly-thrilling rolls of the camel-drums which drowned and refreshed the quavering deep-throated flute-music. 'They are coming. They are coming.' A confused shouting rose and the children darted here and there like mice among the stalls. From the throat of a narrow alley, spilled like a widening circle of fire upon the darkness, burst a long tilting gallery of human beings headed by the leaping acrobats and dwarfs of Alexandria, and followed at a dancing measure by the long grotesque cavalcade of gonfalons, rising and falling in a tide of mystical light, treading the peristaltic measures of the wild music—nibbled out everywhere by the tattling flutes and the pang of drums or the long shivering orgasm of tambourines struck by the dervishes in their habits as they moved towards the site of the festival. 'All-*ah* All-*ah*' burst from every throat.

Narouz took a stick of sugar-cane from a stall and nibbled it as he watched the wave moving forward to engulf him. Here came the Rifiya dervishes, who could in their trances walk upon embers or drink molten glass or eat live scorpions — or dance the turning measure of the universe out, until reality ran down like an overwound spring and they fell gasping to the earth, dazed like birds. The banners and torches, the great openwork braziers full of burning wood, the great paper lanterns inscribed with texts, they made staggering loops and patterns of light upon the darkness of the Alexandrian night, rising and falling, and now the pitches were swollen with spectators, worrying at the procession like mastiffs, screaming and pulling; and still the flood poured on with its own wild music (perhaps the very music that the dying Antony in Cavafy's poem heard) until it engulfed the darkness of the great *meidan*, spreading around it the fitful contours of robes and faces and objects without context but whose colours sprang up and darkened the edges of the sky with colour. Human beings were setting fire to each other.

Somewhere in that black hinterland of smashed and tumbled masonry, of abandoned and disembowelled houses, was a small garden with a tomb in it marking the site which was the sum and meaning of this riot. And here, before a glimmering taper would be read a Christian prayer for a Christian saint, while all around rode the dark press and flood of Alexandria. The dozen faiths and religions shared a celebration which time had sanctified, which was made common to all and dedicated to a season and a landscape, completely obliterating its canon referents in lore and code. To a religious country all religions were one and while the faithful uttered prayers for a chosen saint, the populace enjoyed the fair which had grown up around the celebration, a rocking carnival of light and music.

And through it all (sudden reminders of the city itself and the full-grown wants and powers of a great *entrepôt*) came the whistle of steam-engines from the dark goods-yards or a sniff of sound from the siren of a liner, negotiating the tortuous fairways of the harbour as it set off for India. The night accommodated them all — a prostitute singing in the harsh chipped accents of the land to the gulp and spank of a finger-drum, the cries of children on the swings and sweating roundabouts and goose-nests, the cock-shies and snake-charmers, the freaks (Zubeida the bearded woman and the calf with five legs), the great canvas theatre outside which the muscle-dancers stood, naked except for loin-cloths, to advertise their skill, and motionless, save for the incredible rippling of their bodies — the flickering and toiling of pectoral, abdominal and dorsal muscles, deceptive as summer lightning.

Narouz was rapt and looked about him with the air of a drunkard, revelling in it all, letting his footsteps follow the haphazard meanderings of this township of light. At the end of one long gallery, having laughingly shaken off the grasp of a dozen girls who plied their raucous trade in painted canvas booths among the stalls, he came to the brilliantly lighted circumcision booths of which the largest and most colourful was that of Abdul's master, Mahmoud Enayet Allah, splendid with lurid cartoons of the ceremony, painted and framed, and from whose lintel hung a great glass jar cloying with leeches. The doyen himself was there tonight, haranguing the crowd and promising free circumcision to any of the faithful too poor to pay the ordinary fee. His great voice rolled out and boomed, while his two assistants stood at attention behind the ancient brass-bound shoe-black's chair with their razors at the alert. Inside the booth, two elderly men in dark suits sipped coffee with the air of philologists at a congress.

Business was slack. 'Come along, come along, be purified, ye faithful' boomed the old man, his thumbs behind the lapels of his ancient frock-coat, the sweat pouring down his face under his red tarbush. A little to one side, rapt in the performance of his trade sat a cousin of Mahmoud, tattooing the breast of a magnificent-looking male prostitute whose oiled curls hung down his back and whose eyes and lips were heavily painted. A glass panel of great brilliance hung beside him, painted with a selection of designs from which his clients could choose — purely geometric for Moslems, or Texts, or the record of a vow, or simply beloved names. Touch by touch he filled in the pores of his subject's skin, like a master of needlecraft, smiling from time to time as if at a private joke, building up his *pointilliste* picture while the old *doyen* roared and boomed from the step above him 'Come along, come along, ye faithful!'

Narouz bent to the tattooist and said in a hoarse voice: 'Is the Magzub here tonight?' and the man raised his startled eye and paused. 'Yes' he said, 'I think. By the tombs.'

Narouz thanked him and turned back once more to the crowded booths, picking his way haphazardly among the narrow thorough-fares until he reached the outskirts of the light. Somewhere ahead of him in the darkness lay a small cluster of abandoned shrines shadowed by leaning palms, and here the gaunt and terrible figure of the famous religious maniac stood, shooting out the thunderbolts of hypnotic personality on to a fearful but fascinated crowd.

Even Narouz shuddered as he gazed upon that ravaged face, the eyes of which had been painted with crayon so that they looked glaring, inhuman, like the eyes of a monster in a cartoon. The holy man hurled oaths and imprecations at the circle of listeners, his fingers curling and uncurling into claws as he worked upon them, dancing this way and that like a bear at bay, turning and twirling, advancing and retreating upon the crowd with grunts and roars and screams until it trembled before him, fascinated by his powers. He had 'come already into his hour', as the Arabs say, and the power of the spirit had filled him.

The holy man stood in an island of the fallen bodies of those he had hypnotized, some crawling about like scorpions, some screaming or bleating like goats, some braying. From time to time he would leap upon one of them uttering hideous screams and ride him across the ring, thrashing at his buttocks like a maniac, and then suddenly turning, with the foam bursting from between his teeth, he would dart into the crowd and pick upon some unfortunate victim, shouting: 'Are you mocking me?' and catching him by his nose or an ear or an arm, drag him with superhuman force into the ring where with a sudden quick pass of his talons he would 'kill his light' and hurl him down among the victims already crawling about in the sand at his feet, to utter shrill cries for mercy which were snuffled out by the braying and hooting of those already under his spell. One felt the power of his personality shooting out into the tense crowd like sparks from an anvil.

Narouz sat down on a tombstone to watch, in the darkness outside the circle. 'Fiends, unclean ones' shrieked the Magzub, thrusting forward his talons so that the circle gave before each onslaught. 'You and You and You and You' his voice rising to a terrible roar. He feared and respected no-one when he was 'in his hour'.

A respectable-looking sheik with the green turban which proclaimed him to be of the seed of the Prophet was walking across the outskirts of the crowd when the Magzub caught sight of him and with flying robes burst through the crowd to the old man's side, shouting: 'He is impure.' The old sheik turned upon his accuser with angry eyes and started to expostulate, but the fanatic thrust his face close to him and sank those terrible eyes into him. The old sheik suddenly went dull, his head wobbled on his neck and with a shout the Magzub had him down on all fours, grunting like a boar, and dragged him by the turban to hurl him among the others. 'Enough' cried the crowd, outraged at this indifference to a man of holiness, but the Magzub twisted round and with flickering fingers rushed back towards the crowd, shrieking: 'Who cries "enough", who cries "enough"?'

And now, obedient to the commands of this terrible nightmare-mystic, the old sheik rose to his feet and began to perform a lonely little ceremonial dance, crying in thin bird-like tones: 'Allah. Allah!' as he trod a shaky measure round the circle of bodies, his voice suddenly breaking into the choking cries of a dying animal. 'Desist' called the crowd, 'desist, O Magzub.' And the hypnotist made a few blunt passes and thrust the old sheik out of the ring, heaping horrible curses upon him.

The old man staggered and recovered himself. He was wide awake now and seemed little the worse for his experience. Narouz came to his side as he was readjusting his turban and dusting his robes. He saluted him and asked him the name of the Magzub, but the old sheik did not know. 'But he is a very good man, a holy man' he said. 'He was once alone in the desert for years.' He walked serenely off into the night and Narouz went back to his tombstone to meditate on the beauty of his surroundings and to wait until he might approach the Magzub whose animal shrieks still sounded upon the night, piercing the blank hubbub of the fair and the drone of the holy men from some nearby shrine. He had as yet not decided how best to deal with the strange personage of the darkness. He waited upon the event, meditating.

It was late when the Magzub ended his performance, releasing the imprisoned menagerie about his feet and driving the crowd away by smacking his hands together — for all the world as if they were geese. He stood for a while shouting imprecations after them and then turned abruptly back among the tombs. 'I must be careful' thought Narouz, who intended using force upon him 'not to get within his eyes.' He had only a small dagger which he now loosened in its sheath. He began to follow, slowly and purposefully.

The holy man walked slowly, as if bowed down by the weight of preoccupations too many to number and almost too heavy for a mortal to bear. He still groaned and sobbed under his breath, and once he fell to his knees and crawled along the ground for a few paces, muttering. Narouz watched all this with head on one side, like a gun-dog, waiting. Together they skirted the ragged confines of the festival in the half-darkness of the hot night, and at last the Magzub came to a long broken wall of earth-bricks which had once demarcated gardens now abandoned and houses now derelict. The noise of the fair had diminished to a hum, but a steam-engine still pealed from somewhere near at hand. They walked now in a peninsula of darkness, unable to gauge relative distances, like wanderers in an unknown desert. But the Magzub had become more erect now, and walked more quickly, with the eagerness of a fox that is near its earth. He turned at last into a great deserted yard, slipping through a hole in the mud-brick wall. Narouz was afraid he might lose trace of him among these shattered fragments of dwellings and dust-blown tombs. He came around a corner full upon him — the figure of a man now swollen by darkness into a mirage of a man, twelve foot high. 'O Magzub' he called softly, 'give praise to God,' and all of a sudden his apprehension gave place, as it always did when there was violence to be done, to a savage exultation as he stepped forward into the radius of this holy man's power, loosening the dagger and half-drawing it from the sheath.

The fanatic stepped back once and then twice; and suddenly they were in a shaft of light which, leaking across the well of darkness from some distant street-lamp, set them both alive, giving to each other only a lighted head like a medallion. Dimly Narouz saw the man's arms raised in doubt, perhaps in fear, like a diver, and resting upon some rotten wooden beam which in some forgotten era must have been driven into the supporting wall of a byre as a foundation for a course of the soft earth-brick. Then the Magzub turned half sideways to join his hands, perhaps in prayer, and with precise and deft calculation Narouz performed two almost simultaneous acts. With his right hand he drove his dagger into the wood, pinning the Magzub's arms to it through the long sleeves of his coarse gown; with his left he seized the beard of the man, as one might seize a cobra above its hood to prevent it striking. Lastly, instinctively, he thrust his face forward, spreading his split lip to the full, and hissing (for deformity also confers magical powers in the East) in almost the form of an obscene kiss, as he whispered 'O beloved of the Prophet.'

They stood like this for a long moment, like effigies of a forgotten action entombed in clay or bronze, and the silence of the night about them took up its palpitating proportions once more. The Magzub breathed heavily, almost plaintively, but he said nothing; but now staring into those terrible eyes, which he had seen that evening burning like live coals, Narouz could discern no more power. Under the cartoon image of the crayon, they were blank and lustreless, and their centres were void of meaning, hollow, dead. It was as if he had pinned a man already dead to this corner of the wall in this abandoned yard. A man about to fall into his arms and breathe his last.

The knowledge that he had nothing to fear, now that the Magzub was 'not in his hour', flooded into Narouz' mind on waves of sadness — apologetic sadness: for he knew he could measure the divinity of the man, the religious power from which he took refuge in madness. Tears came into his eyes and he released the saint's beard, but only to rub the matted hair of his head with his hand and whisper in a voice full of loving tears 'Ah, beloved of the Prophet! Ah! Wise one and beloved' — as if he were caressing an animal —

as if the Magzub now had transformed himself into some beloved hunting-dog. Narouz ruffled his ears and hair, repeating the words in the low magical voice he always used with his favourite animals. The magician's eye rolled, focused and became bleary, like that of a child suddenly overcome with self-pity. A single sob broke from his very heart. He sank to a kneeling position on the dry earth with both hands still crucified to the wall. Narouz bowed and fell with him, comforting him with hoarse inarticulate sounds. Nor was this feigned. He was in a passion of reverence for one who he knew had sought the final truths of religion beneath the mask of madness.

But one side of his mind was still busy with the main problem, so that he now said, not in the tender voice of a hunter wheedling a favourite, but in the tone of a man who carries a dagger: 'Now you will tell me what I wish to know, will you not?' The head of the magician still lolled wearily, and he turned his eyes upwards into his skull with what seemed to be a fatigue which almost resembled death. 'Speak' he said hoarsely; and quickly Narouz leaped up to reclaim his dagger, and then, kneeling beside him with one hand still laid about his neck, told him what he wanted to know.

'They will not believe me' moaned the man. 'And I have seen it by my own scope. Twice I have told them. I did not touch the child.' And then with a sudden flashing return in voice and glance to his own lost power, he cried: 'Shall I show you too? Do you wish to see?' — but sank back again. 'Yes' cried Narouz, who trembled now from the shock of the encounter, 'yes.' It was as if an electric current were passing in his legs, making them tremble. 'Show me.'

The Magzub began to breathe heavily, letting his head fall back on his bosom after every breath. His eyes were closed. It was like watching an engine charge itself, from the air. Then he opened his eyes and said, 'Look into the ground.'

Kneeling upon that dry baked earth he made a circle in the dust with his index finger, and then smoothed out the sand with the palm of his hand. 'Here where the light is' he whispered, touching the dust slowly, purposefully; and then 'look with your eye into the breast of the earth' indicating with his finger a certain spot. 'Here.'

Narouz knelt down awkwardly and obeyed. 'I see nothing' he said quietly after a moment. The Magzub blew his breath out slowly in a series of long sighs. '*Think* to see in the ground' he insisted. Narouz allowed his eyes to enter the earth and his mind to pour through them into the spot under the magician's finger. All was still. 'I conceive' he admitted at last. Now suddenly, clearly, he saw a corner of the great lake with its interlinking network of canals and the old palm-shaded house of faded bricks where once Arnauti and Justine had lived — where indeed he had started *Moeurs* and where the child.... 'I see her' he said at last. 'Ah!' said the Magzub. 'Look well.'

Narouz felt as if he were subtly drugged by the haze rising from the water of the canals. 'Playing by the river' he went on. 'She has fallen'; he could hear the breathing of his mentor becoming deeper. She has fallen' intoned the Magzub. Narouz went on: 'No-one is near her. She is alone. She is dressed in blue with a butterfly brooch.' There was a long silence; then the magician groaned softly before saying in a thick, almost gurgling tone: 'You have seen — to the very place. Mighty is God. In Him is my scope.' And he took a pinch of dust and rubbed it upon his forehead as the vision faded.

Narouz, deeply impressed by these powers, kissed and embraced the Magzub, never for one moment doubting the validity of the information he had been granted in the vision. He rose to his feet and shook himself like a dog. They greeted one another now in low whispers and parted. He left the magician sitting there, as if exhausted, upon the ground, and turned his steps once more towards the fair-lights. His body was still shaking with the reaction as if afflicted by pins and needles — or as if an electric current were discharging through his loins and thighs. He had, he realised, been very much afraid. He yawned and shivered as he walked and struck his arms against his legs for warmth — as if to restore a sluggish circulation.

In order to reach the carpenter's yard where his horse was stabled, he had to traverse the eastern corner of the festival ground, where despite the lateness of the hour there was a good deal of hubbub around the swings, and the lights still blazed. It was the time when the prostitutes came into their own, the black, bronze and citron women, impenitent seekers for the money-flesh of men; flesh of every colour, ivory or gold or black. Sudanese with mauve gums and tongues as blue as chows'. Waxen Egyptians. Circassians golden-haired and blue of eye. Earth-blue negresses, pungent as wood-smoke. Every variety of the name of flesh, old flesh quailing upon aged bones, or the unquenched flesh of boys and women on limbs infirm with the desires that could be represented in effigy but not be slaked except in mime — for they were desires engendered in the forests of the mind, belonging not to themselves but to remote ancestors speaking through them. Lust belongs to the egg and its seat is below the level of psyche.

The hot blank Alexandrian night burned as brightly as a cresset, reaching up through the bare soles of the black feet to warm the incorrigible hearts and minds. In all this frenzy and loveliness Narouz felt himself borne along, buoyant as a lily floating on a river, yet burrowing deeply into the silence of his own mind as he went to where the archetypes of these marvellous images waited for him.

It was now that he saw, idly, a short scene enacted before his eyes — a scene whose meaning he did not grasp, and which indeed concerned someone he had never met and would never meet: except in the pages of this writing — Scobie.

Somewhere in the direction of the circumcision booths a riot had started. The frail canvas and paper walls with their lurid iconography trembled and shook, voices snarled and screamed and hobnailed boots thundered upon the impermanent flooring of duckboards; and then, bursting through those paper walls into the white light, holding a child wrapped in a blanket, staggered an old man dressed in the uniform of an Egyptian Police Officer, his frail puttееd shanks quavering under him as he ran. Behind him streamed a crowd of Arabs yelling and growling like savage but cowardly dogs. This whole company burst in a desperate sortie right across Narouz' tracks. The old man in uniform was shouting in a frail voice, but what he shouted was lost in the hubbub; he staggered across the road to an ancient cab and climbed into it. It set off at once at a ragged trot followed by a fusillade of stones and curses. That was all.

As Narouz watched this little scene, his curiosity aroused by it, a voice spoke out of the shadows at his side — a voice whose sweetness and depth could belong to one person only: Clea. He was stabbed to the quick — drawing his breath sharply, painfully, and joining his hands in a sudden gesture of childish humility at the sound. The voice was the voice of the woman he loved but it came from a hideous form, seated in half-shadow — the greasefolded body of a Moslem woman who sat unveiled before her paper hut on a three-legged stool. As she spoke, she was eating a sesame cake with the air of some huge caterpillar nibbling a lettuce — and at the same time speaking in the veritable accents of Clea!

Narouz went to her side at once, saying in a low wheedling voice: 'O my mother, speak to me'; and once more he heard those perfectly orchestrated tones murmuring endearments and humble blandishments to draw him towards the little torture-chamber. (Petesouchos the crocodile goddess, no less.)

Blind now to everything but the cadences of the voice he followed her like an addict, standing inside the darkened room with eyes closed, his hands upon her great quivering breasts — as if to drink up the music of these slowly falling words of love in one long wholesome draught. Then he sought her mouth feverishly, as if he would suck the very image of Clea from her breath — from that sesame-laden breath. He trembled with excitement — the perilous feeling of one about to desecrate a sacred place by some irresistible obscenity whose meaning flickered like lightning in the mind with a horrible beauty of its own. (Aphrodite permits every conjugation of the mind and sense in love.)

He loosened his clothing and pressed this great doll of flesh slowly down upon the dirty bed, coaxing from her body with his powerful hands the imagined responses he might have coaxed perhaps from another and better-loved form. 'Speak, my mother' he whispered hoarsely, 'speak while I do it. Speak.' Expressing from this great white caterpillar-form one rare and marvellous image, rare perhaps as an Emperor moth, the beauty of Clea. Oh, but how horrible and beautiful to lie there at last, squeezed out like an old paint-tube among the weeping ruins of intestate desires: himself, his own inner man, thrown finally back into the isolation of a personal dream, transitory as childhood, and not less heartbreaking: Clea!

But he was interrupted, yes; for now as I refashion these scenes in the light of the Interlinear, my memory revives something which it had forgotten; memories of a dirty booth with a man and woman lying together in a bed and myself looking down at them, half-drunk, waiting my turn. I have described the whole scene in another place — only then I took the man to be Mnemjian. I now wonder if it was Narouz. 'They lay there like the victims of some terrible accident, clumsily engaged, as if in some incoherent experimental fashion they were the first partners in the history of the human race to think out this peculiar means of communication.'

And this woman, with her 'black spokes of toiling hair', that lay in Narouz' arms — would Clea or Justine recognize themselves in a mother-image of themselves woven out of moneyed flesh? Narouz was drinking Clea thirstily out of this old body hired for pleasure, just as I myself wished only to drink Justine. Once again 'the austere, mindless primeval face of Aphrodite!'

Yes, but thirst *can* be quenched like this, by inviting a succubus to one's bed; and Narouz later wandered about in the darkness, incoherent as a madman, swollen with a relief he could barely stand. He felt like singing. Indeed, if one cannot say that he had completely forgotten Clea at this moment, one can at least assert that the act had delivered him from her image. He was wholly purged of her — and indeed would have had at this moment even the courage to *hate* her. Such is the polarity of love. 'True' love.

He went back slowly, by winding ways, to his carpenter friend and claimed his horse, after first rousing the family to reassure them that it was not a thief who was making a noise in the stable at this hour.

Then he rode back to his lands, the happiest young man alive, and reached the manor as the first streaks of dawn were in the sky. As no-one was about he wrapped himself in a cloak and rested on the balcony until the sun should wake him up. He wanted to tell his brother the news.

But Nessim listened quietly and seriously to his whole story the next morning, wondering that the human heart makes no sound when the blood drains out of it drop by drop — for he thought he saw in this piece of information a vital check to the growth of the confidence he wished to foster in his wife. 'I do not suppose' said Narouz 'that after so long we could find the body but I'll go over with Faraj and some grapnels and see — there can be no harm in trying. Shall I?' Nessim's shoulders had contracted. His brother paused for a moment and then went on in the same level tone: 'Now I did not know anything before about how the child was dressed. But I will describe what I saw in the ground. She had a blue frock with a brooch in the shape of a butterfly.' Nessim said, almost impatiently: 'Yes. Perfectly true. It was the description Justine gave to the Parquet. I remember the description. So, well, Narouz ... what can I say? It is true. I want to thank you. But as for the dragging — it has been done at least a dozen times by the Parquet. Yes, without result. There is a cut there in the canal and a runaway with a strong undercurrent.'

'I see' said Narouz, cast down.

'It is difficult to know.' But Nessim's voice sharpened its edge as he added: 'But one thing, promise me. She must never know the truth from your lips. Promise.'

'I promise you that' said his brother as Nessim turned aside from the hall telephone and came face to face with his wife. Her face was pale and her great eyes searched his with suspense and curiosity. 'I must go now' said Nessim hurriedly and put down the receiver as he turned to face her and take her hands in his. In memory, I always see them like this, staring at each other with clasped hands, so near together, so far apart. The telephone is a modern symbol for communications which never take place.

* * * * *

VIII

'I told you of Scobie's death (so wrote Balthazar) but I did not tell you in detail the manner of it. I myself did not know him very well but I knew of your affection for him. It was not a very pleasant business and I was concerned in it entirely by accident — indeed, only because Nimrod, who runs the Secretariat, and was Scobie's chief at three removes, happened to be dining with me on that particular evening.

'You remember Nimrod? Well, we had recently been competing for the favours of a charming young Athenian actor known by the delightful name of Socrates Pittakakis, and as any serious rivalry might have caused a bad feeling between us which neither could afford on the official level (I am in some sense a consultant to his department) we had sensibly decided to bury our jealousy and frankly share the youth — as all good Alexandrians should. We were therefore dining *à trois* at the Auberge Bleue with the young man between us like the filling in a meat sandwich. I must admit that I had a slight advantage over Nimrod whose Greek is poor, but in general the spirit of reason and measure reigned. The actor, who drank champagne in stout all evening — he was recovering he explained from a wasting malady by this method — in the last analysis refused to have anything to do with either of us, and indeed turned out to be passionately in love with a heavily moustached Armenian girl in my clinic. So all this effort was wasted — I must say Nimrod was particularly bitter as he had had to pay for this grotesque dinner. Well, as I say, here we all were when the great man was called away to the telephone.

'He came back after a while, looking somewhat grave, and said: "It was from the Police Station by the docks. Apparently an old man has been kicked to death by the ratings of H.M.S. *Milton*. I have reason to believe that it might be one of the eccentrics of Q branch — there is an old Bimbashi employed there. . . ." He stood irresolutely on one leg. "At any rate" he went on "I must go down and make sure. You never know. Apparently" he lowered his voice and drew me to one side in confidence "he was dressed in woman's clothes. There may be a scandal."

329

'Poor Nimrod! I could see that while his duty pressed him hard, he was most reluctant that I should be left alone with the actor. He hovered and pondered heavily. At last, however, my finer nature came to my rescue just when I had given up hope. I too rose. Undying sportsmanship! "I had better come with you" said I. The poor man broke into troubled smiles and thanked me warmly for the gesture. We left the young man eating fish (this time for brain fag) and hurried to the car park where Nimrod's official car was waiting for him. It did not take us very long to race along the Corniche and turn down into the echoing darkness of the dock-area with its cobbled alleys and the flickering gas light along the wharves which makes it seem so like a corner of Marseilles circa 1850. I have always hated the place with its smells of sea-damp and urinals and sesame.

'The police post was a red circular building like a Victorian post office consisting of a small charge-room and two dark sweating dungeons, airless and terrible in that summer night. It was packed with jabbering and sweating policemen all showing the startled whites of their eyes like horses in the gloom. Upon a stone bench in one of the cells lay the frail and ancient figure of an old woman with a skirt dragged up above the waist to reveal thin legs clad in green socks held by suspenders and black naval boots. The electric light had failed and a wavering candle on the sill above the body dripped wax on to one withered old hand, now beginning to settle with the approach of the rigor into a histrionic gesture — as of someone warding off a stage blow. It was your friend Scobie.

'He had been battered to death in ugly enough fashion. A lot of broken crockery inside that old skin. As I examined him a phone started to nag somewhere. Keats had got wind of something: was trying to locate the scene of the incident. It could only be a matter of time before his battered old Citroën drew up outside. Obviously a grave scandal might well be the upshot and fear lent wings to Nimrod's imagination. "He must be got out of these clothes" he hissed and started beating out right and left with his cane, driving the policemen out into the corridor and clearing the cell. "Right" I said, and while Nimrod stood with sweating averted face, I got the body out of its clothes as best I could. Not pleasant, but at last the old reprobate lay there "naked as a psalm" as they say in Greek. That was stage one. We mopped our faces. The little cell was like an oven.

' "He must" said Nimrod hysterically "be somehow got back

330

into uniform. Before Keats comes poking around here. I tell you what, let's go to his digs and get it. I know where he lives." So we locked the old man into his cell: his smashed glass eye gave him a reproachful, mournful look — as if he had been subjected to an amateur taxidermist's art. Anyway, we jumped into the car and raced across the docks to Tatwig Street while Nimrod examined the contents of the natty little leatherette handbag with which the old man had equipped himself before setting out on his adventure. In it he found a few coins, a small missal, a master's ticket, and a packet of those old-fashioned rice-papers (one hardly ever sees them now) resembling a roll of cigarette paper. That was all. "The bloody old fool" Nimrod kept saying as we went. "The bloody old fool."

'We were surprised to find that all was chaos in the old man's lodgings, for in some mysterious way the neighbourhood had already got to hear of his death. At least, so I presumed. All the doors of his rooms had been burst open and cupboards rifled. In a sort of lavatory there was a bathtub full of some brew which smelt like *arak* and the local people had apparently been helping themselves freely, for there were prints from countless wet feet on the stairs and wet hands on the walls. The landing was awash. In the courtyard, a boab dancing round his stave and singing — a most unusual sight. Indeed, the whole neighbourhood seemed to wear an air of raffish celebration. It was most uncanny. Though most of Scobie's things had been stolen, his uniform was hanging quite safely behind the door and we grabbed it. As we did so, we got a tremendous start for a green parrot in a cage in the corner of the room said in what Nimrod swore was a perfect imitation of Scobie's voice:

> "*Come the four corners of the world in arms,*
> *We'll (hic) shock 'em.*"

'It was clear that the bird was drunk. Its voice sounded so strange in that dismal empty room. (I have not told Clea any of this, for fear that it would upset her, as she too cared for him very much.)

'Well, back to the police post with the uniform, then. We were in luck, for there was no sign of Keats. We locked ourselves into the cell again, gasping at the heat. The body was setting so fast that it seemed impossible to get the tunic on without breaking his arms — which, God knows, were so frail that they would have snapped off like celery, or so it seemed: so I compromised by wrapping it round him. The trousers were easier. Nimrod tried to help me but was overtaken by violent nausea and spent most of the time retching in a corner. He was indeed much moved by the whole thing and kept repeating under his breath "Poor old bugger". Anyway, by a smart bit of work, the scandal he feared was averted, and hardly had we brought your Scobie into line with the general proprieties than we heard the unmistakable rumble of the *Globe* car at the door and the voice of Keats in the charge-room.

'Must not forget to add that during the following few days there were two deaths and over twenty cases of acute *arak* poisoning in the area around Tatwig Street so that Scobie may be said to have left his mark in the neighbourhood. We tried to get an analysis of the stuff he was brewing, but the Government analyst gave up after testing several samples. God knows what the old man was up to.

'Nevertheless the funeral was a great success (he was buried with full honours as an officer killed in the execution of his duty) and everyone turned out for it. There was quite a contingent of Arabs from around his home. It is rare to hear Moslem ululations at a Christian graveside, and the R.C. Chaplain, Father Paul, was most put out, fearing perhaps the *afreets* of Eblis conjured up by home-made *arak* — who knows? Also there were the usual splendid inadvertencies, so characteristic of life here (grave too small, grave-diggers strike for more pay in the middle of widening it, Greek consul's carriage runs away with him and deposits him in a bush, etc., etc.) I think I described all this in a letter. It was just what Scobie would have desired — to lie covered with honours while the Police Band blew the Last Post — albeit waveringly and with a strong suggestion of Egyptian quarter-tones — over the grave. And the speeches, the tears! You know how people let themselves go on such occasions. You would have thought he was a saint. I kept remembering the body of the old woman in the police cell!

'Nimrod tells me that once he used to be very popular in his *quartier*, but that latterly he had started to interfere with ritual circumcision among the children and became much hated. You know how the Arabs are. Indeed, that they threatened to poison him more than once. These things preyed upon his mind as one may understand. He had been many years down there and I suppose he had no other life of his own. It happens to so many expatriates, does it not? Anyway, latterly he began to drink and to "walk in his sleep" as the Armenians say. Everyone tried to make allowances for him and two constables were detailed to look after him on these jaunts. But on the night of his death he gave them all the slip.

' "Once they start dressing up" says Nimrod (he is really utterly humourless), "it's the beginning of the end." And so there it is. Don't mistake my tone for flippancy. Medicine has taught me to look on things with ironic detachment and so conserve the powers of feeling which should by rights be directed towards those we love and which are wasted on those who die. Or so I think.

'What on earth, after all, is one to make of life with its grotesque twists and turns? And how, I wonder, has the artist the temerity to try and impose a pattern upon it which he infects with his own meanings? (This is aimed slightly in your direction) I suppose you would reply that it is the duty of the pilot to make comprehensible the shoals and quicksands, the joys and misfortunes, and so give the rest of us power over them. Yes, but. . . .

'I desist for tonight. Clea took in the old man's parrot; it was she who paid the expenses of his funeral. Her portrait of him still stands I believe upon a shelf in her now untenanted room. As for the parrot, it apparently still spoke in his voice and she said she was frequently startled by the things it came out with. Do you think one's soul could enter the body of a green Amazon parrot to carry the memory of one forward a little way into Time? I would like to think so. But this is old history now.'

IX

Whenever Pombal was grievously disturbed about something ('*Mon Dieu!* Today I am decomposed!' he would
say in his quaint English) he would take refuge in a
magistral attack of gout in order to remind himself of his Norman
ancestry. He kept an old-fashioned high-backed court chair,
covered in red velveteen, for such occasions. He would sit with his
wadded leg up on a footstool to read the *Mercure* and ponder on
the possible reproof and transfer which might follow upon his
latest *gaffe* whatever that might happen to be. His whole Chancery,
he knew, was against him and considered his conduct (he drank too
much and chased women) as prejudicial to the service. In fact, they
were jealous because his means, which were not large enough to
free him altogether from the burden of working for a living, permitted him nevertheless to live more or less *en prince* — if you
could call the smoky little flat we shared princely.

As I climbed the stairs today I knew that he was in a decomposed
state from the peevish tone in which he spoke. 'It is *not* news' he
was repeating hysterically. 'I forbid you to publish.' One-eyed
Hamid met me in the hall which smelt of frying, and waved a
tender hand in the air. 'The Miss has gone' he whispered, indicating Melissa's departure, 'back six o'clock. Mr. Pombal very not
good.' He pronounced my friend's name as if it contained no
vowels: thus: Pmbl.

I found Keats was with him in the sitting-room, his large and
perspiring frame stretched awkwardly across the sofa. He was
grinning and his hat was on the back of his head. Pombal was
perched in his gout-chair, looking mournful and peevish. I recognized the signs not only of a hangover but of yet another committed
gaffe. What had Keats got hold of now? 'Pombal' I said, 'what the
devil has happened to your car?' He groaned and clutched his
dewlaps as if imploring me to leave the whole subject alone;
obviously Keats had been teasing him about just that.

The little car in question, so dear to Pombal's heart, now stood
outside the front door, badly buckled and smashed. Keats gave a
snuffle-gulp. 'It was Sveva' he explained, 'and I'm not allowed to

print it.' Pombal moaned and rocked. 'He won't tell me the whole story.'

Pombal began to get really angry. 'Will you please get out?' he said, and Keats, always easily discountenanced before someone whose name appeared on the diplomatic list, rose and pocketed his notebook, wiping the smile off his face as he did so. 'All right' he said, punning feebly '*Chacun à son* gout, I suppose' and clambered slowly down the stairs. I sat down opposite Pombal and waited for him to calm down.

'Another *gaffe*, my dear boy' he said at last; 'the worst yet in the *affaire Sveva*. It was she . . . my poor car . . . you have seen it? Here, feel this bump on my neck. Eh? A bloody rock.'

I asked Hamid for some coffee while he recounted his latest mishap with the usual anguished gesticulations. He had been unwise ever to embark on this affair with the fiery Sveva, for now she loved him. 'Love!' Pombal groaned and twisted in his chair. 'I am so weak about women' he admitted, 'and she was so easy. God, it was like having something put on one's plate which one hadn't ordered — or which someone else had and which had been sent to one's table by mistake; she came into my life like a *bifteck à point*, like a stuffed eggplant. . . . What was I to do?

'And then yesterday I thought: "Taking everything into account, her age, the state of her teeth, and so on, illness might very well intervene and cause me expense." Besides, I don't *want* a mistress in *perpetuum mobile*. So I decided to take her out to a quiet spot on the lake and say good-bye. She went mad. In a flash she was on the bank of the river where she found a huge pile of rocks. Before I knew what to say *Piff Paff Pang Bong*.' His gestures were eloquent. 'The air was full of rocks. Windscreen, headlights, everything . . . I was lying beside the clutch screaming. Feel this lump on my neck. She had gone mad. When all the glass was gone, she picked up a huge boulder and began to stove the car in screaming the word "*Amour, Amour*" to puctuate each bang like a maniac. I never want to hear the word again. Radiator gone, all the wings twisted. You have seen? You would never believe a girl could do such a thing. Then what? Then I'll tell you what. *She threw herself into the river*. Figure to yourself my feelings. She can't swim, nor can I. The *scandal* if she died! I threw myself in after her. We held each other and screamed like a pair of cats making love. The water I swallowed! Some policemen came and pulled us out. Long *procès-*

verbal, etc. I simply dare not ring the Chancery this morning. Life isn't worth living.'

He was on the point of tears. 'This is my third scandal this month' he said. 'And tomorrow is carnival. Do you know what? After long thought I have evolved an idea.' He smiled a wintry smile. 'I shall make sure about the carnival — even if I do drink too much and get in a scrape as I usually do. I shall go in an impenetrable disguise. Yes.' He rinsed his fingers and repeated 'An impenetrable disguise.' Then he considered me for a moment as if to decide whether to trust me or not. His scrutiny seemed to satisfy him for he turned abruptly towards the cupboard and said: 'If I show you, you'll keep my secret, eh? We are friends after all. Fetch me the hat from the top shelf in there. You will get a laugh.'

Inside the cupboard I found an immense, old-fashioned picture-hat of the 1912 variety, trimmed with a bunch of faded osprey feathers and secured by a thick hatpin with a large blue stone head. 'This?' I said incredulously, and he chuckled complacently as he nodded. 'Who will ever recognize me in this? Give it here. . . .'

He looked so funny with it on that I was forced to sit down and laugh. He reminded me of Scobie in his own absurd Dolly Varden. Pombal looked . . . it is quite indescribable what this ridiculous creation did to his fat face. He began to laugh too as he said 'Wonderful, no? My bloody colleagues will never know who the drunk woman was. And if the Consul General isn't in domino I shall . . . make advances to him. I shall drive him out of his mind with passionate kisses. The swine!' His face set in a grimace of hate looked even more ludicrous. As with Scobie, I was forced to plead: 'Take it off, for God's sake!'

He did so and sat grinning at me, consumed by the brilliance of his plan. At least, he thought, such indiscretions as he might commit would not be attributable to him. 'I have a whole costume' he added proudly. 'So look out for me, will you? You are going, aren't you? I hear that there are two full-scale balls going so we shall weave about from one to the other, eh? Good. I am a bit relieved, aren't you?'

But it was this fatal hat of Pombal's which led directly to Toto de Brunel's mysterious death next evening at the Cervonis' — the death which Justine believed her husband had reserved for her and which I. . . But I must follow the Interlinear back upon my tracks.

'The question of the watch-key' writes Balthazar ' — the one you helped me hunt for among the crevices of the Grande Corniche on that winter day — turned out oddly. As you know, my time-piece stopped and I had to order another little gold ankh to be made for it. But in the interval the key was returned under strange circumstances. One day Justine came into the clinic and, kissing me warmly, produced it from her handbag. "Do you recognize this?" she asked me smiling, and then went on apologetically "I am so sorry for your concern, my dear Balthazar. It is the first time in my life that I have been forced to turn pickpocket. You see, there is a wall-safe in the house to which I was determined to gain access. At first glance the keys seemed similar and I wanted to see whether your watch-key fitted the lock. I had intended to return it next morning before you had time to worry, but I found that someone had removed it from my dressing-table. You won't repeat this. I thought that perhaps Nessim himself had caught sight of it, and had suspected my motive, and had therefore con-fiscated it in order to try it in the lock of his safe himself. For-tunately (or unfortunately) it does not fit, and I could not open the little safe. But, nor could I make a fuss about the thing for fear that he had not in fact seen it; I did not want to draw his attention to its existence and its similarity to his own. I asked Fatma discreetly and went through my jewel-cases. No luck. Then two days later Nessim himself produced it and said he had found it in his stud-box; he recognized its similarity to his own but did not mention the safe. He simply asked me to give it back to you, which I herewith do, with genuine apologies for the delay."

'I was of course annoyed, and told her so. "And anyway, why should you wish to poke about in Nessim's private safe?" I said. "It seems to me unlike your normal behaviour, and I must say I feel a good deal of contempt for you after the way Nessim has treated you." She hung her head and said "I only hoped to dis-cover something about the child — something which I think he is hiding from me." '

*　　*　　*　　*　　*

337

PART III

X

'I suppose (writes Balthazar) that if you wished somehow to incorporate all I am telling you into your own Justine manuscript now, you would find yourself with a curious sort of book — the story would be told, so to speak, in layers. Unwittingly I may have supplied you with a form, something out of the way! Not unlike Pursewarden's idea of a series of novels with "sliding panels" as he called them. Or else, perhaps, like some medieval palimpsest where different sorts of truth are thrown down one upon the other, the one obliterating or perhaps supplementing another. Industrious monks scraping away an elegy to make room for a verse of Holy Writ!

'I don't suppose such an analogy would be a bad one to apply to the reality of Alexandria, a city at once sacred and profane; between Theocritus, Plotinus, and the Septuagint one moves on intermediate levels which are those of race as much as anything — like saying Copt, Greek and Jew or Moslem, Turk and Armenian. . . . Am I wrong? These are the slow accretions of time itself on place. Just as life on the individual face lays down, wash by successive wash, the wrinkles of experiences in which laughter and tears are utterly indistinguishable. Wormcasts of experience on the sands of life. . . .'

So writes my friend, and he is right; for the Interlinear now raises for me much more than the problem of objective 'truth to life', or if you like 'to fiction'. It raises, as life itself does — whether one makes or takes it — the harder-grained question of form. How then am I to manipulate this mass of crystallized data in order to work out the meaning of it and so give a coherent picture of this impossible city of love and obscenity?

I wish I knew. I wish I knew. So much has been revealed to me by all this that I feel myself to be, as it were, standing upon the threshold of a new book — a new Alexandria. The old evocative outlines which I drew, intertwining them with the names of the city's exemplars — Cavafy, Alexander, Cleopatra and the rest — were subjective ones. I had made the image my own jealous personal property, and it was true yet only within the limitations of a truth only partially perceived. Now, in the light of all these new treasures — for truth, though merciless as love, must always be a treasure — what should I do? Extend the frontiers of original truth, filling in with the rubble of this new knowledge the foundations upon which to build a new Alexandria? Or should the dispositions remain the same, the characters remain the same — and is it only truth *itself* which has changed in contradiction?

All this spring on my lonely island I have been weighed down by this grotesque information, which has so altered my feelings about things — oddly enough even about things past. Can emotions be retrospective, retroactive?

So much I wrote was based upon Justine's fears of Nessim — genuine fears, genuinely expressed. I have seen with my own eyes that cold speechless jealousy upon his face — and seen the fear written on hers. Yet now Balthazar says that Nessim would never have done her harm. What am I to believe?

We dined so often together, the four of us; and there I sat speechless and drunk upon the memory of her actual kisses, believing (only because she told me so) that the presence of the fourth — Pursewarden — would lull Nessim's jealous brain and offer us the safety of chaperonage! Yet if now I am to believe Balthazar, it was I who was the decoy. (Do I remember, or only imagine, a special small smile which from time to time would appear at the corner of Pursewarden's lips, perhaps cynical or perhaps comminatory?) I thought then that I was sheltering behind the presence of the writer while he was in fact sheltering behind mine! I am prevented from fully believing this by . . . what? The quality of a kiss from the lips of one who could murmur, like a being submitting its body to the rack, the words 'I love you.' Of course, of course. I am an expert in love — every man believes himself to be one: but particularly the Englishman. So I am to believe in the kiss rather than in the statements of my friend? Impossible, for Balthazar does not lie. . . .

Is love by its very nature a blindness? Of course, I know I averted my face from the thought that Justine might be unfaithful to me while I possessed her — who does not? It would have been too painful a truth to accept, although in my heart of hearts I knew full well, that she could never be faithful to me for ever. If I ever dared to whisper the thought to myself I hastily added, like every husband, every lover, 'But of course, whatever she does, I am the one she truly loves!' The sophistries which console — the lies which keep love going!

Not that she herself ever gave me direct reason to doubt. I do however remember an occasion on which the faintest breath of suspicion roused itself against Pursewarden, only to be immediately stilled. He walked out of the studio one day towards us with some lipstick on his mouth. But almost immediately I caught sight of the cigarette in his hand — he had obviously picked up a cigarette which Justine had left burning in an ashtray (a common habit with her) for the end of it was red. In matters of love everything is easy to explain.

The wicked Interlinear, freighted with these doubts, presses like a blunt thumb, here and here, always in bruised places. I have begun to copy it whole — the whole of it — slowly and painfully; not only to understand more clearly wherein it differs from my own version of reality, but also to catch a glimpse of it as a separate entity — as a manuscript existing in its own right, as the determined view of another eye upon events which I interpreted in my own way, because that was the way in which I lived them — or they lived me. Did I really miss so much that was going on around me — the connotation of smiles, of chance words and gestures, messages scribbled with a finger in wine spilt upon a table-top, addresses written in the corner of newspapers and folded over? Must I now rework my own experiences in order to come to the heart of the truth? 'Truth has no heart' writes Pursewarden. 'Truth is a woman. That is why it is enigmatic. Of women, the most we can say, not being Frenchmen, is that they are burrowing animals.'

According to Balthazar, I have misread the order of Justine's fears in so far as they concerned Nessim. The incident of the car I have recorded elsewhere; how she was racing towards Cairo one night to meet Pursewarden when the lights of the great moth-coloured Rolls went out. Blinded by darkness she lost control of it and it swarmed off the road, bouncing from dune to dune and throwing up spouts of sand like the spray thrown up by the death-agonies of a whale. Then 'whistling like an arrow' it buried itself to the windscreens in a dune and lay trembling and murmuring. Fortunately, she was not hurt and had the presence of mind to switch off the engine. But how had the accident come about? In telling me of it she said that when the car was examined the wiring was found to have been filed down — by whom?

This was, as far as I know, the first time that her fears concerning Nessim, and a possible attempt on her own life, became articulate. She had spoken of his jealousy before, yes; but not of anything like this, not of anything so concrete — so truly Alexandrian. My own alarm may well be imagined.

Yet now Balthazar in his notes says that some ten days before this incident, she had seen Selim from the studio window walk across the lawn towards the car, and there believing himself unobserved, lift the bonnet to take out from under it one of the little wax rollers which she thought she recognized as part of the equipment belonging to the dictaphone which Nessim often used in the office. He had wrapped the object in a cloth and carried it indoors. She sat at the window for a long time, musing and smoking before acting. Then she took the car out on to the desert road to a lonely place the better to examine it. Under the bonnet she found a small apparatus which she did not recognize but which seemed to her to be possibly a recording machine. Presumably a wire lead connected it to a small microphone buried somewhere among the coloured coils of the dashboard wiring, but she could not trace it. With her nail file, however, she cut the wire at several points while leaving the whole contrivance in place and apparently in working order. It was now, according to Balthazar, that she must by accident have disturbed or half-severed one of the leads to the car's headlights. At least, this is what she told him, though she gave me no such explanation. If I am to believe him, all this time, while she went on and on about the heedless folly of our public behaviour and the risks we were taking, she was really drawing me on — trailing me before the eyes of Nessim like a cape before a bull!

But this was only at first; later, says my friend, came something which really made her feel that some action against her was contemplated by her husband: namely the murder of Toto de Brunel during the carnival ball at the Cervonis'. Why have I never mentioned this? It is true that I was even there at the time, and yet somehow the whole incident though it belonged to the atmosphere of the moment escaped me in the press of other matters. Alexandria had many such unsolved mysteries at that time. And while I knew the interpretation Justine put upon it I did not myself believe it at the time. Nevertheless, it is strange that I should not have mentioned it, even in passing. Of course, the true explanation of the matter was only given to me months later: almost when I myself was on the point of leaving Alexandria for ever as I thought.

The carnival in Alexandria is a purely social affair — having no calendar relationship to the other religious festivals of the city. I suppose it must have been instituted by the three or four great Catholic families in the place — perhaps vicariously they enjoyed through it a sense of identity with the other side of the Mediterranean, with Venice and Athens. Nevertheless, there is today no rich family which does not keep a cupboard full of velvet dominoes against the three days of folly — be it Copt, Moslem or Jewish. After New Year's Eve it is perhaps the greatest Christian celebration of the year — for the ruling spirit of the three days and nights is — utter anonymity: the anonymity conferred by the grim black velvet domino which shrouds identity and sex, prevents one distinguishing between man and woman, wife and lover, friend and enemy.

The maddest aberrations of the city now come boldly forward under the protection of the invisible lords of Misrule who preside at this season. No sooner has darkness fallen than the maskers begin to appear in the streets — first in ones and twos then in small companies, often with musical instruments or drums, laughing and singing their way to some great house or to somen ight-club where already the frosty air is bathed in the nigger warmth of jazz — the cloying grunting intercourse of saxophones and drums. Everywhere they spring up in the pale moonlight, cowled like monks. The disguise gives them all a gloomy fanatical uniformity of outline which startles the white-robed Egyptians and fills them with alarm — the thrill of a fear which spices the wild laughter pouring out of the houses, carried by the light offshore winds towards the cafes on the sea-front; a gaiety which by its very shrillness seems to tremble always upon the edge of madness.

Slowly the bluish spring moon climbs the houses, sliding up the minarets into the clicking palm-trees, and with it the city seems to uncurl like some hibernating animal dug out of its winter earth, to stretch and begin to drink in the music of the three-day festival.

The jazz pouring up from the cellars displaces the tranquil winter air in the parks and thoroughfares, mingling as it reaches the sealine with the drumming perhaps of a liner's screws in the deepwater reaches of the estuary. Or you may hear and see for a brief moment the rip and slither of fireworks against a sky which for a moment curls up at the edges and blushes, like a sheet of burning carbon paper: wild laughter which mixes with the hoarse mooing of an old ship outside the harbour bar — like a cow locked outside a gate.

'The lover fears the carnival' says the proverb. And with the emergence of these black-robed creatures of the night everywhere, all is subtly altered. The whole temperature of life in the city alters, grows warm with the subtle intimations of spring. *Carni vale* — the flesh's farewell to the year, unwinding its mummy wrappings of sex, identity and name, and stepping forward naked into the futurity of the dream.

All the great houses have thrown open their doors upon fabulous interiors warm with a firelight which bristles upon china and marble, brass and copper, and upon the blackleaded faces of the servants as they go about their duties. And down every street now, glittering in the moonlit gloaming, lounge the great limousines of the brokers and gamblers, like liners in dock, the patient and impressive symbols of a wealth which is powerless to bring true leisure or peace of mind for it demands everything of the human soul. They lie webbed in a winter light, expressing only the silence and power of all machinery which waits for the fall of man, looking on at the maskers as they cross and recross the lighted windows of the great houses, clutching each other like black bears, dancing to the throb of nigger music, the white man's solace.

Snatches of music and laughter must rise to Clea's window where she sits with a board on her knees, patiently drawing while her little cat sleeps in its basket at her feet. Or perhaps in some sudden lull the chords of a guitar may be plucked to stay and wallow in the darkness of the open street until they are joined by a voice raised in remote song, as if from the bottom of a well. Or screams, cries for help.

But what stamps the carnival with its spirit of pure mischief is the velvet domino — conferring upon its wearers the disguise which each man in his secret heart desires above all. To become anonymous in an anonymous crowd, revealing neither sex nor relationship nor even facial expression — for the mask of this demented friar's habit leaves only two eyes, glowing like the eyes of a Moslem woman or a bear. Nothing else to distinguish one by; the thick folds of the blackness conceal even the countours of the body. Everyone becomes hipless, breastless, faceless. And concealed beneath the carnival habit (like a criminal desire in the heart, a temptation impossible to resist, an impulse which seems preordained) lie the germs of something: of a freedom which man has seldom dared to imagine for himself. One feels free in this disguise to do whatever one likes without prohibition. All the best murders in the city, all the most tragic cases of mistaken identity, are the fruit of the yearly carnival; while most love affairs begin or end during these three days and nights during which we are delivered from the thrall of personality, from the bondage of ourselves. Once inside that velvet cape and hood, and wife loses husband, husband wife, lover the beloved. The air becomes crisp with the saltpetre of feuds and follies, the fury of battles, of agonizing night-long searches, of despairs. You cannot tell whether you are dancing with a man or a woman. The dark tides of Eros, which demand full secrecy if they are to overflow the human soul, burst out during carnival like something long dammed up and raise the forms of strange primeval creatures — the perversions which are, I suppose, the psyche's ailment — in forms which you would think belonged to the Brocken or to Eblis. Now hidden satyr and maenad can rediscover each other and unite. Yes, who can help but love carnival when in it all debts are paid, all crimes expiated or committed, all illicit desires sated — without guilt or premeditation, without the penalties which conscience or society exact?

But I am wrong about one thing — for there is one distinguishing mark by which your friend or enemy may still identify you: your hands. Your lover's hands, if you have ever noticed them at all, will lead you to her in the thickest press of maskers. Or by arrangement she may wear, as Justine does, a familiar ring — the ivory intaglio taken from the tomb of a dead Byzantine youth — worn upon the fore-finger of the right hand. But this is all, and it is only just enough. (Pray that you are not as unlucky as Amaril who found the perfect woman during carnival but could not persuade her to raise her hood and stand identified. They talked all night, lying in the grass by the fountain, making love together with their velvet faces touching, their eyes caressing each other. For a whole year now, he has gone about the city trying to find a pair of human hands, like a madman. But hands are so alike! She swore, this woman of his, that she would come back next year to the same place, wearing the same ring with its small yellow stone. And so tonight he will wait trembling for a pair of hands by the lily-pond — hands which will perhaps never appear again in his life. Perhaps she was after all an *afreet* or a vampire — who knows? Yet years later, in another book, in another context, he will happen upon her again, almost by accident, but not here, not in these pages too tangled already by the record of ill-starred loves. . . .)

So then you walk the dark streets, serene as a murderer unidentified, all your traces covered by the black cowl, feeling the fresh wintry airs of the city upon your eyelids. The Egyptians you pass look askance at you, not knowing whether to smile or be afraid at your appearance. They hover in an indeterminate state of mind when carnival comes on — wondering how it should be taken. Passing, you give them a burning stare from the depths of your cowl, glad to see them flinch and avert their faces. Other dominoes like yourself emerge from every corner, some in groups laughing and singing as they walk towards some great house or to neighbouring night-clubs.

Walking like this towards the Cervonis', across the network of streets by the Greek Patriarchate you are reminded of other carnivals, perhaps even in other cities, distinguished by the same wildness and gaiety which is the gift of lost identities. Strange adventures which befell you once. At one corner in the Rue Bartout last year the sound of running feet and cries. A man presents a dagger to your throat, crying, like a wounded animal, 'Helen, if you try and run away tonight I swear I'll kill . . .' but the words die as you raise your mask and show your face, and he stammers an apology as he turns away only to burst into sobs and throw himself against an iron railing. Helen has already disappeared, and he will search for her the whole night through!

At a gate into a yard, weirdly lit by the feeble street-lamps, two figures in black are grappling each other, fighting with a tremendous silent fury. They fall, rolling over and over from darkness into light and then back into darkness. Without a word spoken. At the Etoile there is a man hanging from a beam with his neck broken; but when you get close enough you see that it is only a black domino hanging from a nail. How strange that in order to free oneself from guilt by a disguise one should choose the very symbol of the Inquisitor, the cape and hood of the Spanish Inquisition.

But they are not all in domino — for many people are superstitious about the dress and, besides, it can be hot to wear in a crowded room. So you will see many a harlequin and shepherdess, many an Antony and Cleopatra as you walk the streets of the city, many an Alexander. And as you turn into the great iron gates of the Cervonis' house to present your card and climb into the warmth and light and drunkenness within, you will see outlined upon the darkness the feared and beloved shapes and outlines of friends and familiars now distorted into the semblances of clowns and zanies, or clothed in the nothingness of black capes and hoods, infernally joined in a rare and disoriented gaiety.

As if under pressure the laughter squirts up to the ceiling or else, like feathers from a torn quilt, drifts about in clumps in that fevered air. The two string bands, muted by the weight of human voices, labour on in the short staggered rhythms of a maniac jazz — like the steady beating of an airpump. Here on the ballroom floor a million squeakers and trumpets squash and distort the sound while already the dense weight of the coloured paper streamers, hanging upon the shoulders of the dancers, sways like tropical seaweed upon rock-surfaces and trails in ankle-high drifts about the polished floors.

On the night in question, the first night of carnival, there was a dinner-party at the great house. On the long hall sofas the dominoes waited for their tenants while the candlelight still smouldered upon the faces of a Justine and Nessim now framed among the portraits which lined the ugly but imposing dining-room. Faces painted in oils matched by human faces lined by preoccupations and maladies of the soul — all gathered together, made one in the classical brilliance of candlelight. After dinner Justine and Nessim were to go together to the Cervoni ball according to the yearly custom. According to custom too, Narouz at the last moment had excused himself. He would arrive upon the stroke of ten, just in time to claim a domino before the whole party set off, laughing and chattering, for the ball.

As always, he himself had preferred to ride into the city on his horse and to stable it with his friend the carpenter, but as a concession to the event he had struggled into an ancient suit of blue serge and had knotted a tie at his collar. Undress did not matter, since he too would later be wearing a domino. He walked lightly, swiftly across the ill-lit Arab quarter, drinking in the familiar sights and sounds, yet eager for the first sight of the maskers as he reached the end of Rue Fuad and found himself on the confines of the modern town.

At one corner stood a group of shrill-chattering women in domino bent upon mischief. From their language and accent he could detect at once that they were society women, Greeks. These black harpies caught hold of every passer-by to shout jests at him and to pluck at his hood if he were masked. Narouz too had to run the gauntlet: one caught hold of his hand and pretended to tell his fortune; another whispered a proposition in Arabic, setting his hand upon her thigh; the third cackled like a hen and shouted 'Your wife has a lover' and other unkindnesses. He could not tell if they recognized him or not.

Narouz flinched, shook himself and burst smiling through their number, fending them off good-naturedly and roaring with laughter at the sally about his wife. 'Not tonight, my doves' he cried hoarsely in Arabic, thinking suddenly of Clea; and as they showed some disposition to capture him for the evening, be began to run. They chased him a little way, shouting and laughing incoherently down the long dark street, but he easily outdistanced them, and so turned the corner to the great house, still smiling but a little out of breath, and flattered by these attentions which seemed to set the key for the evening's enjoyment. In the silent hall his eye caught the black of dominoes and he put one on before edging open the door of the drawing-room behind which he could hear their voices. It disguised his shabby suit. The cape lay back upon his shoulders.

They were all there by the fire, waiting for him, and he took their cries of welcome greedily and seriously, making his round to kiss Justine on the cheek and to shake hands with the rest in an agony of awkward silence. He put on an artificially sincere expression, looking with distaste into the myopic eyes of Pierre Balbz (he hated him for the goatee and spats) and those of Toto de Brunel (an old lady's lap-dog); but he liked the overblown rose, Athena Trasha, for she used the same scent as his mother; and he was sorry for Drusilla Banubula because she was so clever that she hardly seemed to be a woman at all. With Pursewarden he shared a smile of easy complicity. 'Well' he said, expelling his breath at last in relief. His brother handed him a whisky with mild tenderness, which he drank slowly but all in one draught, like a peasant.

'We were waiting for you, Narouz.'

'The Hosnani exile' glittered Pierre Balbz ingratiatingly.

'The farmer' cried little Toto.

The conversation which had been interrupted by his sudden appearance closed smoothly over his head once more and he sat down by the fire until they should be ready to leave for the Cervoni house, folding his strong hands one upon the other in a gesture of finality, as if to lock up once and for all his powers. The skin at Nessim's temples appeared to be stretched, he noticed, an old sign of anger or strain. The fullness of Justine's dark beauty in her dress (the colour of hare's blood) glowed among the ikons, seeming to enjoy the semi-darkness of the candlelight — to feed upon it and give back the glitter of her barbaric jewellery. Narouz felt full of a marvellous sense of detachment, of unconcern; what these small portents of trouble or stress meant, he did not know. It was only Clea who flawed his self-sufficiency, who darkened the edges of his thought. Each year he hoped that when he arrived at his brother's house he would find she had been included in the party. Yet each year she was not, and in consequence he was forced to drift about all night in the darkness, searching for her as aimlessly as a ghost not even really hoping to encounter her: and yet living upon the attenuated wraith of his fond hope as a soldier upon an iron ration.

They had been talking that night of Amaril and his unhappy passion for a pair of anonymous hands and a carnival voice, and Pursewarden was telling one of his famous stories in that crisp uninflected French of his which was just a shade too perfect.

'When I was twenty, I went to Venice for the first time at the invitation of an Italian poet with whom I had been corresponding, Carlo Negroponte. For a middle-class English youth this was a great experience, to live virtually by candlelight in this huge tumbledown palazzo on the Grand Canal with a fleet of gondolas at my disposal — not to mention a huge wardrobe of cloaks lined with silk. Negroponte was generous and spared no effort to entertain a fellow-poet in the best style. He was then about fifty, frail and rather beautiful, like a rare kind of mosquito. He was a prince and a diabolist, and his poetry happily married the influences of Byron and Baudelaire. He went in for cloaks and shoes with buckles and silver walking-sticks and encouraged me to do the same. I felt I was living in a Gothic novel. Never have I written worse poetry.

'That year we went to the carnival together and got separated though we each wore something to distinguish each other by; you know of course that carnival is the one time of the year when vampires walk freely abroad, and those who are wise carry a pig of garlic in their pockets to drive them off — if by chance one were to be encountered. Next morning I went into my host's room and found him lying pale as death in bed, dressed in the white night-shirt with lace cuffs, with a doctor taking his pulse. When the doctor had gone he said: "I have met the perfect woman, masked; I went home with her and she proved to be a vampire." Then drawing up his nightshirt he showed me with exhausted pride that his body was covered with great bites, like the marks of a weasel's teeth. He was utterly exhausted but at the same time excited — and frightening to relate, very much in love. "Until you have experienced it" he said "you have no idea what it is like. To have one's blood sucked in darkness by someone one adores." His voice broke. "Sade could not begin to describe it. I did not see her face, but I had the impression she was fair, of a northern fairness; we met in the dark and separated in the dark. I have only the impression of white teeth, and a voice — never have I heard any woman say the things she says. She is the very lover for whom I have been waiting all these years. I am meeting her again tonight by the marble griffin at the Footpads' Bridge. O my friend, be happy for me. The real world has become more and more meaningless to me. Now at last, with this vampire's love, I feel I can live again, feel again, write again!" He spent all that day at his papers, and at nightfall set off, cloaked, in his gondola. It was not my business to say anything. The next day once more I found him, pale and deathly tired. He had a high fever, and again these terrible bites. But he could not speak of his experience without weeping — tears of love and exhaustion. And it was now that he had begun his great poem which begins — you all know it ——

> *"Lips not on lips, but on each other's wounds*
> *Must suck the envenomed bodies of the loved*
> *And through the tideless blood draw nourishment*
> *To feed the love that feeds upon their deaths. . . ."*

'The following week I left for Ravenna where I had some studies to make for a book I was writing and where I stayed two months. I heard nothing from my host, but I got a letter from his sister to say that he was ill with a wasting disease which the doctors could not diagnose and that the family was much worried because he insisted on going out at night in his gondola on journeys of which he would not speak but from which he returned utterly exhausted. I did not know what to reply to this.

'From Ravenna, I went down to Greece and it was not until the following autumn that I returned. I had sent a card to Negroponte saying I hoped to stay with him, but had no reply. As I came down the Grand Canal a funeral was setting off in choppy water, by twilight, with the terrible plumes and emblems of death. I saw that they were coming from the Negroponte Palazzo. I landed and ran to the gates just as the last gondola in the procession was filling up with mourners and priests. I recognized the doctor and joined him in the boat, and as we rowed stiffly across the canal, dashed with spray and blinking at the stabs of lightning, he told me what he knew. Negroponte had died the day before. When they came to lay out the body, they found the bites: perhaps of some tropical insect? The doctor was vague. "The only such bites I have seen" he said, "were during the plague of Naples when the rats had been at the bodies. They were so bad we had to dust him down with talcum powder before we could let his sister see the body."

Pursewarden took a long sip from his glass and went on wickedly. 'The story does not end there; for I should tell you how I tried to avenge him, and went myself at night to the Bridge of the Footpads — where according to the gondolier this woman always waited in the shadow. . . . But it is getting late, and anyway, I haven't made up the rest of the story as yet.'

There was a good deal of laughter and Athena gave a well-bred shudder, drawing her shawl across her shoulders. Narouz had been listening open-mouthed, with reeling senses, to this recital: he was spellbound. 'But' he stammered 'is all this true?' Fresh laughter greeted his question.

'Of course it's true' said Pursewarden severely, and added: 'I have never been in Venice in my life.'

And he rose, for it was time for them to be going, and while the impassive black servants waited they put on the velveteen capes and adjusted their masks like the actors they were, comparing their identical reflections as they stood side by side in the two swollen mirrors among the palms. Giggles from Pierre and sallies of wit from Toto de Brunel; and so they stepped laughing into the clear night air, the inquisitors of pleasure and pain, the Alexandrians. . . .

The cars engulfed them while the solicitous domestics and chauffeurs tucked them in, carefully as bales of precious merchandise or spices, tenderly as flowers. 'I feel fragile' squeaked Toto at these attentions. 'This side up with care, eh? Which side up, I ask myself?' He must have been the only person in the city not to know the answer to his own question.

When they had started, Justine leaned forward in the car and plucked his sleeve. 'I want to whisper' she said hoarsely though there was little need for Nessim and Narouz were discussing something in harsh tones (Narouz' voice with the characteristic boyish break in it) and Athena was squibbling to Pierre like a flute. 'Toto . . . listen. One great service tonight, if you will. I have put a chalk-mark on your sleeve, here, at the back. Later on in the evening, I want to give you my ring to wear. Shh. I want to disappear for an hour or so on my own. Hush . . . don't giggle.' But there were squeaks from the velvet hood. 'You will have adventures in my name, dear Toto, while I am gone. Do you agree?'

He threw back his cape to show a delighted face, dancing eyes and that grim little procurer's smile. 'Of course' he whispered back, enraptured by the idea and full of admiration. The feature-less hood at his side from which the voice of Justine had issued like an oracle glowed with a sort of death's-head beauty of its own, nodding at him in the light from the passing street-lamps. The conversation and laughter around them sealed them in a conspiracy of private silence. 'Do you agree?' she said.

'Darling, of course.'

The two masked men in the front seats of the car might have been abbots of some medieval monastery, discussing theological niceties. Athena, consumed by her own voice, still babbled away to Pierre. 'But of course.'

Justine took his arm and turned back the sleeve to show him the chalk-mark she had made. 'I count on you' she said, with some of the hoarse imperiousness of her speaking-voice, yet still in a whis-per. 'Don't let me down!' He took her hand and raised it to his Cupid's lips, kissing the ring from the dead finger of the Byzantine youth as one might kiss the holy picture which had performed a miracle long desired; he was to be turned from a man into a woman. Then he laughed and cried: 'And my indiscretions will be on your head. You will spend the rest of your days. . . .'

'Hush.'

'What is all this?' cried Athena Trasha, scenting a joke or a scandal worth repetition. 'What indiscretions?'

'My own' cried Toto triumphantly into the darkness. 'My very own.' But Justine lay back in the dark car impassively hooded, and did not speak. 'I can't wait to get there' said Athena, and turned back to Pierre. As the car turned into the gate of the Cervoni house, the light caught the intaglio, throwing into relief (colour of burnt milk) a Pan raping a goat, his hands grasping its horns, his head thrown back in ecstasy. 'Don't forget' Justine said once more, for the last time, allowing him to maul her hand with gratitude for such a wonderful idea. 'Don't forget' allowing her ringed fingers to lie in his, cool and unfeeling as a cow which allows itself to be milked. 'Only tell me all the interesting conversations you have, won't you?' He could only mutter 'Darling, darling, darling' as he

kissed the ring with the ovarian passion of the sexually dispossessed.

Almost at once, like the Gulf Stream breaking up an iceberg
with its warm currents, dispersing it, their party disintegrated as it
reached the ballroom and merged with the crowd. Abruptly
Athena was dragged screaming into the heart of the press by a
giant domino who gobbled and roared incomprehensible blas-
phemies in his hood. Nessim, Narouz, Pierre, they suddenly found
themselves turned to ciphers, expelled into a formless world of
adventitious meetings, mask to dark mask, like a new form of insect
life. Toto's chalk-mark gave him a few fugitive moments of identity
as he was borne away like a cork on a stream, and Justine's ring
as well (for which I myself was hunting all that evening in vain).

But everything now settled into the mindless chaotic dance-
figures of the black jazz supported only by the grinding drums and
saxophones, the voices. The spirits of the darkness had taken over
you'd think, disinheriting the daylight hearts and minds of the
maskers, plunging them ever deeper into the loneliness of their
own irrecoverable identities, setting free the polymorphous desires
of the city. The tide washed them up now onto the swampy littorals
of their own personalities — symbols of Alexandria, a dead brackish lake surrounded by the silent, unjudging, wide-eyed desert
which stretches away into Africa under a dead moon.

Locked in our masks now we prowled about despairingly among
the company, hunting from room to room, from floor to lighted
floor of the great house, for an identifiable object to direct our love:
a rose pinned to a sleeve, a ring, a scarf, a coloured bead. Something, anything, to discover our lovers by. The hoods and masks
were like the outward symbols of our own secret minds as we
walked about — as single-minded and as dispossessed as the desert
fathers hunting for their God. And slowly but with irresistible
momentum the great carnival ball gathered pace around us. Here
and there, like patches of meaning in an obscure text, one touched
upon a familiar identity: a bullfighter drinking whisky in a corridor
greeted one in the lisping accents of Tony Umbada, or Pozzo di
Borgo unmasked for an instant to identify himself to his trembling
wife. Outside in the darkness on the grass by the lily pond sat
Amaril, also trembling and waiting. He did not dare to remain unmasked lest the sight of his face might disgust or disappoint her,
should she return this year to the promised assignation. If one falls
in love with a mask when one is masked oneself . . . which of you

will first have the courage to raise it? Perhaps such lovers would go through life together, remaining masked? (Racing thoughts in Amaril's sentimental brain. . . . Love rejoices in self-torture.)

An expressive washerwoman dressed in a familiar picture-hat and recognizable boots (Pombal, as ever was), had pinned a meagre-looking Roman centurion to a corner of the mantelpiece and was cursing him in a parrot-voice. I caught the word '*salaud*'. The little figure of the Consul-General managed to mime his annoyance with choppy gestures and struggles, but it was all in vain, for Pombal held him fast in his great paws. It was fascinating to watch. The centurion's casque fell off, and pushing him to the bandstand Pombal began to beat his behind rhythmically upon the big drum and at the same time to kiss him passionately. He was certainly getting his own back. But as I watched this brief scene, the crowd closed down upon it in a whirl of streamers and confetti and obliterated it. We were packed body to body, cowl to cowl, eye to eye. The music drove us round and round the floor. Still no Justine.

> Old Tiresias
> No-one half so breezy as,
> Half so free and easy as
> Old Tiresias.

It must have been about two o'clock that the fire started in one of the chimneys on the first floor, though its results were not serious and it caused more delight than alarm by its appropriateness. Servants scurried officiously everywhere; I caught a glimpse of Cervoni, running unmasked upstairs, and then a telephone rang. There were pleasing clouds of smoke, suggesting whiffs of brimstone from the bottomless pit. Then within minutes a fire-engine arrived with its siren pealing, and the hall was full of fancy-dress figures of *pompiers* with hatchets and buckets. They were greeted with acclamation as they made their way up to the scene of the fireplace which they virtually demolished with their axes. Others of the tribe had climbed on the roof and were throwing buckets of water down the chimney. This had the effect of filling the first floor with a dense cloud of soot like a London fog. The maskers crowded in shouting with delight, dancing like dervishes. These are the sort of inadvertencies which make a party go. I found myself shouting with them. I suppose I must have been rather drunk by now.

In the great tapestried hall the telephone rang and rang again, needling the uproar. I saw a servant answer it, lay the receiver down, and quest about like a gun-dog until presently he returned with Nessim, smiling and unmasked, who spoke into it quickly and with an air of impatience. Then he too put the receiver down and came to the edge of the dance-floor, staring about him keenly. 'Is anything wrong?' I asked, lifting my own hood as I joined him. He smiled and shook his head. 'I can't see Justine anywhere. Clea wants to speak to her. Can you?' Alas! I had been trying to pick up the distinguishing ring all evening without success. We waited, watching the slow rotation of the dancers, keenly as fishermen waiting for a bite. 'No' he said and I echoed 'No.' Pierre Balbz came up and joined us, lifting his cowl, and said 'A moment ago I was dancing with her. She went out, perhaps.'

Nessim returned to the telephone and I heard him say. 'She's here somewhere. Yes, quite sure. No. Nothing has happened. Pierre had the last dance with her. Such a crowd. She may be in the garden. Any message? Can I ask her to ring you? Very well. No, it was simply a fire in a chimney. It's out now.' He put down the receiver and turned back to us. 'Anyway' he said 'we have a rendezvous in the hall unmasked at three.'

And so the great ball rolled on around us, and the firemen who had done their duty now joined the throng of dancers. I caught a glimpse of a large washerwoman being carried, apparently insensible, out into the conservatory by four demons with breasts amid great applause. Pombal had evidently succumbed to his favourite brand of whisky once more. He had lost his hat but had had the forethought to wear under it an immense wig of yellow hair. It is doubtful whether anyone could have recognized him in such a rig.

Punctually at three Justine appeared in the hall from the garden and unmasked herself: Pierre and I had decided not to accept Nessim's offer of a lift home but to stay on and lend our energy to the ball which was beginning to flag now. Little parties were meeting and leaving, cars were being rallied. Nessim kissed her tenderly and said 'Where's your ring?' a question which I myself had been burning to put to her though I had not dared. She smiled that innocent and captivating smile as she said: 'Toto pinched it from my finger a few minutes ago, during a dance. Where is the little brute? I want it back.' We raked the floor for Toto but there was no sign of him and at last Nessim who was tired decided to give him up for lost. But he did not forget to give Justine Clea's message, and I saw my lover go obediently to the telephone and dial her friend's number. She spoke quietly and with an air of mystification for a few moments, and I heard her say: 'Of course I'm all right' before bidding Clea a belated good night. Then they stepped down together into the waning moonlight arm in arm, and Pierre and I helped to tuck them into the car. Selim, impassive and hawk-featured, sat at the wheel. 'Good night!' cried Justine, and her lips brushed my cheek. She whispered 'Tomorrow' and the word sang on in my mind like the whistle of a bullet as we turned together into the lighted house. Nessim's face had been full of a curious impish serenity as of someone resting after a great expenditure of energy.

Someone had heard a ghost murmuring in the conservatory. Much laughter. 'No, but I assure you' squealed Athena. 'We were sitting on the sofa, Jacques and I, weren't we, Jacques?' A masked figure appeared, blew a squeaker in her face and retired. Something told me it was Toto. I dragged his cowl back and up bobbed the features of Chloë Martinengo. 'But I assure you' said Athena, 'it moaned a word — something like . . .' she set her face in a grim scowl of concentration and after a pause sang out in a lullaby voice the expiring words '*Justice . . . Justice.*' Everyone laughed heartily and several voices mimicked her: '*Justice*' roared a domino rushing away up the stairs. '*Justice!*'

Alone once more, I found that my irresolution and despondency had turned to physical hunger, and I traversed the dance-floor cautiously in the direction of the supper-room from which I could hear the thirsty snap of champagne corks. The ball itself was still in full swing, and dancers swaying like wet washing in a high wind, the saxophones wailing like a litter of pigs. In an alcove Drusilla Banubula sat with her dress drawn up to her shapely knees, allowing a pair of contrite harlequins to bandage a sprained ankle. She had fallen down or been knocked down it would seem. An African witch-doctor wearing a monocle lay fast asleep on the couch behind her. In the second room a maudlin woman in evening dress was playing jazz on a grand piano and singing to herself while great tears coursed down her cheeks. An old fat man with hairy legs hung over her, dressed as the Venus de Milo. He was crying too. His belly trembled.

The supper-room however was comparatively quiet, and here I found Pursewarden, uncowled and apparently rather tipsy, talking to Mountolive as the latter walked with his curious gliding, limping walk round the table, loading a plate with slices of cold turkey and salad. Pursewarden was inveighing somewhat incoherently against the Cervonis for serving Spumante instead of champagne. 'I should watch it' he called out to me, 'there's a headache in every mouthful.' But he had his glass refilled almost at once, holding it with exaggerated steadiness. Mountolive turned a speculative and gentle eye upon me as I seized a plate, and then greeted me by name with evident relief. 'Ah, Darley' he said, 'for a moment I thought you were one of my secretaries. They've been following me around all evening. Spoiling my fun. Errol simply refuses to violate protocol and leave before his Chief of Mission; so I had to hide in the garden until they thought I had left, poor dears. As a junior I have so often cursed my Minister for keeping me up on boring evenings that I made a vow never to make my juniors suffer in the same way if I should ever become Head of Mission.' His light effortless conversation with its unaffectedness of delivery always made him seem immediately sympathetic, though I realized that his manner was a professional one, the bedside manner of the trained diplomat. He had spent so many years in putting his inferiors at their ease, and in hiding his spirit's condescension, that he had at last achieved an air of utterly professional sincerity which while seeming true to nature could not, in reality, have been less false. It had all the fidelity of great acting. But it was annoying that I should always find myself liking him so much. We circled the table slowly together, talking and filling our plates.

'What did you see in the garden, David?' said Pursewarden in a teasing tone, and the Minister's eye rested speculatively on him for a minute, as if to warn him against saying something which would be indiscreet or out of place. 'I saw' said Mountolive smiling and reaching for a glass, 'I saw the amorous Amaril by the lake — talking to a woman in a domino. Perhaps his dreams have come true?' Amaril's passion was well-known to everyone. 'I do hope so.'

'And what *else*?' said Pursewarden in a challenging, rather vulgar tone, as if he shared a private secret with him. 'What else, *who* else did you see, David?' He was slightly tipsy and his voice, though friendly, had a bullying note. Mountolive flushed and looked down at his plate.

At this I left them and made my way back, equipped with loaded plate and glass. I felt a certain scorn in my heart for Pursewarden, and a rush of sympathy for Mountolive at the thought of him being put out of countenance. I wanted to be alone, to eat in silence and think about Justine. My cargo of food was nearly upset by three heavily-rouged Graces, all of them men to judge by the deep voices, who were scuffling in the hall. They were attacking each others' private parts with jocular growls, like dogs. I had the sudden idea of going up to the library which would surely be empty at this time. I wondered if the new Cavafy manuscripts would be there, and whether the collection was unlocked, for Cervoni was a great collector of books.

On the first floor, a fat man with spindly legs, dressed in the costume of Red Riding Hood, was hammering on a lavatory door; servants were sucking the soot from the carpets of the rooms with Hoovers and talking in undertones. The library was on the floor above. There was a noise in one of the bedrooms, and from the bathroom below I could hear someone being chromatically sick. I reached the landing and pressed the airtight door with my foot, and it sucked open to admit me. The long room with its gleaming shelves of books was empty save for a Mephistopheles sitting in an armchair by the fire with a book on his knees. He took his spectacles off in order to identify me and I saw that it was Capodistria. He could not have chosen a more suitable costume. It suited his great ravening beak of a nose and those small, keen eyes, set so close together. 'Come in' he cried. 'I was afraid it might be someone wanting to make love in which case . . . *toujours la politesse*, I should have felt bound. . . . What are you eating? The fire is lovely. I was just looking up a quotation which has been worrying me all evening.'

I joined him and placed my loaded plate as an offering between us to be shared. 'I came to see the new Cavafy manuscript' I said.

'All locked up, the manuscripts' he said.

'Well.'

The fire crackled brightly and the room was silent and welcoming with its lining of fine books. I took off my cape and sat down after a preliminary quest along the walls, during which Da Capo finished copying something out on to a piece of paper. 'Curious thing about Mountolive's father' he said absently. 'This huge eight-volume edition of Buddhist texts. Did you know?'

'I had heard' I said vaguely.

'The old man was a judge in India. When he retired he stayed on there, is still there; foremost European scholar on Pali texts. I must say. . . . Mountolive hasn't seen him for years. He dresses like a *saddhu* he says. You English are eccentrics through and through. Why shouldn't the old man work on his texts in Oxford, eh?'

'Climate, perhaps?'

'Perhaps.' He agreed. 'There. That's what I was hunting for — I knew it was somewhere in the fourth volume.' He banged his book shut.

'What is it?'

He held his paper out to the fire and read slowly with an air of puzzled pleasure the quotation he had copied out: 'The fruit of the tree of good and evil is itself but flesh; yes, and the apple itself is but an apple of the dust.'

'That's not Buddhist, surely' I said.

'No, it's Mountolive père himself, from the introduction.'

'I think that. . . .'

But now there came a confused screaming from somewhere near at hand, and Capodistria sighed. 'I don't know why the devil I take part in this damned carnival year after year' he said peevishly, draining his whisky. 'It is an unlucky time astrologically. For me, I mean. And every year there are ugly accidents. It makes one uneasy. Two years ago Arnelh was found hanging in the musicians' gallery at the Fontanas' house. Funny eh? Damned inconsiderate if he did it himself. And then Martin Fery fought that duel with Jacomo Forte. . . . It brings out the devil. That is why I am dressed as the devil. I hang about waiting for people to come and sell me their souls. Aha!' He sniffed and rubbed his hands with a parchment sound and gave his little dry cachinnation. And then, standing up and finishing the last slice of turkey, 'God, have you seen the time? I must be going home. Beelzebub's bedtime.'

'So should I' I said, disappointed that I could not get a look at the handwriting of the old poet. 'So should I.'

'Can I lift you?' he said, as the sucking door expelled us once more into the trampled musical air of the landing. 'Useless to expect to say good-bye to our hosts. Cervoni is probably in bed by now.'

We went down slowly chatting into the great hall where the music rolled on in an unbroken stream of syncopated sound. Da Capo had adjusted his mask now and looked like some weird bird-like demon. We stood for a moment watching the dancers, and then yawning he said: 'Well, this is where to quote Cavafy the God abandons Antony. Good night. I can't stay awake any longer, though I am afraid the evening will be full of surprises yet. It always is.'

Nor was he to be proved wrong. I hovered for a while, watching the dance, and then walked down the stairs into the dark coolness of the night. There were a few limousines and sleepy servants waiting by the gates, but the streets had begun to empty and my own footfalls sounded harsh and exotic as they smacked up from the pavements. At the corner of Fuad there were a couple of European whores leaning dispiritedly against a wall and smoking. They called once hoarsely after me. They wore magnolia blossoms in their hair.

Yawning, I passed the Etoile to see if perhaps Melissa was still working, but the place was empty except for a drunk family which had refused to go home despite the fact that Zoltan had stacked up the chairs and tables around them on the dance-floor. 'She went off early' the little man explained. 'Band gone. Girls gone. Everyone gone. Only these *canaille* from Assuan. His brother is a policeman; we dare not close.' A fat man began to belly-dance with sugary movements of the hips and pelvis and the company began to mark the time. I left and walked past Melissa's shabby lodgings in the vague hope that she might still be awake. I felt I wanted to talk to someone; no, I wanted to borrow a cigarette. That was all. Afterwards would come the desire to sleep with her, to hold that slender cherished body in my arms, inhaling its sour flavours of alcohol and tobacco-smoke, thinking all the time of Justine. But her window was dark; either she was asleep or was not yet home. Zoltan had said that she left with a party of business-men disguised as admirals. '*Des petits commerçants quelconques*' he had added contemptuously, and then turned at once apologetic.

No, it was to be an empty night, with the frail subfusc moonlight glancing along the waves of the outer harbour, the sea licking and relicking the piers, the coastline thinning away in whiteness, glittering away into the greyness like mica. I stood for a while on the Corniche snapping a paper streamer in my fingers, bit by bit, each fragment breaking off with a hard dry finality, like a human relationship. Then I turned sleepily home, repeating in my mind the words of Da Capo: 'The evening will be full of surprises.'

Indeed, they were already beginning in the house which I had just left, though of course I was not to learn about them until the following day. And yet, surprises though they were, their reception was perfectly in keeping with the city — a city of resignation so deep as almost to be Moslem. For nobody in Alexandria can ever be shocked deeply; among us tragedy exists only to flavour conversation. Death and life are both simply the hazards of a chance which cannot be averted, and merit only smiles and conversations made more animated by the consciousness of their intrusion. No sooner do you tell an Alexandrian a piece of bad news than the words come out of his mouth: 'I knew. Something like this was bound to happen. It always does.' This, then, is what happened.

In the conservatory of the Cervoni house there were several old-fashioned *chaises-longues* on which a mountain of overcoats and evening-wraps had been piled; as the dancers began to go home there came the usual shedding of dominoes and the hunt for furs and capes. I think it was Pierre who must have made the discovery while hunting in this great tumulus of coats for the velvet smoking-jacket which he had shed earlier in the evening. At any rate, I myself had already left and started to walk home by this time.

Toto de Brunel was discovered, still warm in his velvet domino, with his paws raised like two neat little cutlets, in the attitude of a dog which had rolled over to have its belly scratched. He was buried deep in the drift of coats. One hand had half-tried to move towards the fatal temple but the impulse had been cut off at source before the action was complete, and it had stayed there raised a little higher than the other, as if wielding an invisible baton. The hatpin from Pombal's picture hat had been driven sideways into his head with terrific force, pinning him like a moth into his velvet headpiece. Athena had been making love to Jacques while she was literally lying upon his body — a fact which would under normal circumstances have delighted him thoroughly. But he was dead, *le pauvre Toto*, and what is more he was still wearing the ring of my lover. "*Justice!*"

'Of course, something like this happens every year.'

'Of course.' I was still dazed.

'But Toto — that is rather unexpected, really.'

Balthazar rang me up about eleven o'clock the next morning to tell me the whole story. In my stupefied and sleepy condition it sounded not merely improbable, but utterly incomprehensible. 'There will be the *procès-verbal* — that's why I'm ringing. Nimrod is making it as easy as he can. One dinner-party witness only — Justine thought perhaps you if you don't mind? Good. Of course. No, I was got out of bed at a quarter to four by the Cervonis. They were in rather a state about it. I went along to . . . do the needful. I'm afraid they can't quite sort it all out as yet. The pin belonged to the hat — yes, your friend Pombal . . . diplomatic immunity, naturally. Nevertheless, he was very drunk too. . . . Of course it is inconceivable that he did it, but you know what the Police are like.

Is he up yet?' I had not dared to try and wake him at such an early hour, and I said so. 'Well anyway' said Balthazar 'his death has fluttered a lot of dovecotes, not least at the French Legation.'

'But he was wearing Justine's ring' I said thickly, and all the premonitions of the last few months gathered in force at my elbow, crowding in upon me. I felt quite ill and feverish and had to lean for a moment against the wall by the telephone. Balthazar's measured tone and cheerful voice sounded to me like an obscenity. There was a long silence. 'Yes, I know about the ring' he said, and added with a quiet chuckle 'but that too is hard to think of as a possible reason. Toto was also the lover of the jealous Amar, you know. Any number of reasons. . . .'

'Balthazar' I said, and my voice broke.

'I'll ring you if there's anything else. The *procès* is at seven down in Nimrod's office. See you there, eh?'

'Very well.'

I put down the phone and burst like a bomb into Pombal's bedroom. The curtains were still drawn and the bed was in a terrible mess suggesting a recent occupancy, but there was no other sign of him. His boots and various items from the washerwoman's fancy dress lay about the room in various places, enabling me to discern that he had in fact got home the night before. Actually his wig lay on the landing outside the front door: I know this because much later, towards midday, I heard his heavy step climbing the stairs and he entered the flat holding it in his hand.

'I am quite finished' he said briefly, at once. 'Finished, *mon ami*.' He looked more plethoric than ever as he made for his gout chair as if anticipating a sudden attack of his special and private malady. 'Finished' he repeated, sinking into it with a sigh and distending. I was confused and bewildered, standing there in my pyjamas. Pombal sighed heavily.

'My Chancery has discovered everything' he said grimly setting his jaw. 'I first behaved very badly . . . yes . . . the Consul General is having a nervous breakdown today. . . .' And then all of a sudden real tears of mixed rage, confusion and hysteria sprang up in his eyes. 'Do you know what?' he sneezed. 'The *Deuxième* think I went specially to the ball to stick a pin in de Brunel, the best and most trusted agent we have ever had here!'

He burst out sobbing like a donkey now, and in some fantastic way his tears kept running into laughter; he mopped his streaming eyes and panted as he sobbed and laughed at one and the same time. Then, still blown up by these overmastering paroxysms he rolled out of his chair like a hedgehog on to the carpet and lay there for a while still shaking; and then began to roll slowly to the wainscot where, shaken still with tears and laughter, he began to bang his head rhythmically against the wall, shouting at every bang the pregnant and magnificent word — the *summa* of all despair: '*Merde. Merde. Merde. Merde. Merde.*'

'Pombal' I said weakly, 'for God's sake!'

'Go away' he cried from the floor. 'I shall never stop unless you go away. Please go away.' And so taking pity on him I left the room and ran myself a cold bath in which I lay until I heard him helping himself to bread and butter from the larder. He came to the bathroom door and tapped. 'Are you there?' he said. 'Yes.' 'Then forget every word I said' he shouted through the panel. 'Please, eh?'

'I have forgotten already.'

'Good. Thank you, *mon ami.*'

And I heard his heavy footfalls retreating in the direction of his room. We lay in bed until lunch-time that day, both of us, silent. At one-thirty, Hamid arrived and set out a lunch which neither of us had the appetite to eat. In the middle of it, the telephone rang and I went to answer it. It was Justine. She must have assumed that I had heard about Toto de Brunel for she made no direct mention of the business. 'I want' she said 'my dreadful ring back. Balthazar has reclaimed it from the Police. The one Toto took, yes. But apparently someone has to identify and sign for it. At the *procès.* A thousand thanks for offering to go. As you can imagine, Nessim and I . . . it's a question of witnessing only. And then perhaps my darling we could meet and you could give it back to me. Nessim has to fly to Cairo this afternoon on business. Shall we say in the garden of the Aurore at nine? That will give you time. I'll wait in the car. So much want to speak to you. Yes. I must go now. Thank you again. Thank you.'

We sat once more to our meal, fellow bondsmen, heavy with a sense of guilt and exhaustion. Hamid waited upon us with solicitude and in complete silence. Did he know what was preoccupying us both? It was impossible to read anything on those gentle pockmarked features, in that squinting single eye.

* * * * *

XI

It was already dark when I dismissed my taxi at Mohammed Ali Square and set out to walk to the sub-department of the Prefecture where Nimrod's office was. I was still dazed by the turn events had taken, and weighed down by the dispiriting possibilities they had raised in my mind — the warnings and threatenings of the last few months during which I had lived only for one person — Justine. I burned with impatience to see her again.

The shops were already lit up and the money-changers' counters were crowded with French sailors turning their francs into food and wine, silks, women, boys or opium — every kind of understandable forgetfulness. Nimrod's office was at the back of a grey old-fashioned building set back at an angle to the road. It seemed deserted now, full of empty corridors and open offices. All the clerks had gone off duty at six. My lagging footfalls echoed past the empty porter's lodge and the open doors. It seemed strange to walk about so freely in a Police building unchallenged. At the end of the third long corridor I came to Nimrod's own door and knocked. There were voices inside. His office was a large, indeed rather grandiose room befitting his rank, whose windows gave out on to a bare courtyard where some chickens clucked and picked all day in the dried mud floor. A single tattered palm stood in the middle offering some summer shade.

There was no sign from within the room so I opened the door and stepped in — only to stop short; for the brilliant light and darkness suggested that a cinema-show was taking place. But it was only the huge epidiascope which threw upon the farther wall the blazing and magnified images of the photographs which Nimrod himself was feeding into it one by one from an envelope. Dazzled, I stepped forward and identified Balthazar and Keats in that phosphorescent penumbra around the machine, their profiles magnetically lighted by the powerful bulb.

'Good' said Nimrod, half-turning, and 'sit you down' as he abstractedly pushed out a chair for me. Keats smiled at me, full of a mysterious self-satisfaction and excitement. The photographs which they were studying with such care were his own flashlight pictures of the Cervoni ball. At such magnification they looked like grotesque frescoes materializing and vanishing again upon the white wall. 'See if you can help on identification' said Nimrod, and I sat down and obediently turned my face to the blaze in which sprawled the silhouettes of a dozen demented monks dancing together. 'Not that one' said Keats. The white light of the magnesium had set fire to the outlines of the robed figures.

Blown up to such enormous size the pictures suggested a new art-form, more macabre than anything a Goya could imagine. This was a new iconography — painted in smoke and lightning flashes. Nimrod changed them slowly, dwelling upon each one. 'No comment?' he would ask before passing another bloated facsimile of real life before our eyes. 'No comment?'

For identification purposes they were quite useless. There were eight in all — each a fearful simulacrum of a death-feast celebrated by satyr-monks in some medieval crypt, each imagined by Sade! 'There's the one with the ring' said Balthazar as the fifth picture came up and hovered before us on the wall. A group of hooded figures, frenziedly swaying with linked arms, wallowed before us, expressionless as cuttlefish, or those other grotesque monsters one sometimes sees lurking in the glooms of aquaria. Their eyes were slits devoid of meaning, their gaiety a travesty of everything human. So this is how Inquisitors behave when they are off duty! Keats sighed in despair. One of the figures had a hand upon another's black-robed arm. The hand bore a just recognizable dash of white to indicate Justine's unlucky ring. Nimrod described it all carefully to himself with the air of a man reading a gauge. 'Five maskers ... somewhere near the buffet, you can see the corner. ... But the hand. Is it de Brunel's? What do you think?' I stared at it. 'I think it must be' I said. 'Justine wears the ring on another finger.'

Nimrod said 'Hah' triumphantly and added 'A good point there.' Yes, but who were the other figures, snatched thus fortuitously out of nothingness by the flash-bulb? We stared at them and they stared expressionlessly back at us through their velvet slits like snipers.

'No good' said Balthazar at last with a sigh, and Nimrod switched off the humming machine. After an instant's darkness the ordinary electric light came up in the room. His desk was stacked up with typed papers for signature — the *procès-verbal* I had no doubt. On a square of grey silk lay several objects with a direct relationship to our brimming thoughts — the great hatpin with its ugly blue stone head, and the eburnine ring of my lover which I could not see even now without a pang.

'Sign up' said Nimrod, indicating the paper 'when you've read your copy, will you?' He coughed behind his hand and added in a lower tone 'And you can take the ring.'

Balthazar handed it to me. It felt cold, and it was faintly dusted with fingerprint powder. I cleaned it on my tie and put it in my fob-pocket. 'Thank you' I said, and took a seat at the desk to read through the Police formula, while the others lit cigarettes and talked in low voices. Beside the typewritten papers lay another, written in the nervous shallow hand of General Cervoni. It was the invitation list to the carnival ball, still echoing with the majestic poetry of the names which had come to mean so much to me, the names of the Alexandrians. Listen:

Pia dei Tolomei, Benedict Dangeau, Dante Borromeo, Colonel Neguib, Toto de Brunel, Wilmot Pierrefeu, Mehmet Adm, Pozzo di Borgo, Ahmed Hassan Pacha, Delphine de Francueil, Djam-boulat Bey, Athena Trasha, Haddad Fahmy Amin, Gaston Phipps, Pierre Balbz, Jacques de Guéry, Count Banubula, Onouphrios Papas, Dmitri Randidi, Paul Capodistria, Claude Amaril, Nessim Hosnani, Tony Umbada, Baldassaro Trivizani, Gilda Ambron. . . .

I murmured the names as I read through the list, mentally adding the word 'murderer' after each, simply to see whether it sounded appropriate. Only when I reached the name of Nessim did I pause and raise my eyes to the dark wall — to throw his mental image there and study it as we had studied the pictures. I still saw the expression on his face as I had helped to tuck him into the great car — an expression of curious impish serenity, as of some-one resting after a great expenditure of energy.

* * * * *

PART IV

XII

Despite the season the seafront of the city was gay with light — the long sloping lines of the Grande Corniche curving away to a low horizon; a thousand lighted panels of glass in which, like glorious tropical fish, the inhabitants of the European city sat at glittering tables stocked with glasses of mastic, aniseed or brandy. Watching them (I had eaten little lunch) my hunger overcame me, and as there was some time in hand before my meeting with Justine, I turned into the glittering doors of the Diamond Sutra and ordered a ham sandwich and a glass of whisky. Once again, as always when the drama of external events altered the emotional pattern of things, I began to see the city through new eyes — to examine the shapes and contours made by human beings with the detachment of an entomologist studying a hitherto unknown species of insect. Here it was, the race, each member of it absorbed in the solution of individual preoccupations, loves, hates and fears. A woman counting money on to a glass table, an old man feeding a dog, an Arab in a red flowerpot drawing a curtain.

Aromatic smoke poured from the small sailor taverns along the seafront where the iron spits loaded with a freight of entrails and spices turned monotonously back and forth, or bellied from under the lids of shining copper cauldrons, giving off hot gusts of squid, cuttlefish and pigeon. Here one drank from the blue cans and ate with one's fingers as they do in the Cyclades even today.

I picked up a decrepit horse-cab and jogged along by the sighing sea towards the Aurore, drinking in the lighted darkness with regrets and fears so fugitive as to be beyond analysis; but underneath (like a toad under a cool stone, the surface airs of night) I still felt the stirrings of horror at the thought that Justine herself might be endangered by the love which 'we bore one another'. I turned the thought this way and that in my mind, like a prisoner pressing with all his weight upon doors which denied him an exit from an intolerable bondage, trying to devise an issue from a situation which, it seemed, might as well end in her death as in mine.

The great car was waiting, drawn up off the road in the darkness under the pepper-trees. She opened the door for me silently and I got in, spellbound by my fears.

'Well' she said at last, and giving a little groan which expressed everything, sank into my arms and pressed her warm mouth on mine. 'Did you go? Is it over?'

'Yes.'

She let in the clutch and the driving wheels spurned the gravel as the car moved out into the pearly nightfall and began to follow the coast road to the outer desert. I studied her harsh Semitic profile in the furry light flung back by the headlights from the common objects of the roadside. It belonged so much to the city which I now saw as a series of symbols stretching away from us on either side — minarets, pigeons, statues, ships, coins, camels and palms; it lived in a heraldic relation to the exhausted landscapes which enclosed it — the loops of the great lake: as proper to the scene as the Sphinx was to the desert.

'My ring' she said. 'You brought it?'

'Yes.' I polished it once more on my tie and slipped it back once more on to its appropriate finger. Involuntarily I said now: 'Justine, what is to become of us?'

She gave me a wild frowning look like a Bedouin woman, and then smiled that warm smile. 'Why?'

'Surely you see? We shall have to stop this altogether. I can't bear to think you might be in danger. . . . Or else I should go straight to Nessim and confront him with. . . .' With what? I did not know.

'No' she said softly, 'no. You could not do it. You are an Anglo-Saxon . . . you couldn't step outside the law like that, could you? You are not one of us. Besides, you could tell Nessim nothing he does not guess if not actually know. . . . Darling' she laid her warm hand upon mine, 'simply wait . . . simply love, above all . . . and we shall see.'

It is astonishing now for me to realize, as I record this scene, that she was carrying within her (invisible as the already conceived foetus of a child) Pursewarden's death: that her kisses were, for all I know, falling upon the graven image of my friend — the death-mask of the writer who himself did not love her, indeed regarded her with derision. But such a demon is love that I would not be surprised if in a queer sort of way his death actually enriched our own love-making, filling it with the deceits on which the minds of women feed — the compost of secret pleasures and treacheries which are an inseparable part of every human relation.

Yet what have I to complain of? Even this half-love filled my heart to overflowing. It is she, if anyone, who had cause for complaint. It is very hard to understand these things. Was she already planning her flight from Alexandria then? 'The power of woman is such' writes Pursewarden 'that a single kiss can paraphrase the reality of man's life and turn it . . .' but why go on? I was happy sitting beside her, feeling the warmth of her hand as it lay in mine.

The blue night was hoary with stars and the attentive desert stretched away on either side with its grotesque amphitheatres — like the empty rooms in some great cloud-mansion. The moon was late and wan tonight, the air still, the dunes wind-carved. 'What are you thinking?' said my lover.

What was I thinking? Of a passage in Proclus which says that Orpheus ruled over the silver race, meaning those who led a 'silver' life; on Balthazar's mantelpiece presumably among the pipe-cleaners and the Indian wood-carving of monkeys which neither saw, spoke nor heard evil, under a magic pentacle from Pythagoras. What was I thinking? The foetus in its waxen wallet, the locust squatting in the horn of the wheat, an Arab quoting a proverb which reverberated in the mind. 'The memory of man is as old as misfortune.' The quails from the burst cage spread upon the ground softly like honey, having no idea of escape. In the Scent Bazaar the flavour of Persian lilac.

'Fourteen thousand years ago' I said aloud, 'Vega in Lyra was the Pole Star. Look at her where she burns.'

The beloved head turned with its frowning deep-set eyes and once more I see the long boats drawing in to the Pharos, the tides running, the minarets a-glitter with dew; noise of the blind Hodja crying in the voice of a mole assaulted by sunlight; a shuffle-pad of a camel-train clumping to a festival carrying dark lanterns. An Arab woman makes my bed, beating the pillows till they fluff out like white egg under a whisk; a passage in Pursewarden's book which reads: 'They looked at each other, aware that there was neither youth nor strength enough between them to prevent their separation.' When Melissa was pregnant by Nessim Amaril could not perform the abortion Nessim so much desired because of her illness and her weak heart. 'She may die anyway' he said, and Nessim nodded curtly and took up his overcoat. But she did not die then, she bore the child. . . .

Justine is quoting something in Greek which I do not recognize:

> Sand, dog-roses and white rocks
> Of Alexandria, the mariner's sea-marks,
> Some sprawling dunes falling and pouring
> Sand into water, water into sand,
> Never into the wine of exile
> Which stains the air it is poured through;
> Or a voice which stains the mind,
> Singing in Arabic: 'A ship without a sail
> Is a woman without breasts.' Only that. Only that.

We walked hand in hand across the soft sand-dunes, laboriously as insects, until we reached Taposiris with its rumble of shattered columns and capitals among the ancient weather-eroded sea-marks. ('Reliques of sensation' says Coleridge 'may exist for an indefinite time in a latent state in the very same order in which they were impressed.') Yes, but the order of the imagination is not that of memory. A faint wind blew off the sea from the Grecian archipelago. The sea was smooth as a human cheek. Only at the edges it stirred and sighed. Those warm kisses remain there, amputated from before and after, existing in their own right like the frail transparencies of ferns or roses pressed between the covers of old books — unique and unfading as the memories of the city they exemplified and evoked: a plume of music from a forgotten carnival-guitar echoing on in the dark streets of Alexandria for as long as silence lasts. . . .

I see all of us not as men and women any longer, identities swollen with their acts of forgetfulness, follies, and deceits — but as beings unconsciously made part of place, buried to the waist among the ruins of a single city, steeped in its values; like those creatures of whom Empedocles wrote 'Solitary limbs wandered, seeking for union with one another,' or in another place, 'So it is that sweet lays hold of sweet, bitter rushes to bitter, acid comes to acid, warm couples with warm.' All members of a city whose actions lay just outside the scope of the plotting or conniving spirit: Alexandrians.

Justine, lying back against a fallen column at Taposiris, dark head upon the darkness of the sighing water, one curl lifted by the sea-winds, saying: 'In the whole of English only one phrase means something to me, the words "Time Immemorial".'

Seen across the transforming screens of memory, how remote

that forgotten evening seems. There was so much as yet left for us all to live through until we reached the occasion of the great duckshoot which so abruptly, concisely, precipitated the final change — and the disappearance of Justine herself. But all this belongs to another Alexandria — one which I created in my mind and which the great Interlinear of Balthazar has, if not destroyed, changed out of all recognition.

'To intercalate realities' writes Balthazar 'is the only way to be faithful to Time, for at every moment in Time the possibilities are endless in their multiplicity. Life consists in the act of choice. The perpetual reservations of judgement and the perpetual choosing.'

From the vantage-point of this island I can see it all in its doubleness, in the intercalation of fact and fancy, with new eyes; and re-reading, re-working reality in the light of all I now know, I am surprised to find that my feelings themselves have changed, have grown, have deepened even. Perhaps then the destruction of my private Alexandria was necessary ('the artifact of a true work of art never shows a plane surface'); perhaps buried in all this there lies the germ and substance of a truth — time's usufruct — which, if I can accommodate it, will carry me a little further in what is really a search for my proper self. We shall see.

*   *   *   *   *

XIII

'Clea and her old father, whom she worships. White-haired, erect, with a sort of haunted pity in his eyes for the young unmarried goddess he has fathered. Once a year, however, on New Year's eve, they dance at the Cecil, stately, urbanely. He waltzes like a clockwork man.' Somewhere I once wrote down these words. They bring to mind another scene, another sequence of events.

The old scholar comes to sit at my table. He has a particular weakness for me, I do not know why, but he always talks to me with humorous modesty as we sit and watch his beautiful daughter move around the room in the arms of an admirer, so graceful and so composed. 'There is so much of the schoolgirl still about her — or the artist. Tonight her cape had some wine on it so she put a mackintosh over her ball gown and ate the toffees which she found in the pockets. I don't know what her mother would say if she were alive.' We drank quietly and watched the coloured lights flickering among the dancers. He said 'I feel like an old procurer. Always looking out for someone to marry her. . . . Her happiness seems so important, somehow . . . I am going the right way about to spoil it I know, by meddling . . . yet I can't leave it alone . . . I've scraped a dowry together over the years. . . . The money burns my pocket. . . . When I see a nice Englishman like you my instinct is to say: "For God's sake take her and look after her." . . . It has been a bitter pleasure bringing her up without a mother. Eh? No fool like an old fool.' And he walks stiffly away to the bar, smiling.

Presently that evening Clea herself came and sat beside me in the alcove, fanning herself and smiling. 'Quarter of an hour to midnight. Poor Cinderella. I must get my father home before the clock strikes or he'll lose his beauty-sleep!'

We spoke then of Amar whose trial for the murder of de Brunel had ended that afternoon with his acquittal due to lack of direct evidence.

'I know,' said Clea softly. 'And I'm glad. It has saved me from a *crise de conscience*. I would not have known what to do if he had been convicted. You see, I know he didn't do it. Why? Because, my dear, I know who did and why. . . .' She narrowed those splendid eyes and went on. 'A story of Alexandria — shall I tell you? But only if you keep it a secret. Would you promise me? Bury it with the old year — all our misfortunes and follies. You must have had a surfeit of them by now, must you not? All right. Listen. On the night of the carnival I lay in bed thinking about a picture — the big one of Justine. It was all wrong and I didn't know where. But I suspected the hands — those dark and shapely hands. I had got their position quite faithfully, but, well, something in the composition didn't go; it had started to trouble me at this time — months after the thing was finished. I can't think why. Suddenly I said to myself "Those hands want thinking about," and I had the thing lugged back to my room from the studio where I stood it against a wall. Well, to no effect, really; I'd spent the whole evening smoking over it, and sketching the hands in different positions from memory. Somehow I thought it might be that beastly Byzantine ring which she wears. Anyway, all my thinking was of no avail so about midnight I turned in, and lay smoking in bed with my cat asleep on my feet.

'From time to time a small group of people passed outside in the street, singing or laughing, but gradually the town was draining itself of life, for it was getting late.

'Suddenly in the middle of the silence I heard feet running at full speed. I have never heard anyone run so fast, so lightly. Only danger or terror or distress could make someone put on such a mad burst of speed, I thought, as I listened. Down Rue Fuad came the footsteps at the same breakneck pace and turned the corner into St Saba, getting louder all the time. They crossed over, paused, and then crossed back to my side of the street. Then came a wild pealing at my bell.

'I sat up in some surprise and switched on the light to look at the clock. Who could it be at such a time? While I was still sitting there irresolutely, it came again: a long double peal. Well! The electric switch on the front door is shut off at midnight so there was no help for it but to go down and see who it was. I put on a dressing-gown and slipping my little pistol into the pocket I went down to see. There was a shadow on the glass of the front door which was too thick to challenge anyone through, so I had to open it. I stood back a bit. "Who's there?"

'There was a man standing there, hanging in the corner of the door like a bat. He was breathing heavily for I saw his breast rising and falling, but he made no sound. He wore a domino, but the headpiece was turned back so that I could see his face in the light of the street-lamp. I was of course rather frightened for a moment. He looked as if he were about to faint. It took me about ten seconds before I could put a name to the ugly face with its cruel great harelip. Then relief flooded me and my feet got pins and needles. Do you know who it was? His hair was matted with sweat and in that queer light his eyes looked enormous — blue and childish. I realized that it was that strange brother of Nessim's — the one nobody ever sees. Narouz Hosnani. Even this was rather a feat of memory: I only remembered him vaguely from the time when Nessim took me riding on the Hosnani lands. You can imagine my concern to see him like this, unexpectedly, in the middle of the night.

'I did not know what to say, and he for his part was trying to articulate something, but the words would not come. It seemed he had two sentences jammed together in the front of his mind, like cartridges in the muzzle of a gun, and neither would give place to the other. He leaned inwards upon me with a ghastly incoherence, his hands hanging down almost below his knees which gave him an ape-like silhouette, and croaked something at me. You mustn't laugh. It was horrifying. Then he drew a great breath and forced his muscles to obey him and said in a small marionette's voice: "I have come to tell you that I love you because I have killed Justine." For a moment I almost suspected a joke. "What?" I stammered. He repeated in an even smaller voice, a whisper, but mechanically as a child repeating a lesson: "I have come to tell you that I love you because I have killed Justine." Then in a deep voice he added "Oh, Clea, if you but knew the agony of it." And he gave a sob and fell on his knees in the hall, holding the edge of my dressing-gown, his head bowed while the tears trickled down his nose.

'I didn't know what to do. I was at once horrified and disgusted, and yet I couldn't help feeling sorry. From time to time he gave a small harsh cry — the noise of a she-camel crying, or of some dreadful mechanical toy, perhaps. It was unlike anything I have seen or heard before or since. His trembling was communicated to me through the fringe of my gown which he held in two fingers.

' "Get up" I said at last, and raising his head he croaked: "I swear I did not mean to do it. It happened before I could think.

She put her hand upon me, Clea, she made advances to me. Horrible. Nessim's own wife."

'I did not know what to make of all this. Had he really harmed Justine? "You just come upstairs" I said, keeping tight hold of my little pistol, for his expression was pretty frightening. "Get up now." He got up at once, quite obediently, and followed me back up the stairs, but leaning heavily against the wall and whispering something incoherently to himself, Justine's name, I think, though it sounded more like "Justice".

' "Come in while I telephone" I said, and he followed me slowly, half-blinded by the light. He stood by the door for a moment, accustoming himself to it, and then he saw the portrait. He exclaimed with great force: "This Jewish fox has eaten my life," and struck his fists against his thighs several times. Then he put his hands over his face and breathed deeply. We waited like this facing one another, while I thought what there was to be done. They had all gone to the Cervoni ball, I knew. I would telephone them to find out if there was any truth in this story.

'Meanwhile Narouz opened his fingers and peeped at me. He said: "I only came to tell you I loved you before giving myself up to my brother." Then he spread his hands in a hopeless gesture. "That is all."

'How disgusting, how unfair love is! Here I had been loved for goodness knows how long by a creature — I cannot say a fellow-creature — of whose very existence I had been unaware. Every breath I drew was unconsciously a form of his suffering, without my ever having been aware of it. How had this disaster come about? You will have to make room in your thoughts for this variety of the animal. I was furious, disgusted and wounded in one and the same moment. I felt almost as if I owed him an apology; and yet I also felt insulted by the intrusiveness of a love which I had never asked him to owe me.

'Narouz looked now as if he were in a high fever. His teeth chattered in his head and he was shaken by spasms of violent shivering. I gave him a glass of cognac which he drained at one gulp, and then another even larger one. Drinking it he sank slowly down to the carpet and doubled his legs under him like an Arab. "It is better at last" he whispered, and looking sadly round him added: "So this is where you live. I have wanted to see it for years. I have been imagining it all." Then he frowned and coughed and combed his hair back with his fingers.

'I rang the Cervoni house and almost at once got hold of Nessim. I questioned him tactfully, without giving anything away. But there seemed nothing wrong, as far as could be judged, though he could not at that moment locate Justine. She was somewhere on the dance-floor. Narouz listened to all this with staring surprised eyes, incredulous. "She is due to meet them in the hall in ten minutes' time. Finish your drink and wait until she rings up. Then you will know that there has been some mistake." He closed his eyes and seemed to pray.

'I sat down opposite him on the sofa, not knowing quite what to say. "What exactly happened?" I asked him. All of a sudden his eyes narrowed and grew small, suspicious-looking. Then he sighed and hung his head, tracing the design of the carpet with his finger. "It is not for you to hear" he whispered, his lips trembling.

'We waited like this, and all of a sudden, to my intense embarrassment and disgust, he began to talk of his love for me, but in the tone of a man talking to himself. He seemed almost oblivious of me, never once looking up into my face. And I felt all the apologetic horror that comes over me when I am admired or desired and cannot reciprocate the feeling. I was somehow ashamed too, looking at that brutal tear-stained face, simply because I could not feel the slightest stirring of sympathy within my heart. He sat there on the carpet like some great brown toad, talking; like some story-book troglodyte. What the devil was I to do? "When have you seen me?" I asked him. He had only seen me three times in his life, though frequently at night he passed through the street to see if my light was on. I swore under my breath. It was so unfair. I had done nothing to merit this grotesque passion.

'Then at last came a reprieve. The telephone rang, and he trembled all over like a hound as he heard the unmistakable hoarse tones of the woman he thought he had killed. There was nothing wrong that she knew of, and she was on her way home with Nessim. Everything was as it should be at the Cervoni house and the ball was still going on at full blast. As I said good night I felt Narouz clasp my slippers and begin kissing them with gratitude. "Thank you. Thank you" he repeated over and over again.

' "Come on. Get up. It's time to go home." I was deathly tired by now. I advised him to go straight back home and to confide his story to nobody. "Perhaps you have imagined the whole thing" I said, and he gave me a tired but brilliant smile.

'He walked slowly and heavily downstairs before me, still shaken by his experience, it was clear, but the hysteria had left him. I opened the front door, and he tried once more to express his incoherent gratitude and affection. He seized my hands and kissed them repeatedly with great wet hairy kisses. Ugh! I can feel them now. And then, before turning into the night, he said in a low voice, smiling: "Clea, this is the happiest day of my life, to have seen and touched you and to have seen your little room." '

Clea sipped her drink, nodding into the middle distance for a moment with a sad smile on her face. Then she looked at her own brown hands and gave a little shudder. 'Ugh! The kisses' she said under her breath and with an involuntary movement began to rub her hands, palms upward, upon the red plush arm of the chair, as if to obliterate the kisses once and for all, to expunge the memory of them.

But now the band had begun to play a Paul Jones (perhaps the very dance in which Arnauti first met Justine?) and the warm lighted gallery of faces began to fan out once more from the centre of the darkness, the brilliance of flesh and cloth and jewels in the huge gaunt ballroom where the palms splintered themselves in the shivering mirrors: leaking through the windows to where the moonlight waited patiently among the deserted public gardens and highways, troubling the uneasy water of the outer harbour with its glittering heartless gestures. 'Come' said Clea, 'why do you never play a part in these things? Why do you prefer to sit apart and study us all?'

But I was thinking as I watched the circle of lovely faces move forward and reverse among the glitter of jewellery and the rustle of silks, of the Alexandrians to whom these great varieties of experience meant only one more addition to the sum of an infinite knowledge husbanded by their world-weariness. Round and round the floor we went, the women unconsciously following the motion of the stars, of the earth as it curved into space; and then suddenly like a declaration of war, like an expulsion from the womb, silence came, and a voice crying: 'Take your partners please.' And the lights throbbed down the spectrum to purple and a waltz began. For a brief moment at the far end of the darkness I caught a glimpse of Nessim and Justine dancing together, smiling into each other's eyes. The shapely hand on his shoulder still wore the great ring taken from the tomb of a Byzantine youth. Life is short, art long.

Clea's father was dancing with her, stiffly, happily like a clockwork mouse; and he was kissing the gifted hand upon which the unwanted kisses of Narouz had fallen on that forgotten evening. A daughter is closer than a wife.

'At first' writes Pursewarden 'we seek to supplement the emptiness of our individuality through love, and for a brief moment enjoy the illusion of completeness. But it is only an illusion. For this strange creature, which we thought would join us to the body of the world, succeeds at last in separating us most thoroughly from it. Love joins and then divides. How else would we be growing?'

How else indeed? But relieved to find myself once more partnerless I have already groped my way back to my dark corner where the empty chairs of the revellers stand like barren ears of corn.

★   ★   ★   ★   ★

XIV

In the early summer I received a letter from Clea with which this brief memorial to Alexandria may well be brought to a close. It was unexpected.

'*Tashkent, Syria*

'Your letter, so unexpected after a silence which I feared might endure all through life, followed me out of Persia to this small house perched high on a hillside among the cedars and pines. I have taken it for a few months in order to try my hand and brush on these odd mountains — rocks bursting with fresh water and Mediterranean flowers. Turtle doves by day and nightingales by night. What a relief after the dust. How long is it? Ah, my dear friend, I trembled a little as I slit open the envelope. Why? I was afraid that what you might have to say would drag me back by the hair to old places and scenes long since abandoned; the old stations and sites of the personality which belonged to the Alexandrian Clea you knew — not to me any longer, or at any rate, not wholly. I've changed. A new woman, certainly a new painter is emerging, still a bit tender and shy like the horns of a snail — but new. A whole new world of experience stands between us. . . . How could you know all this? You would perhaps be writing to Clea, the old Clea; what would I find to say to you in reply? I put off reading your letter until tonight. It touched me and reply I must: so here it is — my own letter written at odd times, between painting sessions, or at night when I light the stove and make my dinner. Today is a good day to begin it for it is raining — and the whole mountain side is under the hush of the rain and the noise of swollen springs. The trees are alive with giant snails.

'So Balthazar has been disturbing you with his troublesome new information? I am not sure that I approve. It may be good for you, but surely not for your book or books which must, I suppose, put us all in a very special position regarding reality. I mean as "characters" rather than human beings. No? And why, you ask me, did I never tell you a tithe of the things you know now? One never does, you know, one never does. As a spectator standing equidistant between two friends or lovers one is always torn by friendship to intervene, to interfere — but one never does. Rightly. How could I tell you what I knew of Justine — or for that matter what I felt about your neglect of Melissa? The very range of my sympathies for the three of you precluded it. As for love, it is so paradoxical a creature and so satisfying in itself that it would not have been much altered by the intervention of truths from outside. I am sure now, if you analyse your feelings, you will find you love Justine *better* because she betrayed you! The whore is man's true darling, as I once told you, and we are born to love those who most wound us. Am I wrong? Besides, my own affection for you lay in another quarter. I was jealous of you as a writer — and as a writer I wanted you to myself and did so keep you. Do you see?

'There is nothing I can do to help you now — I mean help your book. You will either have to ignore the data which Balthazar has so wickedly supplied, or to "rework reality" as you put it.

'And you say you were unjust to Pursewarden; yes, but it is not important. He was equally unjust to you. Unknown to either of you, you joined hands in me! As writers. My only regret is that he did not manage to finish the last volume of *God is a Humorist* according to plan. It is a loss — though it cannot detract from his achievement. You, I surmise, will soon be coming into the same degree of self-possession — perhaps through this cursed city of ours, Alexandria, to which we most belong when we most hate it. By the way, I have a letter from Pursewarden about the missing volume which I have carried around with me among my papers for ages, like a talisman. It helps not only to revive the man himself a bit, but to revive me also when I fall into a depression about my work. (I must go to the village to buy eggs. I shall copy it out tonight for you.)

'Later. Here is the letter I spoke about, harsh and crabbed if you like, but none the less typical of our friend. Don't take his remarks about you too seriously. He admired you and believed in you — so he once told me. Perhaps he was lying. Anyway.

'*Mount Vulture Hotel*
'*Alexandria*

'My dear Clea:

'A surprise and delight to find your letter waiting for me. Clement reader thank you — not for the blame or praise (one shrinks from both equally) but for being there, devoted and watchful, a true reader between the lines — where all real writing is done! I have just come hotfoot from the Café Al Aktar after listening to a long discursion on "the novel" by old Lineaments and Keats and Pombal. They talk as if every novel wasn't *sui generis* — it is as meaningless to me as Pombal generalizing about "les femmes" as a race; for after all it isn't the family relationship which really matters. Well, Lineaments was saying that Redemption and Original Sin were the new topics and that the writer of today. . . . Ouf! I fled, feeling like the writer of the day before yesterday, and unwilling to help them build this sort of mud-pie.

'I'm sure old Lineaments will do a lovely novel about Original Sin and score what I always privately call a suck-eggs *d'estime* (it means not covering one's advance). In fact, I was in such despair at the thought of his coming fame that I thought I would go straight off to a brothel and expiate my unoriginal sense of sin right away. But the hour was early, and besides, I felt that I smelt of sweat for it has been a hot day. I therefore returned to the hotel for a shower and a change of shirt and so found your letter. There is a little gin in the bottle and as I don't know where I shall be later on I think I'll just sit down and answer you now as best I can until six when the brothels start to open.

'The questions you ask me, my dear Clea, are the very questions I am putting myself. I must get them a little clearer before I tidy up the last volume in which I want above all to combine, resolve and harmonize the tensions so far created. I feel I want to sound a note of . . . affirmation — though not in the specific terms of a philosophy or religion. It should have the curvature of an embrace, the wordlessness of a lover's code. It should convey some feeling that the world we live in is founded in something too simple to be over-described as cosmic law — but as easy to grasp as, say, an act of tenderness, simple tenderness in the primal relation between animal and plant, rain and soil, seed and trees, man and God. A relationship so delicate that it is all too easily broken by the inquiring mind and *conscience* in the French sense which of course has its own rights and its own field of deployment. I'd like to think of my work simply as a cradle in which philosophy could rock itself to sleep, thumb in mouth. What do you say to this? After all, this is not simply what we most need in the world, but really what describes the state of pure process in it. Keep silent awhile and you feel a comprehension of this act of tenderness — not power or glory: and certainly not Mercy, that vulgarity of the

Jewish mind which can only imagine man as crouching under the whip. No, for the sort of tenderness I mean is utterly merciless! "A law unto itself" as we say. Of course, one must always remember that truth itself is always halved in utterance. Yet I must in this last book insist that there is hope for man, scope for man, within the boundaries of a simple law; and I seem to see mankind as gradually appropriating to itself the necessary information through mere attention, *not reason*, which may one day enable it to live within the terms of such an idea — the true meaning of "joy unconfined". How could joy be anything else? This new creature we artists are hunting for will not "live" so much as, like time itself, simply "elapse". Damn, it's hard to say these things. Perhaps the key lies in laughter, in the Humorous God? It is after all the serious who disturb the peace of the heart with their antics — like Justine. (Wait. I must fix myself a ration of gin.)

'I think it better for us to steer clear of the big oblong words like Beauty and Truth and so on. Do you mind? We are all so silly and feeble-witted when it comes to living, but giants when it comes to pronouncing on the universe. *Sufflaminandus erat*. Like you, I have two problems which interconnect: my art and my life. Now in my life I am somewhat irresolute and shabby, but in my art I am free to be what I most desire to seem — someone who might bring resolution and harmony into the dying lives around me. In my art, indeed, through my art, I want really to achieve myself by shedding the work, which is of no *importance*, as a snake sheds its skin. Perhaps that's why writers at heart want to be loved for their work rather than for themselves — do you think? But then this presupposes a new order of woman too. Where is she?

'These, my dear Clea, are some of the perplexities of your omniscient friend, the classical head and romantic heart of Ludwig Pursewarden.

'Ouf! It is late and the oil in the lamp is low. I must leave this letter for tonight. Tomorrow perhaps, if I am in the mood after my shopping, I shall write a little more; if not, not. Wise one, how much better it would be if we could *talk*. I feel I have whole conversations stacked inside me, lying unused! I think it is perhaps the only real lack of which one is conscious in living alone; the mediating power of a friend's thoughts to place beside one's own, just to see if they match! The lonely become autocratic, as they must, and their judgements *ex cathedra* in the very nature of things:

and perhaps this is not altogether good for the work. But here at least we will be well-matched, you on your island — which is only a sort of metaphor like Descartes' oven, isn't it? — and I in my fairy-tale hut among the mountains.

'Last week a man appeared among the trees, also a painter, and my heart began to beat unwontedly fast. I felt the sudden predisposition to fall in love — reasoning thus, I suppose: "If one has gone so far from the world and one finds a man in that place, must he not be the one person destined to share one's solitude, brought to this very place by the invisible power of one's selfless longing and destined specially for oneself?" Dangerous self-delusive tricks the heart plays on itself, always tormented by the desire to be loved! Balthazar claimed once that he could induce love as a control-experiment by a simple action: namely telling each of two people who had never met that the other was dying to meet them, had never seen anyone so attractive, and so on. This was, he claimed infallible as a means of making them fall in love: they always did. What do you say?

'At any rate, my own misgivings saved me from the youth who was, I will admit, handsome and indeed quite intelligent, and would have done me good, I think, as a lover — perhaps for a single summer. But when I saw his *paintings* I felt my soul grow hard and strong and separate again; through them I read his whole personality as one can read a handwriting or a face. I saw weakness and poverty of heart and a power to do mischief. So I said good-bye there and then. The poor youth kept repeating: "Have I done anything to offend you, have I said anything?" What could I reply — for there was nothing he could do about the offence except live it out, paint it out; but that presupposed becoming conscious of its very existence within himself.

'I returned to my hut and locked myself in with real relief. He came at midnight and tried the door. I shouted "Go away," and he obeyed. This morning I saw him leaving on the bus, but I did not even wave good-bye. I found myself whistling happily, nay, almost dancing, as I walked to town across the forest to get my provisions. It is wonderful whenever one can overcome one's treacherous heart. Then I went home and was hardly in the door when I picked up a brush and started on the painting which has been holding me up for nearly a month; all the ways were clear, all the relations in play. The mysterious obstacle had vanished. Who can say it was not due to our painter friend and the love affair I did not have? I am still humming a tune as I write these words to you. . . .

'Later: re-reading your letter, why do you go on so, I wonder, about Pursewarden's death? It puzzles me, for in a way it is a sort of vulgarity to do so. I mean that surely it is not within your competence or mine to pass an open judgement on it? All we can say is that his art overleaps the barrier. For the rest, it seems to me to be his own private property. We should not only respect his privacy in such matters but help him to defend it against the unfeeling. They are his own secrets, after all, for what we actually saw in him was only the human disguise that the artist wore (as in his own character, old Parr, the hopeless sensualist of volume two who turns out in the end to be the one who painted the disputed fresco of the Last Supper — remember?)

'In much the same sort of way, Pursewarden carried the secret of his everyday life over into the grave with him, leaving us only his books to marvel at and his epitaph to puzzle over: "Here lies an intruder from the East."

'No. No. The death of an artist is quite unassailable. One can only smile and bow.

'As for Scobie, you are right in what you say. I was terribly upset when Balthazar told me that he had fallen down those stairs at the central Quism and killed himself. Yes, I took his parrot, which by the way was inhabited by the old man's spirit for a long time afterwards. It reproduced with perfect fidelity the way he got up in the morning singing a snatch of "*Taisez-vous, petit babouin*' (do you remember) and even managed to imitate the dismal cracking of the old man's bones as he got out of bed. But then the memory gradually wore out, like an old disc, and he seemed to do it less often and with less sureness of voice. It was like Scobie himself dying very gradually into silence: this is how I suppose one dies to one's friends and to the world, wearing out like an old dance tune or a memorable conversation with a philosopher under a cherry-tree. Being refunded into silence. And finally the bird itself went into a decline and died with its head under its wing. I was so sorry, yet so glad.

'For us, the living, the problem is of a totally different order: how to harness time in the cultivation of a style of heart — something like that? I am only trying to express it. Not to force time, as the weak do, for that spells self-injury and dismay, but to harness its rhythms and put them to our own use. Pursewarden used to say:

"God give us artists resolution and tact"; to which I myself would say a very hearty Amen.

'But by now you will think that I have simply become an opinionated old shrew. Perhaps I have. What does it matter, provided one can get a single idea across to oneself?

'There is so little time; with the news from Europe becoming worse every day I feel an autumnal quality in the days — as if they were settling towards an unpredictable future. And side by side with this feeling, I also feel the threads tightening in our sleeves, so to speak, drawing us slowly back towards the centre of the stage once more. Where could this be but to Alexandria? But perhaps it will prove to be a new city, different to the one which has for so long imposed itself on our dreams. I would like to think that, for the old one and all it symbolized is, if not dead, at least meaningless to the person I now feel myself to be. Perhaps you too have changed by the same token. Perhaps your book too has changed. Or perhaps you, more than any of us, need to see the city again, need to see us again. We, for our part, very much need to see you again and refresh the friendship which we hope exists the other side of the writing — if indeed an author can ever be just a friend to his "characters". I say "we", writing in the Imperial Style as if I were a Queen, but you will guess that I mean, simply, both the old Clea and the new — for both have need of you in a future which. . . .'

There are a few more lines and then the affectionate superscription.

CONSEQUENTIAL DATA

*   *   *

Some shorthand notes of Keats's, recording the Obiter Dicta of Pursewarden in fragmentary fashion:

(a)

'I know my prose is touched with plum pudding, but then all the prose belonging to the poetic continuum is; it is intended to give a stereoscopic effect to character. And events aren't in serial form but collect here and there like quanta, like real life.'

(b)

'Nessim hasn't got the resources we Anglo-Saxons have; all our women are nurses at heart. In order to secure the lifelong devotion of an Anglo-Saxon woman one has only to get one's legs cut off above the waist. I've always thought Lady Chatterley weak in symbolism from this point of view. Nothing should have earned the devotion of his wife more surely than Clifford's illness. Anglo-Saxons may not be interested in love like other Europeans but they can get just as ill. Characteristically, it is to his English Kate that Laforgue cries out: "*Une Garde-malade pour l'amour de l'art!*" He detected the nurse.'

(c)

'The classical in art is what marches by intention with the cosmology of the age.'

(d)

'A state-imposed metaphysic or religion should be opposed, if necessary at pistol-point. We must fight for variety if we fight at all. The uniform is as dull as a sculptured egg.'

(e)

Of Da Capo: 'Gamblers and lovers really play to lose.'

(f)

'Art like life is an open secret.'

(*g*)

'Science is the poetry of the intellect and poetry the science of the heart's affections.'

(*h*)

'Truth is independent of fact. It does not mind being disproved. It is already dispossessed in utterance.'

(*i*)

'I love the French edition with its uncut pages. I would not want a reader too lazy to use a knife on me.'

(*j*)

In a book of poems: 'One to be taken from time to time as needed and allowed to dissolve in the mind.'

(*k*)

'We must always defend Plato to Aristotle and vice versa because if they should lose touch with each other we should be lost. The dimorphism of the psyche produced them both.'

(*l*)

'To the medieval world-picture of the World, the Flesh and the Devil (each worth a book) we moderns have added Time: a fourth dimension.'

(*m*)

'New critical apparatus: le roman bifteck, guignol or cafard.'

(*n*)

'The real ruins of Europe are its great men.'

(*o*)

'I have always believed in letting my reader sink or skim.'

(*p*)

On reading a long review of *God is a Humorist*: 'Good God! At last they are beginning to take me seriously. This imposes a terrible burden on me. I must redouble my laughter.'

(*q*)

'Why do I always choose an epigraph from Sade? Because he demonstrates pure rationalism — the ages of sweet reason we have lived through in Europe since Descartes. He is the final flower of reason, and the typic of European behaviour. I hope to live to see him translated into Chinese. His books would bring the house down and would read as pure humour. But his spirit has already brought the house down around our ears.'

(*r*)

'Europe: a Logical Positivist trying to prove to himself by logical deduction that he exists.'

(*s*)

'My objects in the novels? To interrogate human values through an honest representation of the human passions. A desirable end, perhaps a hopeless objective.'

(*t*)

'My unkindest critics maintain that I am making lampshades out of human skin. This puzzles me. Perhaps at the bottom of the Anglo-Saxon soul there is a still small voice forever whispering: "Is this Quaite Naice?" and my books never seem to pass the test.'

SCOBIE'S COMMON USAGE

Expressions noted from Scobie's quaint conversation, his use of certain words, as:

Vivid, meaning 'angry', ex.: 'Don't be so vivid, old man.'

Mauve, meaning 'silly', ex.: 'He was just plain mauve when it came to, etc.'

Spoof, meaning 'trick', ex.: 'Don't spoof me, old boy.'

Ritual, meaning 'habit, form', ex.: 'We all wear them. It's ritual for the police.'

Squalid, meaning 'very elated', ex.: 'Toby was squalid with joy when the news came.'

Septic, meaning 'unspeakable', ex.: 'What septic weather today!'

Saffron Walden, meaning 'male brothel', ex.: 'He was caught in a Saffron Walden, old man, covered in jam.'

Cloud Cuckoo, meaning 'male prostitute', ex.: 'Budgie says there's not a cloud cuckoo in the whole of Horsham. He's advertised.'

WORKPOINTS

'How many lovers since Pygmalion have been able to build their beloved's face out of flesh, as Amaril has?' asked Clea. The great folio of noses so lovingly copied for him to choose from — Nefertiti·to Cleopatra. The readings in a darkened room.

*   *   *

Narouz always held in the back of his consciousness the memory of the moonlit room; his father sitting in the wheel-chair at the mirror, repeating the one phrase over and over again as he pointed the pistol at the looking-glass.

*   *   *

Mountolive was swayed by the dangerous illusion that now at last he was free to conceive and act — the one misjudgement which decides the fate of a diplomat.

*   *   *

Nessim said sadly: 'All motive is mixed. You see, from the moment I married her, a Jewess, all their reservations disappeared and they ceased to suspect me. I do not say it was the only reason. Love is a wonderfully luxuriant plant, but unclassifiable really, fading as it does into mysticism on the one side and naked cupidity on the other.'

*   *   *

This now explained something to me which had hitherto puzzled me; namely that after his death Da Capo's huge library was moved over to Smyrna, book by book. Balthazar did the packing and posting.

NOTE IN THE TEXT

* *Page* 298
From Eugène Marais's *The Soul of The White Ant.*

MOUNTOLIVE

A
CLAUDE
τὸ ὄνομα τοῦ ἀγαθοῦ διάμονος

NOTE

All the characters and situations described in this book (a sibling to *Justine* and *Balthazar* and the third volume of a quartet) are purely imaginary. I have exercised a novelist's right in taking a few necessary liberties with modern Middle Eastern history and the staff-structure of the Diplomatic Service.

The dream dissipated, were one to recover one's commonsense mood, the thing would be of but mediocre import — 'tis the story of mental wrongdoing. Everyone knows very well and it offends no one. But alas! one sometimes carries the thing a little further. What, one dares wonder, what would not be the idea's realization if its mere abstract shape thus exalted has just so profoundly moved one? The accursed reverie is vivified and its existence is a crime.

D. A. F. DE SADE: *Justine*

Il faut que le roman raconte.

STENDHAL

I

As a junior of exceptional promise, he had been sent to Egypt for a year in order to improve his Arabic and found himself attached to the High Commission as a sort of scribe to await his first diplomatic posting; but he was already conducting himself as a young secretary of legation, fully aware of the responsibilities of future office. Only somehow today it was rather more difficult than usual to be reserved, so exciting had the fish-drive become.

He had in fact quite forgotten about his once-crisp tennis flannels and college blazer and the fact that the wash of bilge rising through the floor-boards had toe-capped his white plimsolls with a black stain. In Egypt one seemed to forget oneself continually like this. He blessed the chance letter of introduction which had brought him to the Hosnani lands, to the rambling old-fashioned house built upon a network of lakes and embankments near Alexandria. Yes.

The punt which now carried him, thrust by slow thrust across the turbid water, was turning slowly eastward to take up its position in the great semicircle of boats which was being gradually closed in upon a target-area marked out by the black reed spines of fish-pans. And as they closed in, stroke by stroke, the Egyptian night fell — the sudden reduction of all objects to bas-reliefs upon a screen of gold and violet. The land had become dense as tapestry in the lilac afterglow, quivering here and there with water mirages from the rising damps, expanding and contracting horizons, until one thought of the world as being mirrored in a soap-bubble trembling on the edge of disappearance. Voices too across the water sounded now loud, now soft and clear. His own cough fled across the lake in sudden wing-beats. Dusk, yet it was still hot; his shirt stuck to his back. The spokes of darkness which reached out to them only outlined the shapes of the reed-fringed islands, which punctuated the water like great pin-cushions, like paws, like hassocks.

Slowly, at the pace of prayer or meditation, the great arc of boats was forming and closing in, but with the land and the water liquefying at this rate he kept having the illusion that they were travelling across the sky rather than across the alluvial

397

waters of Mareotis. And out of sight he could hear the splatter of geese, and in one corner water and sky split apart as a flight rose, trailing its webs across the estuary like seaplanes, honking crassly. Mountolive sighed and stared down into the brown water, chin on his hands. He was unused to feeling so happy. Youth is the age of despairs.

Behind him he could hear the hare-lipped younger brother Narouz grunting at every thrust of the pole while the lurch of the boat echoed in his loins. The mud, thick as molasses, dripped back into the water with a slow *flob flob*, and the pole sucked lusciously. It was very beautiful, but it all stank so: yet to his surprise he found he rather enjoyed the rotting smells of the estuary. Draughts of wind from the far sea-line ebbed around them from time to time, refreshing the mind. Choirs of gnats whizzed up there like silver rain in the eye of the dying sun. The cobweb of changing light fired his mind. 'Narouz' he said, 'I am so happy' as he listened to his own unhurried heart-beats. The youth gave his shy hissing laugh and said: 'Good, good' ducking his head. 'But this is nothing. Wait. We are closing in.' Mountolive smiled. 'Egypt' he said to himself as one might repeat the name of a woman. 'Egypt.'

'Over there' said Narouz in his hoarse, melodious voice 'the ducks are not *rusés*, do you know?' (His English was imperfect and stilted.) 'For the poaching of them, it is easy (you say 'poaching' don't you?) You dive under them and take them by the legs. Easier than shooting, eh? If you wish, tomorrow we will go.' He grunted again at the pole and sighed.

'What about snakes?' said Mountolive. He had seen several large ones swimming about that afternoon.

Narouz squared his stout shoulders and chuckled. 'No snakes' he said and laughed once more.

Mountolive turned sideways to rest his cheek on the wood of the prow. Out of the corner of his eye he could see his companion standing up as he poled, and study the hairy arms and hands, the sturdy braced legs. 'Shall I take a turn?' he asked in Arabic. He had already noticed how much pleasure it gave his hosts when he spoke to them in their native tongue. Their answers, smilingly given, were a sort of embrace. 'Shall I?'

'Of course not' said Narouz, smiling his ugly smile which was only redeemed by magnificent eyes and a deep voice. Sweat dripped down from the curly black hair with its widow's peak.

And then lest his refusal might seem impolite, he added: 'The drive will start with darkness. I know what to do; and you must look and see the fish.' The two little pink frills of flesh which edged his unbasted lip were wet with spittle. He winked lovingly at the English youth.

The darkness was racing towards them now and the light expiring. Narouz suddenly cried: 'Now is the moment. Look there.' He clapped his hands loudly and shouted across the water, startling his companion who followed his pointed finger with raised head. 'What?' the dull report of a gun from the furtherest boat shook the air and suddenly the skyline was sliced in half by a new flight, rising more slowly and dividing earth from air in a pink travelling wound; like the heart of a pomegranate staring through its skin. Then, turning from pink to scarlet, flushed back into white and fell to the lake-level like a shower of snow to melt as it touched the water — 'Flamingo' they both cried and laughed, and the darkness snapped upon them, extinguishing the visible world.

For a long moment now they rested, breathing deeply, to let their eyes grow accustomed to it. Voices and laughter from the distant boats floating across their path. Someone cried 'Ya Narouz' and again 'Ya Narouz'. He only grunted. And now there came the short syncopated tapping of a finger-drum, music whose rhythms copied themselves instantly in Mountolive's mind so that he felt his own fingers begin to tap upon the boards. The lake was floorless now, the yellow mud had vanished — the soft cracked mud of prehistoric lake-faults, or the bituminous mud which the Nile drove down before it on its course to the sea. All the darkness still smelt of it. 'Ya Narouz' came the cry again, and Mountolive recognized the voice of Nessim the elder brother borne upon a sea-breath as it spaced out the words. 'Time . . . to . . . light . . . up.' Narouz yelped an answer and grunted with satisfaction as he fumbled for matches. 'Now you'll see' he said with pride.

The circle of boats had narrowed now to encompass the pans and in the hot dusk matches began to spark, while soon the carbide lamps attached to the prows blossomed into trembling yellow flowers, wobbling up into definition, enabling those who were out of line to correct their trim. Narouz bent over his guest with an apology and groped at the prow. Mountolive smelt the sweat of his strong body as he bent down to test the rubber tube and shake the old bakelite box of the lamp, full of rock-carbide. Then he turned a key, struck a match, and for a moment the dense fumes engulfed them both where they sat, breath held, only to clear swiftly while beneath them also flowered, like some immense coloured crystal, a semicircle of lake water, candent and faithful as a magic lantern to the startled images of fish scattering and re-forming with movements of surprise, curiosity, perhaps even pleasure. Narouz expelled his breath sharply and retired to his place. 'Look down' he urged, and added 'But keep your head well down.' And as Mountolive, who did not understand this last piece of advice, turned to question him, he said 'Put a coat around your head. The kingfishers go mad with the fish and they are not night-sighted. Last time I had my cheek cut open; and Sobhi lost an eye. Face forwards and down.'

Mountolive did as he was bidden and lay there floating over the nervous pool of lamplight whose floor was now peerless crystal not mud and alive with water-tortoises and frogs and sliding fish—a whole population disturbed by this intrusion from the overworld. The punt lurched again and moved while the cold bilge came up around his toes. Out of the corner of his eye he could see that now the great half-circle of light, the chain of blossoms, was closing more rapidly; and as if to give the boats orientation and measure, there arose a drumming and singing, subdued and melancholy, yet authoritative. He felt the tug of the turning boat echoed again in his backbone. His sensations recalled nothing he had ever known, were completely original.

The water had become dense now, and thick; like an oatmeal soup that is slowly stirred into thickness over a slow fire. But when he looked more closely he saw that the illusion was caused not by the water but by the multiplication of the fish themselves. They had begun to swarm, darting in schools, excited by the very consciousness of their own numbers, yet all sliding and skirmishing one way. The cordon too had tightened like a noose and only twenty feet now separated them from the next boat, the next pool of waxen light. The boatmen had begun to utter hoarse cries and pound the waters around them, themselves excited by the pre-monition of those fishy swarms which crowded the soft lake bottom, growing more and more excited as the shallows began and they recognized themselves trapped in the shining circle. There was something like delirium in their swarming and circling now.

Vague shadows of men began to unwind hand-nets in the boats and the shouting thickened. Mountolive felt his blood beating faster with excitement. 'In a moment' cried Narouz. 'Lie still.'

The waters thickened to glue and silver bodies began to leap into the darkness only to fall back, glittering like coinage, into the shallows. The circles of light touched, overlapped, and the whole ceinture was complete, and from all around it there came the smash and crash of dark bodies leaping into the shallows, furling out the long hand-nets which were joined end to end and whose dark loops were already bulging like Christmas stockings with the squirming bodies of fish. The leapers had taken fright too and their panic-stricken leaps ripped up the whole surface of the pan, flashing back cold water upon the stuttering lamps, falling into the boats, a shuddering harvest of cold scales and drumming tails. Their exciting death-struggles were as contagious as the drumming had been. Laughter shook the air as the nets closed. Mountolive could see Arabs with their long white robes tucked up to the waist pressing forwards with steadying hands held to the dark prows beside them, pushing their linked nets slowly forward. The light gleamed upon their dark thighs. The darkness was full of their barbaric blitheness.

And now came another unexpected phenomenon — for the sky itself began to thicken above them as the water had below. The darkness was suddenly swollen with unidentifiable shapes for the jumpers had alerted the sleepers from the shores of the lakes, and with shrill incoherent cries the new visitants from the sedge-lined outer estuary joined in the hunt — hundreds of pelican, flamingo, crane and kingfisher — coming in on irregular trajectories to careen and swoop and snap at the jumping fish. The waters and the air alike seethed with life as the fishermen aligned their nets and began to scoop the swarming catch into the boats, or turned out their nets to let the rippling cascades of silver pour over the gunwales until the helmsmen were sitting ankle-deep in the squirming bodies. There would be enough and to spare for men and birds, and while the larger waders of the lake folded and unfolded awkward wings like old-fashioned painted parasols, or hovered in ungainly parcels above the snapping, leaping water, the kingfishers and herring-gulls came in from every direction at the speed of thunderbolts, half mad with greed and excitement, flying on suicidal courses, some to break their necks outright upon the decks of the boats, some to flash beak forward into the dark body of a fisherman to split open a cheek or a thigh in their terrifying cupidity. The splash of water, the hoarse cries, the snapping of beaks and wings, and the mad tattoo of the finger-drums gave the whole scene an unforgettable splendour, vaguely recalling to the mind of Mountolive forgotten Pharaonic frescoes of light and darkness.

Here and there too the men began to fight off the birds, striking at the dark air around them with sticks until amid the swarming scrolls of captured fish one could see surprisingly rainbow feathers of magical hue and broken beaks from which blood trickled upon the silver scales of the fish. For three-quarters of an hour the scene continued thus until the dark boats were brimming. Now Nessim was alongside, shouting to them in the darkness. 'We must go back.' He pointed to a lantern waving across the water, creating a warm cave of light in which they glimpsed the smooth turning flanks of a horse and the serrated edge of palm-leaves. 'My mother is waiting for us' cried Nessim. His flawless head bent down to take the edge of a light-pool as he smiled. His was a Byzantine face such as one might find among the frescoes of Ravenna — almond-shaped, dark-eyed, clear-featured. But Mountolive was looking, so to speak, through the face of Nessim and into that of Leila who was so like him, his mother. 'Narouz' he called hoarsely, for the younger brother had jumped into the water to fasten a net. 'Narouz!' One could hardly make oneself heard in the commotion. 'We must go back.'

And so at last the two boats each with its Cyclops-eye of light turned back across the dark water to the far jetty where Leila waited patiently for them with the horses in the mosquito-loud silence. A young moon was up now.

Her voice came laughingly across the variable airs of the lake, chiding them for being late, and Narouz chuckled. 'We've brought lots of fish' cried Nessim. She stood, slightly darker than the darkness, and their hands met as if guided by some perfected instinct which found no place in their conscious minds. Mount-olive's heart shook as he stood up and climbed on to the jetty with her help. But no sooner were the two brothers ashore than Narouz cried: 'Race you home, Nessim' and they dived for their horses which bucked and started at the laughing onslaught. 'Careful' she cried sharply, but before a second had passed they were off, hooves drumming on the soft rides of the embankment, Narouz chuckling like a Mephistopheles. 'What is one to do?' she said with mock resignation, and now the factor came forward with their own horses.

They mounted and set off for the house. Ordering the servant to ride on before with the lantern, Leila brought her horse close in so that they might ride knee-to-knee, solaced by the touch of each other's bodies. They had not been lovers for very long — barely ten days — though to the youthful Mountolive it seemed a century, an eternity of despair and delight. He had been formally educated in England, educated not to wish to feel. All the other valuable lessons he had already mastered, despite his youth — to confront the problems of the drawing-room and the street with sang-froid; but towards personal emotions he could only oppose the nervous silence of a national sensibility almost anaesthetized into clumsy taciturnity: an education in selected reticences and shames. Breeding and sensibility seldom march together, though the breach can be carefully disguised in codes of manners, forms of address towards the world. He had heard and read of passion, but had regarded it as something which would never impinge on him, and now here it was, bursting into the secret life which, like every overgrown schoolboy, lived on autonomously behind the indulgent screen of everyday manners and transactions, everyday talk and affections. The social man in him was overripe before the inner man had grown up. Leila had turned him out as one might turn out an old trunk, throwing everything into confusion. He suspected himself now to be only a mawkish and callow youth, his reserves depleted. With indignation almost, he realized that here at last there was something for which he might even be prepared to die — something whose very crudity carried with it a winged message which pierced to the quick of his mind. Even in the darkness he could feel himself wanting to blush. It was absurd. To *love* was absurd, like being knocked off the mantelpiece. He caught himself wondering what his mother would think if she could picture them riding among the spectres of these palm-trees by a lake which mirrored a young moon, knee touching knee. 'Are you happy?' she whispered and he felt her lips brush his wrist. Lovers can find nothing to say to each other that has not been said and unsaid a thousand times over. Kisses were invented to translate such nothings into wounds. 'Mountolive' she said again, 'David darling.' — 'Yes.' — 'You are so quiet. I thought you must be asleep.' Mountolive frowned, confronting his own dispersed inner nature. 'I was thinking' he said. Once more he felt her lips on his wrist.

'Darling.'

'Darling.'

They rode on knee-to-knee until the old house came into view, built four-square upon the network of embankments which carved up the estuary and the sweet-water canals. The air was full of fruit-bats. The upper balconies of the house were brightly lit and here the invalid sat crookedly in his wheel-chair, staring jealously out at the night, waiting for them. Leila's husband was dying of some obscure disease of the musculature, a progressive atrophy which cruelly emphasized the already great difference in their ages. His infirmity had hollowed him out into a cadaverous shell composed of rugs and shawls from which protruded two long sensitive hands. Saturnine of feature and with an uncouthness of mien which was echoed in his younger son's face, his head was askew on his shoulders and in some lights resembled those carnival masks which are carried on poles. It only remains to be added that Leila loved him!

'*Leila loved him.*' In the silence of his own mind Mountolive could never think the words without mentally shrieking them like a parrot. How could she? He had asked himself over and over again. How could she?

As he heard the hooves of the horses on the cobbles of the courtyard, the husband urged his wheel-chair forward to the balcony's edge, calling testily: 'Leila, is that you?' in the voice of an old child ready to be hurt by the warmth of her smile thrown upwards to him from the ground and the deep sweet contralto in which she answered him, mixing oriental submissiveness with the kind of comfort which only a child could understand. 'Darling'. And running up the long wooden flights of stairs to embrace him, calling out 'We are all safely back.' Mountolive slowly dismounted in the courtyard, hearing the sick man's sigh of relief. He busied himself with an unnecessary tightening of a girth rather than see them embrace. He was not jealous, but his incredulity pierced and wounded him. It was hateful to be young, to be maladroit, to feel carried out of one's depth. How had all this come about? He felt a million miles away from England; his past had sloughed from him like a skin. The warm night was fragrant with jasmine and roses. Later if she came to his room he would become as still as a needle, speechless and thoughtless, taking that strangely youthful body in his arms almost without desire or regrets; his eyes closed then, like a man standing under an icy waterfall. He climbed the stairs slowly; she had made him aware that he was tall, upright and handsome.

'Did you like it, Mountolive?' croaked the invalid, with a voice in which floated (like oil in water) pride and suspicion. A tall negro servant wheeled a small table forward on which the decanter of whisky stood — a world of anomalies: to drink 'sundowners' like colonials in this old rambling house full of magnificent carpets, walls covered with assegais captured at Omdurman, and weird Second Empire furniture of a Turkish cast. 'Sit' he said, and Mountolive, smiling at him, sat, noticing that even here in the reception rooms there were books and periodicals lying about — symbols of the unsatisfied hunger for thought which Leila had never allowed to master her. Normally, she kept her books and papers in the *harim*, but they always overflowed into the house. Her husband had no share of this world. She tried as far as possible not to make him conscious of it, dreading his jealousy which had become troublesome as his physical incapacity increased. His sons were washing — somewhere Mountolive heard the sound of pouring water. Soon he would excuse himself and retire to change into a white suit for dinner. He drank and talked to the crumpled man in the wheel-chair in his low melodious voice. It seemed to him terrifying and improper to be the lover of his wife; and yet he was always breathless with surprise to see how naturally and simply Leila carried off the whole deception. (Her cool honeyed voice, etc.; he should try not to think of her too much.) He frowned and sipped his drink.

It had been quite difficult to find his way out to the lands to present his letter of introduction: the motor road still only ran as far as the ford, after which horses had to be used to reach the house among the canals. He had been marooned for nearly an hour before a kindly passer-by had offered him a horse on which he reached his destination. That day there had been nobody at home save the invalid. Mountolive noticed with some amusement that in reading the letter of introduction, couched in the flowery high style of Arabic, the invalid muttered aloud the conventional politenesses of reciprocity to the compliments he was reading just as if the writer of the letter had himself been present. Then at once he looked up tenderly into the face of the young Englishman and spoke, and Mountolive softly answered. 'You will come and stay with us — it is the only way to improve your Arabic. For two months if you wish. My sons know English and will be delighted to converse with you; my wife also. It would be a blessing to them to have a new face, a stranger in the house. And my dear Nessim, though still so young, is in his last year at Oxford.' Pride and pleasure glowed in his sunken eyes for a minute and flickered out to give place to the customary look of pain and chagrin. Illness invites contempt. A sick man knows it.

Mountolive had accepted, and by renouncing both home and local leave had obtained permission to stay for two months in the house of this Coptic squire. It was a complete departure from everything he had known to be thus included in the pattern of a family life based in and nourished by the unconscious pageantry of a feudalism which stretched back certainly as far as the Middle Ages, and perhaps beyond. The world of Burton, Beckford, Lady Hester. . . . Did they then still exist? But here, seen from the vantage point of someone inside the canvas his own imagination had painted, he had suddenly found the exotic becoming completely normal. Its poetry was irradiated by the unconsciousness with which it was lived. Mountolive who had already found the open sesame of language ready to hand, suddenly began to feel himself really penetrating a foreign country, foreign *moeurs*, for the first time. He felt as one always feels in such a case, namely the vertiginous pleasure of losing an old self and growing a new one to replace it. He felt he was slipping, losing so to speak the contours of himself. Is this the real meaning of education? He had begun transplanting a whole huge intact world from his imagination into the soil of his new life.

The Hosnani family itself was oddly assorted. The graceful Nessim and his mother were familiars of the spirit, belonging to the same intense world of intelligence and sensibility. He, the eldest son, was always on the watch to serve his mother, should she need a door opened or a handkerchief recovered from the ground. His English and French were perfect, impeccable as his manners, graceful and strong as his physique. Then, facing them across the candle-light, sat the other two: the invalid in his rugs, and the younger son, tough and brutish as a mastiff and with an indefinable air of being ready at any moment to answer a call to arms. Heavily built and ugly, he was nevertheless gentle; but you could see from the loving way he drank in each word uttered by his father where his love-allegiance lay. His simplicity shone in his eyes, and he too was ready to be of service, and indeed, when the work of the lands did not take him from the house, was always quick to dismiss the silent boy-servant who stood behind the wheel-chair and to serve his father with a glowing pride, glad even to pick him up bodily and take him tenderly, almost gloatingly to the lavatory. He regarded his mother with something like the pride and childish sadness which shone in the eyes of the cripple. Yet, though the brothers were divided in this way like twigs of olive, there was no breach between them — they were of the same branch and felt it, and they loved one another dearly, for they were in truth complementaries, the one being strong where the other was weak. Nessim feared bloodshed, manual work and bad manners: Narouz rejoiced in them all. And Leila? Mountolive of course found her a beautiful enigma when he might, had he been more experienced, have recognized in her naturalness a perfect simplicity of spirit and in her extravagant nature a temperament which had been denied its true unfolding, had fallen back with good grace among compromises. This marriage, for example, to a man so much older than herself had been one of arrangement — this was still Egypt. The fortunes of her family had been matched against the fortunes of the Hosnanis — it resembled, as all such unions do, a merger between two great companies. Whether she was happy or unhappy she herself had never thought to consider. She was hungry, that was all, hungry for the world of books and meetings which lay forever outside this old house and the heavy charges of the land which supported their fortunes. She was obedient and pliant, loyal as a finely-bred animal. Only a disorienting monotony beset her. When young she had completed her studies in Cairo brilliantly and for a few years nourished the hope of going to Europe to continue them. She had wanted to be a doctor. But at this time the women of Egypt were lucky if they could escape the black veil — let alone the narrow confines of Egyptian thought and society. Europe for the Egyptians was simply a shopping centre for the rich to visit. Naturally, she went several times to Paris with her parents and indeed fell in love with it as we all do, but when it came to attempting to breach the barriers of Egyptian habit and to escape the parental net altogether — escape into a life which might have nourished a clever brain — there she struck upon the rock of her parents' conservatism. She must marry and make Egypt her home, they said coldly, and selected for her among the rich men of their acquaintance the kindliest and the most able they could find. Standing upon the cliff edge of these dreams, still beautiful and rich (and indeed, in Alexandrian society she was known as 'the dark swallow') Leila found everything becoming shadowy and insubstantial. She must conform. Of course, nobody would mind her visiting Europe with her husband every few years to shop or have a holiday. . . . But her life must belong to Egypt.

She gave in, responding at first with despair, later with resignation, to the life they had designed for her. Her husband was kind and thoughtful, but mentally something of a dullard. The life sapped her will. Her loyalty was such that she immersed herself in his affairs, living because he wished it far from the only capital which bore the remotest traces of a European way of life — Alexandria. For years now she had surrendered herself to the blunting airs of the Delta, and the monotony of life on the Hosnani lands. She lived mostly through Nessim who was being educated largely abroad and whose rare visits brought some life to the house. But to allay her own active curiosity about the world, she subscribed to books and periodicals in the four languages which she knew as well as her own, perhaps better, for nobody can think or feel only in the dimensionless obsolescence of Arabic. So it had been for many years now, a battle of resignations in which the element of despair only arose in the form of nervous illnesses for which her husband prescribed a not unintelligent specific — a ten-day holiday in Alexandria which always brought the colour back into her cheeks. But even these visits became in time more rare: she had insensibly slipped out of society and found herself less and less practised in the small talk and small ideas upon which it is based. The life of the city bored her. It was shallow as the waters of the great lake itself, derived; her powers of introspection sharpened with the years, and as her friends fell away only a few names and faces remained — Balthazar the doctor, for example, and Amaril and a few others. But Alexandria was soon to belong more fully to Nessim than to herself. When his studies ended he was to be conscripted into the banking house with its rapidly ramifying ancillaries, roots pushing out into shipping and oil and tungsten, roots needing water. . . . But by this time she would have become virtually a hermit.

This lonely life had made her feel somewhat unprepared for Mountolive, for the arrival of a stranger in their midst. On that first day she came in late from a desert ride and slipped into her place between her husband and his guest with some pleasurable excitement. Mountolive hardly looked at her, for the thrilling voice alone set up odd little vibrations in his heart which he registered but did not wish to study. She wore white jodhpurs and a yellow shirt with a scarf. Her smooth small hands were white and ringless. Neither of her sons appeared at lunch that day, and after the meal it was she who elected to show him round the house and gardens, already pleasantly astonished by the young man's respectable Arabic and sound French. She treated him with the faintly apprehensive solicitude of a woman towards her only man-child. His genuine interest and desire to learn filled her with the emotions of a gratitude which surprised her. It was absurd; but then never had a stranger shown any desire to study and assess them, their language, religion and habits. And Mountolive's manners were as perfect as his self-command was weak. They both walked about the rose-garden hearing each other's voices in a sort of dream. They felt short of breath, almost as if they were suffocating.

When he said good-bye that night and accepted her husband's invitation to return and stay with them, she was nowhere to be found. A servant brought a message to say that she was feeling indisposed with a headache and was lying down. But she waited for his return with a kind of obstinate and apprehensive attention.

He did, of course, meet both the brothers on the evening of that first day, for Nessim appeared in the afternoon from Alexandria and Mountolive instantly recognized in him a person of his own kind, a person whose life was a code. They responded to each other nervously, like a concord in music.

And Narouz. 'Where is this old Narouz?' she asked her husband as if the second son were his concern rather than hers, his stake in the world. 'He has been locked in the incubators for forty days. Tomorrow he will return.' Leila looked faintly embarrassed. 'He is to be the farmer of the family, and Nessim the banker' she explained to Mountolive, flushing slightly. Then, turning to her husband again, she said 'May I take Mountolive to see Narouz at work?' 'Of course.' Mountolive was enchanted by her pronunciation of his name. She uttered it with a French intonation, 'Montolif', and it sounded to him a most romantic name. This thought also was new. She took his arm and they walked through the rose-gardens and across the palm-plantations to where the incubators were housed in a long low building of earth-brick, constructed well below ground level. They knocked once or twice on a sunken door, but at last Leila impatiently pushed it open and they entered a narrow corridor with ten earthen ovens ranged along each side facing each other.

'Close the door' shouted a deep voice as Narouz rose from among a nest of cobwebs and came through the gloom to identify the intruders. Mountolive was somewhat intimidated by his scowl and hare-lip and the harshness of his shout; it was as if, despite his youth, they had intruded upon some tousled anchorite in a cliff-chapel. His skin was yellow and his eyes wrinkled from this long vigil. But when he saw them Narouz apologized and appeared delighted that they had troubled to visit him. He became at once proud and anxious to explain the workings of the incubators, and Leila tactfully left him a clear field. Mountolive already knew that the hatching of eggs by artificial heat was an art for which Egypt had been famous from the remotest antiquity and was delighted to be informed about the process. In this underground fairway full of ancient cobwebs and unswept dirt they talked techniques and temperatures with the equivocal dark eyes of the woman upon them, studying their contrasting physiques and manners, their voices. Narouz' beautiful eyes were now alive and brilliant with pleasure. His guest's lively interest seemed to thrill him too, and he explained everything in detail, even the strange technique by which egg-heats are judged in default of the thermometer, simply by placing the egg in the eye-socket.

Later, walking back through the rose-garden with Leila, Mountolive said: 'How very nice your son is.' And Leila, unexpectedly, blushed and hung her head. She answered in a low tone, with emotion: 'It is so much on our conscience that we did not have his hare-lip sewn up in time. And afterwards the village children teased him, calling him a camel, and that hurt him. You know that a camel's lip is split in two? No? It is. Narouz has had much to contend with.' The young man walking at her side felt a sudden pang of sympathy for her. But he remained tongue-tied. And then, that evening, she had disappeared.

At the outset his own feelings somewhat confused him, but he was unused to introspection, unfamiliar so to speak with the entail of his own personality — in a word, as he was young he successfully dismissed them. (All this he repeated in his own mind afterwards, recalling every detail gravely to himself as he shaved in the old-fashioned mirror or tied a tie. He went over the whole business obsessively time and again, as if vicariously to provoke and master the whole new range of emotions which Leila had liberated in him. At times he would utter the imprecation 'Damn' under his breath, between set teeth, as if he were recalling in his own memory some fearful disaster. It was unpleasant to be forced to grow. It was thrilling to grow. He gravitated between fear and grotesque elation.)

They often rode together in the desert at her husband's suggestion, and there one night of the full moon, lying together in a dune dusted soft by the wind to the contours of snow or snuff, he found himself confronted by a new version of Leila. They had eaten their dinner and talked by ghost-light. 'Wait' she said suddenly. 'There is a crumb on your lip.' And leaning forward she took it softly upon her own tongue. He felt the small warm tongue of an Egyptian cat upon his underlip for a moment. (This is where in his mind he always said the word 'Damn'.) At this he turned pale and felt as if he were about to faint. But she was there so close, harmlessly close, smiling and wrinkling up her nose, that he could only take her in his arms, stumbling forward like a man into a mirror. Their muttering images met now like reflections on a surface of lake-water. His mind dispersed into a thousand pieces, winging away into the desert around them. The act of becoming lovers was so easy and was completed with such apparent lack of premeditation, that for a while he hardly knew himself what had happened. When his mind caught up with him he showed at once how young he was, stammering: 'But why me, Leila?' as if there was all the choice in the wide world before her, and was astonished when she lay back and repeated the words after him with what seemed like a musical contempt; the puerility of his question indeed annoyed her. 'Why you? Because.' And then, to Mountolive's amazement, she recited in a low sweet voice a passage from one of her favourite authors.

'There is a destiny now possible to us — the highest ever set before a nation to be accepted or refused. We are still undegenerate in race; a race mingled of the best northern blood. We are not yet dissolute in temper, but still have the firmness to govern, and the grace to obey. We have been taught a religion of pure mercy which we must now finally betray or learn to defend by fulfilling. And we are rich in an inheritance of honour, bequeathed to us through a thousand years of noble history, which it should be our daily thirst to increase with splendid avarice, so that Englishmen, if it be a sin to covet honour, should be the most offending souls alive.'

Mountolive listened to her voice with astonishment, pity and shame. It was clear that what she saw in him was something like a prototype of a nation which existed now only in her imagination. She was kissing and cherishing a painted image of England. It was for him the oddest experience in the world. He felt the tears come into his eyes as she continued the magnificent peroration, suiting her clear voice to the melody of the prose. 'Or will you, youths of England, make your country again a royal throne of kings, a sceptred isle, for all the world a source of light, a centre of peace; mistress of learning and the arts; faithful guardian of great memories in the midst of irreverent and ephemeral visions; a faithful servant of time-tried principles, under temptation from fond experiments and licentious desires; and amidst the cruel and clamorous jealousies of the nations, worshipped in her strange valour, of goodwill towards men?' The words began to vibrate in his skull.

'Stop. Stop' he cried sharply. 'We are not like that any longer, Leila.' It was an absurd book-fed dream this Copt had discovered and translated. He felt as if all those magical embraces had been somehow won under false pretences — as if her absurd thoughts were reducing the whole thing, diminishing the scale of it to something as shadowy and unreal as, say, a transaction with a woman of the streets. Can you fall in love with the stone effigy of a dead crusader?

'You asked me *why*' she said, still with contempt. 'Because' with a sigh 'you are English, I suppose.' (It surprised him each time he went over this scene in his mind and only an oath could express the astonishment of it. 'Damn'.)

And then, like all the inexperienced lovers since the world began, he was not content to let things be; he must explore and evaluate them in his conscious mind. None of the answers she gave him was expected. If he mentioned her husband she at once became angry, interrupting him with withering directness: 'I *love* him. I will *not* have him lightly spoken of. He is a noble man and I would never do anything to wound him.'

'But . . . but . . . ' stammered the young Mountolive; and now, laughing at his perplexity, she once more put her arms about him saying 'Fool. David, *fool*! It is he who told me to take you for a lover. Think — is he not wise in his way? Fearing to lose me altogether by a mischance? Have you never starved for love? Don't you know how dangerous love is?' No, he did not know.

What on earth was an Englishman to make of these strange patterns of thought, these confused and contending loyalties? He was struck dumb. 'Only I must not fall in love and I won't.' Was this why she had elected to love Mountolive's England through him rather than Mountolive himself? He could find no answer to this. The limitations of his immaturity tongue-tied him. He closed his eyes and felt as if he were falling backwards into black space. And Leila, divining this, found in him an innocence which was itself endearing: in a way she set herself to make a man of him, using every feminine warmth, every candour. He was both a lover to her and a sort of hapless man-child who could be guided by her towards his own growth. Only (she must have made the reservation quite clearly in her own mind) she must beware of any possible resentment which he might feel at this tutelage. So she hid her own experience and became for him almost a companion of his own age, sharing a complicity which somehow seemed so innocent, so beyond reproach, that even his sense of guilt was almost lulled, and he began to drink in through her a new resolution and self-confidence. He told himself with equal resolution that he also must respect her reservations and not fall in love, but this kind of dissociation is impossible for the young. He could not distinguish between his own various emotional needs, between passion-love and the sort of romance fed on narcissism. His desire strangled him. He could not qualify it. And here his English education hampered him at every step. He could not even feel happy without feeling guilty. But all this he did not know very clearly: he only half-guessed that he had discovered more than a lover, more than an accomplice. Leila was not only more experienced; to his utter chagrin he found that she was even better read, in his own language, than he was, and better instructed. But, as a model companion and lover, she never let him feel it. There are so many resources open to a woman of experience. She took refuge always in a tenderness which expressed itself in teasing. She chided his ignorance and provoked his curiosity. And she was amused by the effect of her passion on him — those kisses which fell burning like spittle upon a hot iron. Through her eyes he began to see Egypt once more — but extended through a new dimension. To have a grasp of the language was nothing, he now realized; for Leila exposed the hollowness of the knowledge when pitted against understanding.

An inveterate note-taker by habit, he found his little pocket diary now swollen with the data which emerged from their long rides together, but it was always data which concerned the country, for he did not dare to put down a single word about his feelings or so much as record even Leila's name. In this manner:

'*Sunday. Riding through a poor fly-blown village my companion points to marks like cuneiform scratched on the walls of houses and asks if I can read them. Like a fool I say no, but perhaps they are Amharic? Laughter. Explanation is that a venerable pedlar who travels through here every six months carries a special henna from Medina, much esteemed here by virtue of its connection with the holy city. People are mostly too poor to pay, so he extends credit, but lest he or they forget, marks his tally on the clay wall with a sherd.*

'*Monday. Ali says that shooting stars are stones thrown by the angels in heaven to drive off evil djinns when they try to eavesdrop on the conversations in Paradise and learn the secrets of the future. All Arabs terrified of the desert, even Bedouin. Strange.*

'*Also: the pause in conversation which we call "Angels Passing" is greeted another way. After a moment of silence one says: "Wahed Dhu" or "One is God" and then the whole company repeats fervently in response "La Illah Illa Allah" or "No God but one God" before normal conversation is resumed. These little habits are extremely taking.*

'*Also: my host uses a curious phrase when he speaks of retiring from business. He calls it "making his soul".*

'*Also: have never before tasted the Yemen coffee with a speck of ambergris to each cup. It is delicious.*

'*Also: Mohammed Shebab offered me on meeting a touch of jasmine-scent from a phial with a glass stopper — as we would offer a cigarette in Europe.*

'*Also: they love birds. In a tumbledown cemetery I saw graves with little drinking-wells cut in the marble for them which my companion told me were filled on Friday visits by women of the village.*

'*Also: Ali, the Negro factor, an immense eunuch, told me that they feared above all blue eyes and red hair as evil signs. Odd that the examining angels in the Koran as their most repulsive features have blue eyes.*'

So the young Mountolive noted and pondered upon the strange ways of the people among whom he had come to live, painstakingly as befitted a student of manners so remote from his own; yet also in a kind of ecstasy to find a sort of poetic correspondence between the reality and the dream-picture of the East which he had constructed from his reading. There was less of a disparity here than between the twin images which Leila appeared to nurse — a poetic image of England and its exemplar the shy and in many ways callow youth she had taken for a lover. But he was not altogether a fool; he was learning the two most important lessons in life: to make love honestly and to reflect.

Yet there were other episodes and scenes which touched and excited him in a different way. One day they all rode out across the plantations to visit the old nurse Halima, now living in honourable retirement. She had been the boys' chief nurse and companion during their infancy. 'She even suckled them when my milk dried up' explained Leila.

Narouz gave a hoarse chuckle. 'She was our "chewer" ' he explained to Mountolive. 'Do you know the word?' In Egypt at this time young children were fed by servants whose duty it was to chew the food up first before spoon-feeding them with it.

Halima was a freed black slave from the Sudan, and she too was 'making her soul' now in a little wattle house among the fields of sugar-cane, happily surrounded by innumerable children and grandchildren. It was impossible to judge her age. She was delighted out of all measure at the sight of the Hosnani youths, and Mountolive was touched by the way they both dismounted and raced into her embrace. Nor was Leila less affectionate. And when the old negress had recovered herself she insisted on executing a short dance in honour of their visit; oddly it was not without grace. They all stood around her affectionately clapping their hands in time while she turned first upon one heel and then upon the other; and as she ended her song their embraces and laughter were renewed. This unaffected and spontaneous tenderness delighted Mountolive and he looked upon his mistress with shining eyes in which she could read not only his love but a new respect. He was dying now to be alone with her, to embrace her; but he listened patiently while old Halima told him of the family's qualities and how they had enabled her to visit the holy city twice as a recognition of her services. She kept one hand tenderly upon Narouz' sleeve as she spoke, gazing into his face from time to time with the affection of an animal. Then when he unpacked from the dusty old game-bag he always carried all the presents they had brought for her, the smiles and dismays played over her old face successively like eclipses of the moon. She wept.

But there were other scenes, less palatable perhaps, but none-theless representative of the *moeurs* of Egypt. One morning early he had witnessed a short incident which took place in the courtyard under his window. A dark youth stood uneasily here before a different Narouz, scowling fiercely yet with ebbing courage into those blue eyes. Mountolive had heard the words 'Master, it was no lie' spoken twice in a low clear voice as he lay reading; he rose and walked to the window in time to see Narouz, who was repeating in a low, obstinate voice, pressed between his teeth into a hiss, the words 'You lied again', perform an act whose carnal brutality thrilled him; he was in time to see his host take out a knife from his belt and sever a portion of the boy's ear-lobe, but slowly, and indeed softly, as one might sever a grape from its stalk with a fruit-knife. A wave of blood flowed down the servant's neck but he stood still. 'Now go' said Narouz in the same diabolical hiss, 'and tell your father that for every lie I will cut a piece of your flesh until we come to the true part, the part which does not lie.' The boy suddenly broke into a staggering run and disappeared with a gasp. Narouz wiped his knife-blade on his baggy trousers and walked up the stairs into the house, whistling. Mountolive was spellbound!

And then (the variety of these incidents was the most bewildering thing about them) that very afternoon while out riding with Narouz they had reached the boundaries of the property where the desert began, and had here come upon a huge sacred tree hung with every manner of *ex-voto* by the childless or afflicted villagers; every twig seemed to have sprouted a hundred fluttering rags of cloth. Nearby was the shrine of some old hermit, long since dead, and whose name even had been forgotten except perhaps by a few aged villagers. The tumbledown tomb, however, was still a place of pilgrimage and intercession to Moslem and Copt alike; and it was here that, dismounting, Narouz said in the most natural manner in the world: 'I always say a prayer here — let us pray together, eh?' Mountolive felt somewhat abashed, but he dismounted without a word and they stood side by side at the dusty little tomb of the lost saint, Narouz with his eyes raised to the sky and an expression of demonic meekness upon his face. Mountolive imitated his pose exactly, forming his hands into a cup shape and placing them on his breast. Then they both bowed their heads and prayed for a long moment, after which Narouz expelled his breath in a long slow hiss, as if with relief, and made the gesture of drawing his fingers downwards across his face to absorb the blessing which flowed from the prayer. Mountolive imitated him, deeply touched.

'Good. We have prayed now' said Narouz with finality as they remounted and set off across the fields which lay silent under the sunlight save where the force-pumps sucked and wheezed as they pumped the lake-water into the irrigation channels. At the end of the long shady plantations, they encountered another, more familiar, sound, in the soughing of the wooden water-wheels, the *sakkia* of Egypt, and Narouz cocked an appreciative ear to the wind. 'Listen' he said, 'listen to the *sakkias*. Do you know their story? At least, what the villagers say? Alexander the Great had asses' ears though only one person knew his secret. That was his barber who was a Greek. Difficult to keep a secret if you are Greek! So the barber to relieve his soul went out into the fields and told it to a *sakkia*; ever since the *sakkias* are crying sadly to each other "Alexander has asses' ears." Is that not strange? Nessim says that in the museum at Alexandria there is a portrait of Alexander wearing the horns of Ammon and perhaps this tale is a survival. Who can tell?'

They rode in silence for a while. 'I hate to think I shall be leaving you next week' said Mountolive. 'It has been a wonderful time.' A curious expression appeared on Narouz' face, compounded of doubt and uneasy pleasure, and somewhere in between them a kind of animal resentment which Mountolive told himself was perhaps jealousy — jealousy of his mother? He watched the stern profile curiously, unsure quite how to interpret these matters to himself. After all, Leila's affairs were her own concern, were they not? Or perhaps their love-affair had somehow impinged upon the family feeling, so tightly were the duties and affections of the Hosnani family bound? He would have liked to speak freely to the brothers. Nessim at least would understand and sympathize with him, but thinking of Narouz he began to doubt. The younger brother — one could not quite trust him somehow. The early atmosphere of gratitude and delight in the visitor had subtly changed — though he could not trace an open hint of animosity or reserve. No, it was more subtle, less definable. Perhaps, thought Mountolive all at once, he had manufactured this feeling entirely out of his own sense of guilt? He wondered, watching the darkly bitter profile of Narouz. He rode beside him, deeply bemused by the thought.

He could not of course identify what it was that preoccupied the younger brother, for indeed it was a little scene which had taken place without his knowledge one night some weeks previously, while the household slept. At certain times the invalid took it into his head to stay up later than usual, to sit on the balcony in his wheel-chair and read late, usually some manual of estate management, or forestry, or whatnot. At such times the dutiful Narouz would settle himself upon a divan in the next room and wait, patiently as a dog, for the signal to help his father away to bed; he himself never read a book or paper if he could help it. But he enjoyed lying in the yellow lamplight, picking his teeth with a match and brooding until he heard the hoarse waspish voice of his father call his name.

On the night in question he must have dozed off, for when he woke he found to his surprise that all was dark. A brilliant moonlight flooded the room and the balcony, but the lights had been extinguished by an unknown hand. He started up. Astonishingly, the balcony was empty. For a moment, Narouz thought he must be dreaming, for never before had his father gone to bed alone. Yet standing there in the moonlight, battling with this sense of incomprehension and doubt, he thought he heard the sound of the wheel-chair's rubber tyres rolling upon the wooden boards of the invalid's bedroom. This was an astonishing departure from accepted routine. He crossed the balcony and tiptoed down the corridor in amazement. The door of his father's room was open. He peered inside. The room was full of moonlight. He heard the bump of the wheels upon the chest of drawers and a scrabble of fingers groping for a knob. Then he heard a drawer pulled open, and a sense of dismay filled him for he remembered that in it was kept the old Colt revolver which belonged to his father. He suddenly found himself unable to move or speak as he heard the breech snapped open and the unmistakable sound of paper rustling — a sound immediately interpreted by his memory. Then the small precise click of the shells slipping into the chambers. It was as if he were trapped in one of those dreams where one is running with all one's might and yet unable to move from the same spot. As the breech snapped home and the weapon was assembled, Narouz gathered himself together to walk boldly into the room but found that he could not move. His spine got pins and needles and he felt the hair bristle up on the back of his neck. Overcome by one of the horrifying inhibitions of early childhood he could do no more than take a single slow step forward and halt in the doorway, his teeth clenched to prevent them chattering.

The moonlight shone directly on to the mirror, and by its

reflected light he could see his father sitting upright in his chair, confronting his own image with an expression on his face which Narouz had never before seen. It was bleak and impassive, and in that ghostly derived light from the pierglass it looked denuded of all human feeling, picked clean by the emotions which had been steadily sapping it. The younger son watched as if mesmerized. (Once, in early childhood, he had seen something like it — but not quite as stern, not quite as withdrawn as this: yet something like it. That was when his father was describing the death of the evil factor Mahmoud, when he said grimly: So they came and tied him to a tree. *Et on lui a coupé les choses and stuffed them into his mouth.*' As a child it was enough just to repeat the words and recall the expression on his father's face to make Narouz feel on the point of fainting. Now this incident came back to him with redoubled terror as he saw the invalid confronting himself in a moonlight image, slowly raising the pistol to point it, not at his temple, but at the mirror, as he repeated in a hoarse croaking voice: 'And now if she should fall in love, you know what you must do.')

Presently there was a silence and a single dry weary sob. Narouz felt tears of sympathy come into his eyes but still the spell held him; he could neither move nor speak nor even sob aloud. His father's head sank down on his breast, and his pistol-hand fell with it until Narouz heard the faint tap of the barrel on the floor. A long thrilling silence fell in the room, in the corridor, on the balcony, the gardens everywhere — the silence of a relief which once more let the imprisoned blood flow in his heart and veins. (Somewhere sighing in her sleep Leila must have turned, pressing her disputed white arms to a cool place among the pillows.) A single mosquito droned. The spell dissolved.

Narouz retired down the corridor to the balcony where he stood for a moment fighting with his tears before calling 'Father'; his voice was squeaky and nervous — the voice of a schoolboy. At once the light went on in his father's room, a drawer closed, and he heard the noise of rubber rolling on wood. He waited for a long second and presently came the familiar testy growl 'Narouz' which told him that everything was well. He blew his nose in his sleeve and hurried into the bedroom. His father was sitting facing the door with a book upon his knees. 'Lazy brute' he said, 'I could not wake you.'

'I'm sorry' said Narouz. He was all of a sudden delighted. So great was his relief that he suddenly wished to abase himself, to be sworn at, to be abused. 'I am a lazy brute, a thoughtless swine, a grain of salt' he said eagerly, hoping to provoke his father into still more wounding reproaches. He was smiling. He wanted to bathe voluptuously in the sick man's fury.

'Get me to bed' said the invalid shortly, and his son stooped with lustful tenderness to gather up that wasted body from the wheel-chair, inexpressibly relieved that there was still breath in it. . . .

But how indeed was Mountolive to know all this? He only recognized a reserve in Narouz which was absent from the gently smiling Nessim. As for the father of Narouz, he was quite frankly disturbed by him, by his sick hanging head, and the self-pity which his voice exuded. Unhappily, too, there was another conflict which had to find an issue somehow, and this time Mountolive un-wittingly provided an opening by committing one of those *gaffes* which diplomats, more than any other tribe, fear and dread; the memory of which can keep them awake at nights for years. It was an absurd enough slip, but it gave the sick man an excuse for an outburst which Mountolive recognized as characteristic. It all happened at table, during dinner one evening, and at first the company laughed easily enough over it — and in the expanding circle of their communal amusement there was no bitterness, only the smiling protest of Leila: 'But my dear David, we are not Moslems, but Christians *like yourself*.' Of course he had known this; how could his words have slipped out? It was one of those dreadful remarks which once uttered seem not only inexcusable but also impossible to repair. Nessim, however, appeared delighted rather than offended, and with his usual tact, did not permit himself to laugh aloud without touching his friend's wrist with his hand, lest by chance Mountolive might think the laughter directed at him rather than at his mistake. Yet, as the laughter itself fell away, he became consciously aware that a wound had been opened from the flinty features of the man in the wheel-chair who alone did not smile. 'I see nothing to smile at.' His fingers plucked at the shiny arms of the chair. 'Nothing at all. The slip exactly expresses the British point of view — the view with which we Copts have always had to contend. There were never any differences between us and the Moslems in Egypt before they came. The British have taught the Moslems to hate the Copts and to discriminate against them. Yes, Mountolive, the British. Pay heed to my words.'

'I am sorry' stammered Mountolive, still trying to atone for his *gaffe*.

'I am not' said the invalid. 'It is good that we should mention these matters openly because we Copts feel them in here, in our deepest hearts. The British have made the Moslems oppress us. Study the Commission. Talk to your compatriots there about the Copts and you will hear their contempt and loathing of us. They have inoculated the Moslems with it.'

'Oh, surely, Sir!' said Mountolive, in an agony of apology.

'Surely' asseverated the sick man, nodding his head upon that sprained stalk of neck. 'We *know* the truth.' Leila made some small involuntary gesture, almost a signal, as if to stop her husband before he was fully launched into a harangue, but he did not heed her. He sat back chewing a piece of bread and said indistinctly: 'But then what do you, what does any Englishman know or care of the Copts? An obscure religious heresy, they think, a debased language with a liturgy hopelessly confused by Arabic and Greek. It has always been so. When the first Crusade captured Jerusalem it was expressly ruled that no Copt enter the city — *our Holy City*. So little could those Western Christians distinguish between Moslems who defeated them at Askelon and the Copts — the only branch of the Christian Church which was thoroughly integrated into the Orient! But then your good Bishop of Salisbury openly said he considered these Oriental Christians as worse than infidels, and your Crusaders massacred them joyfully.' An expression of bitterness translated into a cruel smile lit up his features for a moment. Then, as his customary morose hangdog expression appeared, licking his lips he plunged once more into an argument the matter of which, Mountolive suddenly realized, had been preying upon his secret mind from the first day of his visit. He had indeed carried the whole of this conversation stacked up inside him, waiting for the moment to launch it. Narouz gazed at his father with sympathetic adoration, his features copying their expression from what was said — pride, at the words 'Our Holy City', anger at the words 'worse than infidels'. Leila sat pale and absorbed, looking out towards the balcony; only Nessim looked serious yet easy in spirit. He watched his father sympathetically and respectfully but without visible emotion. He was still almost smiling.

'Do you know what they call us — the Moslems?' Once more his head wagged. 'I will tell you. *Gins Pharoony*. Yes, we are *genus Pharaonicus* — the true descendants of the ancients, the true

o

marrow of Egypt. We call ourselves *Gypt* — ancient Egyptians. Yet we are Christians like you, only of the oldest and purest strain. And all through we have been the brains of Egypt — even in the time of the Khedive. Despite persecutions we have held an honoured place here; our Christianity has always been respected. *Here* in Egypt, not *there* in Europe. Yes, the Moslems who have hated Greek and Jew have recognized in the Copt the true inheritor of the ancient Egyptian strain. When Mohammed Ali came to Egypt he put all the financial affairs of the country into the hands of the Copts. So did Ismail his successor. Again and again you will find that Egypt was to all intents and purposes ruled by us, the despised Copts, because we had more brains and more integrity than the others. Indeed, when Mohammed Ali first arrived he found a Copt in charge of all state affairs and made him his Grand Vizier.'

'Ibrahim E. Gohari' said Narouz with the triumphant air of a schoolboy who can recite his lesson correctly.

'Exactly' echoed his father, no less triumphantly. 'He was the only Egyptian permitted to smoke his pipe in the presence of the first of the Khedives. A *Copt*!'

Mountolive was cursing the slip which had led him to receive this curtain lecture, and yet at the same time listening with great attention. These grievances were obviously deeply felt. 'And when Gohari died where did Mohammed Ali turn?'

'To Ghali Doss' said Narouz again, delightedly.

'Exactly. As Chancellor of the Exchequer he had full powers over revenue and taxation. A Copt. Another *Copt*. And *his* son Basileus was made a Bey and a member of the Privy Council. These men ruled Egypt with honour; and there were many of them given great appointments.'

'Sedarous Takla in Esneh' said Narouz, 'Shehata Hasaballah in Assiout, Girgis Yacoub in Beni Souef.' His eyes shone as he spoke and he basked like a serpent in the warmth of his father's approbation. 'Yes,' cried the invalid, striking his chair-arm with his hand. 'Yes. And even under Said and Ismail the Copts played their part. The public prosecutor in every province was a Copt. Do you realize what that means? The reposing of such a trust in a *Christian* minority? The Moslems knew us, they knew we were Egyptians first and Christians afterwards. *Christian Egyptians* — have you British with your romantic ideas about Moslems ever thought what the words mean? The only *Christian Orientals* fully integrated into a Moslem state? It would be the dream of Germans to discover such a key to Egypt, would it not? Everywhere Christians in positions of trust, in key positions as mudirs, Governors, and so on. Under Ismail a Copt held the Ministry of War.'

'Ayad Bey Hanna' said Narouz with relish.

'Yes. Even under Arabi a Coptic Minister of Justice. And a Court Master of Ceremonies. Both Copts. And others, many others.'

'How did all this change?' said Mountolive quietly, and the sick man levered himself up in his rugs to point a shaking finger at his guest and say: 'The British changed it, with their hatred of the Copts. Gorst initiated a diplomatic friendship with Khedive Abbas, and as a result of his schemes not a single Copt was to be found in the entourage of the Court or even in the services of its departments. Indeed, if you spoke to the men who surrounded that corrupt and bestial mán, supported by the British, you would have been led to think that the enemy was the Christian part of the nation. At this point, let me read you something.' Here Narouz, swiftly as a well-rehearsed acolyte, slipped into the next room and returned with a book with a marker in it. He laid it open on the lap of his father and returned in a flash to his seat. Clearing his throat the sick man read harshly: ' "When the British took control of Egypt the Copts occupied a number of the highest positions in the State. In less than a quarter of a century almost all the Coptic Heads of Departments had disappeared. They were at first fully represented in the bench of judges, but gradually the number was reduced to *nil*; the process of removing them and shutting the door against fresh appointments has gone on until they have been reduced to a state of discouragement bordering on despair!" These are the words of an Englishman. It is to his honour that he has written them.' He snapped the book shut and went on. 'Today, with British rule, the Copt is debarred from holding the position of Governor or even of *Mamur* — the administrative magistrate of a province. Even those who work for the Government are compelled to work on Sunday because, in deference to the Moslems, Friday has been made a day of prayer. No provision has been made for the Copts to worship. They are not even properly represented on Government Councils and Committees. They pay large taxes for education — but no provision is made that such money goes towards Christian education. It is all Islamic. But I will not weary you with the rest of our grievances. Only that you should understand why we feel that Britain hates us and wishes to stamp us out.'

'I don't think that *can* be so' said Mountolive feebly, now rendered somewhat breathless by the forthrightness of the criticism but unaware how to deal with it. All this matter was entirely new to him for his studies had consisted only in reading the conventional study by Lane as the true Gospel on Egypt. The sick man nodded again, as if with each nod he drove his point home a little deeper. Narouz, whose face like a mirror had reflected the various feelings of the conversation, nodded too. Then the father pointed at his eldest son. 'Nessim' he said, 'look at *him*. A true Copt. Brilliant, reserved. What an ornament he would make to the Egyptian diplomatic service. Eh? As a diplomat-to-be you should judge better than I. But no. He will be a businessman because we Copts know that it is useless, *useless*.' He banged the arm of his wheel-chair again, and the spittle came up into his mouth.

But this was an opportunity for which Nessim had been waiting, for now he took his father's sleeve and kissed it submissively, saying at the same time with a smile: 'But David will learn all this anyway. It is enough now.' And smiling round at his mother sanctioned the relieved signal she made to the servants which called an end to the dinner.

They took their coffee in uncomfortable silence on the balcony where the invalid sat gloomily apart staring out at the darkness, and the few attempts at general conversation fell flat. To do him justice, the sick man himself was feeling ashamed of his outburst now. He had sworn to himself not to introduce the topic before his guest, and was conscious that he had contravened the laws of hospitality in so doing. But he too could now see no way of repairing the conversation in which the good feeling they had reciprocated and enjoyed until now had temporarily foundered.

Here once more Nessim's tact came to the rescue; he took Leila and Mountolive out into the rose-garden where the three of them walked in silence for a while, their minds embalmed by the dense night-odour of the flowers. When they were out of earshot of the balcony the eldest son said lightly: 'David, I hope you didn't mind my father's outburst at dinner. He feels very deeply about all this.'

'I know.'

'And you know' said Leila eagerly, anxious to dispose of the whole subject and return once more to the normal atmosphere of friendliness, 'he really isn't wrong *factually*, however he expresses himself. Our position is an unenviable one, and it is due entirely to you, the British. We do live rather like a secret society — the most brilliant, indeed, once the key community in our own country.'

'I cannot understand it' said Mountolive.

'It is not so difficult' said Nessim lightly. 'The clue is the Church militant. It is odd, isn't it, that for us there was no real war between Cross and Crescent? That was entirely a Western European creation. So indeed was the idea of the cruel Moslem infidel. The Moslem was never a persecutor of the Copts on religious grounds. On the contrary, the Koran itself shows that Jesus is respected as a true Prophet, indeed a precursor of Mohammed. The other day Leila quoted you the little portrait of the child Jesus in one of the *suras* — remember? Breathing life into the clay models of birds he was making with other children. . . . .'

'I remember.'

'Why, even in Mohammed's tomb' said Leila 'there has always been that empty chamber which waits for the body of Jesus. According to the prophecy he is to be buried in Medina, the fountain of Islam, remember? And here in Egypt no Moslem feels anything but respect and love for the Christian God. Even today. Ask anyone, ask any *muezzin*.' (This was as if to say 'Ask anyone who speaks the truth' — for no unclean person, drunkard, madman or woman is regarded as eligible for uttering the Moslem call to prayer.)

'You have remained Crusaders at heart' said Nessim softly, ironically but still with a smile on his lips. He turned and walked softly away between the roses, leaving them alone. At once Leila's hand sought his familiar clasp. 'Never mind this' she said lightly, in a different voice. 'One day we will find our way back to the centre with or without your help! We have long memories!'

They sat together for a while on a block of fallen marble, talking of other things, these larger issues forgotten now they were alone. 'How dark it is tonight. I can only see one star. That means mist. Did you know that in Islam every man has his own star which appears when he is born and goes out when he dies? Perhaps that is your star, David Mountolive.'

'Or yours?'

'It is too bright for mine. They pale, you know, as one gets older. Mine must be quite pale, past middle age by now. And when you leave us, it will become paler still.' They embraced.

They spoke of their plans to meet as often as possible; of his intention to return whenever he could get leave. 'But you will not be long in Egypt' she said with her light fatalistic glance and smile. 'You will be posted soon? Where to, I wonder? You will forget us — but no, the English are always faithful to old friends, are they not? Kiss me.'

'Let us not think of that now' said Mountolive. Indeed, he felt quite deprived of any power to confront this parting coolly. 'Let us talk of other things. Look, I went into Alexandria yesterday and hunted about until I found something suitable to give Ali and the other servants.'

'What was it?'

In his suitcase upstairs he had some Mecca water in sealed blue bottles from the Holy Well of Zem Zem. These he proposed to give as *pourboires*. 'Do you think it will be well taken coming from an infidel?' he asked anxiously, and Leila was delighted. 'What a good idea, David. How typical and how tactful! Oh what are we going to do with ourselves when you have gone?' He felt quite absurdly pleased with himself. Was it possible to imagine a time when they might no longer embrace like this or sit hand in hand in the darkness to feel each other's pulses marking time quietly away into silence — the dead reaches of experience past? He averted his mind from the thought — feebly resisting the sharply-pointed truth. But now she said: 'But fear nothing. I have already planned our relations for years ahead; don't smile — it may even be better when we have stopped making love and started . . . what? I don't know — somehow thinking about each other from a neutral position; as lovers, I mean, who have been forced to separate; who perhaps never should have become lovers; I shall write to you often. A new sort of relationship will begin.'

'Please stop' he said, feeling hopelessness steal over him.

'Why?' she said, and smiling now lightly kissed his temples. 'I am more experienced than you are. We shall see.' Underneath her lightness he recognized something strong, resistant and durable — the very character of an experience he lacked. She was a gallant creature, and it is only the gallant who can remain light-hearted in adversity. But the night before he left she did not, despite her promises, come to his room. She was woman enough to wish to sharpen the pangs of separation, to make them more durable. And his tired eyes and weary air at breakfast filled her with an undiminished pleasure at his obvious suffering.

She rode to the ferry with him when he left, but the presence of Narouz and Nessim made private conversation impossible, and once again she was almost glad of the fact. There was, in fact, nothing left for either to say. And she unconsciously wished to avoid the tiresome iteration which goes with all love-making and which in the end stales it. She wanted his image of her to remain sharply in focus, and stainless; for she alone recognized that this parting was the pattern, a sample so to speak, of a parting far more definitive and final, a parting which, if their communication was to remain only through the medium of words and paper, might altogether lose her Mountolive. You cannot write more than a dozen love-letters without finding yourself gravelled for fresh matter. The richest of human experiences is also the most limited in its range of expression. Words kill love as they kill everything else. She had already planned to turn their intercourse away upon another plane, a richer one; but Mountolive was still too young to take advantage of what she might have to offer him — the treasures of the imagination. She would have to give him time to grow. She realized quite clearly that she both loved him dearly, and could resign herself to never seeing him again. Her love had already encompassed and mastered the object's disappearance — its own death! This thought, defined so sharply in her own mind, gave her a stupendous advantage over him — for he was still wallowing in the choppy sea of his own illogical and entangled emotions, desire, self-regard, and all the other nursery troubles of a teething love, whereas she was already drawing strength and self-assurance from the very hopelessness of her own case. Her pride of spirit and intelligence lent her a new and unsuspected strength. And though she was sorry with one part of her mind to see him go so soon, though she was glad to see him suffer, and prepared never to see him return, yet she knew she already possessed him, and in a paradoxical way, to say good-bye to him was almost easy.

They said good-bye at the ferry and all four participated in the long farewell embrace. It was a fine, ringing morning, with low mists trammelling the outlines of the great lake. Nessim had ordered a car which stood under the further palm-tree, a black, trembling dot. Mountolive took one wild look around him as he stepped into the boat — as if he wished to furnish his memory forever with details of this land, these three faces smiling and wishing him good luck in his own tongue and theirs. 'I'll be back!' he shouted, but in his tone she could detect all his anxiety and pain. Narouz raised a crooked arm and smiled his crooked smile; while Nessim put his arm about Leila's shoulder as he waved, fully aware of what she felt, though he would have been unable to find words for feelings so equivocal and so true.

The boat pulled away. It was over. Ended.

* * * * *

II

Late that autumn his posting came through. He was somewhat surprised to find himself accredited to the Mission in Prague, as he had been given to understand that after his lengthy refresher in Arabic he might expect to find himself a lodgement somewhere in the Levant Consular where his special knowledge would prove of use. Yet despite an initial dismay he accepted his fate with good grace and joined in the elaborate game of musical chairs which the Foreign Office plays with such eloquent impersonality. The only consolation, a meagre one, was to find that everyone in his first mission knew as little as he did about the language and politics of the country. His Chancery consisted of two Japanese experts and three specialists in Latin American affairs. They all twisted their faces in melancholy unison over the vagaries of the Czech language and gazed out from their office windows on snow-lit landscapes: they felt full of a solemn Slav foreboding. He was in the Service now.

He had only managed to see Leila half a dozen times in Alexandria — meetings made more troubling and incoherent than thrilling by the enforced secrecy which surrounded them. He ought to have felt like a young dog — but in fact he felt rather a cad. He only returned to the Hosnani lands once, for a spell of three days' leave — and here at any rate the old spiteful magic of circumstance and place held him; but so briefly — like a fugitive afterglow from the conflagration of the previous spring. Leila appeared to be somehow fading, receding on the curvature of a world moving in time, detaching herself from his own memories of her. The foreground of his new life was becoming crowded with the expensive coloured toys of his professional life — banquets and anniversaries and forms of behaviour new to him. His concentration was becoming dispersed.

For Leila, however, it was a different matter; she was already so intent upon the recreation of herself in the new role she had planned that she rehearsed it every day to herself, in her own private mind, and to her astonishment realized that she was waiting with actual impatience for the parting to become final, for the old links to snap. As an actor uncertain of a new part might wait in a fever of anxiety for his cue to be spoken. She longed for what she most dreaded, the word 'Good-bye'.

But with his first sad letter from Prague, she felt something like a new sense of elation rising in her, for now at last she would be free to possess Mountolive as she wished — greedily in her mind. The difference in their ages — widening like the chasms in floating pack-ice — were swiftly carrying their bodies out of reach of each other, out of touch. There was no permanence in any of the records to be made by the flesh with its language of promises and endearments, these were all already compromised by a beauty no longer in its first flower. But she calculated that her inner powers were strong enough to keep him to herself in the one special sense most dear to maturity, if only she could gain the courage to substitute mind for heart. Nor was she wrong in realizing that had they been free to indulge passion at will, their relationship could not have survived more than a twelvemonth. But the distance and the necessity to transfer their commerce to new ground had the effect of refreshing their images in one another. For him the image of Leila did not dissolve but suffered a new and thrilling mutation as it took shape on paper. She kept pace with his growth in those long, well-written, ardent letters which betrayed only the hunger which is as poignant as anything the flesh is called upon to cure: the hunger for friendship, the fear of being forgotten.

From Prague, Oslo, Berne, this correspondence flowed backwards and forwards, the letters swelling or diminishing in size but always remaining constant to the mind directing it — the lively, dedicated mind of Leila. Mountolive, growing, found these long letters in warm English or concise French an aid to the process, a provocation. She planted ideas beside him in the soft ground of a professional life which demanded little beyond charm and reserve — just as a gardener will plant sticks for a climbing sweet-pea. If the one love died, another grew up in its place. Leila became his only mentor and confidant, his only source of encouragement. It was to meet these demands of hers that he taught himself to write well in English and French. Taught himself to appreciate things which normally would have been outside the orbit of his interests — painting and music. He informed himself in order to inform her.

'You say you will be in Zagreb next month. Please visit and describe to me . . . ' she would write, or 'How lucky you will be in passing through Amsterdam; there is a retrospective Klee which has received tremendous notices in the French press. *Please* pay it a visit and describe your impressions honestly to me, even if unfavourable. I have never seen an original myself.' This was Leila's parody of love, a flirtation of minds, in which the roles were now reversed; for she was deprived of the riches of Europe and she fed upon his long letters and parcels of books with the double gluttony. The young man strained every nerve to meet these demands, and suddenly found the hitherto padlocked worlds of paint, architecture, music and writing opening on every side of him. So she gave him almost a gratuitous education in the world which he would never have been able to compass by himself. And where the old dependence of his youth slowly foundered, the new one grew. Mountolive, in the strictest sense of the words, had now found a woman after his own heart.

The old love was slowly metamorphosed into admiration, just as his physical longing for her (so bitter at first) turned into a consuming and depersonalized tenderness which fed upon her absence instead of dying from it. In a few years she was able to confess: 'I feel somehow nearer to you today, on paper, than I did before we parted. Why is this?' But she knew only too well. Yet she added at once, for honesty's sake: 'Is this feeling a little unhealthy perhaps? To outsiders it might even seem a little pathetic or ludicrous — who can say? And these long long letters, David — are they the bitter-sweet of a Sanseverina's commerce with her nephew Fabrizio? I often wonder if they were lovers — their intimacy is so hot and close? Stendhal never actually says so. I wish I knew Italy. Has your lover turned aunt in her old age? Don't answer even if you know the truth. Yet it is lucky in a way that we are both solitaries, with large blank unfilled areas of heart — like the early maps of Africa? — and need each other still. I mean, you as an only child with only your mother to think of, and I — of course, I have many cares, but live within a very narrow cage. Your description of the ballerina and your love-affair was amusing and touching; thank you for telling me. Have a care, dear friend, and do not wound yourself.'

It was a measure of the understanding which had grown up between them that he was now able to confide in her without reserve details of the few personal histories which occupied him: the love-affair with Grishkin which almost entangled him in a premature marriage; his unhappy passion for an Ambassador's mistress which exposed him to a duel, and perhaps disgrace. If she felt any pangs, she concealed them, writing to advise and console him with the warmth of an apparent detachment. They were frank with each other, and sometimes her own deliberate exchanges all but shocked him, dwelling as they did upon the self-examinations which people transfer to paper only when there is no one to whom they can talk. As when she could write: 'It was a shock, I mean, to suddenly see Nessim's naked body floating in the mirror, the slender white back so like yours and the loins. I sat down and, to my own surprise, burst into tears, because I wondered suddenly whether my attachment for you wasn't lodged here somehow among the feeble incestuous desires of the inner heart, I know so little about the penetralia of sex which they are exploring so laboriously, the doctors. Their findings fill me with misgivings. Then I also wondered whether there wasn't a touch of the vampire about me, clinging so close to you for so long, always dragging at your sleeve when by now you must have outgrown me quite. What do you think? Write and reassure me, David, even while you kiss little Grishkin, will you? Look, I am sending you a recent photo so you can judge how much I have aged. Show it to her, and tell her that I fear nothing so much as her unfounded jealousy. But one glance will set her heart at rest. I must not forget to thank you for the telegram on my birthday — it gave me a sudden image of you sitting on the balcony talking to Nessim. He is now so rich and independent that he hardly ever bothers to visit the land. He is too occupied with great affairs in the city. Yet . . . he feels the depth of my absence as I would wish you to; more strongly than if we were living in each other's laps. We write often and at length; our minds understudy each other, yet we leave our hearts free to love, to grow. Through him I hope that one day we Copts will regain our place in Egypt — but no more of this now. . . .' Clear-headed, self-possessed and spirited the words ran on in that tall fluent hand upon different-coloured stationery, letters that he would open eagerly in some remote Legation garden, reading them with an answer half-formulated in his mind which must be written and sealed up in time to catch the outgoing bag. He had come to depend on this friendship which still dictated, as a form, the words 'My dearest love' at the head of letters concerned solely with, say, art, or love (his love) or life (his life).

And for his part, he was scrupulously honest with her — as for instance in writing about his ballerina: 'It is true that I even considered at one time marrying her. I was certainly very much in love. But she cured me in time. You see, her language which I did not know, effectively hid her commonness from me.

Fortunately she once or twice risked a public familiarity which froze me; once when the whole ballet was invited to a reception I got myself seated next to her believing that she would behave with discretion since none of my colleagues knew of our liaison. Imagine their amusement and my horror when all of a sudden while we were seated at supper she passed her hand up the back of my head to ruffle my hair in a gesture of coarse endearment! It served me right. But I realized the truth in time, and even her wretched pregnancy when it came seemed altogether too transparent a ruse. I was cured.'

When at last they parted Grishkin taunted him saying: 'You are only a diplomat. You have no politics and no religion!' But it was to Leila that he turned for an elucidation of this telling charge. And it was Leila who discussed it with him with the blithe disciplined tenderness of an old lover.

So in her skilful fashion she held him year by year until his youthful awkwardness gave place to a maturity which matched her own. Though it was only a dialect of love they spoke, it sufficed her and absorbed him; yet it remained for him impossible to classify or analyse.

And punctually now as the calendar years succeeded each other, as his posts changed, so the image of Leila was shot through with the colours and experiences of the countries which passed like fictions before his eyes: cherry-starred Japan, hook-nosed Lima. But never Egypt, despite all his entreaties for postings which he knew were falling or had fallen vacant. It seemed that the Foreign Office would never forgive him for having learned Arabic, and even deliberately selected posts from which leave taken in Egypt was difficult or impossible. Yet the link held. Twice he met Nessim in Paris, but that was all. They were delighted with each other, and with their own worldliness.

In time his annoyance gave place to resignation. His profession which valued only judgement, coolness and reserve, taught him the hardest lesson of all and the most crippling — never to utter the pejorative thought aloud. It offered him too something like a long Jesuitical training in self-deception which enabled him to present an ever more highly polished surface to the world without deepening his human experience. If his personality did not become completely diluted it was due to Leila; for he lived surrounded by his ambitious and sycophantic fellows who taught him only how to excel in forms of address, and the elaborate kindnesses which, in pleasing, pave the way to advancement. His real life became a buried stream, flowing on underground, seldom emerging into that artificial world in which the diplomat lives — slowly suffocating like a cat in an air-pump. Was he happy or unhappy? He hardly knew any longer. He was alone, that was all. And several times, encouraged by Leila, he thought to solace his solitary concentration (which was turning to selfishness) by marrying. But somehow, surrounded as he was by eligible young women, he found that his only attraction lay among those who were already married, or who were much older than himself. Foreigners were beyond consideration for even at that time mixed marriages were regarded as a serious bar to advancement in the service. In diplomacy as in everything else there is a right and a wrong kind of marriage. But as the time slipped by he found himself climbing the slow gyres — by expediency, compromise and hard work — towards the narrow anteroom of diplomatic power: the rank of councillor or minister. Then one day the whole bright mirage which lay buried and forgotten reawoke, re-emerged, substantial and shining from the past; in the fullness of his powers he woke one day to learn that the coveted 'K' was his, and something else even more desirable — the long-denied Embassy to Egypt. . . .

But Leila would not have been a woman had she not been capable of one moment of weakness which all but prejudiced the whole unique pattern of their relationship. It came with her husband's death. But it was swiftly followed by a romantic punishment which drove her further back into the solitude which, for one wild moment, she dreamed of abandoning. It was perhaps as well, for everything might have been lost by it.

There was a silence after her telegram announcing Faltaus' death; and then a letter unlike anything she had written before, so full of hesitations and ambiguities was it. 'My indecision has become to my surprise such an agony. I am really quite distraught. I want you to think most carefully about the proposal I am about to make. Analyse it, and if the least trace of disgust arises in your mind, the least reservation, we will banish it and never speak of it again. David! Today as I looked in my mirror, as critically and cruelly as I could, I found myself entertaining a thought which for years now I have rigorously excluded. The thought of *seeing you again*. Only I could not for the life of me see the terms and conditions of such a meeting. My vision of it was covered by a black cloud of doubt. Now that Faltaus is dead and buried the whole of *that* part of my life has snapped off short. I have no other except the one I shared with you — a paper life. Crudely, we have been like people drifting steadily apart in age as each year passed. Subconsciously I must have been waiting for Faltaus' death, though I never wished it, for how else should this hope, this delusion suddenly rise up in me now? It suddenly occurred to me last night that we might still have six months or a year left to spend together before the link snaps for good in the old sense. Is this rubbish? Yes! Would I in fact only encumber you, embarrass you by arriving in Paris as I plan to do in two months' time? For goodness' sake write back at once and dissuade me from my false hopes, from such folly — for I recognize deep within myself that it is a folly. But . . . to enjoy you for a few months before I return here to take up this life: how hard it is to abandon the hope. Scotch it, please, at once; so that when I do come I will be at peace, simply regarding you (as I have all these years) as something more than my closest friend.'

She knew it was unfair to put him in such a position; but she could not help herself. Was it fortunate then that fate prevented him from having to make such an elaborate decision — for her letter arrived on his desk in the same post as Nessim's long telegram announcing the onset of her illness? And while he was still hesitating between a choice of answers there came her post-card, written in a new sprawling hand, which absolved him finally by the words: 'Do not write again until I can read you; I am bandaged from head to foot. Something very bad, very definitive has happened.'

During the whole of that hot summer the confluent smallpox — invented perhaps as the cruellest remedy for human vanity — dragged on, melting down what remained of her once celebrated beauty. It was useless to pretend even to herself that her whole life would not be altered by it. But how? Mountolive waited in an agony of indecision until their correspondence could be renewed, writing now to Nessim, now to Narouz. A void had suddenly opened at his feet.

Then: 'It is an odd experience to look upon one's own features full of pot-holes and landslides — like a familiar landscape blown up. I fear that I must get used to the new sensation of being a hag. But by my own force. Of course, all this may strengthen other sides of my character — as acids can — I've lost the metaphor! Ach! what sophistry it is, for there is no way out. And how bitterly ashamed I am of the proposals contained in my last long letter. *This* is not the face to parade through Europe, nor would one dare to shame you by letting it claim your acquaintance at close range. Today I ordered a dozen black veils such as the poor people of my religion still wear! But it seemed so painful an act that I ordered my jeweller to come and measure me afresh for some new bracelets and rings. I have become so thin of late. A reward for bravery too, as children are bribed with a sweet for facing a nasty medicine. Poor little Hakim. He wept bitterly as he showed me his wares. I felt his tears on my fingers. Yet somehow, I was able to laugh. My voice too has changed. I have been so sick of lying in darkened rooms. The veils will free me. Yes, and of *course* I have been debating suicide — who does not at such times? No, but if I live on it won't be to pity myself. Or perhaps woman's vanity is not, as we think, a mortal matter — a killing business? I must be confident and strong. Please don't turn solemn and pity me. When you write, let your letters be gay as always, will you?'

But thereafter came a silence before their correspondence was fully resumed, and her letters now had a new quality — of bitter resignation. She had retired, she wrote, to the land once more, where she lived alone with Narouz. 'His gentle savagery makes him an ideal companion. Besides, at times I am troubled in mind now, not quite *compos mentis*, and then I retire for days at a time to the little summer-house, remember? At the end of the garden. There I read and write with only my snake — the genius of the house these days is a great dusty cobra, tame as a cat. It is company enough. Besides, I have other cares now, other plans. Desert without and desert within!

> '*The veil's a fine and private place:*
> *But none, I think, do there embrace.*

'If I should write nonsense to you during the times when the *afreet* has bewitched my mind (as the servants say) don't answer. These attacks only last a day or two at most.'

And so the new epoch began. For years she sat, an eccentric and veiled recluse in Karm Abu Girg, writing those long marvellous letters, her mind still ranging freely about the lost worlds of Europe in which he still found himself a traveller. But there were fewer imperatives of the old eager kind. She seldom looked outward now towards new experiences, but mostly backwards into the past as one whose memory of small things needed to be refreshed. Could one hear the cicadas on the Tour Magne? Was the Seine corn-green at Bougival? At the Pallio of Siena were the costumes of silk? The cherry-trees of Navarra. . . . She wanted to verify the past, to look back over her shoulder, and patiently Mountolive undertook these reassurances on every journey. Rembrandt's little monkey — had she seen or only imagined it in his canvases? No, it existed, he told her sadly. Very occasionally a request touching the new came up. 'My interest has been aroused by some singular poems in Values (Sept) signed Ludwig Pursewarden. Something new and harsh here. As you are going to London next week, please enquire about him for me. Is he German? Is he the novelist who wrote those two strange novels about Africa? The name is the same.'

It was this request which led directly to Mountolive's first meeting with the poet who later was to play a part of some importance in his life. Despite the almost French devotion he felt (copied from Leila) for artists, he found Pursewarden's name an awkward, almost comical one to write upon the postcard which he addressed to him care of his publishers. For a month he heard nothing; but as he was in London on a three-months' course of instruction he could afford to be patient. When his answer came it was surprisingly enough, written upon the familiar Foreign Office notepaper; his post, it appeared, was that of a junior in the Cultural Department! He telephoned him at once and was agreeably surprised by the pleasant, collected voice. He had half-expected someone aggressively underbred, and was relieved to hear a civilized note of self-collected humour in Pursewarden's voice. They agreed to meet for a drink at the 'Compasses' near Westminster Bridge that evening, and Mountolive looked forward to the meeting as much for Leila's sake as his own, for he intended to write her an account of it, carefully describing her artist for her.

It was snowing with light persistence, the snow melting as it touched the pavements, but lingering longer on coat-collars and hats. (A snowflake on the eyelash suddenly bursts the world asunder into the gleaming component colours of the prism.) Mountolive bent his head and came round the corner just in time to see a youthful-looking couple turn into the bar of the 'Compasses'. The girl, who turned to address a remark to her companion over her shoulder as the door opened, wore a brilliant tartan shawl with a great white brooch. The warm lamplight splashed upon her broad pale face with its helmet of dark curling hair. She was strikingly beautiful with a beauty whose somehow shocking placidity took Mountolive a full second to analyse. Then he saw that she was blind, her face slightly upcast to her companion's in the manner of those whose expressions never fully attain their target — the eyes of another. She stayed thus a full second before her companion said something laughingly and pressed her onwards into the bar. Mountolive entered on their heels and found himself at once grasping the warm steady hand of Pursewarden. The blind girl, it seemed, was his sister. A few moments of awkwardness ensued while they disposed themselves by the blazing coke fire in the corner and ordered drinks.

Pursewarden, though in no way a striking person, seemed agreeably normal. He was of medium height and somewhat pale in colouring with a trimmed moustache which made a barely noticeable circumflex above a well-cut mouth. He was, however, so completely unlike his sister in colouring that Mountolive concluded that the magnificent dark hair of the sightless girl must perhaps be dyed, though it seemed natural enough, and her slender eyebrows were also dark. Only the eyes might have given one a clue to the secret of this Mediterranean pigmentation, and they, of course, were spectacularly missing. It was the head of a Medusa, its blindness was that of a Greek statue — a blindness perhaps brought about by intense concentration through centuries upon sunlight and blue water? Her expression, however, was not magistral but tender and appealing. Long silken fingers curled and softened at the butts like the fingers of a concert pianist moved softly upon the oaken table between them, as if touching, confirming, certifying — hesitating to ascribe qualities to his voice. At times her own lips moved softly as if she were privately repeating the words they spoke to herself in order to recapture their resonance and meaning; then she was like someone following music with a private score.

'Liza, my darling?' said the poet.

'Brandy and soda.' She replied with her placid blankness in a voice at once clear and melodious — a voice which might have given some such overtone to the words 'Honey and nectar'. They seated themselves somewhat awkwardly while the drinks were dispensed. Brother and sister sat side by side, which gave them a somewhat defensive air. The blind girl put one hand in the brother's pocket. So began, in rather a halting fashion, the conversation which lasted them far into the evening and which he afterwards transcribed so accurately to Leila, thanks to his formidable memory.

'He was somewhat shy at first and took refuge in a pleasant diffidence. I found to my surprise that he was earmarked for a Cairo posting next year and told him a little about my friends there, offering to give him a few letters of introduction, notably to Nessim. He may have been a little intimidated by my rank but this soon wore off; he hasn't much of a head for drinks and after the second began to talk in a most amusing and cutting fashion. A rather different person now emerged — odd and equivocal as one might expect an artist to be — but with pronounced views on a number of subjects, some of them not at all to my taste. But they had an oddly personal ring. One felt they were deduced from experience and not worked out simply to *épater*. He is, for example, rather an old-fashioned reactionary in his outlook, and is consequently rather *mal vu* by his brother craftsmen who suspect him of Fascist sympathies; the prevailing distemper of left-wing thought, indeed all radicalism is repugnant to him. But his views were expressed humorously and without heat. I could not, for example, rouse him on the Spanish issue. ("All those little *beige* people trooping off to die for the Left Book Club!")'

Mountolive had indeed been rather shocked by opinions as clear-cut as they were trenchant, for he at the time shared the prevailing egalitarian sympathies of the day — albeit in the anodyne liberalized form then current in The Office. Pursewarden's royal contempts made him rather a formidable person. 'I confess' Mountolive wrote 'that I did not feel I had exactly placed him in any one category. But he expressed views rather than attitudes, and I must say he said a number of striking things which I memorized for you, as: "The artist's work constitutes the only satisfactory relationship he can have with his fellow-men since he seeks his real friends among the dead and the unborn. That is why he can't dabble in politics, it isn't his job. He must concentrate on values rather than policies. Today it all looks to me like a silly shadow-play, for ruling is an art, not a science, just as a society is an organism, not a system. Its smallest unit is the family and really royalism is the right structure for it — for a Royal Family is a mirror image of the human, a legitimate idolatry. I mean, for us, the British, with our essentially quixotic temperament and mental sloth. I don't know about the others. As for capitalism, its errors and injustices are all remediable, by fair taxation. We should be hunting not for an imaginary equality among men, but simply for a decent equity. But then Kings should be manufacturing a philosophy of sorts, as they did in China; and absolute Monarchy is hopeless for us today because the philosophy of kingship is at a low ebb. The same goes for a dictatorship.

' "As for Communism, I can see that is hopeless too; the analysis of man in terms of economic behaviourism takes all the fun out of living, and to divest him of a personal psyche is madness." And so on. He has visited Russia for a month with a cultural delegation and did not like what he felt there; other *boutades* like "Sad Jews on whose faces one could see all the melancholia of a secret arithmetic; I asked an old man in Kiev if Russia was a happy place. He drew his breath sharply and after looking around him furtively said: 'We say that once Lucifer had good intentions, a change of heart. He decided to perform a good act for a change — just one. So hell was born on earth, and they named it Soviet Russia.' "

'In all this, his sister played no part but sat in eloquent silence with her fingers softly touching the table, curling like tendrils of vine, smiling at his aphorisms as if at private wickednesses. Only once, when he had gone out for a second, she turned to me and said: "He shouldn't concern himself with these matters really. His one job is to learn how to submit to despair." I was very much struck by this oracular phrase which fell so naturally from her lips and did not know what to reply. When he returned he resumed his place and the conversation at one and the same time as if he had been thinking it over by himself. He said "No, they are a biological necessity, Kings. Perhaps they mirror the very constitution of the psyche? We have compromised so admirably with the question of their divinity that I should hate to see them replaced by a dictator or a Workers' Council and a firing squad." I had to protest at this preposterous view, but he was quite serious. "I assure you that this is the way the left-wing tends; its object is civil war, though it does not realize it — thanks to the cunning with which the sapless puritans like Shaw and company have presented their case. Marxism is the revenge of the Irish and the Jews!" I had to laugh at this, and so — to do him justice — did he. "But at least it will explain why I am *mal vu*" he said, "and why I am always glad to get out of England to countries where I feel no moral responsibility and no desire to work out such depressing formulations. After all, what the hell! I am a writer!"

'By this time he had had several drinks and was quite at his ease. "Let us leave this barren field! Oh, how much I want to get away to the cities which were created by their women; a Paris or Rome built in response to the female lusts. I never see old Nelson's soot-covered form in Trafalgar Square without thinking: poor Emma had to go all the way to Naples to assert the right to be pretty, feather-witted and *d'une splendeur* in bed. What am I, Pursewarden, doing here among people who live in a frenzy of propriety? Let me wander where people have come to terms with their own human obscenity, safe in the poet's cloak of invisibility. I want to learn to respect nothing while despising nothing — crooked is the path of the initiate!"

' "My dear, you are tipsy!" cried Liza with delight.

' "Tipsy and sad. Sad and tipsy. But joyful, joyful!"

'I must say this new and amusing vein in his character seemed to bring me much nearer to the man himself. "Why the stylized emotions? Why the fear and trembling? All those gloomy lavatories with mackintoshed policewomen waiting to see if one pees straight or not? Think of all the passionate adjustment of dress that goes on in the kingdom! the keeping off the grass: is it any wonder that I absent-mindedly take the entrance marked Aliens Only whenever I return?"

' "You are tipsy" cried Liza again.

' "No. I am happy." He said it seriously. "And happiness can't be induced. You must wait and ambush it like a quail or a girl with tired wings. Between art and contrivance there is a gulf fixed!"

'On he went in this new and headlong strain; and I must confess that I was much taken by the effortless play of a mind which was no longer conscious of itself. Of course, here and there I stumbled against a coarseness of expression which was boorish, and looked anxiously at his sister, but she only smiled her blind smile, indulgent and uncritical.

'It was late when we walked back together towards Trafalgar Square in the falling snow. There were few people about and the snowflakes deadened our footsteps. In the Square itself your poet stopped to apostrophize Nelson Stylites in true calf-killing fashion. I have forgotten exactly what he said, but it was sufficiently funny to make me laugh very heartily. And then he suddenly changed his mood and turning to his sister said: "Do you know what has been upsetting me all day, Liza? Today is Blake's birthday. Think of it, the birthday of codger Blake. I felt I ought to see some signs of it on the national countenance, I looked about me eagerly all day. But there was nothing. Darling Liza, let *us* celebrate the old b . . .'s birthday, shall we? You and I and David Mountolive here — as if we were French or Italian, as if it meant something." The snow was falling fast, the last sodden leaves lying in mounds, the pigeons uttering their guttural clotted noises. "Shall we, Liza?" A spot of bright pink had appeared in each of her cheeks. Her lips were parted. Snowflakes like dissolving jewels in her dark hair. "How?" she said. "Just how?"

' "We will dance for Blake" said Pursewarden, with a comical look of seriousness on his face, and taking her in his arms he started to waltz, humming the Blue Danube. Over his shoulder, through the falling snowflakes, he said: "This is for Will and Kate Blake." I don't know why I felt astonished and rather touched. They moved in perfect measure gradually increasing in speed until they were skimming across the square under the bronze lions, hardly heavier than the whiffs of spray from the fountains. Like pebbles skimming across a smooth lake or stones across an ice-bound pond. . . . It was a strange spectacle. I forgot my cold hands and the snow melting on my collar as I watched them. So they went, completing a long gradual ellipse across the open space, scattering the leaves and the pigeons, their breath steaming on the night-air. And then, gently, effortlessly spinning out the arc to bring them back to me — to where I stood now with a highly doubtful-looking policeman at my side. It was rather amusing. "What's goin' on 'ere?" said the bobby, staring at them with a distrustful admiration. Their waltzing was so perfect that I think even he was stirred by it. On they went and on, magnificently in accord, the dark girl's hair flying behind her, her sightless face turned up towards the old admiral on his sooty perch. "They are celebrating Blake's birthday" I explained in rather a shamefaced fashion, and the officer looked a shade more relieved as he followed them with an admiring eye. He coughed and said "Well, he can't be drunk to dance like that, can he? The things people get up to on their birthdays!"

'At long last they were back, laughing and panting and kissing one another. Pursewarden's good humour seemed to be quite restored now, and he bade me the warmest of good-nights as I put

442

them both in a taxi and sent them on their way. There! My dear
Leila, I don't know what you will make of all this. I learned
nothing of his private circumstances or background, but I shall
be able to look him up; and you will be able to meet him when he
comes to Egypt. I am sending you a small printed collection of his
newest verses which he gave me. They have not appeared anywhere as yet.'

In the warm central heating of the club bedroom, he turned the
pages of the little book, more with a sense of duty than one of
pleasure. It was not only modern poetry which bored him, but
all poetry. He could never get the wave-length, so to speak,
however hard he tried. He was forced to reduce the words to
paraphrase in his own mind, so that they stopped their dance.
This inadequacy in himself (Leila had taught him to regard it
as such) irritated him. Yet as he turned the pages of the little
book he was suddenly interested by a poem which impinged upon
his memory, filling him with a sudden chill of misgiving. It was
inscribed to the poet's sister and was unmistakingly a love-poem
to ' a blind girl whose hair is painted black'. At once he saw the
white serene face of Liza Pursewarden rising up from the text.

> *Greek statues with their bullet holes for eyes*
> *Blinded as Eros by surprise,*
> *The secrets of the foundling heart disguise,*
> *Lover and loved. . . .*

It had a kind of savage deliberate awkwardness of surface;
but it was the sort of poem a modern Catullus might have written.
It made Mountolive extremely thoughtful. Swallowing, he read
it again. It had the simple beauty of shamelessness. He stared
gravely at the wall for a long time before slipping the book into
an envelope and addressing it to Leila.

There were no further meetings during that month, though once
or twice Mountolive tried to telephone to Pursewarden at his
office. But each time he was either on leave or on some obscure
mission in the north of England. Nevertheless he traced the sister
and took her out to dinner on several occasions, finding her a
delightful and somehow moving companion.

Leila wrote in due course to thank him for his information,
adding characteristically: 'The poems were splendid. But of
course I would not wish to meet an artist I admired. The work
has no connection with the man, I think. But I am glad he is

coming to Egypt. Perhaps Nessim can help him — perhaps he can help Nessim? We shall see.'

Mountolive did not know what the penultimate phrase meant.

The following summer, however, his leave coincided with a visit to Paris by Nessim, and the two friends met to enjoy the galleries and plan a painting holiday in Brittany. They had both recently started to try their hands at painting and were full of the fervour of amateurs in a new medium. It was here in Paris that they ran into Pursewarden. It was a happy accident, and Mountolive was delighted at the chance of making his path smooth for him by this lucky introduction. Pursewarden himself was quite transfigured and in the happiest of moods, and Nessim seemed to like him immensely. When the time came to say good-bye, Mountolive had the genuine conviction that a friendship had been established and cemented over all this good food and blithe living. He saw them off at the station and that very evening reported to Leila on the notepaper of his favourite café: 'It was a real regret to put them on the train and to think that this week I shall be back in Russia! My heart sinks at the thought. But I have grown to like P. very much, to understand him better. I am inclined to put down his robust scolding manners not to boorishness as I did, but to a profoundly hidden shyness, almost a feeling of guilt. His conversation this time was quite captivating. You must ask Nessim. I believe he liked him even more than I did. And so . . . what? An empty space, a long frozen journey. Ah! my dear Leila, how much I miss you — what you stand for. When will we meet again, I wonder? If I have enough money on my next leave I may fly down to visit you. . . .'

He was unaware that quite soon he would once more find his way back to Egypt — the beloved country to which distance and exile lent a haunting brilliance as of tapestry. Could anything as rich as memory be a cheat? He never asked himself the question.

*   *   *   *   *

III

The central heating in the Embassy ballroom gave out a thick furry warmth which made the air taste twice-used; but the warmth itself was a welcome contrast to the frigid pine-starred landscapes outside the tall windows where the snow fell steadily, not only over Russia, it seemed, but over the whole world. It had been falling now for weeks on end. The numb drowsiness of the Soviet winter had engulfed them all. There seemed so little motion, so little sound in the world outside the walls which enclosed them. The tramp of soldiers' boots between the shabby sentry-boxes outside the iron gates had died away now in the winter silence. In the gardens the branches of the trees bowed lower and lower under the freight of falling whiteness until one by one they sprang back shedding their parcels of snow, in soundless explosions of glittering crystals; then the whole process began again, the soft white load of the tumbling snow-flakes gathering upon them, pressing them down like springs until the weight became unendurable.

Today it was Mountolive's turn to read the lesson. Looking up from the lectern from time to time he saw the looming faces of his staff and fellow secretaries in the shadowy gloom of the ball-room as they followed his voice; faces gleaming white and sunless — he had a sudden image of them all floating belly upwards in a snowy lake, like bodies of trapped frogs gleaming upwards through the mirror of ice. He coughed behind his hand, and the contagion spread into a ripple of coughing which subsided once more into that spiritless silence, with only the susurrus of the pipes echoing through it. Everyone today looked morose and ill. The six Chancery guards looked absurdly pious, their best suits awkwardly worn, their jerks of hair pasted to their brows. All were ex-Marines and clearly showed traces of vodka hangovers. Mountolive sighed inwardly as he allowed his quiet melodious voice to enunciate the splendours — incomprehensible to them all — of the passage in the Gospel of St. John which he had found under the marker. The eagle smelt of camphor — why, he could not imagine. As usual, the Ambassador had stayed in bed; during the last year he had become very lax in his duties and was prepared to depend on Mountolive who was luckily always there to perform them with grace and lucidity. Sir Louis had given up even the pretence of caring about the welfare physical or spiritual of his little flock. Why should he not? In three months he would have retired for good.

It was arduous to replace him on these public occasions but it was also useful, thought Mountolive. It gave him a clear field in the exploitation of his own talents for administration. He was virtually running the whole Embassy now, it was in his hands. Nevertheless. . . .

He noticed that Cowdell, the Head of Chancery, was trying to catch his eye. He finished the lesson unfalteringly, replaced the markers, and made his way slowly back to his seat. The chaplain uttered a short catarrhal sentence and with a riffling of pages they found themselves confronting the banal text of 'Onward Christian Soldiers' in the eleventh edition of the Foreign Service Hymnal. The harmonium in the corner suddenly began to pant like a fat man running for a bus; then it found its voice and gave out a slow nasal rendering of the first two phrases in tones whose harshness across the wintry hush was like the pulling out of entrails. Mountolive repressed a shudder, waiting for the instrument to subside on the dominant as it always did — as if about to burst into all-too-human sobs. Raggedly they raised their voices to attest to . . . to what? Mountolive found himself wondering. They were a Christian enclave in a hostile land, a country which had become like a great concentration camp owing to a simple failure of the human reason. Cowdell was nudging his elbow and he nudged back to indicate a willingness to receive any urgent communication not strictly upon religious matters. The Head of Chancery sang:

> '*Someone's lucky dáy today*
> *Marching as to war* (fortissimo, with piety)
> *Ciphers have an urgent*
> *Going on before,* (fortissimo, with piety).

Mountolive was annoyed. There was usually little to do on a Sunday, though the Cipher office remained open with a skeleton staff on duty. Why had they not, according to custom, telephoned to the villa and called him in? Perhaps it was something about the new liquidations? He started the next verse plaintively:

> '*Someone should have told me*
> *How was I to know?*
> *Who's the duty cipherine?*'

446

Cowdell shook his head and frowned as he added the rider: '*She is still at work-ork-ork.*'

They wheeled round the corner, so to speak, and drew collective breath while the music started to march down the aisle again. This respite enabled Cowdell to explain hoarsely: 'No, it's an urgent *Personal*. Some groups corrupt still.'

They smoothed their faces and consciences for the rest of the hymn while Mountolive grappled with his perplexity. As they knelt on the uncomfortable dusty hassocks and buried their faces in their hands, Cowdell continued from between his fingers: 'You've been put up for a "K" and a mission. Let me be the first to congratulate you, etc.'

'Christ!' said Mountolive in a surprised whisper, to himself rather than to his Maker. He added 'Thank you.' His knees suddenly felt weak. For once he had to study to achieve his air of imperturbability. Surely he was still too young? The ramblings of the Chaplain, who resembled a swordfish, filled him with more than the usual irritation. He clenched his teeth. Inside his mind he heard himself repeating the words: 'To get out of Russia!' with ever-growing wonder. His heart leaped inside him.

At last the service ended and they trailed dolorously out of the ballroom and across the polished floors of the Residence, coughing and whispering. He managed to counterfeit a walk of slow piety, though it hardly matched his racing mind. But once in the Chancery, he closed the padded door slowly behind him, feeling it slowly suck up the air into its valve as it sealed, and then, drawing a sharp breath, clattered down the three flights of stairs to the wicket-gate which marked the entry to Archives. Here a duty-clerk dispensed tea to a couple of booted couriers who were banging the snow from their gloves and coats. The canvas bags were spread everywhere on the floor waiting to be loaded with the mail and chained up. Hoarse good-mornings followed him to the cipher-room door where he tapped sharply and waited for Miss Steele to let him in. She was smiling grimly. 'I know what you want' she said. 'It's in the tray — the Chancery copy. I've had it put in your tray and given a copy to the Secretary for H.E.'

She bent her pale head once more to her codes. There it was, the flimsy pink membrane of paper with its neatly typed message. He sat down in a chair and read it over slowly twice. Lit a cigarette. Miss Steele raised her head. 'May I congratulate you, sir?' — 'Thank you' said Mountolive vaguely. He reached his hands to the electric fire for a moment to warm his fingers as he thought deeply. He was beginning to feel a vastly different person. The sensation bemused him.

After a while he walked slowly and thoughtfully upstairs to his own office, still deep in this new and voluptuous dream. The curtains had been drawn back — that meant that his secretary had come in; he stood for a while watching the sentries cross and recross the snowlit entrance to the main gate with its ironwork piled heavily with ice. While he stood there with his dark eyes fixed upon an imagined world lying somewhere behind this huge snowscape, his secretary came in. She was smiling with jubilance. 'It's come at last' she said. Mountolive smiled slowly back. 'Yes. I wonder if H.E. will stand in my way?'

'Of course not' she said emphatically. 'Why should he?'

Mountolive sat once more at his familiar desk and rubbed his chin. 'He himself will be off in three months or so' said the girl. She looked at him curiously, almost angrily, for she could read no pleasure, no self-congratulation in his sober expression. Even good fortune could not pierce that carefully formulated reserve. 'Well' he said slowly, for he was still swaddled by his own amazement, the voluptuous dream of an unmerited success. 'We shall see.' He had been possessed now by another new and even more vertiginous thought. He opened his eyes widely as he stared at the window. Surely now, he would at long last be free to *act*? At last the long discipline of self-effacement, of perpetual delegation, was at an end? This was frightening to contemplate, but also exciting. He felt as if now his true personality would be able to find a field of expression in acts; and still full of this engrossing delusion he stood up and smiled at the girl as he said: 'At any rate, I must ask H.E.'s blessing before we answer. He is not on deck this morning, so lock up. Tomorrow will do.' She hovered disappointedly for a moment over him before gathering up his tray and taking out the key to his private safe. 'Very well' she said.

'There's no hurry' said Mountolive. He felt that his real life now stretched before him; he was about to be reborn. 'I don't see my *exequatur* coming through for a time yet. And so on.' But his mind was already racing upon a parallel track, saying: 'In summer the whole Embassy moves to Alexandria, to summer quarters. If I could time my arrival. . . .'

And then, side by side with this sense of exhilaration, came a twinge of characteristic meanness. Mountolive like most people who have nobody on whom to lavish affection, tended towards meanness in money matters. Unreasonable as it was, he suddenly felt a pang of depression at the thought of the costly dress uniform which his new position would demand. Only last week there had been a catalogue from Skinners showing a greatly increased scale for Foreign Service uniforms.

He got up and went into the room next door to see the private secretary. It was empty. An electric fire glowed. A lighted cigarette smoked in the ashtray beside the two bells marked respectively 'His Ex.' and 'Her Ex'. On the pad beside them the Secretary had written in his round feminine hand 'Not to be woken before eleven.' This obviously referred to 'His Ex.', As for 'Her Ex.', she had only managed to last six months in Moscow before retiring to the amenities of Nice where she awaited her husband upon his retirement. Mountolive stubbed out the cigarette.

It would be useless to call on his Chief before midday, for the morning in Russia afflicted Sir Louis with a splenetic apathy which often made him unresponsive to ideas; and while he could not, in all conscience, do anything to qualify Mountolive's good fortune, he might easily show pique at not having been consulted according to custom by the Principal Private Secretary. Anyway. He retired to his now empty office and plunged into the latest copy of *The Times*, waiting with ill-concealed impatience for the Chancery clock to mark out midday with its jangling whirrs and gasps. Then he went downstairs and slipped into the Residence again through the padded door, walking with his swift limping walk across the polished floors with their soft archipelagos of neutral rug. Everything smelt of disuse and Mansion polish; in the curtains a smell of cigar-smoke. At every window a screen of tossing snowflakes.

Merritt the valet was starting up the staircase with a tray containing a cocktail shaker full of Martini and a single glass. He was a pale heavily-built man who cultivated the gravity of a churchwarden while he moved about his tasks in the Residence. He stopped as Mountolive drew level and said hoarsely: 'He's just up and dressing for a duty lunch, sir.' Mountolive nodded and passed him, taking the stairs two at a time. The servant turned back to the buttery to add a second glass to his tray.

Sir Louis whistled dispiritedly at his own reflection in the great mirror as he dressed himself. 'Ah, my boy' he said vaguely as Mountolive appeared behind him. 'Just dressing. I know, I know.

449

It's my unlucky day. Chancery rang me at eleven. So you have done it at last. Congratulations.'

Mountolive sat down at the foot of the bed with relief to find the news taken so lightly. His Chief went on wrestling with a tie and a starched collar as he said: 'I suppose you'll want to go off at once, eh? It's a loss to us.'

'It would be convenient' admitted Mountolive slowly.

'A pity. I was hoping you'd see me out. But anyway' he made a flamboyant gesture with a disengaged hand 'you've done it. From tricorne and dirk to bicorne and sword — the final apotheosis.' He groped for cuff-links and went on thoughtfully. 'Of course, you could stay a bit; it'll take time to get *agrément*. Then you'll have to go to the Palace and kiss hands and all that sort of thing. Eh?'

'I have quite a lot of leave due' said Mountolive with the faintest trace of firmness underlying his diffident tone. Sir Louis retired to the bathroom and began scrubbing his false teeth under the tap. 'And the next Honours List?' he shouted into the small mirror on the wall. 'You'll wait for that?'

'I suppose.' Merritt came in with the tray and the old man shouted 'Put it anywhere. An extra glass?'

'Yes sir.'

As the servant retired closing the door softly behind him, Mountolive got up to pour the cocktail. Sir Louis was talking to himself in a grumbling tone. 'It's damn hard on the Mission. Well, anyway, David, I bet your first reaction to the news was: now I'm free to act, eh?' He chuckled like a fowl and returned to his dressing-table in a good humour. His junior paused in the act of pouring out, startled by such unusual insight. 'How on earth did you know that?' he said, frowning. Sir Louis gave another self-satisfied cluck.

'We all do. We all do. The final delusion. Have to go through it like the rest of us, you know. It's a tricky moment. You find yourself throwing your weight about — committing the sin against the Holy Ghost if you aren't careful.'

'What would that be?'

'In diplomacy it means trying to build a policy on a minority view. Everyone's weak spot. Look how often we are tempted to build something on the Right here. Eh? Won't do. Minorities are no use unless they're prepared to *fight*. That's the thing.' He accepted his drink in rosy old fingers, noting with approval the breath of dew upon the cold glasses. They toasted each other and smiled affectionately. In the last two years they had become the greatest of friends. 'I shall miss you. But then, in another three months I shall be out of this . . . this place myself.' He said the words with undisguised fervour. 'No more nonsense about Objectivity. Eastern can find some nice impartial products of the London School of Economics to do their reporting.' Recently the Foreign Office had complained that the Mission's despatches were lacking in balance. This had infuriated Sir Louis. He was fired even by the most fugitive memory of the slight. Putting down his empty glass he went on to himself in the mirror: 'Balance! If the F.O. sent a mission to Polynesia they would expect their despatches to begin (he put on a cringing whining tone to enunciate it): "While it is true that the inhabitants eat each other, nevertheless the food consumption per head is remarkably high." ' He broke off suddenly and sitting down to lace his shoes said: 'Oh, David my boy, who the devil am I going to be able to talk to when you go? Eh? You'll be walking about in your ludicrous uniform with an osprey feather in your hat looking like the mating plumage of some rare Indian bird and I — I shall be trotting backwards and forwards to the Kremlin to see those dull beasts.'

The cocktails were rather strong. They embarked upon a second, and Mountolive said: 'Actually, I came wondering if I could buy your old uniform, unless it's bespoke. I could get it altered.'

'Uniform?' said Sir Louis. 'I hadn't thought of that.'

'They are so fearfully expensive.'

'I know. And they've gone up. But you'd have to send mine back to the taxidermist for an overhaul. And they never fit round the neck, you know. All that braid stuff. I'm a frogging or two loose I think. Thank God this isn't a monarchy — one good thing. Frock coats in order, what? Well I don't know.'

They sat pondering upon the question for a long moment. Then Sir Louis said: 'What would you offer me?' His eye narrowed. Mountolive deliberated for a few moments before saying 'Thirty pounds' in an unusually energetic and decisive tone. Sir Louis threw up his hands and simulated incoherence. 'Only thirty? It cost me. . . .'

'I know' said Mountolive.

'Thirty pounds' meditated his Chief, hovering upon the fringes of outrage. 'I think, dear boy ——"

'The sword is a bit bent' said Mountolive obstinately.

'Not too badly' said Sir Louis. 'The King of Siam pinched it in the door of his private motor-car. Honourable scar.' He smiled once more and continued dressing, humming to himself. He took an absurd delight in this bargaining. Suddenly he turned round.

'Make it fifty' he said. Mountolive shook his head thoughtfully.

'That is too much, sir.'

'Forty-five.'

Mountolive rose and took a turn up and down the room, amused by the old man's evident delight in this battle of wills. 'I'll give you forty' he said at last and sat down once more with deliberation. Sir Louis brushed his silver hair furiously with his heavy tortoiseshell-backed brushes. 'Have you any drink in your cellar?'

'As a matter of fact, yes, I have."

'Well then, you can have it for forty if you throw in a couple of cases of . . . what have you? Have you a respectable champagne?'

'Yes.'

'Very well. Two — no, *three* cases of same.'

They both laughed and Mountolive said 'It's a hard bargain you drive.' Sir Louis was delighted by the compliment. They shook hands upon it and the Ambassador was about to turn back to the cocktail tray when his junior said: 'Forgive me, sir. Your third.'

'Well?' said the old diplomat with a well-simulated start and a puzzled air. 'What of it?' He knew perfectly well. Mountolive bit his lip. 'You expressly asked me to warn you.' He said it reproachfully. Sir Louis threw himself further back with more simulated surprise. 'What's wrong with a final boneshaker before lunch, eh?'

'You'll only hum' said Mountolive sombrely.

'Oh, pouf, dear boy!' said Sir Louis.

'You will, sir.'

Within the last year, and on the eve of retirement, the Ambassador had begun to drink rather too heavily — though never quite reaching the borders of incoherence. In the same period a new and somewhat surprising tic had developed. Enlivened by one cocktail too many he had formed the habit of uttering a low continuous humming noise at receptions which had earned him a rather questionable notoriety. But he himself had been unaware of this habit, and indeed at first indignantly denied its existence. He found to his surprise that he was in the habit of humming,

452

over and over again, in *basso profundo*, a passage from the Dead March in Saul. It summed up, appropriately enough, a lifetime of acute boredom spent in the company of friendless officials and empty dignitaries. In a way, it was his response perhaps to a situation which he had subconsciously recognized as intolerable for a number of years; and he was grateful that Mountolive had had the courage to bring the habit to his notice and to help him overcome it. Nevertheless, he always felt bound to protest in spite of himself at his junior's reminder. '*Hum?*' he repeated now, indignantly pouting, 'I never heard such nonsense.' But he put down the glass and returned to the mirror for a final criticism of his toilet. 'Well, anyway' he said, 'time is up.' He pressed a bell and Merritt appeared with a gardenia on a plate. Sir Louis was somewhat pedantic about flowers and always insisted on wearing his favourite one in his buttonhole when in *tenue de ville*. His wife flew up boxes of them from Nice and Merritt kept them in the buttery refrigerator, to be rationed out religiously.

'Well, David' he said, and patted Mountolive's arm with affection. 'I owe you many a good turn. No humming today, however appropriate.'

They walked slowly down the long curving staircase and into the hall where Mountolive saw his Chief gloved and coated before signalling the official car by house-telephone. 'When do you want to go?' The old voice trembled with genuine regret.

'By the first of next month, sir. That leaves time to wind up and say good-bye.'

'You won't stay and see me out?'

'If you order me to, sir.'

'You know I wouldn't do that' said Sir Louis, shaking his white head, though in the past he had done worse things. 'Never.'

They shook hands warmly once more while Merritt walked past them to throw back the heavy front door, for his ears had caught the slither and scrape of tyre-chains on the frosty drive outside. A blast of snow and wind burst upon them. The carpets rose off the floor and subsided again. The Ambassador donned his great fur helmet and thrust his hands into the carmuff. Then, bowed double, he stalked out to the wintry greyness. Mountolive sighed and heard the Residence clock clear its dusty throat carefully before striking one.

Russia was behind him.

* * * * *

Berlin was also in the grip of snow, but here the sullen goaded helplessness of the Russias was replaced by a malignant euphoria hardly less dispiriting. The air was tonic with gloom and uncertainty. In the grey-green lamplight of the Embassy he listened thoughtfully to the latest evaluations of the new Attila, and a valuable summary of the measured predictions which for months past had blackened the marbled minute-papers of German Department, and the columns of the P.E. printings — political evaluations. Was it really by now so obvious that this nation-wide exercise in political diabolism would end by plunging Europe into bloodshed? The case seemed overwhelming. But there was one hope — that Attila might turn eastwards and leave the cowering west to moulder away in peace. If the two dark angels which hovered over the European subconscious could only fight and destroy each other. . . . There was some real hope of this. 'The *only* hope, sir' said the young attaché quietly, and not without a certain relish, so pleasing to a part of the mind is the prospect of total destruction, as the only cure for the classical *ennui* of modern man. 'The only hope' he repeated. Extreme views, thought Mountolive, frowning. He had been taught to avoid them. It had become second nature to remain uncommitted in his mind.

That night he was dined somewhat extravagantly by the youthful Chargé d'Affaires, as the Ambassador was absent on duty, and after dinner was taken to the fashionable Tanzfest for the cabaret. The network of candle-lit cellars, whose walls were lined with blue damask, was filled with the glow of a hundred cigarettes, twinkling away like fireflies outside the radius of white lights where a huge hermaphrodite with the face of a narwhal conducted the measures of the 'Fox Macabre Totentanz'. Bathed in the pearly sweat of the nigger saxophonists the refrain ran on with its hysterical coda:

> *Berlin, dein Tanzer ist der Tod!*
> *Berlin, du wuhlst mit Lust im Kot!*
> *Halt ein! lass sein! und denk ein bischen nach:*
> *Du tanzt dir doch vom Leibe nicht die Schmach.*
> *denn du boxt, und du jazzt, und du foxt auf dem Pulverfass!*

It was an admirable commentary on the deliberations of the afternoon and underneath the frenetic licence and fervour of the singing he seemed to catch the drift of older undertones —

passages from Tacitus, perhaps? Or the carousings of death-dedicated warriors heading for Valhalla? Somehow the heavy smell of the abattoir clung to it, despite the tinsel and the streamers. Thoughtfully Mountolive sat among the white whorls of cigar-smoke and watched the crude peristaltic movements of the Black Bottom. The words repeated themselves in his mind over and over again. 'You won't dance the shame out of your belly,' he repeated to himself as he watched the dancers break out and the lights change from green and gold to violet.

Then he suddenly sat up and said 'My Goodness!' He had caught sight of a familiar face in a far corner of the cellar: that of Nessim. He was seated at a table among a group of elderly men in evening-dress, smoking a lean cheroot and nodding from time to time. They were taking scant notice of the cabaret. A magnum of champagne stood upon the table. It was too far to depend upon signals and Mountolive sent over a card, waiting until he saw Nessim follow the waiter's pointing finger before he smiled and raised a hand. They both stood up, and Nessim at once came over to his table with his warm shy smile to utter the conventional exclamations of surprise and delight. He was, he said, in Berlin on a two-day business visit. 'Trying to market tungsten' he added quietly. He was flying back to Egypt at dawn next morning. Mountolive introduced him to his own host and persuaded him to spend a few moments at their table. 'It is such a rare pleasure — and now.' But Nessim had already heard the rumour of his impending appointment. 'I know it isn't confirmed yet,' he said, 'but it leaked just the same — needless to say via Pursewarden. You can imagine our delight after so long.'

They talked on for a while, Nessim smiling as he answered Mountolive's questions. Only Leila was at first not mentioned. After a while Nessim's face took on a curious expression — a sort of chaste cunning, and he said with hesitation: 'Leila will be so delighted.' He gave him a swift upward glance from under his long lashes and then looked hastily away. He stubbed out his cheroot and gave Mountolive another equivocal glance. He stood up and glanced anxiously back in the direction of his party at the far table. 'I must go' he said.

They discussed plans for a possible meeting in England before Mountolive should fly out to his new appointment. Nessim was vague, unsure of his movements. They would have to wait upon the event. But now Mountolive's host had returned from the cloak-room, a fact which effectively prevented any further private exchanges. They said good-bye with good grace and Nessim walked slowly back to his table.

'Is your friend in armaments?' asked the Chargé d'Affaires as they were leaving. Mountolive shook his head. 'He's a banker. Unless tungsten plays a part in armaments — I don't really know.'

'It isn't important. Just idle curiosity. You see, the people at his table are all from Krupps, and so I wondered. That was all.'

★ ★ ★ ★ ★

IV

To London he always returned with the tremulous eagerness of a lover who has been separated a long time from his mistress; he returned, so to speak, upon a note of interrogation. Had life altered? Had anything been changed? Perhaps the nation had, after all, woken up and begun to live? The thin black drizzle over Trafalgar Square, the soot-encrusted cornices of Whitehall, the slur of rubber tyres spinning upon macadam, the haunting conspiratorial voice of river traffic behind the veils of mist — they were both a reassurance and a threat. He loved it inarticulately, the melancholy of it, though he knew in his heart he could no longer live here permanently, for his profession had made an expatriate of him. He walked in the soft clinging rain towards Downing Street, muffled in his heavy overcoat, comparing himself from time to time, not without a certain complacence, to the histrionic Grand Duke who smiled at him from the occasional hoardings advertising De Reszke cigarettes.

He smiled to himself as he remembered some of Pursewarden's acid strictures on their native capital, repeating them in his own mind with pleasure, as compliments almost. Pursewarden transferring his sister's hand from one elbow to another in order to complete a vague gesture towards the charred-looking figure of Nelson under its swarming troops of pigeons befluffed against the brute cold. 'Ah, Mountolive! Look at it all. Home of the eccentric and the sexually disabled. London! Thy food as appetizing as a barium meal, thy gloating discomforts, thy causes not lost but gone before.' Mountolive had protested laughingly. 'Never mind, It is *our own* — and it is greater than the sum of its defects.' But his companion had found such sentiments uncongenial. He smiled now as he remembered the writer's wry criticisms of gloom, discomfort and the native barbarism. As for Mountolive, it nourished him, the gloom; he felt something like the fox's love for its earth. He listened with a comfortable smiling indulgence while his companion perorated with mock fury at the image of his native island, saying: 'Ah, England! England where the members of the R.S.P.C.A. eat meat twice a day and the nudist devours imported fruit in the snow. The only country which is ashamed of poverty.'

Big Ben struck its foundering plunging note. Lamps had begun to throw out their lines of prismatic light. Even in the rain there was the usual little cluster of tourists and loungers outside the gates of Number Ten. He turned sharply away and entered the silent archways of the Foreign Office, directing his alien steps to the bag-room, virtually deserted now, where he declared himself and gave instructions about the forwarding of his mail, and left an order for the printing of new and more resplendent invitation cards.

Then in a somewhat more thoughtful mood, and a warier walk to match it, he climbed the cold staircase smelling of cobwebs and reached the embrasures in the great hall patrolled by the uniformed janitors. It was late, and most of the inhabitants of what Pursewarden always called the 'Central Dovecot' had surrendered their tagged keys and vanished. Here and there in the great building were small oases of light behind barred windows. The clink of teacups sounded somewhere out of sight. Someone fell over a pile of scarlet despatch boxes which had been stacked in a corridor against collection. Mountolive sighed with familiar pleasure. He had deliberately chosen the evening hours for his first few interviews because there was Kenilworth to be seen and . . . his ideas were not very precise upon the point; but he might atone for his dislike of the man by taking him to his club for a drink? For somewhere along the line he had made an enemy of him, he could not guess how, for it had never been marked by any open disagreement. Yet it was there, like a knot in wood.

They had been near-contemporaries at school and university, though never friends. But while he, Mountolive, had climbed smoothly and faultlessly up the ladder of promotion the other had been somehow faulted, had always missed his footing; had drifted about among the departments of little concern, collecting the routine honours, but never somehow catching a favourable current. The man's brilliance and industry were undeniable. Why had he never succeeded? Mountolive asked himself the question fretfully, indignantly. Luck? At any rate here was Kenilworth now heading the new department concerned with Personnel, innocuous enough, to be sure, but his failure embarrassed Mountolive. For a man of his endowment it was really a shame to be merely in charge of one of those blank administrative constructs which offered no openings into the worlds of policy. A dead end. And if he could not develop positively he would soon develop the negative powers of obstruction which always derive from a sense of failure.

As he was thinking this he was climbing slowly to the third floor to report his presence to Granier, moving through the violet crepuscule towards the tall cream doors behind which the Under-Secretary sat in a frozen bubble of green light, incising designs on his pink blotter with a paper-knife. Congratulations weighed something here, for they were spiced with professional envy. Granier was a clever, witty and good-tempered man with some of the mental agility and drive of a French grandmother. It was easy to like him. He spoke rapidly and confidently, marking his sentences with little motions of the ivory paper-weight. Mountolive fell in naturally with the charm of his language — the English of fine breeding and polish which carried those invisible diacritical marks, the expression of its caste.

'You looked in on the Berlin mission, I gather? Good. Anyway, if you've been following P.E. you will see the shape of things to come perhaps, and be able to judge the extent of our preoccupations with your own appointment. Eh?' He did not like to use the word 'war'. It sounded theatrical. 'If the worst comes to the worst we don't need to emphasize a concern for Suez — indeed, for the whole Arab complex of states. But since you've served out there I won't pretend to lecture you about it. But we'll look forward to your papers with interest. And moreover as you know Arabic.'

'My Arabic has all gone, rusted away.'

'Hush' said Granier, 'not too loud. You owe your appointment in a very large measure to it. Can you get it back swiftly?'

'If I am allowed the leave I have accrued.'

'Of course. Besides, now that the Commission is wound up, we shall have to get *agrément* and so on. And of course the Secretary of State will want to confer when he gets back from Washington. Then what about investiture, and kissing hands and all that? Though we regard every appointment of the sort as urgent . . . well, you know as well as I do the mandarin calm of F.O. movements' He smiled his clever and indulgent smile, lighting a Turkish cigarette. 'I'm not so sure it isn't a good philosophy either' he went on. 'At any rate, as a bias for policy. After all, we are always facing the inevitable, the irremediable; more haste, more muddle! More panic and less confidence. In diplomacy one can only propose, never dispose. That is up to God, don't you think?' Granier was one of those worldly Catholics who regarded God as a congenial club-member whose motives are above question. He sighed and was silent for a moment before adding: 'No, we'll have to set the chessboard up for you properly. It's not everyone who'd consider Egypt a plum. All the better for you.'

Mountolive was mentally unrolling a map of Egypt with its green central spine bounded by deserts, the dusty anomalies of its peoples and creeds; and then watching it fade in three directions into incoherent desert and grassland; to the north Suez like a caesarian section through which the East was untimely ripped; then again the sinuous complex of mountains and dead granite, orchards and plains which were geographically distributed about the map at hazard, boundaries marked by dots. . . . The metaphor from chess was an apposite one. Cairo lay to the centre of this cobweb. He sighed and took his leave, preparing a new face with which to greet the unhappy Kenilworth.

As he walked thoughtfully back to the janitors on the first floor he noted with alarm that he was already ten minutes late for his second interview and prayed under his breath that this would not be regarded as a deliberate slight.

'Mr. Kenilworth has phoned down twice, sir. I told him where you were.'

Mountolive breathed more freely and addressed himself once more to the staircase, only to turn right this time and wind down several cold but odourless corridors to where Kenilworth waited, tapping his rimless pince-nez against a large and shapely thumb. They greeted one another with a grotesque effusion which effectively masked a reciprocal distaste. 'My *dear* David'. . . . Was it, Mountolive wondered, simply an antipathy to a physical type? Kenilworth was of a large and porcine aspect, over two hundred pounds of food-and-culture snob. He was prematurely grey. His fat, well-manicured fingers held a pen with a delicacy suggesting incipient crewel-work or crochet. 'My *dear* David!' They embraced warmly. All the fat on Kenilworth's large body hung down when he stood up. His flesh was knitted in a heavy cable stitch. 'My *dear* Kenny' said Mountolive with apprehension and self-disgust. 'What splendid news. I flatter myself' Kenilworth put on an arch expression 'that I may have had something, quite small, quite insignificant, to do with it. Your Arabic weighed with the S. of S. and it was I who remembered it! A long memory. Paper

work.' He chuckled confusedly and sat down motioning Mountolive to a chair. They discussed commonplaces for a while and at
last Kenilworth joined his fingers into a gesture reminiscent of a
pout and said: 'But to our *moutons*, dear boy. I've assembled all
the personal papers for you to browse over. It is all in order. It's
a well-found mission, you'll find, very well-found. I've every
confidence in your Head of Chancery, Errol. Of course, your own
recommendations will weigh. You will look into the staff structure,
won't you, and let me know? Think about an A.D.C. too, eh?
And I don't know how you feel about a P.A. unless you can rob
the typists' pool. But as a bachelor, you'll need someone for the
social side, won't you? I don't think your third secretary would be
much good.'

'Surely I can do all this on the spot?'

'Of course, of course. I was just anxious to see you settled in as
comfortably as possible.'

'Thank you.'

'There is only one change I was contemplating on my own.
That was Pursewarden as first political.'

'Pursewarden?' said Mountolive with a start.

'I am transferring him. He has done statutory time, and he
isn't really happy about it. Needs a change in my view.'

'Has he said so?'

'Not in so many words.'

Mountolive's heart sank. He took out the cigarette holder which
he only used in moments of perplexity, charged it from the silver
box on the desk, and sat back in the heavy old-fashioned chair.
'Have you any other reasons?' he asked quietly. 'Because I should
personally like to keep him, at least for a time.' Kenilworth's
small eyes narrowed. His heavy neck became contused by the
blush of annoyance which was trying to find its way up to his face.
'To be frank with you, yes' he said shortly.

'Do tell me.'

'You will find a long report on him by Errol in the papers I've
assembled. I don't think he is altogether suitable. But then contract
officers have never been as dependable as officers of the career.
It's a generalization, I know. I won't say that our friend isn't faithful
to the firm — far from it. But I can say that he is opinionated and
difficult. Well, *soit!* He's a writer, isn't he?' Kenilworth ingratiated
himself with the image of Pursewarden by a brief smile of unconscious contempt. 'There has been endless friction with Errol.

You see, since the gradual break-up of the High Commission after the signing of the Treaty, there has been a huge gap created, a hiatus; all the agencies which have grown up there since 1918 and which worked to the Commission have been cut adrift now that the parent body is giving place to an Embassy. There will be some thorough-going decisions for you to make. Everything is at sixes and sevens. Suspended animation has been the keynote of the last year and a half — and unsuspended hostilities between an Embassy lacking a Chief, and all these parentless bodies struggling against their own demise. Do you see? Now Pursewarden may be brilliant but he has put a lot of backs up — not only in the mission; people like Maskelyne, for example, who runs the War Office I.C. Branch and has this past five years. They are at each other's throats.'

'But what has an I. Branch to do with us?'

'Exactly, nothing. But the High Commissioner's Political Section depended on Maskelyne's Intelligence reports. I.C. Intelligence Collation was the central agency for the Middle East Central Archives and all that sort of thing.'

'Where's the quarrel?'

'Pursewarden as political feels that the Embassy has also in a way inherited Maskelyne's department from the Commission. Maskelyne refuses to countenance this. He demands parity or even complete freedom for his show. It is military after all.'

'Then set it under a military attaché for the time being.'

'Good, but Maskelyne refuses to agree to become part of your mission as his seniority is greater than your attaché designate's.'

'What rubbish all this is. What is his rank?'

'Brigadier. You see, since the end of the '18 show, Cairo has been the senior post office of the intelligence network and all intelligence was funnelled through Maskelyne. Now Pursewarden is trying to appropriate him, bring him to heel. Battle royal, of course. Poor Errol, who I admit is rather weak in some ways, is flapping between them like a loose sail. That is why I thought your task would be easier if you shed Pursewarden.'

'Or Maskelyne.'

'Good, but he's a War Office body. You couldn't. At any rate, he is most eager for you to arrive and arbitrate. He feels sure you will establish his complete autonomy.'

'I can't tolerate an autonomous War Office Agency in a territory to which I am accredited, can I?'

'I agree. I agree, my dear fellow.'

'What does the War Office say?'

'You know the military! They will stand by any decision you choose to make. They'll have to. But they have been dug in there for years now. Own staff branches and their transmitter up in Alexandria. I think they would like to stay.'

'Not independently. How could I?'

'Exactly. That is what Pursewarden maintains. Good, but someone will have to go in the interests of equity. We can't have all this pin-pricking.'

'What pin-pricking?'

'Well, Maskelyne withholding reports and being forced to disgorge them to Political Branch. Then Pursewarden criticizing their accuracy and questioning the value of I.C. Branch. I tell you, real fireworks. No joke. Better shed the fellow. Besides, you know, he's something of a . . . , 'keeps odd company. Errol is troubled about his security. Mind you, there is nothing *against* Pursewarden. It's simply that's he's, well . . . a bit of a vulgarian, would you say? I don't know how to qualify it. It's Errol's paper.'

Mountolive sighed. 'It's surely only the difference between, say, Eton and Worthing, isn't it?' They stared at one another. Neither thought the remark was funny. Kenilworth shrugged his shoulders with obvious pique. 'My dear chap' he said, 'if you propose to make an issue of it with the S. of S. I can't help it; you will get my proposals overruled. But my views have gone on record now. You'll forgive me if I let them stay like that, as a comment upon Errol's reports. After all, he has been running the show.'

'I know.'

'It is hardly fair on him.'

Stirring vaguely in his subconscious Mountolive felt once more the intimations of power now available to him — a power to take decisions in factors like these which had hitherto been left to fate, or the haphazard dictation of mediating wills; factors which had been unworth the resentments and doubts which their summary resolution by an act of thought would have bred. But if he was ever to claim the world of action as his true inheritance he must begin somewhere. A Head of Mission had the right to propose and sponsor the staff of his choice. Why should Pursewarden suffer through these small administrative troubles, endure the discomfort of a new posting to some uncongenial place?

'I'm afraid the F.O. will lose him altogether if we play about with him' he said unconvincingly; and then, as if to atone for a proposition so circuitous, added crisply: 'At any rate, I propose to keep him for a while.'

The smile on Kenilworth's face was one in which his eyes played no part. Mountolive felt the silence close upon them like the door of a vault. There was nothing to be done about it. He rose with an exaggerated purposefulness and extruded his cigarette-end into the ugly ashtray as he said: 'At any rate, those are my views; and I can always send him packing if he is no use to me.'

Kenilworth swallowed quietly, like a toad under a stone, his expressionless eyes fixed upon the neutral wall-paper. The quiet susurrus of the London traffic came welling up between them. 'I must go' said Mountolive, by now beginning to feel annoyed with himself. 'I am collecting all the files to take down to the country tomorrow evening. Today and tomorrow I'll clear off routine interviews, and then . . . some leave I hope. Good-bye, Kenny.'

'Good-bye.' But he did not move from his desk. He only nodded smilingly at the door as Mountolive closed it; then he turned back with a sigh to Errol's neatly-typed memoranda which had been assembled in the grey file marked *Attention of Ambassador Designate*. He read a few lines, and then looked up wearily at the dark window before crossing the room to draw the curtains and pick up the phone. 'Give me Archives, please.'

It would be wiser for the moment not to press his view.

This trifling estrangement, however, had the effect of making Mountolive set aside his plan to take Kenilworth back to his club with him. It was in its way a relief. He rang up Liza Pursewarden instead and took her out to dinner.

It was only two hours down to Dewford Mallows but once they were outside London it was clear that the whole countryside was deeply under snow. They had to slow down to a crawl which delighted Mountolive but infuriated the driver of the duty-car. 'We'll be there for Christmas, sir' he said, 'if at all!'

Ice-Age villages, their thatched barns and cottages perfected by the floury whiteness of snow, glistening as if from the tray of an expert confectioner; curving white meadows printed in cuneiform with the small footmarks of birds or otters, or the thawing blotches of cattle. The car windows sealing up steadily, gummed by the frost. They had no chains and no heater. Three miles from the village they came upon a wrecked lorry with a couple of villagers and an A.A. man standing idly about it, blowing on their perished fingers. The telegraph poles were down hereabouts. There was a dead bird lying on the glittering grey ice of Newton's Pond — a hawk. They would never get over Parson's Ridge, and Mountolive took pity on his driver and turned him back summarily on to the main road by the foot-bridge. 'I live just over the hill' he said. 'It'll take me just twenty-five minutes to walk it.' The man was glad to turn back and unwilling to accept the tip Mountolive offered. Then he reversed slowly and turned the car away northward, while his passenger stepped forward into the brilliance, his condensing breath rising before him in a column.

He followed the familiar footpath across fields which tilted ever more steeply away towards an invisible sky-line, describing (his memory had to do duty for his eyesight) something as perfected in its simplicity as Cavendish's first plane. A ritual landscape made now overwhelmingly mysterious by the light of an invisible sun, moving somewhere up there behind the opaque screens of low mist which shifted before him, withdrawing and closing. It was a walk full of memories — but in default of visibility he was forced to imagine the two small hamlets on the hill-crown, the intent groves of beeches, the ruins of a Norman castle. His shoes cut a trembling mass of raindrops from the lush grass at every scythe-like step, until the bottoms of his trousers were soaked and his ankles turned to ice.

Out of the invisible marched shadowy oaks, and suddenly there came a rattling and splattering — as if their teeth were chattering with the cold; the thawing snow was dripping down upon the carpet of dead leaves from the upper branches.

Once over the crown all space was cut off. Rabbits lobbed softly away on all sides. The tall plumed grass had been starched into spikes by frost. Here and there came glimpses of a pale sun, its furred brilliance shining through the mist like a gas mantle burning brightly but without heat. And now he heard the click of his own shoes upon the macadam of the second-class road as he hastened his pace towards the tall gates of the house. Hereabouts the oaks were studded with brilliants; as he passed two fat pigeons rushed out of them and disappeared with the sharp wingflap of a thousand closing books. He was startled and then amused. There was the 'form' of a hare in the paddock, quite near the house. Fingers of ice tumbled about the trees with a ragged clatter — a thousand broken wineglasses. He groped for the old Yale key and smiled again as he felt it turn, admitting him to an unforgotten warmth which smelt of apricots and old books, polish and flowers; all the memories which led him back unerringly towards Piers Plowman, the pony, the fishing-rod, the stamp album. He stood in the hall and called her name softly.

His mother was sitting by the fire, just as he had last left her with a book open upon her knees, smiling. It had become a convention between them to disregard his disappearance and returns: to behave as if he had simply absented himself for a few moments from this companionable room where she spent her life, reading or painting or knitting before the great fireplace. She was smiling now with the same smile — designed to cement space and time, and to anneal the loneliness which beset her while he was away. Mountolive put down his heavy briefcase and made a funny little involuntary gesture as he stepped towards her. 'Oh dear' he said, 'I can see from your face that you've heard. I was so hoping to surprise you with my news!'

They were both heartbroken by the fact; and as she kissed him she said: 'The Graniers came to tea last week. Oh, David, I'm so sorry. I did so want you to have your surprise. But I pretend so badly.'

Mountolive felt an absurd disposition towards tears of sheer vexation: he had invented the whole scene in his mind, and made up question and answer. It was like tearing up a play into which one had put a lot of imagination and hard work. 'Damn' he said, 'how thoughtless of them!'

'They were trying to please me — and of course it did. You can imagine how much, can't you?'

But from this point he stepped once more, lightly and effortlessly back into the current of memories which the house evoked around her and which led back almost to his eleventh birthday, the sense of well-being and plenitude as the warmth of the fire came out to greet him.

'Your father will be pleased,' she said later, in a new voice, sharper for being full of an unrealized jealousy — tidemarks of a passion which had long since refunded itself into an unwilling acquiescence. 'I put all your mail in his study for you.' 'His' study — the study which his father had never seen, never inhabited.

The defection of his father stood always between them as their closest bond, seldom discussed yet somehow always there — the invisible weight of his private existence, apart from them both, in another corner of the world: happy or unhappy, who can say? 'For those of us who stand upon the margins of the world, as yet unsolicited by any God, the only truth is that work itself is Love.' An odd, a striking phrase for the old man to embed in a scholarly preface to a Pali text! Mountolive had turned the green volume over and over in his hands, debating the meaning of the words and measuring them against the memory of his father — the lean brown figure with the spare bone-structure of a famished sea-bird: dressed in an incongruous pith-helmet. Now, apparently he wore the robes of an Indian *fakir*! Was one to smile? He had not seen his father since his departure from India on his eleventh birthday; he had become like someone condemned *in absentia* for a crime . . . which could not be formulated. A friendly withdrawal into the world of Eastern scholarship on which his heart had been set for many years. It was perplexing.

Mountolive senior had belonged to the vanished India, to the company of its rulers whose common devotion to their charge had made them a caste; but a caste which was prouder of a hostage given to Buddhist scholarship than of one given to an Honours List. Such disinterested devotions usually ended by a passionate self-identification with the subject of them — this sprawling subcontinent with its castes and creeds, its monuments and faiths and ruins. At first he had been simply a judge in the service, but within a few years he had become pre-eminent in Indian scholarship, an editor and interpreter of rare and neglected texts. The young Mountolive and his mother had been comfortably settled in England on the understanding that he would join them on retirement; to this end had this pleasant house been furnished with the trophies, books and pictures of a long working career. If it now had something of the air of a museum, it was because it had been deserted by its real author who had decided to stay on in India to complete the studies which (they both now recognized) would last him the rest of his life. This was not an uncommon phenomenon among the officials of the now vanished and disbanded corps. But it had come gradually. He had deliberated upon it for years before arriving at the decision, so that the letter he wrote announcing it all had the air of a document long meditated. It was in fact the last letter either of them received from him. From time to time, however, a passer-by who had visited him in the Buddhist Lodge near Madras to which he had retired, brought a kindly message from him. And of course the books themselves arrived punctually, one after the other, resplendent in their rich uniforms and bearing the grandiose imprints of University Presses. The books were, in a way, both his excuse and his apology.

Mountolive's mother had respected this decision; and nowadays hardly ever spoke of it. Only now and again the invisible author of their joint lives here in this snowy island emerged thus in a reference to 'his' study; or in some other remark like it which, uncommented upon, evaporated back into the mystery (for them) of a life which represented an unknown, an unresolved factor. Mountolive could never see below the surface of his mother's pride in order to judge how much this defection might have injured her. Yet a common passionate shyness had grown up between them on the subject, for each secretly believed the other wounded.

Before dressing for dinner that evening, Mountolive went into the book-lined study, which was also a gun-room, and took formal possession of 'his father's' desk which he used whenever he was at home. He locked his files away carefully and sorted out his mail. Among the letters and postcards was a bulky envelope with a Cyprus stamp addressed to him in the unmistakable hand of Pursewarden. It suggested a manuscript at first and he cracked the seal with his finger in some perplexity. 'My dear David' it read. 'You will be astonished to get a letter of such length from me, I don't doubt. But the news of your appointment only reached me lately in rumoured form, and there is much you should know about the state of affairs here which I could not address to you formally as Ambassador Designate (Confidential: Under Flying Seal) ahem!'

There would be time enough, thought Mountolive with a sigh, to study all this accumulation of memoranda, and he unlocked the desk again to place it with his other papers.

He sat at the great desk for a while in the quietness, soothed by the associations of the room with its *bric-à-brac*; the mandala paintings from some Burmese shrine, the Lepcha flags, the framed drawings for the first edition of the Jungle Book, the case of Emperor moths, the votive objects left at some abandoned temple. Then the rare books and pamphlets—early Kipling bearing the imprint of Thacker and Spink, Calcutta, Edwards Thompson's fascicules, Younghusband, Mallows, Derby. . . . Some museum would be glad of them one day. Under a pressmark they would revert back to anonymity.

He picked up the old Tibetan prayer-wheel which lay on the desk and twirled it once or twice, hearing the faint scrape of the revolving drum, still stuffed with the yellowing fragments of paper on which devout pens had long ago scribbled the classical invocation *Om Mani Padme Hum*. This had been an accidental parting gift. Before the boat left he had pestered his father for a celluloid aeroplane and together they had combed the bazaar for one without avail. Then his father had suddenly stopped at a pedlar's stall and bought the wheel for a few rupees, thrusting it into his unwilling fingers as a substitute. It was late. They had to rush. Their good-byes had been perfunctory.

Then after that, what? A tawny river-mouth under a brazen sun, the iridescent shimmer of heat blurring the faces, the smoke from the burning ghats, the dead bodies of men, blue and swollen, floating down the estuary. . . . That was as far as his memory went. He put down the heavy wheel and sighed. The wind shook the windows, whirling the snow against them, as if to remind him where he was. He took out his bundle of Arabic primers and the great dictionary. These must live beside his bed for the next few months.

That night he was once more visited by the unaccountable affliction with which he always celebrated his return home — a crushing ear-ache which rapidly reduced him to a shivering pain-racked ghost of himself. It was a mystery, for no doctor had so far managed to allay — or even satisfactorily to diagnose — this onslaught of the *petit mal*. It never attacked him save when he was at home. As always, his mother overheard his groans and knew from old experience what they meant; she materialized out of the darkness by his bed bringing the comfort of ancient familiarity and the one specific which, since childhood, she had used to combat his distress. She always kept it handy now, in the cupboard beside her bed. Salad oil, warmed in a teaspoon over a candle-flame. He felt the warmth of the oil penetrate and embalm his brain, while his mother's voice upon the darkness soothed him with its promises of relief. In a little while the tide of agony receded to leave him, washed up so to speak, on the shores of sleep — a sleep stirred vaguely by those comforting memories of childhood illnesses which his mother had always shared — they fell ill together, as if by sympathy. Was it so that they might lie in adjoining rooms talking to each other, reading to each other, sharing the luxury of a common convalescence? He did not know.

He slept. It was a week before he addressed himself to his official papers and read the letter from Pursewarden.

★ ★ ★ ★ ★

V

My dear David,

You will be astonished to get a letter of such length from me, I don't doubt. But the news of your appointment only reached me lately in rumoured form, and there is much you should know about the state of affairs here which I could not address to you formally as Ambassador Designate (Confidential: Under Flying Seal) ahem!

Ouf! What a bore! I hate writing letters as you well know. And yet . . . I myself shall almost certainly be gone by the time you arrive, for I have taken steps to get myself transferred. After a long series of calculated wickednesses I have at *last* managed to persuade poor Errol that I am unsuitable for the Mission which I have adorned these past months. Months! A lifetime! And Errol himself is so good, so honest, so worthy; a curious goat-like creature who nevertheless conveys the impression of being a breech-delivery! He has put in his paper against me with the greatest reluctance. *Please do nothing to countermand the transfer which will result from it*, as it squares with my own private wishes. I implore you.

The deciding factor has been my desertion of my post for the past five weeks which has caused grave annoyance and finally decided Errol. I will explain everything. Do you remember, I wonder, the fat young French diplomat of the Rue du Bac? Nessim took us round once for drinks? Pombal by name? Well, I have taken refuge with him—he is serving here. It is really quite gay *chez lui*. The summer over, the headless Embassy retired with the Court to winter in Cairo, but this time without Yours Truly. I went underground. Nowadays we rise at eleven, turn out the girls, and after having a hot bath play backgammon until lunch-time; then an *arak* at the Café Al Aktar with Balthazar and Amaril (who send their love) and lunch at the Union Bar. Then perhaps we call on Clea to see what she is painting, or go to a cinema. Pombal is doing all this legitimately; he is on local leave. I am *en retraite*. Occasionally the exasperated Errol rings up long distance in an attempt to trace me and I answer him in the voice of a *poule* from the Midi. It rattles him badly because he guesses it is me, but isn't quite sure. (The point about a Wykehamist is that he cannot *risk* giving offence.) We have lovely, lovely conversations. Yesterday I told him that I, Pursewarden, was under treatment for a glandular condition chez Professor Pombal but was now out of danger. Poor Errol! One day I shall apologize to him for all the trouble I have caused him. Not now. Not until I get my transfer to Siam or Santos.

All this is very wicked of me, I know, but . . . the tedium of this Chancery with all these un-grown-up people! The Errols are formidably Britannic. They are, for example, *both* economists. Why *both*, I ask myself? One of them must feel permanently redundant. They make love to two places of decimals only. Their children have all the air of vulgar fractions!

Well. The only nice ones are the Donkins; he is clever and high-spirited, she rather common and fast-looking with too much rouge. But . . . poor dear, she is over-compensating for the fact that her little husband has grown a beard and turned Moslem! She sits with a hard aggressive air on his desk, swinging her leg and smoking swiftly. Mouth too red. Not quite a lady and hence insecure? Her husband is a clever youth but far too serious. I do not dare to ask if he intends to put in for the extra allowance of wives to which he is entitled.

But let me tell you in my laboured fashion what lies behind all this nonsense. I was sent here, as you know, under contract, and I fulfilled my original task faithfully — as witness the giant roll of paper headed (in a lettering usually reserved for tomb-stones) *Instruments for a Cultural Pact Between the Governments of His Britannic Majesty etc.* Blunt instruments indeed — for what can a Christian culture have in common with a Moslem or a Marxist? Our premises are hopelessly opposed. Never mind! I was told to do it and I done it. And much as I love what they've got here I don't understand the words in relation to an educational system based on the abacus and a theology which got left behind with Augustine and Aquinas. Personally I think we both have made a mess of it, and I have no *parti-pris* in the matter. And so on. I just don't see what D. H. Lawrence has to offer a pasha with seventeen wives, though I believe I know which one of them is happiest. . . . However, I done it, the Pact I mean.

This done I found myself rapidly sent to the top of the form as a Political and this enabled me to study papers and evaluate the whole Middle Eastern complex as a coherent whole, as a policy venture. Well, let me say that after prolonged study I have come to the reluctant conclusion that it is neither coherent nor even a policy — at any rate a policy capable of withstanding the pressures which are being built up here.

These rotten states, backward and venal as they are, must be seriously thought about; they cannot be held together just by encouraging what is weakest and most corrupt in them, as we appear to be doing. This approach would presuppose another fifty years of peace and no radical element in the electorate at home: that given, the *status quo* might be maintained. But given this prevailing trend, can England be as short-sighted as this? Perhaps. I don't know. It is not my job to know these things, *as an artist*; as a political I am filled with misgiving. To encourage Arab unity while at the same time losing the power to use the poison-cup seems to me to be a very dubious thing: not policy but lunacy. And to add Arab unity to all the other currents which are running against us seems to me to be an engaging folly. Are we still beset by the doleful dream of the Arabian Nights, fathered on us by three generations of sexually disoriented Victorians whose subconscious reacted wholeheartedly to the thought of more than one legal wife? Or the romantic Bedouin-fever of the Bells and Lawrences? Perhaps. But the Victorians who fathered this dream on us were people who believed in *fighting* for the value of their currency; they knew that the world of politics was a jungle. Today the Foreign Office appears to believe that the best way to deal with the jungle is to turn Nudist and conquer the wild beast by the sight of one's nakedness. I can hear you sigh. 'Why can't Pursewarden be *more precise*. All these *boutades!*'

Very well. I spoke of the pressures. Let us divide them into internal and external, shall we, in the manner of Errol? My views may seem somewhat heretical, but here they are.

Well then, first, the abyss which separates the rich from the poor — it is positively Indian. In Egypt today, for example, six per cent of the people own over three-quarters of the land, thus leaving under a *feddan* a head for the rest to live on. Good! Then the population is doubling itself every second generation — or is it third? But I suppose any economic survey will tell you this. Meanwhile there is the steady growth of a vocal and literate middle-class whose sons are trained at Oxford among our comfy liberalisms — and who find no jobs waiting for them when they come back here. The *babu* is growing in power, and the dull story is being repeated here as elsewhere. 'Intellectual coolies of the world unite.'

To these internal pressures we are gracefully adding by direct encouragement, the rigour of a nationalism based in a fanatical religion. I personally admire it, but never forget that it is a fighting religion with no metaphysics, only an ethic. The Arab Union, etc. . . . My dear chap, why are we thinking up these absurd constructs to add to our own discomfiture — specially as it is clear to me that we have lost the basic power to act which alone would ensure that our influence remained paramount here? These tottering backward-looking feudalisms could only be supported by arms against these disintegrating elements inherent in the very nature of things today; but to use arms, 'to preach with the sword' in the words of Lawrence, one must have a belief in one's own ethos, one's own mystique of life. What does the Foreign Office believe? I just don't know. In Egypt, for example, very little has been done beyond keeping the peace; the High Commission is vanishing after a rule of — since 1888? — and will not leave behind even the vestiges of a trained civil service to stabilize this rabble-ridden grotesque which we now apparently regard as a sovereign state. How long will fair words and courtly sentiments prevail against the massive discontents these people feel? One can trust a treaty king only as long as he can trust his people. How long remains before a flashpoint is reached? I don't know — and to be frank I don't much *care*. But I should say that some unforeseen outside pressure like a war would tumble over these scarecrow principalities at a breath. Anyway, these are my general reasons for wanting a change. I believe we should re-orient policy and build Jewry into the power behind the scenes here. And quick.

Now for the particular. Very early in my political life I ran up against a department of the War Office specializing in general intelligence, run by a Brigadier who resented the idea that his office should bow the knee to us. A question of rank, or allowances, or some such rot; under the Commission he had been allowed more or less a free hand. Incidentally, this is the remains of the old Arab Bureau left over from 1918 which has been living on quietly like a toad buried under a stone! Obviously in the general re-alignment, his show must (it seemed to me) integrate with somebody. And now there was only an embryonic Embassy in Egypt. As he had worked formerly to the High Commission's Political Branch, I thought he should work to me — and indeed, after a series of sharp battles, bent if not broke him — Maskelyne is the creature's name. He is so typical as to be rather interesting and I have made extensive notes on him for a book in my usual fashion. (One writes to recover a lost innocence!)

Well, since the Army discovered that imagination is a major factor in producing cowardice they have trained the Maskelyne breed in the virtues of counter-imagination: a sort of amnesia which is almost Turkish. The contempt for death has been turned into a contempt for life and this type of man accepts life only on his own terms. A frozen brain alone enables him to keep up a routine of exceptional boredom. He is very thin, very tall, and his skin has been tanned by Indian service to the colour of smoked snakeskin, or a scab painted with iodine. His perfect teeth rest as lightly as a feather upon his pipestem. There is a peculiar gesture he has — I wish I could describe it, it interests me so much — of removing his pipe slowly before speaking, levelling his small dark eyes at one, and almost whispering: 'Oh, do you really think so?' The vowels drawing themselves out infinitely into the lassitude, the boredom of the silence which surrounds him. He is gnawed by the circumscribed perfection of a breeding which makes him uncomfortable in civilian clothes, and indeed he walks about in his well-cut cavalry coat with a *Noli me tangere* air. (Breed for type and you always get anomalies of behaviour.) He is followed everywhere by his magnificent red pointer Nell (named after his wife?) who sleeps on his feet while he works at his files, and on his bed at night. He occupies a room in a hotel in which there is nothing personal — no books, no photographs, no papers. Only a set of silver-backed brushes, a bottle of whisky and a newspaper. (I imagine him sometimes brushing the silent fury out of his own scalp, furiously brushing his dark shiny hair back from the temples, faster and faster. Ah, that's better — that's better!)

He reaches his office at eight having bought his day-late copy of the *Daily Telegraph*. I have never seen him read anything else. He sits at his huge desk, consumed with a slow dark contempt for the venality of the human beings around him, perhaps the human race as a whole; imperturbably he examines and assorts their differing corruptions, their maladies, and outlines them upon marble minute-paper which he always signs with his little silver pen in a small awkward fly's handwriting. The current of his loathing flows through his veins slowly, heavily, like the Nile at flood. Well, you can see what a *numéro* he is. He lives purely in the military imagination for he never sees or meets the subjects of most of his papers; the information he collates comes in from suborned clerks, or discontented valets, or pent-up servants. It does not matter. He prides himself on his readings of it, his I.A. (intelligence appreciation), just like an astrologer working upon charts belonging to unseen, unknown subjects. He is judicial, proud as the Calif, unswerving, I admire him very much. Honestly I do.

Maskelyne has set up two marks between which (as between degree-signs on a calibrated thermometer) the temperatures of his approval and disapproval are allowed to move, expressed in the phrases: 'A good show for the Raj' and 'Not such a good show for the Raj'. He is too single-minded of course, ever to be able to imagine a really Bad Show for the Bloody Raj. Such a man seems unable to see the world around him on open sights; but then his profession and the need for reserve make him a complete recluse, make him inexperienced in the ways of the world upon which he sits in judgement. . . . Well, I am tempted to go on and frame the portrait of our spycatcher, but I will desist. Read my next novel but four, it should also include a sketch of Telford, who is Maskelyne's Number Two — a large blotchy ingratiating civilian with illfitting dentures who manages to call one 'old fruit' a hundred times a second between nervous guffaws. His worship of the cold snaky soldier is marvellous to behold. 'Yes, Brigadier', 'No, Brigadier', falling over a chair in his haste to serve; you would say he was completely in love with his boss. Maskelyne sits and watches his confusion coldly, his brown chin, cleft by a dark dimple, jutting like an arrow. Or he will lean back in his swivel-chair and tap softly on the door of the huge safe behind him with the faintly satisfied air of a gourmet patting his paunch as he says: 'You don't believe me? I have it all in here, all in here.' Those files, you think, watching this superlative, all-comprehending gesture, must contain material enough to indict the world! Perhaps they do.

Well, this is what happened: one day I found a characteristic document from Maskelyne on my desk headed *Nessim Hosnani*, and sub-titled *A Conspiracy Among the Copts* which alarmed me somewhat. According to the paper, our Nessim was busy working up a large and complicated plot against the Egyptian Royal House. Most of the data were rather questionable I thought, knowing Nessim, but the whole paper put me in a quandary for it carried the bland recommendation that the details should be transmitted by the Embassy to the Egyptian Ministry of Foreign Affairs! I can hear you draw your breath sharply. Even supposing this were true, such a course would put Nessim's life in the greatest danger. Have I explained that one of the major characteristics of Egyptian nationalism is the gradually growing envy and hate of the 'foreigners' — the half-million or so of non-Moslems here? And that the moment full Egyptian sovereignty was declared the Moslems started in to bully and expropriate them? The brains of Egypt, as you know, is its foreign community. The capital which flowed into the land while it was safe under our suzerainty, is now at the mercy of these paunchy pashas. The Armenians, Greeks, Copts, Jews — they are all feeling the sharpening edge of this hate; many are wisely leaving, but most cannot. These huge capital investments in cotton, etc., cannot be abandoned overnight. The foreign communities are living from prayer to prayer and from bribe to bribe. They are trying to save their industries, their life-work from the gradual encroachment of the pashas. We have literally thrown them to the lions!

Well, I read and re-read this document, as I say, in a state of considerable anxiety. I knew that if I gave it to Errol he would run bleating with it to the King. So I went into action myself to test the weak points in it — mercifully it was not one of Maskelyne's best papers — and succeeded in throwing doubt upon many of his contentions. But what infuriated him was that I actually *suspended* the paper — I had to in order to keep it out of Chancery's hands! My sense of duty was sorely strained, but then there was no alternative; what would those silly young schoolboys next door have done? If Nessim was really guilty of the sort of plot Maskelyne envisaged, well and good; one could deal with him later according to his lights. But . . . you know Nessim. I felt that I owed it to him to be sure before passing such a paper upwards.

But of course Maskelyne was furious, though he had the grace not to show it. We sat in his office with the conversational temperature well below zero and still falling while he showed me his accumulated evidence and his agents' reports. For the most part they were not as solid as I had feared. 'I have this man Selim suborned' Maskelyne kept croaking 'and I'm convinced his own secretary can't be wrong about it. There is this small secret society with the regular meetings — Selim has to wait with the car and drive them home. Then there is this curious cryptogram which goes out all over the Middle East from Balthazar's clinic, and then the visits to arms manufacturers in Sweden and Germany. . . .' I tell you, my brain was swimming! I could see all our friends neatly laid out on a slab by the Egyptian Secret Police, being measured for shrouds.

I must say too, that *circumstantially* the inferences which Maskelyne drew appeared to hold water. It all looked rather sinister; but luckily a few of the basic points would not yield to analysis — things like the so-called cipher which friend Balthazar shot out once every two months to chosen recipients in the big towns of the Middle East. Maskelyne was still trying to follow these up. But the data were far from complete and I stressed this as strongly as I could, much to the discomfort of Telford, though Maskelyne is too cool a bird of prey to be easily discountenanced. Nevertheless I got him to agree to pend the paper until something more substantial was forthcoming to broaden the basis of the doctrine. He hated me but he swallowed it, and so I felt that I had gained at least a temporary respite. The problem was what to do next — how to use the time to advantage? I was of course convinced that Nessim was innocent of these grotesque charges. But I could not, I admit, supply explanations as convincing as those of Maskelyne. What, I could not help wondering, were they really up to? If I was to deflate Maskelyne, I must find out for myself. Very annoying, and indeed professionally improper — but *que faire?* Little Ludwig must turn himself into a private investigator, a Sexton Blake, in order to do the job! But where to begin?

Maskelyne's only direct lead on Nessim was through the suborned secretary, Selim; through him he had accumulated quite a lot of interesting though not intrinsically alarming data about the Hosnani holdings in various fields — the land bank, shipping line, ginning mills, and so on. The rest was largely gossip and rumour, some of it damaging, but none of it more than circumstantial. But piled up in a heap it did make our gentle Nessim sound somewhat sinister. I felt that I must take it all apart somehow. Specially as a lot of it concerned and surrounded his marriage — the acid gossip of the lazy and envious, so typical of Alexandria — or anywhere else for that matter. In this, of course, the unconscious moral judgements of the Anglo-Saxon were to the fore — I mean in the value-judgements of Maskelyne. As for Justine — well, I know her a bit, and I must confess I rather admire her surly magnificence. Nessim haunted her for some time before getting her to consent, I am told; I cannot say I had misgivings about it all exactly, but . . . even today their marriage feels in some curious way uncemented. They make a perfect pair, but never seem to touch each other; indeed, once I saw her very slightly shrink as he picked a thread from her fur. Probably imagination. Is there perhaps a thundercloud brooding there behind the dark satin-eyed wife? Plenty nerves, certainly. Plenty hysteria. Plenty Judaic melancholy. One recognizes her vaguely as the girl-friend of the man whose head was presented on a charger. . . . What do I mean?

Well, Maskelyne says with his dry empty contempt: 'No sooner does she marry than she starts an affair with another man, and a foreigner to boot.' This of course is Darley, the vaguely amiable bespectacled creature who inhabits Pombal's box-room at certain times. He teaches for a living and writes novels. He has that nice round babyish back to the head which one sees in cultural types; slight stoop, fair hair, and the shyness that goes with Great Emotions imperfectly kept under control. A fellow-romantic quotha! Looked at hard, he starts to stammer. But he's a good fellow, gentle and resigned . . . I confess that he seems unlikely material for someone as dashing as Nessim's wife to work upon. Can it be benevolence in her, or simply a perverse taste for innocence? There is a small mystery here. Anyway, it was Darley and Pombal who introduced me to the current Alexandrian *livre de chevet* which is a French novel called *Moeurs* (a swashing study in the grand manner of nymphomania and psychic impotence) written by Justine's last husband. Having written it he wisely divorced her and decamped but she is popularly supposed to be the central subject of the book and is regarded with grave sympathy by society. I must say, when you think that everyone is both polymorph and perverse here, it seems hard luck to be singled out like this as the main character in a *roman vache*. Anyway, this lies in the past, and now Nessim has carried her into the ranks of *le monde* where she acquits herself with a sharply defined grace and savagery. They suit her looks and the dark but simple splendours of Nessim himself. Is he happy? But wait, let me put the question another way. Was he ever happy? Is he unhappier now than he was? Hum! I think he could do a lot worse, for the girl is neither too innocent nor too unintelligent. She plays the piano really well, albeit with a sulky emphasis, and reads widely. Indeed, the novels of Yours Truly are much admired — with a disarming wholeheartedness. (Caught! Yes, this is why I am disposed to like her.)

On the other hand, what she sees in Darley I cannot credit. The poor fellow flutters on a slab like a skate at her approach; he and Nessim are, however, great frequenters of each other, great friends. These modest British types — do they all turn out to be Turks secretly? Darley at any rate must have some appeal because he has also got himself regally entangled with a rather nice little cabaret dancer called Melissa. You would never think, to look at him, that he was capable of running a tandem, so little self-possession does he appear to have. A victim of his own fine sentiment? He wrings his hands, his spectacles steam up, when he mentions either name. Poor Darley! I always enjoy irritating him by quoting the poem by his minor namesake to him:

> *O blest unfabled Incense Tree*
> *That burns in glorious Araby,*
> *With red scent chalicing the air,*
> *Till earth-life grows Elysian there.*

He pleads with me blushingly to desist, though I cannot tell which Darley he is blushing for; I continue in magistral fashion:

> *Half-buried in her flaming breast*
> *In this bright tree she makes her nest*
> *Hundred-sunned Phoenix! When she must*
> *Crumble at length to hoary dust!*

It is not a bad conceit for Justine herself. 'Stop' he always cries.

> *Her gorgeous death-bed! Her rich pyre*
> *Burn up with aromatic fire!*
> *Her urn, sight-high from spoiler men!*
> *Her birth-place when self-born again!*

'Please. Enough.'

'What's wrong with it? It's not such a bad poem, is it?'

And I conclude with Melissa, disguised as an 18th Century Dresden China shepherdess.

> *The mountainless green wilds among,*
> *Here ends she her unechoing song*
> *With amber tears and odorous sighs*
> *Mourned by the desert where she dies!*

So much for Darley! But as for Justine's part in the matter I can find no rhyme, no reason, unless we accept one of Pombal's epigrams at its face value. He says, with fat seriousness: '*Les femmes sont fidèles au fond, tu sais? Elles ne trompent que les autres femmes!*' But it seems to me to offer no really concrete reason for Justine wishing to *tromper* the pallid rival Melissa. This would be *infra dig* for a woman with her position in society. See what I mean?

Well, then, it is upon Darley that our Maskelyne keeps his baleful ferret's eyes fixed; apparently Selim tells us that all the real information on Nessim is kept in a little wall-safe at the house and not in the office. There is only one key to this safe which Nessim always carries on his person. The private safe, says Selim, is full of papers. But he is vague as to what the papers can be. Love letters? Hum. At any rate, Selim has made one or two attempts to get at the safe, but without any luck. One day the bold Maskelyne himself decided to examine it at close range and take, if necessary, a wax squeeze. Selim let him in and he climbed the back stairs — and nearly ran into Darley, our cicisbeo, and Justine in the bedroom! He just heard their voices in time. Never tell me after this that the English are puritans. Some time later I saw a short story Darley published in which a character exclaims: 'In his arms I felt mauled, chewed up, my fur coated with saliva, as if between the paws of some great excited cat.' I reeled. 'Crumbs!' I thought. 'This is what Justine is doing to the poor bugger — eating him alive!'

I must say, it gave me a good laugh. Darley is so typical of my compatriots — snobbish and parochial in one. And so *good!* He lacks devil. (Thank God for the Irishman and the Jew who spat in my blood.) Well, why should I take this high and mighty line? Justine must be awfully good to sleep with, must kiss like a rainbow and squeeze out great sparks — yes. But out of Darley? It doesn't hold water. Nevertheless 'this rotten creature' as Maskelyne calls her is certainly his whole attention, or was when I was last there. Why?

All these factors were tumbling over and over in my mind as I drove up to Alexandria, having secured myself a long duty week-end which even the good Errol found unexceptionable. I never dreamed then, that within a year you might find yourself engaged by these mysteries. I only knew that I wanted, if possible, to demolish the Maskelyne thesis and stay the Chancery's hand in the matter of Nessim. But apart from this I was somewhat at a loss. I am no spy, after all; was I to creep about Alexandria dressed in a pudding-basin wig with concealed earphones, trying to clear the name of our friend? Nor could I very well present myself to Nessim and, clearing my throat, say nonchalantly:

'Now about this spy-net you've got here. . . . ' However, I drove steadily and thoughtfully on. Egypt, flat and unbosomed, flowed back and away from me on either side of the car. The green changed to blue, the blue to peacock's eye, to gazelle-brown, to panther-black. The desert was like a dry kiss, a flutter of eyelashes against the mind. Ahem! The night became horned with stars like branches of almond-blossom. I gibbered into the city after a drink or two under a new moon which felt as if it were drawing half its brilliance from the open sea. Everything smelt good again. The iron band that Cairo puts round one's head (the consciousness of being completely surrounded by burning desert?) dissolved, relaxed — gave place to the expectation of an open sea, an open road leading one's mind back to Europe. . . . Sorry. Off the point.

I telephoned the house, but they were both out at a reception; feeling somewhat relieved I betook myself to the Café Al Aktar in the hope of finding congenial company and found: only our friend Darley. I like him. I like particularly the way he sits on his hands with excitement when he discusses art, which he insists on doing with Yours Truly — why? I answer as best I can and drink my *arak*. But this generalized sort of conversation puts me out of humour. For the artist, I think, as for the public, no such thing as art exists; it only exists for the critics and those who live in the forebrain. Artist and public simply register, like a seismograph, an electromagnetic charge which can't be rationalized. One only knows that a transmission of sorts goes on, true or false, successful or unsuccessful, according to chance. But to try to break down the elements and nose them over — one gets nowhere. (I suspect this approach to art is common to all those who cannot surrender themselves to it!) Paradox. Anyway.

Darley is in fine voice this eve, and I listen to him with grudging pleasure. He really *is* a good chap, and a sensitive one. But it is with relief that I hear Pombal is due to appear shortly after a visit to the cinema with a young woman he is besieging. I am hoping he will offer to put me up as hotels are expensive and I can then spend my travel allowance on drink. Well, at last old P. turns up, having had his face smacked by the girl's mother who caught them in the foyer. We have a splendid evening and I stay *chez* him as I had hoped.

The next morning I was up betimes though I had decided on nothing, was still bedevilled in mind about the whole issue. However, I thought I could at least visit Nessim in his office as I had so often done, to pass the time of day and cadge a coffee. Whispering up in the huge glass lift, so like a Byzantine sarcophagus, I felt confused. I had prepared no conversation for the event. The clerks and typists were all delighted and showed me straight through into the great domed room where he sat. . . . Now here is the curious thing. He not only seemed to be expecting me, but to have divined my reasons for calling! He seemed delighted, relieved and full of an impish sort of serenity. 'I've been waiting for ages' he said with dancing eyes, 'wondering when you were finally going to come and beard me, to ask me questions. At last! What a relief!' Everything melted between us after this and I felt I could take him on open sights. Nothing could exceed the warmth and candour of his answers. They carried immediate conviction with me.

The so-called secret society, he told me, was a student lodge of the Cabala devoted to the customary mumbo-jumbo of parlour mysticism. God knows, this is the capital of superstition. Even Clea has her horoscope cast afresh every morning. Sects abound. Was there anything odd in Balthazar running such a small band of would-be hermetics — a study group? As for the cryptogram it was a sort of mystical calculus — the old *boustrophedon* no less — with the help of which the lodge-masters all over the Middle East could keep in touch. Surely no more mysterious than a stock-report or a polite exchange between mathematicians working on the same problem? Nessim drew one for me and explained roughly how it was used. He added that all this could be effectively checked by consulting Darley who had taken to visiting these meetings with Justine to suck up hermetical lore. *He* would be able to say just how subversive they were! So far so good. 'But I can't disguise from you' he went on 'the existence of another movement, purely political, with which I am directly concerned. This is purely Coptic and is designed simply to rally the Copts — not to revolt against anyone (how could we?) but simply to band themselves together; to strengthen religious and political ties in order that the community can find its way back to a place in the sun. Now that Egypt is free from the Copt-hating British, we feel freer to seek high offices for our people, to get some Members of Parliament elected and so on. There is nothing in all this which should make an intelligent Moslem tremble. We seek nothing illegitimate or harmful; simply our rightful place in our own land as the most intelligent and able community in Egypt.'

There was a good deal more about the back history of the Coptic community and its grievances — I won't bore you with it as you probably know it all. But he spoke it all with a tender shy fury which interested me as being so out of keeping with the placid Nessim we both knew. Later, when I met the mother, I understood; she is the driving force behind this particular minority-dream, or so I believe. Nessim went on: 'Nor need France and Britain fear anything from us. We love them both. Such modern culture as we have is modelled on both. We ask for no aid, no money. We think of ourselves as Egyptian patriots, but knowing how stupid and backward the Arab National element is, and how fanatical we do not think it can be long before there are violent differences between the Egyptians and yourselves. They are already flirting with Hitler. In the case of a war . . . who can tell? The Middle East is slipping out of the grasp of England and France day by day. We minorities see ourselves in peril as the process goes on. Our only hope is that there is some respite, like a war, which will enable you to come back and retake the lost ground. Otherwise, we will be expropriated, enslaved. But we still place our faith in you both. Now, from this point of view, a compact and extremely rich little group of Coptic bankers and businessmen could exercise an influence out of all proportion to its numbers. *We are your fifth column in Egypt, fellow Christians.* In another year or two, when the movement is perfected, we could bring immediate pressure to bear on the economic and industrial life of the country — if it served to push through a policy which you felt to be necessary. That is why I have been dying to tell you about us, for England should see in us a bridgehead to the East, a friendly enclave in an area which daily becomes more hostile, to you.' He lay back, quite exhausted, but smiling.

'But of course I realize' he said 'that this concerns you as an official. Please treat the matter as a secret, for friendship's sake. The Egyptians would welcome any chance to expropriate us Copts — confiscate the millions which we control: perhaps even kill some of us. They must not know about us. That is why we meet secretly, have been building up the movement so slowly, with such circumspection. There must be no slips, you see. Now my dear Pursewarden. I fully realize that you cannot be expected to take all I tell you on trust, without proof. So I am going to take a rather unusual step. Day after tomorrow is Sitna Damiana and we are having a meeting in the desert. I would like you to come with me so that you can see everything, hear the proceedings and have your mind quite clear about our composition and our intentions. Later we may be of the greatest service to Britain here; I want to drive the fact home. Will you come?'

Would I come!

I went. It was really a great experience which made me realize that I had hardly seen Egypt — the true Egypt underlying the fly-tormented airless towns, the drawing-rooms of commerce, the bankers' sea-splashed villas, the Bourse, the Yacht Club, the Mosque. . . . But wait.

We set off in a cold mauve dawn and drove a little way down the Aboukir road before turning inland; thence across dust roads and deserted causeways, along canals and abandoned trails which the pashas of old had constructed to reach their hunting-boxes on the lake. At last we had to abandon the car, and here the other brother was waiting with horses — the troglodyte with the *gueule cassée*, Narouz of the broken face. What a contrast, this black peasant, compared to Nessim! And what power! I was much taken by him. He was caressing a swashing great hippo's backbone made into a whip — the classical *kurbash*. Saw him pick dragon-flies off the flowers at fifteen paces with it; later in the desert he ran down a wild dog and cut it up with a couple of strokes. The poor creature was virtually dismembered in a couple of blows, by this toy! Well, we rode sombrely along to the house. You went there ages ago, didn't you? I had a long session with the mother, an odd imperious bundle of a woman in black, heavily veiled, who spoke arresting English in a parched voice which had the edge of hysteria in it. Nice, somehow, but queer and somewhat on edge — voice of a desert father or desert sister? I don't know. Apparently the two sons were to take me across to the monastery in the desert. Apparently Narouz was due to speak. It was his maiden over — his first try at it. I must say, I couldn't see this hirsute savage being able to. Jaws working all the time pressing the muscles around his temples! He must, I reflected, grind his teeth in sleep. But somehow also the shy blue eyes of a girl. Nessim was devoted to him. And God what a rider!

Next morning we set off with a bundle of Arab horses which they rode sweetly and a train of shuffle-footed camels which were a present for the populace from Narouz — they were to be cut up and devoured. It was a long exhausting trek with the heat mirages playing havoc with concentration and eyesight and the water tepid and horrible in the skins, and yours truly feeling baleful and fatigued. The sun upon one's brainpan! My brains were sizzling in my skull by the time we came upon the first outcrop of palms — the jumping and buzzing image of the desert monastery where poor Damiana had her Diocletian head struck from her shoulders for the glory of our Lord.

By the time we reached it dusk had fallen, and here one entered a brilliantly-coloured engraving which could have illustrated . . . what? *Vathek!* A huge encampment of booths and houses had grown up for the festival. There must have been six thousand pilgrims camped around in houses of wattle and paper, of cloth and carpet. A whole township had grown up with its own lighting and primitive drainage — but a complete town, comprising even a small but choice brothel quarter. Camels pounded everywhere in the dusk, lanterns and cressets flapped and smoked. Our people pitched us a tent under a ruined arch where two grave bearded dervishes talked, under gonfalons folded like the brilliant wings of moths, and by the light of a great paper lantern covered in inscriptions. Dense darkness now, but brilliantly lit sideshows with all the fun of the fair. I was itching to have a look round and this suited them very well as they had things to arrange within the church, so Nessim gave me a rendezvous at the home tent in an hour and a half. He nearly lost me altogether, I was so enraptured by this freak town with its mud streets, and long avenues of sparkling stalls — food of every sort, melons, eggs, bananas, sweets, all displayed in that unearthly light. Every itinerant pedlar from Alexandria must have trekked out across the sand to sell to the pilgrims. In the dark corners were the children playing and squeaking like mice, while their elders cooked food in huts and tents, lit by tiny puffing candles. The sideshows were going full blast with their games of chance. In one booth a lovely prostitute sang heart-breakingly, chipped quartertones and plangent headnotes as she turned in her sheath of spiral sequins. She had her price on the door. It was not excessive, I thought, being a feeble-minded man, and I rather began to curse my social obligations. In another corner a story-teller was moaning out the sing-song romance of El Zahur. Drinkers of sherbet, of cinnamon, were spread at ease on the seats of makeshift cafés in these beflagged and lighted thoroughfares. From within the walls of the monastery came the sound of priests chanting. From without the unmistakable clatter of men playing at single-stick with the roar of the crowd acclaiming every stylish manœuvre. Tombs full of *flowers*, water-melons shedding a buttery light, trays of meat perfuming the air — sausages and cutlets and entrails buzzing on spits. The whole thing welded into one sharply fused picture of light and sound in my brain. The moon was coming up hand over fist.

In the Ringa-booths there were groups of glistening mauve abstracted Sudanese dancing to the odd music of the wobbling little harmonium with vertical keys and painted gourds for pipes; but they took their step from a black buck who banged it out with a steel rod upon a section of railway line hanging from the tent-pole. Here I ran into one of Cervoni's servants who was delighted to see me and pressed upon me some of the curious Sudanese beer they call *merissa*. I sat and watched this intent, almost maniacal form of dance — the slow revolutions about a centre and the queer cockroach-crushing steps, plunging the toe down and turning it in the earth. Until I was woken by the ripple of drums and saw a dervish pass holding one of the big camel-drums — a glowing hemisphere of copper. He was black — a Rifiya — and as I had never seen them do their fire-walking, scorpion-eating act, I thought I might follow him and see it tonight. (It was touching to hear Moslems singing religious songs to Damiana, a Christian saint; I heard voices ululating the words '*Ya Sitt Ya Bint El Wali*' over and over again. Isn't that odd? 'O Lady, Lady of the Viceroy'.) Across the darkness I tracked down a group of dervishes in a lighted corner between two great embrasures. It was the end of a dance and they were turning one of their number into a human chandelier, covered in burning candles, the hot wax dripping all over him. His eyes were vague and tranced. Last of all comes an old boy and drives a huge dagger through both cheeks. On each end of the dagger he hoists a candlestick with a branch of lighted candles in each. Transfixed thus the boy rises slowly to his toes and revolves in a dance — like a tree on fire. After the dance, they simply whipped the sword out of his jaw and the old man touched his wounds with a finger moistened with spittle. Within a second there was the boy standing there smiling again with nothing to show for his pains. But he looked awake now.

Outside all this — the white desert was turning under the moon to a great field of skulls and mill-stones. Trumpets and drums sounded and there came a rush of horsemen in conical hats waving wooden swords and shrieking in high voices, like women. The camel-and-horse races were due to start. Good, thought I, I shall have a look at that; but treading unwarily I came upon a grotesque scene which I would gladly have avoided if I had been able. The camels of Narouz were being cut up for the feast. Poor things, they knelt there peacefully with their forelegs folded under them like cats while a horde of men attacked them with axes in the moonlight. My blood ran cold, yet I could not tear myself away from this extraordinary spectacle. The animals made no move to avoid the blows, uttered no cries as they were dismembered. The axes bit into them, as if their great bodies were made of cork, sinking deep under every thrust. Whole members were being hacked off as painlessly, it seemed, as when a tree is pruned. The children were dancing about in the moonlight picking up the fragments and running off with them into the lighted town, great gobbets of bloody meat. The camels stared hard at the moon and said nothing. Off came the legs, out came the entrails; lastly the heads would topple under the axe like statuary and lie there in the sand with open eyes. The men doing the axeing were shouting and bantering as they worked. A huge soft carpet of black blood spread into the dunes around the group and the barefoot boys carried the print of it back with them into the township. I felt frightfully ill of a sudden and retired back to the lighted quarter for a drink; and sitting on a bench watched the passing show for a while to recover my nerve. Here at last Nessim found me and together we walked inside the walls, past the grouped cells called 'combs'. (Did you know that all early religions were built up on a cell pattern, imitating who-knows-what biological law? . . .) So we came at last to the church.

Wonderfully painted sanctuary screen, and ancient candles with waxen beards burning on the gold lectern, the light now soft and confused by incense to the colour of pollen; and the deep voices running like a river over the gravel-bottomed Liturgy of St Basil. Moving softly from gear to gear, pausing and resuming, starting lower down the scale only to be pressed upwards into the throats and minds of these black shining people. The choir passed across us like swans, breath-catching in their high scarlet helmets and white robes with scarlet crossbands. The light on their glossy black curls and sweating faces! Enormous frescoed eyes with whites gleaming. It was pre-Christian, this; each of these young men in his scarlet biretta had become Rameses the Second. The great chandeliers twinkled and fumed, puffs of snowy incense rose. Outside you could hear the noises of the camel-racing crew, inside only the grumble of the Word. The long hanging lamps had ostrich-eggs suspended under them. (This has always struck me as being worth investigating.)

I thought that this was our destination but we skirted the crowd and went down some stairs into a crypt. And this was it at last. A series of large beehive rooms, lime-washed white and spotless. In one, by candlelight, a group of about a hundred people sat upon rickety wooden benches waiting for us. Nessim pressed my arm and pushed me to a seat at the very back among a group of elderly men who gave me place. 'First I will talk to them,' he whispered, 'and then Narouz is to speak to them — for the first time.' There was no sign of the other brother as yet. The men next to me were wearing robes but some of them had European suits on underneath. Some had their heads wrapped in wimples. To judge by their well-kept hands and nails, none were workmen. They spoke Arabic but in low tones. No smoking.

Now the good Nessim rose and addressed them with the cool efficiency of someone taking a routine board meeting. He spoke quietly and as far as I could gather contented himself with giving them details about recent events, the election of certain people to various committees, the arrangements for trust funds and so on. He might have been addressing shareholders. They listened gravely. A few quiet questions were asked which he answered concisely. Then he said: 'But this is not all, these details. You will wish to hear something about our nation and our faith, something that even our priests cannot tell you. My brother Narouz, who is known to you, will speak a little now.'

What on earth could the baboon Narouz have to tell them, I wondered? It was most interesting. And now, from the outer darkness of the cell next door came Narouz, dressed in a white robe and looking pale as ashes. His hair had been smeared down on his forehead in an oiled quiff, like a collier on his day off. No, he looked like a terrified curate in a badly-ironed surplice; huge hands joined on his chest with the knuckles squeezed white. He took his place at a sort of wooden lectern with a candle burning on it, and stared with obvious wild terror at his audience, squeezing the muscles out all over his arms and shoulders. I thought he was going to fall down. He opened his clenched jaws but nothing came. He appeared to be paralysed.

There came a stir and a whisper, and I saw Nessim looking somewhat anxiously at him, as if he might need help. But Narouz stood stiff as a javelin, staring right through us as if at some terrifying scene taking place behind the white walls at our backs. The suspense was making us all uncomfortable. Then he made a queer motion with his mouth, as if his tongue were swollen, or as if he was surreptitiously swallowing a soft palate, and a hoarse cry escaped him. '*Meded! Meded!*' It was the invocation for divine strength you sometimes hear desert preachers utter before they fall into a trance — the dervishes. His face worked. And then came a change — all of a sudden it was as if an electric current had begun to pour into his body, into his muscles, his loins. He relaxed his grip on himself and slowly, pantingly began to speak, rolling those amazing eyes as if the power of speech itself was half-involuntary and causing him physical pain to support. . . . It was a terrifying performance, and for a moment or two I could not understand anything, he was articulating so badly. Then all of a sudden he broke through the veil and his voice gathered power, vibrating in the candle-light like a musical instrument.

'Our Egypt, our beloved country' drawing out the words like toffee, almost crooning them. It was clear that he had nothing prepared to say — it was not a speech, it was an invocation uttered extempore such as one has sometimes heard — the brilliant spontaneous flight of drunkards, ballad singers, or those professional mourners who follow burial processions with their shrieks of death-divining poetry. The power and the tension flooded out of him into the room; all of us were electrified, even myself whose Arabic was so bad! The tone, the range and the bottled ferocity and tenderness his words conveyed hit us, sent us sprawling, like music. It didn't seem to matter whether we understood them or not. It does not even now. Indeed, it would have been impossible to paraphrase the matter. 'The Nile . . . the green river flowing in our hearts hears its children. They will return to her. Descendants of the Pharaohs, children of Ra, offspring of St Mark. They will find the birthplace of light.' And so on. At times the speaker closed his eyes, letting the torrent of words pour on unhindered. Once he set his head back, smiling like a dog, still with eyes closed, until the light shone upon his back teeth. That voice! It went on autonomously, rising to a roar, sinking to a whisper, trembling and crooning and wailing. Suddenly snapping out words like chainshot, or rolling them softly about like honey. We were absolutely captured — the whole lot of us. But it was something comical to see Nessim's concern and wonder. He had expected nothing like this apparently for he was trembling like a leaf and quite white. Occasionally he was swept away himself by the flood of rhetoric and I saw him dash away a tear from his eye almost impatiently.

It went on like this for about three-quarters of an hour and suddenly, inexplicably, the current was cut off, the speaker was snuffed out. Narouz stood there gasping like a fish before us — as if thrown up by the tides of inner music on to a foreign shore. It was as abrupt as a metal shutter coming down — a silence impossible to repair again. His hands knotted again. He gave a startled groan and rushed out of the place with his funny scrambling motion. A tremendous silence fell — the silence which follows some great performance by an actor or orchestra — the germinal silence in which you can hear the very seeds in the human psyche stirring, trying to move towards the light of self-recognition. I was deeply moved and utterly exhausted. Fecundated!

At last Nessim rose and made an indefinite gesture. He too was exhausted and walked like an old man; took my hand and led me up into the church again, where a wild hullabaloo of cymbals and bells had broken out. We walked through the great puffs of incense which now seemed to blow up at us from the centre of the earth — the angel and demon-haunted spaces below the world of men. In the moonlight he kept repeating: 'I never knew, I never guessed this of Narouz. He is a *preacher*. I asked him only to talk of our history — but he made it . . . ' He was at a loss for words. Nobody had apparently suspected the existence of this spell-binder in their midst — the man with the whip! 'He could lead a great religious movement' I thought to myself. Nessim walked wearily and thoughtfully by my side among the palms. 'He is a *preacher*, really' he said with amazement. 'That is *why* he goes to see Taor.' He explained that Narouz often rode into the desert to visit a famous woman saint (alleged by the way to have three breasts) who lives in a tiny cave near Wadi Natrun; she is famous for her wonder-working cures, but won't emerge from obscurity. 'When he is away' said Nessim, 'he has either gone to the island to fish with his new gun or to see Taor. Always one or the other.'

When we got back to the tent the new preacher was lying wrapped in his blanket sobbing in a harsh voice like a wounded she-camel. He stopped when we entered, though he went on

491

shaking for a while. Embarrassed, we said nothing and turned in that night in a heavy silence. A momentous experience indeed!

I couldn't sleep for quite a while, going over it all in my mind. The next morning we were up at dawn (bloody cold for May — the tent stiff with frost) and in the saddle by the earliest light. Narouz had completely come to himself. He twirled his whip and played tricks on the factors in a high good humour. Nessim was rather thoughtful and withdrawn, I thought. The long ride galled our minds and it was a relief to see the crested palms grow up again. We rested and spent the night again at Karm Abu Girg. The mother was not available at first and we were told to see her in the evening. Here an odd scene took place for which Nessim appeared as little prepared as I. As the three of us advanced through the rose-garden towards her little summer-house, she came to the door with a lantern in her hand and said: 'Well, my sons, how did it go?' At this Narouz fell upon his knees, reached out his arms to her. Nessim and I were covered with confusion. She came forward and put her arms round this snorting and sobbing peasant, at the same time motioning us to leave. I must say I was relieved when Nessim sneaked off into the rose-garden and was glad to follow him. 'This is a new Narouz' he kept repeating softly, with genuine mystification. 'I did not know of these powers.'

Later Narouz came back to the house in the highest of spirits and we all played cards and drank *arak*. He showed me, with immense pride, a gun he had had made for him in Munich. It fires a heavy javelin under water and is worked by compressed air. He told me a good deal of this new method of fishing under water. It sounded a thrilling game and I was invited to visit his fishing island with him one week-end to have a pot. The preacher had vanished altogether by now; the simple-minded second son had returned.

Ouf! I am trying to get all the salient detail down as it may be of use to you later when I am gone. Sorry if it is a bore. On the way back to the town I talked at length to Nessim and got all the facts clear in my head. It did seem to me that from the policy point of view the Coptic group might be of the greatest use to us; and I was certain that this interpretation of things would be swallowed if properly explained to Maskelyne. High hopes!

So I rode back happily to Cairo to rearrange the chess-board accordingly. I went to see Maskelyne and tell him the good news.

To my surprise he turned absolutely white with rage, the corners of his nose pinched in, his ears moving back about an inch like a greyhound. His voice and eyes remained the same. 'Do you mean to tell me that you have tried to supplement a secret intelligence paper by consulting the subject of it? It goes against every elementary rule of intelligence. And how can you believe a word of so obvious a cover story? I have never heard of such a thing. You deliberately suspend a War Office paper, throw my fact-finding organization into disrepute, pretend we don't know our jobs, etc. . . .' You can gather the rest of the tirade. I began to get angry. He repeated dryly: 'I have been doing this for fifteen years. I tell you it smells of arms, of subversion. You won't believe my I.A. and I think yours is ridiculous. Why not pass the paper to the *Egyptians* and let them find out for themselves?' Of course I could not afford to do this, and he knew it. He next said that he had asked the War Office to protest in London and was writing to Errol to ask for 'redress'. All this, of course, was to be expected. But then I tackled him upon another vector. 'Look here' I said. 'I have seen all your sources. They are all Arabs and as such unworthy of confidence. How about a gentlemen's agreement? There is no hurry — we can investigate the Hosnanis at leisure — but how about choosing a new set of sources — English sources? If the interpretations still match, I promise you I'll resign and make a full recantation. Otherwise I shall fight this thing right through.'

'What sort of sources do you have in mind?'

'Well, there are a number of Englishmen in the Egyptian Police who speak Arabic and who know the people concerned. Why not use some of them?'

He looked at me for a long time. 'But they are as corrupt as the Arabs. Nimrod *sells* his information to the press. The Globe pay him a retainer of twenty pounds a month for confidential information.'

'There must be others.'

'By God there are. You should see them!'

'And then there's Darley who apparently goes to these meetings which worry you so much. Why not ask him to help?'

'I won't compromise my net by introducing characters like that. It is not worth it. It is not secure.'

'Then why not make a separate net — let Telford build it up. Specially for this group, for no other. And having no access to your main organization. Surely you could do that?'

He stared at me slowly, drop by drop. 'I could if I chose to' he admitted. 'And if I thought it would get us anywhere. But it won't.'

'At any rate, why not try? Your own position here is rather equivocal until an Ambassador comes to define it and arbitrate between us. Suppose I do pass this paper out and this whole group gets swept up?'

'Well, what?'

'Supposing it is, as I believe it to be, something which could help British policy in this area, you'll get no thanks for having allowed the Egyptians to nip it in the bud. And indeed, if that did prove to be the case, you would find. . . .'

'I'll think about it.' He had no intention of doing so, I could see, but he must have. He changed his mind; next day he rang up and said he was doing as I suggested, though 'without prejudice'; the war was still on between us. Perhaps he had heard of your appointment and knew we were friends. I don't know.

Ouf! that is about as much as I can tell you; for the rest, the country is still here — everything that is heteroclyte, devious, polymorph, anfractuous, equivocal, opaque, ambiguous, many-branched, or just plain dotty. I wish you joy of it when I am far away! I know you will make your first mission a resounding success. Perhaps you won't regret these tags of information from

Yours sincerely,
Earwig van Beetfield.

*   *   *   *   *

Mountolive studied this document with great care. He found the tone annoying and the information mildly disturbing. But then, every mission was riven with faction; personal annoyances, divergent opinions, they were always coming to the fore. For a moment he wondered whether it would not be wiser to allow Pursewarden the transfer he desired; but he restrained the thought by allowing another to overlap it. If he was to act, he should not at this stage show irresolution — even with Kenilworth. He walked about in that wintry landscape waiting for events to take definite shape around his future. Finally, he composed a tardy note to Pursewarden, the fruit of much rewriting and thought, which he despatched through the bag room.

My dear P.,

I must thank you for your letter with the interesting data. I feel I cannot make any decisions before my own arrival. I don't wish to prejudge issues. I have however decided to keep you attached to the Mission for another year. I shall ask for a greater attention to discipline than your Chancery appears to do; and I know you won't fail me however disagreeable the prospect of staying seems to you. There is much to do this end, and much to decide before I leave.

Yours sincerely,

David Mountolive.

It conveyed, he hoped, the right mixture of encouragement and censure. But of course, Pursewarden would not have written flippantly had he visualized serving under him. Nevertheless, if his career was to take the right shape he must start at the beginning.

But in his own mind he had already planned upon getting Maskelyne transferred and Pursewarden elevated in rank as his chief political adviser. Nevertheless a hint of uneasiness remained. But he could not help smiling when he received a postcard from the incorrigible. 'My dear Ambassador' it read. 'Your news has worried me. You have so many great big bushy Etonians to choose from. . . . Nevertheless. At your service.'

* * * * *

VI

The airplane stooped and began to slant slowly downwards, earthwards into the violet evening. The brown desert with its monotony of windcarved dunes had given place now to a remembered relief-map of the delta. The slow loops and tangents of the brown river lay directly below, with small craft drifting about upon it like seeds. Deserted estuaries and sand-bars — the empty unpopulated areas of the hinterland where the fish and birds congregated in secret. Here and there the river split like a bamboo, to bend and coil round an island with fig-trees, a minaret, some dying palms — the feather-softness of the palms furrowing the flat exhausted landscape with its hot airs and mirages and humid silences. Squares of cultivation laboriously darned it here and there like a worn tweed plaid; between segments of bituminous swamp embraced by slow contours of the brown water. Here and there too rose knuckles of rosy limestone.

It was frightfully hot in the little cabin of the airplane. Mountolive wrestled in a desultory tormented fashion with his uniform. Skinners had done wonders with it — it fitted like a glove; but the *weight* of it. It was like being dressed in a boxing-glove. He would be parboiled. He felt the sweat pouring down his chest, tickling him. His mixed elation and alarm translated itself into queasiness. Was he going to be airsick — and for the first time in his life? He hoped not. It would be awful to be sick into this impressive refurbished hat. 'Five minutes to touchdown'; words scribbled on a page torn from an operations pad. Good. Good. He nodded mechanically and found himself fanning his face with this musical-comedy object. At any rate, it became him. He was quite surprised to see how handsome he looked in a mirror.

They circled softly down and the mauve dusk rose to meet them. It was as if the whole of Egypt were settling softly into an inkwell. Then flowering out of the golden whirls sent up by stray dust-devils he glimpsed the nippled minarets and towers of the famous tombs; the Moquattam hills were pink and nacreous as a fingernail.

On the airfield were grouped the dignitaries who had been detailed to receive him officially. They were flanked by the members of his own staff with their wives — all wearing garden-party hats and gloves as if they were in the paddock at Long-champs. Everyone was nevertheless perspiring freely, indeed in streams. Mountolive felt *terra firma* under his polished dress shoes and drew a sigh of relief. The ground was almost hotter than the plane; but his nausea had vanished. He stepped foward tentatively to shake hands and realized that with the donning of his uniform everything had changed. A sudden loneliness smote him — for he realized that now, as an Ambassador, he must forever renounce the friendship of ordinary human beings in exchange for their *deference*. His uniform encased him like a suit of chain-armour. It shut him off from the ordinary world of human ex-changes. 'God!' he thought. 'I shall be forever soliciting a normal human reaction from people who are bound to defer to my *rank!* I shall become like that dreadful parson in Sussex who always feebly swears in order to prove that he is really quite an ordinary human being despite the dog-collar!'

But the momentary spasm of loneliness passed in the joys of a new self-possession. There was nothing to do now but to exploit his charm to the full; to be handsome, to be capable, surely one had the right to enjoy the consciousness of these things without self-reproach? He proved himself upon the outer circle of Egyptian officials whom he greeted in excellent Arabic. Smiles broke out everywhere, at once merging into a confluence of self-congratulatory looks. He knew also how to present himself in half-profile to the sudden stare of flash-bulbs as he made his first speech — a tissue of heart-warming platitudes pronounced with charming diffidence in Arabic which won murmurs of delight and excitement from the raffish circle of journalists.

A band suddenly struck up raggedly, playing woefully out of key; and under the plaintive iterations of a European melody played somehow in quartertones he recognized his own National Anthem. It was startling, and he had difficulty in not smiling. The police mission had been diligently training the Egyptian force in the uses of the slide-trombone. But the whole performance had a desultory and impromptu air, as if some rare form of ancient music (Palestrina?) were being interpreted on a set of fire-irons. He stood stiffly to attention. An aged Bimbashi with a glass eye stood before the band, also at attention — albeit rather shakily. Then it was over. 'I'm sorry about the band' said Nimrod Pasha under his breath. 'You see, sir, it was a scratch team. Most of the musicians are ill.' Mountolive nodded gravely, sympathetically, and addressed himself to the next task. He walked with profuse keenness up and down a guard of honour to inspect their bearing; the men smelt strongly of sesame oil and sweat and one or two smiled affably. This was delightful. He restrained the impulse to grin back. Then, turning, he completed his devoirs to the Protocol section, warm and smelly too in its brilliant red flower-pot hats. Here the smiles rolled about, scattered all over the place like slices of unripe water-melon. An Ambassador who spoke Arabic! He put on the air of smiling diffidence which he knew best charmed. He had learned this. His crooked smile was appealing — even his own staff was visibly much taken with him, he noted with pride; but particularly the wives. They relaxed and turned their faces towards him like flower-traps. He had a few words for each of the secretaries.

Then at last the great car bore him smoothly away to the Residence on the banks of the Nile. Errol came with him to show him around and make the necessary introductions to the house-staff. The size and elegance of the building were exciting, and also rather intimidating. To have all these rooms at one's disposal was enough to deter any bachelor. 'Still, for entertaining' he said almost sorrowfully 'I suppose they are necessary.' But the place echoed around him as he walked about the magnificent ball-room, across the conservatories, the terraces, peering out on the grassy lawns which went right down to the bank of the cocoa-coloured Nile water. Outside, goose-necked sprinklers whirled and hissed night and day, keeping the coarse emerald grass fresh with moisture. He heard their sighing as he undressed and had a cold shower in the beautiful bathroom with its vitreous glass baubles; Errol was soon dismissed with an invitation to return after dinner and discuss plans and projects. 'I'm tired' said Mountolive truthfully, 'I want to have a quiet dinner alone. This heat — I should remember it; but I'd forgotten.'

The Nile was rising, filling the air with the dank summer moisture of its yearly inundations, climbing the stone wall at the bottom of the Embassy garden inch by slimy inch. He lay on his bed for half an hour and listened to the cars drawing up at the Chancery entrance and the sound of voices and footsteps in the hall. His staff were busily autographing the handsome red visitors' book, bound in expensive morocco. Only Pursewarden had not put in an appearance. He was presumably still in hiding? Mountolive planned to give him a shaking-up at the first opportunity; he could not now afford absurdities which might put him in a difficult position with the rest of the staff. He hoped that his friend would not force him to become authoritative and unpleasant — he shrank from the thought. Nevertheless. . . .

After a rest he dined alone on a corner of the long terrace, dressed only in trousers and a shirt, his feet clad in sandals. Then he shed the latter and walked barefoot across the floodlit lawns down to the river, feeling the brilliant grass spiky under his bare feet. But it was of a coarse, African variety and its roots were dusty, even under the sprays, as if it were suffering from dandruff. There were three peacocks wandering in the shadows with their brilliant Argus-eyed tails. The black soft sky was powdered with stars. Well, he had arrived — in every sense of the word. He remembered a phrase from one of Pursewarden's books: 'The writer, most solitary of animals. . . .' The glass of whisky in his hand was icy-cold. He lay down in that airless darkness on the grass and gazed straight upwards into the sky, hardly thinking any more, but letting the drowsiness gradually creep up over him, inch by inch, like the rising tide of the river-water at the garden's end. Why should he feel a sadness at the heart of things when he was so confident of powers, so full of resolution? He did not know.

Errol duly returned after a hastily eaten dinner and was charmed to find his chief spread out like a starfish on the elegant lawn, almost asleep. The informalities were excellent signs. 'Ring for drink' said Mountolive benevolently 'and come and sit out here: it is more or less cool. There's a breath of wind off the river.' Errol obeyed and came to seat himself diffidently on the grass. They talked about the general design of things. 'I know' said Mountolive 'that the whole staff is trembling with anticipation about the summer move to Alexandria. I used to when I was a junior in the Commission. Well, we'll move out of this swelter just as soon as I've presented my credentials. The King will be in Divan three days hence? Yes, I gathered from Abdel Latif at the airport. Good. Then tomorrow I want to bid all Chancery secretaries and wives to tea; and in the evening the junior staff for a cocktail. Everything else can wait until you fix the special train and load up the despatch boxes. How about Alexandria?'

Errol smiled mistily. 'It is all in order, sir. There has been the usual scramble with incoming missions; but the Egyptians

499

have been very good. Protocol has found an excellent residence with a good summer Chancery and other offices we could use. Everything is splendid. You'll only need a couple of Chancery staff apart from the house; I've fixed a duty roster so that we all get a chance to spend three weeks up there in rotation. The house staff can go ahead. You'll be doing some entertaining I expect. The Court will leave in about another fortnight. No problems.'

No problems! It was a cheering phrase. Mountolive sighed and fell silent. On the darkness across the expanse of river-water a faint noise broke out, as with a patter like a swarming of bees, laughter and singing mingled with the harsh thrilling rattle of the sistrum. 'I had forgotten' he said with a pang. 'The tears of Isis! It is the Night of the Drop, isn't it?' Errol nodded wisely. 'Yes, sir.' The river would be alive with slender feluccas full of singers and loud with guitars and voices. Isis-Diana would be bright in the heavens, but here the floodlit lawns created a cone of white light which dimmed the night-sky outside it. He gazed vaguely round, searching for the constellations. 'Then that is all' he said, and Errol stood up. He cleared his throat and said: 'Pursewarden didn't appear because he had 'flu.' Mountolive thought this kind of loyalty a good sign. 'No' he said smiling, 'I know he is giving you trouble. I'm going to see he stops it.' Errol looked at him with delighted surprise. 'Thank you, sir.' Mountolive walked him slowly to the house. 'I also want to dine Maskelyne. Tomorrow night, if convenient.'

Errol nodded slowly. 'He was at the airport, sir.' 'I didn't notice. Please get my secretary to make out a card for tomorrow night. But ring him first and tell him if it is inconvenient to let me know. For eight-fifteen, black tie.'

'I will, sir.'

'I want particularly to talk to him as we are taking up some new dispositions and I want his co-operation. He is a brilliant officer, I have been told.'

Errol looked doubtful. 'He has had some rather fierce exchanges with Pursewarden. Indeed, this last week he has more or less besieged the Embassy. He is clever, but . . . somewhat hard-headed?' Errol was tentative, appeared unwilling to go too far. 'Well' said Mountolive, 'let me talk to him and see for myself. I think the new arrangement will suit everyone, even Master Pursewarden.'

They said goodnight.

The next day was full of familiar routines for Mountolive, but conducted, so to speak, from a new angle — the unfamiliar angle of a position which brought people immediately to their feet. It was exciting and also disturbing; even up to the rank of councillor he had managed to have a comfortably-based relationship with the junior staff at every level. Even the hulking Marines who staffed the section of Chancery Guards were friendly and equable towards him in the happiest of colloquial manners. Now they shrank into postures of reserve, almost of self-defence. These were the bitter fruits of power, he reflected, accepting his new role with resignation.

However, the opening moves were smoothly played; and even his staff party of the evening went off so well that people seemed reluctant to leave. He was late in changing for his dinner-party and Maskelyne had already been shown into the anodyne drawing-room when he finally appeared, bathed and changed. 'Ah, Mountolive!' said the soldier, standing up and extending his hand with a dry expressionless calm. 'I have been waiting for your arrival with some anxiety.' Mountolive felt a sudden sting of pique after all the deference shown to him during the day to be left thus untitled by this personage. ('Heavens' he thought, 'am I really a provincial at heart?')

'My dear Brigadier,' his opening remarks carried a small but perceptible coolness as a result. Perhaps the soldier simply wished to make it clear that he was a War Office body, and not a Foreign Office one? It was a clumsy way to do it. Nevertheless, and somewhat to his own annoyance, Mountolive felt himself rather drawn to this lean and solitary-looking figure with its tired eyes and lustreless voice. His ugliness had a certain determined elegance. His ancient dinner-clothes were not very carefully pressed and brushed, but the quality of the material and cut were both excellent. Maskelyne sipped his drink slowly and calmly, lowering his greyhound's muzzle towards his glass circumspectly. He scrutinized Mountolive with the utmost coolness. They exchanged the formal politeness of host and guest for a while, and somewhat to his own annoyance, Mountolive found himself liking him despite the dry precarious manner. He suddenly seemed to see in him one who, like himself, had hesitated to ascribe any particular meaning to life.

The presence of servants excluded any but the most general exchanges during the dinner they shared, seated out upon the lawn, and Maskelyne seemed content to bide his time. Only once the name of Pursewarden came up and he said with his offhand air: 'Yes. I hardly know him, of course, except officially. The odd thing is that his father — surely the name is too uncommon for me to be wrong? — his father was in my company during the war. He picked up an M.C. Indeed, I actually composed the citation which put him up for it: and of course, I had the disagreeable next-of-kin jobs. The son must have been a mere child then, I suppose. Of course, I may be wrong — not that it matters.'

Mountolive was intrigued. 'As a matter of fact' he said, 'I think you *are* right — he mentioned something of the kind to me once. Have you ever talked to him about it?'

'Good Heavens, no! Why should I?' Maskelyne seemed very faintly shocked. 'The son isn't really . . . my kind of person' he said quietly but without animus, simply as a statement of fact. 'He . . . I . . . well, I read a book of his once.' He stopped abruptly as if everything had been said; as if the subject had been disposed of for all time.

'He must have been a brave man' said Mountolive after an interval.

'Yes — or perhaps not' said his guest slowly, thoughtfully. He paused. 'One wonders. He wasn't a real soldier. One saw it quite often at the front. Sometimes acts of gallantry come as much out of cowardice as bravery — that is the queer thing. His act, particularly, I mean, was really an unsoldierly one. Oddly enough.'

'But ——' protested Mountolive.

'Let me make myself clear. There is a difference between a necessary act of bravery and an unnecessary one. If he had remembered his training as a soldier, he would not have done what he did. It may sound like a quibble. He lost his head, quite literally, and acted without thinking. I admire him enormously as a man, but not as a soldier. Our life is a good deal more exacting — it is a science, you know, or should be.'

He spoke thoughtfully in his dry, clearly enunciated way. It was clear that the topic was one which he had often debated in his own mind.

'I wonder' said Mountolive.

'I may be wrong' admitted the soldier.

The soft-footed servants had withdrawn at last, leaving them to their wine and cigars, and Maskelyne felt free to touch upon the real subject of his visit. 'I expect you've studied all the differences which have arisen between ourselves and your political branch. They have been extremely sharp; and we are all waiting for you to resolve them.'

Mountolive nodded. 'They have all been resolved as far as I am concerned' he said with the faintest tinge of annoyance (he disliked being hurried). 'I had a conference with your General on Tuesday and set out a new grouping which I am sure will please you. You will get a confirming signal this week ordering you to transfer your show to Jerusalem, which is to become the senior post and headquarters. This will obviate questions of rank and precedence; you can leave a staging post here under Telford, who is a civilian, but it will of course be a junior post. For convenience it can work to us and liaise with our Service Departments.'

A silence fell. Maskelyne studied the ash of his cigar while the faintest trace of a smile hovered at the edges of his mouth.

'So Pursewarden wins' he said quietly. 'Well, well!' Mountolive was both surprised and insulted by his smile, though in truth it seemed entirely without malice.

'Pursewarden' he said quietly 'has been reprimanded for suppressing a War Office paper; on the other hand, I happen to know the subject of the paper rather well and I agree that you should supplement it more fully before asking us to take action.'

'We are trying, as a matter of fact; Telford is putting down a grid about this Hosnani man — but some of the candidates put forward by Pursewarden seem to be rather . . . well, prejudicial, to put it mildly. However, Telford is trying to humour him by engaging them. But . . . well, there's one who sells information to the Press, and one who is at present consoling the Hosnani lady. Then there's another, Scobie, who spends his time dressed as a woman walking about the harbour at Alexandria — it would be a charity to suppose him in quest of police information. Altogether, I shall be quite glad to confide the net to Telford and tackle something a bit more serious. What people!'

'As I don't know the circumstances yet' said Mountolive quietly 'I can't comment. But I shall look into it.'

'I'll give you an example' said Maskelyne 'of their general efficiency. Last week Telford detailed this policeman called Scobie to do a routine job. When the Syrians want to be clever, they don't use a diplomatic courier; they confide their pouch to a lady, the vice-consul's niece, who takes it down to Cairo by train. We wanted to see the contents of one particular pouch — details of arms shipments, we thought. Gave Scobie some doped chocolates — with the doped one clearly marked. His job was to send the lady to sleep for a couple of hours and walk off with her pouch. Do you know what happened? He was found doped in the train when it got to Cairo and couldn't be wakened for nearly twenty-four hours. We had to put him into the American hospital. Apparently as he sat down in the lady's compartment, the train gave a sudden jolt and all the chocolates turned over in their wrappers. The one we had so carefully marked was now upside down; he could not remember which it was. In his panic, he ate it himself. Now I ask you. . . .' Maskelyne's humourless eye flashed as he retailed this story. 'Such people are not to be trusted' he added, acidly.

'I promise you I'll investigate the suitability of anyone proposed by Pursewarden; I also promise that if you mark papers to me there will be no hitch, and no repetition of this unauthorized behaviour.'

'Thank you.' He seemed genuinely grateful as he rose to take his leave. He waved away the beflagged duty car at the front door, muttering something about 'an evening constitutional', and walked off down the drive, putting on a light overcoat to hide his dinner-jacket. Mountolive stood at the front door and watched his tall, lean figure moving in and out of the yellow pools of lamplight, absurdly elongated by distance. He sighed with relief and weariness. It had been a heavy day. 'So much for Maskelyne.'

He returned to the deserted lawns to have one last drink in the silence before he retired to bed. Altogether, the work completed that day had not been unsatisfactory. He had disposed of a dozen disagreeable duties of which telling Maskelyne about his future had been perhaps the hardest. Now he could relax.

Yet before climbing the staircase, he walked about for a while in the silent house, going from room to room, thinking; hugging the knowledge of his accession to power with all the secret pride of a woman who has discovered that she is pregnant.

* * * * *

VII

Once his official duties in the capital had been performed to his private satisfaction, Mountolive felt free to anticipate the Court by transferring his headquarters to the second capital, Alexandria. So far everything had gone quite smoothly. The King himself had praised his fluency in Arabic and he had won the unusual distinction of press popularity by his judicious public use of the language. From every newspaper these days pictures of himself stared out, always with that crooked, diffident smile. Sorting out the little mound of press cuttings he found himself wondering: 'My God, am I slowly becoming irresistible to myself?' They were excellent pictures; he was undeniably handsome with his greying temples and crisply cut features. 'But the mere habit of culture is not enough to defend one from one's own charm. I shall be buried alive among these soft, easy aridities of a social practice which I do not even enjoy.' He thought with his chin upon his wrist: 'Why does not Leila write? Perhaps when I am in Alexandria I shall have word?' But he could at least leave Cairo with a good following wind. The other foreign missions were mad with envy at his success!

The move itself was completed with exemplary despatch by the diligent Errol and the Residence staff. He himself could afford to saunter down late when the special train had been loaded with all the diplomatic impedimenta which would enable them to make a show of working while they were away . . . suitcases and crates and scarlet despatch-boxes with their gold monograms. Cairo had by this time become unbearably hot. Yet their hearts were light as the train rasped out across the desert to the coast.

It was the best time of the year to remove, for the ugly spring khamseens were over and the town had put on its summer wear — coloured awnings along the Grande Corniche, and the ranks of coloured island craft which lay in shelves below the black turrets of the battleships and framed the blue Yacht Club harbour, atwinkle with sails. The season of parties had also begun and Nessim was able to give his long-promised reception for his returning friend. It was a barbaric spread and all Alexandria turned out to do Mountolive honour, for all the world as if he were a prodigal son returning, though in fact he knew few people apart from Nessim and his family. But he was glad to renew his acquaintance with Balthazar and Amaril, the two doctors who were always together, always chaffing each other; and with Clea whom he had once met in Europe. The sunlight, fading over the evening sea, blazed in upon the great brass-framed windows, turning them to molten diamonds before it melted and softened once more into the aquamarine twilight of Egypt. The curtains were drawn and now a hundred candles' breathing shone softly upon the white napery of the long tables, winking among the slender stems of the glasses. It was the season of ease, for the balls and rides and swimming-parties had started or were about to be planned. The cool sea-winds kept the temperature low, the air was fresh and invigorating.

Mountolive sank back into the accustomed pattern of things with a sense of sureness, almost of beatitude. Nessim had, so to speak, gone back into place like a picture into an alcove built for it, and the companionship of Justine — this dark-browed, queenly beauty at his side — enhanced rather than disturbed his relations with the outer world. Mountolive liked her, liked to feel her dark appraising eyes upon him lit with a sort of compassionate curiosity mixed with admiration. They made a splendid couple, he thought, with almost a touch of envy: like people trained to work together from childhood, instinctively responding to each other's unspoken needs and desires, moving up unhesitatingly to support one another with their smiles. Though she was handsome and reserved and appeared to speak little, Mountolive thought he detected an endearing candour cropping up the whole time among her sentences — as if from some hidden spring of secret warmth. Was she pleased to find someone who valued her husband as deeply as she herself did? The cool, guileless pressure of her fingers suggested that, as did her thrilling voice when she said 'I have known you so long from hearsay as David that it will be hard to call you anything else.' As for Nessim, he had lost nothing during the time of separation, had preserved all his graces, adding to them only the weight of a worldly judgement which made him seem strikingly European in such provincial surroundings. His tact, for example, in never mentioning any subject which might have an official bearing to Mountolive was deeply endearing — and this despite the fact that they rode and shot together frequently, swam, sailed and painted. Such information upon political affairs as he had to put forward was always scrupulously

relayed through Pursewarden. He never compromised their friendship by mixing work with pleasure, or forcing Mountolive to
struggle between affection and duty.

Best of all, Pursewarden himself had reacted most favourably
to his new position of eminence and was wearing what he called
'his new leaf'. A couple of brusque minutes in the terrible red
ink — the use of which is the prerogative only of Heads of Mission
— had quelled him and drawn from him a promise to 'turn over
a new fig-leaf', which he had dutifully done. His response had
indeed been wholehearted and Mountolive was both grateful and
relieved to feel that at last he could rely upon a judgement which
was determined not to overrun itself, or allow itself to founder
among easy dependences and doubts. What else? Yes, the new
Summer Residence was delightful and set in a cool garden full
of pines above Roushdi. There were two excellent hard courts
which rang all day to the pang of racquets. The staff seemed happy
with their new head of mission. Only . . . Leila's silence was still an
enigma. Then one evening Nessim handed him an envelope on
which he recognized her familiar hand. Mountolive put it in his
pocket to read when he was alone.

'Your reappearance in Egypt — you perhaps have guessed? —
has upset me somehow: upset my apple-cart. I am all over the
place and cannot pick up the pieces as yet. It puzzles me, I
admit. I have been living with you so long in my imagination —
quite *alone* there — that now I must almost reinvent you to bring
you back to life. Perhaps I have been traducing you all these years,
painting your picture to myself? You may be now simply a figment
instead of a flesh and blood dignitary, moving among people and
lights and policies. I can't find the courage to compare the truth
to reality as yet; I'm scared. Be patient with a silly headstrong
woman who never seems to know her own mind. Of course, we
should have met long since — but I shrank like a snail. Be patient.
Somewhere inside me I must wait for a tide to turn. I was so
angry when I heard you were coming that I cried with sheer rage.
Or was it panic? I suppose that really I had managed to forget . . .
my own face, all these years. Suddenly it came back over me like
an Iron Mask. Bah! soon my courage will come back, never fear.
Sooner or later we must meet and shock one another. When?
I don't know as yet. I don't know.'

Disconsolately reading the words as he sat upon the terraces
at dusk he thought: 'I cannot assemble my feelings coherently

enough to respond to her intelligently. What should I say or do? Nothing.' But the word had a hollow ring. 'Patience' he said softly to himself, turning the word this way and that in his mind the better to examine it. Later, at the Cervonis' ball among the blue lights and the snapping of paper streamers, it seemed easy once more to be patient. He moved once more in a glad world in which he no longer felt cut off from his fellows — a world full of friends in which he could enjoy the memory of the long rides with Nessim, conversations with Amaril, or the troubling pleasure of dancing with the blonde Clea. Yes, he could be patient here, so close at hand. The time, place and circumstances were all of them rewards for patience. He felt no omens rising from the unclouded future, while even the premonitions of the slowly approaching war were things which he could share publicly with the others. 'Can they really raze whole capitals, these bombers?' asked Clea quietly. 'I've always believed that our inventions mirror our secret wishes, and we wish for the end of the city-man, don't we? All of us? Yes, but how hard to surrender London and Paris. What do you think?'

What did he think? Mountolive wrinkled his fine brows and shook his head. He was thinking of Leila draped in a black veil, like a nun, sitting in her dusty summerhouse at Karm Abu Girg, among the splendid roses, with only a snake for company. . . .

So the untroubled, unhurried summer moved steadily onwards — and Mountolive found little to daunt him professionally in a city so eager for friendship, so vulnerable to the least politeness, so expert in taking pleasure. Day after day the coloured sails fluttered and loitered in the harbour mirror among the steel fortresses, the magical white waves moved in perfect punctuation over desert beaches burnt white as calx by the African suns. By night, sitting above a garden resplendent with fireflies, he heard the deep booming tread of screws as the Eastern-bound liners coasted the deeper waters outside the harbour, heading for the ports on the other side of the world. In the desert they explored oases of greenness made trembling and insubstantial as dreams by the water mirages, or stalked the bronze knuckles of the sandstone ridges around the city on horses, which, for all their fleetness, carried food and drink to assuage their talkative riders.

He visited Petra and the strange coral delta along the Red Sea coast with its swarming population of rainbow-coloured tropical fish. The long cool balconies of the summer residence echoed night after night to the clink of ice in tall glasses, the clink of platitudes and commonplaces made thrilling to him by their position in place and time, by their appositeness to a city which knew that pleasure was the only thing that made industry worth while; on these balconies, hanging out over the blue littoral of the historic coast, warmly lit by candle-light, these fragmentary friendships flowered and took shape in new affections whose candour made him no longer feel separated from his fellow-men by the powers he wielded. He was popular and soon might be well-beloved. Even the morbid spiritual lassitude and self-indulgence of the city was delightful to one who, secure in income, could afford to live outside it. Alexandria seemed to him a very desirable summer cantonment, accessible to every affection and stranger-loving in the sense of the Greek word. But why should he not feel at home?

The Alexandrians themselves were strangers and exiles to the Egypt which existed below the glittering surface of their dreams, ringed by the hot deserts and fanned by the bleakness of a faith which renounced worldly pleasure: the Egypt of rags and sores, of beauty and desperation. Alexandria was still Europe — the capital of Asiatic Europe, if such a thing could exist. It could never be like Cairo where his whole life had an Egyptian cast, where he spoke ample Arabic; here French, Italian and Greek dominated the scene. The ambience, the social manner, everything was different, was cast in a European mould where somehow the camels and palm-trees and cloaked natives existed only as a brilliantly coloured frieze, a backcloth to a life divided in its origins.

Then the autumn came and his duties drew him back once more to the winter capital, albeit puzzled and indeed a little aggrieved by the silence of Leila; but back to the consuming interests of a professional life which he found far from displeasing. There were papers to be constructed, miscellaneous reports, economic-social and military, to be made. His staff had shaken down well now, and worked with diligence and a will; even Pursewarden gave of his best. The enmity of Errol, never very deep, had been successfully neutralized, converted into a long-term truce. He had reason to feel pleased with himself.

Then at carnival time there came a message to say that Leila had at last signified her intention of meeting him — but both of them, it was understood, were to wear the conventional black domino of the season — the mask in which the Alexandrians revelled. He understood her anxiety. Nevertheless he was delighted by the thought and spoke warmly to Nessim on the telephone as he accepted the invitation, planning to remove his whole Chancery up to Alexandria for the carnival, so that his secretaries might enjoy the occasion with him. Remove he did, to find the city now basking under crisp winter skies as blue as a bird's egg and hardly touched at night by the desert frosts.

But here another disappointment awaited him; for when in the midst of the hubbub at the Cervoni ball Justine took his arm and piloted him through the garden to the place of rendezvous among the tall hedges, all they found was an empty marble seat with a silk handbag on it containing a note scrawled in lipstick. 'At the last moment my nerve fails me. Forgive.' He tried to hide his chagrin and discomfiture from Justine. She herself seemed almost incredulous, repeating: 'But she came in from Karm Abu Girg specially for the meeting. I cannot understand it. She has been with Nessim all day.' He felt a sympathy in the warm pressure of her hand upon his elbow as they returned, downcast, from the scene, brushing impatiently past the laughing masked figures in the garden.

By the pool he caught a glimpse of Amaril, sitting uncowled before a slender masked figure, talking in low, pleading tones, and leaning forward from time to time to embrace her. A pang of envy smote him, though God knew there was nothing he recognized as passional now in his desire to see Leila. It was, in a paradoxical way, that Egypt itself could not fully come alive for him until he had seen her — for she represented something like a second, almost mythical image of the reality which he was experiencing, expropriating day by day. He was like a man seeking to marry the twin images in a camera periscope in order to lay his lens in true focus. Without having gone through the experience of having seen her once more, he felt vaguely helpless, unable either to confirm his own memories of this magical landscape, or fully assess his newest impressions of it. Yet he accepted his fate with philosophical calm. There was, after all, no real cause for alarm. Patience — there was ample room for patience now, to wait upon her courage.

Besides, other friendships had ripened now to fill the gap — friendships with Balthazar (who often came to dine and play chess), friendships with Amaril, Pierre Balbz, the Cervoni family.

Clea too had begun her slow portrait of him at this time. His mother had been begging him to have a portrait in oils made for her; now he was able to pose in the resplendent uniform which Sir Louis had so obligingly sold him. The picture would make a surprise gift for Christmas, he thought, and was glad to let Clea dawdle over it, reconstructing the portions which displeased her. Through her (for she talked as she worked in order to keep her subjects' faces alive) he learned much during that summer about the lives and pre-occupations of the Alexandrians — the fantastic poetry and grotesque drama of life as these exiles of circumstance lived it; tales of the modern lake-dwellers, inhabitants of the stone skyscrapers which stared out over the ruins of the Pharos towards Europe.

One such tale struck his fancy — the love-story of Amaril (the elegant, much beloved doctor) for whom he had come to feel a particular affection. The very name on Clea's lips sounded with a common affection for this diffident and graceful man, who had so often sworn that he would never have the luck to be loved by a woman. 'Poor Amaril!' sighing and smiling as she painted she said: 'shall I tell you his story? It is somehow typical. It has made all his friends happy, for we were always apt to think that he had left the matter of love in this world until too late — had missed the bus.'

'But Amaril is going abroad to England,' said Mountolive. 'He has asked us for a visa. Am I to assume that his heart is broken? And who is Semira? Please tell me.'

'The virtuous Semira!' Clea smiled again tenderly, and pausing on her work, put a portfolio into his hands. He turned the pages. 'All noses' he said with surprise, and she nodded. 'Yes, noses. Amaril has kept me busy for nearly three months, travelling about and collecting noses for her to choose from; noses of the living and the dead. Noses from the Yacht Club, the Etoile, from frescoes in the Museum, from coins. . . . It has been hard work assembling them all for comparative study. Finally, they have ` chosen the nose of a soldier in a Theban fresco.'

Mountolive was puzzled. 'Please, Clea, tell me the story.'

'Will you promise to sit still, not to move?'

'I promise.'

'Very well, then. You know Amaril quite well now; well, this romantic, endearing creature — so true a friend and so wise a doctor — has been our despair for years. It seemed that he could

never, would never fall in love. We were sad for him — you know
that despite our hardness of surface we Alexandrians are sentimental people, and wish our friends to enjoy life. Not that he was
unhappy — and he has had lovers from time to time: but never
une amie in our special sense. He himself bemoaned the fact
frequently — I think not entirely to provoke pity or amusement,
but to reassure himself that there was nothing wrong: that he was
sympathetic and attractive to the race of women. Then last year
at the Carnival, the miracle happened. He met a slender masked
domino. They fell madly in love — indeed went farther than is
customary for so cautious a lover as Amaril. He was completely
transformed by the experience, but . . . the girl disappeared, still
masked, without leaving her name. A pair of white hands and a
ring with a yellow stone was all he knew of her — for despite
their passion she had refused to unmask so that oddly enough, he
had been denied so much as a kiss, though granted . . . other
favours. Heavens, I am gossiping! Never mind.

'From then on Amaril became insupportable. The romantic
frenzy, I admit, suited him very well — for he is a romantic to
his finger-tips. He hunted through the city all year long for those
hands, sought them everywhere, beseeched his friends to help
him, neglected his practice, became almost a laughing-stock. We
were amused and touched by his distress, but what could we do?
How could we trace her? He waited for Carnival this year with
burning impatience for she had promised to return to the place
of rendezvous. Now comes the fun. She did reappear, and once
more they renewed their vows of devotion; but this time Amaril
was determined not to be given the slip — for she was somewhat
evasive about names and addresses. He became desperate and
bold, and refused to be parted from her which frightened her very
much indeed. (All this he told me himself — for he appeared at
my flat in the early morning, walking like a drunkard and with his
hair standing on end, elated and rather frightened.)

'The girl made several attempts to give him the slip but he
stuck to her and insisted on taking her home in one of those old
horse-drawn cabs. She was almost beside herself, indeed, and
when they reached the eastern end of the city, somewhat shabby
and unfrequented, with large abandoned properties and decaying
gardens, she made a run for it. Demented with romantic frenzy,
Amaril chased the nymph and caught her up as she was slipping
into a dark courtyard. In his eagerness he snatched at her cowl

when the creature, her face at last bared, sank to the doorstep in tears. Amaril's description of the scene was rather terrifying. She sat there, shaken by a sort of snickering and whimpering and covering her face with her hands. *She had no nose.* For a moment he got a tremendous fright for he is the most superstitious of mortals, and knows all the beliefs about vampires appearing during carnival. But he made the sign of the cross and touched the clove of garlic in his pocket — but she didn't disappear. And then the doctor in him came to the fore, and taking her into the courtyard (she was half-fainting with mortification and fear) he examined her closely. He tells me he heard his own brain ticking out possible diagnoses clearly and watchfully, while at the same time he felt that his heart had stopped beating and that he was suffocating. . . . In a flash he reviewed the possible causes of such a feature, repeating with terror words like syphilis, leprosy, lupus, and turning her small distorted face this way and that. He cried angrily: "What is your name?" And she blurted out "Semira — the virtuous Semira." He was so unnerved that he roared with laughter.

'Now this is an oddity. Semira is the daughter of a very old deaf father. The family was once rich and famous, under the Khedives, and is of Ottoman extraction. But it was plagued by misfortunes and the progressive insanity of the sons, and has so far today decayed as to be virtually forgotten. It is also poverty-stricken. The old half-mad father locked Semira away in this rambling house, keeping her veiled for the most part. Vaguely, in society, one had heard tales of her — of a daughter who had taken the veil and spent her life in prayer, who had never been outside the gates of the house, who was a mystic; or who was deaf, dumb and bed-ridden. Vague tales, distorted as tales always are in Alexandria. But while the faint echo remained of the so-called virtuous Semira — she was really completely unknown to us and her family forgotten. Now it seemed that at carnival-time her curiosity about the outer world overcame her and she gate-crashed parties in a domino!

'But I am forgetting Amaril. Their footsteps had brought down an old manservant with a candle. Amaril demanded to see the master of the house. He had already come to a decision. The old father lay asleep in an old-fashioned four-poster bed, in a room covered in bat-droppings, at the top of the house. Semira was by now practically insensible. But Amaril had come to a great decision. Taking the candle in one hand and the small Semira in the crook of his arm, he walked the whole way up to the top and kicked open the door of the father's room. It must have been a strange and unfamiliar scene for the old man to witness as he sat up in bed — and Amaril describes it with all the touching flamboyance of the romantic, even moving himself in the recital so that he is in tears as he recalls it. He is touched by the magnificence of his own fancy, I think; I must say, loving him as much as I do, I felt tears coming into my own eyes as he told me how he put down the candle beside the bed, and kneeling down with Semira, said "I wish to marry your daughter and take her back into the world." The terror and incomprehension of the old man at this unexpected visit took some time to wear off, and for a while it was hard to make him understand. Then he began to tremble and wonder at this handsome apparition kneeling beside his bed holding up his noseless daughter with his arm and proposing the impossible with so much pride and passion.

' "But" the old man protested "no-one will take her, for she has no nose." He got out of bed in a stained nightshirt and walked right round Amaril, who remained kneeling, studying him as one might an entomological specimen. (I am quoting.) Then he touched him with his bare foot — as if to see whether he was made of flesh and blood — and repeated: "Who are you to take a woman without a nose?" Amaril replied: "I am a doctor from Europe and I will give her a new nose," for the idea, the fantastic idea, had been slowly becoming clear in his own mind. At the words, Semira gave a sob and turned her beautiful, horrible face to his, and Amaril thundered out: "Semira, will you be my wife?" She could hardly articulate her response and seemed little less doubtful of the whole issue than was her father. Amaril stayed and talked to them, convincing them.

'The next day when he went back, he was received with a message that Semira was not to be seen and that what he proposed was impossible. But Amaril was not to be put off, and once more he forced his way in and bullied the father.

'This, then, is the fantasy in which he has been living. For Semira, as loving and eager as ever, cannot leave her house for the open world until he fulfils his promise. Amaril offered to marry her at once, but the suspicious old man wants to make sure of the nose. But what nose? First Balthazar was called in and together they examined Semira, and assured themselves that the illness was due neither to leprosy nor syphilis but to a rare form of lupus — a peculiar skin T.B. of rare kind of which many cases have been recorded from the Damietta region. It had been left untreated over the years and had finally collapsed the nose. I must say, it is horrible — just a slit like the gills of a fish. For I too have been sharing the deliberations of the doctors and have been going regularly to read to Semira in the darkened rooms where she has spent most of her life. She has wonderful dark eyes like an odalisque and a shapely mouth and well-modelled chin: and then the gills of a fish! It is too unfair. And it has taken her ages to actually believe that surgery can restore the defect. Here again Amaril has been brilliant, in getting her interested in her restoration, conquering her self-disgust, allowing her to choose the nose from that portfolio, discuss the whole project with him. He has let her choose her nose as one might let one's mistress choose a valuable bracelet from Pierantoni. It was just the right approach, for she is beginning to conquer her shame, and feel almost proud of being free to choose this valuable gift — the most treasured feature of a woman's face which aligns every glance and alters every meaning: and without which good eyes and teeth and hair become useless treasures.

'But now they have run into other difficulties, for the restoration of the nose itself requires techniques of surgery which are still very new; and Amaril, though a surgeon, does not wish there to be any mistake about the results. You see, he is after all building a woman of his own fancy, a face to a husband's own specifications; only Pygmalion had such a chance before! He is working on the project as if his life depended on it — which in a way I suppose it does.

'The operation itself will have to be done in stages, and will take ages to complete. I have heard them discussing it over and over again in such detail that I feel I could almost perform it myself. First you cut off a strip of the costal cartilage, here, where the rib joins the breastbone, and make a graft from it. Then you cut out a triangular flap of skin from the forehead and pull downwards to cover the nose — the Indian technique, Balthazar calls it; but they are still debating the removal of a section of flesh and skin from inside the thigh. . . . You can imagine how fascinating this is for a painter and sculptor to think about. But meanwhile Amaril is going to England to perfect the operative technique under the best masters. Hence his demand for a visa. How many months he will be away we don't know yet, but he is setting out with all the air of a knight in search of the Holy Grail. For he intends to complete the operation himself. Meanwhile, Semira will wait for him here, and I have promised to visit her frequently and keep her interested and amused if I can. It is not difficult, for the real world outside the four walls of her house sounds to her strange and cruel and romantic. Apart from a brief glimpse of it at carnival-time, she knows little of our lives. For her, Alexandria is as brilliantly coloured as a fairy-story. It will be some time before she sees it as it really is — with its harsh, circumscribed contours and its wicked, pleasure-loving and unromantic in-habitants. But you have moved!'

Mountolive apologized and said: 'Your use of the word "unromantic" startled me, for I was just thinking how romantic it all seems to a newcomer.'

'Amaril is an exception, though a beloved one. Few are as generous, as unmercenary as he. As for Semira — I cannot at present see what the future holds for her beyond romance.' Clea sighed and smiled and lit a cigarette.

'*Espérons*' she said quietly.

*　　*　　*　　*　　*

VIII

'A hundred times I've asked you not to use my razor' said Pombal plaintively 'and you do so again. You *know* I am afraid of syphilis. Who knows what spots, when you cut them, begin to leak?'

'*Mon cher collègue*' said Pursewarden stiffly (he was shaving his lip), and with a grimace which was somewhat intended to express injured dignity, 'what can you mean? I am British. *Hein?*'

He paused, and marking time with Pombal's cut-throat declaimed solemnly:

> '*The British who perfected the horseless carriage*
> *Are now working hard on the sexless marriage.*
> *Soon the only permissible communion*
> *Will be by agreement with one's Trade Union.*'

'Your blood may be infected' said his friend between grunts as he ministered to a broken suspender with one fat calf exposed upon the *bidet*. 'You never know, after all.'

'I am a writer' said Pursewarden with further and deeper dignity. 'And therefore I *do* know. There is no blood in my veins. Plasma' he said darkly, wiping his ear-tip, 'that is what flows in my veins. How else would I do all the work I do? Think of it. On the *Spectator* I am *Ubique*, on the *New Statesman* I am *Mens Sana*. On the *Daily Worker* I sign myself as *Corpore Sano*. I am also *Paralysis Agitans* on *The Times* and *Ejaculatio Praecox* in *New Verse*. I am . . .' But here his invention failed him.

'I never see you working' said Pombal.

'Working little, I earn less. If my work earned more than one hundred pounds a year I should not be able to take refuge in being misunderstood.' He gave a strangled sob.

'*Compris*. You have been drinking. I saw the bottle on the hall table as I came in. Why so early?'

'I wished to be quite honest about it. It is your wine, after all. I wished to hide nothing. I *have* drunk a tot or so.'

'Celebration?'

'Yes. Tonight, my dear Georges, I am going to do something rather unworthy of myself. I have disposed of a dangerous enemy and advanced my own position by a large notch. In our service, this would be regarded as something to crow about. I am going to offer myself a dinner of self-congratulation.'

'Who will pay it?'

'I will order, eat and pay for it myself.'

'That is not much good.'

Pursewarden made an impatient face in the mirror.

'On the contrary' he said. 'A quiet evening is what I most need. I shall compose a few more fragments of my autobiography over the good oysters at Diamandakis.'

'What is the title?'

'*Beating about the Bush*. The opening words are "I first met Henry James in a brothel in Algiers. He had a naked houri on each knee."'

'Henry James was a pussy, I think.'

Pursewarden turned the shower on full and stepped into it crying: 'No more literary criticism from the French, please.'

Pombal drove a comb through his dark hair with a laborious impatience and then consulted his watch. '*Merde*' he said, 'I am going to be retarded again.'

Pursewarden gave a shriek of delight. They adventured freely in each other's languages, rejoicing like schoolboys in the mistakes which cropped up among their conversations. Each blunder was greeted with a shout, was turned into a war-cry. Pursewarden hopped with pleasure and shouted happily above the hissing of the water: 'Why not stay in and enjoy a nice little *nocturnal emission* on the short hairs?' (Pombal had described a radio broadcast thus the day before and had not been allowed to forget it.) He made a round face now to express mock annoyance. 'I did *not* say it' he said.

'You bloody well did.'

'I did not say "the short hairs" but the "short undulations"—*des ondes courtes*.'

'Equally dreadful. You Quai d'Orsay people shock me. Now my French may not be perfect, but I have never made a ——'

'If I begin with your mistakes — ha! ha!'

Pursewarden danced up and down in the bath, shouting 'Nocturnal emissions on the short hairs'. Pombal threw a rolled towel at him and lumbered out of the bathroom before he could retaliate effectively.

Their abusive conversation was continued while the Frenchman made some further adjustments to his dress in the bedroom mirror. 'Will you go down to Etoile later for the floor-show?'

'I certainly will' said Pursewarden. 'I shall dance a Fox-Macabre with Darley's girl-friend or Sveva. Several Fox-Macabres, in fact. Then, later on, like an explorer who has run out of pemmican, purely for body-warmth, I shall select someone and conduct her to Mount Vulture. There to sharpen my talons on her flesh.' He made what he imagined to be the noise a vulture makes as it feeds upon flesh — a soft, throaty croaking. Pombal shuddered.

'Monster' he cried. 'I go — good-bye.'

'Good-bye. *Toujours la maladresse!*'

'*Toujours*.' It was their war-cry.

Left alone, Pursewarden whistled softly as he dried himself in the torn bath-towel and completed his toilet. The irregularities in the water system of the Mount Vulture Hotel often drove him across the square to Pombal's flat in search of a leisurely bath and a shave. From time to time too, when Pombal went on leave, he would actually rent the place and share it, somewhat uneasily, with Darley who lived a furtive life of his own in the far corner of it. It was good from time to time to escape from the isolation of his hotel-room, and the vast muddle of paper which was growing up around his next novel. To escape — always to escape. . . . The desire of a writer to be alone with himself —'the writer, most solitary of human animals'; 'I am quoting from the great Pursewarden himself' he told his reflection in the mirror as he wrestled with his tie. Tonight he would dine quietly, self-indulgently, alone! He had gracefully refused a halting dinner invitation from Errol which he knew would involve him in one of those gauche, haunting evenings spent in playing imbecile paper-games or bridge. 'My God' Pombal had said, 'your compatriots' methods of passing the time! Those rooms which they fill with their sense of guilt! To express *one* idea is to stop a dinner party dead in its tracks and provoke an *awkwardness*, a *silence*. . . . I try my best, but always feel I've put my foot in it. So I always automatically send flowers the next morning to my hostess. . . . What a nation you are! How intriguing for us French because how *repellent* is the way you live!'

Poor David Mountolive! Pursewarden thought of him with compassion and affection. What a price the career diplomat had to pay for the fruits of power! 'His dreams must forever be awash with the memories of fatuities endured — deliberately endured in the name of what was most holy in the profession, namely the desire to please, the determination to captivate in order to influence. Well! It takes all sorts to unmake a world.'

Combing his hair back he found himself thinking of Maskelyne, who must at this moment be sitting in the Jerusalem express
jogging stiffly, sedately down among the sand-dunes and orange-
groves, sucking a long pipe; in a hot carriage, fly-tormented
without and roasted within by the corporate pride of a tradition
which was dying. . . . Why should it be allowed to die? Maskelyne,
full of the failure, the ignominy of a new post which carried
advancement with it. The final cruel thrust. (The idea gave him a
twinge of remorse for he did not underestimate the character of
the unself-seeking soldier.) Narrow, acid, desiccated as a human
being, nevertheless the writer somewhere treasured him while the
man condemned him. (Indeed, he had made extensive notes upon
him — a fact which would certainly have surprised Maskelyne had
he known.) His way of holding his pipe, of carrying his nose high,
his reserves. . . . It was simply that he might want to use him one
day. 'Are real human beings becoming simply extended humours
capable of use, and does this cut one off from them a bit? Yes. For
observation throws down a field about the observed person or
object. Yes. Makes the unconditional response more difficult —
the response to the common ties, affections, love and so on. But
this is not only the writer's problem — it is everyone's problem.
Growing up means separation in the interests of a better, more
lucid joining up. . . . Bah!' He was able to console himself against
his furtive sympathy with Maskelyne by recalling a few of the
man's stupidities. His arrogance! 'My dear fellow, when you've
been in "I" as long as I have you develop *intuition*. You can see
things a mile off.' The idea of anyone like Maskelyne developing
intuition was delightful. Pursewarden gave a long crowing laugh
and reached for his coat.

He slipped lightly downstairs into the dusky street, counting
his money and smiling. It was the best hour of the day in Alexandria — the streets turning slowly to the metallic blue of carbon
paper but still giving off the heat of the sun. Not all the lights
were on in the town, and the large mauve parcels of dusk moved
here and there, blurring the outlines of everything, repainting the
hard outlines of buildings and human beings in smoke. Sleepy
cafés woke to the whine of mandolines which merged in the shrilling
of heated tyres on the tarmac of streets now crowded with life,
with white-robed figures and the scarlet dots of tarbushes. The
window-boxes gave off a piercing smell of slaked earth and urine.
The great limousines soared away from the Bourse with softly

crying horns, like polished flights of special geese. To be half-blinded by the mauve dusk, to move lightly, brushing shoulders with the throng, at peace, in that dry inspiriting air . . . these were the rare moments of happiness upon which he stumbled by chance, by accident. The pavements still retained their heat just as water-melons did when you cut them open at dusk; a damp heat slowly leaking up through the thin soles of one's shoes. The sea-winds were moving in to invest the upper town with their damp coolness, but as yet one only felt them spasmodically. One moved through the dry air, so full of static electricity (the crackle of the comb in his hair), as one might swim through a tepid summer sea full of creeping cold currents. He walked towards Baudrot slowly through little isolated patches of smell — a perfume shed by a passing woman, or the reek of jasmine from a dark archway — knowing that the damp sea air would soon blot them all out. It was the perfect moment for an *apéritif* in the half-light.

The long wooden outer balconies, lined with potted plants which exhaled the twilight smell of watered earth, were crowded now with human beings, half melted by the mirage into fugitive cartoons of gestures swallowed as soon as made. The coloured awnings trembled faintly above the blue veils which shifted uneasily in the darkening alleys, like the very nerves of the lovers themselves who hovered here, busy on the assignations, their gestures twinkling like butterflies full of the evening promises of Alexandria. Soon the mist would vanish and the lights would blaze up on cutlery and white cloth, on ear-rings and flashing jewellery, on sleek oiled heads and smiles made brilliant by their darkness, brown skins slashed by white teeth. Then the cars would begin once more to slide down from the upper town with their elegant precarious freight of diners and dancers. . . . This was the best moment of the day. Sitting here, with his back against a wooden trellis, he could gaze sleepily into the open street, unrecognized and ungreeted. Even the figures at the next table were unrecognizable, the merest outlines of human beings. Their voices came lazily to him in the dusk, the mauve-veiled evening voices of Alexandrians uttering stockyard quotations or the lazy verses from Arabic love-poems — who could tell?

How good the taste of Dubonnet with a *zeste de citron*, with its concrete memory of a Europe long-since abandoned yet living on unforgotten below the surface of this unsubstantial life in

Alexander's shabby capital! Tasting it he thought enviously of Pombal, of the farmhouse in Normandy to which his friend hoped one day to return heart-whole. How marvellous it would be to feel the same assured relations with his own country, the same certainty of return! But his gorge rose at the mere thought of it; and at the same time the pain and regret that it should be so. (She said: 'I have read the books so slowly — not because I cannot read fast as yet in Braille; but because I wanted to surrender to the power of each word, even the cruelties and the weaknesses, to arrive at the grain of the thought.') The *grain!* It was a phrase which rang in one's ear like the whimper of a bullet which passes too close. He saw her — the marble whiteness of the sea-goddess' face, hair combed back upon her shoulders, staring out across the park where the dead autumn leaves and branches flared and smoked; a Medusa among the snows, dressed in her old tartan shawl. The blind spent all day in that gloomy subterranean library with its pools of shadow and light, their fingers moving like ants across the perforated surfaces of books engraved for them by a machine. ('I so much wanted to understand, but I could not.') Good, this is where you break into a cold sweat; this is where you turn through three hundred and sixty-five degrees, a human earth, to bury your face in your pillow with a groan! (The lights were coming on now, the veils were being driven upwards into the night, evaporating. The faces of human beings. . . .) He watched them intently, almost lustfully, as if to surprise their most inward intentions, their basic designs in moving here, idle as fireflies, walking in and out of the bars of yellow light; a finger atwinkle with rings, a flashing ear, a gold tooth set firmly in the middle of an amorous smile. 'Waiter, *kaman wahed*, another please.' And the half-formulated thoughts began to float once more across his mind (innocent, purged by the darkness and the alcohol): thoughts which might later dress up, masquerade as verses. . . . Visitants from other lives.

Yes, he would do another year — one more whole year, simply out of affection for Mountolive. He would make it a good one, too. Then a transfer — but he averted his mind from this, for it might result in disaster. Ceylon? Santos? Something about this Egypt, with its burning airless spaces and its unrealized vastness — the grotesque granite monuments to dead Pharaohs, the tombs which became cities — something in all this suffocated him. It was no place for memory — and the strident curt reality of the day-world was almost more than a human being could bear. Open sores, sex, perfumes, and money.

They were crying the evening papers in a soup-language which was deeply thrilling — Greek, Arabic, French were the basic ingredients. The boys ran howling through the thoroughfares like winged messengers from the underworld, proclaiming . . . the fall of Byzantium? Their white robes were tucked up about their knees. They shouted plaintively, as if dying of hunger. He leaned from his wooden porch and bought an evening paper to read over his solitary meal. Reading at meals was another self-indulgence which he could not refuse himself.

Then he walked quietly along the arcades and through the street of the cafés, past a mauve mosque (sky-floating), a library, a temple (grilled: 'Here once lay the body of the great Alexander'); and so down the long curving inclines of the street which took one to the seashore. The cool currents were still nosing about hereabouts, tantalizing to the cheek.

He suddenly collided with a figure in a mackintosh and belatedly recognized Darley. They exchanged confused pleasantries, weighed down by a mutual awkwardness. Their politenesses got them, so to speak, suddenly stuck to each other, suddenly stuck to the street as if it had turned to flypaper. Then at last Darley managed to break himself free and turn back down the dark street saying: 'Well, I mustn't keep you. I'm dead tired myself. Going home for a wash.' Pursewarden stood still for a moment looking after him, deeply puzzled by his own confusion and smitten by the memory of the damp bedraggled towels which he had left lying about Pombal's bathroom, and the rim of shaving-soap grey with hairs around the washbasin. . . . Poor Darley! But how was it that, liking and respecting the man, he could not feel natural in his presence? He at once took on a hearty, unnatural tone with him purely out of nervousness. This must seem rude and contemptuous. The brisk hearty tone of some country medico rallying a patient . . . damn! He must some time take him back to the hotel for a solitary drink and try to get to know him a little. And yet, he had tried to get to know him on several occasions on those winter walks together. He rationalized his dissatisfaction by saying to himself 'But the poor bastard is still interested in *literature*.'

But his good humour returned when he reached the little Greek oyster-tavern by the sea whose walls were lined with butts and barrels of all sizes, and from whose kitchens came great gusts of smoke and smell of whitebait and octopus frying in olive oil. Here he sat, among the ragged boatmen and schooner-crews of the Levant, to eat his oysters and dip into the newspaper, while the evening began to compose itself comfortably around him, untroubled by thought or the demands of conversation with its wicked quotidian platitudes. Later he might be able to relate his ideas once more to the book which he was trying to complete so slowly, painfully, in these hard-won secret moments stolen from an empty professional life, stolen even from the circumstances which he built around himself by virtue of laziness, of gregariousness. ('Care for a drink?' — 'Don't mind if I do.' How many evenings had been lost like this?)

And the newspapers? He dwelt mostly upon the *Faits Divers* — those little oddities of human conduct which mirrored the true estate of man, which lived on behind the wordier abstractions, pleading for the comic and miraculous in lives made insensitive by drabness, by the authority of bald reason. Beside a banner headline which he would have to interpret in a draft despatch for Mountolive the next day — ARAB UNION APPEALS AGAIN — he could find the enduring human frailties in GREAT RELIGIOUS LEADER TRAPPED IN LIFT or LUNATIC BREAKS MONTE CARLO BANK which reflected the macabre unreason of fate and circumstance.

Later, under the influence of the excellent food at the Coin de France he began to smoke his evening more enjoyably still — like a pipe of opium. The inner world with its tensions unwound its spools inside him, flowing out and away in lines of thought which flickered intermittently into his consciousness like morse. As if he had become a real receiving apparatus — these rare moments of good dictation!

At ten he noted on the back of a letter from his bank a few of the gnomic phrases which belonged to his book. As 'Ten. No attacks by the hippogriff this week. Some speeches for Old Parr?' And then, below it, disjointedly, words which, condensing now in the mind like dew, might later be polished and refashioned into the armature of his characters' acts.

(*a*) With every advance from the known to the unknown, the mystery increases.

(*b*) Here I am, walking about on two legs with a name — the whole intellectual history of Europe from Rabelais to de Sade.

(*c*) Man will be happy when his Gods perfect themselves.

(d) Even the Saint dies with all his imperfections on his head.

(e) Such a one as might be above divine reproach, beneath human contempt.

(f) Possession of a human heart — disease without remedy.

(g) All great books are excursions into pity.

(h) The yellow millet dream is everyman's way.

Later these oracular thoughts would be all brushed softly into the character of Old Parr, the sensualist Tiresias of his novel, though erupting thus, at haphazard, they offered no clue as to the order in which they would really be placed finally.

He yawned. He was pleasantly tipsy after his second Armagnac. Outside the grey awnings, the city had once more assumed the true pigmentation of night. Black faces now melted into blackness; one saw apparently empty garments walking about, as in *The Invisible Man*. Red pill-boxes mounted upon cancelled faces, the darkness of darkness. Whistling softly, he paid his bill and walked lightly down to the Corniche again to where, at the end of a narrow street, the green bubble of the Etoile flared and beckoned; he dived into the narrow bottleneck staircase to emerge into an airless ballroom, half blinded now by the incandescent butcher's light and pausing only to let Zoltan take his mackintosh away to the cloakroom. For once he was not irked by the fear of his unpaid drink-chits — for he had drawn a substantial advance upon his new salary. 'Two new girls' said the little waiter hoarsely in his ear, 'both from Hungary.' He licked his lips and grinned. He looked as if he had been fried very slowly in olive oil to a rich dark brown.

The place was crowded, the floor-show nearly over. There were no familiar faces to be seen around, thank God. The lights went down, turned blue, black — and then with a shiver of tambourines and the roll of drums threw up the last performer into a blinding silver spot. Her sequins caught fire as she turned, blazing like a Viking ship, to jingle down the smelly corridor to the dressing-rooms.

He had seldom spoken to Melissa since their initial meeting months before, and her visits to Pombal's flat now rarely if ever coincided with his. Darley too was painstakingly secretive — perhaps from jealousy, or shame? Who could tell? They smiled and greeted one another in the street when their paths crossed, that was all. He watched her reflectively now as he drank a couple of whiskies and slowly felt the lights beginning to burn more brightly inside him, his feet respond to the dull sugared beat of the nigger jazz. He enjoyed dancing, enjoyed the comfortable shuffle of the four-beat bar, the rhythms that soaked into the floor under one's toes. Should he dance?

But he was too good a dancer to be adventurous, and holding Melissa in his arms thus he hardly bothered to do more than move softly, lightly round the floor, humming to himself the tune of *Jamais de la vie*. She smiled at him and seemed glad to see a familiar face from the outer world. He felt her narrow hand with its slender wrist resting upon his shoulder, fingers clutching his coat like the claw of a sparrow. 'You are *en forme*' she said. 'I am *en forme*' he replied. They exchanged the meaningless pleasantries suitable to the time and place. He was interested and attracted by her execrable French. Later she came across to his table and he stood her a couple of *coups de champagne* — the statutory fee exacted by the management for private conversations. She was on duty that night, and each dance cost the dancer a fee; therefore this interlude won her gratitude, for her feet were hurting her. She talked gravely, chin on hand, and watching her he found her rather beautiful in an etiolated way. Her eyes were good — full of small timidities which recorded perhaps the shocks which too great an honesty exacts from life? But she looked, and clearly was, ill. He jotted down the words: 'The soft bloom of phthisis.' The whisky had improved his sulky good humour, and his few jests were rewarded by an unforced laughter which, to his surprise, he found delightful. He began to comprehend dimly what Darley must see in her — the *gamine* appeal of the city, of slenderness and neatness: the ready street-arab response to a hard world. Dancing again he said to her, but with drunken irony: '*Melissa, comment vous défendez-vous contre la foule?*' Her response, for some queer reason, cut him to the heart. She turned upon him an eye replete with all the candour of experience and replied softly: '*Monsieur, je ne me défends plus.*' The melancholy of the smiling face was completely untouched by self-pity. She made a little gesture, as if indicating a total world, and said 'Look' — the shabby wills and desires of the Etoile's patrons, clothed in bodily forms, spread around them in that airless cellar. He understood and suddenly felt apologetic for never having treated her seriously. He was furious at his own complacency. On an impulse, he pressed his cheek to hers, affectionately as a brother. She was completely *natural!*

A human barrier dissolved now and they found that they could talk freely to each other, like old friends. As the evening wore on he found himself dancing with her more and more often. She seemed to welcome this, even though on the dance-floor itself he danced silently now, relaxed and happy. He made no gestures of intimacy, yet he felt somehow accepted by her. Then towards midnight a fat and expensive Syrian banker arrived and began to compete seriously for her company. Much to his annoyance, Pursewarden felt his anxiety rise, form itself almost into a proprietary jealousy. This made him swear under his breath! But he moved to a table near the floor the better to be able to claim her as soon as the music started. Melissa herself seemed oblivious to this fierce competition. She was tired. At last he asked her 'What will you do when you leave here? Will you go back to Darley tonight?' She smiled at the name, but shook her head wearily. 'I need some money for — never mind' she said softly, and then abruptly burst out, as if afraid of not being taken for sincere, with 'For my winter coat. We have so little money. In this business, one has to dress. You understand?' Pursewarden said: 'Not with that horrible Syrian?' Money! He thought of it with a pang. Melissa looked at him with an air of amused resignation. She said in a low voice, but without emphasis, without shame: 'He has offered me 500 piastres to go home with him. I say no now, but later — I expect I shall have to.' She shrugged her shoulders.

Pursewarden swore quietly. 'No' he said. 'Come with me. I shall give you 1,000 if you need it.'

Her eyes grew round at the mention of so great a sum of money. He could see her telling it over coin by coin, fingering it, as if on an abacus, dividing it up into food, rent and clothes. 'I mean it' he said sharply. And added almost at once: 'Does Darley know?'

'Oh yes' she said quietly. 'You know, he is very good. Our life is a struggle, but he knows me. He *trusts* me. He never asks for any details. He knows that one day when we have enough money to go away I will stop all this. It is not important for us.' It sounded quaint, like some fearful blasphemy in the mouth of a child. Pursewarden laughed. 'Come now' he said suddenly; he was dying to possess her, to cradle and annihilate her with the disgusting kisses of a false compassion. 'Come now, Melissa darling' he said, but she winced and turned pale at the word and he saw that he had made a mistake, for any sexual transaction must be made strictly outside the bounds of her personal affection for Darley. He was disgusted by himself and yet rendered powerless to act otherwise; 'I tell you what' he said 'I shall give Darley a lot of money later this month — enough to take you away.' She did not seem to be listening. 'I'll get my coat' she said in a small mechanical voice 'and meet you in the hall.' She went to make her peace with the manager, and Pursewarden waited for her in an agony of impatience. He had hit upon the perfect way to cure these twinges of a puritan conscience which lurked on underneath the carefree surface of an amoral life.

Several weeks before, he had received through Nessim a short note from Leila, written in an exquisite hand, which read as follows:

Dear Mr. Pursewarden,

I am writing to ask you to perform an unusual service for me. A favourite uncle of mine has just died. He was a great lover of England and the English language which he knew almost better than his own; in his will he left instructions that an epitaph in English should be placed upon his tomb, in prose or verse, and if possible original. I am anxious to honour his memory in this most suitable way and to carry out his last wishes, and this is why I write: to ask you if you would consider such an undertaking, a common one for poets to perform in ancient China, but uncommon today. I would be happy to commission you in the sum of £500 for such a work.

The epitaph had been duly delivered and the money deposited in his bank, but to his surprise he found himself unable to touch it. Some queer superstition clung to him. He had never written poetry to order before, and never an epitaph. He smelt something unlucky almost about so large a sum. It had stayed there in his bank, untouched. Now he was suddenly visited by the conviction that he must give it away to Darley! It would, among other things, atone for his habitual neglect of his qualities, his clumsy awkwardness.

She walked back to the hotel with him, pressed as close as a scabbard to his thigh — the professional walk of a woman of the streets. They hardly spoke. The streets were empty.

The old dirty lift, its seats trimmed with dusty brown braid and its mirrors with rotting lace curtains, jerked them slowly upwards into the cobwebbed gloom. Soon, he thought to himself, he would drop through the trap-door feet first, arms pinioned by arms, lips by lips, until he felt the noose tighten about his throat and the stars explode behind his eyeballs. Surcease, forgetfulness, what else should one seek from an unknown woman's body?

Outside the door he kissed her slowly and deliberately, pressing into the soft cone of her pursed lips until their teeth met with a slight click and a jar. She neither responded to him nor withdrew, presenting her small expressionless face to him (sightless in the gloom) like a pane of frosted glass. There was no excitement in her, only a profound and consuming world-weariness. Her hands were cold. He took them in his own, and a tremendous melancholy beset him. Was he to be left once more alone with himself? At once he took refuge in a comic drunkenness which he well knew how to simulate, and which would erect a scaffolding of words about reality, to disorder and distemper it. *'Viens, viens!'* he cried sharply, reverting almost to the false jocularity he assumed with Darley, and now beginning to feel really rather drunk again. *'Le maître vous invite.'* Unsmiling, trustful as a lamb, she crossed the threshold into the room, looking about her. He groped for the bed-lamp. It did not work. He lit a candle which stood in a saucer on the night-table and turned to her with the dark shadows dancing in his nostrils and in the orbits of his eyes. They looked at one another while he conducted a furious mercenary patter to disguise his own unease. Then he stopped, for she was too tired to smile. Then, still unspeaking and unsmiling, she began to undress, item by item, dropping her clothes about her on the ragged carpet.

For a long moment he lay, simply exploring her slender body with its slanting ribs (structure of ferns) and the small, immature but firm breasts. Troubled by his silence, she sighed and said something inaudible. *'Laissez. Laissez parler les doigts . . . comme ça'* he whispered to silence her. He would have liked to say some simple and concrete word. In the silence he felt her beginning to struggle against the luxurious darkness and the growing powers of his lust, struggling to compartment her feelings, to keep them away from her proper life among the bare transactions of existence. 'A separate compartment' he thought; and 'Is it marked Death?' He was determined to exploit her weakness, the tenderness he felt ebbing and flowing in her veins, but his own moral strength ebbed now and guttered. He turned pale and lay with his bright feverish eyes turned to the shabby ceiling, seeing backwards into time. A clock struck coarsely somewhere, and the sound of the hours woke Melissa, driving away her lassitude, replacing it once more with anxiety, with a desire to be done, to be poured back into the sleep with which she struggled.

They played with each other, counterfeiting a desultory passion which mocked its own origins, could neither ignite nor extinguish itself. (You can lie with lips apart, legs apart, for numberless eternities, telling yourself it is something you have forgotten, it is on the tip of your tongue, the edge of your mind. For the life of you you cannot remember what it is, the name, the town, the day, the hour . . . the biological memory fails.) She gave a small sniff, as if she were crying, holding him in those pale, reflective fingers, tenderly as one might hold a fledgling fallen from the nest. Expressions of doubt and anxiety flitted across her face — as if she were herself guilty for the failure of the current, the broken communication. Then she groaned — and he knew that she was thinking of the money. Such a large sum! His improvidence could never be repeated by other men! And now her crude solicitude, her roughness began to make him angry.

'*Chéri.*' Their embraces were like the dry conjunction of wax-works, of figures modelled in *gesso* for some classical tomb. Her hands moved now charmlessly upon the barrel-vaulting of his ribs, his loins, his throat, his cheek; her fingers pressing here and there in darkness, finger of the blind seeking a secret panel in a wall, a forgotten switch which would slide back, illuminate another world, out of time. It was useless, it seemed. She gazed wildly around her. They lay under a nightmarish window full of sealight, against which a single curtain moved softly like a sail, reminding her of Darley's bed. The room was full of the smell of stale joss, decomposing manuscripts, and the apples he ate while he worked. The sheets were dirty.

As usual, at a level far below the probings of self-disgust or humiliation, he was writing, swiftly and smoothly in his clear mind. He was covering sheet upon sheet of paper. For so many years now he had taken to writing out his life in his own mind — the living and the writing were simultaneous. He transferred the moment bodily to paper as it was lived, warm from the oven, naked and exposed. . . .

'Now' she said angrily, determined not to lose the piastres which in her imagination she had already spent, already owed, 'now I will make you *La Veuve*' and he drew his breath in an exultant literary thrill to hear once more this wonderful slang expression stolen from the old nicknames of the French guillotine, with its fearful suggestion of teeth reflected in the concealed metaphor for the castration complex. *La Veuve!* The shark-infested seas of love which closed over the doomed sailor's head in a voiceless paralysis of the dream, the deep-sea dream which dragged one slowly downwards, dismembered and dismembering . . . until with a vulgar snick the steel fell, the clumsy thinking head ('use your loaf') smacked dully into the basket to spurt and wriggle like a fish. . . . '*Mon coeur*' he said hoarsely, '*mon ange*'; simply to taste the commonest of metaphors, hunting through them a tenderness lost, torn up, cast aside among the snows. '*Mon ange.*' A sea-widow into something rich and strange!

Suddenly she cried out in exasperation: 'Ah God! But what is it? You do not want to?' her voice ending almost in a wail. She took his soft rather womanish hand upon her knee and spread it out like a book, bending over it a despairing curious face. She moved the candle the better to study the lines, drawing up her thin legs. Her hair fell about her face. He touched the rosy light on her shoulder and said mockingly 'You tell fortunes.' But she did not look up. She answered shortly 'Everyone in the city tells fortunes.' They stayed like this, like a tableau, for a long moment. 'The *caput mortuum* of a love-scene' he thought to himself. Then Melissa sighed, as if with relief, and raised her head. 'I see now' she said quietly. 'You are all closed in, your heart is closed in, completely so.' She joined index finger to index finger, thumb to thumb in a gesture such as one might use to throttle a rabbit. Her eyes flashed with sympathy. 'Your life is dead, closed up. Not like Darley's. His is wide . . . very wide . . . open.' She spread her arms out for a moment before dropping them to her knee once more. She added with the tremendous unconscious force of veracity: '*He* can still love.' He felt as if he had been hit across the mouth. The candle flickered. 'Look again' he said angrily. 'Tell me some more.' But she completely missed the anger and the chagrin in his voice and bent once more to that enigmatic white hand. 'Shall I tell you everything?' she whispered, and for a minute his breath stopped. 'Yes' he said curtly. Melissa smiled a stranger, private smile.

'I am not very good' she said softly, 'I'll tell you only what I see.' Then she turned her candid eyes to him and added: 'I see death very close.' Pursewarden smiled grimly. 'Good' he said. Melissa drew her hair back to her ear with a finger and bent to his hand once more. 'Yes, very close. You will hear about it in a matter of hours. What rubbish!' She gave a little laugh. And then, to his complete surprise she went on to describe his sister. 'The blind one — *not* your wife.' She closed her eyes and spread her repellent arms out before her like a sleep-walker. 'Yes' said Pursewarden, 'that is her. That is my sister.' 'Your sister?' Melissa was astounded. She dropped his hand. She had never in playing this game made an accurate prediction before. Pursewarden told her gravely: 'She and I were lovers. We shall never be able to love other people.' And now, with the recital begun he suddenly found it easy to tell the rest, to tell her everything. He was completely master of himself and she gazed at him with pity and tenderness. Was it easy because they spoke French? In French the truth of passion stood up coldly and cruelly to the scrutiny of human experience. In his own curious phrase he had always qualified it as 'an unsniggerable language'. Or was it simply that the fugitive sympathy of Melissa made these events easy to speak of? She herself did not judge, everything was known, had been experienced. She nodded gravely as he spoke of his love and his deliberate abandoning of it, of his attempt at marriage, of its failure.

Between pity and admiration they kissed, but passionately now, united by the ties of recorded human experience, by the sensation of having shared something. 'I saw it in the hand' she said, 'in your hand.' She was somewhat frightened by the unwonted accuracy of her own powers. And he? He had always wanted someone to whom he could speak freely — *but it must be someone who could not fully understand!* The candle flickered. On the mirror with shaving soap he had written the mocking verses for Justine which began:

> *Oh Dreadful is the check!*
> *Intense the agony.*
> *When the ear begins to hear*
> *And the eye begins to see!*

He repeated them softly to himself, in the privacy of his own mind, as he thought of the dark composed features which he had seen here, by candle-light — the dark body seated in precisely the pose which Melissa now adopted, watching him with her chin on her knee, holding his hand with sympathy. And as he went on in his quiet voice to speak of his sister, of his perpetual quest for satisfactions which might be better than those he could remember, and which he had deliberately abandoned, other verses floated through his mind; the chaotic commentaries thrown up by his reading no less than by his experiences. Even as he saw once again the white marble face with its curling black hair thrown back about the nape of a slender neck, the ear-points, chin cleft by a dimple — a face which led him back always to those huge empty eye-sockets — he heard his inner mind repeating:

> *Amors par force vos demeine!*
> *Combien durra vostre folie?*
> *Trop avez mene ceste vie.*

He heard himself saying things which belonged elsewhere. With a bitter laugh, for example: 'The Anglo-Saxons invented the word "fornication" because they could not believe in the variety of love.' And Melissa, nodding so gravely and sympathetically, began to look more important — for here was a man at last confiding in her things she could not understand, treasures of that mysterious male world which oscillated always between sottish sentimentality and brutish violence! 'In my country almost all the really delicious things you can do to a woman are criminal offences, grounds for divorce.' She was frightened by his sharp, cracked laugh. Of a sudden he looked so ugly. Then he dropped his voice again and continued pressing her hand to his cheek softly, as one presses upon a bruise; and inside the inaudible commentary continued:

> *'What meaneth Heaven by these diverse laws?*
> *Eros, Agape* — *self-division's cause?'*

Locked up there in the enchanted castle, between the terrified kisses and intimacies which would never now be recovered, they had studied La Lioba! What madness! Would they ever dare to enter the lists against other lovers? *Jurata fornicatio* — those verses dribbling away in the mind; and her body, after Rudel, *'gras, delgat et gen'*. He sighed, brushing away the memories like a cobweb and saying to himself: 'Later, in search of an *askesis* he followed the desert fathers to Alexandria, to a place between two deserts, between the two breasts of Melissa. *O morosa delectatio.* And he buried his face there among the dunes, covered by her quick hair.'

Then he was silent, staring at her with his clear eyes, his trembling lips closing for the first time about endearments which were now alight, now truly passionate. She shivered suddenly, aware that she would not escape him now, that she would have to submit to him fully.

'Melissa' he said triumphantly.

They enjoyed each other now, wisely and tenderly, like friends long sought for and found among the commonplace crowds which thronged the echoing city. And here was a Melissa he had planned to find — eyes closed, warm open breathing mouth, torn from sleep with a kiss by the rosy candle-light. 'It is time to go.' But she pressed nearer and nearer to his body, whimpering with weariness. He gazed down fondly at her as she lay in the crook of his arm. 'And the rest of your prophecy?' he said gaily. 'Rubbish, all rubbish' she answered sleepily. 'I can sometimes learn a character from a hand — but the future! I am not so clever.'

The dawn was breaking behind the window. On a sudden impulse he went to the bathroom and turned on the bathwater. It flowed boiling hot, gushing into the bath with a swish of steam! How typical of the Mount Vulture Hotel, to have hot bathwater at such an hour and at no other. Excited as a schoolboy he called her. 'Melissa, come and soak the weariness out of your bones or I'll never get you back to your home.' He thought of ways and means of delivering the five hundred pounds to Darley in such a way as to disguise the source of the gift. He must never know that it came from a rival's epitaph on a dead Copt! 'Melissa' he called again, but she was asleep.

He picked her up bodily and carried her into the bathroom. Lying snugly in the warm bath, she woke up, uncurled from sleep like one of those marvellous Japanese paper-flowers which open in water. She paddled the warmth luxuriously over her shallow pectorals and glowed, her thighs beginning to turn pink. Pursewarden sat upon the *bidet* with one hand in the warm water and talked to her as she woke from sleep. 'You mustn't take too long' he said, 'or Darley will be angry.'

'Darley! Bah! He was out with Justine again last night.' She sat up and began to soap her breasts, breathing in the luxury of soap and water like someone tasting a rare wine. She pronounced her rival's name with small cringing loathing that seemed out of character. Pursewarden was surprised. 'Such people — the Hosnanis' she said with contempt. 'And poor Darley believes in them, in her. She is only using him. He is too good, too simple.'

'*Using him?*'

She turned on the shower and revelling in the clouds of steam nodded a small pinched-up face at him. 'I know all about *them*.'

'What do you know?'

He felt inside himself the sudden stirring of a discomfort so pronounced that it had no name. She was about to overturn his world as one inadvertently knocks over an inkpot or a goldfish-bowl. Smiling a loving smile all the time. Standing there in the clouds of steam like an angel emerging from heaven in some seventeenth-century engraving.

'What do you know?' he repeated.

Melissa examined the cavities in her teeth with a handmirror, her body still wet and glistening. 'I'll tell you. I used to be the mistress of a very important man, Cohen, very important and very rich.' There was something pathetic about such boasting. 'He was working with Nessim Hosnani and told me things. He also talked in his sleep. He is dead now. I think he was poisoned because he knew so much. He was helping to take arms into the Middle East, into Palestine, for Nessim Hosnani. Great quantities. He used to say "*Pour faire sauter les Anglais!*"' She ripped out the words vindictively, and all of a sudden, after a moment's thought added: 'He used to do this.' It was grotesque, her imitation of Cohen bunching up his fingers to kiss them and then waving them in a gesture as he said '*Tout à toi, John Bull!*' Her face crumpled and screwed up into an imitation of the dead man's malice.

'Dress now' said Pursewarden in a small voice. He went into the other room and stood for a moment gazing distractedly at the wall above the bookshelf. It was as if the whole city had crashed down about his ears.

'*That* is why I don't like the Hosnanis' cried Melissa from the bathroom in a new, brassy fishwife's voice. 'They secretly hate the British.'

'Dress' he called sharply, as if he were speaking to a horse. 'And get a move on.'

Suddenly chastened she dried herself and tiptoed out of the bathroom saying 'I am ready immediately.' Pursewarden stood quite still staring at the wall with a fixed, dazed expression. He might have fallen there from some other planet. He was so still that his body might have been a statue cast in some heavy metal. Melissa shot small glances at him as she dressed. 'What is it?' she said. He did not answer. He was thinking furiously.

When she was dressed he took her arm and together they walked in silence down the staircase and into the street. The dawn was beginning to break. There were still street-lamps alight and they still cast shadows. She looked at his face from time to time, but it was expressionless. Punctually as they approached each light their shadows lengthened, grew narrower and more contorted, only to disappear into the half-light before renewing their shape. Purse-warden walked slowly, with a tired, deliberate trudge, still holding her arm. In each of these elongated capering shadows he saw now quite clearly the silhouette of the defeated Maskelyne.

At the corner by the square he stopped and with the same abstracted expression on his face said: '*Tiens!* I forgot. Here is the thousand I promised you.'

He kissed her upon the cheek and turned back towards the hotel without a word.

★　　★　　★　　★　　★

IX

Mountolive was away on an official tour of the cotton-ginning plants in the Delta when the news was phoned through to him by Telford. Between incredulity and shock, he could hardly believe his ears. Telford spoke self-importantly in the curious slushy voice which his ill-fitting dentures conferred upon him; death was a matter of some importance in his trade. But the death of an enemy! He had to work hard to keep his tone sombre, grave, sympathetic, to keep the self-congratulation out of it. He spoke like a county coroner. 'I thought you'd like to know, sir, so I took the liberty of interrupting your visit. Nimrod Pasha phoned me in the middle of the night and I went along. The police had already sealed up the place for the Parquet inquiry; Dr Balthazar was there. I had a look around while he issued the certificate of death. I was allowed to bring away a lot of personal papers belonging to the . . . the deceased. Nothing of much interest. Manuscript of a novel. The whole business came as a complete surprise. He had been drinking very heavily — as usual, I'm afraid. Yes.'

'But . . .' said Mountolive feebly, the rage and incredulity mixing in his mind like oil and water. 'What on earth. . . .' His legs felt weak. He drew up a chair and sat down at the telephone crying peevishly: 'Yes, yes, Telford — go on. Tell me what you can.'

Telford cleared his throat, aware of the interest his news was creating, and tried to marshal the facts in his fuddled brain. 'Well, sir, we have traced his movements. He came up here, very unshaven and haggard (Errol tells me) and asked for you. But you had just left. Your secretary says that he sat down at your desk and wrote something — it took him some time — which he said was to be delivered to you personally. He insisted on her franking it "Secret" and sealing it up with wax. It is in your safe now. Then he appears to have gone off on a . . . well, a binge. He spent all day at a tavern on the seashore near Montaza which he often visited. It's just a shack down by the sea — a few timbers with a palm-leaf roof, run by a Greek. He spent the whole day there writing and drinking. He drank quite a lot of *zibib* according to the proprietor. He had a table set right down by the sea-shore in the sand. It was windy and the man suggested he would be better off in the shelter. But no. He sat there by the sea. In the late afternoon he ate a sandwich and took a tram back to town. He called on me.'

'Good: well.'

Telford hesitated and gasped. 'He came to the office. I must say that although unshaven he seemed in very good spirits. He made a few jokes. But he asked me for a cyanide tablet — you know the kind. I won't say any more. This line isn't really secure. You will understand, sir.'

'Yes, yes' cried Mountolive. 'Go on, man.'

Reassured Telford continued breathlessly: 'He said he wanted to poison a sick dog. It seemed reasonable enough, so I gave him one. That is probably what he used according to Dr Balthazar. I hope you don't feel, sir, that I was in any way. . . .'

Mountolive felt nothing except a mounting indignation that anyone in his mission should confer such annoyance by a public act so flagrant! No, this was silly. 'It is stupid' he whispered to himself. But he could not help feeling that Pursewarden had been guilty of something. Damn it, it was inconsiderate and underbred — as well as being mysterious. Kenilworth's face floated before him for a moment. He joggled the receiver to get a clear contact, and shouted: 'But what does it all mean?'

'I don't know' said Telford, helplessly. 'It's rather mysterious.'

A pale Mountolive turned and made some muttered apologies to the little group of pashas who stood about the telephone in that dreary outhouse. Immediately they spread self-deprecating hands like a flock of doves taking flight. There was no inconvenience. An Ambassador was expected to be entrained in great events. They could wait.

'Telford' said Mountolive, sharply and angrily.

'Yes, sir.'

'Tell me what else you know.'

Telford cleared his throat and went on in his slushy voice:

'Well, there isn't anything of exceptional importance from my point of view. The last person to see him alive was that man Darley, the schoolteacher. You probably don't know him, sir. Well, he met him on the way back to the hotel. He invited Darley in for a drink and they stayed talking for some considerable time and drinking gin. In the hotel. The deceased said nothing of any special interest — and certainly nothing to suggest that he was planning to take his own life. On the contrary, he said he was going to take the night train to Gaza for a holiday. He showed

Darley the proofs of his latest novel, all wrapped up and addressed, and a mackintosh full of things he might need for the journey — pyjamas, toothpaste. What made him change his mind? I don't know, sir, but the answer may be in your safe. That is why I rang you.'

'I see' said Mountolive. It was strange, but already he was beginning to get used to the idea of Pursewarden's disappearance from the scene. The shock was abating, diminishing: only the mystery remained. Telford still spluttered on the line. 'Yes' he said, recovering mastery of himself. 'Yes.'

It was only a matter of moments before Mountolive recovered his demure official pose and reoriented himself to take a benign interest in the mills and their thumping machinery. He worked hard not to seem too abstracted and to seem suitably impressed by what was shown to him. He tried too to analyse the absurdity of his anger against Pursewarden having committed an act which seemed . . . a gross solecism! How absurd. Yet, as an act, it was somehow typical because so inconsiderate: perhaps he should have anticipated it? Profound depression alternated with his feelings of anger.

He motored back in haste, full of an urgent expectancy, an unease. It was almost as if he were going to take Pursewarden to task, demand an explanation of him, administer a well-earned reproof. He arrived to find that the Chancery was just closing, though the industrious Errol was still busy upon State papers in his office. Everyone down to the cipher clerks seemed to be afflicted by the air of gravid depression which sudden death always confers upon the uncomfortably living. He deliberately forced himself to walk slowly, talk slowly, not to hurry. Haste, like emotion, was always deplorable because it suggested that impulse or feeling was master where only reason should rule. His secretary had already left but he obtained the keys to his safe from Archives and sedately walked up the two short flights to his office. Heartbeats are mercifully inaudible to anyone but oneself.

The dead man's 'effects' (the poetry of causality could not be better expressed than by the word) were stacked on his desk, looking curiously disembodied. A bundle of papers and manuscript, a parcel addressed to a publisher, a mackintosh and various odds and ends conscripted by the painstaking Telford in the interests of truth (though they had little beauty for Mountolive). He got a tremendous start when he saw Pursewarden's bloodless features staring up at him from his blotter — a death-mask in plaster of Paris with a note from Balthazar saying 'I took the liberty of making an impression of the face after death. I trust this will seem sensible.' Pursewarden's face! From some angles death can look like a fit of the sulks. Mountolive touched the effigy with reluctance, superstitiously, moving it this way and that. His flesh crept with a small sense of loathing; he realized suddenly that he was afraid of death.

Then to the safe with its envelope whose clumsy seals he cracked with a trembling thumb as he sat at his desk. Here at least he should find some sort of rational exegesis for this gross default of good manners! He drew a deep breath.

My dear David,

I have torn up half a dozen other attempts to explain this in detail. I found I was only making literature. There is quite enough about. My decision has to do with life. Paradox! I am terribly sorry, old man.

Quite by accident, in an unexpected quarter, I stumbled upon something which told me that Maskelyne's theories about Nessim were right, mine wrong. I do not give you my sources, and will not. But I now realize Nessim is smuggling arms into Palestine and has been for some time. He is obviously the unknown source, deeply implicated in the operations which were described in Paper Seven — you will remember. (Secret Mandate File 341. Intelligence.)

But I simply am not equal to facing the simpler moral implications raised by this discovery. I know what has to be done about it. But the man happens to be my friend. Therefore . . . a *quietus*. (This will solve other deeper problems too.) Ach! what a boring world we have created around us. The slime of plot and counter-plot. I have just recognized that it is not my world at all. (I can hear you swearing as you read.)

I feel in a way a cad to shelve my own responsibilities like this, and yet, in truth, I know that they are not really mine, never have been mine. *But they are yours!* And jolly bitter you will find them. But . . . you are of the career . . . and you must act where I cannot bring myself to!

I know I am wanting in a sense of duty, but I have let Nessim know obliquely that his game has been spotted and the information passed on. Of course, in this vague form you could also be right in suppressing it altogether, forgetting it. I don't envy you your temptations. Mine, however, not to reason why. I'm tired, my dear chap; sick unto death, as the living say.

And so . . .

Will you give my sister my love and say that my thoughts were with her? Thank you.

Affectionately yours,

L. P.

Mountolive was aghast. He felt himself turning pale as he read. Then he sat for a long time staring at the expression on the face of the death-mask — the characteristic air of solitary impertinence which Pursewarden's profile always wore in repose; and still obstinately struggling with the absurd sense of diplomatic outrage which played about his mind, flickering like stabs of sheet-lightning.

'It is folly!' he cried aloud with vexation, as he banged the desk with the flat of his hand. 'Utter folly! Nobody kills himself for an official reason!' He cursed the stupidity of the words as he uttered them. For the first time complete confusion overtook his mind.

In order to calm it he forced himself to read Telford's typed report slowly and carefully, spelling out the words to himself with moving lips, as if it were an exercise. It was an account of Pursewarden's movements during the twenty-four hours before his death with depositions by the various people who had seen him. Some of the reports were interesting, notably that of Balthazar who had seen him during the morning in the Café Al Aktar where Pursewarden was drinking *arak* and eating a *croissant*. He had apparently received a letter from his sister that morning and was reading it with an air of grave preoccupation. He put it in his pocket abruptly when Balthazar arrived. He was extremely unshaven and haggard. There seemed little enough of interest in the conversation which ensued save for one remark (probably a jest?) which stayed in Balthazar's memory. Pursewarden had been dancing with Melissa the evening before and said something about her being a desirable person to marry. ('This must have been a joke' added Balthazar.) He also said that he had started another book 'all about Love'. Mountolive sighed as he slowly ran his eye down the typed page. Love! Then came an odd thing. He had bought a printed Will form and filled it in, making his sister his literary executor, and bequeathing five hundred pounds to the schoolteacher Darley and his mistress. This, for some reason, he had antedated by a couple of months — perhaps he forgot the date? He had asked two cipher clerks to witness it.

The letter from his sister was there also, but Telford had tactfully put it into a separate envelope and sealed it. Mountolive read it, shaking his bewildered head, and then thrust it into his pocket shamefacedly. He licked his lips and frowned heavily at the wall. Liza!

Errol put his head timidly round the door and was shocked to surprise tears upon the cheek of his Chief. He ducked back tactfully and retreated hastily to his office, deeply shaken by a sense of diplomatic inappropriateness somewhat similar to the feelings which Mountolive himself had encountered when Telford telephoned him. Errol sat at his desk with attentive nervousness thinking: 'A good diplomat should never show feeling.' Then he lit a cigarette with sombre deliberation. For the first time he realized that his Ambassador had feet of clay. This increased his sense of self-respect somewhat. Mountolive was, after all, only a man. . . . Nevertheless, the experience had been disorienting.

Upstairs Mountolive too had lighted a cigarette in order to calm his nerves. The accent of his apprehension was slowly transferring itself from the bare *act* of Pursewarden (this inconvenient plunge into anonymity) — was transferring itself to the central meaning of the act — to the tidings it brought with it. Nessim! And here he felt his own soul shrink and contract and a deeper, more inarticulate anger beset him. He had trusted Nessim! ('Why?' said the inner voice. 'There was no need to do so.') And then, by this wicked somersault, Pursewarden had, in effect, transferred the whole weight of the moral problem to Mountolive's own shoulders. He had started up the hornets' nest: the old conflict between duty, reason and personal affection which every political man knows is his cross, the central weakness of his life! What a swine, he thought (almost admiringly), Pursewarden had been to transfer it all so easily — the enticing *ease* of such a decision: withdrawal! He added sadly: 'I trusted Nessim because of Leila!' Vexation upon vexation. He smoked and stared now, seeing in the dead white plaster face (which the loving hands of Clea had printed from Balthazar's clumsy negative) the warm living face of Leila's son: the dark abstract features from a Ravenna fresco! The face of his friend. And then, his very thoughts uttered themselves in whispers: 'Perhaps after all Leila is at the bottom of everything.'

('Diplomats have no real friends' Grishkin had said bitterly, trying to wound him, to rouse him. 'They use everyone.' He had used, she was implying, her body and her beauty: and now that she was pregnant. . . .)

He exhaled slowly and deeply, invigorated by the nicotine-laden oxygen which gave his nerves time to settle, his brain time to clear. As the mist lifted he discerned something like a new landscape opening before him; for here was something which could not help but alter all the dispositions of chance and friendship, alter every date on the affectionate calendar his mind had compiled about his stay in Egypt: the tennis and swimming and riding. Even these simple motions of joining with the ordinary world of social habit and pleasure, of relieving the *taedium vitae* of his isolation, were all infected by the new knowledge. Moreover, what was to be done with the information which Pursewarden had so unceremoniously thrust into his lap? It must be of course reported. Here he was able to pause. *Must* it be reported? The data in the letter lacked any shred of supporting evidence — except perhaps the overwhelming evidence of a death which. . . . He lit a cigarette and whispered the words: 'While the balance of his mind was disturbed.' That at least was worth a grim smile! After all, the suicide of a political officer was not such an uncommon event; there had been that youth Greaves, in love with a cabaret-girl in Russia. . . . Somehow he still felt aggrieved at so malicious a betrayal of his friendship for the writer.

Very well. Suppose he simply burnt the letter, disposing with the weight of moral onus it bore? It could be done quite simply, in his own grate, with the aid of a safety-match. He could continue to behave as if no such revelation had ever been made — except for the fact that Nessim knew it had! No, he was trapped.

And here his sense of duty, like ill-fitting shoes, began to pinch him at every step. He thought of Justine and Nessim dancing together, silently, blindly, their dark faces turned away from each other, eyes half-closed. They had attained a new dimension in his view of them already — the unsentimental projection of figures in a primitive fresco. Presumably they also struggled with a sense of duty and responsibility — to whom? 'To themselves, perhaps' he whispered sadly, shaking his head. He would never be able to meet Nessim eye to eye again.

It suddenly dawned on him. Up to now their personal relationship had been forced from any prejudicial cast by Nessim's tact

— *and Pursewarden's existence.* The writer, in supplying the official link, had freed them in the personal lives. Never had the two men been forced to discuss anything remotely connected with official matters. Now they could not meet upon this happy ground. In this context too Pursewarden had traduced his freedom. As for Leila, perhaps here lay the key to her enigmatic silence, her inability to meet him face to face.

Sighing, he rang for Errol. 'You'd better glance at this' he said. His Head of Chancery sat himself down and began to read the document greedily. He nodded slowly from time to time. Mountolive cleared his throat: 'It seems pretty incoherent to me' he said, despising himself for so trying to cast a doubt upon the clear words, to influence Errol in a judgement which, in his own secret mind, he had already made. Errol read it twice slowly, and handed it back across the desk. 'It seems pretty extraordinary' he said tentatively, respectfully. It was not his place to offer evaluations of the message. They must by rights come from his Chief. 'It all seems a bit out of proportion' he added helpfully, feeling his way.

Mountolive said sombrely: 'I'm afraid it is typical of Pursewarden. It makes me sorry that I never took up your original recommendations about him. I was wrong, it seems, and you were right about his suitability.'

Errol's eye glinted with modest triumph. He said nothing, however, as he stared at Mountolive. 'Of course,' said the latter, 'as you well know, Hosnani has been suspect for some time.'

'I know, sir.'

'But there is no *evidence* here to support what he says.' He tapped the letter irritably twice. Errol sat back and breathed through his nose. 'I don't know' he said vaguely. 'It sounds pretty conclusive to me.'

'I don't think' said Mountolive 'it would support a paper. Of course we'll report it to London as it stands. But I'm inclined not to give it to the Parquet to help them with their inquest. What do you say?'

Errol cradled his knees. A slow smile of cunning crept around his mouth. 'It might be the best way of getting it to the Egyptians' he said softly, 'and they might choose to act on it. Of course, it would obviate the diplomatic pressure we might have to bring if . . . later on, the whole thing came out in a more concrete form. I know Hosnani was a friend of yours, sir.'

Mountolive felt himself colouring slightly. 'In matters of business, a diplomat has no friends' he said stiffly, feeling that he spoke in the very accents of Pontius Pilate.

'Quite, sir.' Errol gazed at him admiringly.

'Once Hosnani's guilt is established we shall have to act. But without supporting evidence we should find ourselves in a weak position. With Memlik Pasha — you know he isn't very pro-British . . . I'm thinking. . . .'

'Yes, sir?'

Mountolive waited, drinking the air like a wild animal, scenting that Errol was beginning to approve his judgement. They sat silently in the dusk for a while, thinking. Then, with a histrionic snap, the Ambassador switched on the desk-light and said decisively: 'If you agree, we'll keep this out of Egyptian hands until we are better documented. London must have it. Classified of course. But not private persons, even next-of-kin. By the way, are you capable of undertaking the next-of-kin correspondence? I leave it to you to make up something.' He felt a pang as he saw Liza Pursewarden's face rise up before him.

'Yes. I have his file here. There is only a sister at the Imperial Institute for the Blind, I think, apart from his wife.' Errol fussily consulted a green folder, but Mountolive said 'Yes, yes. I know her.' Errol stood up.

Mountolive added: 'And I think in all fairness we should copy to Maskelyne in Jerusalem, don't you?'

'Most certainly, sir.'

'And for the moment keep our own counsel?'

'Yes, sir.'

'Thank you very much' said Mountolive with unusual warmth. He felt all of a sudden very old and frail. Indeed he felt so weak that he doubted if his limbs could carry him downstairs to the Residence. 'That is all at present.' Errol took his leave, closing the door behind him with the gravity of a mute.

Mountolive telephoned to the buttery and ordered himself a glass of beef-tea and biscuits. He ate and drank ravenously, staring the while at the white mask and the manuscript of a novel. He felt both a deep disgust and a sense of enormous bereavement — he could not tell which lay uppermost. Unwittingly, too, Pursewarden had, he reflected, separated him forever from Leila. Yes, that also, and perhaps forever.

That night, however, he made his witty prepared speech

(written by Errol) to the Alexandrian Chamber of Commerce, delighting the assembled bankers by his fluent French. The clapping swelled and expanded in the august banquet room of the Mohammed Ali Club. Nessim, seated at the opposite end of the long table, undertook the response with gravity and a calm address. Once or twice during the dinner Mountolive felt the dark eyes of his friend seeking his own, interrogating them, but he evaded them. A chasm now yawned between them which neither would know how to bridge. After dinner, he met Nessim briefly in the hall as he was putting on his coat. He suddenly felt the almost irresistible desire to refer to Pursewarden's death. The subject obtruded itself so starkly, stuck up jaggedly into the air between them. It shamed him as a physical deformity might; as if his handsome smile were disfigured by a missing front tooth. He said nothing and neither did Nessim. Nothing of what was going on beneath the surface showed in the elastic and capable manner of the two tall men who stood smoking by the front door, waiting for the car to arrive. But a new watchful, obdurate knowledge had been born between them. How strange that a few words scribbled on a piece of paper should make them enemies!

Then leaning back in his beflagged car, drawing softly on an excellent cigar, Mountolive felt his innermost soul become as dusty, as airless as an Egyptian tomb. It was strange too that side by side with these deeper preoccupations the shallower should coexist; he was delighted by the extent of his success in captivating the bankers! He had been undeniably brilliant. Discreetly circulated copies of his speech would, he knew, be printed verbatim in tomorrow's papers, illustrated by new photographs of himself. The Corps would be envious as usual. Why had nobody thought of making a public statement about the Gold Standard in this oblique fashion? He tried to keep his mind effervescent, solidly anchored to this level of self-congratulation, but it was useless. The Embassy would soon be moving back to its winter quarters. He had not seen Leila. Would he ever see her again?

Somewhere inside himself a barrier had collapsed, a dam had been broached. He had engaged upon a new conflict with himself which gave a new tautness to his features, a new purposeful rhythm to his walk.

That night he was visited by an excruciating attack of the earache with which he always celebrated his return home. This was the first time he had ever been attacked while he was outside the stockade of his mother's security, and the attack alarmed him. He tried ineffectually to doctor himself with the homely specific she always used, but he heated the salad oil too much by mistake and burnt himself severely in the process. He spent three restless days in bed after this incident, reading detective stories and pausing for long moments to stare at the whitewashed wall. It at least obviated his attendance at Pursewarden's cremation — he would have been sure to meet Nessim there. Among the many messages and presents which began to flow in when the news of his indisposition became known, was a splendid bunch of flowers from Nessim and Justine, wishing him a speedy recovery. As Alexandrians and friends, they could hardly do less!

He pondered deeply upon them during those long sleepless days and nights and for the first time he saw them, in the light of this new knowledge, as enigmas. They were puzzles now, and even their private moral relationship haunted him with a sense of something he had never properly understood, never clearly evaluated. Somehow his friendship for them had prevented him from thinking of them as people who might, like himself, be living on several different levels at once. As conspirators, as lovers — what was the key to the enigma? He could not guess.

But perhaps the clues that he sought lay further back in the past — further than either he or Pursewarden could see from a vantage-point in the present time.

There were many facts about Justine and Nessim which had not come to his knowledge — some of them critical for an understanding of their case. But in order to include them it is necessary once more to retrace our steps briefly to the period immediately before their marriage.

    * * * * *

X

The blue Alexandrian dusk was not yet fully upon them. "But do you . . . how shall one say it? . . . Do you really *care* for her, Nessim? I know of course how you have been haunting her; and she knows what is in your mind.'

Clea's golden head against the window remained steady, her gaze was fixed upon the chalk drawing she was doing. It was nearly finished; a few more of those swift, flowing strokes and she could release her subject. Nessim had put on a striped pullover to model for her. He lay upon her uncomfortable little sofa holding a guitar which he could not play, and frowning. 'How do you spell love in Alexandria?' he said at last, softly. 'That is the question. Sleeplessness, loneliness, *bonheur*, *chagrin* — I do not want to harm or annoy her, Clea. But I feel that somehow, somewhere, she must need me as I need her. Speak, Clea.' He knew he was lying. Clea did not.

She shook her head doubtfully, still with her attention on the paper, and then shrugged her shoulders. 'Loving you both as I do, who could wish for anything better? And I *have* spoken to her, as you asked me, tried to provoke her, probe her. It seems hopeless.' Was this strictly true, she asked herself? She had too great a tendency to believe what people said.

'False pride?' he said sharply.

'She laughs hopelessly and' Clea imitated a gesture of hopelessness 'like that! I think she feels that she has had all the clothes stripped off her back in the street by that book *Moeurs*. She thinks herself no longer able to bring anyone peace of mind! Or so she says.'

'Who asks for that?'

'She thinks you would. Then of course, there is your social position. And then she is, after all, a Jew. Put yourself in her place.' Clea was silent for a moment. Then she added in the same abstract tone: 'If she needs you at all it is to use your fortune to help her search for the child. And she is too proud to do that. But . . . you have read *Moeurs*. Why repeat myself?'

'I have never read *Moeurs*' he said hotly, 'and she knows that I never will. I have told her that. Oh, Clea dear!' He sighed. This was another lie.

Clea paused, smiling, to consider his dark face. Then she

continued, rubbing at the corner of the drawing with her thumb as she said: '*Chevalier sans peur*', etc. That is like you, Nessim. But is it wise to idealize us women so? You are a bit of a baby still, for an Alexandrian.'

'I don't idealize; I know exactly how sad, mad or bad she is. Who does not? Her past and her present . . . they are known to everyone. It is just that I feel she would match perfectly my own. . . .'

'Your own what?'

'*Aridity*' he said surprisingly, rolling over, smiling and frowning at the same time. 'Yes, I sometimes think I shall never be able to fall in love properly until after my mother dies — and she is still comparatively young. Speak, Clea!'

The blonde head shook slowly. Clea took a puff from the cigarette burning in the ashtray beside the easel and bent once more to the work in hand. 'Well' said Nessim, 'I shall see her myself this evening and make a serious attempt to make her understand.'

'You do not say "make her love"!'

'How could I?'

'If she *cannot* love, it would be dishonourable to pretend.'

'I do not know whether I can yet either; we are both *âmes veuves* in a queer way, don't you see?'

'Oh, la, la!' said Clea, doubtfully but still smiling.

'Love may be for a time *incognito* with us' he said, frowning at the wall and setting his face. 'But it is there. I must try to make her see.' He bit his lip. 'Do I really present such an enigma?' He really meant 'Do I succeed in deluding you?'

'Now you've moved' she said reproachfully; and then after a moment went on quietly: 'Yes. It is an enigma. Your passion sounds so *voulue*. A *besoin d'aimer* without a *besoin d'être aimé?* Damn!' He had moved again. She stopped in vexation and was about to reprove him when she caught sight of the clock on the mantelpiece. 'It's time to go' she said. 'You must not keep her waiting.'

'Good' he said sharply, and rising, stripped off the pullover and donned his own well-cut coat, groping in the pocket for the keys of the car as he turned. Then, remembering, he brushed his dark hair back swiftly, impatiently, in the mirror, trying suddenly to imagine how he must look to Justine. 'I wish I could say exactly what I mean. Do you not believe in love-contracts for those whose souls aren't yet up to loving? A *tendresse* against an *amour-passion*, Clea? If she had parents I would have bought her from them unhesitatingly. If she had been thirteen she would have had nothing to say or feel, eh?'

'Thirteen!' said Clea in disgust; she shuddered and pulled his coat down at the back for him. 'Perhaps' he went on ironically, 'unhappiness is a *diktat* for me. . . . What do you think?'

'But then you would believe in *passion*. You don't.'

'I do . . . but. . . .'

He gave his charming smile and made a tender hopeless gesture in the air, part resignation, part anger. 'Ah, you are no use' he said. 'We are all waiting for an education of sorts.'

'Go' said Clea, 'I'm sick of the subject. Kiss me first.'

The two friends embraced and she whispered: 'Good luck' while Nessim said between his teeth 'I must stop this childish interrogation of you. It is absurd. I must do something decisive about her myself.' He banged a doubled fist into the palm of his hand, and she was surprised at such unusual vehemence in one so reserved. 'Well' she said, with surprise opening her blue eyes, 'this is new!' They both laughed.

He pressed her elbow and turning ran lightly down the darkening staircase to the street. The great car responded to his feather-deftness of touch on the controls; it bounded crying its klaxon-warnings, down Saad Zaghloul and across the tramlines to roll down the slope towards the sea. He was talking to himself softly and rapidly in Arabic. In the gaunt lounge of the Cecil Hotel she would perhaps be waiting, gloved hands folded on her handbag, staring out through the windows upon which the sea crawled and sprawled, climbing and subsiding, across the screen of palms in the little municipal square which flapped and creaked like loose sails.

As he turned the corner, a procession was setting out raggedly for the upper town, its brilliant banners pelted now by a small rain mixed with spray from the harbour; everything flapped confusedly. Chanting and the noise of triangles sounded tentatively on the air. With an expression of annoyance he abandoned the car, locked it, and looked anxiously at his watch, ran the last hundred yards to the circular glass doors which would admit him upon the mouldering silence of the great lounge. He entered breathless but very much aware of himself. This siege of Justine had been going on for months now. How would it end — with victory or defeat?

He remembered Clea saying: 'Such creatures are not human beings at all, I think. If they live, it is only inasmuch as they represent themselves in human form. But then, anyone possessed by a single ruling passion presents the same picture. For most of us, life is a *hobby*. But she seems like a tense and exhaustive pictorial representation of nature at its most superficial, its most powerful. She is possessed — and the possessed can neither learn nor be taught. It doesn't make her less lovely for all that it is death-propelled; but my dear Nessim — from what angle are you to accept her?'

He did not as yet know; they were sparring still, talking in different languages. This might go on forever, he thought despairingly.

They had met more than once, formally, almost like business partners to discuss the matter of this marriage with the detachment of Alexandrian brókers planning a cotton merger. But this is the way of the city.

With a gesture which he himself thought of as characteristic he had offered her a large sum of money saying: 'Lest an inequality of fortune may make your decision difficult, I propose to make you a birthday present which will enable you to think of yourself as a wholly independent person — simply as a woman, Justine. This hateful stuff which creeps into everyone's thoughts in the city, poisoning everything! Let us be free of it before deciding anything.'

But this had not answered; or rather had provoked only the insulting, uncomprehending question: 'Is it that you really want to sleep with me? You may. Oh, I would do anything for you, Nessim.' This disgusted and angered him. He had lost himself. There seemed no way forward along this line. Then suddenly, after a long moment of thought, he saw the truth like a flashing light. He whispered to himself with surprise: 'But that is why I am not understood; I am not being really honest.' He recognized that though he might have initially been swayed by his passion, he could think of no way to stake a claim on her attention, except, first, by the gift of money (ostensibly to 'free' her but in fact only to try and bind her to him) — and then, as his desperation increased, he realized that there was nothing to be done except to place himself entirely at her mercy. In one sense it was madness — but he could think of no other way to create in her the sense of obligation on which every other tie could be built. In this way a child may sometimes endanger itself in order to canvass a mother's love and attention which it feels is denied to it.

'Look' he said in a new voice, full of new vibrations, and now he had turned very pale. 'I want to be frank. I have no interest in *real life.*' His lips trembled with his voice. 'I am visualizing a relationship far closer in a way than anything passion could invent — a bond of a common belief.' She wondered for a moment whether he had some strange new religion, whether this was what was meant. She waited with interest, amused yet disturbed to see how deeply moved he was. 'I wish to make you a confidence now which, if betrayed, might mean irreparable harm to myself and my family; and indeed to the cause I am serving. I wish to put myself utterly in your power. Let us suppose we are both dead to love . . . I want to ask you to become part of a dangerous. . . .'

The strange thing was that as he began to talk thus, about what was nearest to his thoughts, she began to *care*, to really notice him as a man for the first time. For the first time he struck a responsive chord in her by a confession which was paradoxically very far from a confession of the heart. To her surprise, to her chagrin and to her delight, she realized that she was not being asked merely to share his bed — but his whole life, the monomania upon which it was built. Normally, it is only the artist who can offer this strange and selfless contract — but it is one which no woman worth the name can ever refuse. He was asking, not for her hand in marriage (here his lies had created the misunderstanding) but for her partnership in allegiance to his ruling *daimon*. It was in the strictest sense, the only meaning he could put upon the word 'love'. Slowly and quietly he began, passionately collecting his senses now that he had decided to tell her, marshalling his words, husbanding them. 'You know, we all know, that our days are numbered since the French and the British have lost control in the Middle East. We, the foreign communities, with all we have built up, are being gradually engulfed by the Arab tide, the Moslem tide. Some of us are trying to work against it; Armenians, Copts, Jews, and Greeks here in Egypt, while others elsewhere are organizing themselves. Much of this work I have undertaken here. . . . To defend ourselves, that is all, defend our lives, defend the right to belong here only. You know this, everyone knows it. But to those who see a little further into history. . . .'

Here he smiled crookedly — an ugly smile with a trace of complacency in it. 'Those who see further know this to be but a shadow-play; we will never maintain our place in this world except it be by virtue of a nation strong and civilized enough to dominate the whole area. The day of France and England is over — much as we love them. Who, then, can take their place?' He drew a deep breath and paused, then he squeezed his hands together between his knees, as if he were squeezing out the unuttered thought, slowly, luxuriously from a sponge.

He went on in a whisper: 'There is only one nation which can determine the future of everything in the Middle East. Everything — and by a paradox, even the standard of living of the miserable Moslems themselves depends upon it, its power and resources. Have you understood me, Justine? Must I utter its name? Perhaps you are not interested in these things?' He gave her a glittering smile. Their eyes met. They sat staring at each other in the way that only those who are passionately in love can stare. He had never seen her so pale, so alert, with all her intelligence suddenly mobilized in her looks. 'Must I say it?' he said, more sharply; and suddenly expelling her breath in a long sigh she shook her head and whispered the single word.

'Palestine.'

There was a long silence during which he looked at her with a triumphant exultation. 'I was not wrong' he said at last, and she suddenly knew what he meant: that his long-formulated judgement of her had not been at fault. 'Yes, Justine, Palestine. If only the Jews can win their freedom, we can all be at ease. It is the only hope for us . . . the dispossessed *foreigners*.' He uttered the word with a slight twist of bitterness. They both slowly lit cigarettes now with shaking fingers and blew the smoke out towards each other, enwrapped by a new atmosphere of peace, of understanding. 'The whole of our fortune has gone into the struggle which is about to break out there' he said under his breath. 'On that depends everything. Here, of course, we are doing other things which I will explain to you. The British and French help us, they see no harm. I am sorry for them. Their condition is pitiable because they have no longer the will to fight or even to think.' His contempt was ferocious, yet full of controlled pity. 'But with the Jews — there is something *young* there: the cockpit of Europe in these rotten marshes of a dying race.' He paused and suddenly said in a sharp, twanging tone: 'Justine.' Slowly and thoughtfully, at the same moment they put out their hands to each other. Their cold fingers locked and squeezed hard. On the faces of both there was expressed an exultant determination of purpose, almost of terror!

His image had suddenly been metamorphosed. It was now lit with a new, a rather terrifying grandeur. As she smoked and watched him, she saw someone different in his place — an adventurer, a corsair, dealing with the lives and deaths of men; his power too, the power of his money, gave a sort of tragic backcloth to the design. She realized now that he was not seeing her — the Justine thrown back by polished mirrors, or engraved in expensive clothes and fards — but something even closer than the chambermate of a passional life.

This was a Faustian compact he was offering her. There was something more surprising: for the first time she felt desire stir within her, in the loins of that discarded, pre-empted body which she regarded only as a pleasure-seeker, a mirror-reference to reality. There came over her an unexpected lust to sleep with him — no, with his plans, his dreams, his obsessions, his money, his death! It was as if she had only now understood the nature of the love he was offering her; it was his all, his only treasure, this pitiable political design so long and so tormentingly matured in his heart that it had forced out every other impulse or wish. She felt suddenly as if her feelings had become caught up in some great cobweb, imprisoned by laws which lay beneath the level of her conscious will, her desires, the self-destructive flux and reflux of her human personality. Their fingers were still locked, like a chord in music, drawing nourishment from the strength transmitted by their bodies. Just to hear him say: 'Now my life is in your keeping' set her brain on fire, and her heart began to beat heavily in her breast. 'I must go now' she said, with a new terror — one that she had never experienced before — 'I really must go.' She felt unsteady and faint, touched as she was by the coaxings of a power stronger than any physical attraction could be. 'Thank God' he said under his breath, and again 'Oh Thank God.' Everything was decided at last.

But his own relief was mixed with terror. How had he managed at last to turn the key in the lock? By sacrificing to the truth, by putting himself at her mercy. His unwisdom had been the only course left open. He had been forced to take it. Subconsciously he knew too, that the oriental woman is not a sensualist in the European sense; there is nothing mawkish in her constitution. Her true obsessions are power, politics and possessions — however much she might deny it. The sex ticks on in the mind, but its motions are warmed by the kinetic brutalities of money. In this response to a common field of action, Justine was truer to herself than she had ever been, responding as a flower responds to light. And it was now, while they talked quietly and coldly, their heads bent towards each other like flowers, that she could at last say, magnificently: 'Ah, Nessim, I never suspected that I should agree. How did you know that I only exist for those who believe in me?'

He stared at her, thrilled and a little terrified, recognizing in her the perfect submissiveness of the oriental spirit — the absolute feminine submissiveness which is one of the strongest forces in the world.

They went out to the car together and Justine suddenly felt very weak, as if she had been carried far out of her depth and abandoned in mid-ocean. 'I don't know what more to say.'

'Nothing. You must start living.' The paradoxes of true love are endless. She felt as if she had received a smack across the face. She went into the nearest coffee-shop and ordered a cup of hot chocolate. She drank it with trembling hands. Then she combed her hair and made up her face. She knew her beauty was only an advertisement and kept it fresh with disdain.

It was some hours later, when he was sitting at his desk, that Nessim, after a long moment of thought, picked up the polished telephone and dialled Capodistria's number. 'Da Capo' he said quietly, 'you remember my plans for marrying Justine? All is well. We have a new ally. I want you to be the first to announce it to the committee. I think now they will show no more reservation about my not being a Jew — since I am to be married to one. What do you say?' He listened with impatience to the ironical congratulations of his friend. 'It is impertinent' he said at last, coldly 'to imagine that I am not motivated by feelings as well as by designs. As an old friend I must warn you not to take that tone with me. My private life, my private feelings, are my own. If they happen to square with other considerations, so much the better. But do not do me the injustice of thinking me without honour. I love her.' He felt quite sick as he said the words: sick with a sudden self-loathing. Yet the word was utterly exact — love.

Now he replaced the receiver slowly, as if it weighed a ton, and sat staring at his own reflection in the polished desk. He was telling himself: 'It is all that I *am not* as a man which she thinks she can love. Had I no such plans to offer her, I might have pleaded with her for a century. What is the meaning of this little four-letter word we shake out of our minds like poker-dice — love?' His self-contempt almost choked him.

That night she arrived unexpectedly at the great house just as the clocks were chiming eleven. He was still up and dressed and sitting by the fire, sorting his papers. 'You did not telephone?' he cried with delight, with surprise. 'How wonderful!' She stood in grave silence at the door until the servant who had showed her in retired. Then she took a step forward letting her fur cape slide from her shoulders. They embraced passionately, silently. Then, turning her regard upon him in the firelight, that look at once terrified and exultant, she said: 'Now at last I know you, Nessim Hosnani.' Love is every sort of conspiracy. The power of riches and intrigue stirred within her now, the deputies of passion. Her face wore the brilliant look of innocence which comes only with conversion to a religious way of life! 'I have come for your directions, for further instructions' she said. Nessim was transfigured. He ran upstairs to his little safe and brought down the great folders of correspondence — as if to show that he was honest, that his words could be verified there and then, on the spot. He was now revealing to her something which neither his mother nor his brother knew — the extent of his complicity in the Palestine conspiracy. They crouched down before the fire talking until nearly dawn.

'You will see from all this my immediate worries. You can deal with them. First the doubts and hesitations of the Jewish Committee. I want *you* to talk to them. They think that there is something questionable about a Copt supporting them while the local Jews are staying clear, afraid of losing their good name with the Egyptians. We must convince them, Justine. It will take a little while at least to complete the arms build-up. Then, all this must be kept from our well-wishers here, the British and the French. I know they are busy trying to find out about me, my underground activities. As yet, I think they don't suspect. But among them all there are two people who particularly concern us. Darley's liaison with the little Melissa is one *point néuralgique*; as I told you she was the mistress of old Cohen who died this year. He was our chief agent for arms shipments, and knew all about us. Did he tell her anything? I don't know. Another person even more equivocal is Pursewarden; he clearly belongs to the political agency of the Embassy. We are great friends and all that but . . . I am not sure what he suspects. We must if necessary reassure him, try and sell him an innocent community movement among the Copts! What else does he, might he, know or fear? You can help me here. Oh, Justine, I knew you would understand!' Her dark intent features, so composed in the firelight, were full of a new clarity, a new power. She nodded. In her hoarse voice she said 'Thank you, Nessim Hosnani. I see now what I have to do.'

Afterwards they locked the tall doors, put away the papers, and in the dead of night lay down before the fire in each other's arms, to make love with the passionate detachment of succubi. Savage and exultant as their kisses were, they were but the lucid illustrations of their human case. They had discovered each other's inmost weakness, the true site of love. And now at last there were no reserves and no inhibitions in Justine's mind, and what may seem wantonness in other terms was really the powerful co-efficient of a fully realized abandonment to love itself — a form of true identity she had never shared with anyone else! The secret they shared made her free to act. And Nessim foundering in her arms with his curiously soft — almost virginal — femininity, felt shaken and banged by her embrace like a rag doll. The nibbling of her lips reminded him of the white Arab mare he had owned as a child; confused memories flew up like flocks of coloured birds. He felt exhausted, on the point of tears, and yet irradiated by a tremendous gratitude and tenderness. In these magnificent kisses all his loneliness was expurgated. He had found someone to share his secret — a woman after his own special heart. Paradox within paradox!

As for her, it was as if she had rifled the treasury of his spiritual power symbolized so queerly in the terms of his possessions; the cold steel of rifles, the cold nipples of bombs and grenades which had been born from tungsten, gum arabic, jute, shipping, opals, herbs, silks and trees.

He felt her on top of him, and in the plunge of her loins he felt the desire to add to him — to fecundate his actions; and to fructify him through these fatality-bearing instruments of his power, to give life to those death-burdening struggles of a truly barren woman. Her face was expressionless as a mask of Siva. It was neither ugly nor beautiful, but naked as power itself. It seemed coeval (this love) with the Faustian love of saints who had mastered the chilly art of seminal stoppage in order the more clearly to recognize themselves — for its blue fires conveyed not heat but cold to the body. But will and mind burned up as if they had been dipped in quicklime. It was a true sensuality with nothing of the civilized poisons about it to make it anodyne, palatable to a human society constructed upon a romantic idea of truth. Was it the less love for that? Paracelsus had described such relationships among the Caballi. In all this one may see the austere mindless primeval face of Aphrodite.

And all the time he was thinking to himself: 'When all this is over, when I have found her lost child — by that time we shall be so close that there will never be any question of leaving me.' The passion of their embraces came from *complicity*, from something deeper, more wicked, than the wayward temptings of the flesh or the mind. He had conquered her in offering her a married life which was both a pretence and yet at the same time informed by a purpose which might lead them both to *death!* This was all that sex could mean to her now! How thrilling, sexually thrilling, was the expectation of their death!

He drove her home in the first faint trembling light of dawn; waited to hear the lift climb slowly, painfully, to the third floor and return again. It stopped with a slight bounce before him and the light went out with a click. The personage had gone, but her perfume remained.

It was a perfume called *'Jamais de la vie'*.

*   *   *   *   *

XI

Throughout that summer and autumn the conspirators had worked together to mount entertainments on a scale seldom seen in the city. The big house was seldom quiet now for hours together. It was perpetually alive to the cool fern-like patterns of a quartet, or to the foundering plunge of saxophones crying to the night like cuckolds. The once cavernous and deserted kitchens were now full of the echoing bustle of servants preparing for a new feast or clearing up after one which had ended. In the city it was said that Nessim had deliberately set himself to launch Justine in society — as if the provincial splendours of Alexandria held any promise or charm to one who had become at heart a European, as he had. No, these planned assaults upon the society of the second capital were both exploratory and diversionary. They offered a backcloth against which the conspirators could move with a freedom necessary to their work. They worked indefatigably — and only when the pressure of things became too great stole short holidays in the little summer lodge which Nessim had christened 'Justine's Summer Palace'; here they could read and write and bathe, and enjoy those friends who were closest to them — Clea and Amaril and Balthazar.

But always after these long evenings spent in a wilderness of conversation, a forest of plates and wine-bottles, they locked the doors, shot the great bolts themselves and turned sighing back to the staircase, leaving the sleepy domestics to begin the task of clearing up the *débris*; for the house must be completely set to rights by morning; they walked slowly arm in arm, pausing to kick off their shoes on the first landing and to smile at each other in the great mirror. Then, to quieten their minds, they would take a slow turn up and down the picture-gallery, with its splendid collection of Impressionists, talking upon neutral topics while Nessim's greedy eyes explored the great canvases slowly, mute testimony to the validity of private worlds and secret wishes.

So at last they came to those warm and beautifully furnished private bedrooms, adjoining one another, on the cool north side of the house. It was always the same; while Nessim lay down on the bed fully dressed, Justine lit the spirit-lamp to prepare the infusion of valerian which he always took to soothe his nerves before he slept. Here too she would set out the small card-table by the bed, and together they played a hand or two of cribbage or picquet as they talked, obsessively talked about the affairs which occupied their waking minds. At such times their dark, passionate faces glowed in the soft light with a sort of holiness conferred by secrecy, by the appetites of a shared will, by desires joined at the waist. Tonight it was the same. As she dealt the first hand, the telephone by the bed rang. Nessim picked up the receiver, listened for a second, and then passed it to her without a word. Smiling, she raised her eyebrows in interrogation and her husband nodded. 'Hullo' the hoarse voice counterfeited sleepiness, as if she had been woken from her bed. 'Yes, my darling. Of course. No, I was awake. Yes, I am alone.' Nessim quietly and methodically fanned out his hand and studied the cards without visible expression. The conversation ran stutteringly on and then the caller said good-night and rang off. Sighing, Justine replaced the receiver, and then made a slow gesture, as of someone removing soiled gloves, or of someone disembarrassing herself of a skein of wool. 'It was poor Darley' she said, picking up her cards. Nessim raised his eyes for a moment, put down a card, and uttered a bid. As the game began, she started to talk again softly, as if to herself. 'He is absolutely fascinated by the diaries. Remember? I used to copy out all Arnauti's notes for *Moeurs* in my own handwriting when he broke his wrist. We had them bound up. All the parts which he did not use in the end. I have given them to Darley as my diary.' She depressed her cheeks in a sad smile. 'He accepts them as mine, and says, not unnaturally, that I have a masculine mind! He also says my French is not very good — that would please Arnauti, wouldn't it?'

'I am sorry for him' said Nessim quietly, tenderly. 'He is so good. One day I will be quite honest, explain everything to him.'

'But I don't see your concern for the little Melissa' said Justine, again as if engaged in a private debate rather than a conversation. 'I have tried to sound him in every way. He knows nothing. I am convinced that she knows nothing. Just because she was Cohen's mistress . . . I don't know.'

Nessim laid down his cards and said: 'I cannot get rid of a feeling she knows something. Cohen was a boastful and silly man and he certainly knew all that there was to know.'

'But why should he tell her?'

'It is simply that after his death, whenever I ran across her, she would look at me in a new way — as if *in the light* of something she had heard about me, a piece of new knowledge. It's hard to describe.'

They played in silence until the kettle began to whine. Then Justine put down her cards, went across to prepare the valerian. As he sipped it she went into the other room to divest herself of her jewellery. Sipping the cup, and staring reflectively at the wall, Nessim heard the small snap of her ear-rings as she plucked them off, and the small noise of the sleeping-tablets falling into a glass. She came back and sat down at the card-table.

'Then if you feared her, why did you not get her removed somehow?' He looked startled and she added: 'I don't mean to harm her, but to get her sent away.'

Nessim smiled. 'I thought I would, but then when Darley fell in love with her, I . . . had a sympathy for him.'

'There is no room for such ideas' she said curtly, and he nodded, almost humbly. 'I know' he said. Justine dealt the cards once more, and once more they consulted their hands in silence.

'I am working now to get her sent away — by Darley himself. Amaril says that she is really seriously ill and has already recommended that she go to Jerusalem for special treatment. I have offered Darley the money. He is in a pitiable state of confusion. Very English. He is a good person, Nessim, though now he is very much afraid of you and invents all sorts of bogies with which to frighten himself. He makes me feel sad, he is so helpless.'

'I know.'

'But Melissa must go. I have told him so.'

'Good.' Then, in a totally different voice, raising his dark eyes to hers, he said: 'What about Pursewarden?'

The question hung between them in the still air of the room, quivering like a compass needle. Then he slung his eyes once more to the cards in his hand. Justine's face took on a new expression, both bitter and haggard. She lit a cigarette carefully and said: 'As I told you, he is someone quite out of the ordinary — *c'est un personnage*. It would be quite impossible to get a secret out of him. It's hard to describe.'

She stared at him for a long time, studying those dark averted features with an expression of abstraction. 'What I am trying to say is this: about the difference between them. Darley is so sentimental and so loyal to me that he constitutes no danger at all.

Even if he came into the possession of information which might harm us, he would not use it, he would bury it. Not Pursewarden!' Now her eyes glittered. 'He is somehow cold and clever and self-centred. Completely amoral — like an Egyptian! He would not deeply care if we died tomorrow. I simply cannot reach him. But potentially he is an enemy worth reckoning with.'

He raised his eyes to her and they sat for a long moment staring sightlessly into each other's minds. His eyes were now full of a burning passionate sweetness like the eyes of some strange noble bird of prey. He moistened his lips with his tongue but did not speak. He had been on the point of blurting out the words: 'I am terrified that you may be falling in love with him.' But a queer feeling of pudicity restrained him.

'Nessim.'

'Yes.'

She stubbed out her cigarette now and, deep in thought, rose to walk up and down the room, her hands hugged in her armpits. As always when she was thinking deeply, she moved in a strange, almost awkward way — a prowling walk which reminded him of some predatory animal. His eye had become vague now, and lustreless. He picked up the cards mechanically and shuffled them once, twice. Then he put them down and raised his palms to his burning cheeks.

At once she was at his side with her warm hand upon his brow. 'You have a temperature again.'

'I don't think so' he said rapidly, mechanically.

'Let me take it.'

'No.'

She sat down opposite him, leaning forward, and stared once more into his eyes. 'Nessim, what has been happening? Your health . . . these temperatures, and you don't sleep?' He smiled wearily and pressed the back of her hand to his hot cheek.

'It is nothing' he said. 'Just strain now that everything is coming to an end. Also having to tell Leila the whole truth. It has alarmed her to understand the full extent of our plans. Also it has made her relationship with Mountolive much harder. I think that is the reason she refused to see him at the Carnival meeting, remember? I had told her everything that morning. Never mind. Another few months and the whole build-up is complete. The rest is up to them. But of course Leila does not like the idea of going away. I knew she wouldn't. And then, I have other serious problems.'

'What problems?'

But he shook his head, and getting up started to undress. Once in bed he finished his valerian and lay, hands and feet folded like the effigy of a Crusader. Justine switched off the light and stood in the doorway in silence. At last she said: 'Nessim. I am afraid that something is happening to you which I don't understand. These days . . . are you ill? Please speak to me!'

There was a long silence. Then she said: 'How is all this going to turn out?'

He raised himself slightly on the pillows and stared at her. 'By the autumn, when everything is ready, we shall have to take up new dispositions. It may mean a separation of perhaps a year, Justine. I want you to go there and stay there while it all happens. Leila must go to the farm in Kenya. There will certainly be sharp reactions here which I must stay to face.'

'You talk in your sleep.'

'I am exhausted' he cried shortly, angrily.

Justine stood still, motionless in silhouette, in the lighted doorway. 'What about the others?' she asked softly, and once more he raised himself on the pillows to answer peevishly. 'The only one who concerns us at the moment is Da Capo. He must be apparently killed, or must disappear, for he is very much compromised. I have not worked out the details properly. He wants me to claim his insurance, anyway, as he is completely in debt, ruined, so his disappearance would fit in. We will speak of this later. It should be comparatively easy to arrange.'

She turned thoughtfully back into the lighted room and began to prepare for sleep. She could hear Nessim sighing and turning restlessly in the next room. In the great mirror she studied her own sorrowful, haunted face, stripping it of its colours, and combing her black hair luxuriously. Then she slipped naked between the sheets and snapped out the light, tumbling lightly, effortlessly into sleep in a matter of moments.

It was almost dawn when Nessim came barefoot into her room. She woke to feel his arms about her shoulders; he was kneeling by the bed, shaken by a paroxysm which at first she took to be a fit of weeping. But he was trembling, as if with a fever, and his teeth were chattering. 'What is it?' she began incoherently, but he put a hand over her mouth to silence her. 'I simply must tell you why I have been acting so strangely. I cannot bear the strain any longer. Justine, I have been brought face to face with another problem. I am faced with the terrible possibility of having to do away with Narouz. That is why I have been feeling half-mad. He has got completely out of hand. And I don't know what to do. I don't know what to do!'

This conversation took place some little time before the unexpected suicide of Pursewarden in the Mount Vulture Hotel.

*   *   *   *   *

XII

But it was not only for Mountolive that all the dispositions on the chessboard had been abruptly altered now by Pursewarden's solitary act of cowardice — and the unexpected discovery which had supplied its motive, the mainspring of his death. Nessim too, so long self-deluded by the same dreams of a perfect finite action, free and heedless as the impulse of a directed will, now found himself, like his friend, a prey to the gravitational forces which lie inherent in the time-spring of our acts, making them spread, ramify and distort themselves; making them spread as a stain will spread upon a white ceiling. Indeed, now the masters were beginning to find that they were, after all, the servants of the very forces which they had set in play, and that nature is inherently ungovernable. They were soon to be drawn along ways not of their choosing, trapped in a magnetic field, as it were, by the same forces which unwind the tides at the moon's bidding, or propel the glittering forces of salmon up a crowded river — actions curving and swelling into futurity beyond the powers of mortals to harness or divert. Mountolive knew this, vaguely and uneasily, lying in bed watching the lazy spirals of smoke from his cigar rise to the blank ceiling; Nessim and Justine knew it with greater certainty, lying brow to cold brow, eyes wide open in the magnificent darkened bedroom, whispering to each other. Beyond the connivance of the will they knew it, and felt the portents gathering around them — the paradigms of powers unleashed which must fulfil themselves. But how? In what manner? That was not as yet completely clear.

Pursewarden, before lying down on that stale earthly bed beside the forgotten muttering images of Melissa or Justine — and whatever private memories besides — had telephoned to Nessim in a new voice, full of a harsh resignation, charged with the approaching splendours of death. 'It is a matter of life and death, as they say in books. Yes, please, come at once. There is a message for you in an appropriate place: the mirror.' He rang off with a simple chuckle which frightened the alert, frozen man at the other end of the line; at once Nessim had divined the premonition of a possible disaster. On the mirror of that shabby hotel-room, among the quotations which belonged to the private workshop of the writer's life, he found the following words written in capitals with a wet shaving-stick:

NESSIM. COHEN PALESTINE ETC. ALL DISCOVERED AND REPORTED.

This was the message which he had all but managed to obliterate before there came the sound of voices in the hall and the furtive rapping at the panels of the door; before Balthazar and Justine had tiptoed softly into the room. But the words and the memory of that small parting chuckle (like a sound of some resurrected Pan) were burned forever into his mind. His expression was one of neuralgic vacancy as he repeated all these facts to Justine in later times for the exposure of the act itself had numbed him. It would be impossible to sleep, he had begun to see; it was a message which must be discussed at length, sifted, unravelled where they lay, motionless as the effigies upon Alexandrian tombs, side by side in the dark room, their open eyes staring into each other with the sightlessness of inhuman objects, mirrors made of quartz, dead stars. Hand in hand they sighed and murmured, and even as he whispered: 'I told you it was Melissa . . . The way she always looked at me. . . . I suspected it.' The other troubling problems of the case interlocked and overlapped in his mind, the problem of Narouz among them.

He felt as a beleaguered knight must feel in the silence of a fortress who suddenly hears the click of spades and mattocks, the noise of iron feet, and divines that the enemy sappers are burrowing inch by inch beneath the walls. What would Mountolive feel *bound* to do now, supposing he had been told? (Strange how the very phrase betrayed them both as having moved out of the orbit of human free will.) They were both *bound* now, tied like bondsmen to the unrolling action which illustrated the personal predispositions of neither. They had embarked on a free exercise of the will only to find themselves shackled, bricked up by the historical process. And a single turn of the kaleidoscope had brought it about. Pursewarden! The writer who was so fond of saying 'People will realize one day that it is only the artist who can make things really *happen*; that is why society should be founded upon him.' A *deus ex machina!* In his dying he had used them both like . . . a public convenience, as if to demonstrate the truth of his own aphorism! There would have been many other issues to take without separating them by the act of his death, and setting them at odds by the dispensation of a knowledge which could benefit neither! Now everything hung upon a hair — the thinnest terms of a new probability. Act Mountolive would, but *if he must*; and his one word to Memlik Pasha would entrain new forces, new dangers. . . . .

The city with its obsessive rhythms of death twanged round them in the darkness — the wail of tyres in empty squares, the scudding of liners, the piercing whaup of a tug in the inner harbour; he felt the dusty, deathward drift of the place as never before, settling year by year more firmly into the barren dunes of Mareotis. He turned his mind first this way and then that, like an hourglass; but it was always the same sand which sifted through it, the same questions which followed each other unanswerably at the same leaden pace. Before them stretched the potential of a disaster for which — even though they had evaluated the risk so thoroughly and objectively — they had summoned up no reserves of strength. It was strange. Yet Justine, savagely brooding with her brows drawn down and her knuckle against her teeth, seemed still unmoved, and his heart went out to her, for the dignity of her silence (the unmoved sibyl's eye) gave him the courage to think on, assess the dilemma. They must continue as if nothing had changed when, in fact, everything had changed. The knowledge of the fact that they must, expressionless as knights nailed into suits of armour, continue upon a predetermined course, constituted both a separation and a new, deeper bond; a more passionate comradeship, such as soldiers enjoy upon the field of battle, aware that they have renounced all thought of human continuity in terms of love, family, friends, home — become servants of an iron will which exhibits itself in the mailed mask of duty. 'We must prepare for every eventuality' he said, his lips dry from the cigarettes he had smoked 'and hold on until things are complete. We may have more time in hand than we imagine; indeed, nothing whatsoever may come of it all. Perhaps Mountolive has not been told.' But then he added in a smaller voice, full of the weight of realization: 'But if he has been, we shall know; his manner will show it at once.'

He might suddenly find himself, at any street corner, face to face with a man armed with a pistol — in any dark corner of the town; or else he might find his food poisoned some day by some suborned servant. Against these eventualities he could at least react, by a study of them, by a close and careful attention to probabilities. Justine lay silent, with wide eyes. 'And then' he said 'tomorrow I must speak to Narouz. He must be made to see.'

Some weeks before he had walked into his office to find the grave, silver-haired Serapamoun sitting in the visitor's chair, quietly smoking a cigarette. He was by far the most influential and important of the Coptic cotton-kings, and had played a decisive role in supporting the community movement which Nessim had initiated. They were old friends though the older man was of another generation. His serene mild face and low voice carried the authority of an education and a poise which spoke of Europe. His conversation had the quick pulse of a reflective mind. 'Nessim' he said softly, 'I am here as a representative of our committee, not just as myself. I have a rather disagreeable task to perform. May I speak to you frankly, without heat or rancour? We are very troubled.'

Nessim closed and locked the door, unplugged his telephone and squeezed Serapamoun's shoulder affectionately as he passed behind his visitor's chair to reach his own. 'I ask nothing better' he said. 'Speak.'

'Your brother, Narouz.'

'Well, what of him?'

'Nessim, in starting this community movement you had no idea of initiating a *jehad* — a holy war of religion — or of doing anything subversive which might unsettle the Egyptian Government? Of course not. That is what we thought, and if we joined you it was from a belief in your convictions that the Copts should unite and seek a larger place in public affairs.' He smoked in silence for a minute, lost in deep thought. Then he went on: 'Our community patriotism in no way qualified our patriotism as Egyptians, did it? We were glad to hear Narouz preach the truths of our religion and race, yes, very glad, for these things needed saying, needed *feeling*. But . . . you have not been to a meeting for nearly three months. Are you aware what a change has come about? Narouz has been so carried away by his own powers that he is saying things today which could seriously compromise us all. We are most alarmed. He is filled now with some sort of mission. His head is a jumble of strange fragments of knowledge, and when he preaches all sorts of things pour out of him in a torrent which would look bad on paper if they were to reach Memlik Pasha.' Another long silence. Nessim found himself growing gradually pale with apprehension. Serapamoun continued in his low smoothly waxed voice. 'To say that the Copts will find a place in the sun is one thing; but to say that they will sweep away the

corrupt régime of the pashas who own ninety per cent of the land
... to talk of taking over Egypt and setting it to rights. ....'

'Does he?' stammered Nessim, and the grave man nodded.

'Yes. Thank God our meetings are still secret. At the last he
started raving like someone *melboos* (possessed) and shouted
that if it was necessary to achieve our ends he would arm the
Bedouin. Can you improve on that?'

Nessim licked his dry lips. 'I had no idea' he said.

'We are very troubled and concerned about the fate of the
whole movement with such preaching. We are counting on you
to act in some way. He should, my dear Nessim, be restrained;
or at least given some understanding of our role. He is seeing
too much of old Taor — he is always out there in the desert with
her. I don't think she has any political ideas, but he gets religious
fervour from these meetings with her. He spoke of her and said
that they kneel together for hours in the sand, under the blazing
sun, and pray together. "I see her visions now and she sees mine."
That is what he said. Also, he has begun to drink very heavily. It
is something which needs urgent attention.'

'I shall see him at once' Nessim had said, and now, turning
to stare once more into the dark, untroubled gaze of a Justine
he knew to be much stronger than himself, he repeated the phrase
softly, trying it with his mind as one might try the blade of a knife
to test its keenness. He had put off the meeting on one pretext or
another, though he knew that sooner or later it would have to be,
he would have to assert himself over Narouz — but over a different
Narouz to the one he had always known.

And now Pursewarden had clumsily intervened, interpolated
his death and betrayal, to load him still more fully with the
preoccupations with all that concerned affairs about which Narouz
himself knew nothing; setting his fevered mind to run upon
parallel tracks towards an infinity. ... He had the sensation of
things closing in upon him, of himself beginning slowly to suffocate
under the weight of the cares he had himself invented. It had all
begun to happen suddenly — within a matter of weeks. Helplessness began to creep over him, for every decision now seemed no
longer a product of his will but a response to pressures built up
outside him; the exigencies of the historical process in which
he himself was being sucked as if into a quicksand.

But if he could no longer control events, it was necessary that
he should take control of himself, his own nerves. Sedatives had

for weeks now taken the place of self-control, though they only exorcized the twitchings of the subconscious temporarily; pistol-practice, so useless and childish a training against assassination, offered little surcease. He was possessed, assailed by the dreams of his childhood, erupting now without reason or consequence, almost taking over his waking life. He consulted Balthazar, but was of course unable to let him share the true preoccupations which burdened him, so that his wily friend suggested that he should record the dreams whenever possible on paper, and this also was done. But psychic pressures are not lifted unless one faces them squarely and masters them, does battle with the perils of the quivering reason. . . .

He had put off the interview with Narouz until he should feel stronger and better able to endure it. Fortunately the meetings of the group were infrequent. But daily he felt less and less equal to confronting his brother and it was in fact Justine who, with a word spoken in season at last, drove him out to Karm Abu Girg. Holding the lapels of his coat she said slowly and distinctly: 'I would offer to go out and kill him myself, if I did not know that it would separate us forever. But if you have decided that it must be done, I have the courage to give the orders for you.' She did not mean it, of course. It was a trick to bring him to his senses and in a trice his mind cleared, the mist of his irresolution dissolved. These words, so terrible and yet so quietly spoken, with not even the pride of resolution in them, reawakened his passionate love for her, so that the tears almost started to his eyes. He gazed upon her like a religious fanatic gazing upon an ikon — and in truth her own features, sullen now and immobile, her smouldering eyes, were those of some ancient Byzantine painting.

'Justine' he said with trembling hands.

'Nessim' she said hoarsely, licking her dry lips, but with a barbaric resolution gleaming in her eyes. It was almost exultantly (for the impediment had gone) that he said: 'I shall be going out this evening, never fear. Everything will be settled one way or the other.' He was all of a sudden flooded with power, determined to bring his brother to his senses and avert the danger of a second compromising order to his people, the Copts.

Nor had the new resolute mood deserted him that afternoon when he set off in the great car, driving with speed and deliberation along the dusty causeways of the canals to where the horses for which he had telephoned would be waiting for him. He was positively eager to see his brother, now, to outface him, to reassert himself, restore himself in his own eyes. Ali the factor met him at the ford with the customary politeness which seemed comfortably to reaffirm this new mood of resolution. He was after all the elder son. The man had brought Narouz' own white Arab and they cantered along the edge of the canals at great speed, with their reflections racing beside them in the tumbled water. He had asked only if his brother were now at home and had received a taciturn admission of the fact that he was. They exchanged no further word on the ride. The violet light of dusk was already in the air and the earth-vapours were rising from the lake. The gnats rose into the eye of the dying sun in silver streams, to store the last memories of the warmth upon their wings. The birds were collecting their families. How peaceful it all seemed! The bats had begun to stitch and stitch slowly across the darker spaces. The *bats!*

The Hosnani house was already in cool violet half-darkness, tucked as it was under the shoulder of the low hillock, in the shadow of the little village whose tall white minaret blazed still in the sunset. He heard now the sullen crack of the whip as he dismounted, and caught a glimpse of the man standing upon the topmost balcony of the house, gazing intently down into the blue pool of the courtyard. It was Narouz: and yet somehow also not Narouz. Can a single gesture from someone with whom one is familiar reveal an interior transformation? The man with the whip, standing there, so intently peering into the sombre well of the courtyard, registered in his very stance a new, troubling flamboyance, an authority which did not belong, so to speak, to the repertoire of Narouz' remembered gestures. 'He practises' said the factor softly, holding the bridle of the horse 'every evening now with his whip he practises upon the bats.' Nessim suddenly had a feeling of incoherence. 'The *bats?*' he repeated softly, under his breath. The man on the balcony — the Narouz of this hastily raised impression — gave a sudden chuckle and exclaimed in a hoarse voice: 'Thirteen.' Nessim threw back the doors and stood framed now against the outer light. He spoke upwards in the darkening sky in a quiet, almost conversational voice, casting it like a ventriloquist towards the cloaked figure which stood at the top of the staircase in silhouette, with the long whip coiled at its side, at rest. 'Ya Narouz' he said, uttering the traditional greeting of their common childhood with affection.

'Ya Nessim' came the response after a pause, and then a long ebbing silence fell. Nessim, whose eyes had become accustomed to the dusk, now saw that the courtyard was full of the bodies of bats, like fragments of torn umbrella, some fluttering and crawling in puddles of their own blood, some lying still and torn up. So this was what Narouz did in the evenings — 'practising upon the bats'! He stood for a while unsure of himself, unsure what to say next. The factor closed the great doors abruptly behind him, and at once he stood, black against the darkness now, staring up the stairway to where his unknown brother stood with a kind of watchful impenitent awareness. A bat ripped across the light and he saw Narouz' arm swing with an involuntary motion and then fall to the side again; from his vantage point at the top of the stairway he could shoot, so to speak, downwards upon his targets. Neither said anything for a while; then a door opened with a creak, throwing out a shaft of light across his path, and the factor came out of the outhouse with a broom with which he started to sweep up the fragments of fluttering bodies of Narouz' victims which littered the earthen floor of the courtyard. Narouz leaned forward a little to watch him intently as he did so, and when he had almost swept the pile of tattered bodies to the door of the outhouse, said in a hoarse voice: 'Thirteen, eh?'

'Thirteen.'

His voice gave Nessim a dull neuralgic thrill, for he sounded drugged — the harsh authoritative voice of someone drunk on *hashish*, perhaps, or opium; the voice of someone signalling from a new orbit in an unknown universe. He drew his breath slowly until his lungs were fully inflated and then spoke upwards once more to the figure on the stair. 'Ya Narouz. I have come to speak to you on a matter of great urgency.'

'Mount' said Narouz gruffly, in the voice of a sheepdog. 'I wait for you here, Nessim.' The voice made many things clear to Nessim, for never before had the voice of his brother been completely free from a note of welcome, of joy even. At any other time he would have run down the stairs in clumsy welcome, taking them two at a time and calling out 'Nessim, how *good* you have come!' Nessim walked across the courtyard and placed his hand upon the dusty wooden rail. 'It is important' he said sharply, crisply, as if to establish his own importance in this tableau — the shadowy courtyard with the solitary figure standing up against the sky in silhouette, holding the long whip lightly, effortlessly, and watching him. Narouz repeated the word 'Mount' in a lower key, and suddenly sat down putting his whip beside him on the top stair. It was the first time, thought Nessim, that there had been no greeting for him on his return to Karm Abu Girg. He walked up the steep stairs slowly, peering upwards.

It was much lighter on the first floor, and at the top of the second there was enough light to see his brother's face. Narouz sat quite still, in cloak and boots. His whip lay lightly coiled over the balustrade with its handle upon his knees. Beside him on the dusty wooden floor stood a half-empty bottle of gin. His chin was sunk upon his chest and he stared crookedly up under shaggy brows at the approaching stranger with an expression which combined truculence with a queer, irresolute sorrow. He was at his old trick of pressing his back teeth together and releasing them so that the cords of muscle at his temples expanded and contracted as if a heavy pulse were beating there. He watched his brother's slow ascent with this air of sombre self-divided uncertainty into which there crept from time to time the smouldering glow of an anger banked up, held under control. As Nessim reached the final landing and set foot upon the last flight of stairs, Narouz stirred and gave a sudden gargling bark — a sound such as one might make to a hound — and held out a hairy hand. Nessim paused and heard his brother say: 'Stay there, Nessim' in a new and authoritative voice, but which contained no particular note of menace. He hesitated, leaning forward keenly the better to interpret this unfamiliar gesture — the square hand thrown out in an attitude almost of imprecation, fingers stretched, but not perfectly steady.

'You have been drinking' he said at last, quietly but with a profound ringing disgust. 'Narouz, this is new for you.' The shadow of a smile, as if of self-contempt, played upon the crooked lips of his brother. It broadened suddenly to a slow grin which displayed his hare-lip to the full: and then vanished, was swallowed up, as if abruptly recalled by a thought which it could not represent. Narouz now wore a new air of unsteady self-congratulation, of pride at once mawkish and dazed. 'What do you wish from me?' he said hoarsely. 'Say it here, Nessim. I am practising.'

'Let us go indoors to speak privately.'

Narouz shook his head slowly and after consideration said crisply:

'You can speak here.'

'*Narouz*' cried Nessim sharply, stung by these unfamiliar responses, and in the voice one would use to awaken a sleeper. '*Please.*' The seated man at the head of the stairs stared up at him with the strange inflamed but sorrowful air and shook his head again. 'I have spoken, Nessim' he said indistinctly. Nessim's voice broke, it was pitched so sharply against the silence of the courtyard. He said, almost pitifully now, 'I simply must speak to you, do you understand?'

'Speak now, here. I am listening.' This was indeed a new and unexpected personage, the man in the cloak. Nessim felt the colour rising in his cheeks. He climbed a couple of steps more and hissed assertively: 'Narouz, I come from *them*. In God's name what have you been saying to them? The committee has become terrified by your words.' He broke off and irresolutely waved the memorandum which Serapamoun had deposited with him, crying: 'This . . . this paper is from them.'

Narouz' eyes blazed up for a second with a maudlin pride made somehow regal by the outward thrust of his chin and a straightening of the huge shoulders. 'My words, Nessim?' he growled, and then nodding: 'And Taor's words. When the time comes we will know how to act. Nobody needs to fear. We are not dreamers.'

'*Dreamers!*' cried Nessim with a gasp, almost beside himself now with apprehension and disgust and mortified to his very quick by this lack of conventional address in a younger brother. 'You are the dreamers! Have I not explained a thousand times what we are trying to do . . . what we mean by all this? Peasant, idiot that you are. . . . .' But these words which once might have lodged like goads in Narouz' mind seemed blunt, ineffectual. He tightened his mouth hard and made a slow cutting movement with his palm, cutting the air from left to right before his own body. 'Words' he cried harshly. 'I know you now, my brother.' Nessim glanced wildly about him for a moment, as if to seek help, as if to seek some instrument heavy enough to drive the truth of what he had to say into the head of the seated man. A hysterical fury had beset him, a rage against this sottish figure which raised so incomprehending a face to his pleas. He was trembling; he had certainly anticipated nothing like this when he set out from Alexandria with his resolution bright and his mind composed.

'Where is Leila?' he cried sharply, as if he might invoke her aid, and Narouz gave a short clicking chuckle. He raised his finger to his temple gravely and muttered: 'In the summer-house, as you know. Why not go to her if you wish?' He chuckled again, and then added, nodding his head with an absurdly childish expression. 'She is angry with *you*, now. For once it is with *you*, not with *me*. You have made her cry, Nessim.' His lower lip trembled.

'Drunkard' hissed Nessim helplessly. Narouz' eyes flashed. He gave a single jarring laugh, a short bark, throwing his head right back. Then suddenly, without warning, the smile vanished and he put on once more his watchful, sorrowing expression. He licked his lips and whispered 'Ya Nessim' under his breath, as if he were slowly recovering his sense of proportion. But Nessim, white with rage, was now almost beside himself with frustration. He stepped up the last few stairs and shook Narouz by the shoulder, almost shouting now: 'Fool, you are putting us all in danger. Look at these, from Serapamoun. The committee will disband unless you stop talking like this. Do you understand? You are mad, Narouz. In God's name, Narouz, understand what I am saying. . . .' But the great head of his brother looked dazed now, beset by the flicker of contradictory expressions, like the lowered crest of a bull badgered beyond endurance. 'Narouz, *listen* to me.' The face that was slowly raised to Nessim's seemed to have grown larger and more vacant, the eyes more lustreless, yet full of the pain of a new sort of knowledge which owed little to the sterile revolutions of reason; it was full too of a kind of anger and incomprehension, confused and troubling, which was seeking expression. They stared angrily at each other. Nessim was white to the lips and panting, but his brother sat simply staring at him, his lips drawn back over his white teeth as if he were hypnotized.

'Do you hear me? Are you deaf?' Nessim shook, but with a motion of his broad shoulders Narouz shook off the importunate hand while his face began to flush. Nessim ran on, heedless, carried away by the burning preoccupations which poured out of him clothed in a torrent of reproaches. 'You have put us all in danger, even Leila, even yourself, even Mountolive.' Why should chance have led him to that fatal name? The utterance of it seemed to electrify Narouz and fill him with a new, almost triumphant desperation.

'Mountolive' he shouted the word in a deep groaning voice and ground his teeth together audibly; he seemed as if he were about to go berserk. Yet he did not move, though his hand moved in-voluntarily to the handle of the great whip which lay in his lap.

'That British swine!' he brought out with a thunderous vehemence, almost spitting the words.

'Why do you say that?'

And then another transformation occurred with unexpected suddenness, for Narouz' whole body relaxed and subsided; he looked up with a sly air now, and said with a little chuckle, in a tone pitched barely above a whisper: '*You* sold our mother to him, Nessim. You knew it would cause our father's death.'

This was too much. Nessim fell upon him, flailing at him with his doubled fists, uttering curse after guttural curse in Arabic, beating him. But his blows fell like chaff upon the huge body. Narouz did not move, did not make any attempt to avert or to respond to his brother's blows — here at least Nessim's seniority held. He could not bring himself to strike back at his elder brother. But sitting doubled up and chuckling under the futile rain of blows, he repeated venomously over and over again the words: '*You* sold our *mother!*'

Nessim beat him until his own knuckles were bruised and aching. Narouz stooped under this febrile onslaught, bearing it with the same composed smile of maudlin bitterness, repeating the triumphant phrase over and over again in that thrilling whisper. At last Nessim shrieked '*Stop*' and himself desisted, falling against the rail of the balustrade and sinking under the weight of his own exhaustion down to the first landing. He was trembling all over. He shook his fist upwards at the dark seated figure and said incoherently 'I shall go to Serapamoun myself. You will see who is master.' Narouz gave a small contemptuous chuckle, but said nothing.

Putting his dishevelled clothes to rights, Nessim tottered down the stairway into the now darkened courtyard. His horse and Ali's had been tethered to the iron hitching post outside the great front door. As he mounted, still trembling and muttering, the factor raced out of the arches and unbolted the doors. Narouz was standing up now, visible only against the yellow light of the living-room. Flashes of incoherent rage still stormed Nessim's mind — and with them irresolution, for he realized that the mission he had set himself was far from completed, indeed, had gone awry. With some half-formulated idea of offering the silent figure another chance to open up a discussion with him or seek a *rapprochement*, he rode his horse into the courtyard and sat there, looking up into the darkness. Narouz stirred.

'Narouz' said Nessim softly. 'I have told you once and for all now. You will see who is going to be master. It would be wise for you. . . .'

But the dark figure gave a bray of laughter.

'Master and servant' he cried contemptuously. 'Yes, Nessim. We shall see. And now—' He leaned over the rail and in the darkness Nessim heard the great whip slither along the dry boards like a cobra and then lick the still twilight air of the courtyard. There was a crack and a snap like a giant mousetrap closing, and the bundle of papers in his arm was flicked out peremptorily and scattered over the cobbles. Narouz laughed again, on a more hysterical note. Nessim felt the heat of the whipstroke on his hand though the lash had not touched him.

'Now go' cried Narouz, and once more the whip hissed in the air to explode menacingly behind the buttocks of his horse. Nessim rose in his stirrups and shaking his fist once more at his brother, cried 'We shall see!'

But his voice sounded thin, choked by the imprecations which filled his mind. He drove his heels in the horse's flanks and twisted suddenly about to gallop abruptly out of the courtyard throwing up sparks from the stone threshold, bending low in the saddle. He rode back to the ford now, where the car awaited, like a madman his face distorted with rage; but as he rode his pulse slowed and his anger emptied itself into the loathsome disgust which flooded up into his mind in slow coils, like some venomous snake. Unexpected waves of remorse, too, began to invade him, for something had now been irreparably damaged, irreparably broken, in the iron ceinture of the family relation. Dispossessed of the authority vested in the elder son by the feudal pattern of life, he felt all at once a prodigal, almost an orphan. In the heart of his rage there was also guilt; he felt unclean, as if he had debauched himself in this unexpected battle with one of his own kin. He drove slowly back to the city, feeling the luxurious tears of a new exhaustion, a new self-pity, rolling down his cheeks.

How strange it was that he had somehow, inexplicably, foreseen this irreparable break with his brother — from the first discreet phrases of Serapamoun he had divined it and feared it. It raised once more the spectre of duties and responsibilities to causes which he himself had initiated and must now serve. Ideally, then, he should be prepared in such a crisis to disown Narouz, to depose Narouz, even if necessary to . . . him! (He slammed on the brakes of the car, brought it to a standstill, and sat muttering. He had censored the thought in his mind, for the hundredth time. But the nature of the undertaking should be clear enough to anyone in a similar situation. He had never understood Narouz, he thought wistfully. But then, you do not have to understand someone in order to love them. His hold had not really been deep, founded in understanding: it had been conferred by the family conventions to which both belonged. And now the tie had suddenly snapped.) He struck the wheel of the car with aching palms and cried 'I shall never harm him.'

He threw in the clutch, repeating 'Never' over and over again in his mind. Yet he knew this decision to be another weakness, for in it his love traduced his own ideal of duty. But here his *alter ego* came to his rescue with soothing formulations such as: 'It is really not so serious. We shall, of course, have to disband the movement temporarily. Later I shall ask Serapamoun to start something similar. We can isolate and expel this . . . fanatic.' He had never fully realized before how much he loved this hated brother whose mind had now become distended by dreams whose religious poetry conferred upon their Egypt a new, an ideal future. 'We must seek to embody the frame of the eternal in nature here upon earth, in our hearts, in this very Egypt of ours.' That is what Narouz had said, among so many other things which filled the fragmentary transcription which Serapamoun had ordered to be made. 'We must wrestle here on earth against the secular injustice, and in our hearts against the injustice of a divinity which respects only man's struggle to possess his own soul.' Were these simply the ravings of Taor, or were they part of a shared dream of which the ignorant fanatic had spoken? Other phrases, barbed with the magnificence of poetry, came into his mind. 'To rule is to be ruled; but ruler and ruled must have a divine consciousness of their role, of their inheritance in the Divine. The mud of Egypt rises to choke our lungs, the lungs with which we cry to living God.'

He had a sudden picture of that contorted face, the little gasping voice in which Narouz had, that first day of his possession, invoked the divine spirit to visit him with a declared truth. '*Meded! Meded!*' He shuddered. And then it slowly came upon him that in a paradoxical sort of way Narouz was right in his desire to inflame the sleeping will — for he saw the world, not so much as a political chessboard but as a pulse beating within a greater will which only the poetry of the psalms could invoke and body forth. To awaken not merely the impulses of the forebrain with its limited formulations, but the sleeping beauty underneath — the poetic consciousness which lay, coiled like a spring, in the heart of everyone. This thought frightened him not a little; for he suddenly saw that his brother might be a religious leader, but for the prevailing circumstances of time and place — *these*, at least, Nessim could judge. He was a prodigy of nature but his powers were to be deployed in a barren field which could never nourish them, which indeed would stifle them forever.

He reached the house, abandoned the car at the gate, and raced up the staircase, taking the steps three at a time. He had been suddenly assailed by one of the customary attacks of diarrhoea and vomiting which had become all too frequent in recent weeks. He brushed past Justine who lay wide-eyed upon the bed with the reading-lamp on and the piano-score of a concerto spread upon her breast. She did not stir, but smoked thoughtfully, saying only, under her breath, 'You are back so soon.' Nessim rushed into the bathroom, turning on the taps of the washbasin and the shower at the same time to drown his retching. Then he stripped his clothes off with disgust, like dirty bandages, and climbed under the hail of boiling water to wash away all the indignities which flooded his thoughts. He knew she would be listening thoughtfully, smoking thoughtfully, her motions as regular as a pendulum, waiting for him to speak, lying at length under the shelf of books with the mask smiling down ironically at her from the wall. Then the water was turned off and she heard him scrubbing himself vigorously with a towel.

'Nessim' she called softly.

'It was a failure' he cried at once. 'He is quite mad, Justine, I could get nothing out of him. It was ghastly.'

Justine continued to smoke on silently, with her eyes fixed upon the curtains. The room was full of the scent of the pastels burning in the great rose-bowl by the telephone. She placed her score beside the bed. 'Nessim' she said in the hoarse voice which he had come to love so much.

'Yes.'

'I am thinking.'

He came out at once, his hair wet and straggly, his feet bare, wearing the yellow silk dressing-gown, his hands thrust deep into the pockets, a lighted cigarette smouldering in the corner of his mouth. He walked slowly up and down at the foot of her bed. He said with an air of considered precision: 'All this unease comes from my fear that we may have to do him harm. But, even if we are endangered by him, we must never harm him, *never*. I have told myself that. I have thought the whole thing out. It will seem a failure of duty, but we must be clear about it. Only then can I become calm again. Are you with me?'

He looked at her once more with longing, with the eyes of his imagination. She lay there, as if afloat upon the dark damascened bed-spread, her feet and hands crossed in the manner of an effigy, her dark eyes upon him. A lock of dark hair curled upon her forehead. She lay in the silence of a room which had housed (if walls have ears) their most secret deliberations, under a Tibetan mask with lighted eyeballs. Behind her gleamed the shelves of books which she had gathered though not all of which she had read. (She used their texts as omens for the future, riffling the pages to place her finger at hazard upon a quotation — 'bibliomancy' the art is called.) Schopenhauer, Hume, Spengler, and oddly enough some novels, including three of Pursewarden's. Their polished bindings reflected the light of the candles. She cleared her throat, extinguished her cigarette, and said in a calm voice: 'I can be resigned to whatever you say. At the moment, this weakness of yours is a danger to both of us. And besides, your health is troubling us all, Balthazar not least. Even unobservant people like Darley are beginning to notice. That is not good.' Her voice was cold and toneless.

'Justine' his admiration overflowed. He came and sat down beside her on the bed, putting his arms around her to embrace her fiercely. His eyes glittered with a new elation, a new gratitude. 'I am so weak' he said.

He extended himself beside her, put his arms behind his head, and lay silent, thinking. For a long time now they lay thus, silently side by side. At last she said:

'Darley came to dinner tonight and left just before you arrived. I heard from him that the Embassies will all be packing up next week to return to Cairo. Mountolive won't get back to Alexandria much before Christmas. This is also our chance to take a rest and recuperate our forces. I've told Selim that we are going out to Abousir next week for a whole month. You must rest now, Nessim. We can swim and ride in the desert and think about nothing, do you hear? After a while I shall invite Darley to come and stay with us for a while so that you have someone to talk to apart from me. I know you like him and find him a pleasant companion. It will do us both good. From time to time I can come in here for a night and see what is happening . . . what do you say?'

Nessim groaned softly and turned his head. 'Why?' she whispered softly, her lips turned away from him. 'Why do you do that?'

He sighed deeply and said: 'It is not what you think. You know how much I like him and how well we get on. It is only the pretence, the eternal play-acting one has to indulge in even with one's friends. If only we did not have to keep on acting a part, Justine.'

But he saw that she was looking at him wide-eyed now, with an expression suggesting something that was close to horror or dismay. 'Ah' she said thoughtfully, sorrowfully after a moment, closing her eyes, 'ah, Nessim! Then I should not know who I was.'

*   *   *   *   *.

The two men sat in the warm conservatory, silently facing each other over the magnificent chessboard with its ivories — in perfect companionship. The set was a twenty-first birthday gift, from Mountolive's mother. As they sat, each occasionally mused aloud, absently. It wasn't conversation, but simply thinking aloud, a communion of minds which were really occupied by the grand strategy of chess: a by-product of friendship which was rooted in the fecund silences of the royal game. Balthazar spoke of Pursewarden. 'It annoys me, his suicide. I feel I had somehow missed the point. I take it to have been an expression of contempt for the world, contempt for the conduct of the world.'

Mountolive glanced up quickly. 'No, no. A conflict between duty and affection.' Then he added swiftly 'But I can't tell you very much. When his sister comes, she will tell you more, perhaps, if she can.' They were silent. Balthazar sighed and said 'Truth naked and unashamed. That's a splendid phrase. But we always see her as she seems, never as she is. Each man has his own interpretation.'

Another long silence. Balthazar *loquitur*, musingly, to himself. 'Sometimes one is caught pretending to be God and learns a bitter lesson. Now I hated Dmitri Randidi, though not his lovely daughter; but just to humiliate him (I was disguised as a gipsy woman at the carnival ball), I told her fortune. Tomorrow, I said, she would have a life-experience which she must on no account miss — a man sitting in the ruined tower at Taposiris. "You will not speak" I said "but walk straight into his arms, your eyes closed. His name begins with an L, his family name with J." (I had in fact already thought of a particularly hideous young man with these initials, and he was across the road at the Cervonis' ball. Colourless eyelashes, a snout, sandy hair.) I chuckled when she believed me. Having told her this prophecy — everyone believes the tale of a gipsy, and with my black face and hook nose I made a splendid gipsy — having arranged this, I went across the road and sought out L. J., telling him I had a message for him. I knew him to be superstitious. He did not recognize me. I told him of the part he should play. Malign, spiteful, I suppose. I only planned to annoy Randidi. And it all turned out as I had planned. For the lovely girl obeyed the gipsy and fell in love with this freckled toad with the red hair. A more unsuitable conjunction cannot be imagined. But that was the idea — to make Randidi hop! It did, yes, very much, and I was so pleased by my own cleverness. He of course forbade the marriage. The lovers — which *I* invented, *my* lovers — were separated. Then Gaby Randidi, the beautiful girl, took poison. You can imagine how clever I felt. This broke her father's health and the neurasthenia (never very far from the surface in the family) overwhelmed him at last. Last autumn he was found hanging from the trellis which supports the most famous grapevine in the city and from which. . . .'

In the silence which followed he could be heard to add the words: 'It is only another story of our pitiless city. But check to your Queen, unless I am mistaken. . . .'

* * * * *

XIII

With the first thin effervescence of autumn rain Mount-olive found himself back for the winter spell in Cairo with nothing of capital importance as yet decided in the field of policy; London was silent on the revelations contained in Pursewarden's farewell letter and apparently disposed rather to condole with a Chief of Mission whose subordinates proved of doubtful worth than to criticize him or subject the whole matter to any deep scrutiny. Perhaps the feeling was best expressed in the long and pompous letter in which Kenilworth felt disposed to discuss the tragedy, offering assurances that everyone 'at the Office' was sad though not surprised. Pursewarden had always been considered rather *outré*, had he not? Apparently some such outcome had long been suspected. 'His charm' wrote Kenilworth in the august prose style reserved for what was known as 'a balanced appraisal', 'could not disguise his aberrations. I do not need to dilate on the personal file which I showed you. *In Pace Requiescat*. But you have our sympathy for the loyal way in which you brushed aside these considerations to give him another chance with a Mission which had already found his manners insupportable, his views unsound.' Mountolive squirmed as he read; yet his repugnance was irrationally mixed with a phantom relief for he saw, cowering behind these deliberations as it were, the shadows of Nessim and Justine, the outlaws.

If he had been reluctant to leave Alexandria, it was only because the unresolved problem of Leila nagged him still. He was afraid of the new thoughts he was forced to consider concerning her and her possible share in the conspiracy — if such it was — he felt like a criminal harbouring the guilt for some as yet undiscovered deed. Would it not be better to force his way in upon her — to arrive unannounced at Karm Abu Girg one day and coax the truth out of her? He could not do it. His nerve failed him at this point. He averted his mind from the ominous future and packed with many a sigh for his journey, planning to plunge once more into the tepid stream of his social activities in order to divert his mind.

For the first time now the aridities of his official duty seemed almost delightful, almost enticing. Time-killers and pain-killers at once, he followed out the prescribed round of entertainments with a concentration and attention that made them seem almost a narcotic. Never had he radiated such calculated charm, such attentiveness to considered trifles which turned them into social endearments. A whole colony of bores began to seek him out. It was a little time before people began to notice how much and in how short a time he had been aged, and to attribute the change to the unceasing round of pleasure into which he cast himself with such ravenous enthusiasm. What irony! His popularity expanded around him in waves. But now it began to seem to him that there was little enough behind the handsome indolent mask which he exposed to the world save a terror and uncertainty which were entirely new. Cut off in this way from Leila, he felt dispossessed, orphaned. All that remained was the bitter drug of duties to which he held desperately.

Waking in the morning to the sound of his curtains being drawn by the butler — slowly and reverently as one might slide back the curtains of Juliet's tomb — he would call for the papers and read them eagerly as he tackled a breakfast-tray loaded with the prescribed delicacies to which his life had made him accustomed. But already he was impatient for the tapping on the door which would herald the appearance of his young bearded third secretary, bringing him his appointments book and other impedimenta of his work. He would hope frantically that the day would be a full one, and felt almost anguish on those rare occasions when there were few engagements to be met. As he lay back on his pillows with controlled impatience Donkin would read the day's agenda in the manner of someone embarking on a formal recitation of the Creed. Dull as they always sounded, these official engagements, they rang in Mountolive's ear with a note of promise, a prescription for boredom and unease. He listened like an anxious voluptuary to the voice reciting: 'There is a call on Rahad Pasha at eleven to deliver an *aide-mémoire* on investment by British subjects. Chancery have the data. Then Sir John and Lady Gilliatt are coming to lunch. Errol met the plane. Yes, we sent the flowers to the hotel for her. They will sign the book at eleven today. Their daughter is indisposed which rather mucked up the lunch-seating, but as you already had Haida Pasha and the American Minister, I took the liberty of popping in Errol and wife; the *placement* works out like this. I didn't need to consult protocol because Sir John is here on a private visit — this has been publicly announced in the Press.' Laying down all the beautifully-typed memoranda on its stiff crested paper, Mountolive sighed and said 'Is the new *chef* any good? You might send him to me later in my office. I know a favourite dish of the Gilliatts'.'

Donkin nodded and scribbled a note before continuing in his toneless voice: 'At six there is a cocktail party for Sir John at Haida's. You have accepted to dine at the Italian Embassy — a dinner in honour of Signor Maribor. It will be a tight fit.'

'I shall change before' said Mountolive thoughtfully.

'There are also one or two notes here in your hand which I couldn't quite decipher, sir. One mentions the Scent Bazaar, Persian Lilac.'

'Good, yes. I promised to take Lady Gilliatt. Arrange transport for the visit please, and let them know I am coming. After lunch — say, three-thirty.'

'Then there is a note saying "Luncheon gifts".'

'Aha, yes' said Mountolive, 'I am becoming quite an oriental. You see, Sir John may be most useful to us in London, at the Office, so I thought I would make his visit as memorable as possible, knowing his interests. Will you be good enough to go down to Karda in Suleiman Pasha and shop me a couple of those little copies of the Tel Al Aktar figurines, the coloured ones? I'd be most grateful. They are pretty toys. And see that they are wrapped with a card to put beside their plates? Thank you very much.'

Once more alone he sipped his tea and committed himself mentally to the crowded day which he saw stretching before him, rich in the promise of distractions which would leave no room for the more troubling self-questionings. He bathed and dressed slowly, deliberately, concentrating his mind on a choice of clothes suitable for his mid-morning official call, tying his tie carefully in the mirror. 'I shall soon have to change my life radically' he thought 'or it will become completely empty. How best should that be done?' Somewhere in the link of cause and effect he detected a hollow space which crystallized in his mind about the word 'companionship'. He repeated it aloud to himself in the mirror. Yes, there was where a lack lay. 'I shall have to get myself a dog' he thought, somewhat pathetically 'to keep me company. It will be something to look after. I can take it for walks by the Nile.' Then a sense of absurdity beset him and he smiled. Nevertheless, in the course of his customary tour of the Embassy offices that morning, he stuck his head into the Chancery and asked Errol very seriously what sort of dog would make a good house pet. They had a long and pleasurable discussion of the various breeds and decided that some sort of fox-terrier might be the most suitable pet for a bachelor. A fox-terrier! He repeated the words as he crossed the landing to visit the Service attachés, smiling at his own asininity. 'What next!'

His secretary had neatly stacked his papers in their trays and placed the red despatch cases against the wall; the single bar of the electric fire kept the office at a tepid norm suitable for the routine work of the day. He settled to his telegrams with an exaggerated attention, and to the draft replies which had already been dictated by his team of juniors. He found himself chopping and changing phrases, inverting sentences here and there, adding marginalia; this was something new, for he had never had excessive zeal in the matter of official English and indeed dreaded the portentous circumlocutions which his own drafts had been forced to harbour when he himself had been a junior, under a Minister who fancied himself as a stylist — are there any exceptions in the Foreign Service? No. He had always been undemanding in this way, but now the forcible concentration with which he lived and worked had begun to bear fruit in a series of meddlesome pedantries which had begun mildly to irritate the diligent Errol and his staff. Though he knew this, nevertheless Mountolive persisted unshrinkingly; he criticized, quizzed and amended work which he knew to be well enough done already, working with the aid of the Unabridged Oxford Dictionary and a Skeat — for all the world like some medieval scholar splitting theological hairs. He would light a cheroot and smoke thoughtfully as he jotted and scored on the marbled minute-paper.

Today at ten there came the customary welcome clinking of cups and saucers and Bohn, the Chancery Guard, presented himself somewhat precariously with the cup of Bovril and a plate of rusks to announce a welcome interval for refreshment. Mountolive relaxed in an armchair for a quarter of an hour as he sipped, staring heavily at the white wall with its group of neutral Japanese prints — the standard decoration chosen by the Ministry of Works for the offices of Ambassadors. In a little while it would be time to deal with the Palestine bag; already it was being sorted in the Archives Department — the heavy canvas ditty-bags lying about the floor with their mouths agape, the clerks sorting swiftly upon trestle tables, covered with green baize, the secretaries of the various departments waiting patiently outside the wooden pen each for her share of the spoils. . . . He felt a small premonitory unease this morning as he waited, for Maskelyne had not as yet shown any sign of life. He had not even acknowledged, let alone commented upon, Pursewarden's last letter. He wondered why.

There was a tap at the door, and Errol entered with his diffident ungainly walk, holding a bulky envelope impressively sealed and superscribed. 'From Maskelyne, sir' he said, and Mountolive rose and stretched with an elaborate show of nonchalance. 'Good Lord!' he said, weighing the parcel in his hand before handing it back to Errol. 'So this came by pigeon-post, eh? Wonder what it can be? It looks like a novel, eh?'

'Yes, sir.'

'Well, open it up, dear boy' (he had picked up a lot of avuncular tricks of speech from Sir Louis, he noted sadly; he must make a note to reform the habit before it was too late.)

Errol slit the huge envelope clumsily with the paper-knife. A fat memorandum and a bundle of photostats tumbled out on to the desk between them. Mountolive felt a small sense of shrinking as he recognized the spidery handwriting of the soldier upon the crowned notepaper of the covering letter. 'What have we here?' he said, settling himself at his desk. 'My dear Ambassador'; the rest of the letter was faultlessly typed in Primer. As Errol turned over the neatly stapled photostats with a curious finger, reading a few words here and there, he whistled softly. Mountolive read:

My dear Ambassador,

I am sure you will be interested in the enclosed data, all of which has been recently unearthed by my department in the course of a series of widespread investigations here in Palestine.

I am able to supply a very large fragment of a detailed correspondence carried on over the last few years between Hosnani, the subject of my original *pended* paper, and the so-called Jewish Underground Fighters in Haifa and Jerusalem. One glance at it should convince any impartial person that my original appraisal of the gentleman in question erred on the side of moderation. The quantities of arms and ammunition detailed in the attached check-list are so considerable as to cause the Mandate authorities grave alarm. Everything is being done to locate and confiscate these large dumps, so far however with little success.

This of course raises once more, and far more urgently, the political question of how to deal with this gentleman. My original view, as you know, was that a timely word to the Egyptians would meet the case. I doubt if even Memlik Pasha would care to prejudice Anglo-Egyptian relations and Egypt's new-found freedom, by refusing to act if pressure were applied. Nor need we enquire too closely into the methods he might employ. Our hands would at least be clean. But obviously Hosnani must be stopped — and soon.

I am copying this paper to W.O. and F.O. The London copy leaves under flying seal with an Urgent Personal from the Commissioner to the F.S. urging action in these terms. Doubtless you will have a reaction from London before the end of the week.

Comment on the letter of Mr. Pursewarden which you copied to me seems superfluous at this stage. The enclosures to this Memorandum will be sufficient explanation. It is clear that he could not look his duty in the face.

> I am, Sir, Your Most Obedient Servant,
>
> Oliver Maskelyne, Brigadier.

The two men sighed simultaneously and looked at one another. 'Well' said Errol at last, thumbing over the glossy photostats with a voluptuous finger. 'At last we have proof positive.' He was beaming with pleasure. Mountolive shook his head weakly and lit another cheroot. Errol said: 'I've only flicked over the correspondence, sir, but each letter is signed Hosnani. They are all typescripts, of course. I expect you'll want to mull them over at leisure, so I'll retire for an hour until you need me. Is that all?'

Mountolive fingered the great wad of paper with nausea, with a sense of surfeit, and nodded speechlessly.

'Right' said Errol briskly and turned. As he reached the door, Mountolive found his voice, though to his own ears it sounded both husky and feeble. 'Errol' he said, 'there's only one thing; signal London to say that we have received Maskelyne's Memorandum and are *au courant*. Say we are standing by for instructions.' Errol nodded and backed smiling into the passage. Mountolive settled to his desk and turned a vague and bilious eye upon the facsimiles. He read one or two of the letters slowly, almost uncomprehendingly, and was suddenly afflicted by a feeling of vertigo. He felt as if the walls of the room were slowly closing in upon him. He breathed deeply through his nose with his eyes fast closed. His fingers began involuntarily to drum softly upon the blotter, copying the syncopated rhythms of the Arab finger-drum, the broken-loined rhythms which one might hear any evening floating over the waters of the Nile from some distant boat. As he sat, softly tapping out this insidious dance measure of Egypt, with his eyes closed like a blind man, he asked himself over and over again: 'Now what is to happen?'

But what could possibly happen?

'I should expect an action telegram this afternoon' he mumbled. This was where he found his duty so useful a prop. Despite his interior preoccupations, he allowed it to drag him along now, to drag his aberrant attention along like a dog on a lead. The morning was a relatively busy one. His lunch-party was an unqualified success, and the surprise visit to the Scent Bazaar afterwards confirmed his powers as a brilliant and thoughtful host. After it was over, he lay down for half an hour in his bedroom with the curtains drawn, sipping a cup of tea, and conducting the usual debate with himself which always began with the phrase: 'Would I rather be a dunce than a fop — that is the question?' The very intensity of his self-contempt kept his mind off the issue concerned with Nessim until six when the Chancery opened once more. He had a cold shower and changed before sauntering down from the Residence.

When he reached his office it was to find the desk-lamp burning and Errol seated in the armchair, smiling benignly and holding the pink telegram in his fingers. 'It has just come in, sir' he said, passing it to his Chief as if it were a bouquet of flowers specially gathered for him. Mountolive cleared his throat loudly — attempting by the physical action to clear his mind and attention at the same time. He was afraid that his fingers might tremble as he held it, so he placed it elaborately on his blotter, thrust his hands into his trouser-pockets, and leaned down to study it, registering (he hoped) little beyond polite nonchalance. 'It is pretty clear, sir' said Errol hopefully, as if to strike an echoing spark of enthusiasm from his Chief. But Mountolive read it slowly and thoughtfully twice before looking up. He suddenly wanted to go to the lavatory very much. 'I must do a pee' he said hastily, practically driving the younger man out of the door 'and I'll come down in a little while to discuss it. It seems clear enough, though. I shall have to act tomorrow. In a minute, eh?' Errol disappeared with an air of disappointment. Mountolive rushed to the toilet; his knees were shaking. Within a quarter of an hour, however, he had composed himself once more and was able to walk lightly down the staircase to where Errol's office was; he entered softly with the telegram in his hand. Errol sat at his desk; he had just put the telephone down and was smiling.

Mountolive handed over the pink telegram and sank into an armchair noticing with annoyance the litter of untidy personal objects on Errol's desk — a china ashtray in the likeness of a Sealyham terrier, a Bible, a pin-cushion, an expensive fountain-pen whose holder was embedded in a slab of green marble, a lead paperweight in the shape of a statue of Athene. . . . It was the sort of jumble one would find in an old lady's work-basket; but then, Errol was something of an old lady. He cleared his throat. 'Well, sir' said Errol, taking off his glasses, 'I've been on to Protocol and said you would like an interview with the Foreign Minister tomorrow on a matter of great urgency. I suppose you'll wear uniform?'

'Uniform?' said Mountolive vaguely.

'The Egyptians are always impressed if one puts on a Tiger Tim.'

'I see. Yes, I suppose so.'

'They tend to judge the importance of what you have to say by the style in which you dress to say it. Donkin is always rubbing it into us and I expect it's true.'

'It is, my dear boy.' (There! The avuncular note again! Damn.)

'And I suppose you'll want to support the verbal side with a definitive *aide-mémoire*. You'll have to give them all the information to back up our contention, won't you, sir?'

Mountolive nodded briskly. He had been submerged suddenly by a wave of hate for Nessim so unfamiliar that it surprised him. Once again, of course, he recognized the root of his anger — that he should be forced into such a position by his friend's indiscretion: forced to proceed against him. He had a sudden little series of mental images — Nessim fleeing the country, Nessim in Hadra Prison, Nessim in chains, Nessim poisoned at his lunchtable by a servant. . . . With the Egyptians one never knew where one was. Their ignorance was matched by an excess of zeal which might land one anywhere. He sighed.

'Of course I shall wear uniform' he said gravely.

'I'll draft the *aide-mémoire*.'

'Very good.'

'I should have a definite time for you within half an hour.'

'Thank you. And I'd like to take Donkin with me. His Arabic is much better than mine and he can take minutes of the meeting so that London can have a telegram giving a full account of it. Will you send him up when he has seen the brief? Thank you.'

All the next morning he hung about in his office, turning over papers in a desultory fashion, forcing himself to work. At mid-day the youthful bearded Donkin arrived with the typed *aide-mémoire* and the news that Mountolive's appointment was for twelve-thirty the next day. His small nervous features and watery eyes made him look more than ever a youthful figure, masquerading in a goatee. He accepted a cigarette and puffed it quickly, like a girl, not inhaling the smoke. 'Well' said Mountolive with a smile, 'your considered views on my brief, please. Errol has told you ——?'

'Yes, sir.'

'What do you think of this . . . vigorous official protest?'

Donkin drew a deep breath and said thoughtfully: 'I doubt if you'll get any direct action at the moment, sir. The internal stresses and strains of the Government since the King's illness have put them all at sixes and sevens. They are all afraid of each other, all pulling different ways. I'm sure that Nur will agree and try hard to get Memlik to act on your paper . . . but. . . .' He drew his lips back thoughtfully about his cigarette. 'I don't know. You know Memlik's record. He hates Britain.'

Mountolive's spirits suddenly began to rise, despite himself. 'Good Lord' he said, 'I hadn't thought of it that way. But they simply can't ignore a protest in these terms. After all, my dear boy, the thing is practically a veiled threat.'

'I know, sir.'

'I really don't see *how* they could ignore it.'

'Well, sir, the King's life is hanging by a hair at present. He might, for example, die tonight. He hasn't sat in Divan for nearly six months. Everyone is at jealousies nowadays, personal dislikes and rivalries have come very close to the surface, and with a vengeance. His death would completely alter things — and everyone knows it. Nur above all. By the way, sir, I hear that he is not on speaking terms with Memlik. There has been some serious trouble about the bribes which people have been paying Memlik.'

'But Nur himself doesn't take bribes?'

Donkin smiled a small sardonic smile and shook his head slowly and doubtfully. 'I don't know, sir' he said primly. 'I suspect that they all do and all would. I may be wrong. But in Hosnani's shoes I should certainly manage to get a stay of action by a handsome bribe to Memlik. His susceptibility to a bribe is . . . almost legendary in Egypt.'

Mountolive tried hard to frown angrily. 'I hope you are wrong' he said. 'Because H.M.G. are determined to get some action on this and so am I. Anyway, we'll see, shall we?'

Donkin was still pursuing some private thoughts in silence and gravity. He sat on for a moment smoking and then stood up. He said thoughtfully: 'Errol said something which suggested that Hosnani knew we were up to his game. If that is so, why has he not cleared out? He must have a clear idea about our own line of attack, must he not? If he has not moved it must mean that he is confident of holding Memlik in check somehow. I am only thinking aloud, sir.'

Mountolive stared at him for a long time with open eyes. He was trying hard to disperse a sudden and, it seemed to him, almost treacherous feeling of optimism. 'Most interesting' he said at last. 'I must confess I hadn't thought of it in those terms.'

'I personally wouldn't take it to the Egyptians at all' said Donkin slyly. He was not averse to teasing his chief of Mission. 'Though it is not my place to say so. I should think that Brigadier Maskelyne has more ways than one of settling the issue. In my view we'd be better advised to leave diplomatic channels alone and simply pay to have Hosnani shot or poisoned. It would cost less than a hundred pounds.'

'Well, thank you very much' said Mountolive feebly, his optimism giving place once more to the dark turmoil of half-rationalized emotions in which he seemed doomed to live perpetually. 'Thank you, Donkin.' (Donkin, he thought angrily, looked awfully like Lenin when he spoke of poison or the knife. It was easy for third secretaries to commit murder by proxy.) Left alone once more he paced his green carpet, balanced between conflicting emotions which were the shapes of hope and despair alternately. Whatever must follow was now irrevocable. He was committed to policies whose outcome, in human terms, was not to be judged. Surely there should be some philosophical resignation to be won from the knowledge? That night he stayed up late listening to his favourite music upon the huge gramophone and drinking rather more heavily than was his wont. From time to time he went across the room and sat at the Georgian writing-desk with his pen poised above a sheet of crested notepaper.

'My dear Leila: At this moment it seems more necessary than ever that I should see you and I must ask you to overcome your. . . .'

But it was a failure. He crumpled up the letters and threw them regretfully into the wastepaper basket. Overcome her what? Was he beginning to hate Leila too, now? Somewhere, stirring in the hinterland of his consciousness was the thought, almost certain knowledge now, that it was she and not Nessim who had initiated these dreadful plans. She was the prime mover. Should he not tell Nur so? Should he not tell his own Government so? Was it not likely that Narouz, who was the man of action in the family, was even more deeply implicated in the conspiracy than Nessim himself? He sighed. What could any of them hope to gain from a successful Jewish insurrection? Mountolive believed too firmly in the English mystique to realize fully that anyone could have lost faith in it and the promise it might hold of future security, future stability.

No, the whole thing seemed to him simply a piece of gratuitous madness; a typical hare-brained business venture with a chance of large profits! How typical of Egypt! He stirred his own contempt slowly with the thought, as one might stir a mustard-pot. How typical of Egypt! Yet, strangely, how un-typical of Nessim!

Sleep was impossible that night. He slipped on a light over-coat, more as a disguise than anything, and went for a long walk by the river in order to settle his thoughts, feeling a foolish regretfulness that there was not a small dog to follow him and occupy his mind. He had slipped out of the servants' quarters, and the resplendent *kawass* and the two police guards were most surprised to see him re-enter the front gate at nearly two o'clock, walking on his own two legs as no Ambassador should ever be allowed to do. He gave them a civil good-evening in Arabic and let himself into the Residence door with his key. Shed his coat and limped across the lighted hall still followed by an imaginary dog which left wet footprints everywhere upon the polished parquet floors. . . .

On his way up to bed he found the now finished painting of himself by Clea standing forlornly against the wall on the first landing. He swore under his breath, for the thing had slipped his mind; he had been meaning to send it off to his mother for the past six weeks. He would make a special point of getting the Bag Room to deal with it tomorrow. They would perhaps have some qualms because of its size, he debated, but nevertheless: he would insist, in order to obviate the trouble of obtaining an export licence for a so-called 'work of art'. (It was certainly not that.) But ever since a German archaeologist had stolen a lot of Egyptian statuary and sold it to the Museums of Europe the Government had been very sensitive about letting works of art out of the country. They would certainly delay a licence for months while the whole thing was debated. No, the Bag Room must attend to it; his mother would be pleased. He thought of her with a sentimental pang, sitting reading by the fire in that snowbound landscape. He owed her a really long letter. But not now. 'After all this is over' he said, and gave a small involuntary shiver.

Once in bed he entered a narrow maze of shallow and unrefreshing dreams in which he floundered all night long — images of the great network of lakes with their swarming fish and clouds of wild birds, where once more the youthful figures of himself and Leila moved, spirited by the soft concussion of oars in water, to the punctuation of a single soft finger-drum across a violet nightscape; on the confines of the dream there moved another boat, in silhouette, with two figures in it — the brothers: both armed with long-barrelled rifles. Soon he would be overtaken; but warm in the circle of Leila's arms, as if he were Antony at Actium, he could hardly bring himself to feel fear. They did not speak, or at least, he heard no voices. As for himself, he felt only the messages to and from the woman in his arms — transmitted it seemed only by the ticking blood. They were past speech and reflection — the diminished figures of an unforgotten, unregretted past, infinitely dear now because irrecoverable. In the heart of the dream itself, he knew he was dreaming, and awoke with surprise and anguish to find tears upon the pillow. Breakfasting according to established custom, he suddenly felt as if he had a fever, but the thermometer refused to confirm his belief. So he rose reluctantly and presented himself in full fig, punctual upon the instant, to find Donkin nervously pacing the hall with the bundle of papers under his arm. 'Well' said Mountolive, with a gesture vaguely indicating his rig, 'here I am at last.'

In the black car with its fluttering pennant they slid smoothly across the town to the Ministry where the timid and ape-like Egyptian waited for them full of uneasy solicitudes and alarms. He was visibly impressed by the dress uniform and by the fact that the two best Arabists of the British Mission had been detailed to call upon him. He gleamed and bowed, automatically playing the opening hand — an exchange of formal politenesses — with his customary practice. He was a small sad man with tin cuff-links and matted hair. His anxiety to please, to accommodate, was so great that he fell easily into postures of friendship, almost of mawkishness. His eyes watered easily. He pressed ceremonial coffee and Turkish delight upon them as if the gesture itself represented a confession of love almost. He mopped his brow continually, and gave his ingratiating pithecanthropoid grimace. 'Ah! Ambassador' he said sentimentally as the compliments gave place to business. 'You know our language and our country well. We trust you.' Paraphrased, his words meant: 'You know our venality to be ineradicable, the mark of an ancient culture, therefore we do not feel ashamed in your presence.'

Then he sat with his paws folded over his neat grey waistcoat, glum as a foetus in a bottle, as Mountolive delivered his strongly worded protest and produced the monument to Maskelyne's industry. Nur listened, shaking his head doubtfully from time to time, his visage lengthening. When Mountolive had done, he said impulsively, standing up: 'Of course. At once. At once.' And then, as if plunged into doubt, unsteadily sat down once more and began to play with his cuff-links. Mountolive sighed as he stood up. 'It is a disagreeable duty' he said, 'but necessary. May I assure my Government that the matter will be prosecuted with speed?'

'With speed. With speed.' The little man nodded twice and licked his lips; one had the impression that he did not quite understand the words he was using. 'I shall see Memlik today' he added in lower tones. But the timbre of his voice had changed. He coughed and ate a sweetmeat, dusting the castor sugar off his fingers with a silk handkerchief. 'Yes' he said. If he was interested in the massive document lying before him it was (or so it seemed to Mountolive) only that the photostats intrigued him. He had not seen things like these before. They belonged to the great foreign worlds of science and illusion in which these Western peoples lived — worlds of great powers and responsibilities — out of which they sometimes descended, clad in magnificent uniforms, to make the lot of the simple Egyptians harder than it was at the best of times. 'Yes. Yes. Yes' said Nur again, as if to give the conversation stability and depth, to give his visitor confidence in his good intentions.

Mountolive did not like it at all; the whole tone lacked directness, purpose. The absurd sense of optimism rose once more in his breast and in order to punish himself for it (also because he was extremely conscientious) he stepped forward and pressed the matter forward another inch. 'If you like, Nur, and if you expressly authorize me, I am prepared to lay the facts and recommendations before Memlik Pasha myself. Only speak.' But here he was pressing upon the shallow, newly-grown skin of protocol and national feeling. 'Cherished Sir' said Nur with a beseeching smile and the gesture of a beggar importuning a rich man, 'that would be out of order. For the matter is an internal one. It would not be proper for me to agree.'

And he was right there, reflected Mountolive, as they drove uneasily back to the Embassy; they could no longer give orders in Egypt as once the High Commission had been able to do. Donkin sat with a quizzical and reflective smile, studying his own fingers. The pennant on the car's radiator fluttered merrily, reminding Mountolive of the quivering burgee of Nessim's thirty-foot cutter as it slit the harbour waters. . . . 'What did you make of it, Donkin?' he said, putting his arm on the elbow of the bearded youth.

'Frankly, sir, I doubted.'

'So did I, really.' Then he burst out: 'But they will have to act, simply have to; I am not going to be put aside like this.' (He was thinking: 'London will make our lives a misery until I can give them some sort of satisfaction.') Hate for an image of Nessim whose features had somehow — as if by a trick of double-exposure — become merged with those of the saturnine Maskelyne, flooded him again. Crossing the hall he caught sight of his own face in the great pierglass and was surprised to notice that it wore an expression of feeble petulance.

That day he found himself becoming more and more short-tempered with his staff and the Residence servants. He had begun to feel almost persecuted.

*　　*　　*　　*　　*

XIV

If Nessim had the temerity to laugh softly now to himself as he studied the invitation: if he propped the florid thing against his inkstand the better to study it, laughing softly and uneasily into the space before him; it was because he was thinking to himself:

'To say that a man is unscrupulous implies that he was born with inherent scruples which he now chooses to disregard. But does one visualize a man *born* patently conscienceless? A man *born* without a common habit of soul? (Memlik).'

Yes, it would be easy if he were legless, armless, blind, to visualize him; but a particular deficit of a glandular secretion, a missing portion of soul, that would make him rather a target for wonder, perhaps even commiseration. (Memlik). There were men whose feelings dispersed in spray — became as fine as if squeezed through an atomizer: those who had frozen them — 'pins and needles of the heart'; there were others born without a sense of value — the morally colour-blind ones. The very powerful were often like that — men walking inside a dream-cloud of their actions which somehow lacked meaning to them. Was this also Memlik? Nessim felt all the passionate curiosity about the man which an entomologist might have for an unclassified specimen.

Light a cigarette. Get up and walk about the room, pausing from time to time to read the invitation and laugh again silently. The relief kept displacing anxiety, the anxiety relief. He lifted the telephone and spoke to Justine quietly, with a smiling voice: 'The Mountain has been to Mahomet.' (Code for Mountolive and Nur.) 'Yes, my dear. It is a relief to know for certain. All my toxicology and pistol-practice! It looks silly now, I know. This is the way I would have wanted it to happen; but of course, one had to take precautions. Well, pressure is being put upon Mahomet, and he has delivered a small mouse in the form of an invitation to a *Wird*.' He heard her laugh incredulously. 'Please, my darling' he said, 'obtain one of the finest Korans you can get and send it to the office. There are some old ones with ivory covers in the library collection. Yes, I shall take it to Cairo on Wednesday. He must certainly have his Koran.' (Memlik.) It was all very well to joke. The respite would only be a temporary one; but at least he need not for the moment fear poison or the stealthy figure lurking in an alley which *might* have. . . . No. The situation seemed not without a promise of fruitful delay.

Today in the sixties the house of Memlik Pasha has become famous in the remotest capitals of the world chiefly because of the distinctive architecture of the Banks which bear their founder's name; and indeed their style has all the curious marks of this mysterious man's taste — for they are all built to the same grotesque pattern, a sort of travesty of an Egyptian tomb, adapted by a pupil of Corbusier! Irresistibly one is forced to stop short and wonder at their grim façades, whether one is walking in Rome or Rio. The squat pillars suggest a mammoth stricken by sudden elephantiasis, the grotesque survival, or perhaps revival, of something inherently macabre — a sort of Ottoman-Egyptian-Gothic? For all the world as if Euston Station had multiplied by binary fission! But by now the power of the man has gone out through these strange funnels into the world at large — all that power condensed and deployed from the small inlaid coffee-table upon which (if ever) he wrote, from the tattered yellow divan to which his lethargy held him tethered day by day. (For interviews of particular importance, he wore his tarbush and yellow suède gloves. In his hand he held a common market fly-whisk which his jeweller had embellished with a design in seed-pearls.) He never smiled. A Greek photographer who had once implored him in the name of art to do so had been unceremoniously carted out into the garden under the clicking palms and dealt twelve lashes to atone for his insult.

Perhaps the strange mixture of heredities had something to do with it; for his blood was haunted by an Albanian father and a Nubian mother, whose dreadful quarrels tormented his childhood sleep. He was an only son. This was perhaps how simple ferocity contrived to be matched against an apparent apathy, a whispering voice raised sometimes to a woman's pitch but employed without the use of gesture. Physically too, the long silky head-hair with its suggestion of kink, the nose and mouth carved flatly in dark Nubian sandstone and set in bas-relief upon a completely round Alpine head — they gave the show away. If indeed he had smiled he would have shown a half-circumference of nigger whiteness under nostrils flattened and expanded like rubber. His skin was full of dark beauty-spots, and of a colour much admired in Egypt — that of cigar-leaf. Depilatories such as *halawa* kept his body free from hair, even his hands and forearms. But his eyes were small and set in puckers, like twin cloves. They transmitted their uneasiness by an expression of perpetual drowsiness — the discoloured whites conveying a glaucous absence of mind — as if the soul inhabiting that great body were perpetually away on a private holiday. His lips too were very red, the underlip particularly so; and their contused-looking ripeness suggested: epilepsy?

How had he risen so swiftly? Stage by stage, through slow and arduous clerkships in the Commission (which had taught him his contempt for his masters) and lastly by nepotism. His methods were choice and studied. When Egypt became free, he surprised even his sponsors by gaining the Ministry of the Interior at a single bound. Only then did he tear off the disguise of mediocrity which he had been wearing all these years. He knew very well how to strike out echoes around his name with the whip — for he was now wielding it. The timorous soul of the Egyptian cries always for the whip. 'O want easily supplied by one who has trained himself to see men and women as flies.' So says the proverb. Within a matter of a year his name had become a dreaded one; it was rumoured that even the old King feared to cross him openly. And with his country's new-found freedom he himself was also magnificently free — at least with Egyptian Moslems. Europeans had still the right, by treaty, to submit their judicial problems or answer charges against them at Les Tribunaux Mixtes, European courts with European lawyers to prosecute or defend. But the Egyptian judicial system (if one could dare to call it that) was run directly by men of Memlik's stamp, the anachronistic survivals of a feudalism as terrible as it was meaningless. The age of the Cadi was far from over for them and Memlik acted with all the authority of someone with a Sultan's *firman* or dispensation in his hands. There was, in truth, nobody to gainsay him. He punished hard and often, without asking questions and often purely upon hearsay or the most remote suspicion. People disappeared silently, leaving no trace, and there was no court of appeal to heed their appeals — if they made any — or else they reappeared in civil life elegantly maimed or deftly blinded — and somehow curiously unwilling to discuss their misfortunes in public. ('Shall we see if he can sing?' Memlik was reputed to say; the reference was to the putting out of a canary's eyes with a red-hot wire — an operation much resorted to and alleged to make the bird sing more sweetly.)

An indolent yet clever man, he depended for his staff work upon

Greeks and Armenians for the most part. He hardly ever visited his office in the Ministry but left its running to his minions, explaining and complaining that he was always besieged there by time-wasting petitioners. (In fact he feared that one day he might be assassinated there — for it was a vulnerable sort of place. It would have been easy, for example, to place a bomb in one of the unswept cupboards where the mice frolicked among the yellowing files. Hakim Effendi had put the idea into his head so that he himself could have a free play in the Ministry. Memlik knew this, but did not care.)

Instead he had set aside the old rambling house by the Nile for his audiences. It was surrounded by a dense grove of palms and orange-trees. The sacred river flowed outside his windows. there was always something to see, to watch: feluccas plying up or down-river, pleasure parties passing, an occasional motor-boat. . . . Also it was too far for petitioners to come and bother him about imprisoned relations. (Hakim shared the office bribes anyway.) Here Memlik would only see people who were relatively too important to dismiss: struggling upright into a seated position on the yellow divan and placing his neat shoes (with their pearl-grey spats) upon a damask footstool before him, his right hand in his breast pocket, his left holding the common market fly-whisk as if to confer an absolution with it. The staff attending to his daily business transactions here consisted of an Armenian secretary (Cyril) and the little doll-like Italian Rafael (by profession a barber and procurer) who kept him company and sweetened the dullness of official work by suggesting pleasures whose perversity might ignite a man who appeared to have worn away every mental appetite save that for money. I say that Memlik never smiled, but sometimes when he was in good humour, he stroked Rafael's hair thoughtfully and placed his fingers over his mouth to silence his laughter. This was when he was thinking deeply before lifting the receiver of the old-fashioned goose-necked telephone to have a conversation with someone in that low voice, or to ring the Central Prison for the pleasure of hearing the operator's obvious alarm when he uttered his name. At this, Rafael particularly would break into sycophantic giggles, laughing until the tears ran down his face, stuffing a handkerchief into his mouth. But Memlik did not smile. He depressed his cheeks slightly and said: 'Allah! you laugh.' Such occasions were few and far between.

Was he indeed as terrible as his reputation made him? The

truth will never be known. Legends collect easily around such a personage because he belongs more to legend than to life. ('Once when he was threatened by impotence he went down to the prison and ordered two girls to be flogged to death before his eyes while a third was obliged' — how picturesque are the poetical figures of the Prophet's tongue — 'to refresh his lagging spirits.' It was said that he personally witnessed every official execution, and that he trembled and spat continuously. Afterwards he called for a siphon of soda-water to quench his thirst. . . . But who shall ever know the truth of these legends?)

He was morbidly superstitious and incurably venal — and indeed was building an immense fortune upon bribery; yet how shall we add to the sum of this the fact of his inordinate religiosity — a fanatical zeal of observance which might have been puzzling in anyone who was not an Egyptian? This is where the quarrel with the pious Nur had arisen; for Memlik had established almost a court-form for the reception of bribes. His collection of Korans was a famous one. They were housed upstairs in a ramshackle gallery of the house. By now it was known far and wide that the polite form in which to approach him was to interleave a particularly cherished copy of the Holy Book with notes or other types of currency and (with an obeisance) to present him with a new addition to his great library. He would accept the gift and reply, with thanks that he must repair at once upstairs to see if he already had a copy. On his return, the petitioner knew that he had succeeded if Memlik thanked him once more and said that he had put the book in his library; but if Memlik claimed to possess a copy already and handed back the book (albeit the money had inevitably been extracted) the petitioner knew that his plea had failed. It was this little social formula which Nur had characterized as 'bringing discredit upon the Prophet' — and had so earned Memlik's quiet hate.

The long-elbowed conservatory in which he held his private Divan was also something of a puzzle. The coloured fanlights in cheap cathedral glass transformed visitors into harlequins, squirting green and scarlet and blue upon their faces and clothes as they walked across the long room to greet their host. Outside the murky windows ran the cocoa-coloured river on whose further bank stood the British Embassy with its elegant gardens in which Mountolive wandered on the evenings when he found himself alone. The wall-length of Memlik's great reception-room was almost covered by two enormous and incongruous Victorian paintings by some forgotten master which, being too large and heavy to hang, stood upon the floor and gave something of the illusion of framed tapestries. But the subject-matter! In one, the Israelites crossed the Red Sea which was gracefully piled up on either side to admit their fearful passage, in the other a hirsute Moses struck a stage rock with a shepherd's crook. Somehow these attenuated Biblical subjects matched the rest of the furniture perfectly — the great Ottoman carpets and the stiff ugly-backed chairs covered in blue damask, the immense contorted brass chandelier with its circles of frosted electric light bulbs which shone night and day. On one side of the yellow divan stood a life-size bust of Fouché which took the eye of the petitioner at once by its incongruity. Once Memlik had been flattered by a French diplomat who had said: 'You are regarded as the best Minister of Interior in modern history — indeed, since Fouché there has been no-one to equal you.' The remark may have been barbed, but nevertheless it struck Memlik's fancy, and he at once ordered the bust from France. It looked faintly reproachful amidst all that Egyptian flummery, for the dust had settled thick upon it. The same diplomat had once described Memlik's reception-room as a cross between an abandoned geological museum and a corner of the old Crystal Palace — and this also was apt though cruel.

All this detail Nessim's polite eye took in with many a hidden gleam of amusement as he stood in the doorway and heard his name announced. It appealed richly to him to be thus invited to share a prayer-meeting or *Wird* with the redoubtable Memlik. Nor were these functions uncommon, strange though it seems to relate, for Memlik frequently enjoyed these so-called 'Nights of God' and his piety did not seem inconsistent with the rest of his mysterious character; he listened attentively, unwaveringly to the reciter, often until two or three in the morning, with the air of a hibernating snake. Sometimes he even joined in the conventional gasp 'Allah' with which the company expressed its joy in some particularly felicitous passage of the Gospel. . . .

Nessim crossed the chamber with a light and lively walk, conventionally touching breast and lip, and seated himself before Memlik to express gratitude for an invitation which did him great honour. On the evening of his appearance there were nine or ten other guests only, and he felt certain that this was because Memlik wished to study him, if possible even to hold some private conversation with him. He carried the exquisite little Koran wrapped in soft tissue paper; he had carefully larded the pages with bank drafts negotiable in Switzerland. 'O Pasha' he said softly, 'I have heard of your legendary library and ask only the pleasure of a book-lover in offering you an addition to it.' He laid his present down on the little table and accepted the coffee and sweetmeats which were placed before him. Memlik neither answered nor moved his position on the divan for a long moment, allowing him to sip his coffee, and then said negligently: 'The host is honoured. These are my friends.' He performed some rather perfunctory introductions to his other visitors who seemed rather an odd collection to gather together for a recitation of the Gospel; there was nobody here of any obvious standing in the society of Cairo, this much Nessim noticed. Indeed, he knew none of them though he was attentively polite to all. Then he permitted himself a few generalized comments on the beauty and appropriateness of the reception chamber and the high quality of the paintings against the wall. Memlik was not displeased by this and said lazily: 'It is both my work-room and my reception-room. Here I live.'

'I have often heard it described' said Nessim with his courtier's air 'by those lucky enough to visit you either for work or pleasure.'

'My work' said Memlik with a glint 'is done on Tuesdays only. For the rest of the week I take pleasure with my friends.'

Nessim was not deaf to the menace in the words; Tuesday for the Moslem is the least favoured day for human undertakings, for he believes that on Tuesday God created all the unpleasant things. It is the day chosen for the execution of criminals; no man dares marry on a Tuesday for the proverb says: 'Married on Tuesday, hanged on Tuesday.' In the words of the Prophet: 'On Tuesday God created darkness absolute.'

'Happily' said the smiling Nessim 'today is Monday, when God created the trees.' And he led the conversation around to the lovely palm-trees which nodded outside the window: a conversational turn which broke the ice and won the admiration of the other visitors.

The wind changed now, and after half an hour of desultory talk, the sliding doors at the far end of the chamber were set aside to admit them to a banquet laid out upon two great tables. The room was decorated with magnificent flowers. Here at least over the expensive delicacies of Memlik's supper table, the hint of animation and friendship became a little more obvious. One or two people talked, and Memlik himself, though he ate nothing, moved slowly from group to group uttering laboured politenesses in a low voice. He came upon Nessim in a corner and said quite simply, indeed with an air of candour: 'I wished particularly to see you, Hosnani.'

'I am honoured, Memlik Pasha.'

'I have seen you at receptions; but we have lacked common friends to present us to each other. Great regrets.'

'Great regrets.'

Memlik sighed and fanned himself with his fly-whisk, complaining that the night was hot. Then he said, in a tone of a man debating something with himself, hesitantly almost: 'Sir, the Prophet has said that great power brings greater enemies. I know you are powerful.'

'My power is insignificant, yet I have enemies.'

'Great regrets.'

'Indeed.'

Memlik shifted his weight to his left leg and picked his teeth thoughtfully for a moment; then he went on:

'I think we shall understand each other perfectly soon.'

Nessim bowed formally and remained silent while his host gazed speculatively at him, breathing slowly and evenly through his mouth. Memlik said: 'When they wish to complain, they come to me, the very fountain-head of complaints. I find it wearisome, but sometimes I am forced to act on behalf of those who complain. You take my meaning?'

'Perfectly.'

'At some moments, I am not bound to commit myself to particular action. But at others, I may be so bound. Therefore, Nessim Hosnani, the wise man removes the grounds for complaints.'

Nessim bowed again gracefully and once more remained silent. It was useless to pursue the dialectics of their relative positions until he had obtained acceptance of his proffered gift. Memlik perhaps sensed this, for he sighed and moved away to another group of visitors, and presently the dinner ended and the company retired once more to the long reception-room. Now Nessim's pulse beat faster, for Memlik picked up the tissue-wrapped package and excused himself, saying 'I must compare this with the books in my collection. The sheik of tonight — he of Imbabi — will come soon now. Seat yourselves and take your leisure. I will join you soon.' He left the room. A desultory conversation began now, in which Nessim tried his best to take part though he realized that his heart was beating uncomfortably fast and his fingers felt shaky as they raised a cigarette to his lips. After a while, the doors were once more opened to admit an old blind sheik who had come to preside over this 'Night Of God'. The company surrounded him, shaking his hands and uttering compliments. And then Memlik entered abruptly and Nessim saw that his hands were empty: he uttered a prayer of thanksgiving under his breath and mopped his brow.

It did not take him long to compose himself once more. He was standing rather apart from the press of dark-coated gentlemen in whose midst stood the old blind preacher, whose vacant, bewildered face turned from voice to voice with the air of some mechanical contrivance built to register sound-waves; his air of mild confusion suggested all the ghostly contentment of an absolute faith in something which was the more satisfying for not being fully apprehended by the reason. His hands were joined on his breast; he looked as shy as some ancient child, full of the kinetic beauty of a human being whose soul has become a votive object.

The pasha who entered once more made his way slowly to Nessim's side, but by stages so delayed that it seemed to the latter he would never reach him. This slow progress was prolonged by compliments and an air of elaborate disinterestedness. At last he was there, at Nessim's elbow, his long clever fingers still holding the bejewelled fly-whisk. 'Your gift is a choice one' the low voice said at last, with the faintest suggestion of honey in its tones. 'It is most acceptable. Indeed, sir, your knowledge and discrimination are both legendary. To show surprise would betoken vulgar ignorance of the fact.'

The formula which Memlik invariably used was so smooth and remarkably well-turned in Arabic that Nessim could not help looking surprised and pleased. It was a choice turn of speech such as only a really cultivated person would have used. He did not know that Memlik had carefully memorized it against such occasions. He bowed his head as one might to receive an accolade, but remained silent. Memlik flirted his fly-whisk for a moment, before adding in another tone: 'Of course, there is only one thing.

I have already spoken of the complaints which come to me, *effendi* mine. In all such cases I am bound sooner or later to investigate causes. Great regrets.'

Nessim turned his smooth black eye upon the Egyptian and still smiling said in a low voice: 'Sir, by the European Christmastide — a matter of months — there will be no further grounds for complaint.' There was a silence.

'Then time is important' said Memlik reflectively.

'Time is the air we breathe, so says a proverb.'

The pasha half turned now and, speaking as if to the company in general, added: 'My collection has need of your most discriminating knowledge. I hope you may discover for me many other treasures of the Holy Word.' Again Nessim bowed.

'As many as may be found acceptable, pasha.'

'I am sorry we did not meet before. Great regrets.'

'Great regrets.'

But now he became the host again and turned aside. The wide circle of uncomfortable stiff-backed chairs had been almost filled by his other visitors. Nessim selected one at the end of the line as Memlik reached his yellow divan and climbed slowly upon it with the air of a swimmer reaching a raft in mid-ocean. He gave a signal and the servants came forward to remove the coffee-cups and sweetmeats; they brought with them a tall and elegant high-backed chair with carved arms and green upholstery which they set for the preacher a little to one side of the room. A guest rose and with mutterings of respect led the blind man to his seat. Retiring in good order the servants closed and bolted the tall doors at the end of the room. The *Wird* was about to begin. Memlik formally opened the proceedings with a quotation from Ghazzali the theologian — a surprising innovation for someone, like Nessim, whose picture of the man had been formed entirely from hearsay. 'The only way' said Memlik 'to become united with God is by constant intercourse with him.' Having uttered the words he leaned back and closed his eyes, as if exhausted by the effort. But the phrase had the effect of a signal, for as the blind preacher raised his scraggy neck and inhaled deeply before commencing, the company responded like one man. At once all cigarettes were extinguished, every leg was uncrossed, coat buttons formally done up, every negligent attitude of body and address corrected.

They waited now with emotion for that old voice, melodious

and worn with age, to utter the opening strophes of the Holy Book, and there was nothing feigned in the adoring attention of the circle of venal faces. Some licked their lips and leaned forward eagerly, as if to take the phrases upon their lips; others lowered their heads and closed their eyes as if against a new experience in music. The old preacher sat with his waxen hands folded in his lap and uttered the first *sura*, full of the soft warm colouring of a familiar understanding, his voice a little shaky at first but gathering power and assurance from the silence as he proceeded. His eyes now were as wide and lustreless as a dead hare's. His listeners followed the notation of the verses as they fell from his lips with care and rapture, gradually seeking their way together out into the main stream of the poetry, like a school of fish following a leader by instinct out into the deep sea. Nessim's own constraint and unease gave place to a warmth about the heart, for he loved the *suras*, and the old preacher had a magnificent speaking voice, although the tone was as yet furry and unaccentuated. But it was a 'voice of the inmost heart' — his whole spiritual presence coursed like a bloodstream in the magnificent verses, filling them with his own ardour, and one could feel his audience tremble and respond, like the rigging of a ship in the wind. '*Allah!*' they sighed at every newly remembered felicity of phrasing, and these little gasps increased the confidence of the old voice with its sweet high register. 'A voice whose melody is sweeter than charity' says the proverb. The recitation was a dramatic one and very varied in style, the preacher changing his tone to suit the substance of the words, now threatening, now pleading, now declaiming, now admonishing. It was no surprise that he should be word-perfect, for in Egypt the blind preachers have a faculty for memorizing which is notorious, and moreover the whole length of the Koran is about two-thirds that of the New Testament. Nessim listened to him with tenderness and admiration, staring down upon the carpet, half-entranced by the ebb and flow of the poetry which distracted his mind from the tireless speculations he had been entertaining about Memlik's possible response to the pressures which Mountolive had been forced to bring upon him.

Between each *sura* there came a few moments of silence in which nobody stirred or uttered a word, but appeared sunk in contemplation of what had gone before. The preacher then sank his chin upon his breastbone as if to regain his strength and softly linked his fingers. Then once more he would look upwards towards the sightless light and declaim, and once more one felt the tension of the words as they sped through the attentive consciousness of his listeners. It was after midnight when the Koran reading was complete and some measure of relaxation came back to the audience as the old man embarked upon the stories of tradition; these were no longer listened to as if they were a part of music, but were followed with the active proverbial mind: for they were the dialectics of revelation — its ethic and application. The company responded to the changed tone by letting their expression brighten to the keenness of habitual workers in the world, bankers, students, or business men.

It was two o'clock before the evening ended and Memlik showed his guests to the front door where their cars awaited them, with a white dew upon their wheels and chromium surfaces. To Nessim he said in a quiet deliberate voice — a voice which went down to the heart of their relationship like some heavy plumb-line: 'I will invite you again, sir, for as long as may be possible. But reflect.' And with his finger he gently touched the coat-button of his guest as if to underline the remark.

Nessim thanked him and walked down the drive among the palm-trees to where he had left the great car; his naked relief was by no means unmixed with doubt. He had at best, he reflected, gained a respite which did not fundamentally alter the enmity of the forces ranged against him. But even a respite was something to be grateful for; for how long though? It was at this stage impossible to judge.

Justine had not gone to bed. She was sitting in the lounge of Shepheards Hotel under the clock with an untouched Turkish coffee before her. She stood up eagerly as he passed through the swing doors with his usual gentle smile of welcome; she did not move but stared at him with a peculiar strained intensity — as if she were trying to decipher his feelings from his carriage. Then she relaxed and smiled with relief. 'I'm so relieved! Thank God! I could see from your face as you came in.' They embraced gently and he sank into a chair beside her whispering: 'My goodness, I thought it would never end. I spent part of the time being rather anxious too. Did you dine alone?'

'Yes. I saw David.'

'Mountolive?'

'He was at some big dinner. He bowed frigidly but did not

stop to speak to me. But then, he had people with him, bankers or something.'

Nessim ordered a coffee and as he drank it gave an account of his evening with Memlik. 'It is clear' he said thoughtfully 'that the sort of pressure the British are bringing is based upon those files of correspondence they captured in Palestine. The Haifa office told Capodistria so. It would be a good angle to present these to Nur and press him to . . . take action.' He drew a tiny gallows in pencil on the back of an envelope with a small fly-like victim hanging from it. 'What I gathered from Memlik suggested that he can *delay* action but that the sort of pressure is too strong to ignore indefinitely; sooner or later he will be forced to satisfy Nur. I virtually told him that by Christmas I would be able . . . I would be out of the danger zone. His investigations would lead nowhere.'

'*If* everything goes according to plan.'

'Everything *will* go according to plan.'

'Then what?'

'Then what!' Nessim stretched his long arms over his head, yawning, and nodded sideways at her. 'We will take up new dispositions. Da Capo will disappear; you will go away. Leila will go down to Kenya for a long holiday together with Narouz. That is what!'

'And you?'

'I shall stay on a little while to keep things in place here. The Community needs me. There is a lot to be done politically still. Then I shall come to you and we can have a long holiday in Europe or anywhere you choose. . . .'

She was staring unsmilingly at him. 'I am nervous' she said at last with a little shiver. 'Nessim, let us drive by the Nile for an hour and collect our thoughts before we go to bed.'

He was glad to indulge her, and for an hour the car nosed softly along the noble tree-lined roads of the Nile river-bank under the jacarandas, its engine purring, while they talked intermittently in low voices. 'What worries me' she said, 'is that you will have Memlik's hand upon your shoulder. How will you ever shake it off? If he has firm evidence against you, he will never relax his grip until you are squeezed dry.'

'Either way' said Nessim quietly 'it would be bad for us. For if he proceeded with an open enquiry, you know very well that it would give the Government a chance to sequestrate our properties. I would rather satisfy his private cupidity as long as I can. Afterwards, we shall see. The main thing is to concentrate on this coming . . . battle.'

As he uttered the word they were passing the brilliantly lighted gardens of the British Embassy. Justine gave a little start and plucked his sleeve, for she had caught sight of a slender pyjama-clad figure walking about the green lawns with an air of familiar distraction. 'Mountolive' she said. Nessim looked sorrowfully across the gardens at his friend, suddenly possessed by a temptation to stop the car and enter the gardens to surprise him. Such a gesture would have been in keeping with their behaviour towards each other — not three months before. What had happened to everything now? 'He'll catch cold' said Justine; 'he is barefooted. Holding a telegram.'

Nessim increased speed and the car curved on down the avenue. 'I expect' he said 'that he suffers from insomnia and wanted to cool his feet in the grass before trying to get to sleep. You often used to do that. Remember?'

'But the telegram?'

There was really no great mystery about the telegram which the sleepless Ambassador held in his hand and which he studied from time to time as he walked slowly about in his own demesne, smoking a cigar. Once a week he played a game of chess with Balthazar by telegram — an event which nowadays gave him great solace, and some of the refreshment which tired men of affairs draw from crossword puzzles. He did not see the great car as it purred on past the gardens and headed for the town.

* * * * *

XV

They were to stay like this for many weeks now, the actors: as if trapped once and for all in postures which might illustrate how incalculable a matter naked providence can be. To Mountolive, more than the others, came a disenchanting sense of his own professional inadequacy, his powerlessness to act now save as an instrument (no longer a factor), so strongly did he feel himself gripped by the gravitational field of politics. Private humours and impulses were alike disinherited, counting for nothing. Did Nessim also feel the mounting flavour of stagnation in everything? He thought back bitterly and often to the casually spoken words of Sir Louis as he was combing his hair in the mirror. 'The illusion that you are free to act!' He suffered from excruciating headaches now from time to time and his teeth began to give him trouble. For some reason or another he took the fancy that this was due to over-smoking and tried to abandon the habit unsuccessfully. The struggle with tobacco only increased his misery.

Yet if he himself were powerless, now, how much more so the others? Like the etiolated projections of a sick imagination, they seemed, drained of meaning, empty as suits of clothes; taking up emplacements in this colourless drama of contending wills. Nessim, Justine, Leila — they had an unsubstantial air now — as of dream projections acting in a world populated by expressionless waxworks. It was difficult to feel that he owed them even love any longer. Leila's silence above all suggested, even more clearly, the guilt of her complicity.

Autumn drew to an end and still Nur could produce no proof of action. The life-lines which tied Mountolive's Mission to London became clogged with longer and longer telegrams full of the shrewish iterations of minds trying to influence the operation of what Mountolive now knew to be not merely chance, but in fact destiny. It was interesting, too, in a paradoxical sort of way, this first great lesson which his profession had to teach him; for outside the circumscribed area of his personal fears and hesitations, he watched the whole affair with a kind of absorbed attention, with almost a sense of dreadful admiration. But it was like some fretful mummy that he now presented himself to the gaze of Nur, almost ashamed of the splendours of that second-hand uniform, so clearly was it intended to admonish or threaten the Minister. The old man was full of a feverish desire to accommodate him; he was like a monkey jumping enthusiastically on the end of a chain. But what could he do? He made faces to match his transparent excuses. The investigations undertaken by Memlik were not as yet complete. It was essential to verify the truth. The threads were still being followed up. And so forth.

Mountolive did what he had never done before in his official life, colouring up and banging the dusty table between them with friendly exasperation. He adopted the countenance of a thundercloud and predicted a rupture of diplomatic relations. He went so far as to recommend Nur for a decoration . . . realizing that this was his last resort. But in vain.

The broad contemplative figure of Memlik squatted athwart the daylight, promising everything, performing nothing; immovable, imperturbable, and only faintly malign. Each was now pressing the other beyond the point of polite conciliation: Maskelyne and the High Commissioner were pressing London for action; London, full of moralizing grandeurs, pressed Mountolive; Mountolive pressed Nur, overwhelming the old man with a sense of his own ineffectuality, for he too was powerless to grapple with Memlik without the help of the King: and the King was ill, very ill. At the bottom of this pyramid sat the small figure of the Minister for Interior, with his priceless collection of Korans locked away in dusty cupboards.

Constrained nevertheless to keep up the diplomatic pressure, Mountolive was now irradiated by an appalling sense of futility as he sat (like some ageing *jeune premier*) and listened to the torrent of Nur's excuses, drinking the ceremonial coffee and prying into those ancient and imploring eyes. 'But what more evidence do you need, Pasha, than the papers I brought you?' The Minister's hands spread wide, smoothing the air between them as if he were rubbing cold-cream into it; he exuded a conciliatory and apologetic affection, like an unguent. 'He is going into the matter' he croaked helplessly. 'There is more than one Hosnani, to begin with' he added in desperation. Backwards and forwards moved the tortoise's wrinkled head, regular as a pendulum. Mountolive groaned inside himself as he thought of those long telegrams following one another, endless as a tapeworm. Nessim had now, so to speak, wedged himself neatly in between his various adversaries, in a position where neither could reach him — for the time being. The game was in baulk.

Donkin alone derived a quizzical amusement from these exchanges — so characteristic of Egypt. His own affection for the Moslem had taught him to see clearly into his motives, to discern the play of childish cupidities underneath the histrionic silence of a Minister, under his facile promises. Even Mountolive's gathering hysteria in the face of these checks was amusing for a junior secretary. His Chief had become a puffy and petulant dignitary, under all this stress. Who could have believed such a change possible?

The observation that there was more than one Hosnani was a strange one, and it was a fruit of the prescient Rafael's thought as he quietly shaved his master one morning, according to custom; Memlik paid great attention to what the barber said — was he not a European? While the little barber shaved him in the morning they discussed the transactions of the day. Rafael was full of ideas and opinions, but he uttered them obliquely, simplifying them so that they presented themselves in readily understandable form. He knew that Memlik had been troubled by Nur's insistence, though he had not shown it; he knew, moreover, that Memlik would act only if the King recovered enough to grant Nur an audience. It was a matter of luck and time; meanwhile, why not pluck Hosnani as far as possible? It was only one of a dozen such matters which lay gathering dust (and perhaps bribes) while the King was ill.

One fine day His Majesty would feel much better under his new German doctors and would grant audience once again. He would send for Nur. That is the manner in which the matter would fall out. The next thing: the old goose-necked telephone by the yellow divan would tingle and the old man's voice (disguising its triumphant tone) would say, 'I am Nur, speaking from the very Divan of the Very King, having received audience. That matter of which we spoke concerning the British Government. It must now be advanced and go forward. Give praise to God!'

'Give praise to God!' and from this point forward Memlik's hands would be tied. But for the moment he was still a free agent, free to express his contempt for the elder Minister by inaction.

'There are two brothers, Excellence,' Rafael had said, putting on a story-book voice and casting an expression of gloomy maturity upon his little doll's face. 'Two brothers Hosnani, not one, Excellence.' He sighed as his white fingers took up small purses of Memlik's dark skin for the razor to work upon. He proceded slowly, for to register an idea in a Moslem mind is like trying to paint a wall: one must wait for the first coat to dry (the first idea) before applying a second. 'Of the two brothers, one is rich in land, and the other rich in money — he of the Koran. Of what good are lands to my Excellence? But one whose purse is fathomless. . . .' His tone suggested all the landless man's contempt for good ground.

'Well, well, but. . . .' said Memlik with a slow, unemphatic impatience, yet without moving his lips under the kiss of the crisp razor. He was impatient for the theme to be developed. Rafael smiled and was silent for a moment. 'Indeed' he said thoughtfully, 'the papers you received from his Excellence were signed Hosnani — in the family name. Who is to say which brother signed them, which is guilty and which innocent? If you were wise in deed would you sacrifice a moneyed man to a landed one? I not, Excellence, I not.'

'What would you do, my Rafael?'

'For people like the British it could be made to seem that the poor one was guilty, not the rich. I am only thinking aloud, Excellence, a small man among great affairs.'

Memlik breathed quietly through his mouth, keeping his eyes shut. He was skilled in never showing surprise. Yet the thought, suspended idly in his mind, filled him with a reflective astonishment. In the last month he had received three additions to his library which had left in little doubt the comparative affluence of his client, the elder Hosnani. It was getting on for the Christian Christmastide. He pondered heavily. To satisfy both the British and his own cupidity. . . . That would be very clever!

Not eight hundred yards away from the chair in which Memlik sprawled, across the brown Nile water, sat Mountolive at his papers. On the polished desk before him lay the great florid invitation card which enjoined his participation in one of the great social events of the year — Nessim's annual duckshoot on Lake Mareotis. He propped it against his inkwell in order to read it again with an expression of fugitive reproach.

But there was another communication of even greater importance; even after this long silence he recognized Leila's nervous handwriting on the lined envelope smelling of *chypre*. But inside it he found a page torn from an exercise book scrawled over with words and phrases set down anyhow, as if in great haste.

'David, I am going abroad, perhaps long perhaps short, I cannot tell; against my will. Nessim insists. But I must see you before I leave. I must take courage and meet you the evening before. Don't fail. I have something to ask, something to tell. "This business"! I knew nothing about it till carnival I swear; now only you can save. . . . .'

So the letter ran on pell-mell; Mountolive felt a queer mixture of feelings — an incoherent relief which somehow trembled on the edge of indignation. After all this time she would be waiting for him after dark near the *Auberge Bleue* in an old horse-drawn cab pulled back off the road among the palms! That plan was at least touched with something of her old fantasy. For some reason Nessim was not to know of this meeting — why should he disapprove? But the information that she at least had had no part in the conspiracies fostered by her son — that flooded him with relief and tenderness. And all this time he had been seeing Leila as a hostile extension of Nessim, had been training himself to hate her! 'My poor Leila' he said aloud, holding the envelope to his nose to inhale the fragrance of *chypre*. He picked up the phone and spoke softly to Errol: 'I suppose the whole Chancery has been invited to the Hosnani shoot? Yes? I agree, he has got rather a nerve at such a time. . . . I shall, of course, have to decline, but I would like you chaps to accept and apologize for me. To keep up a public appearance of normality merely. Will you then? Thank you very much. Now one more thing. I shall go up the evening before the shoot for private business and return the next day — we shall probably pass each other on the desert road. No, I'm *glad* you fellows have the chance. By all means, and good hunting.'

The next ten days passed in a sort of dream, punctuated only by the intermittent stabbings of a reality which was no longer a drug, a dissipation which gagged his nerves; his duties were a torment of boredom. He felt immeasurably expended, used-up, as he confronted his face in the bathroom mirror, presenting it to the razor's edge with undisguised distaste. He had become quite noticeably grey now at the temples. From somewhere in the servants' quarters a radio burred and scratched out the melody of an old song which had haunted a whole Alexandrian summer: *'Jamais de la vie'*. He had come to loathe it now. This new epoch — a limbo filled with the dispersing fragments of habit, duty and circumstance — filled him with a gnawing impatience; underneath it all he was aware that he was gathering himself together for this long-awaited meeting with Leila. Somehow it would determine, not the physical tangible meaning of his return to Egypt so much as the psychic meaning of it in relation to his inner life. God! that was a clumsy way to put it — but how else could one express these things? It was a sort of barrier in himself which had to be crossed, a puberty of the feelings which had to be outgrown.

He drove up across the crackling desert in his pennoned car, rejoicing in the sweet whistle of its cooled engine, and the whickering of wind at the side-screens. It had been some time since he had been able to travel across the desert alone like this — it reminded him of older and happier journeys. Flying across the still white air with the speedometer hovering in the sixties, he hummed softly to himself, despite his distaste, the refrain:

> *Jamais de la vie,*
> *Jamais dans la nuit*
> *Quand ton coeur se démange de chagrin.* . . .

How long was it since he had caught himself singing like this? An age. It was not really happiness, but an overmastering relief of mind. Even the hateful song helped him to recover the lost image of an Alexandria he had once found charming. Would it, could it be so again?

It was already late afternoon by the time he reached the desert fringe and began the slow in-curving impulse which would lead him to the city's bristling outer slums. The sky was covered with clouds. A thunderstorm was breaking over Alexandria. To the east upon the icy green waters of the lake poured a rainstorm — flights of glittering needles pocking the waters; he could dimly hear the hush of rain above the whisper of the car. He glimpsed the pearly city through the dark cloud-mat, its minarets poked up against the cloud bars of an early sunset; linen soaked in blood. A sea-wind chaffered and tugged at the sea-limits of the estuary. Higher still roamed packages of smoking, blood-stained cloud throwing down a strange radiance into the streets and squares of the white city. Rain was a rare and brief winter phenomenon in Alexandria. Presently the sea-wind would rise, alter inclination, and peel the sky clear in a matter of minutes, rolling up the heavy cumulus like a carpet. The glassy freshness of the winter sky would resume its light, polishing the city once more till it glittered against the desert like quartz, like some beautiful artifact. He was no longer impatient. Dusk was beginning to swallow the sunset. As he neared the ugly ribbons of cabins and warehouses by the outer harbour, his tyres began to smoke and seethe upon the wet tarmac, its heat now slaked by a light rain. Time to throttle down. . . .

He entered the penumbra of the storm slowly, marvelling at the light, at the horizon drawn back like a bow. Odd gleams of sunshine scattered rubies upon the battleships in the basin (squatting under their guns like horned toads). It was the ancient city again; he felt its pervading melancholy under the rain as he crossed it on his way to the Summer Residence. The brilliant unfamiliar lighting of the thunder-storm re-created it, giving it a spectral, story-book air — broken pavements made of tinfoil, snail-shells, cracked horn, mica; earth-brick buildings turned to the colour of ox-blood; the lovers wandering in Mohammed Ali Square, disoriented by the unfamiliar rain, disconsolate as untuned instruments; the clicking of violet trams along the sea-front among the tatting of palm-fronds. The desuetude of an ancient city whose streets were plastered with the wet blown dust of the surrounding desert. He felt it all anew, letting it extend panoramically in his consciousness — the moan of a liner edging out towards the sunset bar, or the trains which flowed like a torrent of diamonds towards the interior, their wheels chattering among the shingle ravines and the powder of temples long since abandoned and silted up. . . .

Mountolive saw it all now with a world-weariness which he at last recognized as the stripe which maturity lays upon the shoulders of an adult — the stigma of the experiences which age one. The wind spouted in the harbour. The corridors of wet rigging swayed and shook like the foliage of some great tree. Now the tears were trickling down the windscreen under the diligent and noiseless wipers. . . . A little period in this strange contused darkness, fitfully lit by lightning, and then the wind would come — the magistral north wind, punching and squeezing the sea into its own characteristic plumage of white crests, knocking open the firmament until the faces of men and women once more reflected the open winter sky. He was in plenty of time.

He drove to the Summer Residence to make sure that the

staff had been warned of his arrival; he intended to stay the night and return to Cairo on the morrow. He let himself into the front door with his own key, having pressed the bell, and stood listening for the shuffle of Ali. And as he heard the old man's step approaching, the north wind arrived with a roar, stiffening the windows in their frames, and the rain stopped abruptly as if it had been turned off.

He had still an hour or so before the rendezvous: comfortable time in which to have a bath and change his clothes. To his own surprise, he felt perfectly at ease now, no longer tormented by doubts or elated by a sense of relief. He had put himself unreservedly in the hands of chance.

He ate a sandwich and drank two strong whiskies before setting out and letting the great car slide softly down the Grande Corniche towards the *Auberge Bleue* which lay towards the outskirts of the town, fringed by patches of dune and odd clusters of palm. The sky was clear again now and the whitecaps were racing ashore to bang themselves in showers of spray upon the metal piers of Chatby. At the horizon's edge flickered the intermittent lightning still, but dimly. These faint gleams suggested perhaps the gun flashes of distant warships in a naval engagement.

He edged the car softly off the road and into the deserted car park of the Auberge, switching off the side-lamps as he did so. He sat for a moment, accustoming himself to the bluish dusk. The Auberge was empty — it was still too early for dancers and diners to throng its elegant floor and bars. Then he saw it. Just off the road, on the opposite side of the park, there was a bare patch of sand-dune with a few leaning palms. A gharry stood there. Its old-fashioned oil-lamps were alight and wallowed feebly like fireflies in the light sea-airs. There was a dim figure on the jarvey's box in a tarbush — apparently asleep.

He crossed the gravel with a light and joyous step, hearing it squeak under his shoes, and as he neared the gharry called, in a soft voice: 'Leila!' He saw the silhouette of the driver turn against the sky and register attention; from inside the cab he heard a voice — Leila's voice — say something like: 'Ah! David, so at last we meet. I have come all this way to tell you. . . .'

He leaned forward with a puzzled air, straining his eyes, but could not see more than the vague shape of someone in the far corner of the cab. 'Get in' she cried imperiously. 'Get in and we shall talk.'

And it was here that a sense of unreality overtook Mount-olive; he could not exactly fathom why. But he felt as one does in dreams when one walks without touching the ground, or else appears to rise deliberately through the air like a cork through water. His feelings, like antennae, were reaching out towards the dark figure, trying to gather and assess the meaning of these tumbling phrases and to analyse the queer sense of disorientation which they carried, buried in them, like a foreign intonation creeping into familiar voices; somewhere the whole context of his impressions foundered.

The thing was this: he did not quite recognize the voice. Or else, to put it another way, he could identify Leila but not quite believe in the evidence of his own ears. It was, so to speak, not the precious voice which, in his imagination, had lived on, in-habiting the remembered figure of Leila. She spoke now with a sort of gobbling inconsistency, an air of indiscretion, in a voice which had a slightly clipped edge on it. He supposed this to be the effect of excitement and who knows what other emotions? But . . . phrases which petered out, only to start again in the middle, phrases which lapsed and subsided in the very act of joining two thoughts? He frowned to himself in the darkness as he tried to analyse this curious unreal quality of distraction in the voice. It was not the voice that belonged to Leila — or was it? Presently, a hand fell upon his arm and he was able to study it eagerly in the puddle of soft light cast by the oil-lamp in the brass holder by the cabby's box. It was a chubby and unkempt little hand, with short, unpainted fingernails and unpressed cuticles. 'Leila — is it really you?' he asked almost involuntarily, still invaded by this sense of unreality, of disorientation; as of two dreams overlapping, displacing one another. 'Get in' said the new voice of an invisible Leila.

As he obeyed and stepped forward into the swaying cab he smelt her strange confusion of scents on the night air — again a troubling departure from the accepted memory. But orange-water, mint, Eau de Cologne, and sesame; she smelt like some old Arab lady! And then he caught the dull taint of whisky. She too had had to string her nerves for the meeting with alcohol! Sympathy and indecision battled within him; the old image of the brilliant, resourceful and elegant Leila refused somewhere to fix itself in the new. He simply must see her face. As if she read his thoughts, she said: 'So I came at last, *unveiled*, to meet you.'

He suddenly thought, bringing himself up with a start, 'My God! I simply haven't stopped to think how old Leila might be!'

She made a small sign and the old jarvey in the tarbush drew his nag slowly back on to the lighted macadam of the Grande Corniche and set the gharry moving at walking pace. Here the sharp blue street-lamps came up one after the other to peer into the cab, and with the first of these intrusive gleams of light Mountolive turned to gaze at the woman beside him. He could very dimly recognize her. He saw a plump and square-faced Egyptian lady of uncertain years, with a severely pock-marked face and eyes drawn grotesquely out of true by the antimony-pencil. They were the mutinous sad eyes of some clumsy cartoon creature: a cartoon of animals dressed up and acting as human beings. She had indeed been brave enough to unveil, this stranger who sat facing him, staring at him with the painted eye one sees in frescoes with a forlorn and pitiable look of appeal. She wore an air of unsteady audacity as she confronted her lover, though her lips trembled and her large jowls shook with every vibration of the solid rubber tyres on the road. They stared at each other for a full two seconds before the darkness swallowed the light again. Then he raised her hand to his lips. It was shaking like a leaf. In the momentary light he had seen her uncombed and straggly hair hanging down the back of her neck, her thoughtless and disordered black dress. Her whole appearance had a rakish and improvised air. And the dark skin, so cruelly botched and cicatriced by the smallpox, looked coarse as the skin of an elephant. *He did not recognize her at all!* 'Leila!' he cried (it was almost a groan) pretending at last to identify and welcome the image of his lover (now dissolved or shattered forever) in this pitiable grotesque — a fattish Egyptian lady with all the marks of eccentricity and age written upon her appearance. Each time the lamps came up he looked again, and each time he saw himself confronting something like an animal cartoon figure — an elephant, say. He could hardly pay attention to her words, so intent was he upon his racing feelings and memories. 'I knew we should meet again some day. I knew it.' She pressed his hand, and again he tasted her breath, heavy with sesame and mint and whisky.

She was talking now and he listened uneasily, but with all the attention one gives to an unfamiliar language; and each time the street lamps came up to peer at them, he gazed at her anxiously — as if to see whether there had been any sudden and magical change in her appearance. And then he was visited by another thought: 'What if I too have changed as much as she has — if indeed this is she?' What indeed? Sometime in the distant past they had exchanged images of one another like lockets; now his own had faded, changed. What might she see upon his face — traces of the feebleness which had overrun his youthful strength and purpose? He had now joined the ranks of those who compromise gracefully with life. Surely his ineffectuality, his unmanliness must be written all over his foolish, weak, good-looking face? He eyed her mournfully, with a pitiful eagerness to see whether she indeed really recognized him. He had forgotten that women will never surrender the image of their hearts' affections; no, she would remain forever blinded by the old love, refusing to let it be discountenanced by the new. 'You have not changed by a day' said this unknown woman with the disagreeable perfume. 'My beloved, my darling, my angel.' Mountolive flushed in the darkness at such endearments coming from the lips of an unknown personage. And the known Leila? He suddenly realized that the precious image which had inhabited his heart for so long had now been dissolved, completely wiped out! He was suddenly face to face with the meaning of love and time. They had lost forever the power to fecundate each other's minds! He felt only self-pity and disgust where he should have felt love! And these feelings were simply not permissible. He swore at himself silently as they went up and down the dark causeway by the winter sea, like invalids taking the night air, their hands touching each other, in the old horse-drawn cab. She was talking faster, now, vaguely, jumping from topic to topic. Yet it all seemed an introduction to the central statement which she had come to make. She was to leave tomorrow evening: 'Nessim's orders. Justine will come back from the lake and pick me up. We are disappearing together. At Kantara we'll separate and I shall go on to Kenya to the farm. Nessim won't say, can't say for how long as yet. I *had* to see you. I *had* to speak to you once. Not for myself — never for myself, my own heart. It was what I learned about Nessim at the carnival time. I was on the point of coming to meet you; but what he told me about Palestine! My blood ran cold. To do something against the British! How could I! Nessim must have been mad. I didn't come because I would not have known what to say to you, how to face you. But now you know all.'

She had begun to draw her breath sharply now, to hurry

onward as if all this were introductory matter to her main speech. Then suddenly she came out with it. 'The Egyptians will harm Nessim, and the British are trying to provoke them to do so. David, you must use your power to stop it. I am asking you to save my son. I am asking you to save him. You must listen, must help me. I have never asked you a favour before.'

The tear- and crayon-streaked cheeks made her look even more of a stranger in the street-lights. He began to stammer. She cried aloud: 'I implore you to help' and suddenly, to his intense humiliation, began to moan and rock like an Arab, pleading with him. '*Leila!*' he cried. '*Stop it!*' But she swayed from side to side repeating the words 'Only you can save him now' more, it seemed, to herself, than to anyone else. Then she showed some disposition to go down on her knees in the cab and kiss his feet. By this time Mountolive was trembling with anger and surprise and disgust. They were passing the Auberge for the tenth time. 'Unless you stop at once' he cried angrily, but she wailed once more and he jumped awkwardly down into the road. It was hateful to have to end their interview like this. The cab drew to a halt. He said, feeling stupid, and in a voice which seemed to come from far away and to have no recognizable expression save a certain old-fashioned waspishness: 'I cannot discuss an official matter with a private person.' Could anything be more absurd than these words? He felt bitterly ashamed as he uttered them. 'Leila, good-bye' he said hurriedly under his breath, and squeezed her hand once more before he turned. He took to his heels. He unlocked his car and climbed into it panting and overcome by a sense of ghastly folly. The cab moved off into the darkness. He watched it curve slowly along the Corniche and disappear. Then he lit a cigarette and started his engine. All of a sudden there seemed nowhere in particular to go. Every impulse, every desire had faltered and faded out.

After a long pause, he drove slowly and carefully back to the Summer Residence, talking to himself under his breath. The house was in darkness and he let himself in with his key. He walked from room to room switching on all the lights, feeling all of a sudden quite light-headed with loneliness; he could not accuse the servants of desertion since he had already told Ali that he would be dining out. But he walked up and down the drawing-room with his hands in his pockets for a long time. He smelt the damp unheated rooms around him; the blank reproachful face of the clock told him that it was only just after nine. Abruptly, he went over to the cocktail cabinet and poured himself a very strong whisky and soda which he drank in one movement — gasping as if it were a dose of fruit salts. His mind was humming now like a high-tension wire. He supposed that he would have to go out and have some dinner by himself. But where? Suddenly the whole of Alexandria, the whole of Egypt, had become distasteful, burden-some, wearisome to his spirit.

He drank several more whiskies, enjoying the warmth they brought to his blood — so unused was he to spirits which usually he drank very sparingly. Leila had suddenly left him face to face with a reality which, he supposed, had always lain lurking behind the dusty tapestry of his romantic notions. In a sense, she had *been* Egypt, his own private Egypt of the mind; and now this old image had been husked, stripped bare. 'It would be intemperate to drink any more' he told himself as he drained his glass. Yes, that was it! He had never been intemperate, never been natural, outward-going in his attitude to life. He had always hidden behind measure and compromise; and this defection had somehow lost him the picture of the Egypt which had nourished him for so long. Was it, then, all a lie?

He felt as if somewhere inside himself a dam were threatened, a barrier was on the point of giving way. It was with some idea of restoring this lost contact with the life of this embodied land that he hit upon the idea of doing something he had never done since his youth: he would go out and dine in the Arab quarter, humbly and simply, like a small clerk in the city, like a tradesman, a merchant. Somewhere in a small native restaurant he would eat a pigeon and some rice and a plate of sweetmeats; the food would sober and steady him while the surroundings would restore in him the sense of contact with reality. He could not remember ever having felt so tipsy and leaden-footed before. His thoughts were awash with inarticulate self-reproaches.

Still with this incoherent, half-rationalized desire in mind he suddenly went out to the hall cupboard to unearth the red felt tarbush which someone had left behind after a cocktail party last summer. He had suddenly remembered it. It lay among a litter of golf-clubs and tennis racquets. He put it on with a chuckle. It transformed his appearance completely. Looking at himself un-steadily in the hall mirror, he was quite surprised by the trans-formation: he was confronting not a distinguished foreign visitor to Egypt now, but — *un homme quelconque*: a Syrian business-man, a broker from Suez, an airline representative from Tel Aviv. Only one thing was necessary to lay claim to the Middle East properly — dark glasses, worn indoors, in winter! There was a pair of them in the top drawer of the writing desk.

He drove the car slowly down to the little square by Ramleh Station, quite absurdly pleased by his fancy dress, and eased it neatly into the car park by the Cecil Hotel; then he locked it and walked quietly off with the air of someone abandoning a lifetime's habit — walked with a new and quite delightful feeling of self-possession towards the Arab quarters of the town where he might find the dinner he sought. As he skirted the Corniche he had one moment of unpleasant fear and doubt — for he saw a familiar figure cross the road further down and walk towards him along the sea-wall. It was impossible to mistake Balthazar's characteristic prowling walk; Mountolive was overcome with a sheepish sense of shame, but he held his course. To his delight, Balthazar glanced once at him and looked away without recognizing his friend. They passed each other in a flash, and Mountolive expelled his breath loudly with relief; it was really odd the anonymity conferred by this ubiquitous red flower-pot of a hat, which so much altered the outlines of the human face. And the dark glasses! He chuckled quietly as he turned away from the sea-front, choosing the tangle of little lanes which might lead him towards the Arab bazaars and the eating houses round the commercial port.

Hereabouts it would be a hundred to one that he would ever be recognized — for few Europeans ever came into this part of the city. The quarter lying beyond the red lantern belt, populated by the small traders, money-lenders, coffee-speculators, ships' chandlers, smugglers; here in the open street one had the illusion of time spread out flat — so to speak — like the skin of an ox; the map of time which one could read from one end to the other, filling it in with known points of reference. This world of Moslem time stretched back to Othello and beyond — cafés sweet with trilling of singing birds whose cages were full of mirrors to give them the illusion of company. The love-songs of birds to companions they imagined — which were only reflections of themselves! How heartbreakingly they sang, these illustrations of human love! Here too in the ghastly breath of the naphtha flares the old eunuchs sat at *trictrac*, smoking the long *narguilehs* which at every drawn breath loosed a musical bubble of sound like a dove's sob; the walls of the old cafés were stained by the sweat from the tarbushes hanging on the pegs; their collections of coloured *narguilehs* were laid up in rows in a long rack, like muskets, for which each tobacco-drinker brought his cherished personal holder. Here too the diviners, cartomancers — or those who would deftly fill your palm with ink and for half a piastre scry the secrets of your inmost life. Here the pedlars carried magic loads of variegated and dissimilar objects of *vertu* from the thistle-soft carpets of Shiraz and Baluchistan to the playing cards of the Marseilles Tarot; incense of the Hejaz, green beads against the evil eye, combs, seeds, mirrors for birdcages, spices, amulets and paper fans . . . the list was endless; and each, of course, carried in his private wallet — like a medieval pardoner — the fruit of the world's great pornographies in the form of handkerchiefs and post-cards on which were depicted, in every one of its pitiful variations, the one act we human beings most dream of and fear. Mysterious, underground, the ever-flowing river of sex, trickling easily through the feeble dams set up by our fretful legislation and the typical self-reproaches of the unpleasure-loving . . . the broad underground river flowing from Petronius to Frank Harris. (The drift and overlap of ideas in Mountolive's fuddled mind, rising and disappearing in pretty half-formulated figures, iridescent as soap-bubbles.) He was perfectly at his ease, now; he had come to terms with his unfamiliar state of befuddlement and no longer felt that he was drunk; it was simply that he had become inflated now by a sense of tremendous dignity and self-importance which gave him a grandiose deliberation of movement. He walked slowly, like a pregnant woman nearing term, drinking in the sights and sounds.

At long last he entered a small shop which took his fancy because of its flaring ovens from which great draughts of smoke settled in parcels about the room; the smell of thyme, roasting pigeon and rice gave him a sudden stab of hunger. There were only one or two other diners, hardly to be seen through the clouds of smoke. Mountolive sat down with the air of someone making a grudging concession to the law of gravity and ordered a meal in his excellent Arabic, though he still kept his dark glasses and tarbush on. It was clear now that he could pass easily for a Moslem. The café owner was a great bald Tartar-faced Turk who served his visitor at once and without comment. He also set up a tumbler beside Mount-olive's plate and without uttering a word filled it to the brim with the colourless *arak* made from the mastic-tree which is called *mastika*. Mountolive choked and spluttered a bit over it, but he was highly delighted — for it was the first drink of the Levant he had ever tasted and he had forgotten its existence for years now. Forgetting also how strong it was, and overcome with nostalgia, he ordered himself a second glass to help him finish the excellent hot pilaff and the pigeon (so hot from the spit that he could hardly bear to pick it up with his fingers). But he was in the seventh heaven of delight now. He was on the way to recovering, to restoring the blurred image of an Egypt which the meeting with Leila had damaged or somehow stolen from him.

The street outside was full of the shivering of tambourines and the voices of children raised in a chanting sort of litany; they were going about the shops in groups, repeating the same little verse over and over again. After three repetitions he managed to disentangle the words. Of course!

> *Lord of the shaken tree*
> *Of Man's extremity*
> *Keep thou our small leaves firm*
> *On branches free from harm*
> *For we thy little children be!*

'Well I'm damned' he said, swallowing a fiery mouthful of *arak* and smiling as the meaning of the little processions became clear. There was a venerable old sheik sitting opposite by the window and smoking a long-shanked *narguileh*. He waved towards the din with his graceful old hand and cried: 'Allah! The noise of the children!' Mountolive smiled back at him and said: 'Inform me if I err, sir, but it is for *El Sird* they cry, is it not?' The old man's face lit up and he nodded, smiling his saintly smile. 'You have guessed it truly, sir.' Mountolive was pleased with himself and filled ever more deeply with nostalgia for those half-forgotten years. 'Tonight then' he said 'it must be mid-Shaaban and the Tree of Extremity is to be shaken. Is that not so?'

Once more a delighted nod. 'Who knows' said the old sheik 'but that both our names may be written on the falling leaves?' He puffed softly and contentedly, like a toy train. 'Allah's will be done.'

The belief is that on the eve of mid-Shaaban the Lote Tree of Paradise is shaken, and the falling leaves of the tree bear the names of all who will die in the coming year. This is called the

Tree of Extremity in some texts. Mountolive was so pleased by the identification of the little song that he called for a final glass of *arak* which he drank standing up as he paid his reckoning. The old sheik abandoned his pipe and came slowly towards him through the smoke. He said: 'Effendi mine, I understand your purpose here. What you seek will be revealed to you by me.' He placed two brown fingers on Mountolive's wrist, speaking modestly and softly, as one who had secrets to impart. His face had all the candour and purity of some desert saint. Mountolive was delighted by him. 'Honoured sheik' he said 'divulge your sense, then, to an unworthy Syrian visitor.' The old man bowed twice, looked circumspectly round the place, and then said: 'Be good enough to follow me, honoured sir.' He kept his two fingers on Mountolive's wrist as a blind man might. They stepped into the street together; Mountolive's romantic heart was beating wildly — was he now to be vouchsafed some mystical vision of religious truth? He had so often heard stories of the bazaars and the religious men who lurked there, waiting to fulfil secret missions on behalf of that unseen world, the numinous, carefully guarded world of the hermetic doctors. They walked in a soft cloud of unknowing with the silent sheik swaying and recovering himself at every few paces and smiling a maudlin smile of beatitude. They passed together at this slow pace through the dark streets — now turned by the night to long shadowy tunnels or shapeless caverns, still dimly echoing to muffled bagpipe music or skirmishing voices muted by thick walls and barred windows.

Mountolive's heightened sense of wonder responded to the beauty and mystery of this luminous township of shadows carved here and there into recognizable features by a single naphtha lamp or an electric bulb hanging from a frail stalk, rocking in the wind. They turned at last down a long street spanned with coloured banners and thence into a courtyard which was completely dark where the earth smelt vaguely of the stale of camels and jasmine. A house loomed up, set within thick walls; one caught a glimpse of its silhouette on the sky. They entered a sort of rambling barrack of a place passing through a tall door which was standing ajar, and plunged into a darkness still more absolute. Stood breathing for half a second in silence. Mountolive felt rather than saw the worm-eaten staircases which climbed the walls to the abandoned upper floors, heard the chirrup and scramble of the rats in the deserted galleries, together with something else —

a sound vaguely reminiscent of human beings, but in what context he could not quite remember. They shuffled slowly down a long corridor upon woodwork so rotten that it rocked and swayed under their feet, and here, in a doorway of some sort, the old sheik said kindly: 'That our simple satisfactions should not be less than those of your homeland, effendi mine, I have brought you here.' He added in a whisper, 'Attend me here a moment, if you will.' Mountolive felt the fingers leave his wrist and the breath of the door closing at his shoulder. He stayed in composed and trustful silence for a moment or two.

Then all at once the darkness was so complete that the light, when it did come, gave him the momentary illusion of something taking place very far away, in the sky. As if someone had opened and closed a furnace-door in Heaven. It was only the spark of a match. But in the soft yellow flap he saw that he was standing in a gaunt high chamber with shattered and defaced walls covered in *graffiti* and the imprint of dark palms — signs which guard the superstitious against the evil eye. It was empty save for an enormous broken sofa which lay in the centre of the floor, like a sarcophagus. A single window with all the panes of glass broken was slowly printing the bluer darkness of the starry sky upon his sight. He stared at the flapping, foundering light, and again heard the rats chirping and the other curious susurrus composed of whispers and chuckles and the movement of bare feet on boards. . . . Suddenly he thought of a girls' dormitory at a school: and as if invented by the very thought itself, through the open door at the end of the room trooped a crowd of small figures dressed in white soiled robes, like defeated angels. He had stumbled into a house of child prostitutes, he realized with a sudden spasm of disgust and pity. Their little faces were heavily painted, their hair scragged in ribbons and plaits. They wore green beads against the evil eye. Such little creatures as one has seen incised on Greek vases — floating out of tombs and charnel houses with the sad air of malefactors fleeing from justice. It was the foremost of the group who carried the light — a twist of string burning in a saucer of olive oil. She stooped to place this feeble will-o-the-wisp on the floor in the corner and at once the long spiky shadows of these children sprawled on the ceiling like an army of frustrated wills. 'No, by Allah' said Mountolive hoarsely, and turned to grope at the closed door. There was a wooden latch with no means of opening it on his side. He put his face to a hole in the panel and called softly 'O sheik, where are you?' The little figures had advanced and surrounded him now, murmuring the pitiable obscenities and endearments of their trade in the voices of heart-broken angels; he felt their warm nimble fingers on his shoulders, picking at the sleeves of his coat. 'O sheik' he called again, shrinking up, 'it was not for this.' But there was a silence beyond the door. He felt the children's sharp arms twining round his waist like lianas in a tropical jungle, their sharp little fingers prying for the buttons of his coat. He shook them off and turned his pale face to them, making a half-articulate sound of protest. And now someone inadvertently kicked over the saucer with its floating wick and in the darkness he felt the tension of anxiety sweep through them like a fire through brushwood. His protests had made them fear the loss of a lucrative client. Anxiety, anger and a certain note of terror were in their voices now as they spoke to him, wheedling and half-threatening; heaven only knew what punishments might attend them if he escaped! They began to struggle, to attack him; he felt the concussion of their starved little bodies as they piled round him, panting and breathless with importunity, but determined that he should not retreat. Fingers roved over him like ants — indeed, he had a sudden memory, buried from somewhere back in his remembered reading, of a man staked down upon the burning sand over a nest of white ants which would soon pick the flesh from his very bones.

'No' he cried incoherently again; some absurd inhibition prevented him from striking out, distributing a series of brutal cuffs which alone might have freed him. (The smallest were so very small.) They had his arms now, and were climbing on his back — absurd memories intruded of pillow fights in a dark dormitory at school. He banged wildly on the door with his elbow, and they redoubled their entreaties in whining voices. Their breath was as hot as wood-smoke. 'O Effendi, patron of the poor, remedy for our affliction. . . .' Mountolive groaned and struggled, but felt himself gradually being borne to the ground; gradually felt his befuddled knees giving way under this assault which had gathered a triumphant fury now.

'No!' he cried in an anguished voice, and a chorus of voices answered 'Yes. Yes, by Allah!' They smelt like a herd of goats as they swarmed upon him. The giggles, the obscene whispers, the cajoleries and curses mounted up to his brain. He felt as if he were going to faint.

Then suddenly everything cleared — as if a curtain had been drawn aside — to reveal him sitting beside his mother in front of a roaring fire with a picture-book open on his knee. She was reading aloud and he was trying to follow the words as she pronounced them; but his attention was always drawn away to the large colour-plate which depicted Gulliver when he had fallen into the hands of the little people of Lilliput. It was fascinating in its careful detail. The heavy-limbed hero lay where he had fallen, secured by a veritable cobweb of guy-ropes which had been wound around him pinioning him to the ground while the ant-people roved all over his huge body securing and pegging more and more guy-ropes against which every struggle of the colossus would be in vain. There was a malign scientific accuracy about it all: wrists, ankles and neck pinioned against movement; tent-pegs driven between the fingers of his huge hand to hold each individual finger down. His pigtails were neatly coiled about tiny spars which had been driven into the ground beside him. Even the tails of his surtout were skilfully pinned to the ground through the folds. He lay there staring into the sky with expressionless wonder, his blue eyes wide open, his lips pursed. The army of Lilliputians wandered all over him with wheel-barrows and pegs and more rope; their attitudes suggested a feverish ant-like frenzy of capture. And all the time Gulliver lay there on the green grass of Lilliput, in a valley full of microscopic flowers, like a captive balloon. . . .

He found himself (though he had no idea how he had finally escaped) leaning upon the icy stone embankment of the Corniche with the dawn sea beneath him, rolling its slow swell up the stone piers, gushing softly into the conduits. He could remember only running in dazed fashion down twisted streets in darkness and stumbling across the road and on to the seafront. A pale rinsed dawn was breaking across the long sea-swell and a light sea-wind brought him the smell of tar and the sticky dampness of salt. He felt like some merchant sailor cast up helpless in a foreign port at the other end of the world. His pockets had been turned inside out like sleeves. He was clad in a torn shirt and trousers. His expensive studs and cuff-links and tie-pin had gone, his wallet had vanished. He felt deathly sick. But as he gradually came to his senses he realized where he was from the glimpse of the Goharri Mosque as it stood up to take the light of dawn among its clumps of palms. Soon the blind *muezzin* would be coming out like ancient tortoises to recite the dawn-praise of the only living God. It was perhaps a quarter of a mile to where he had left the car. Denuded now of his tarbush and dark glasses, he felt as if he had been stripped naked. He started off at a painful trot along the stony embankments, glad that there was nobody about to recognize him. The deserted square outside the Hotel was just waking to life with the first tram. It clicked away towards Mazarita, empty. The keys to his car had also disappeared and he now had the ignominious task of breaking the door-catch with a spanner which he took from the boot — terrified all the time that a policeman might come and question or perhaps even arrest him on suspicion. He was seething with self-contempt and disgust and he had a splitting headache. At last he broke the door and drove off wildly — fortunately, the chauffeur's keys were in the car — in the direction of Rushdi through the deserted streets. His latchkey too had disappeared in the mêlée and he was forced to burst open one of the window-catches in the drawing-room in order to get into the house. He thought at first that he would spend the morning asleep in bed after he had bathed and changed his clothes, but standing under the hot shower he realized that he was too troubled in mind; his thoughts buzzed like a swarm of bees and would not let him rest. He decided suddenly that he would leave the house and return to Cairo before even the servants were up. He felt that he could not face them.

He changed his clothes furtively, gathered his belongings together, and set off across the town towards the desert road, leaving the city hurriedly like a common thief. He had come to a decision in his own mind. He would ask for a posting to some other country. He would waste no more time upon this Egypt of deceptions and squalor, this betraying landscape which turned emotions and memories to dust, which beggared friendship and destroyed love. He did not even think of Leila now; tonight she would be gone across the border. But already it was as if she had never existed.

There was plenty of petrol in the tank for the ride back. As he turned through the last curves of the road outside the town he looked back once, with a shudder of disgust at the pearly mirage of minarets rising from the smoke of the lake, the dawn mist. A train pealed somewhere, far away. He turned on the radio of the car at full blast to drown his thoughts as he sped along the silver desert highway to the winter capital. From every side, like startled hares, his thoughts broke out to run alongside the whirling car in a frenzy of terror. He had, he realized, reached a new frontier in himself; life was going to be something completely different from now on. He had been in some sort of bondage all this time; now the links had snapped. He heard the soft hushing of strings and the familiar voice of the city breaking in upon him once again with its perverted languors, its ancient wisdoms and terrors.

> *Jamais de la vie,*
> *Jamais dans ton lit*
> *Quand ton coeur se démange de chagrin. . . .*

With an oath he snapped the radio shut, choked the voice, and drove frowning into the sunlight as it ebbed along the shadowy flanks of the dunes.

He made very good time and drew up before the Embassy to find Errol and Donkin loading the latter's old touring car with all the impedimenta of professional hunters — gun-cases and cartridge bags, binoculars and thermos flasks. He walked slowly and shamefacedly towards them. They both greeted him cheerfully. They were due to start for Alexandria at midday. Donkin was excited and blithe. The newspapers that morning had carried reports that the King had made a good recovery and that audiences were to be granted at the week-end. 'Now, sir' said Donkin, 'is Nur's chance to make Memlik act. You'll see.' Mountolive nodded dully; the news fell flatly on his ear, toneless and colourless and without presage. He no longer cared what was going to happen. His decision to ask for a transfer of post seemed to have absolved him in a curious way from any further personal responsibility as regards his own feelings.

He walked moodily into the Residence and ordered his breakfast tray to be brought into the drawing-room. He felt irritable and abstracted. He rang for his despatch box to see what personal mail there might be. There was nothing of great interest: a long chatty letter from Sir Louis who was happily sunning himself in Nice; it was full of amusing and convivial gossip about mutual friends. And of course the inevitable anecdote of a famous *raconteur* to round off the letter: 'I hope, dear boy, that the uniform still fits you. I thought of you last week when I met Claudel, the French poet who was also an Ambassador, for he told me an engaging anecdote about *his* uniform. It was while

he was serving in Japan. Out for a walk one day, he turned round
to see that the whole residence was a sheet of flame and blazing
merrily; his family was with him so he did not need to fear for
their safety. But his manuscripts, his priceless collection of books
and letters — they were all in the burning house. He hurried back
in a state of great alarm. It was clear that the house would be
burned to the ground. As he reached the garden he saw a small
stately figure walking towards him — the Japanese butler. He
walked slowly and circumspectly towards the Ambassador with
his arms held out before him like a sleepwalker; over them was
laid the dress uniform of the poet. The butler said proudly and
sedately: "There is no cause for alarm, sir. I have saved the
only valuable object." And the half-finished play, and the poems
lying upstairs on the burning desk? I suddenly thought of you,
I don't know why.'

He read on sighing and smiling sadly and enviously; what
would he not give to be retired in Nice at this moment? There
was a letter from his mother, a few bills from his London trades-
men, a note from his broker, and a short letter from Pursewarden's
sister. . . . Nothing of any real importance.

There was a knock and Donkin appeared. He looked somewhat
crestfallen. 'The M.F.A.' he said 'have been on the line with a
message from Nur's office to say that he will be seeing the King
at the weekend. But . . . Gabr hinted that our case is not supported
by Memlik's own investigations.'

'What does he mean by that?'

'He says, in effect, that we have got the wrong Hosnani. The
real culprit is a brother of his who lives on a farm somewhere
outside Alexandria.'

'Narouz' said Mountolive with astonishment and incredulity.

'Yes. Well apparently he ——"

They both burst out laughing with exasperation. 'Honestly' said
Mountolive, banging his fist into his palm, 'the Egyptians really
are incredible. Now how on earth have they arrived at such a
conclusion? One is simply baffled.'

'Nevertheless, that is Memlik's case. I thought you'd like to
know, sir. Errol and I are just off to Alex. There isn't anything
else, is there?'

Mountolive shook his head. Donkin closed the door softly
behind him. 'So now they are going to turn on Narouz. What
a muddle of conflicting policies and diversions.' He sank des-

pairingly into a chair and frowned at his own fingers for a long moment before pouring himself out another cup of tea. He felt incapable now of thought, of making the smallest decision. He would write to Kenilworth and the Foreign Secretary this very morning about his transfer. It was something he should have considered long since. He sighed heavily.

There came another and more diffident rap at the door. 'Come in' he called wearily. It opened and a dispirited-looking sausage-dog waddled into the room followed by Angela Errol who said, in a tone of strident heartiness not untouched by a sort of aggressive archness, 'Forgive the intrusion, but I came on *behalf* of the Chancery *wives*. We thought you seemed rather *lonely* so we decided to put our *heads* together. *Fluke* is the result.' Dog and man looked at each other in a dazed and distrustful silence for a moment. Mountolive struggled for words. He had always loathed sausage-dogs with legs so short that they appeared to flop along like toads rather than walk. Fluke was such an animal, already panting and slavering from its exertions. It sat down at last and, as if to express once and for all its disenchantment with the whole sum of canine existence, delivered itself of a retromingent puddle on the beautiful Shiraz. 'Isn't he jolly?' cried the wife of the Head of Chancery. It cost Mountolive something of an effort to smile, to appear to be overcome with pleasure, to express the appropriate thanks due to a gesture so thoughtful. He was wild with vexation. 'He looks charming' he said, smiling his handsome smile, 'really charming. I am most awfully grateful, Angela. It was a kind thought.' The dog yawned lazily. 'Then I shall *tell* the wives that the *gift* has met with *approval*' she said briskly, and moved towards the door. 'They will be *delighted*. There is *no* companionship like that of a dog, is there?' Mountolive shook his head seriously. 'None' he said. He tried to look as if he meant it.

As the door closed behind her he sat down once more and raised his cup of tea to his lips as he stared unwinkingly and with distaste into the dog's lustreless eyes. The clock chimed softly on the mantelpiece. It was time to be going to the office. There was much to be done. He had promised to finish the definitive economic report in time for this week's bag. He must bully the bag room about that portrait of himself. He must. . . .

Yet he sat on looking at the dispirited little creature on the mat and feeling suddenly as if he had been engulfed in a tidal wave of human contumely — so expressed by his admirers in this unwanted gift. He was to be *garde-malade*, a male nurse to a short-legged lap dog. Was this now the only way left of exorcizing his sadness. . . ? He sighed, and sighing pressed the bell. . . .

*   *   *   *   *

XVI

The day of his death was like any other winter day at Karm Abu Girg; or if it was different it was only in one small and puzzling detail, the significance of which did not strike him at first: the servants suddenly ebbing away to leave him alone in the house. All night long now he lay in troubled sleep among the luxuriant growths of his own fantasy, dense as a tropical vegetation; only waking from time to time to be comforted by the soft whewing of the cranes flying overhead in the darkness. It was full winter and the great bird migrations had begun. The long vitreous expanses of the lake had begun to fill up with their winged visitants like some great terminus. All night long one could hear the flights come in — the thick whirring of mallard-wings or the metallic *kraonk kraonk* of high-flying geese as they bracketed the winter moon. Among the thickets of reed and sedge, in places polished to black or viper-green by the occasional clinging frosts, you could hear the chuckling and gnatting of royal duck. The old house with its mildewed walls where the scorpions and fleas hibernated among the dusty interstices of the earth-brick felt very empty and desolate to him now that Leila had gone. He marched defiantly about it, making as much noise as he could with his boots, shouting at the dogs, cracking his whip across the courtyard. The little toy figures with windmill arms which lined the walls against the ubiquitous evil eye, worked unceasingly, flurried by the winter winds. Their tiny celluloid propellers made a furry sound as they revolved which was somehow comforting.

Nessim had pleaded hard with him to accompany Leila and Justine but he had refused — and indeed behaved like a bear though he knew in truth that without his mother the loneliness of the house would be hard to support. He had locked himself into the egg-incubators, and to his brother's feverish knocking and shouting had opposed a bitter silence. There had been no way of explaining things to Nessim. He would not emerge even when Leila came to plead with him — for fear that his resolve might weaken under her importunities. He had crouched there in silence with his back against the wall, his fist crammed into his mouth to stifle the noiseless sobbing — how heavy was the guilt one bore for filial disobedience! They had abandoned him at last. He heard the horses clatter out of the courtyard. He was alone.

Then after that a whole month of silence before he heard his brother's voice on the telephone. Narouz had walked all day long in a forest of his own heart-beats, attending to the work of the land with a concentrated fury of purpose, galloping along the slow-moving river of his inheritance on horseback, his reflection flying beside him: always with the great whip coiled at his saddle-bow. He felt immeasurably aged now — and yet, at one and the same time, as new to the world as a foetus hanging from the birth-cord. The land, *his* land, now brown and greasy as an old wineskin under the rain, compelled him. It was all he had left now to care for — trees bruised by frost, sand poisoned by desert salt, water-pans stocked with fish and geese; and silences all day except for the sighing and the groaning of the water-wheels with their eternal message ('Alexander has asses' ears') carried away by the winds to the further corners of the land, to pollinate history once more with the infectious memory of the soldier-god; or the suck and pluck of the black 'forehead-smasher' buffalo wallowing in the ooze of the dykes. And then at night the haunting plural syllables of the duck deploying in darkness, calling to one another in anxiety or content — travellers' codes. Screens of mist, low-lying clouds through which the dawns and sunsets burst with unexampled splendour each one the end of a world, a dying into amethyst and nacre.

Normally, this would be the hunter's season which he loved, brisk with great woodfires and roving gun-dogs: time for the dousing of boots with bear's fat, for the tuning in of the long punt-guns, the sorting out of shot, the painting of decoys. . . . This year he had not even the heart to join in the great annual duck-shoot given by Nessim. He felt cut off, in a different world. He wore the bitter revengeful face of a communicant refused absolution. He could no longer exorcize his sadness privately with a dog and gun; he thought only of Taor now, and the dreams he shared with her — the fierce possessive recognition of his dedicated role *here*, among his own lands, and in the whole of Egypt. . . . These confusing dreams interlinked, overlapped, intersected — like so many tributaries of the great river itself. Even Leila's love threatened them now — was like some brilliant parasite ivy which strangles the growth of a tree. He thought vaguely and without contempt of his brother still there in the city

— (he was not to leave until later) — moving among people as insubstantial as waxworks, the painted society women of Alexandria. If he thought at all of his love for Clea it was for a love left now like some shining coin, forgotten in a beggar's pocket. . . . Thus, galloping in savage exultation along moss-green wharves and embankments of the estuary with its rotting palms fretted by the wind, thus he lived.

Once last week Ali had reported the presence of unknown men upon the land, but he had not given the matter a thought. Often a stray Bedouin took a short cut across the plantations or a stranger rode through the property bound for the road to the city. He was more interested when Nessim telephoned to say that he would be visiting Karm Abu Girg with Balthazar who wished to investigate reports of a new species of duck which had been seen on the lake. (From the roof of the house one could sweep the whole estuary with a powerful glass.)

This indeed was what he was doing now, at this very moment. Tree by tree, reed-patch by reed-patch, turning a patient and curious eye upon the land through his ancient telescope. It lay, mysterious, unpeopled and silent in the light of the dawn. He intended to spend the whole day out there among the plantations in order to avoid, if possible, seeing his brother. But now the defection of the servants was puzzling, and indeed, inexplicable. Usually when he woke he roared for Ali who brought him a large copper can with a long spout full of hot water and sluiced him down as he stood in the battered Victorian hip-bath, gasping and hissing. But today? The courtyard was silent, and the room in which Ali slept was locked. The key hung in its place upon the nail outside. There was not a soul about.

With sudden quick strides he climbed to the balcony for his telescope and then mounted the outer wooden staircase to the roof to stand among the turrets of the dovecots and scan the Hosnani lands. A long patient scrutiny revealed nothing out of the ordinary. He grunted and snapped the glass shut. He would have to fend for himself today. He climbed down from his perch and taking the old leather game-bag made his way to the kitchens to fill it with food. Here he found coffee simmering and some pans set to heat upon the charcoal fire, but no trace of the cooks. Grumbling, he helped himself to a snag of bread which he munched while he assembled some food for lunch. Then an idea struck him. In the courtyard, his shrill angry whistle would normally have brought the gun-dogs growling and fawning about his boots from wherever they had taken refuge from the cold; but today the empty echo of his own whistle was all that the wind threw back to him. Had Ali perhaps taken them out on some excursion of his own? It did not seem likely. He whistled again more loudly and waited, his feet set squarely apart in his jackboots, his hands upon his hips. There was no answer. He went round to the stables and found his horse. Everything was perfectly normal here. He saddled and bridled it and led it round to the hitching post. Then he went upstairs for his whip. As he coiled it, another thought struck him. He turned into the living-room and took a revolver from the writing-desk, checking it to see that the chambers were primed. He stuck this in his belt.

Then he set out, riding softly and circumspectly towards the east, for he proposed first of all to make an exploratory circuit of the land before plunging into the dense green plantations where he wished to spend the day. It was crisp weather, rapidly clearing, the marsh-mist full of evanescent shapes and contours but rising fast. Horse and rider moved with smooth deftness along the familiar ways. He reached the desert fringe in half an hour, having seen nothing untoward though he looked about him carefully under his bushy brows. On the soft ground the horse's hooves made little noise. In the eastern corner of the plantation, he halted for a good ten minutes, combing the landscape once more with his telescope. And once more there was nothing of particular importance. He neglected none of the smaller signs which might indicate a foreign visitation, tracks in the desert, footmarks on the soft embankment by the ferry. The sun was rising slowly but the land slept in its thinning mist. At one place he dismounted to check the depth-pumps, listening to their sullen heart-beats with pleasure, greasing a lever here and there. Then he remounted and turned his horse's head towards the denser groves of the plantations with their cherished Tripoli olives and acacia, their humus-giving belts of juniper, the wind-breaks of rattling Indian corn. He was still on the alert, however, and rode in short swift spurts, reining in every now and again to listen for a full minute. Nothing but the distant gabble of birds, the slither of flamingo-wings on the lake-water, the melodious horns of teal or the splendour (as of a tuba in full pomp) of honking geese. All familiar, all known. He was still puzzled but not ill at ease.

He made his way at last to the great *nubk* tree standing up starkly in its clearing, its great trophied branches dripping with condensing mist. Here, long ago, he had stood and prayed with Mountolive under the holy branches, still heavy with their curious human fruitage; everywhere blossomed the *ex votos* of the faithful in strips of coloured cloth, calico, beads. They were tied to every branch and twig and leaf so that it looked like some giant Christmas tree. Here he dismounted to take some cuttings which he wrapped and stowed carefully. Then he straightened up for he had heard the sounds of movement in the green glades around him. Difficult to identify, to isolate — slither of a body among the leaves, or perhaps a pack-saddle catching in a branch as horse and rider moved swiftly out of ambush? He listened and gave a small spicy chuckle, as if at some remembered private joke. He was sorry for anyone coming to molest him in such a place — every glade and ride of which he knew by memory. Here he was on his own ground — the master.

He ran back to his horse with his curious bandy-legged stride, but noiselessly. He mounted and rode slowly out of the shadow of the great branches in order to give his long whip a wide margin for wrist-play and to cover the only two entrances to the plantation. His adversaries, if such there were, would have to come upon him down one of two paths. He had his back to the tree and its great stockade of thorns. He gave a small clicking laugh of pleasure as he sat there attentively, his head on one side like a listening gun-dog; he moved the coils of his whip softly and voluptuously along the ground, drawing circles with them, curling them in the grass like a snake. . . . It would probably turn out to be a false alarm — Ali coming to apologize for his neglect that morning? At any rate, his master's posture of readiness would frighten him, for he had seen the whip in action before. . . . The noise again. A water-rat plopped into the channel and swam quickly away. Among the bushes on two sides of the ride he could see indistinct movements. He sat, as immobile as an equestrian statue, his pistol grasped lightly in the left hand, his whip lying slightly behind him, his arm curved in the position of a fisherman about to make a long cast. So he waited, smiling. His patience was endless.

* * * * *

The sound of distant shooting upon the lake was a commonplace among the vocabulary of lake-sounds; it belonged to the music of the gulls, visitants from the seashore, and the other water-birds which thronged the reed-haunted lagoons. When the big shoots were on the ripple of thirty guns in action at one and the same time flowed tidelessly out into the air of Mareotis like a cadenza. Habit taught one gradually to differentiate between the various sounds and to recognize them — and Nessim too had spent his childhood here with a gun. He could tell the difference between the deep *tang* of a punt gun aimed at highflying geese and the flat biff of a twelve-bore. The two men were standing by their horses at the ferry when it came, a small puckering of the air merely, falling upon the ear-drum in a patter: raindrops sliding from an oar, the drip of a tap in an old house, were hardly less in volume. But it was certainly shooting. Balthazar turned his head and gazed out over the lake. 'That sounded pistolish' he said; Nessim smiled and shook his head. 'Small calibre rifle, I should say. A poacher after sitting duck?' But there were more shots than could be accommodated at one time in the magazine of either weapon. They mounted, a little puzzled that the horses had been sent for them but that Ali had disappeared. He had tied the animals to the hitching-post of the ferry, commending them to the care of the ferryman, and vanished in the mist.

They rode briskly down the embankments side by side. The sun was up now and the whole surface of the lake was rising into the sky like the floor of a theatre, pouring upwards with the mist; here and there reality was withered by mirages, landscapes hanging in the sky upside down or else four or five superimposed on each other with the effect of a multiple exposure. The first indication of anything amiss was a figure dressed in white robes which fled into the mist — an unheard-of action in that peaceful country. Who would fly from two horsemen on the Karm Abu Girg road? A vagabond? They stopped in bemused wonder. 'I thought I heard shouts' said Nessim at last in a small constrained voice, 'towards the house.' As if both were stimulated by the same simultaneous anxiety, they pushed their horses into a brisk gallop, heading them for the house.

A horse, Narouz' horse, now riderless, stood trembling outside the open gates of the manor house. It had been shot through the lips — a profusely-bleeding graze which gave it a weird bloody smile. It whinnied softly as they came up. Before they had time to dismount there came shouts from the palm-grove and a flying figure burst through the trees waving to them. It was Ali. He pointed down among the plantations and shouted the name of

Narouz. The name, so full of omens for Nessim, had a curiously obituary ring already, though he was not as yet dead. 'By the Holy Tree' shouted Ali, and both men drove their heels into their horses' flanks and crashed into the plantation as fast as they could go.

He was lying on the grass underneath the *nubk* tree with his head and neck supported by it, an angle which cocked his face forward so that he appeared to be studying the pistol-wounds in his own body. His eyes alone were movable, but they could only reach up to the knee of his rescuers; and the pain had winced them from the normal periwinkle blue to the dull blue of plumbago. His whip had got coiled round his body in some manner, probably when he fell from the saddle. Balthazar dismounted and walked slowly and deliberately over to him, making the little clucking noise he always made with his tongue; it sounded sympathetic, but it was in fact a reproof to his own curiosity, to the elation with which one part of his professional mind responded to human tragedy. It always seemed to him that he had no right to be so interested. *Tsck, tsck.* Nessim was very pale and very calm but he did not approach the fallen figure of his brother. Yet it had for him a dreadful magnetism — it was as if Balthazar were laying some tremendously powerful explosive which might go off and kill them both. He was merely helping by holding the horse. Narouz said in a small peevish voice — the voice of a feverish child which can count on its illness for the indulgence it seeks — something unexpected. 'I want to see Clea.' It ran smoothly off his tongue, as if he had been rehearsing the one phrase in his mind for centuries. He licked his lips and repeated it more slowly. It seemed from Balthazar's angle of vision that a smile settled upon his lips, but he recognized that the contraction was a grimace of pain. He hunted swiftly for the old pair of surgical scissors which he had brought to use upon the soft wire duck-seals and slit the vest of Narouz stiffly from North to South. At this Nessim drew nearer and together they looked down upon the shaggy and powerful body on which the blue and bloodless bullet-holes had sunk like knots in an oak. But they were many, very many. Balthazar made his characteristic little gesture of uncertainty which parodied a Chinaman shaking hands with himself.

Other people had now entered the clearing. Thinking became easier. They had brought an enormous purple curtain with which to carry him back to the house. And now, in some strange way, the place was full of servants. They had ebbed back like a tide. The air was dark with their concern. Narouz ground his teeth and groaned as they lifted him to the great purple cloak and bore him back, like a wounded stag, through the plantations. Once as he neared the house, he said in the same clear child's voice: 'To see Clea' and then subsided into a feverish silence punctuated by occasional quivering sighs.

The servants were saying: 'Praise be to God that the doctor is here! All will be well with him!'

Balthazar felt Nessim's eyes turned upon him. He shook his head gravely and hopelessly and repeated his clucking sound softly. It was a matter of hours, of minutes, of seconds. So they reached the house like some grotesque religious procession bearing the body of the younger son. Softly mewing and sobbing, but with hope and faith in his recovery, the women gazed down upon the jutting head and the sprawled body in the purple curtain which swelled under his weight like a sail. Nessim gave directions, uttering small words like 'Gently here' and 'Slowly at the corner'. So they gradually got him back to the gaunt bedroom from which he had sallied forth that morning, while Balthazar busied himself, breaking open a packet of medical supplies which were kept in a cupboard against lake-accidents, hunting for a hypodermic needle and a phial of morphia. Small croaks and groans were now issuing from the mouth of Narouz. His eyes were closed. He could not hear the dim conversation which Nessim, in another corner of the house, was having with Clea on the telephone.

'But he is dying, Clea.'

Clea made an inarticulate moaning noise of protest. 'What can I do, Nessim? He is nothing to me, never was, never will be. Oh, it is so *disgusting* — please do not make me come, Nessim.'

'Of course not. I simply thought as he is dying ——'

'But if you think I should I will feel obliged to.'

'I think nothing. He has not long to live, Clea.'

'I hear from your voice that I must come. Oh, Nessim, how disgusting that people should love without consent! Will you send the car or shall I telephone Selim? My flesh quails on my bones.'

'Thank you, Clea' said Nessim shortly and with sadly downcast head; for some reason the word 'disgusting' had wounded him. He walked slowly back to the bedroom, noticing on the way that the courtyard was thronged with people — not only the house servants but many new curious visitors. Calamity draws people as an open wound draws flies, Nessim thought. Narouz was in a doze. They sat for a while talking in whispers. 'Then he must really die?' asked Nessim sadly, 'without his mother?' It seemed to him an added burden of guilt that it was through his agency that Leila had been forced to leave. 'Alone like this.' Balthazar made a grimace of impatience. 'It is amazing he's alive at all still' he said. 'And there is absolutely nothing. . . .' Slowly and gravely Balthazar shook that dark intelligent head. Nessim stood up and said: 'Then I should tell them that there is no hope of recovery. They will want to prepare for his death.'

'Do as you wish.'

'I must send for Tobias the priest. He must have the last sacraments — the Holy Eucharist. The servants will know the truth from him.'

'Act as seems good to you' said Balthazar dryly, and the tall figure of his friend slipped down the staircase into the courtyard to give instructions. A rider was to be despatched at once to the priest with instructions to consecrate the holy elements in the church and then come post-haste to Karm Abu Girg to administer the last sacraments to Narouz. As this intelligence went abroad there went up a great sigh of dreadful expectancy and the faces of the servants lengthened with dread. 'And the doctor?' they cried in tones of anguish. 'And the doctor?'

Balthazar smiled grimly as he sat on the chair beside the dying man. He repeated to himself softly, under his breath, 'And the doctor?' What a mockery! He placed his cool palm on Narouz' forehead for a moment, with an air of certitude and resignation. A high temperature, a dozen bullet-holes. . . . . 'And the doctor?'

Musing upon the futility of human affairs and the dreadful accidents to which life exposed the least distrustful, the most innocent of creatures, he lit a cigarette and went out on to the balcony. A hundred eager glances sought his, imploring him by the power of his magic to restore the patient to health. He frowned heavily at one and all. If he had been able to resort to the old-fashioned magic of the Egyptian fables, of the New Testament, he would gladly have told Narouz to rise. But . . . 'And the doctor?'

Despite the internal haemorrhages, the drumming of the pulses in his ears, the fever and pain, the patient was only resting — in a sense — husbanding his energies for the appearance of Clea. He mistook the little flutter of voices and footsteps upon the staircase which heralded the appearance of the priest. His eyelashes fluttered and then sank down again, exhausted to hear the fat voice of the goose-shaped young man with the greasy face and the air of just having dined on sucking-pig. He returned to his own remote watchfulness, content that Tobias should treat him as insensible, as dead even, provided he could husband a small share of his dying space for the blonde image — intractable and remote as ever now to his mind — yet an image which might respond to all this hoarded suffering. Even from pity. He was swollen with desire, distended like a pregnant woman. When you are in love you know that love is a beggar, shameless as a beggar; and the responses of merely human pity can console one where love is absent by a false travesty of an imagined happiness. Yet the day dragged on and still she did not come. The anxiety of the house deepened with his own. And Balthazar, whose intuition had guessed rightly the cause of his patience, was tempted by the thought: 'I could imitate Clea's voice — would he know? I could soothe him with a few words spoken in her voice.' He was a ventriloquist and mimic of the first order. But to the first voice a second replied: 'No. One must not interfere with a destiny however bitter by introducing lies. He must die as he was meant to.' And the first voice said bitterly: 'Then why morphia, why the comforts of religion, and not the solace of a desired human voice imitated, the pressure of a hand imitated? You could easily do this.' But he shook his dark head at himself and said 'No' with bitter obstinacy, as he listened to the unpleasant voice of the priest reading passages of scripture upon the balcony, his voice mixing with the murmuring and shuffling of the human beings in the courtyard below. Was not the evangel all that the imitation of Clea's voice might have been? He kissed his patient's brow slowly, sadly as he reflected.

Narouz began to feel the tuggings of the Underworld, the five wild dogs of the sense pulling ever more heavily upon the leash. He opposed to them the forces of his mighty will, playing for time, waiting for the only human revelation he could expect — voice and odour of a girl who had become embalmed by his senses, entombed like some precious image. He could hear the nerves ticking away in their spirals of pain, the oxygen bubbles rising ever more slowly to explode in his blood. He knew that he was running out of funds, running out of time. The slowly gathering weight of a paralysis was settling over his mind, the narcotic of pain.

Nessim went away to the telephone again. He was wax pale now, with a hectic spot of pink in each cheek, and he spoke with the high sweet hysterical voice of his mother. Clea had already started for Karm Abu Girg, but it seemed that a part of the road had been washed away by a broken dyke. Selim doubted whether she could get through to the ferry that evening.

There now began a tremendous struggle in the breast of Narouz — a struggle to maintain an equilibrium between the forces battling within him. His musculature contracted in heavy bunches with the effort of waiting; his veins bunched out, polished to ebony with the strain, controlled by his will. He ground his teeth savagely together like a wild boar as he felt himself foundering. And Balthazar sat like an effigy, one hand upon his brow and the other fiercely holding the contorted muscles of his wrist. He whispered in Arabic: 'Rest, my darling. Easily, my loved one.' His sadness gave him complete mastery of himself, complete calm. Truth is so bitter that the knowledge of it confers a kind of luxury.

So it went for a while. Then lastly there burst from the hairy throat of the dying man a single tremendous word, the name of Clea, uttered in the cavernous voice of a wounded lion: a voice which combined anger, reproof and an overwhelming sadness in its sudden roar. So nude a word, her name, as simple as 'God' or 'Mother' — yet it sounded as if upon the lips of some dying conqueror, some lost king, conscious of the body and breath dissolving within him. The name of Clea sounded through the whole house, drenched by the splendour of his anguish, silencing the little knots of whispering servants and visitors, setting back the ears of the hunting dogs, making them crouch and fawn: ringing in Nessim's mind with a new and terrifying bitterness too deep for tears. And as this great cry slowly faded, the intelligence of his death dawned upon them with a new and crushing weight — like the pressure of some great tomb door closing upon hope.

Immobile, ageless as pain itself, sat the defeated effigy of the doctor at the bedside of pain. He was thinking to himself, full of the bright light of intellection: 'A phrase like "out of the jaws of death" might mean something like that cry of Narouz', its bravery. Or "out of the jaws of Hell". It must mean the hell of a private mind. No, we can do nothing.'

The great voice thinned softly into the the burring comb-and-paper sound of a long death-rattle, fading into the buzz of a fly caught in some remote spider's web.

And now Nessim gave a single sweet sob out there on the balcony — the noise that a bamboo stem makes when it is plucked from the stalk. And like the formal opening bars of some great symphony this small sob was echoed below in the darkness, passed from lip to lip, heart to heart. Their sobs lighted one another — as candles take a light from one another — an orchestral fulfilment of the precious theme of sorrow, and a long quivering ragged moan came up out of the empty well to climb upwards towards the darkening sky, a long hushing sigh which mingled with the hushing of the rain upon Lake Mareotis. The death of Narouz had begun to be borne. Balthazar with lowered head was quoting softly to himself in Greek the lines:

> *Now the sorrow of the knowledge of parting*
> *Moves like wind in the rigging of the ship*
> *Of the man's death, figurehead of the white body,*
> *The sails of the soul being filled*
> *By the Ghost of the Breath, replete and eternal.*

It was the signal for a release, for now the inescapably terrible scenes of a Coptic wake were to be enacted in the house, scenes charged with an ancient terror and abandon.

Death had brought the women into their kingdom, and made them free to deliver each her inheritance of sorrow. They crept forward in a body, gathering speed as they mounted the staircases, their faces rapt and transfigured now as they uttered the first terrible screaming. Their fingers were turned into hooks now, tearing at their own flesh, their breasts, their cheeks, with a lustful abandon as they moved swiftly up the staircase. They were uttering that curious and thrilling ululation which is called the *zagreet*, their tongues rippling on their palates like mandolines. An ear-splitting chorus of tongue trills in various keys.

The old house echoed to the shrieks of these harpies as they took possession of it and invaded the room of death to circle round the silent corpse, still repeating the blood-curdling signal of death, full of an unbearable animal abandon. They began the dances of ritual grief while Nessim and Balthazar sat silent upon their chairs, their heads sunk upon their breasts, their hands clasped — the very picture of human failure. They allowed these fierce quivering screams to pierce them to the very quick of their beings. Only submission now to the ritual of this ancient sorrow was permissible: and sorrow had become an orgiastic frenzy which bordered on madness. The women were dancing now as they circled the body, striking their breasts and howling, but dancing in the slow measured figures of a dance recaptured from long-forgotten friezes upon the tombs of the ancient world. They moved and swayed, quivering from throat to ankles, and they twisted and turned calling upon the dead man to rise. 'Rise, my despair! Rise, my death! Rise, my golden one, my death, my camel, my protector! O beloved body full of seed, arise!' And then the ghastly ululations torn from their throats, the bitter tears streaming from their torn minds. Round and round they moved, hypnotized by their own lamentations, infecting the whole house with their sorrow while from the dark courtyard below came the deeper, darker hum of their menfolk sobbing as they touched hands in consolation and repeated, to comfort one another: '*Ma-a-lesh!* Let it be forgiven! Nothing avails our grief!'

So the sorrow multiplied and proliferated. From everywhere now the women came in numbers. Some had already put on the dress of ritual mourning — the dirty coverings of dark blue cotton. They had smeared their faces with indigo and rubbed ash from the fires into their black loosened tresses. They now answered the shrieks of their sisters above with their own, baring their glittering teeth, and climbed the stairs, poured into the upper rooms with the ruthlessness of demons. Room by room, with a systematic frenzy, they attacked the old house, pausing only to utter the same terrifying screams as they set about their work.

Bedsteads, cupboards, sofas were propelled out upon the balcony and hurled from there into the courtyard. At each new crash a fresh fever of screaming — the long bubbling *zagreet* — would break out and be answered from every corner of the house. Now the mirrors were shivered into a thousand fragments, the pictures turned back to front, the carpets reversed. All the china and glass in the house — save for the ceremonial black coffee set which was kept for funerals — was now broken up, trampled on, shivered to atoms. It was all swept into a great mound on the balcony. Everything that might suggest the order and continuity of earthly life, domestic, personal or social, must be discarded now and obliterated. The systematic destruction of the memory of death itself in plates, pictures, ornaments or clothes. . . . The domestic furnishings of the house were completely wrecked now, and everything that remained had been covered in black drapes.

Meanwhile, down below a great coloured tent had been pitched, a marquee, in which visiting mourners would come and sit through the whole of the 'Night of Loneliness' drinking coffee in silence from the black cups and listening to the deep thrilling moaning up above which swelled up from time to time into a new outbreak of screaming or the noise of a woman fainting, or rolling on the ground in a seizure. Nothing must be spared to make this great man's funeral successful.

Other mourners too had now begun to appear, both personal and professional, so to speak; those who had a personal stake in the funeral of a friend came to spend the night in the coloured marquee under the brilliant light. But there were others, the professional mourners of the surrounding villages for whom death was something like a public competition in the poetry of mourning; they came on foot, in carts, on camel-back. And as each entered the gate of the house she set up a long shivering cry, like an orgasm, that stirred the griefs of the other mourners anew, so that they responded from every corner of the house — the low sobbing notes gradually swelling into a blood-curdling and sustained tongue-trill that pierced the nerves.

These professional mourners brought with them all the wild poetry of their caste, of memories loaded with years of death-practice. They were often young and beautiful. They were singers. They carried with them the ritual drums and tambourines to which they danced and which they used to punctuate their own grief and stimulate the flagging griefs of those who had already been in action. 'Praise the inmate of the House' they cried proudly as with superb and calculated slowness they began their slow dance about the body, turning and twisting in an ecstasy of pity as they recited eulogies couched in the finest poetic Arabic upon Narouz. They praised his character, his rectitude, his beauty, his riches. And these long perfectly turned strophes were punctuated by the sobs and groans of the audience, both above and below; so vulnerable to poetry, even the old men seated on the stiff-backed chairs in the tent below found their throats tightening until a dry sob broke from their lips and they hung their heads, whispering 'Ma-a-lesh.'

Among them, Mohammed Shebab, the old schoolmaster and friend of the Hosnanis, had pride of place. He was dressed in his best and even wore a pair of ancient pearl spats with a new scarlet tarbush. The memory of forgotten evenings which he had spent on the balcony of the old house listening to music with Nessim and Narouz, gossiping to Leila, smote him now with pain which was not feigned. And since the people of the Delta often use a wake as an excuse to discharge private griefs in communal mourning, he too found himself thinking of his dead sister and sobbing, and he turned to the servant, pressing money into his hand as he said: 'Ask Alam the singer to sing the recitative of the Image of Women once more, please. I wish to mourn it through again.' And as the great poem began, he leaned back luxuriously swollen with the refreshment of a sorrow which would achieve catharsis thus in poetry. There were others too who asked for their favourite laments to be sung, offering the singers the requisite payment. In this way the whole grief of the countryside was refunded once again into living, purged of bitterness, reconquered by the living through the dead image of Narouz.

Until morning now it would be kept up, the strange circling dances, the ripple and shiver of tambourines, the tongue-trilling screams, and the slow pulse of the dirges with their magnificent plumage of metaphor and image — poetry of the death-house. Some were early overcome with exhaustion and several among the house-servants had fainted from hysteria after two hours of singing thus; the professional keeners, however, knew their own strength and behaved like the ritual performers they were. When overcome by excess of grief or by a long burst of screams, they would sink to the floor and take a short rest, sometimes even smoking a cigarette. Then they would once more join the circle of dancers, refreshed.

Presently, however, when the first long passion of grief had been expressed, Nessim sent for the priests who would add the light of tall bloodless candles and the noise of the psalms to the sound of water and sponge — for the body must be washed. They came at last. The body-washers were the two beadles of the little Coptic Church — ignorant louts both. Here a hideous altercation broke out, for the dead man's clothes are the perquisites of the layer-out, and the beadles could find nothing in Narouz' shabby wardrobe which seemed an adequate recompense for the trouble. A few old cloaks and boots, a torn nightshirt, and a small embroidered cap which dated from his circumcision — that was all Narouz owned. Nor would the beadles accept money — that would have been unlucky. Nessim began to rage, but they stood there obstinate as mules, refusing to wash Narouz without the ritual payment. Finally both Nessim and Balthazar were obliged to get out of their own suits in order to make them over to the beadles as payment. They put on the tattered old clothes of Narouz with a shiver of dread — cloaks which hung down like a graduate's gown upon their tall figures. But somehow the ceremony must be completed, so that he could be taken to the church at dawn for burial — or else the ceremonial mourners might keep up the performance for days and nights together: in the olden times such mourning lasted forty days! Nessim also ordered the coffin to be made, and the singing was punctuated all night by the sound of hammers and saws in the wheelwright's yard hard by. Nessim himself was completely exhausted by now, and dozed fitfully on a chair, being woken from time to time by a burst of keening or by some personal problem which remained to be solved and which was submitted to his arbitration by the servants of the house.

Sounds of chanting, rosy flickering of candle-light, swish of sponges and the scratching of a razor upon dead flesh. The experience gave no pain now, but an unearthly numbness of spirits. The sound of water trickling and of sponges crushing softly upon the body of his brother, seemed part of an entirely new fabric of thought and emotion. The groans of the washers as they turned him over; the thump of the body on the table as it turned over. The soft thump of a hare's dead body when it is thrown on to a kitchen table. . . . He shuddered.

Narouz at last, washed and oiled and sprinkled with rosemary and thyme, lay at ease in his rough coffin clad in the shroud which he, like every Copt, had preserved against this moment; a shroud made of white flax which had been dipped in the River Jordan. He had no jewels or rich costumes to take to the grave with him, but Balthazar coiled the great bloodstained whip and placed it under his pillow. (The next morning the servants were to carry in the body of a wretch whose whole face had been pulped by the blows of this singular weapon; he had run, it seems, screaming, unrecognizable, across the plantation to fall insensible in a dyke and drown. So thoroughly had the whip done its work that he was unidentifiable.)

The first part of the work was now complete and it only remained to wait for dawn. Once more the mourners were admitted to the room of death where Narouz lay, once more they resumed their passionate dancing and drumming. Balthazar took his leave now, for there was nothing more he could do to help. The two men crossed the courtyard slowly, arm in arm, leaning on each other as if exhausted.

'If you meet Clea at the ferry, take her back' said Nessim.

'Of course I will.'

They shook hands slowly and embraced each other. Then Nessim turned back, yawning and shivering, into the house. He sat dozing on a chair. It would be three days before the house could be purged of sadness and the soul of Narouz 'sent away' by the priestly rituals. First would come the long straggling procession with the torches and banners in the early dawn, before the mist rose, the women with faces blackened now like furies, tearing their hair. The deacons chanting 'Remember me O Lord when Thou hast come to Thy Kingdom' in deep thrilling voices. Then on the cold floor of the church the sods raining down on Narouz' pale face and the voices reciting 'From dust to dust', and the rolling periods of the evangel singing him away to heaven. Squeak of the brass screws as the lid went down. All this he saw, foreshadowed in his mind as he drowsed upon the stiff-backed chair beside the rough-hewn coffin. Of what, he wondered, could Narouz be dreaming now, with the great whip coiled beneath his pillow?

*　　*　　*　　*　　*

CLEA

To
MY FATHER

The Primary and most beautiful of Nature's qualities is motion, which agitates her at all times, but this motion is simply the perpetual consequence of crimes, it is conserved by means of crimes alone.

D. A. F. DE SADE

I

I

The oranges were more plentiful than usual that year. They glowed in their arbours of burnished green leaf like lanterns, flickering up there among the sunny woods. It was as if they were eager to celebrate our departure from the little island — for at last the long-awaited message from Nessim had come, like a summons back to the Underworld. A message which was to draw me back inexorably to the one city which for me always hovered between illusion and reality, between the substance and the poetic images which its very name aroused in me. A memory, I told myself, which had been falsified by the desires and intuitions only as yet half-realized on paper. Alexandria, the capital of memory! All the writing which I had borrowed from the living and the dead, until I myself had become a sort of postscript to a letter which was never ended, never posted. . . .

How long had I been away? I could hardly compute, though calendar-time gives little enough indication of the aeons which separate one self from another, one day from another; and all this time I had been living there, truly, in the Alexandria of my heart's mind. And page by page, heartbeat by heartbeat, I had been surrendering myself to the grotesque organism of which we had all once been part, victors and vanquished alike. An ancient city changing under the brush-strokes of thoughts which besieged meaning, clamouring for identity; somewhere there, on the black thorny promontories of Africa the aromatic truth of the place lived on, the bitter unchewable herb of the past, the pith of memory. I had set out once to store, to codify, to annotate the past before it was utterly lost — that at least was a task I had set myself. I had failed in it (perhaps it was hopeless?) for no sooner had I embalmed one aspect of it in words than the intrusion of new knowledge disrupted the frame of reference, everything flew asunder, only to reassemble again in unforeseen, unpredictable patterns. . . .

'To re-work reality' I had written somewhere; temeritous, presumptuous words indeed — for it is reality which works and reworks us on its slow wheel. Yet if I had been enriched by the experience of this island interlude, it was perhaps because of this total failure to record the inner truth of the city. I had now come face to face with the nature of time, that ailment of the human psyche. I had been forced to admit defeat on paper. Yet curiously enough the act of writing had in itself brought me another sort of increase; by the very *failure* of words, which sink one by one into the measureless caverns of the imagination and gutter out. An expensive way to begin living, yes; but then we artists are driven towards personal lives nourished in these strange techniques of self-pursuit.

But then . . . if I had changed, what of my friends — Balthazar, Nessim, Justine, Clea? What new aspects of them would I discern after this time-lapse, when once more I had been caught up in the ambience of a new city, a city now swallowed by a war? Here was the rub. I could not say. Apprehension trembled within me like a lodestar. It was hard to renounce the hard-won territory of my dreams in favour of new images, new cities, new dispositions, new loves. I had come to hug my own dreams of the place like a monomaniac. . . . Would it not, I wondered, be wiser to stay where I was? Perhaps. Yet I knew I must go. Indeed *this very night* I should be gone! The thought itself was so hard to grasp that I was forced to whisper it aloud to myself.

We had passed the last ten days since the messenger called in a golden hush of anticipation; and the weather had matched it, turning up a succession of perfectly blue days, windless seas. We stood between the two landscapes, unwilling to relinquish the one yet aching to encounter the other. Poised, like gulls upon the side of a cliff. And already the dissimilar images mixed and baulked in my dreams. This island house, for example, its smoke-silvered olives and almonds where the red-footed partridge wandered . . . silent glades where only the goat-face of a Pan might emerge. Its simple and lucent perfection of form and colour could not mix with the other premonitions crowding in upon us. (A sky full of falling-stars, emerald wash of tides on lonely beaches, crying of gulls on the white roads of the south.) This Grecian world was already being invaded by the odours of the forgotten city — promontories where the sweating sea-captains had boozed and eaten until their intestines cracked, had drained their bodies, like kegs, of every lust, foundering in the embrace of black slaves with spaniels' eyes. (The mirrors, the heart-rending sweetness of the voices of blinded canaries, the bubble of *narguilehs* in their rose-water bowls, the smell of patchouli and joss.) They were eating into one another, these irreconcilable dreams. And I saw my friends once again (not as names now), irradiated anew by the knowledge of this departure. They were no longer shadows of my own writing but refreshed anew — even the dead. At night I walked again those curling streets with Melissa (situated now somewhere beyond regrets, for even in my dreams I knew she was dead), walking comfortably arm in arm; her narrow legs like scissors gave her a swaying walk. The habit of pressing her thigh to mine at every step. I could see everything with affection now — even the old cotton frock and cheap shoes which she wore on holidays. She had not been able to powder out the faint blue lovebite on her throat. . . . Then she vanished and I awoke with a cry of regret. Dawn was breaking among the olives, silvering their still leaves.

Somewhere along the road I had recovered my peace of mind. This handful of blue days before saying farewell — I treasured them, luxuriating in their simplicity: fires of olive-wood blazing in the old hearth whose painting of Justine would be the last item to be packed, jumping and gleaming on the battered table and chair, on the blue enamel bowl of early cyclamen. What had the city to do with all this — an Aegean spring hanging upon a thread between winter and the first white puffs of almond blossom? It was a word merely, and meant little, being scribbled on the margins of a dream, or being repeated in the mind to the colloquial music of time, which is only desire expressed in heart-beats. Indeed, though I loved it so much, I was powerless to stay; the city which I now know I hated held out something different for me — a new evaluation of the experience which had marked me. I must return to it once more in order to be able to leave it forever, to shed it. If I have spoken of time it is because the writer I was becoming was learning at last to inhabit those deserted spaces which time misses — beginning to live between the ticks of the clock, so to speak. The continuous present, which is the real history of that collective anecdote, the human mind; when the past is dead and the future represented only by desire and fear, what of that adventive moment which can't be measured, can't be dismissed? For most of us the so-called Present is snatched away like some sumptuous repast, conjured up by fairies — before one can touch a mouthful. Like the dead Pursewarden I hoped I might soon be truthfully able to say: 'I do not write for those who have never asked themselves this question: "at what point does real life begin?" '

Idle thoughts passing through the mind as I lay on a flat rock above the sea, eating an orange, perfectly circumscribed by a solitude which would soon be engulfed by the city, the ponderous azure dream of Alexandria basking like some old reptile in the bronze Pharaonic light of the great lake. The master-sensualists of history abandoning their bodies to mirrors, to poems, to the grazing flocks of boys and women, to the needle in the vein, to the opium-pipe, to the death-in-life kisses without appetite. Walking those streets again in my imagination I knew once more that they spanned, not merely human history, but the whole biological scale of the heart's affections — from the painted ecstasies of Cleopatra (strange that the vine should be discovered here, near Taposiris) to the bigotry of Hypatia (withered vine-leaves, martyr's kisses). And stranger visitors: Rimbaud, student of the Abrupt Path, walked here with a belt full of gold coins. And all those other swarthy dream-interpreters and politicians and eunuchs were like a flock of birds of brilliant plumage. Between pity, desire and dread, I saw the city once more spread out before me, inhabited by the faces of my friends and subjects. I knew that I must re-experience it once more and this time forever.

Yet it was to be a strange departure, full of small unforeseen elements — I mean the messenger being a hunchback in a silver suit, a flower in his lapel, a perfumed handkerchief in his sleeve! And the sudden springing to life of the little village which had for so long tactfully ignored our very existence, save for an occasional gift of fish or wine or coloured eggs which Athena brought us, folded in her red shawl. She, too, could hardly bear to see us go; her stern old wrinkled mask crumpled into tears over each item of our slender baggage. But 'They will not let you leave without a hospitality' she repeated stubbornly. 'The village will not let you go like that.' We were to be offered a farewell banquet!

As for the child I had conducted the whole rehearsal of this journey (of her whole life, in truth) in images from a fairy story. Many repetitions had not staled it. She would sit staring up at the painting and listening attentively. She was more than prepared for it all, indeed almost ravenous to take up her own place in the gallery of images I had painted for her. She had soaked up all the confused colours of this fanciful world to which she had once belonged by right and which she would now recover — a world

peopled by those presences — the father, a dark pirate-prince, the
stepmother a swarthy imperious queen. . . .

'She is like the playing-card?'

'Yes. The Queen of Spades.'

'And her name is Justine.'

'Her name is Justine.'

'In the picture she is smoking. Will she love me more than my
father or less?'

'She will love you both.'

There had been no other way to explain it to her, except in
terms of myth or allegory — the poetry of infant uncertainty. I
had made her word-perfect in this parable of an Egypt which was
to throw up for her (enlarged to the size of gods or magi) the
portraits of her family, of her ancestors. But then is not life itself
a fairy-tale which we lose the power of apprehending as we grow?
No matter. She was already drunk upon the image of her father.

'Yes, I understand everything.' With a nod and a sigh she
would store up these painted images in the treasure-box of her
mind. Of Melissa, her dead mother, she spoke less often, and
when she did I answered her in the same fashion from the story-
book; but she had already sunk, pale star, below the horizon into
the stillness of death, leaving the foreground to those others —
the playing-card characters of the living.

The child had thrown a tangerine into the water and now leaned
to watch it roll softly down to the sandy floor of the grotto. It
lay there, flickering like a small flame, nudged by the swell and fall
of the currents.

'Now watch me fetch it up.'

'Not in this icy sea, you'll die of cold.'

'It isn't cold today. Watch.'

By now she could swim like a young otter. It was easy, sitting
here on the flat rock above the water, to recognize in her the
dauntless eyes of Melissa, slanted a little at the edges; and sometimes, intermittently, like a forgotten grain of sleep in the corners,
the dark supposing look (pleading, uncertain) of her father Nessim.
I remembered Clea's voice saying once, in another world, long ago:
'Mark, if a girl does not like dancing and swimming she will never
be able to make love.' I smiled and wondered if the words were
true as I watched the little creature turn over smoothly in the
water and flow gracefully downwards to the target with the craft
of a seal, toes pressed back against the sky. The glimmer of the

little white purse between her legs. She retrieved the tangerine beautifully and spiralled to the surface with it gripped in her teeth.

'Now run and dry quickly.'

'It isn't cold.'

'Do as you are told. Be off. Hurry.'

'And the man with the hump?'

'He has gone.'

Mnemjian's unexpected appearance on the island had both started and thrilled her — for it was he who brought us Nessim's message. It was strange to see him walking along the shingle beach with an air of grotesque perturbation, as if balancing on corkscrews. I think he wished to show us that for years he had not walked on anything but the finest pavements. He was literally unused to terra firma. He radiated a precarious and overbred finesse. He was clad in a dazzling silver suit, spats, a pearl tie-pin, and his fingers were heavily ringed. Only the smile, the infant smile was unchanged, and the oiled spitcurl was still aimed at the frontal sinus.

'I have married Halil's widow. I am the richest barber in all Egypt today, my dear friend.'

He blurted this out all in one breath, leaning on a silver-knobbed walking-stick to which he was clearly as unaccustomed. His violet eye roved somewhat disdainfully round our somewhat primitive cottage, and he refused a chair, doubtless because he did not wish to crease those formidable trousers. 'You have a hard style of life here, eh? Not much *luxe*, Darley.' Then he sighed and added, 'But now you will be coming to us again.' He made a vague gesture with the stick intended to symbolize the hospitality we should once more enjoy from the city. 'Myself I cannot stay. I am on my way back. I did this purely as a favour to Hosnani.' He spoke of Nessim with a sort of pearly grandeur, as if he were now his equal socially; then he caught sight of my smile and had the grace to giggle once before becoming serious again. 'There is no time, anyway' he said, dusting his sleeves.

This had the merit of being true, for the Smyrna boat stays only long enough to unload mail and occasional merchandise — a few cases of macaroni, some copper sulphate, a pump. The wants of the islanders are few. Together we walked back towards the village, across the olive-groves, talking as we went. Mnemjian still trudged with that slow turtle-walk. But I was glad, for it enabled me to ask him a few questions about the city, and from his answers to gain some inkling of what I was to find there in the matter of changed dispositions, unknown factors.

'There are many changes since the Hosnani intrigue in Palestine? The collapse? The Egyptians are trying to sequestrate. They have taken much away. Yes, they are poor now, and still in trouble. She is still under house-detention at Karm Abu Girg. Nobody has seen her for an age. He works by special permission as an ambulance driver in the docks, twice a week. Very dangerous. And there was a bad air-raid; he lost one eye and a finger.'

'Nessim?' I was startled. The little man nodded self-importantly. This new, this unforeseen image of my friend struck me like a bullet. 'Good God' I said, and the barber nodded as if to approve the appropriateness of the oath. 'It was bad' he said. 'It is the war, Darley.' Then suddenly a happier thought came into his mind and he smiled the infant smile once more which reflected only the iron material values of the Levant. Taking my arm he continued: 'But the war is also good business. My shops are cutting the armies' hair day and night. Three saloons, twelve assistants! You will see, it is superb. And Pombal says, as a joke, "Now you are shaving the dead while they are still alive." ' He doubled up with soundless refined laughter.

'Is Pombal back there?'

'Of course. He is a high man of the Free French now. He has conferences with Sir Mountolive. He is also still there. Many others too have remained from your time, Darley, you will see.'

Mnemjian seemed delighted to have been able to astonish me so easily. Then he said something which made my mind do a double somersault. I stood still and asked him to repeat it, thinking that I had misheard him. 'I have just visited Capodistria.' I stared at him. Capodistria! 'But he *died*!' I exclaimed, though I had not forgotten Balthazar's enigmatic phrase about the false teeth.

The barber leaned far back, as if on a rocking-horse, and tittered profusely. It was a very good joke this time and lasted him a full minute. Then at last, still sighing luxuriously at the memory of it, he slowly took from his breast-pocket a postcard such as one buys upon any Mediterranean seafront and held it out to me, saying: 'Then who is this?'

It was a murky enough photograph with the heavy developing-marks which are a feature of hasty street-photography. It depicted two figures walking along a seafront. One was Mnemjian. The other . . . I stared at it in growing recognition. . . . .

Capodistria was clad in tubular trousers of an Edwardian style and very pointed black shoes. With this he wore a long academician's topcoat with a fur collar and cuffs. Finally, and quite fantastically, he was sporting a *chapeau melon* which made him look rather like a tall rat in some animal cartoon. He had grown a thin Rilkean moustache which drooped a little at the corner of his mouth. A long cigarette-holder was between his teeth. It was unmistakably Capodistria. 'What on earth . . .' I began, but the smiling Mnemjian shut one eye and laid a finger across his lips. 'Always' he said 'there are mysteries'; and in the act of guarding them he swelled up toad-like, staring into my eyes with a mischievous content. He would perhaps have deigned to explain but at that minute a ship's siren rang out from the direction of the village. He was flustered. 'Quickly'; he began his trudging walk. 'I mustn't forget to give you the letter from Hosnani.' It was carried in his breast pocket and he fished it out at last. 'And now good-bye' he said. 'All is arranged. We will meet again.'

I shook his hand and stood looking after him for a moment, surprised and undecided. Then I turned back to the edge of the olive grove and sat down on a rock to read the letter from Nessim. It was brief and contained the details of the travel arrangements he had made for us. A little craft would be coming to take us off the island. He gave approximate times and instructions as to where we should wait for it. All this was clearly set out. Then, as a postcript Nessim added in his tall hand: 'It will be good to meet again, without reserves. I gather that Balthazar has recounted all our misadventures. You won't exact an unduly heavy repentance from people who care for you so much? I hope not. Let the past remain a closed book for us all.'

That was how it fell out.

For those last few days the island regaled us nobly with the best of its weather and those austere Cycladean simplicities which were like a fond embrace — for which I knew I should be longing when once more the miasma of Egypt had closed over my head.

On the evening of departure the whole village turned out to give us the promised farewell dinner of lamb on the spit and gold *rezina* wine. They spread the tables and chairs down the whole length of the small main street and each family brought its own offerings to the feast. Even those two proud dignitaries were there — mayor and priest — each seated at one end of the long table. It was cold to sit in the lamplight thus, pretending that it was really a summer evening, but even the frail spring moon collaborated, rising blindly out of the sea to shine upon the white tablecloths, polish the glasses of wine. The old burnished faces, warmed by drink, glowed like copperware. Ancient smiles, archaic forms of address, traditional pleasantries, courtesies of the old world which was already fading, receding from us. The old sea-captains of the sponge-fleets sucking their bounty of wine from blue enamel cans: their warm embraces smelt like wrinkled crab-apples, their great moustaches tanned by tobacco curled towards their ears.

At first I had been touched, thinking all this ceremony was for me; I was not the less so to find that it was for my country. To be English when Greece had fallen was to be a target for the affection and gratitude of every Greek, and the humble peasants of this hamlet felt it no less keenly than Greeks everywhere. The shower of toasts and pledges echoed on the night, and all the speeches flew like kites, in the high style of Greek, orotund and sonorous. They seemed to have the cadences of immortal poetry — the poetry of a desperate hour; but of course they were only words, the wretched windy words which war so easily breeds and which the rhetoricians of peace would soon wear out of use.

But tonight the war lit them up like tapers, the old men, giving them a burning grandeur. Only the young men were not there to silence and shame them with their hangdog looks — for they had gone to Albania to die among the snows. The women spoke shrilly, in voices made coarsely thrilling with unshed tears, and among the bursts of laughter and song fell their sudden silences — like so many open graves.

It had come so softly towards us over the waters, this war; gradually, as clouds which quietly fill in a horizon from end to end. But as yet it had not broken. Only the rumour of it gripped the heart with conflicting hopes and fears. At first it had seemed to portend the end of the so-called civilized world, but this hope soon proved vain. No, it was to be as always simply the end of kindness and safety and moderate ways; the end of the artist's hopes, of nonchalance, of joy. Apart from this everything else about the human condition would be confirmed and emphasized; perhaps even a certain truthfulness had already begun to emerge from behind appearances, for death heightens every tension and permits us fewer of the half-truths by which we normally live.

This was all we had known of it, to date, this unknown dragon whose claws had already struck elsewhere. All? Yes, to be sure, once or twice the upper sky had swollen with the slur of invisible bombers, but their sounds could not drown the buzzing, nearer at hand, of the island bees: for each household owned a few white-washed hives. What else? Once (this seemed more real) a sub-marine poked up a periscope in the bay and surveyed the coastline for minutes on end. Did it see us bathing on the point? We waved. But a periscope has no arms with which to wave back. Perhaps on the beaches to the north it had discovered something more rare — an old bull seal dozing in the sun like a Moslem on his prayer-mat. But this again could have had little to do with war.

Yet the whole business became a little more real when the little *caique* which Nessim had sent fussed into the dusk-filled harbour that night, manned by three sullen-looking sailors armed with automatics. They were not Greek, though they spoke the tongue with waspish authority. They had tales to tell of shattered armies and death by frostbite, but in a sense it was already too late, for the wine had fuddled the wits of the old men. Their stories palled rapidly. Yet they impressed me, these three leather-faced specimens from an unknown civilization called 'war'. They sat uneasily in such good fellowship. The flesh was stretched tight over their unshaven cheek-bones as if from fatigue. They smoked gluttonously, gushing the blue smoke from mouth and nostrils like voluptuaries. When they yawned they seemed to fetch their yawns up from the very scrotum. We confided ourselves to their care with misgiving for they were the first unfriendly faces we had seen for a long time.

At midnight we slipped out slantwise from the bay upon a high moonlight — the further darkness made more soft, more con-fiding, by the warm incoherent good-byes which poured out across the white beaches towards us. How beautiful are the Greek words of greeting and farewell!

We shuttled for a while along the ink-shadowed line of cliffs where the engine's heartbeats were puckered up and thrown back at us in volleys. And so at last outwards upon the main deep, feeling the soft unction of the water's rhythms begin to breast us up, cradle and release us, as if in play. The night was superlatively warm and fine. A dolphin broke once, twice at the bow. A course was set.

Exultation mixed with a profound sadness now possessed us; fatigue and happiness in one. I could taste the good salt upon my lips. We drank some warm sage-tea without talking. The child was struck speechless by the beauties of this journey — the quivering phosphorescence of our wake, combed out behind us like a comet's hair, flowing and reviving. Above us, too, flowed the plumed branches of heaven, stars scattered as thick as almond-blossom on the enigmatic sky. So at last, happy with these auguries and lulled by pulses of the water and the even vibrations of the engine, she fell asleep with a smile upon parted lips, with the olive-wood doll pressed against her cheek.

How could I help but think of the past towards which we were returning across the dense thickets of time, across the familiar pathways of the Greek sea? The night slid past me, an unrolling ribbon of darkness. The warm sea-wind brushed my cheek — soft as the brush of a fox. Between sleep and waking I lay, feeling the tug of memory's heavy plumb-line: tug of the leaf-veined city which my memory had peopled with masks, malign and beautiful at once. I should see Alexandria again, I knew, in the elusive temporal fashion of a ghost — for once you become aware of the operation of a time which is not calendar-time you become in some sort a ghost. In this other domain I could hear the echoes of words uttered long since in the past by other voices. Balthazar saying: 'This world represents the promise of a unique happiness which we are not well-enough equipped to grasp.' The grim mandate which the city exercised over its familiars, crippling sentiment, steeping everything in the vats of its own exhausted passions. Kisses made more passionate by remorse. Gestures made in the amber light of shuttered rooms. The flocks of white doves flying upwards among the minarets. The pictures seemed to me to represent the city as I would see it again. But I was wrong — for each new approach is different. Each time we deceive ourselves that it will be the same. The Alexandria I now saw, the first vision of it from the sea, was something I could not have imagined.

It was still dark when we lay up outside the invisible harbour with its remembered outworks of forts and anti-submarine nets. I tried to paint the outlines on the darkness with my mind. The boom was raised only at dawn each day. An all-obliterating darkness reigned. Somewhere ahead of us lay the invisible coast of Africa, with its 'kiss of thorns' as the Arabs say. It was intolerable to be so aware of them, the towers and minarets of the city and yet to be unable to will them to appear. I could not see my own fingers before my face. The sea had become a vast empty ante-room, a hollow bubble of blackness.

Then suddenly there passed a sudden breath, a whiff like a wind passing across a bed of embers, and the nearer distance glowed pink as a sea-shell, deepening gradually into the rose-richness of a flower. A faint and terrible moaning came out across the water towards us, pulsing like the wing-beats of some fearful prehistoric bird — sirens which howled as the damned must howl in limbo. One's nerves were shaken like the branches of a tree. And as if in response to this sound lights began to prick out everywhere, sporadically at first, then in ribbons, bands, squares of crystal. The harbour suddenly outlined itself with complete clarity upon the dark panels of heaven, while long white fingers of powder-white light began to stalk about the sky in ungainly fashion, as if they were the legs of some awkward insect struggling to gain a purchase on the slippery black. A dense stream of coloured rockets now began to mount from the haze among the battleships, emptying on the sky their brilliant clusters of stars and diamonds and smashed pearl snuff-boxes with a marvellous prodigality. The air shook in strokes. Clouds of pink and yellow dust arose with the maroons to shine upon the greasy buttocks of the barrage balloons which were flying everywhere. The very sea seemed to tremble. I had no idea that we were so near, or that the city could be so beautiful in the mere saturnalia of a war. It had begun to swell up, to expand like some mystical rose of the darkness, and the bombardment kept it company, overflowing the mind. To our surprise we found ourselves shouting at each other. We were staring at the burning embers of Augustine's Carthage, I thought to myself, we are observing the fall of city man.

It was as beautiful as it was stupefying. In the top left-hand corner of the tableau the searchlights had begun to congregate, quivering and sliding in their ungainly fashion, like daddy-long-legs. They intersected and collided feverishly, and it was clear that some signal had reached them which told of the struggles of some trapped insect on the outer cobweb of darkness. Again and again they crossed, probed, merged, divided. Then at last we saw what they were bracketing: six tiny silver moths moving down the skylanes with what seemed unbearable slowness. The sky had gone mad around them yet they still moved with this fatal langour; and languidly too curled the curving strings of hot diamonds which spouted up from the ships, or the rank lacklustre sniffs of cloudy shrapnel which marked their progress.

And deafening as was the roaring which now filled our ears it was possible to isolate many of the separate sounds which orchestrated the bombardment. The crackle of shards which fell back like a hailstorm upon the corrugated roofs of the waterside cafés: the scratchy mechanical voices of ships' signallers repeating, in the voices of ventriloquists' dummies, semi-intelligible phrases which sounded like 'Three o'clock red, Three o'clock red'. Strangely too, there was music somewhere at the heart of all the hubbub, jagged quartertones which stabbed; then, too, the foundering roar of buildings falling. Patches of light which disappeared and left an aperture of darkness at which a dirty yellow flame might come and lap like a thirsty animal. Nearer at hand (the water smacked the echo out) we could hear the rich harvest of spent cannon-shells pouring upon the decks from the Chicago Pianos: an almost continuous splashing of golden metal tumbling from the breeches of the skypointed guns.

So it went on, feasting the eye yet making the vertebrae quail before the whirlwind of meaningless power it disclosed. I had not realized the impersonality of war before. There was no room for human beings or thought of them under this vast umbrella of coloured death. Each drawn breath had become only a temporary refuge.

Then, almost as suddenly as it had started, the spectacle died away. The harbour vanished with theatrical suddenness, the string of precious stones was turned off, the sky emptied, the silence drenched us, only to be broken once more by that famished crying of the sirens which drilled at the nerves. And then, nothing — a nothingness weighing tons of darkness out of which grew the smaller and more familiar sounds of water licking at the gunwales. A faint shore-wind crept out to invest us with the alluvial smells of an invisible estuary. Was it only in my imagination that I heard from far away the sounds of wild-fowl on the lake?

We waited thus for a long time in great indecision; but meanwhile from the east the dawn had begun to overtake the sky, the city and desert. Human voices, weighted like lead, came softly out, stirring curiosity and compassion. Children's voices — and in the west a sputum-coloured meniscus on the horizon. We yawned, it was cold. Shivering, we turned to one another, feeling suddenly orphaned in this benighted world between light and darkness.

But gradually it grew up from the eastern marches, this familiar dawn, the first overflow of citron and rose which would set the dead waters of Mareotis a-glitter; and fine as a hair, yet so indistinct that one had to stop breathing to verify it, I heard (or thought I heard) the first call to prayer from some as yet invisible minaret.

Were there, then, still gods left to invoke? And even as the question entered my mind I saw, shooting from the harbour-mouth, the three small fishing-boats — sails of rust, liver and blue plum. They heeled upon a freshet and stooped across our bows like hawks. We could hear the rataplan of water lapping their prows. The small figures, balanced like riders, hailed us in Arabic to tell us that the boom was up, that we might enter harbour.

This we now did with circumspection, covered by the apparently deserted batteries. Our little craft trotted down the main channel between the long lines of ships like a *vaporetto* on the Grand Canal. I gazed around me. It was all the same, yet at the same time unbelievably different. Yes, the main theatre (of the heart's affections, of memory, of love?) was the same; yet the differences of detail, of décor stuck out obstinately. The liners now grotesquely dazzle-painted in cubist smears of white, khaki and North-Sea greys. Self-conscious guns, nesting awkwardly as cranes in incongruous nests of tarpaulin and webbing. The greasy balloons hanging in the sky as if from gibbets. I compared them to the ancient clouds of silver pigeons which had already begun to climb in wisps and puffs among the palms, diving upwards into the white light to meet the sun. A troubling counterpoint of the known and the unknown. The boats, for example, drawn up along the slip at the Yacht Club, with the remembered dew thick as sweat upon their masts and cordage. Flags and coloured awnings alike hanging stiffly, as if starched. (How many times had we not put out from there, at this same hour, in Clea's small boat, loaded with bread and oranges and wicker-clothed wine?) How many old sailing-days spent upon this crumbling coast, landmarks of affection now forgotten? I was amazed to see with what affectionate emotion one's eye could travel along a line of inanimate objects tied to a mossy wharf, regaling itself with memories which it was not conscious of having stored. Even the French warships (though now disgraced, their breech-blocks confiscated, their crews in nominal internment aboard) were exactly where I had last seen them in that vanished life, lying belly-down upon the dawn murk like malevolent tomb-stones: and still, as always, backed by the paper-thin mirages of the city, whose fig-shaped minarets changed colour with every lift of the sun.

Slowly we passed down the long green aisle among the tall ships, as if taking part in some ceremonial review. The surprises among so much that was familiar, were few but choice: an iron-clad lying dumbly on its side, a corvette whose upper works had been smeared and flattened by a direct hit — gun-barrels split like carrots, mountings twisted upon themselves in a contortion of scorched agony. Such a large package of grey steel to be squashed at a single blow, like a paper bag. Human remains were being hosed along the scuppers by small figures with a tremendous patience and quite impassively. This was surprising as it might be for someone walking in a beautiful cemetery to come upon a newly dug grave. ('It is beautiful' said the child.) And indeed it was so — the great forests of masts and spires which rocked and inclined to the slight swell set up by water-traffic, the klaxons mewing softly, the reflections dissolving and reforming. There was even some dog-eared jazz flowing out upon the water as if from a waste-pipe somewhere. To her it must have seemed appropriate music for a triumphal entry into the city of childhood. '*Jamais de la vie*' I caught myself humming softly in my own mind, amazed how ancient the tune sounded, how dated, how pre-posterously without concern for myself! She was looking into the sky for her father, the image which would form like a benevolent cloud above us and envelop her.

Only at the far end of the great dock were there evidences of the new world to which we were coming: long lines of trucks and ambulances, barriers, and bayonets, manned by the blue and khaki races of men like gnomes. And here a slow, but purposeful and continuous activity reigned. Small troglodytic figures emerged from iron cages and caverns along the wharves, busy upon errands of differing sorts. Here too there were ships split apart in geo-metrical sections which exposed their steaming intestines, ships laid open in Caesarian section: and into these wounds crawled an endless ant-like string of soldiers and blue-jackets humping canisters, bales, sides of oxen on blood-stained shoulders. Oven doors opened to expose to the firelight white-capped men fever-ishly dragging at oven-loads of bread. It was somehow unbelievably slow, all this activity, yet immense in compass. It belonged to the instinct of a race rather than to its appetites. And while silence here was only of comparative value small sounds became concrete and imperative — sentries stamping iron-shod boots upon the cobbles, the yowl of a tug, or the buzz of a liner's siren like the sound of some giant blue-bottle caught in a web. All this was part of the newly acquired city to which I was henceforth to belong.

We drew nearer and nearer, scouting for a berth among the small craft in the basin; the houses began to go up tall. It was a moment of exquisite delicacy, too, and my heart was in my mouth (as the saying goes) for I had already caught sight of the figure which I knew would be there to meet us — away across the wharves there. It was leaning against an ambulance, smoking. Something in its attitude struck a chord and I knew it was Nessim, though I dared not as yet be sure. It was only when the ropes went out and we berthed that I saw, with beating heart (recognizing him dimly through his disguise as I had with Capodistria), that it was indeed my friend. Nessim!

He wore an unfamiliar black patch over one eye. He was dressed in a blue service greatcoat with clumsy padded shoulders and very long in the knee. A peaked cap pulled well down over his eyes. He seemed much taller and slimmer than I remembered — perhaps it was this uniform which was half chauffeur's livery, half airman's rig. I think he must have felt the force of my recognition pressing upon him for he suddenly stood upright, and after peering briefly about him, spotted us. He threw the cigarette away and walked along the quay with his swift and graceful walk, smiling nervously. I waved but he did not respond, though he half nodded as he moved towards us. 'Look' I said, not without apprehension. 'Here he comes at last, your father.' She watched with wide and frozen eyes following the tall figure until it stood smiling at us, not six feet away. Sailors were busy with ropes. A gangplank went down with a bang. I could not decide whether that ominous black patch over his eye added to or subtracted from the old distinction. He took off his cap and still smiling, shyly and somewhat ruefully, stroked his hair into place before putting it on again. 'Nessim' I called, and he nodded, though he did not respond. A silence seemed to fall upon my mind as the child stepped out upon the plank. She walked with an air of bemused rapture, spellbound by the image rather than the reality. (Is poetry, then, more real than observed truth?) And putting out her arms like a sleepwalker she walked chuckling into his embrace. I came hard on her heels, and as he still laughed and hugged her Nessim handed me the hand with the missing finger. It had become a claw, digging into mine. He uttered a short dry sob disguised as a cough. That was all. And now the child crawled up like a sloth into a tree-trunk and wound her legs about his hips. I did not quite know what to say, gazing into that one all-comprehending dark eye. His hair was quite white at the temples. You cannot squeeze a hand with a missing finger as hard as you would like.

'And so we meet again.'

He backed away briskly and sat down upon a bollard, groping for his cigarette case to offer me the unfamiliar delicacy of a French cigarette. We were both dumb. The matches were damp and only struck with difficulty. 'Clea was to have come' he said at last, 'but she turned tail at the last moment. She has gone to Cairo. Justine is out at Karm!' Then ducking his head he said under his breath 'You know about it eh?' I nodded and he looked relieved. 'So much the less to explain. I came off duty half an hour ago and waited for you to take you out. But perhaps. . . .'

But at this moment a flock of soldiers closed on us, verifying our identities and checking on our destinations. Nessim was busy with the child. I unpacked my papers for the soldiers. They studied them gravely, with a certain detached sympathy even, and hunted for my name upon a long sheet of paper before informing me that I should have to report to the Consulate, for I was a 'refugee national'. I returned to Nessim with the clearance slips and told him of this. 'As a matter of fact it does not fall badly. I had to go there anyway to fetch a suitcase I left with all my respectable suits in it . . . how long ago, I wonder?'

'A lifetime' he smiled.

'How shall we arrange it?'

We sat side by side smoking and reflecting. It was strange and moving to hear around us all the accents of the English shires. A kindly corporal came over with a tray full of tin mugs, steaming with that singular brew, Army tea, and decorated with slabs of white bread smeared with margarine. In the middle distance a stretcher-party walked apathetically offstage with a sagging load from a bombed building. We ate hungrily and became suddenly aware of our swimming knees. At last I said: 'Why don't you go on and take her with you? I can get a tram at the dock-gate and visit the Consul. Have a shave. Some lunch. Come out this evening to Karm if you will send a horse to the ford.'

'Very well' he said, with a certain relief, and hugging the child suggested this plan to her, whispering in her ear. She offered no objection, indeed seemed eager to accompany him — for which I felt thankful. And so we walked, with a feeling of unreality, across the slimy cobbles to where the little ambulance was parked, and Nessim climbed into the driver's seat with the child. She smiled and clapped her hands, and I waved them away, delighted that the transition was working so smoothly. Nevertheless it was strange to find myself thus, alone with the city, like a castaway on a familar reef. 'Familiar' — yes! For once one had left the semicircle of the harbour nothing had changed whatsoever. The little tin tram groaned and wriggled along its rusty rails, curving down those familiar streets which spread on either side of me images which were absolute in their fidelity to my memories. The barbers' shops with their fly-nets drawn across the door, tingling with coloured beads: the cafés with their idlers squatting at the tin tables (by El Bab, still the crumbling wall and the very table where we had sat motionless, weighed down by the blue dusk). Just as he let in the clutch Nessim had peered at me sharply and said: 'Darley, you have changed very much', though whether in reproof or commendation I could not tell. Yes, I had: seeing the old crumbled arch of El Bab I smiled, remembering a now prehistoric kiss upon my fingers. I remembered the slight flinch of the dark eyes as she uttered the sad brave truth: 'One learns nothing from those who return our love.' Words which burnt like surgical spirit on an open wound, but which cleansed, as all truth does. And busy with these memories as I was, I saw with another part of my mind the whole of Alexandria unrolling once more on either side of me — its captivating detail, its insolence of colouring, its crushing poverty and beauty. The little shops, protected from the sun by bits of ragged awning in whose darkness was piled up every kind of merchandise from live quail to honeycombs and lucky mirrors. The fruit-stalls with their brilliant stock made doubly brilliant by being displayed upon brighter papers; the warm gold of oranges lying on brilliant slips of magenta and crimson-lake. The smoky glitter of the coppersmiths' caves. Gaily tasselled camel-saddlery. Pottery and blue jade beads against the Evil Eye. All this given a sharp prismatic brilliance by the crowds milling back and forth, the blare of the café radios, the hawkers' long sobbing cries, the imprecations of street-arabs, and the demented ululations of distant mourners setting forth at a jogtrot behind the corpse of some notable sheik. And here, strolling in the foreground of the painting with the insolence of full possession, came plum-blue Ethiopians in snowy turbans, bronze Sudanese with puffy charcoal lips, pewter-skinned Lebanese and

Bedouin with the profiles of kestrels, woven like brilliant threads upon the monotonous blackness of the veiled women, the dark Moslem dream of the hidden Paradise which may only be glimpsed through the key-hole of the human eye. And lurching down these narrow streets with their packs scraping the mud walls plunged the sumpter camels with cargoes of green clover, putting down their huge soft pads with infinite delicacy. I suddenly remembered Scobie giving me a lesson on the priority of salutation: 'You must realize that it's a question of form. They're regular Britishers for politeness, my boy. No good throwing your *Salaam Aleikum* around just anyhow. It must be given first by a camel-rider to a man on a horse, by a horseman to a man on a donkey, by a donkey-rider to a man on foot, by a man on foot to a man seated, by a small party to a large one, by the younger to the older. . . . It's only in the great schools at home they teach such things. But here every nipper has it at his fingers' ends. Now repeat the order of battle after me!' It was easier to repeat the phrase than to re-member the order at this remove in time. Smiling at the thought, I strove to re-establish those forgotten priorities from memory, while I gazed about me. The whole toybox of Egyptian life was still there, every figure in place — street-sprinkler, scribe, mour-ner, harlot, clerk, priest — untouched, it seemed, by time or by war. A sudden melancholy invaded me as I watched them, for they had now become a part of the past. My sympathy had dis-covered a new element inside itself — detachment. (Scobie used to say, in an expansive moment: 'Cheer up, me boyo, it takes a lifetime to grow. People haven't the patience any more. *My* mother waited nine months for me!' A singular thought.)

Jolting past the Goharri Mosque I remembered finding one-eyed Hamid there one afternoon rubbing a slice of lemon on a pilaster before sucking it. This, he had said, was an infallible specific against the stone. He used to live somewhere in this quarter with its humble cafés full of native splendours like rose-scented drinking water and whole sheep turning on spits, stuffed with pigeons, rice, nuts. All the paunch-beguiling meals which delighted the ventripotent pashas of the city!

Somewhere up here, skirting the edge of the Arab quarter the tram gives a leap and grinds round abruptly. You can for one moment look down through the frieze of shattered buildings into the corner of the harbour reserved for craft of shallow draught. The hazards of the war at sea had swollen their numbers to overflowing. Framed by the coloured domes there lay feluccas and lateen-rig giassas, wine-caiques, schooners, and brigantines of every shape and size, from all over the Levant. An anthology of masts and spars and haunting Aegean eyes; of names and rigs and destinations. They lay there coupled to their reflections with the sunlight on them in a deep water-trance. Then abruptly they were snatched away and the Grande Corniche began to unroll, the magnificent long sea-parade which frames the modern city, the Hellenistic capital of the bankers and cotton-visionaries — all those European bagmen whose enterprise had re-ignited and ratified Alexander's dream of conquest after the centuries of dust and silence which Amr had imposed upon it.

Here, too, it was all relatively unchanged save for the full khaki clouds of soldiers moving everywhere and the rash of new bars which had sprung up everywhere to feed them. Outside the Cecil long lines of transport-trucks had overflowed the taxi-ranks. Outside the Consulate an unfamiliar naval sentry with rifle and bayonet. I could not say it was all irremediably changed, for these visitors had a shiftless and temporary look, like countrymen visiting a capital for a fair. Soon a sluice gate would open and they would be drawn off into the great reservoir of the desert battles. But there were surprises. At the Consulate, for example, a very fat man who sat like a king prawn at his desk, pressing white hands together whose long filbert nails had been carefully polished that morning, and who addressed me with familiarity. 'My task may seem invidious' he fluted, 'yet it is necessary. We are trying to grab anyone who has a special aptitude before the Army gets them. I have been sent your name by the Ambassador who had designated you for the censorship department which we have just opened, and which is grotesquely understaffed.'

'The Ambassador?' It was bewildering.

'He's a friend of yours, is he not?'

'I hardly know him.'

'Nevertheless I am bound to accept his direction, even though I am in charge of this operation.'

There were forms to be filled in. The fat man, who was not unamiable, and whose name was Kenilworth, obliged by helping me. 'It is a bit of mystery' I said. He shrugged his shoulders and spread his white hands. 'I suggest you discuss it with him when you meet.'

'But I had no intention . . .' I said. But it seemed pointless to discuss the matter further until I discovered what lay behind it. How could Mountolive. . . ? But Kenilworth was talking again. 'I suppose you might need a week to find yourself lodgings here before you settle in. Shall I tell the department so?'

'If you wish' I said in bewilderment. I was dismissed and spent some time in the cellars unearthing my battered cabin-trunk and selecting from it a few respectable city-clothes. With these in a brown paper parcel I walked slowly along the Corniche towards the Cecil, where I purposed to take a room, have a bath and shave, and prepare myself for the visit to the country house. This had begun to loom up rather in my mind, not exactly with anxiety but with the disquiet which suspense always brings. I stood for a while staring down at the still sea, and it was while I was standing thus that the silver Rolls with the daffodil hub-cups drew up and a large bearded personage jumped out and came galloping towards me with hands out-stretched. It was only when I felt his arms hugging my shoulders and the beard brushing my cheek in a Gallic greeting that I was able to gasp 'Pombal!'

'Darley'. Still holding my hands as tenderly, and with tears in his eyes, he drew me to one side and sat down heavily on one of the stone benches bordering the marine parade. Pombal was in the most elegant *tenue*. His starched cuffs rattled crisply. The dark beard and moustache gave him an imposing yet somehow forlorn air. Inside all these trappings he seemed quite unchanged. He peered through them, like a Tiberius in fancy-dress. We gazed at each other for a long moment of silence, with emotion. Both knew that the silence we observed was one of pain for the fall of France, an event which symbolized all too clearly the psychic collapse of Europe itself. We were like mourners at an invisible cenotaph during the two minutes' silence which commemorates an irremediable failure of the human will. I felt in his handclasp all the shame and despair of this graceless tragedy and I sought desperately for the phrase which might console him, might reassure him that France itself could never truly die so long as artists were being born into the world. But this world of armies and battles was too intense and too concrete to make the thought seem more than of secondary importance — for art really means freedom, and it was this which was at stake. At last the words came. 'Never mind. Today I've seen the little blue cross of Lorraine flowering everywhere.'

'You understand' he murmured and squeezed my hand again.

'I knew you would understand. Even when you most criticized her you knew that she meant as much to you as to us.' He blew his nose suddenly, with startling loudness, in a clean handkerchief and leaned back on the stone bench. With amazing suddenness he had become his old self again, the timid, fat, irrepressible Pombal of the past. 'There is so much to tell you. You will come with me now. At once. Not a word. Yes, it is Nessim's car. I bought it to save it from the Egyptians. Mountolive has fixed you an excellent post. I am still in the old flat, but now we have taken the building. You can have the whole top floor. It will be like old times again.' I was carried off my feet by his volubility and by the bewildering variety of prospects he described so rapidly and confidently, without apparently expecting comment. His English had become practically perfect.

'Old times' I stammered.

But here an expression of pain crossed his fat countenance and he groaned, pressing his hands between his knees as he uttered the word: 'Fosca!' He screwed up his face comically and stared at me. 'You do not know.' He looked almost terrified. 'I am in love with her.'

I laughed. He shook his head rapidly. 'No. Don't laugh.'

'I must, Pombal.'

'I beseech you.' And leaning forward with a look of despair on his countenance he lowered his voice and prepared to confide something to me. His lips moved. It was clearly something of tragic importance. At last he brought it out, and the tears came into his eyes as he spoke the words: 'You don't understand. *Je suis fidèle malgré moi.*' He gasped like a fish and repeated '*Malgré moi*. It has never happened before, *never*.' And then abruptly he broke into a despairing whinny with the same look of awed bewilderment on his face. How could I forbear to laugh? At a blow he had restored Alexandria to me, complete and intact — for no memory of it could be complete without the thought of Pombal in love. My laughter infected him. He was shaking like a jelly. 'Stop' he pleaded at last with comic pathos, interjecting into the forest of bearded chuckles the words. 'And I have never slept with her, not once. That is the insane thing.' This made us laugh more than ever.

But the chauffeur softly sounded the horn, recalling him to himself abruptly, reminding him that he had duties to perform. 'Come' he cried. 'I have to take a letter to Pordre before nine.

Then I'll have you dropped at the flat. We can lunch together. Hamid is with me, by the way; he'll be delighted. Hurry up.' Once more my doubts were not given time to formulate themselves. Clutching my parcel I accompanied him to the familiar car, noticing with a pang that its upholstery now smelt of expensive cigars and metal-polish. My friend talked rapidly all the way to the French Consulate, and I was surprised to find that his whole attitude to the Chief had changed. All the old bitterness and resentment had vanished. They had both, it seemed, abandoned their posts in different capitals (Pombal in Rome) in order to join the Free French in Egypt. He spoke of Pordre now with tender affection. 'He is like a father to me. He has been marvellous' said my friend rolling his expressive dark eye. This somewhat puzzled me until I saw them both together and understood in a flash that the fall of their country had created this new bond. Pordre had become quite white-haired; his frail and absent-minded gentleness had given place to the calm resolution of someone grappling with responsibilities which left no room for affectation. The two men treated each other with a courtesy and affection which in truth made them seem like father and son rather than colleagues. The hand that Pordre placed so lovingly on Pombal's shoulder, the face he turned to him, expressed a wistful and lonely pride.

But the situation of their new Chancery was a somewhat unhappy one. The broad windows looked out over the harbour, over the French Fleet which lay there at anchor like a symbol of all that was malefic in the stars which governed the destiny of France. I could see that the very sight of it lying there was a perpetual reproach to them. And there was no escaping it. At every turn taken between the high old-fashioned desks and the white wall their eyes fell upon this repellent array of ships. It was like a splinter lodged in the optic nerve. Pordre's eye kindled with self-reproach and the zealot's hot desire to reform these cowardly followers of the personage whom Pombal (in his less diplomatic moments) was henceforward to refer to as '*ce vieux Putain*'. It was a relief to vent feelings so intense by the simple substitution of a letter. The three of us stood there, looking down into the harbour at this provoking sight, and suddenly the old man burst out: 'Why don't you British intern them? Send them to India with the Italians. I shall never understand it. Forgive me. But do you realize that they are allowed to keep their small arms, mount sentries, take shore leave, just as if they were a neutral

fleet? The admirals wine and dine in the town, all intriguing for
Vichy. There are endless *bagarres* in the cafés between our boys
and their sailors.' I could see that it was a subject which was
capable of making them quite beside themselves with fury. I tried
to change it, since there was little consolation I could offer.

I turned instead to Pombal's desk on which stood a large
framed photograph of a French soldier. I asked who it was and
both men replied simultaneously: 'He saved us.' Later of course
I would come to recognize this proud, sad Labrador's head as
that of de Gaulle himself.

Pombal's car dropped me at the flat. Forgotten whispers stirred
in me as I rang the bell. One-eyed Hamid opened to me, and after
a moment of surprise he performed a curious little jump in the
air. The original impulse of this jump must have been an embrace
which he repressed just in time. But he put two fingers on my
wrist and jumped like a solitary penguin on an ice-floe before
retreating to give himself room for the more elaborate and formal
greeting. 'Ya Hamid' I cried, as delighted as he was. We crossed
ourselves ceremonially at each other.

The whole place had been transformed once more, repainted
and papered and furnished in massive official fashion. Hamid
led me gloatingly from room to room while I mentally tried to
reconstruct its original appearance from memories which had by
now become faded and transposed. It was hard to see Melissa
shrieking, for example. On the exact spot now stood a handsome
sideboard crowded with bottles. (Pursewarden had once gesti-
culated from the far corner.) Bits of old furniture came back to
mind. 'Those old things must be knocking about somewhere'
I thought in quotation from the poet of the city.* The only
recognizable item was Pombal's old gout-chair which had mysteriously reappeared in its old place under the window. Had he
perhaps flown back with it from Rome? That would be like him.
The little box-room where Melissa and I. . . . It was now Hamid's
own room. He slept on the same uncomfortable bed which I looked
at with a kind of shrinking feeling, trying to recapture the flavour
and ambience of those long enchanted afternoons when. . . . But
the little man was talking. He must prepare lunch. And then he
rummaged in a corner and thrust into my hand a crumpled snapshot which he must at some time have stolen from Melissa. It
was a street-photograph and very faded. Melissa and I walked arm
in arm talking down Rue Fuad. Her face was half turned away

from me, smiling — dividing her attention between what I was saying so earnestly and the lighted shop-windows we passed. It must have been taken, this snapshot, on a winter afternoon around the hour of four. What on earth could I have been telling her with such earnestness? For the life of me I could not recall the time and place; yet there it was, in black and white, as they say. Perhaps the words I was uttering were momentous, significant — or perhaps they were meaningless! I had a pile of books under my arm and was wearing the dirty old mackintosh which I finally gave to Zoltan. It was in need of a dry-clean. My hair, too, seemed to need cutting at the back. Impossible to restore this vanished afternoon to mind! I gazed carefully at the circumstantial detail of the picture like someone bent upon restoring an irremediably faded fresco. Yes, it was winter, at four o'clock. She was wearing her tatty sealskin and carried a handbag which I had not ever seen in her possession. 'Sometime in August — *was* it August?' I mentally quoted to myself again.*

Turning back to the wretched rack-like bed again I whispered her name softly. With surprise and chagrin I discovered that she had *utterly vanished*. The waters had simply closed over her head. It was as if she had never existed, never inspired in me the pain and pity which (I had always told myself) would live on, transmitted into other forms perhaps — but live triumphantly on forever. I had worn her out *like an old pair of socks*, and the utterness of this disappearance surprised and shocked me. Could 'love' simply wear out like this? 'Melissa' I said again, hearing the lovely word echo in the silence. Name of a sad herb, name of a pilgrim to Eleusis. Was she less now than a scent or a flavour? Was she simply a nexus of literary cross-references scribbled in the margins of a minor poem? And had my love dissolved her in this strange fashion, or was it simply the literature I had tried to make out of her? Words, the acid-bath of words! I felt guilty. I even tried (with that lying self-deception so natural to sentimentalists) to *force* her to appear by an act of will, to re-evoke a single one of those afternoon kisses which had once been for me the sum of the city's many meanings. I even tried deliberately to squeeze the tears into my eyes, to hypnotize memory by repeating her name like a charm. The experiment yielded nothing. Her name had been utterly worn out of use! It was truly shameful not to be able to evoke the faintest tribute to so all-engulfing an unhappiness. Then like the chime of a distant bell I heard the tart voice of the dead Pursewarden saying 'But our unhappiness was sent to regale us. We were intended to revel in it, enjoy it to the full.' Melissa had been simply one of the many costumes of love!

I was bathed and changed by the time Pombal hurried in to an early lunch, full of the incoherent rapture of his new and remarkable state of mind. Fosca, the cause of it, was, he told me, a refugee married to a British officer. 'How could it have come about, this sudden passionate understanding?' He did not know. He got up to look at his own face in the hanging mirror. 'I who believed so many things about love' he went on moodily, half addressing his own reflection and combing his beard with his fingers, 'but never something like this. Even a year ago had you said what I am just saying I would have answered: "*Pouagh!* It is simply a Petrarchian obscenity. Medieval rubbish!" I even used to think that continence was medically unhealthy, that the damned thing would atrophy or fall off if it were not frequently used. Now look at your unhappy — no *happy* friend! I feel bound and gagged by Fosca's very existence. Listen, the last time Keats came in from the desert we went out and got drunk. He took me to Golfo's tavern. I had a sneaking desire — sort of experimental — to *ramoner une poule*. Don't laugh. Just to see what had gone wrong with my feelings. I drank five Armagnacs to liven them up. I began to feel quite like it theoretically. Good, I said to myself, I will crack this virginity. I will *dépuceler* this romantic image once and for all lest people begin to talk and say that the great Pombal is unmanned. But what happened? I became panic-stricken! My feelings were quite *blindés* like a bloody tank. The sight of all those girls made me memorize Fosca in detail. Everything, even her hands in her lap with her knitting! I was cooled as if by an ice cream down my collar. I emptied my pockets on the table and fled in a hail of slippers and a torrent of cat-calls from my old friends. I was swearing, of course. Not that Fosca expects it, no. She tells me to go ahead and have a girl if I must. Perhaps this very freedom keeps me in prison? Who knows? It is a complete mystery to me. It is strange that this girl should drag me by the hair down the paths of honour like this — an unfamiliar place.'

Here he struck himself softly on the chest with a gesture of reproof mixed with a certain doubtful self-commendation. He came and sat down once more saying moodily: 'You see, she is pregnant by her husband and her sense of honour would not permit her to trick a man on active service, who may be killed at any time. Specially when she is bearing his child. *Ça se conçoit.*'

We ate in silence for a few moments, and then he burst out: 'But what have I to do with such ideas? Tell me please. We only talk, yet it is enough.' He spoke with a touch of self-contempt.

'And he?'

Pombal sighed: 'He is an extremely good and *kind* man, with that national kindliness which Pursewarden used to say was a kind of compulsion neurosis brought on by the almost suicidal boredom of English life! He is handsome, gay, speaks three languages. And yet . . . it is not that he is *froid*, exactly, but he is *tiède* — I mean somewhere in his inner nature. I am not sure if he is typical or not. At any rate he seems to embody notions of honour which would do credit to a troubadour. It isn't that we Europeans lack honour, of course, but we don't stress things unnaturally. I mean self-discipline should be more than a concession to a behaviour-pattern. I sound confused. Yes, I am a little confused in thinking of their relationship. I mean something like this: in the depths of his national conceit he really believes foreigners incapable of fidelity in love. Yet in being so truthful and so faithful she is only doing what comes naturally to her, without a false straining after a form. *She acts as she feels.* I think if he really loved her in the sense I mean he would not appear always to have merely condescended to rescue her from an intolerable situation. I think somewhere inside herself, though she is not aware of it, the sense of injustice rankles a little bit; she is faithful to him . . . how to say? Slightly contemptuously? I don't know. But she does love him in this peculiar fashion, the only one he permits. She is a girl of delicate feelings. But what is strange is that our own love — which neither doubts, and which we have confessed and accepted — has been coloured in a curious way by these circumstances. If it has made me happy it has also made me a little uncertain of myself; at times I get rebellious. I feel that our love is beginning to wear a penitential air — this glorious adventure. It gets coloured by his own grim attitude which is like one of atonement. I wonder if love for a *femme galante* should be quite like this. As for him he also is a *chevalier* of the middle class, as incapable of inflicting pain as of giving physical pleasure I should say. Yet withal gentle and quite overwhelming in his kindness and uprightness. But *merde*, one cannot love judicially, out of a sense of justice, can one? Somewhere along the line he fails her without being conscious of the fact. Nor do I think she *knows* this, at any rate in her conscious mind. But when they are together you feel in the presence of something incomplete, something which is not cemented but just soldered together by good manners and convention. I am aware that I sound unkind, but I am only trying to describe exactly what I see. For the rest we are good friends and indeed I really admire him; when he comes on leave we all go out to dinner and talk politics! Ouf!'

He lay back in his chair, exhausted by this exposition, and yawned heavily before consulting his watch. 'I suppose' he went on with resignation 'that you will find it all very strange, these new aspects of people; but then everything sounds strange here, eh? Pursewarden's sister, Liza, for example — you don't know her? She is stone blind. It seems to us all that Mountolive is madly in love with her. She came out originally to collect his papers and also to find materials for a book about him. Allegedly. Anyway she has stayed on at the Embassy ever since. When he is in Cairo on duty he visits her every weekend! He looks somehow unhappy now — perhaps I do too?' He once more consulted the mirror and shook his head decisively. Apparently he did not. 'Well anyway' he conceded 'I am probably wrong.'

The clock on the mantelpiece struck and he started up. 'I must get back to the office for a conference' he said. 'What about you?' I told him of my projected trip to Karm Abu Girg. He whistled and looked at me keenly. 'You will see Justine again, eh?' He thought for a moment and then shrugged his shoulders doubtfully. 'A recluse now, isn't she? Put under house arrest by Memlik. Nobody has seen her for ages. I don't know what's going on with Nessim either. They've quite broken with Mountolive and as an official I have to take his line, so we would never even try to meet: even if it were allowed, I mean. Clea sees him sometimes. I'm sorry for Nessim. When he was in hospital she could not get permission to visit him. It is all a merry-go-round, isn't it? Like a Paul Jones. New partners until the music stops! But you'll come back, won't you, and share this place? Good. Then I'll tell Hamid. I must be off. Good luck.'

I had only intended to lie down for a brief siesta before the car came, but such was my fatigue that I plunged into a heavy sleep the moment my head touched the pillow; perhaps I should have slept the clock round had not the chauffeur awakened me. Half-dazed as yet I sat in the familiar car and watched the unreal lakelands grow up around with their palms and water-wheels — the Egypt which lives outside the cities, ancient, pastoral and veiled by mists and mirages. Old memories stirred now, some bland and pleasing, others rough as old cicatrices. Scar-tissue of old emotions which I should soon be shedding. The first momentous step would be to encounter Justine again. Would she help or hinder me in the task of controlling and evaluating these precious 'reliques of sensation' as Coleridge calls them? It was hard to know. With every succeeding mile I felt anxiety and expectation running neck and neck. The Past!

★　　★　　★　　★　　★

ncient lands, in all their prehistoric intactness: lake-solitudes hardly brushed by the hurrying feet of the centuries where the uninterrupted pedigrees of pelican and ibis and heron evolve their slow destinies in complete seclusion. Clover-patches of green baize swarming with snakes and clouds of mosquitoes. A landscape devoid of songbirds yet full of owls, hoopoes and kingfishers hunting by day, pluming themselves on the banks of the tawny waterways. The packs of half-wild dogs foraging, the blindfolded water-buffaloes circling the water-wheels in an eternity of darkness. The little wayside chancels built of dry mud and floored with fresh straw where the pious traveller might say a prayer as he journeyed. Egypt! The goose-winged sails scurrying among the freshets with perhaps a human voice singing a trailing snatch of song. The click-click of the wind in the Indian corn, plucking at the coarse leaves, shumbling them. Liquid mud exploded by rainstorms in the dust-laden air throwing up mirages everywhere, despoiling perspectives. A lump of mud swells to the size of a man, a man to the size of a church. Whole segments of the sky and land displace, open like a lid, or heel over on their side to turn upside down. Flocks of sheep walk in and out of these twisted mirrors, appearing and disappearing, goaded by the quivering nasal cries of invisible shepherds. A great confluence of pastoral images from the forgotten history of the old world which still lives on side by side with the one we have inherited. The clouds of silver winged ants floating up to meet and incandesce in the sunlight. The clap of a horse's hoofs on the mud floors of this lost world echo like a pulse and the brain swims among these veils and melting rainbows.

And so at last, following the curves of the green embankments you come upon an old house built sideways upon an intersection of violet canals, its cracked and faded shutters tightly fastened, its rooms hung with dervish trophies, hide shields, bloodstained spears and magnificent carpets. The gardens desolate and untended. Only the little figures on the wall move their celluloid wings — scarecrows which guard against the Evil Eye. The silence of complete desuetude. But then the whole countryside of Egypt shares this melancholy feeling of having been abandoned, allowed to run to seed, to bake and crack and moulder under the brazen sun.

Turn under an arch and clatter over the cobbles of a dark courtyard. Will this be a new point of departure or a return to the starting-point?

It is hard to know.

*　　*　　*　　*　　*

III

She stood at the very top of the long outer staircase looking down into the dark courtyard like a sentinel and holding in her right hand a branch of candles which threw a frail circle of light around her. Very still, as if taking part in a *tableau vivant*. It seemed to me that the tone in which she first uttered my name had been deliberately made flat and unemphatic, copied perhaps from some queer state of mind which she had imposed upon herself. Or perhaps, uncertain that it was I, she was merely interrogating the darkness, trying to unearth me from it like some obstinate and troublesome memory which had slipped out of place. But the familiar voice was to me like the breaking of a seal. I felt like someone at last awakened from a sleep which had lasted centuries and as I walked slowly and circumspectly up the creaking wooden stairway I felt, hovering over me, the breath of a new self-possession. I was halfway up when she spoke again, sharply this time, with something almost comminatory in her tone. 'I heard the horses and went all-overish suddenly. I've spilt scent all over my dress. I stink, Darley. You will have to forgive me.'

She seemed to have become very much thinner. Holding the candle high she advanced a step to the stairhead, and after gazing anxiously into my eyes placed a small cold kiss upon my right cheek. It was as cold as an obituary, dry as leather. As she did so I smelt the spilt perfume. She did indeed give off overpowering waves of it. Something in the enforced stillness of her attitude suggested an inner unsteadiness and the idea crossed my mind that perhaps she had been drinking. I was a trifle shocked too to see that she had placed a bright patch of rouge on each cheek-bone which showed up sharply against a dead white, overpowdered face. If she was beautiful still it was the passive beauty of some Propertian mummy which had been clumsily painted to give the illusion of life, or a photograph carelessly colour-tinted. 'You must not look at my eye' she next said, sharply, imperatively: and I saw that her left eyelid drooped slightly, threatening to transform her expression into something like a leer — and most particularly the welcoming smile which she was trying to adopt at this moment. 'Do you understand?' I nodded. Was the rouge, I wondered, designed to distract attention from the drooping eyelid? 'I had a small stroke' she added under her breath, as if explaining to herself. And as she still stood before me with the raised branch of candles she seemed to be listening to some other sound. I took her hand and we stood together for a long moment thus, staring at one another.

'Have I changed very much?'

'Not at all.'

'Of course I have. We all have.' She spoke now with a contemptuous shrillness. She raised my hand briefly and put it to her cheek. Then nodding with a puzzled air she turned and drew me towards the balcony, walking with a stiff proud step. She was clad in a dress of dark taffeta which whispered loudly at every movement. The candlelight jumped and danced upon the walls. We stopped before a dark doorway and she called out 'Nessim' in a sharp tone which shocked me, for it was the tone in which one would call a servant. After a moment Nessim appeared from the shadowy bedroom, obedient as a djinn.

'Darley's here' she said, with the air of someone handing over a parcel, and placing the candles on a low table reclined swiftly in a long wicker chair and placed her hand over her eyes.

Nessim had changed into a suit of a more familiar cut, and he came nodding and smiling towards me with the accustomed expression of affection and solicitude. Yet it was somehow different again; he wore a faintly cowed air, shooting little glances sideways and downwards towards the figure of Justine, and speaking softly as one might in the presence of someone asleep. A constraint had suddenly fallen upon us as we seated ourselves on that shadowy balcony and lit cigarettes. The silence locked like a gear which would not engage.

'The child is in bed, delighted with the palace as she calls it, and the promise of a pony of her own. I think she will be happy.'

Justine suddenly sighed deeply and without uncovering her eyes said slowly: 'He says we have not changed.'

Nessim swallowed and continued as if he had not heard the interruption in the same low voice: 'She wanted to stay awake till you came but she was too tired.'

Once again the reclining figure in the shadowy corner interrupted to say: 'She found Narouz' little circumcision cap in the cupboard. I found her trying it on.' She gave a short sharp laugh like a bark, and I saw Nessim wince suddenly and turn away his face.

'We are short of servants' he said in a low voice, hastily as if to cement up the holes made in the silence by her last remark.

His air of relief was quite patent when Ali appeared and bade us to dinner. He picked up the candles and led us into the house. It had a somewhat funereal flavour — the white-robed servant with his scarlet belt leading, holding aloft the candles in order to light Justine's way. She walked with an air of preoccupation, of remoteness. I followed next with Nessim close behind me. So we went in Indian file down the unlighted corridors, across high-ceilinged rooms with their walls covered in dusty carpets, their floors of rude planks creaking under our feet. And so we came at last to a supper-room, long and narrow, and suggesting a forgotten sophistication which was Ottoman perhaps; say, a room in a forgotten winter palace of Abdul Hamid, its highly carved window-screens of filigree looking out upon a neglected rose-garden. Here the candlelight with its luminous shadows was ideal as an adjunct to furnishings which were, in themselves, strident. The golds and the reds and the violets would in full light have seemed unbearable. By candle-light they had a subdued magnificence.

We seated ourselves at the supper-table and once more I became conscious of the almost cowed expression of Nessim as he gazed around him. It is perhaps not the word. It was as if he expected some sudden explosion, expected some unforeseen reproach to break from her lips. He was mentally prepared to parry it, to fend it off with a tender politeness. But Justine ignored us. Her first act was to pour out a glass of red wine. This she raised to the light as if to verify its colour. Then she dipped it ironically to each of us in turn like a flag and drank it off all in one motion before replacing the glass on the table. The touches of rouge gave her an enflamed look which hardly matched the half-drowsy stupefaction of her glance. She was wearing no jewellery. Her nails were painted with gold polish. Putting her elbows on the table she propped her chin for a long moment as she studied us keenly, first one and then the other. Then she sighed, as if replete, and said: 'Yes, we have all changed', and turning swiftly like an accuser she stabbed her finger at her husband and said: '*He* has lost an eye.'

Nessim pointedly ignored this, passing some item of table fare towards her as if to distract her from so distressing a topic. She sighed again and said: 'Darley, you look much better, but your hands are cracked and calloused. I felt it on my cheek.'

'Wood-cutting, I expect.'

'Ah. So! But you look well, very well.'

(A week later she would telephone Clea and say: 'Dear God, how coarse he has become. What little trace of sensibility he had has been swamped by the peasant.')

In the silence Nessim coughed nervously and fingered the black patch over his eye. Clearly he misliked the tone of her voice, distrusted the weight of the atmosphere under which one could feel, building up slowly like a wave, the pressure of a hate which was the newest element among so many novelties of speech and manner. Had she really turned into a shrew? Was she ill? It was difficult to disinter the memory of that magical dark mistress of the past whose every gesture, however ill-advised and ill-considered, rang with the newly minted splendour of complete generosity. ('So you come back' she was saying harshly 'and find us all locked up in Karm. Like old figures in a forgotten account book. Bad debts, Darley. Fugitives from justice, eh Nessim?')

There was nothing to be said in answer to such bitter sallies. We ate in silence under the quiet ministration of the Arab servant. Nessim addressed an occasional hurried remark to me on some neutral topic, brief, monosyllabic. Unhappily we felt the silence draining out around us, emptying like some great reservoir. Soon we should be left there, planted in our chairs like effigies. Presently the servant came in with two charged thermos flasks and a package of food which he placed at the end of the table. Justine's voice kindled with a kind of insolence as she said: 'So you are going back tonight?'

Nessim nodded shyly and said: 'Yes, I'm on duty again.' Clearing his throat he added to me: 'It is only four times a week. It gives me something to do.'

'Something to do' she cried clearly, derisively. 'To lose his eye and his finger gives him something to do. Tell the truth, my dear, you would do anything to get away from this house.' Then leaning forward towards me she said: 'To get away from me, Darley. I drive him nearly mad with my scenes. That is what he says.' It was horribly embarrassing in its vulgarity.

The servant came in with his duty clothes carefully pressed and ironed, and Nessim rose, excusing himself with a word and a wry smile. We were left alone. Justine poured out a glass of wine. Then, in the act of raising it to her lips she surprised me with a wink and the words: 'Truth will out.'

'How long have you been locked up here?' I asked.

'Don't speak of it.'

'But is there no way. . . .?'

'He has managed to partly escape. Not me. Drink, Darley, drink your wine.'

I drank in silence, and in a few minutes Nessim appeared once more, in uniform and evidently ready for his night journey. As if by common consent we all rose, the servant took up the candles and once more conducted us back to the balcony in lugubrious procession. During our absence one corner had been spread with carpets and divans while extra candlesticks and smoking materials stood upon inlaid side-tables. The night was still, and almost tepid. The candle-flames hardly moved. Sounds of the great lake came ebbing in upon us from the outer darkness. Nessim said a hurried good-bye and we heard the diminishing clip of his horse's hoofs gradually fade as he took the road to the ford. I turned my head to look at Justine. She was holding up her wrists at me, her face carved into a grimace. She held them joined together as if by invisible manacles. She exhibited these imaginary handcuffs for a long moment before dropping her hands back into her lap, and then, abruptly, swift as a snake, she crossed to the divan where I lay and sat down at my feet, uttering as she did so, in a voice vibrating with remorseful resentment, the words: 'Why, Darley? Oh *why?*' It was as if she were interrogating not merely destiny or fate but the very workings of the universe itself in these thrilling poignant tones. Some of the old beauty almost flashed out in this ardour to trouble me like an echo. But the perfume! At such close quarters the spilled perfume was overpowering, almost nauseating.

Yet suddenly now all our constraint vanished and we were at last able to talk. It was as if this outburst had exploded the bubble of listlessness in which we had been enveloped all evening. 'You see a different me' she cried in a voice almost of triumph. 'But once again the difference lies in you, in what you imagine you see!' Her words rattled down like a hail of sods on an empty coffin. 'How is it that you can feel no resentment against me? To forgive such treachery so easily — why, it is unmanly. Not to hate such a vampire? It is unnatural. Nor could you ever understand my sense of humiliation at not being able to regale, yes *regale* you, my dear, with the treasures of my inner nature as a mistress. And yet, in truth, I enjoyed deceiving you, I must not deny it. But also there was regret in only offering you the pitiful simulacrum of a love (Ha! that word again!) which was sapped by deceit. I suppose this betrays the bottomless female vanity again: to desire the worst of two worlds, of both words — love and deceit. Yet it is strange that now, when you know the truth, and I am free to offer you affection, I feel only increased self-contempt. Am I enough of a woman to feel that the real sin against the Holy Ghost is dishonesty in love? But what pretentious rubbish — for love admits of no honesty by its very nature.'

So she went on, hardly heeding me, arguing my life away, moving obsessively up and down the cobweb of her own devising, creating images and beheading them instantly before my eyes. What could she hope to prove? Then she placed her head briefly against my knee and said: 'Now that I am free to hate or love it is comical to feel only fury at this new self-possession of yours! You have escaped me somewhere. But what else was I to expect?'

In a curious sort of way this was true. To my surprise I now felt the power to wound her for the first time, even to subjugate her purely by my indifference! 'Yet the truth' I said 'is that I feel no resentment for the past. On the contrary I am full of gratitude because an experience which was perhaps banal in itself (even disgusting for you) was for me immeasurably enriching!' She turned away saying harshly: 'Then we should both be laughing now.'

Together we sat staring out into the darkness for a long while. Then she shivered, lighted a cigarette and resumed the thread of her interior monologue. 'The post-mortems of the undone! What could you have seen in it all, I wonder? We are after all totally ignorant of one another, presenting selected fictions to each other! I suppose we all observe each other with the same immense ignorance. I used, in my moments of guilt long afterwards, to try and imagine that we might one day become lovers again, on a new basis. What a farce! I pictured myself making it up to you, expiating my deceit, repaying my debt. But . . . I knew that you would always prefer your own mythical picture, framed by the five senses, to anything more truthful. But now, then, tell me — which of us was the greater liar? I cheated you, you cheated yourself.'

These observations, which at another time, in another context, might have had the power to reduce me to ashes, were now vitally important to me in a new way. 'However hard the road, one is forced to come to terms with truth at last' wrote Pursewarden somewhere. Yes, but unexpectedly I was discovering that truth was nourishing — the cold spray of a wave which carried one always a little further towards self-realization. I saw now that my own Justine had indeed been an illusionist's creation, raised upon the faulty armature of misinterpreted words, actions, gestures. Truly there was no blame here; the real culprit was my love which had invented an image on which to feed. Nor was there any question of dishonesty, for the picture was coloured after the necessities of the love which invented it. Lovers, like doctors, colouring an unpalatable medicine to make it easier for the unwary to swallow! No, this could not have been otherwise, I fully realized.

Something more, fully as engrossing: I also saw that lover and loved, observer and observed, throw down a field about each other ('Perception is shaped like an embrace — the poison enters with the embrace' as Pursewarden writes). They then infer the properties of their love, judging it from this narrow field with its huge margins of unknown ('the refraction'), and proceed to refer it to a generalized conception of something constant in its qualities and universal in its operation. How valuable a lesson this was, both to art and to life! I had only been attesting, in all I had written, to the power of an image which I had created involuntarily by the *mere act of seeing* Justine. There was no question of true or false. Nymph? Goddess? Vampire? Yes, she was all of these and none of them. She was, like every woman, everything that the mind of a man (let us define 'man' as a poet perpetually conspiring against himself) — that the mind of man wished to imagine. She was there forever, and she had never existed! Under all these masks there was only another woman, every woman, like a lay figure in a dressmaker's shop, waiting for the poet to clothe her, breathe life into her. In understanding all this for the first time I began to realize with awe the enormous reflexive power of woman — the fecund passivity with which, like the moon, she borrows her second-hand light from the male sun. How could I help but be grateful for such vital information? What did they matter, the lies, deceptions, follies, in comparison to this truth?

Yet while this new knowledge compelled my admiration for her more than ever — as symbol of woman, so to speak — I was puzzled to explain the new element which had crept in here: a flavour of disgust for her personality and its attributes. The scent! Its cloying richness half sickened me. The touch of the dark head against my knee stirred dim feelings of revulsion in me.

I was almost tempted to embrace her once more in order to explore this engrossing and inexplicable novelty of feeling further! Could it be that a few items of information merely, *facts* like sand trickling into the hour-glass of the mind, had irrevocably altered the image's qualities — turning it from something once desirable to something which now stirred disgust? Yes, the same process, the very same love-process, I told myself. This was the grim metamorphosis brought about by the acid-bath of truth — as Pursewarden might say.

Still we sat together on that shadowy balcony, prisoners of memory, still we talked on: and still it remained unchanged, this new disposition of selves, the opposition of new facts of mind.

At last she took a lantern and a velvet cloak and we walked about for a while in that tideless night, coming at last to a great *nubk* tree whose branches were loaded with votive offerings. Here Nessim's brother had been found dead. She held the lantern high to light the tree, reminding me that the 'nubk' forms the great circular palisade of trees which encircles the Moslem Paradise. 'As for Narouz, his death hangs heavy on Nessim because people say that he ordered it himself — the Copts say so. It has become like a family curse to him. His mother is ill, but she will never return to this house, she says. Nor does he wish her to. He gets quite cold with rage when I speak of her. He says he wishes she would die! So here we are cooped up together. I sit all night reading — guess what? — a big bundle of love-letters to her which she left behind! Mountolive's love-letters! More confusion, more unexplored corners!' She raised the lantern and looked closely into my eyes: 'Ah, but this unhappiness is not just ennui, spleen. There is also a desire to swallow the world. I have been experimenting with drugs of late, the sleep-givers!'

And so back in silence to the great rustling house with its dusty smells.

'He says we will escape one day and go to Switzerland where at least he still has money. But when, but when? And now this war! Pursewarden said that my sense of guilt was atrophied. It is simply that I have no power to decide things now, any more. I feel as if my will had snapped. But it will pass.' Then suddenly, greedily she grasped my hand and said: 'But thank God, you are here. Just to talk is a *soulagement*. We spend whole weeks together without exchanging a word.'

We were seated once more on the clumsy divans by the light of candles. She lit a silver-tipped cigarette and smoked with short decisive inspirations as the monologue went on, unrolling on the night, winding away in the darkness like a river.

'When everything collapsed in Palestine, all our dumps discovered and captured, the Jews at once turned on Nessim accusing him of treachery, because he was friendly with Mountolive. We were between Memlik and the hostile Jews, in disgrace with both. The Jews expelled me. This was when I saw Clea again; I so badly needed news and yet I couldn't confide in her. Then Nessim came over the border to get me. He found me like a mad woman. I was in despair! And he thought it was because of the failure of our plans. It was, of course, it was; but there was another and deeper reason. While we were conspirators, joined by our work and its dangers, I could feel truly passionate about him. But to be under house-arrest, compelled to idle away my time alone with him, in his company. . . . I knew I should die of boredom. My tears, my lamentations were those of a woman forced against her will to take the veil. Ah but you will not understand, being a northerner. How could you? To be able to love a man fully, but only in a single posture, so to speak. You see, when he does not act, Nessim is nothing; he is completely flavourless, not in touch with himself at any point. Then he has no real self to interest a woman, to grip her. In a word he is really a pure idealist. When a sense of destiny consumes him he becomes truly splendid. It was as an actor that he magnetized me, illuminated me for myself. But as a fellow prisoner, in defeat — he predisposes to ennui, migraine, thoughts of utter banality like suicide! That is why from time to time I drive my claws into his flesh. In despair!'

'And Pursewarden?'

'Ah! Pursewarden. That is something different again. I cannot think of him without smiling. There my failure was of a totally different order. My feeling for him was — how shall I say? — almost incestuous, if you like; like one's love for a beloved, an incorrigible elder brother. I tried so hard to penetrate into his confidences. He was too clever, or perhaps too egotistical. He defended himself against loving me by *making me laugh!* Yet I achieved with him, even so very briefly, a tantalizing inkling that there might be other ways of living open to me if only I could find them. But he was a tricky one. He used to say "An artist saddled with a woman is like a spaniel with a tick in its ear; it itches, it draws blood, one cannot reach it. Will some kindly grown-up please. . . . ?" Perhaps he was utterly lovable because quite out of reach? It is hard to say these things. One word "love" has to do service for so many different kinds of the same animal. It was he, too, who reconciled me to that whole business of the rape, remember? All that nonsense of Arnauti's in *Moeurs*, all those psychologists! His single observation stuck like a thorn. He said: "Clearly you enjoyed it, as any child would, and probably even invited it. You have wasted all this time trying to come to terms with an imaginary conception of damage done to you. Try dropping this invented guilt and telling yourself that the thing was both pleasurable and meaningless. Every neurosis is made to measure!" It was curious that a few words like this, and an ironic chuckle, could do what all the others could not do for me. Suddenly everything seemed to lift, get lighter, move about. Like cargo shifting in a vessel. I felt faint and rather sick, which puzzled me. Then later on a space slowly cleared. It was like feeling creeping back into a paralysed hand again.'

She was silent for a moment before going on. 'I still do not quite know how he saw us. Perhaps with contempt as the fabricators of our own misfortunes. One can hardly blame him for clinging to his own secrets like a limpet. Yet he hardly kept them, for he had a so-called Check hardly less formidable than mine, something which had plucked and gutted all sensation for him; so really in a way perhaps his strength was really a great weakness! You are silent, have I wounded you? I hope not, I hope your self-esteem is strong enough to face these truths of our old relationship. I should like to get it *all* off my chest, to come to terms with you — can you understand? To confess everything and wipe the slate clean. Look, even that first, that very first afternoon when I came to you — remember? You told me once how momentous it was. When you were ill in bed with sunburn, remember? Well, I had just been kicked out of his hotel-room against my will and was quite beside myself with fury. Strange to think that every word I then addressed to you was spoken mentally to him, to Pursewarden! In your bed it was he I embraced and subjugated in my mind. And yet again, in another dimension, *everything* I felt and did then was really for Nessim. At the bottom of my rubbish heap of a heart there was really Nessim, and the plan. My innermost life was rooted in this crazy adventure. Laugh now, Darley! Let me see you laugh for a change. You look rueful, but why should you? We are all in the grip of the emotional field which we throw down about one another — you yourself have said it. Perhaps our only sickness is to desire a truth which we cannot bear rather than to rest content with the fictions we manufacture out of each other.'

She suddenly uttered a short ironic laugh and walked to the balcony's edge to drop the smouldering stub of her cigarette out into the darkness. Then she turned, and standing in front of me with a serious face, as if playing a game with a child, she softly patted her palms together, intoning the names, 'Pursewarden and Liza, Darley and Melissa, Mountolive and Leila, Nessim and Justine, Narouz and Clea. . . . Here comes a candle to light them to bed, and here comes a chopper to chop off their heads. The sort of pattern we make should be of interest to someone; or is it just a meaningless display of coloured fireworks, the actions of *human* beings or of a set of dusty puppets which could be hung up in the corner of a writer's mind? I suppose you ask yourself the question.'

'Why did you mention Narouz?'

'After he died I discovered some letters to Clea; in his cupboard along with the old circumcision cap there was a huge nosegay of wax flowers and a candle the height of a man. As you know a Copt proposes with these. But he never had the courage to send them! How I laughed!'

'You laughed?'

'Yes, laughed until the tears ran down my cheeks. But I was really laughing at myself, at you, at all of us. One stumbles over it at every turn of the road, doesn't one; under every sofa the same corpse, in every cupboard the same skeleton? What can one do but laugh?'

It was late by now, and she lighted my way to the gaunt guest-bedroom where I found a bed made up for me, and placed the candles on the old-fashioned chest of drawers. I slept almost at once.

It must have been at some time not far off dawn when I awoke to find her standing beside the bed naked, with her hands joined in supplication like an Arab mendicant, like some beggar-woman of the streets. I started up. 'I ask nothing of you' she said, 'nothing at all but only to lie in your arms for the comfort of it. My head is bursting tonight and the medicines won't bring sleep. I do not want to be left to the mercies of my own imagination. Only for the comfort, Darley. A few strokes and endearments, that is all I beg you.'

I made room for her listlessly, still half asleep. She wept and trembled and muttered for a long time before I was able to quieten her. But at last she fell asleep with her dark head on the pillow beside me.

I lay awake for a long time to taste, with perplexity and wonder, the disgust that had now surged up in me, blotting out every other feeling. From where had it come? The perfume! The unbearable perfume and the smell of her body. Some lines from a poem of Pursewarden's drifted through my mind.

> *Delivered by her to what drunken caresses,*
> *Of mouths half eaten like soft rank fruit,*
> *From which one takes a single bite*
> *A mouthful of the darkness where we bleed.*

The once magnificent image of my love lay now in the hollow of my arm, defenceless as a patient on an operating table, hardly breathing. It was useless even to repeat her name which once held so much fearful magic that it had the power to slow the blood in my veins. She had become a woman at last, lying there, soiled and tattered, like a dead bird in a gutter, her hands crumpled into claws. It was as if some huge iron door had closed forever in my heart.

I could hardly wait for that slow dawn to bring me release. I could hardly wait to be gone.

★　　★　　★　　★　　★

IV

Walking about the streets of the summer capital once more, walking by spring sunlight, and a cloudless skirmishing blue sea — half-asleep and half-awake — I felt like the Adam of the medieval legends: the world-compounded body of a man whose flesh was soil, whose bones were stones, whose blood water, whose hair was grass, whose eyesight sunlight, whose breath was wind, and whose thoughts were clouds. And weightless now, as if after some long wasting illness, I found myself turned adrift again to float upon the shallows of Mareotis with its old tide-marks of appetites and desires refunded into the history of the place: an ancient city with all its cruelties intact, pitched upon a desert and a lake. Walking down the remembered grooves of streets which extended on every side, radiating out like the arms of a starfish from the axis of its founder's tomb. Footfalls echoing in the memory, forgotten scenes and conversations springing up at me from the walls, the café tables, the shuttered rooms with cracked and peeling ceilings. Alexandria, princess and whore. The royal city and the *anus mundi*. She would never change so long as the races continued to seethe here like must in a vat; so long as the streets and squares still gushed and spouted with the fermentation of these diverse passions and spites, rages and sudden calms. A fecund desert of human loves littered with the whitening bones of its exiles. Tall palms and minarets marrying in the sky. A hive of white mansions flanking those narrow and abandoned streets of mud which were racked all night by Arab music and the cries of girls who so easily disposed of their body's wearisome baggage (which galled them) and offered to the night the passionate kisses which money could not disflavour. The sadness and beatitude of this human conjunction which perpetuated itself to eternity, an endless cycle of rebirth and annihilation which alone could teach and reform by its destructive power. ('One makes love only to confirm one's loneliness' said Pursewarden, and at another time Justine added like a coda 'A woman's best love letters are always written to the man she is betraying' as she turned an immemorial head on a high balcony, hanging above a lighted city where the leaves of the trees seemed painted by the electric signs, where the pigeons tumbled as if from shelves. . . .) A great honeycomb of faces and gestures.

'We become what we dream' said Balthazar, still hunting among these grey paving stones for the key to a watch which is Time. 'We achieve in reality, in substance, only the pictures of the imagination.' The city makes no answer to such propositions. Unheeding it coils about the sleeping lives like some great anaconda digesting a meal. Among those shining coils the pitiable human world goes its way, unaware and unbelieving, repeating to infinity its gestures of despair, repentance, and love. Demonax the philosopher said: 'Nobody wishes to be evil' and was called a cynic for his pains. And Pursewarden in another age, in another tongue replied: 'Even to be halfawake among sleep-walkers is frightening at first. Later one learns to dissimulate!'

I could feel the ambience of the city in me once more, its etiolated beauties spreading their tentacles out to grasp at my sleeve. I felt more summers coming, summers with fresh despairs, fresh onslaughts of the 'bayonets of time.' My life would rot away afresh in stifling offices to the tepid whirl of electric fans, by the light of dusty unshaded bulbs hanging from the cracked ceilings of renovated tenements. At the Café Al Aktar, seated before a green *menthe*, listening to the sulky bubbles in the *narguilehs* I would have time to catechize the silences which followed the cries of the hawkers and the clatter of backgammon-boards. Still the same phantoms would pass and repass in the Nebi Daniel, the gleaming limousines of the bankers would bear their choice freight of painted ladies to distant bridge-tables, to the synagogue, the fortune-teller, the smart café. Once all this had power to wound. And now? Snatches of a quartet squirted from a café with scarlet awnings reminded me of Clea once saying: 'Music was invented to confirm human loneliness.' But if I walked here with attention and even a certain tenderness it was because for me the city was something which I myself had deflowered, at whose hands I had learned to ascribe some particular meaning to fortune. These patched and faded walls, the lime wash cracking into a million oyster-coloured patches, only imitated the skins of the lepers who whined here on the edge of the Arab quarter; it was simply the hide of the place itself, peeling and caking away under the sun.

Even the war had come to terms with the city, had indeed stimulated its trade with its bands of aimless soldiers walking about with that grim air of unflinching desperation with which Anglo-Saxons embark upon their pleasures; their own demagnetized

women were all in uniform now which gave them a ravenous air —
as if they could drink the blood of the innocents while it was still
warm. The brothels had overflowed and gloriously engulfed a
whole quarter of the town around the old square. If anything the
war had brought an air of tipsy carnival rather than anything else;
even the nightly bombardments of the harbour were brushed aside
by day, shrugged away like nightmares, hardly remembered as
more than an inconvenience. For the rest, nothing had fundamentally changed. The brokers still sat on the steps of the
Mohammed Ali club sipping their newspapers. The old horse-
drawn gharries still clopped about upon their listless errands. The
crowds still thronged the white Corniche to take the frail spring
sunlight. Balconies crowded with wet linen and tittering girls.
The Alexandrians still moved inside the murex-tinted cyclorama
of the life they imagined. ('Life is more complicated than we think,
yet far simpler than anyone dares to imagine'.) Voices of girls,
stabbing of Arab quarter-tones, and from the synagogue a metallic
drone punctuated by the jingle of a sistrum. On the floor of the
Bourse they were screaming like one huge animal in pain. The
money-changers were arranging their currencies like sweets upon
the big squared boards. Pashas in scarlet flower-pots reclining in
immense cars like gleaming sarcophagi. A dwarf playing a man-
dolin. An immense eunuch with a carbuncle the size of a brooch
eating pastry. A legless man propped on a trolley, dribbling. In all
this furious acceleration of the mind I thought suddenly of Clea
— her thick eyelashes fragmenting every glance of the magnificent
eyes — and wondered vaguely when she would appear. But in the
meantime my straying footsteps had led me back to the narrow
opening of the Rue Lepsius, to the worm-eaten room with the cane
chair which creaked all night, and where once the old poet of
the city had recited 'The Barbarians'. I felt the stairs creak again
under my tread. On the door was a notice in Arabic which said
'Silence'. The latch was hooked back.

Balthazar's voice sounded strangely thin and far away as he
bade me to enter. The shutters were drawn and the room was
shrouded in half-darkness. He was lying in bed. I saw with a considerable shock that his hair was quite white which made him
look like an ancient version of himself. It took me a moment or
two to realize that it was not dyed. But how he had changed! One
cannot exclaim to a friend: 'My God, how much you have aged!'
Yet this is what I almost did, quite involuntarily.

'Darley!' he said feebly, and held up in welcome hands swollen to the size of boxing-gloves by the bandages which swathed them.

'What on earth have you been doing to yourself?'

He drew a long sad sigh of vexation and nodded towards a chair. The room was in great disorder. A mountain of books and papers on the floor by the window. An unemptied chamberpot. A chessboard with the pieces all lying in confusion. A newspaper. A cheese-roll on a plate with an apple. The washbasin full of dirty plates. Beside him in a glass of some cloudy fluid stood a glittering pair of false teeth on which his feverish eye dwelt from time to time with confused perplexity. 'You have heard nothing? That surprises me. Bad news, news of a scandal, travels so fast and so far I should have thought that by now you had heard. It is a long story. Shall I tell you and provoke the look of tactful commiseration with which Mountolive sits down to play chess with me every afternoon?'

'But your hands. . . . .'

'I shall come to those in due course. It was a little idea I got from your manuscript. But the real culprits are these, I think, these false teeth in the glass. Don't they glitter bewitchingly? I am sure it was the teeth which set me off. When I found that I was about to lose my teeth I suddenly began to behave like a woman at the change of life. How else can I explain falling in love like a youth?' He cauterized the question with a dazed laugh.

'First the Cabal — which is now disbanded; it went the way of all words. Mystagogues arose, theologians, all the resourceful bigotry that heaps up around a sect and spells dogma! But the thing had to me a special meaning, a mistaken and unconscious meaning, but nevertheless a clear one. I thought that slowly, by degrees, I should be released from the bondage of my appetites, of the flesh. I should at last, I felt, find a philosophic calm and balance which would expunge the passional nature, sterilize my actions. I thought of course that I had no such *préjugés* at the time; that my quest for truth was quite pure. But unconsciously I was using the Cabal to this precise end — instead of letting it use me. First miscalculation! Pass me some water from the pitcher over there.' He drank thirstily through his new pink gums. 'Now comes the absurdity. I found I must lose my teeth. This caused the most frightful upheaval. It seemed to me like a death-sentence, like a confirmation of growing old, of getting beyond the reach of life itself. I have always been fastidious about mouths, always hated rank breath and coated tongues; but most of all false teeth! Unconsciously, then, I must have somehow pushed myself to this ridiculous thing — as if it were a last desperate fling before old age settled over me. Don't laugh. *I fell in love* in a way that I have never done before, at least not since I was eighteen. "Kisses sharp as quills" says the proverb; or as Pursewarden might say "Once more the cunning gonads on the prowl, the dragnet of the seed, the old biological terror". But my dear Darley this was no joke. I still had my own teeth! But the object of my choice, a Greek actor, was the most disastrous that anyone could hit upon. To look like a god, to have a charm like a shower of silver arrows — and yet to be simply a small-spirited, dirty, venal and empty personage: that was Panagiotis! I knew it. It seemed to make no difference whatsoever. I saw in him the personage of Seleucia on whom Cavafy based his poem.* I cursed myself in the mirror. But I was powerless to behave otherwise. And, in truth, all this might have passed off as so much else had he not pushed me to outrageous jealousies, terrific scenes of recrimination. I remember that old Pursewarden used to say: "Ah! you Jews, you have the knack of suffering" and I used to reply with a quotation from Mommsen about the bloody Celts: "They have shaken all states and founded none. They nowhere created a great state or developed a distinctive culture of their own." No, this was not simply an expression of minority-fever: this was the sort of murderous passion of which one has read, and for which our city is famous! Within a matter of months I became a hopeless drunkard. I was always found hanging about the brothels he frequented. I obtained drugs under prescription for him to sell. Anything, lest he should leave me. I became as weak as a woman. A terrific scandal, rather a series of them, made my practice dwindle until it is now nonexistent. Amaril is keeping the clinic going out of kindness until I can pick myself off the floor. I was dragged across the floor of the club, holding on to his coat and imploring him not to leave me! I was knocked down in Rue Fuad, thrashed with a cane outside the French Consulate. I found myself surrounded by long-faced and concerned friends who did everything they could to avert disaster. Useless. I had become quite impossible! All this went on, this ferocious life — and really I enjoyed being debased in a queer way, being whipped and scorned, reduced to a wreck! It was as if I wanted to swallow the world, to drain the sore of love until it healed. I was pushed to the very extremity of myself, yet I myself was doing the pushing: or was it the teeth?' He cast a sulky furious look in their direction and sighed, moving his head about as if with inner anguish at the memory of these misdeeds.

'It is strange to what extent small inanimate objects can sometimes be responsible for the complete breakdown of an affective field; a love based on an eye-tooth, a disgust fathered by shortsight, a passion founded on hairy wrists. It was the green fingerstall that disgusted him finally. He could not bear to feel a hand moving on his body whose index finger was sheathed in a fingerstall. Yet I had to wear it, for my finger had begun to suppurate again; you know I have a little patch of eczema which plays me up from time to time, usually when I am run down or over-excited. It even manages to burst through the thick scab of methylene blue. I tried everything, but without avail. Perhaps unconsciously I was courting his disgust as an adolescent might with an acne? Who can say?

'Then of course it came to an end, as everything does, even presumably life! There is no merit in suffering as I did, dumbly like a pack animal, galled by intolerable sores it cannot reach with its tongue. It was then that I remembered a remark in your manuscript about the ugliness of my hands. Why did I not cut them off and throw them in the sea as you had so thoughtfully recommended? This was the question that arose in my mind. At the time I was so numb with drugs and drink that I did not imagine I would feel anything. However I made an attempt, but it is harder than you imagine, all that gristle! I was like those fools who cut their throats and come bang up against the oesophagus. They always live. But when I desisted with pain I thought of another writer, Petronius. (The part that literature plays in our lives!) I lay down in a hot bath. But the blood wouldn't run, or perhaps I had no more. The colour of bitumen it seemed, the few coarse drops I persuaded to trickle. I was about to try other ways of alleviating the pain when Amaril appeared at his most abusive and brought me to my senses by giving me a deep sedation of some twenty hours during which he tidied up my corpse as well as my room. Then I was very ill, with shame I believe. Yes, it was chiefly shame, though of course I was much weakened by the absurd excess to which I had been pushed. I submitted to Pierre Balbz who removed the teeth and provided me with this set of glittering snappers — *art nouveau*! Amaril tried in his clumsy way to analyse me — but what is one to say of this very approximate science which has carelessly overflowed into anthropology on one side, theology on the other? There is much they do not know as yet: for instance that one kneels in church because one kneels to enter a woman, or that circumcision is derived from the clipping of the vine, without which it will run to leaf and produce no fruit! I had no philosophic system on which to lean as even Da Capo did. Do you remember Capodistria's exposition of the nature of the universe? "The world is a biological phenomenon which will only come to an end when every single man has had all the women, every woman all the men. Clearly this will take some time. Meanwhile there is nothing to do but to help forward the forces of nature by treading the grapes as hard as we can. As for an afterlife — what will it consist of but satiety? The play of shadows in Paradise — pretty *hanoums* flitting across the screens of memory, no longer desired, no longer desiring to be desired. Both at rest at last. But clearly it cannot be done all at once. Patience! *Avanti!*" Yes, I did a lot of slow and careful thinking as I lay here, listening to the creak of the cane chair and the noises from the street. My friends were very good and often visited me with gifts and conversations that left me headaches. So I gradually began to swim up to the surface again, with infinite slowness. I said to myself "Life is the master. We have been living against the grain of our intellects. The real teacher is endurance." I had learned something, but at what a cost!

'If only I had had the courage to tackle my love wholeheartedly I would have served the ideas of the Cabal better. A paradox, you think? Perhaps. Instead of letting my love poison my intellect and my intellectual reservations my love. Yet though I am rehabilitated and ready once more to enter the world, everything in nature seems to have disappeared! I still awake crying out: "He has gone away forever. True lovers exist for the sake of love." '

He gave a croaky sob and crawled out from between the sheets, looking ridiculous in his long woollen combinations, to hunt for a handkerchief in the chest of drawers. To the mirror he said: 'The most tender, the most tragic of illusions is perhaps to believe that our actions can add or subtract from the total quantity of good and evil in the world.' Then he shook his head gloomily and returned to his bed, settling the pillows at his back and adding: 'And that fat brute Father Paul talks of acceptance! Acceptance of the world can only come from a full recognition of its measureless extents of good and evil; and to really inhabit it, explore it to the full uninhibited extent of this finite human understanding — that is all that is necessary in order to accept it. But what a task! One lies here with time passing and wonders about it. Every sort of time trickling through the hour-glass, "time immemorial" and "for the time being" and "time out of mind"; the time of the poet, the philosopher, the pregnant woman, the calendar. . . . Even "time is money" comes into the picture; and then, if you think that money is excrement for the Freudian, you understand that time must be also! Darley you have come at the right moment, for I am to be rehabilitated tomorrow by my friends. It was a touching thought which Clea first had. The shame of having to put in a public appearance again after all my misdeeds has been weighing on me very heavily. How to face the city again — that is the problem. It is only in moments like this that you realize who your friends are. Tomorrow a little group is coming here to find me dressed, my hands less conspicuously bandaged, my new teeth in place. I shall of course wear dark glasses. Mountolive, Amaril, Pombal and Clea, two on each arm. We will walk the whole length of Rue Fuad thus and take a lengthy public coffee on the pavement outside Pastroudi. Mountolive has booked the largest lunch table at the Mohammed Ali and proposes to offer me a lunch of twenty people to celebrate my resurrection from the dead. It is a wonderful gesture of solidarity, and will certainly quell spiteful tongues and sneers. In the evening the Cervonis have asked me to dinner. With such lucky help I feel I may be able in the long run to repair my damaged confidence and that of my old patients. Is it not fine of them — and in the traditions of the city? I may live to smile again, if not to love — a fixed and glittering smile which only Pierre will gaze at with affection — the affection of the artificer for his handiwork.' He raised his white boxing-gloves like a champion entering the ring and grimly saluted an imaginary crowd. Then he flopped back on his pillows once more and gazed at me with an air of benign sorrow.

'Where has Clea gone?' I asked.

'Nowhere. She was here yesterday afternoon asking for you.'

'Nessim said she had gone somewhere.'

'Perhaps to Cairo for the afternoon; where have you been?'

'Out to Karm for the night.'

There was a long silence during which we eyed each other. There were clearly questions in his mind which he tactfully did not wish to inflict on me; and for my part there was little that

I felt I could explain. I picked up an apple and took a bite from it.

'And the writing?' he said after a long silence.

'It has stopped. I don't seem to be able to carry it any further for the moment. I somehow can't match the truth to the illusions which are necessary to art without the gap showing — you know, like an unbasted seam. I was thinking of it at Karm, confronted again by Justine. Thinking how despite the factual falsities of the manuscript which I sent you the portrait was somehow poetically true — psychographically if you like. But an artist who can't solder the elements together falls short somewhere. I'm on the wrong track.'

'I don't see why. In fact this very discovery should encourage rather than hamper you. I mean about the mutability of all truth. Each fact can have a thousand motivations, all equally valid, and each fact a thousand faces. So many truths which have little to do with fact! Your duty is to hunt them down. At each moment of time all multiplicity waits at your elbow. Why, Darley, this should thrill you and give your writing the curves of a pregnant woman.'

'On the contrary, it has faulted me. For the moment anyway. And now that I am back here in the real Alexandria from which I drew so many of my illustrations I don't feel the need for more writing — or at any rate writing which doesn't fulfil the difficult criteria I see lurking behind art. You remember Pursewarden writing: "A novel should be an act of divination by entrails, not a careful record of a game of pat-ball on some vicarage lawn!" '

'Yes.'

'And so indeed it should. But now I am confronted once more with my models I am ashamed to have botched them up. If I start again it will be from another angle. But there is still so much I don't know, and presumably never will, about all of you. Capodistria, for example, where does he fit in?'

'You sound as if you *knew* he was alive!'

'Mnemjian told me so.'

'Yes. The mystery isn't a very complicated one. He was working for Nessim and compromised himself by a serious slip. It was necessary to clear out. Conveniently it happened at a time when he was all but bankrupt financially. The insurance money was most necessary! Nessim provided the setting and I provided the corpse. You know we get quite a lot of corpses of one sort or another. Paupers. People who donate their bodies, or actually sell them in advance for a fixed sum. The medical schools need them. It wasn't hard to obtain a private one, relatively fresh. I tried to hint at the truth to you once but you did not take my meaning. Anyway the thing's worked smoothly. Da Capo now lives in a handsomely converted Martello tower, dividing his time between studying black magic and working on certain schemes of Nessim's about which I know nothing. Indeed I see Nessim only rarely, and Justine not at all. Though guests are permitted by special police order they never invite anyone out to Karm. Justine telephones people from time to time for a chat, that is all. You have been privileged, Darley. They must have got you a permit. But I am relieved to see you cheerful and undesponding. You have made a step forward somewhere, haven't you?'

'I don't know. I worry less.'

'But you will be happy this time, I feel it; much has changed but much has remained the same. Mountolive tells me he has recommended you for a censorship post, and that you will probably live with Pombal, until you have had a chance to look round a bit.'

'Another mystery! I hardly know Mountolive. Why has he suddenly constituted himself my benefactor?'

'I don't know, possibly because of Liza.'

'Pursewarden's sister?'

'They are up at the summer legation for a few weeks. I gather you will be hearing from him, from them both.'

There was a tap at the door and a servant entered to tidy the flat; Balthazar propped himself up and issued his orders. I stood up to take my leave.

'There is only one problem' he said 'which occupies me. Shall I leave my hair as it is? I look about two hundred and seventy when it isn't dyed. But I think on the whole it would be better to leave it to symbolize my return from the dead with a vanity chastened by experience, eh? Yes, I shall leave it. I think I shall definitely leave it.'

'Toss a coin.'

'Perhaps I will. This evening I must get up for a couple of hours and practise walking about; extraordinary how weak one feels simply from lack of practice. After a fortnight in bed one loses the power of one's legs. And I mustn't fall down tomorrow or the people will think I am drunk again and that would never do. As for you, you must find Clea.'

'I'll go round to the studio and see if she is working.'

'I'm glad you are back.'

'In a strange way so am I.'

And in the desultory brilliant life of the open street it was hard not to feel like an ancient inhabitant of the city, returning from the other side of the grave to visit it. Where would I find Clea?

*　　*　　*　　*　　*

She was not at the flat, though her letter-box was empty, which suggested that she had already collected her mail and gone out to read it over a *café crème*, as had been her wont in the past. There was nobody at the studio either. It fitted in with my mood to try and track her down in one of the familiar cafés and so I dutifully walked down Rue Fuad at a leisurely pace towards Baudrot, the Café Zoltan and the Coquin. But there was no sign of her. There was one elderly waiter at the Coquin who remembered me however, and he had seen her walking down Rue Fuad earlier in the morning with a portfolio. I continued my circuit, peering into the shop-windows, examining the stalls of second-hand books, until I reached the Select on the seafront. But she was not there. I turned back to the flat and found a note from her saying that she would not be able to make contact before the later afternoon, but that she would call there for me; it was annoying, for it meant that I should have to pass the greater part of the day alone, yet it was also useful, for it enabled me to visit Mnemjian's redecorated emporium and indulge in a post-Pharaonic haircut and shave. ('The natron-bath' Pursewarden used to call it.) It also gave me time to unpack my belongings.

But we met by chance, not design. I had gone out to buy some stationery, and had taken a short cut through the little square called Bab El Fedan. My heart heeled half-seas over for a moment, for she was sitting where once (that first day) Melissa had been sitting, gazing at a coffee cup with a wry reflective air of amusement, with her hands supporting her chin. The exact station in place and time where I had once found Melissa, and with such difficulty mustered enough courage at last to enter the place and speak to her. It gave me a strange sense of unreality to repeat this forgotten action at such a great remove of time, like unlocking a door which had remained closed and bolted for a generation. Yet it was in truth Clea and not Melissa, and her blonde head was bent with an air of childish concentration over her coffee cup. She was in the act of shaking the dregs three times and emptying them into the saucer to study them as they dried into the contours from which fortune-tellers 'scry' — a familiar gesture.

'So you haven't changed. Still telling fortunes.'

'Darley.' She sprang up with a cry of pleasure and we embraced warmly. It was with a queer interior shock, almost like a new recognition, that I felt her warm laughing mouth on mine, her hands upon my shoulders. As though somewhere a window had been smashed, and the fresh air allowed to pour into a long-sealed room. We stood thus embracing and smiling for a moment. 'You startled me! I was just coming on to the flat to find you.'

'You've had me chasing my tail all day.'

'I had work to do. But Darley, how you've changed! You don't stoop any more. And your spectacles. . . .'

'I broke them by accident ages ago, and then found I didn't really need them.'

'I'm delighted for you. Bravo! Tell me, do you notice my wrinkles? I'm getting some, I fear. Have I changed very much, would you say?'

She was more beautiful than I could remember her to have been, slimmer, and with a subtle range of new gestures and expressions suggesting a new and troubling maturity.

'You've grown a new laugh.'

'Have I?'

'Yes. It's deeper and more melodious. But I must not flatter you! A nightingale's laugh — if they do laugh.'

'Don't make me self-conscious because I so much want to laugh with you. You'll turn it into a croak.'

'Clea, why didn't you come and meet me?'

She wrinkled up her nose for a moment, and putting her hand on my arm, bent her head once more to the coffee grounds which were drying fast into little whorls and curves like sand-dunes. 'Light me a cigarette' she said pleadingly.

'Nessim said you turned tail at the last moment.'

'Yes, I did, my dear.'

'Why?'

'I suddenly felt it might be inopportune. It might have been a complication somehow. You had old accounts to render, old scores to settle, new relationships to explore. I really felt powerless to do anything about you until . . . well, until you had seen Justine. I don't know why. Yes I do, though. I wasn't sure that the cycle would really change, I didn't know how much you had or hadn't changed yourself. You are such a bloody correspondent I hadn't any way of judging about your inside state of mind. Such a long time since you wrote, isn't it? And then the child and all that.

After all, people sometimes get stuck like an old disc and can't move out of a groove. That might have been your fate with Justine. So it wasn't for me to intrude, since my side of you. . . . Do you see? I had to give you air.'

'And supposing I have stuck like some old disc?'

'No it hasn't turned out like that.'

'How can you tell?'

'From your face, Darley. I could tell in a flash!'

'I don't know quite how to explain. . . .'

'You don't *need* to' her voice curved upwards with elation and her bright eyes smiled. 'We have such totally different claims upon each other. We are free to *forget!* You men are the strangest creatures. Listen, I have arranged this first day together like a tableau, like a charade. Come first and see the queer immortality one of us has gained. Will you put yourself in my hands? I have been so looking forward to acting as dragoman on . . . but no, I won't tell you. Just let me pay for this coffee.'

'What does your fortune say in the grounds?'

'Chance meetings!'

'I think you invent.'

The afternoon had been overcast and dusk fell early. Already the sunset violets had begun to tamper with the perspectives of the streets along the seafront. We took an old horse-drawn gharry which was standing forlornly in a taxi rank by Ramleh Station. The ancient jarvey with his badly cicatriced face asked hopefully if we wished for a 'carriage of love' or an 'ordinary carriage', and Clea, giggling, selected the latter variety of the same carriage as being cheaper. 'O son of truth!' she said. 'What woman would take a lusty husband in such a thing when she has a good bed at home which costs nothing.'

'Merciful is God' said the old man with sublime resignation.

So we set off down the white curving Esplanade with its fluttering awnings, the quiet sea spreading away to the right of us to a blank horizon. In the past we had so often come this way to visit the old pirate in his shabby rooms in Tatwig Street.

'Clea, where the devil are we going?'

'Wait and see.'

I could see him so clearly, the old man. I wondered for a moment if his shabby ghost still wandered about those dismal rooms, whistling to the green parrot and reciting: '*Taisez-vous, petit babouin.*' I felt Clea's arm squeeze mine as we sheered off left and entered the smoking ant-heap of the Arab town, the streets choked with smoke from the burning refuse-heaps, or richly spiced with cooking meat and whiffs of baking bread from the bakeries.

'Why on earth are you taking me to Scobie's rooms?' I said again as we started to clip-clop down the length of the familiar street. Her eyes shone with a mischievous delight as putting her lips to my ear she whispered: 'Patience. You shall see.'

It was the same house all right. We entered the tall gloomy archway as we had so often in the past. In the deepening dusk it looked like some old faded·daguerreotype, the little courtyard, and I could see that it had been much enlarged. Several supporting walls of neighbouring tenements had been razed or had fallen down and increased its mean size by about two hundred square feet. It was just a shattered and pock-marked no-man's-land of red earth littered with refuse. In one corner stood a small shrine which I did not remember having remarked before. It was surrounded by a huge ugly modern grille of steel. It boasted a small white dome and a withered tree, both very much the worse for wear. I recognized in it one of the many *maquams* with which Egypt is studded, spots made sacred by the death of a hermit or holy man and where the faithful repair to pray or solicit his help by leaving ex-votos. This little shrine looked as so many do, utterly shabby and forlorn, as if its existence had been overlooked and forgotten for centuries. I stood looking around me, and heard Clea's clear voice call: 'Ya Abdul!' There was a note in it which suggested suppressed amusement but I could not for the life of me tell why. A man advanced towards us through the shadows peering. 'He is almost blind. I doubt if he'll recognize you.'

'But who is it?' I said, almost with exasperation at all this mystery. 'Scobie's Abdul' she whispered briefly and turned away to say: 'Abdul, have you the key of the *Maquam* of El Scob?'

He greeted her in recognition making elaborate passes over his breast, and produced a clutch of tall keys saying in a deep voice: 'At once O lady' rattling the keys together as all guardians of shrines must do to scare the djinns which hang about the entrances to holy places.

'Abdul!' I exclaimed with amazement in a whisper. 'But he was a youth.' It was quite impossible to identify him with this crooked and hunched anatomy with its stooping centenarian's gait and cracked voice. 'Come' said Clea hurriedly, 'explanations later. Just come and look at the shrine.' Still bemused I followed in the guardian's footsteps. After a very thorough rattling and banging to scare the djinns he unlocked the rusty portals and led the way inside. It was suffocatingly hot in that little airless tomb. A single wick somewhere in a recess had been lighted and gave a wan and trembling yellow light. In the centre lay what I presumed must be the tomb of the saint. It was covered with a green cloth with an elaborate design in gold. This Abdul reverently removed for my inspection, revealing an object under it which was so surprising that I uttered an involuntary exclamation. It was a galvanized iron bath-tub on one leg of which was engraved in high relief the words: ' "The Dinky Tub" Crabbe's. Luton.' It had been filled with clean sand and its four hideous crocodile-feet heavily painted with the customary anti-djinn blue colour. It was an astonishing object of reverence to stumble upon in such surroundings, and it was with a mixture of amusement and dismay that I heard the now completely unrecognizable Abdul, who was the object's janitor, muttering the conventional prayers in the name of El Scob, touching as he did so the ex-votos which hung down from every corner of the wall like little white tassels. These were, of course, the slips of cloth which women tear from their underclothes and hang up as offerings to a saint who, they believe, will cure sterility and enable them to conceive! The devil! Here was old Scobie's bath-tub apparently being invoked to confer fertility upon the childless — and with success, too, if one could judge by the great number of the offerings.

'El Scob was a holy one?' I said in my halting Arabic.

The tired, crooked bundle of humanity with its head encircled in a tattered shawl nodded and bowed as he croaked: 'From far away in Syria he came. Here he found his rest. His name enlightens the just. He was a student of harmlessness!'

I felt as if I were dreaming. I could almost hear Scobie's voice say: 'Yes, it's a flourishing little shrine as shrines go. Mind you, I don't make a fortune, but I do give service!' The laughter began to pile up inside me as I felt the trigger of Clea's fingers on my elbow. We exchanged delighted squeezes as we retired from that fuggy little hole into the dusky courtyard, while Abdul reverently replaced the cloth over the bath-tub, attended to the oil wick, and then joined us. Carefully he locked the iron grille, and accepting a tip from Clea with many hoarse gratitudes, shuffled away into the shadows, leaving us to sit down upon a heap of tumbled masonry.

'I didn't come right in' she said. 'I was afraid we'd start laughing and didn't want to risk upsetting Abdul.'

'Clea! Scobie's *bath-tub!*'

'I know.'

'How the devil did this happen?'

Clea's soft laughter!

'You must tell me.'

'It is a wonderful story. Balthazar unearthed it. Scobie is now officially El Yacoub. At least that is how the shrine is registered on the Coptic Church's books. But as you have just heard he is really El Scob! You know how these saints' *maquams* get forgotten, overlooked. They die, and in time people completely forget who the original saint was; sometimes a sand-dune buries the shrine. But they also spring alive again. Suddenly one day an epileptic is cured there, or a prophecy is given by the shrine to some mad woman — and presto! the saint wakes up, revives. Well, all the time our old pirate was living in this house El Yacoub was there, at the end of the garden, though nobody knew it. He had been bricked in, surrounded by haphazard walls — you know how crazily they build here. He was utterly forgotten. Meanwhile Scobie, after his death, had become a figure of affectionate memory in the neighbourhood. Tales began to circulate about his great gifts. He was clever at magic potions (like Mock Whisky?). A cult began to blossom around him. They said he was a necromancer. Gamblers swore by his name. "El Scob spit on this card" became quite a proverb in the quarter. They also said that he had been able to change himself into a woman at will (!) and by sleeping with impotent men regenerate their forces. He could also make the barren conceive. Some women even called their children after him. Well, in a little while he had already joined the legendary of Alexandrian saints, but of course he had no actual shrine — because everyone knew with one half of his mind that Father Paul had stolen his body, wrapped it in a flag, and buried it in the Catholic cemetery. They knew because many of them had been there for the service and much enjoyed the dreadful music of the police band of which I believe Scobie had once been a member. I often wonder whether he played any instrument and if so what. A slide trombone? Anyway, it was during this time, while his sainthood was only, so to speak, awaiting a Sign, a Portent, a Confirmation, that that wall obligingly fell down and revealed the (perhaps indignant?) Yacoub. Yes, but there was no tomb in the shrine. Even the Coptic Church which has at last reluctantly taken Yacoub on their books knows nothing of him except that he came from Syria. They are not even sure whether he was a Moslem or not! He sounds distinctly Jewish to me. However they diligently questioned the oldest inhabitants of the quarter and at least established his name. But nothing more. And so one fine day the neighbourhood found that it had an empty shrine free for Scobie. He must have a local habitation to match the power of his name. A spontaneous festival broke out at which his bath-tub which had been responsible for so many deaths (great is Allah!) was solemnly enshrined and consecrated after being carefully filled with holy sand from the Jordan. Officially the Copts could not concede Scob and insisted on sticking to Yacoub for official purposes; but Scob he remained to the faithful. It might have been something of a dilemma, but being magnificent diplomatists, the clergy turned a blind eye to El Scob's reincarnation; they behave *as if* they thought it was really El Yacoub in a local pronunciation. So everyone's face is saved. They have, in fact, even — and here is that marvellous tolerance which exists nowhere else on earth — formally registered Scobie's birthday, I suppose because they do not know Yacoub's. Do you know that he is even to have a yearly *mulid* in his honour on St George's Day? Abdul must have remembered his birthday because Scobie always hung up from each corner of his bed a string of coloured flags-of-all-nations which he borrowed from the newsagent. And he used to get rather drunk, you told me once, and sing sea-chanties and recite "The Old Red Duster" until the tears flowed! What a marvellous immortality to enjoy.'

'How happy the old pirate must be.'

'How happy! To be the patron saint of his own *quartier!* Oh, Darley, I knew you'd enjoy it. I often come here at this time in the dusk and sit on a stone and laugh inwardly, rejoicing for the old man.'

So we sat together for a long time as the shadows grew up around the shrine, quietly laughing and talking as people should at the shrine of a saint! Reviving the memory of the old pirate with the glass eye whose shade still walked about those mouldering rooms on the second floor. Vaguely glimmered the lights of Tatwig Street. They shone, not with their old accustomed brilliance, but darkly — for the whole harbour quarter had been placed under blackout and one sector of it included the famous street. My thoughts were wandering.

'And Abdul' I said suddenly. 'What of him?'

'Yes, I promised to tell you; Scobie set him up in a barber's shop, you remember. Well, he was warned for not keeping his razors clean, and for spreading syphilis. He didn't heed the warnings perhaps because he believed that Scobie would never report him officially. But the old man did, with terrible results. Abdul was nearly beaten to death by the police, lost an eye. Amaril spent nearly a year trying to tidy him up. Then he got some wasting disease on top of it and had to abandon his shop. Poor man. But I'm not sure that he isn't the appropriate guardian for the shrine of his master.'

'El Scob! Poor Abdul!'

'But he has taken consolation in religion and does some mild preaching and reciting of the Suras as well as this job. Do you know I believe that he has forgotten the real Scobie. I asked him one evening if he remembered the old gentleman on the upper floor and he looked at me vaguely and muttered something; as if he were reaching far back in his memory for something too remote to grasp. The real Scobie had disappeared just like Yacoub, and El Scob had taken his place.'

'I feel rather as one of the apostles must have — I mean to be in on the birth of a saint, a legend; think, we actually knew the real El Scob! We heard his voice. . . . .'

To my delight Clea now began to mimic the old man quite admirably, copying the desultory scattered manner of his conversation to the life; perhaps she was only repeating the words from memory?

'Yes, mind you, on St George's Day I always get a bit carried away for England's sake as well as my own. Always have a sip or two of the blushful, as Toby would say, even bubbly if it comes my way. But, bless you, I'm no horse-drawn conveyance — always stay on my two pins. It's the cup that cheers and not in . . . in . . . inebriates for me. Another of Toby's expressions. He was full of literary illustrations. As well he might be — for why? *Ber*corse he was never without a book under his arm. In the Navy he was considered quite queer, and several times had rows. "What yer got there?" they used to shout, and Toby who could be pert at times used to huff up and answer quite spontaneous. "What d'yer think, Puffy? Why me marriages lines of course." But it was always some heavy book which made *my* head swim though I love reading. One year it was Stringbag's Plays, a Swedish author as I under-

stand it. Another year it was Goitre's "Frowst". Toby said it was a
liberal education. My education just wasn't up to his. The school
of life, as you might say. But then my mum and dad were killed
off early on and we were left, three perishing little orphans. They
had destined us for high things, my father had; one for the church,
one for the army, one for the navy. Quite shortly after this my two
brothers were run over by the Prince Regent's private train near
Sidcup. That was the end of *them*. But it was all in the papers and
the Prince sent a wreath. But there I was left quite alone. I had to
make my own way without influence — otherwise I should have
been an Admiral I expect by now. . . .'

The fidelity of her rendering was absolutely impeccable. The
little old man stepped straight out of his tomb and began to stalk
about in front of us with his lopsided walk, now toying with his
telescope on the cake-stand, now opening and shutting his battered
Bible, or getting down on one creaking knee to blow up his fire with
the tiny pair of bellows. His birthday! I recalled finding him one
birthday evening rather the worse for brandy, but dancing around
completely naked to music of his own manufacture on a comb and
paper.

Recalling this celebration of his Name Day I began, as it were, to
mimic him back to Clea, in order to hear once more this thrilling
new laugh she had acquired. 'Oh! it's you, Darley! You gave me
quite a turn with your knock. Come in, I'm just having a bit of a
dance in my *tou tou* to recall old times. It's my birthday, yes. I
always dwell a bit on the past. In my youth I was a proper spark,
I don't mind admitting. I was a real dab at the Velouta. Want to
watch me? Don't laugh, just *ber*corse I'm *in puris*. Sit on the chair
over there and watch. Now, advance, take your partners, shimmy,
bow, reverse! It looks easy but it isn't. The smoothness is deceptive. I could do them all once, my boy, Lancers, Caledonians,
Circassian Circle. Never seen a *demi-chaine Anglais*, I suppose?
Before your time I think. Mind you, I loved dancing and for years
I kept up to date. I got as far as the Hootchi-Kootchi — have you
ever seen that? Yes, the haitch is haspirated as in 'otel. It's some
fetching little movements they call oriental allurements. Undulations, like. You take off one veil after another until all is
revealed. The suspense is terrific, but you have to waggle as you
glide, see?' Here he took up a posture of quite preposterous
oriental allurement and began to revolve slowly, wagging his
behind and humming a suitable air which quite faithfully copied

the lag and fall of Arab quartertones. Round and round the room he went until he began to feel dizzy and flopped back triumphantly on his bed, chuckling and nodding with self-approval and self-congratulation, and reaching out for a swig of *arak*, the manufacture of which was also among his secrets. He must have found the recipe in the pages of Postlethwaite's Vade Mecum For Travellers in Foreign Lands, a book which he kept under lock and key in his trunk and by which he absolutely swore. It contained, he said, everything that a man in Robinson Crusoe's position ought to know — even how to make fire by rubbing sticks together; it was a mine of marvellous information. ('To achieve Bombay arrack dissolve two scruples of flowers of benjamin in a quart of good rum and it will impart to the spirit the fragrance of arrack.') That was the sort of thing. 'Yes' he would add gravely, 'old Postlethwaite can't be bettered. There's something in him for every sort of mind and every sort of situation. He's a genius I might say.'

Only once had Postlethwaite failed to live up to his reputation, and that was when Toby said that there was a fortune to be made in Spanish fly if only Scobie could secure a large quantity of it for export. 'But the perisher didn't explain what it was or how, and it was the only time Postlethwaite had me beat. D'you know what he says about it, under Cantharides? I found it so mysterious I memorized the passage to repeat to Toby when next he came through. Old Postle says this: "Cantharides when used internally are diuretic and stimulant; when applied externally they are epispastic and rubefacient." Now what the devil can he mean, eh? And how does this fit in with Toby's idea of a flourishing trade in the things? Sort of worms, they must be. I asked Abdul but I don't know the Arabic word.'

Refreshed by the interlude he once more advanced to the mirror to admire his wrinkled old tortoise-frame. A sudden thought cast a gloom over his countenance. He pointed at a portion of his own wrinkled anatomy and said: 'And to think that *that* is what old Postlethwaite describes as "*merely* erectile tissue". Why the *merely*, I always ask myself. Sometimes these medical men are a puzzle in their language. Just a sprig of erectile tissue indeed! And think of all the trouble it causes. Ah me; if you'd seen what I've seen you wouldn't have half the nervous energy I've got today.'

And so the saint prolonged his birthday celebrations by putting on pyjamas and indulging in a short song-cycle which included many old favourites and one curious little ditty which he sang only

on birthdays. It was called 'The Cruel Cruel Skipper' and had a
chorus which ended:

> *So he was an old sky plant, tum tum,*
> *So he was an old meat loaf, tum tum,*
> *So he was an old cantankeroo.*

And now, having virtually exhausted his legs by dancing and
his singing-voice with song, there remained a few brief conun-
drums which he enunciated to the ceiling, his arms behind his
head.

'Where did King Charles's executioner dine, and what did he
order?'

'I don't know.'

'Give in?'

'Yes.'

'Well he took a chop at the King's Head.'

Delighted clucks and chuckles!

'When may a gentleman's property be described as feathers?'

'I don't know.'

'Give in?'

'Yes.'

'When his estates are all entails (hen-tails, see?)'

The voice gradually fading, the clock running down, the eyes
closing, the chuckles trailing away languorously into sleep. And
it was thus that the saint slept at last, with his mouth open, upon
St George's Day.

So we walked back, arm in arm, through the shadowy archway,
laughing the compassionate laughter which the old man's image
deserved — laughter which in a way regilded the ikon, refuelled
the lamps about the shrine. Our footfalls hardly echoed on the
street's floor of tamped soil. The partial blackout of the area had
cut off the electric light which so brilliantly illuminated it under
normal conditions, and had been replaced by the oil lamps which
flickered wanly everywhere, so that we walked in a dark forest by
glow-worm light which made more than ever mysterious the
voices and the activities in the buildings around us. And at the
end of the street, where the rickety gharry stood awaiting us, came
the stirring cool breath of the night-sea which would gradually
infiltrate the town and disperse the heavy breathless damps from
the lake. We climbed aboard, the evening settling itself about us
cool as the veined leaves of a fig.

'And now I must dine you, Clea, to celebrate the new laughter!'

'No. I haven't finished yet. There is another tableau I want you to see, of a different kind. You see, Darley, I wanted to sort of recompose the city for you so that you could walk back into the painting from another angle and feel quite at home — though that is hardly the word for a city of exiles, is it? Anyhow. . . .' And leaning forward (I felt her breath on my cheek) she said to the jarvey, 'Take us to the Auberge Bleue!'

'More mysteries.'

'No. Tonight the Virtuous Semira makes her first appearance on the public stage. It is rather like a *vernissage* for me — you know, don't you, that Amaril and I are the authors of her lovely nose? It has been a tremendous adventure, these long months; and she has been very patient and brave under the bandages and grafts. Now it's complete. Yesterday they were married. Tonight all Alexandria will be there to see her. We shouldn't absent our-selves, should we? It characterizes something which is all too rare in the city and which you, as an earnest student of the matter, will appreciate. *Il s'agit de* Romantic Love with capital letters. My share in it has been a large one so let me be a bit boastful; I have been part duenna, part nurse, part artist, all for the good Amaril's sake. You see, she isn't very clever, Semira, and I have had to spend hours with her sort of preparing her for the world. Also brushing up her reading and writing. In short, trying to educate her a bit. It is curious in a way that Amaril does not regard this huge gap in their different educations as an obstacle. He loves her the more for it. He says: "I know she is rather simple-minded. That is what makes her so exquisite."

'This is the purest flower of romantic logic, no? And he has gone about her rehabilitation with immense inventiveness. I should have thought it somewhat dangerous to play at Pygmalion, but only now I begin to understand the power of the image. Do you know, for example, what he has devised for her in the way of a profession, a skill of her own? It shows brilliance. She would be too simple-minded to undertake anything very specialized so he has trained her, with my help, to be a doll's surgeon. His wedding-present to her is a smart little surgery for children's dolls which has already become tremendously fashionable though it won't officially open until they come back from the honeymoon. But this new job Semira has really grasped with both hands. For months we have been cutting up and repairing dolls together in preparation for this!

No medical student could have studied harder. "It is the only way" says Amaril "to hold a really stupid woman you adore. Give her something of her own to do." '

So we swayed down the long curving Corniche and back into the lighted area of the city where the blue street-lamps came up one by one to peer into the gharry at us as we talked; and all at once it seemed that past and present had joined again without any divisions in it, and that all my memories and impressions had ordered themselves into one complete pattern whose metaphor was always the shining city of the disinherited — a city now trying softly to spread the sticky prismatic wings of a new-born dragon-fly on the night. Romantic Love! Pursewarden used to call it 'The Comic Demon.'

The Auberge had not changed at all. It remained a lasting part of the furniture of my dreams, and here (like faces in a dream) were the Alexandrians themselves seated at flower-decked tables while a band softly punctuated their idleness with the Blues. The cries of welcome recalled vanished generosities of the old city. Athena Trasha with the silver crickets in her ears, droning Pierre Balbz who drank opium because it made the 'bones blossom', the stately Cervonis and the rash dexterous Martinengo girls, they were all there. All save Nessim and Justine. Even the good Pombal was there in full evening-dress so firmly ironed and starched as to give him the air of a monumental relief executed for the tomb of François Premier. With him was Fosca, warm and dark of colouring, whom I had not met before. They sat with their knuckles touching in a curious stiff rapture. Pombal was perched quite upright, attentive as a rabbit, as he gazed into her eyes — the eyes of this handsome young matron. He looked absurd. ('She calls him "Georges-Gaston" which for some reason quite delights him' said Clea.)

So we made our slow way from table to table, greeting old friends as we had often done in the past until we came to the little alcove table with its scarlet celluloid reservation card marked in Clea's name, where to my surprise Zoltan the waiter materialized out of nothing to shake my hand with warmth. He was now the resplendent *maître d'hôtel* and was in full fig, his hair cut *en brosse*. It seemed also that he was fully in the secret for he remarked under his breath to Clea that everything had been prepared in complete secrecy, and even went so far as to wink. 'I have Anselm outside watching. As soon as he sees Dr Amaril's car he will signal. Then the music will play — Madame Trasha has asked for the old "Blue Danube".' He clasped his hands together like a toad. 'Oh what a good idea of Athena's. Bravo!' cried Clea. It was indeed a gesture of affection for Amaril was the best Viennese waltzer in Alexandria, and though not a vain man was always absurdly delighted by his own prowess as a dancer. It could not fail to please him.

Neither had we long to wait; anticipation and suspense had hardly had time to become wearying when the band, which had been softly playing with one ear cocked for the sound of a car, so to speak, fell silent. Anselm appeared at the corner of the vestibule waving his napkin. They were coming! The musicians struck out one long quivering arpeggio such as normally brings a tzigane melody to a close, and then, as the beautiful figure of Semira appeared among the palms, they swung softly and gravely into the waltz measure of "The Blue Danube". I was suddenly quite touched to see the shy way that Semira hesitated on the threshold of that crowded ballroom; despite the magnificence of her dress and grooming those watching eyes intimidated her, made her lose her self-possession. She hovered with a soft indecision which reminded me of the way a sailing boat hangs pouting when the painter is loosed, the jib shaken out — as if slowly meditating for a long moment before she turns, with an almost audible sigh, to take the wind upon her cheek. But in this moment of charming irresolution Amaril came up behind her and took her arm. He himself looked, I thought, rather white and nervous despite the customary foppishness of his attire. Caught like this, in a moment of almost panic, he looked indeed absurdly young. Then he registered the waltz and stammered something to her with trembling lips, at the same time leading her down gravely among the tables to the edge of the floor where with a slow and perfectly turned movement they began to dance. With the first full figure of the waltz the confidence poured into them both — one could almost see it happening. They calmed, became still as leaves, and Semira closed her eyes while Amaril recovered his usual gay, self-confident smile. And everywhere the soft clapping welled up around them from every corner of the ballroom. Even the waiters seemed moved and the good Zoltan groped for a handkerchief, for Amaril was much-beloved.

Clea too looked quite shaken with emotion. 'Oh, quick, let's have a drink' she said 'for I've a huge lump in my throat and if I cry my make-up will run.'

CLEA

The batteries of champagne-bottles opened up from every corner of the ballroom now, and the floor filled with waltzers, the lights changed colour. Now blue now red now green I saw the smiling face of Clea over the edge of her champagne glass turned towards me with an expression of happy mockery. 'Do you mind if I get a little tipsy tonight to celebrate her successful nose? I think we can drink to their future without reserve for they will never leave each other; they are drunk with the knightly love one reads about in the Arthurian legends — knight and rescued lady. And pretty soon there will be children all bearing my lovely nose.'

'Of that you can't be sure.'

'Well, let me believe it.'

'Let's dance a while.'

And so we joined the thronging dancers in the great circle which blazed with spinning prismatic light hearing the soft drum-beats punctuate our blood, moving to the slow grave rhythms like the great wreaths of coloured seaweed swinging in some under-water lagoon, one with the dancers and with each other.

We did not stay late. As we came out into the cold damp air she shivered and half-fell against me, catching my arm.

'What is it?'

'I felt faint all of a sudden. It's passed.'

So back into the city along the windless seafront, drugged by the clop of the horse's hoofs on the macadam, the jingle of harness, the smell of straw, and the dying strains of music which flowed out of the ballroom and dwindled away among the stars. We paid off the cab at the Cecil and walked up the winding deserted street towards her flat arm-in-arm, hearing our own slow steps magnified by the silence. In a bookshop window there were a few novels, one by Pursewarden. We stopped for a moment to peer into the darkened shop and then resumed our leisurely way to the flat. 'You'll come in for a moment?' she said.

Here, too, the air of celebration was apparent, in the flowers and the small supper-table on which stood a champagne-bucket. 'I did not know we'd stay to dine at the Auberge, and prepared to feed you here if necessary' said Clea, dipping her fingers in the ice-water; she sighed with relief. 'At least we can have a night-cap together.'

Here at least there was nothing to disorient or disfigure memory for everything was exactly as I remembered it; I had stepped back into this beloved room as one might step into some favourite painting. Here it all was, the crowded bookshelves, heavy drawing-boards, small cottage piano, and the corner with the tennis racquet and fencing foils; on the writing desk, with its disorderly jumble of letters, drawings and bills, stood the candlesticks which she was now in the act of lighting. A bundle of paintings stood against the wall. I turned one or two round and stared at them curiously.

'My God! You've gone abstract, Clea.'

'I know! Balthazar hates them. It's just a phase I expect, so don't regard it as irrevocable or final. It's a different way of mobilizing one's feelings about paint. Do you loathe them?'

'No, they are stronger I think.'

'Hum. Candle-light flatters them with false chiaroscuro.'

'Perhaps.'

'Come, sit down; I've poured us a drink.'

As if by common consent we sat facing each other on the carpet as we had so often done in the past, cross-legged like 'Armenian tailors', as she had once remarked. We toasted each other in the rosy light of the scarlet candles which stood un-winking in the still air defining with their ghostly radiance the smiling mouth and candid features of Clea. Here, too, at last, on this memorable spot on the faded carpet, we embraced each other with — how to say it? — a momentous smiling calm, as if the cup of language had silently overflowed into these eloquent kisses which replaced words like the rewards of silence itself, perfecting thought and gesture. They were like soft cloud-formations which had distilled themselves out of a novel innocence, the veritable ache of desirelessness. My steps had led me back again, I realized, remembering the night so long ago when we had slept dreamlessly in each other's arms, to the locked door which had once refused me admission to her. Led me back once more to that point in time, that threshold, behind which the shade of Clea moved, smiling and irresponsible as a flower, after a huge arid detour in a desert of my own imaginings. I had not known then how to find the key to that door. Now of its own accord it was slowly opening. Whereas the other door which had once given me access to Justine had now locked irrevocably. Did not Pursewarden say something once about 'sliding-panels'? But he was talking of books, not of the human heart. In her face now there was neither guile nor premeditation mirrored, but only a sort of magnificent mischief which had captured the fine eyes, expressed itself in the firm and thoughtful way she drew my hands up inside her sleeves to offer herself to their embrace with the uxorious gesture of a woman offering her body to some priceless cloak. Or else to catch my hand, place it upon her heart and whisper 'Feel! It has stopped beating!' So we lingered, so we might have stayed, like rapt figures in some forgotten painting, unhurriedly savouring the happiness given to those who set out to enjoy each other without reservations or self-contempts, without the premeditated costumes of selfishness — the invented limitations of human love: but that suddenly the dark air of the night outside grew darker, swelled up with the ghastly tumescence of a sound which, like the frantic wing-beats of some prehistoric bird, swallowed the whole room, the candles, the figures. She shivered at the first terrible howl of the sirens but did not move; and all around us the city stirred to life like an ants' nest. Those streets which had been so dark and silent now began to echo with the sound of feet as people made their way to the air-raid shelters, rustling like a gust of dry autumn leaves whirled by the wind. Snatches of sleepy conversation, screams, laughter, rose to the silent window of the little room. The street had filled as suddenly as a dry river-bed when the spring rains fall.

'Clea, you should shelter.'

But she only pressed closer, shaking her head like someone drugged with sleep, or perhaps by the soft explosion of kisses which burst like bubbles of oxygen in the patient blood. I shook her softly, and she whispered: 'I am too fastidious to die with a lot of people like an old rats' nest. Let us go to bed together and ignore the loutish reality of the world.'

So it was that love-making itself became a kind of challenge to the whirlwind outside which beat and pounded like a thunderstorm of guns and sirens, igniting the pale skies of the city with the magnificence of its lightning-flashes. And kisses themselves became charged with the deliberate affirmation which can come only from the foreknowledge and presence of death. It would have been good to die at any moment then, for love and death had somewhere joined hands. It was an expression of her pride, too, to sleep there in the crook of my arm like a wild bird exhausted by its struggles with a limed twig, for all the world as if it were an ordinary summer night of peace. And lying awake at her side, listening to the infernal racket of gunfire and watching the stabbing and jumping of light behind the blinds I remembered how once in the remote past she had reminded me of the limitations which love illuminated in us: saying something about its capacity being limited to an iron ration for each soul and adding gravely: 'The love you feel for Melissa, the same love, is trying to work itself out through Justine.' Would I, by extension, find this to be true also of Clea? I did not like to think so — for these fresh and spontaneous embraces were as pristine as invention, and not like ill-drawn copies of past actions. They were the very improvisations of the heart itself — or so I told myself as I lay there trying so hard to recapture the elements of the feelings I had once woven around those other faces. Yes, improvisations upon reality itself, and for once devoid of the bitter impulses of the will. We had sailed into this calm water completely without premeditation, all canvas crowded on; and for the first time it felt natural to be where I was, drifting into sleep with her calm body lying beside me. Even the long rolling cannonades which shook the houses so, even the hail of shards which swept the streets, could not disturb the dreaming silence we harvested together. And when we awoke to find everything silent once more she lit a single candle and we lay by its flickering light, looking at each other, and talking in whispers.

'I am always so bad the first time, why is it?'

'So am I.'

'Are you afraid of me?'

'No. Nor of myself.'

'Did you ever imagine this?'

'We must both have done. Otherwise it would not have happened.'

'Hush! Listen.'

Rain was now falling in sheets as it so often did before dawn in Alexandria, chilling the air, washing down the stiffly clicking leaves of the palms in the Municipal Gardens, washing the iron grilles of the banks and the pavements. In the Arab town the earthen streets would be smelling like a freshly dug graveyard. The flower-sellers would be putting out their stocks to catch the freshness. I remembered their cry of 'Carnations, sweet as the breath of a girl!' From the harbour the smells of tar, fish and briny nets flowing up along the deserted streets to meet the scentless pools of desert air which would later, with the first sunlight, enter the town from the east and dry its damp façades. Somewhere, briefly, the hushing of the rain was pricked by the sleepy pang of a mandoline, inscribing on it a thoughtful and melancholy little air. I feared the intrusion of a single thought or idea which, inserting itself between these moments of smiling peace, might inhibit them, turn them to instruments of sadness. I thought too of the long journey we made from this very bed, since last we lay here together, through so many climates and countries, only to return once more to our starting-point, again captured once more by the gravitational field of the city. A new cycle which was opening upon the promise of such kisses and dazed endearments as we could now exchange — where would it carry us? I thought of some words of Arnauti, written about another woman, in another context: 'You tell yourself that it is a woman you hold in your arms, but watching the sleeper you see all her growth in time, the unerring unfolding of cells which group and dispose themselves into the beloved face which remains always and for ever mysterious — repeating to infinity the soft boss of the human nose, an ear borrowed from a sea-shell's helix, an eyebrow thought-patterned from ferns, or lips invented by bivalves in their dreaming union. All this process is human, bears a name which pierces your heart, and offers the mad dream of an eternity which time disproves in every drawn breath. And if human personality is an illusion? And if, as biology tells us, every single cell in our bodies is replaced every seven years by another? At the most I hold in my arms something like a fountain of flesh, continuously playing, and in my mind a rainbow of dust.' And like an echo from another point of the compass I heard the sharp voice of Purse-warden saying: 'There is no Other; there is only oneself facing forever the problem of one's self-discovery!'

I had drifted into sleep again; and when I woke with a start the bed was empty and the candle had guttered away and gone out. She was standing at the drawn curtains to watch the dawn break over the tumbled roofs of the Arab town, naked and slender as an Easter lily. In the spring sunrise, with its dense dew, sketched upon the silence which engulfs a whole city before the birds awaken it, I caught the sweet voice of the blind *muezzin* from the mosque reciting the *Ebed* — a voice hanging like a hair in the palm-cooled upper airs of Alexandria. 'I praise the perfection of God, the Forever existing; the perfection of God, the Desired, the Existing, the Single, the Supreme; the Perfection of God, the One, the Sole'. . . . . The great prayer wound itself in shining coils across the city as I watched the grave and passionate intensity of her turned head where she stood to observe the climbing sun touch the minarets and palms with light: rapt and awake. And listening I smelt the warm odour of her hair upon the pillow beside me. The buoyancy of a new freedom possessed me like a draught from what the Cabal once called 'The Fountain of All Existing Things'. I called 'Clea' softly, but she did not heed me; and so once more I slept. I knew that Clea would share everything with me, withholding nothing — not even the look of complicity which women reserve only for their mirrors.

* * * * *

II

So the city claimed me once more — the same city made now somehow less poignant and less terrifying than it had been in the past by new displacements in time. If some parts of the old fabric had worn away, others had been restored. In the first few weeks of my new employment I had time to experience both a sense of familiarity and one of alienation, measuring stability against change, past against present tense. And if the society of my friends remained relatively the same, new influences had entered, new winds had sprung up; we had all begun, like those figures on revolving turntables in jewellers' shops, to turn new facets of ourselves towards each other. Circumstances also helped to provide a new counterpoint, for the old, apparently unchanged city had now entered the penumbra of a war. For my part I had come to see it as it must always have been — a shabby little seaport built upon a sand-reef, a moribund and spiritless backwater. True this unknown factor 'war' had given it a specious sort of modern value, but this belonged to the invisible world of strategies and armies, not to ourselves, the inhabitants; it had swollen its population by many thousands of refugees in uniform and attracted those long nights of dull torment which were only relatively dangerous, for as yet the enemy was confining his operations strictly to the harbour area. Only a small area of the Arab quarter came under direct fire; the upper town remained relatively untouched, except perhaps for an occasional error of judgement. No, it was only the harbour at which the enemy scratched, like a dog at an inflamed scab. A mile away from it the bankers conducted their affairs by day as if from the immunity of New York. Intrusions into their world were rare and accidental. It came as a painful surprise to confront a shop-front which had been blasted in, or a lodging-house blown inside out with all its inhabitants' clothes hanging in festoons from the neighbouring trees. This was not part of the normal expectation of things; it had the shocking rarity value merely of some terrible street accident.

How had things changed? It was not danger, then, but a less easily analysable quality which made the notion of war distinctive;

a sensation of some change in the specific gravity of things. It was as if the oxygen content of the air we breathed were being steadily, invisibly reduced day by day; and side by side with this sense of inexplicable blood-poisoning came other pressures of a purely material kind brought about by the huge shifting population of soldiers in whom the blossoming of death released the passions and profligacies which lie buried in every herd. Their furious gaiety tried hard to match the gravity of the crisis in which they were involved; at times the town was racked by the frenetic out-bursts of their disguised spleen and boredom until the air became charged with the mad spirit of carnival; a saddening and heroic pleasure-seeking which disturbed and fractured the old har-monies on which personal relationships had rested, straining the links which bound us. I am thinking of Clea, and her loathing for the war and all it stood for. She feared, I think, that the vulgar blood-soaked reality of this war world which spread around her might one day poison and infect our own kisses. 'Is it fastidious to want to keep your head, to avoid this curious sexual rush of blood to the head which comes with war, exciting the women beyond endurance? I would not have thought the smell of death could be so exciting to them! Darley, I don't want to be a part of this mental saturnalia, these overflowing brothels. And all these poor men crowded up here. Alexandria has become a huge orphanage, everyone grabbing at the last chance of life. You haven't been long enough yet to feel the strain. The disorientation. The city was always perverse, but it took its pleasures with style at an old-fashioned tempo, even in rented beds: never up against a wall or a tree or a truck! And now at times the town seems to be like some great public urinal. You step over the bodies of drunk-ards as you walk home at night. I suppose the sunless have been robbed even of sensuality and drink compensates them for the loss! But there is no place in all this for me. I cannot see these soldiers as Pombal does. He gloats on them like a child — as if they were bright lead soldiers — because he sees in them the only hope that France will be freed. I only feel ashamed for them, as one might to see friends in convict garb; out of shame and sympathy I feel like turning my face away. Oh, Darley, it isn't very sensible, and I know I am doing them a grotesque injustice; possibly it is just selfishness. So I force myself to serve them teas at their various canteens, roll bandages, arrange concerts. But inside myself I shrink smaller every day. Yet I always believed that a love of human beings would flower more strongly out of a common misfortune. It isn't true. And now I am afraid that you too will begin to like me the less for these absurdities of thought, these revulsions of feeling. To be here, just the two of us, sitting by candlelight is almost a miracle in such a world. You can't blame me for trying to hoard and protect it against the intrusive world outside, can you? Curiously, what I hate most about it all is the sentimentality which spells violence in the end!'

I understood what she meant, and what she feared; and yet from the depths of my own inner selfishness I was glad of these external pressures, for they circumscribed our world perfectly, penned us up more closely together, isolated us! In the old world I would have had to share Clea with a host of other friends and admirers. Not now.

Curiously, too, some of these external factors around us, involving us in its death-struggles — gave our newest passion a fulfilment not based on desperation yet nevertheless built just as certainly upon the sense of impermanence. It was of the same order, though different in kind to the dull orgiastic rut of the various armies; it was quite impossible to repudiate the truth, namely, that death (not even at hand, but in the air) sharpens kisses, adds unbearable poignance to every smile and handclasp. Even though I was no soldier the dark question mark hovered over our thoughts, for the real issues of the heart were influenced by something of which we were all, however reluctantly, part: a whole world. If the war did not mean a way of dying, it meant a way of ageing, of tasting the true staleness in human things, and of learning to confront change bravely. No-one could tell what lay beyond the closed chapter of every kiss. In those long quiet evenings before the bombardment began we would sit upon that small square of carpet by the light of candles, debating these matters, punctuating our silences with embraces which were the only inadequate answer we could offer to the human situation. Nor, lying in each other's arms during those long nights of fitful sleep broken by the sirens, did we ever (as if by a silent convention) speak of love. To have uttered the word might acknowledge a more rare yet less perfect variety of the state which now bewitched us, perfected in us this quite unpremeditated relationship. Somewhere in *Moeurs* there is a passionate denunciation of the word. I cannot remember into whose mouth the speech has been put — perhaps Justine's. 'It may be defined as a cancerous growth of unknown origin which may take up its site anywhere without the subject knowing or wishing it. How often have you tried to love the "right" person in vain, even when your heart knows it has found him after so much seeking? No, an eyelash, a perfume, a haunting walk, a strawberry on the neck, the smell of almonds on the breath — these are the accomplices the spirit seeks out to plan your overthrow.'

Thinking of such passages of savage insight — and they are many in that strange book — I would turn to the sleeping Clea and study her quiet profile in order to . . . to ingest her, drink the whole of her up without spilling a drop, mingle my very heart-beats with hers. 'However near we would wish to be, so far exactly do we remain from each other' wrote Arnauti. It seemed to be no longer true of our condition. Or was I simply deluding myself once more, refracting truth by the disorders inherent in my own vision? Strangely enough I neither knew nor cared now; I had stopped rummaging through my own mind, had learned to take her like a clear draught of spring water.

'Have you been watching me asleep?'

'Yes.'

'Unfair! But what thinking?'

'Many things.'

'Unfair to watch a sleeping woman, off her guard.'

'Your eyes have changed colour again. Smoke."

(A mouth whose paint blurred slightly under kisses. The two small commas, which were almost cusps, almost ready to turn into dimples when the lazy smiles broke surface. She stretches and places her arms behind her head, pushing back the helmet of fair hair which captures the sheen of the candle-light. In the past she had not possessed this authority over her own beauty. New gestures, new tendrils had grown, languorous yet adept to express this new maturity. A limpid sensuality which was now undivided by hesitations, self-questionings. A transformation of the old 'silly goose' into this fine, indeed impressive, personage, quite at one with her own body and mind. How had this come about?)

I: 'That commonplace book of Pursewarden's. How the devil did you come by it? I took it to the office today.'

She: 'Liza. I asked her for something to remember him by. Absurd. As if one could forget the brute! He's everywhere. Did the notes startle you?'

I: 'Yes. It was as if he had appeared at my elbow. The first thing I fell upon was a description of my new chief, Maskelyne by name. It seems Pursewarden worked with him once. Shall I read it to you?'

She: 'I know it.'

('Like most of my compatriots he had a large hand-illuminated sign hanging up on the front of his mind reading ON NO ACCOUNT DISTURB. At some time in the distant past he had been set going like a quartz clock. He will run his course unfaltering as a metronome. Do not let the pipe alarm you. It is intended to give a judicial air. White man smoke puff puff, white man ponder puff puff. In fact white man is deeply deeply asleep under the badges of office, the pipe, the nose, the freshly starched handkerchief sticking out of his sleeve.')

She: 'Did you read it to Maskelyne?'

I: 'Naturally not.'

She: 'There are wounding things about all of us in it; perhaps that is why I took a fancy to it! I could hear the brute's voice as he uttered them. You know, my dear, I think I am the only person to have loved old Pursewarden for himself while he was alive. I got his wavelength. I loved him for himself, I say, because strictly he *had* no self. Of course he could be tiresome, difficult, cruel — like everyone else. But he exemplified something — a grasp on something. That is why his work will live and go on giving off light, so to speak. Light me a cigarette. He had cut a foothold in the cliff a bit higher than I could dare to go — the point where one looks at the top because one is afraid to look down! You tell me that Justine also says something like this. I suppose she got the same thing in a way — but I suspect her of being merely grateful to him, like an animal whose master pulls a thorn from its paw. His intuition was very feminine and much sharper than hers — and you know that women instinctively like a man with plenty of female in him; *there*, they suspect, is the only sort of lover who can sufficiently identify himself with them to . . . deliver them of being just women, catalysts, strops, oil-stones. Most of us have to be content to play the role of *machine à plaisir!*'

I: 'Why do you laugh, suddenly like that?'

She: 'I was remembering making a fool of myself with Pursewarden. I suppose I should feel ashamed of it! You will see what he says about me in the notebook. He calls me "a juicy Hanoverian goose, the only truly kallipygous girl in the city"! I cannot think what possessed me, except that I was so worried about my painting. It had dried up on me. I couldn't get any further somehow, canvas gave me a headache. I finally decided that the question of my own blasted virginity was the root cause of the business. You know it is a terrible business to be a virgin — it is like not having one's Matric or Bac. You long to be delivered from it yet . . . at the same time this valuable experience should be with someone whom you care for, otherwise it will be without value to your inside self. Well, there I was, stuck. So with one of those characteristic strokes of fancy which in the past confirmed for everyone my stupidity I decided — guess what? To offer myself grimly to the only artist I knew I could trust, to put me out of my misery. Pursewarden, I thought, might have an understanding of my state and some consideration for my feelings. I'm amused to remember that I dressed myself up in a very heavy tweed costume and flat shoes, and wore dark glasses. I was timid, you see, as well as desperate. I walked up and down the corridor of the hotel outside his room for ages in despair and apprehension, my dark glasses firmly on my nose. He was inside. I could hear him whistling as he always did when he was painting a water colour; a maddening tuneless whistle! At last I burst in on him like a fireman into a burning building, startling him, and said with trembling lips: "I have come to ask you to *dépuceler* me, please, because I cannot get any further with my work unless you do." I said it in French. It would have sounded dirty in English. He was startled. All sorts of conflicting emotions flitted across his face for a second. And then, as I burst into tears and sat down suddenly on a chair he threw his head back and roared with laughter. He laughed until the tears ran down his cheeks while I sat there in my dark glasses sniffing. Finally he collapsed exhausted on his bed and lay staring at the ceiling. Then he got up, put his arms on my shoulders, removed my glasses, kissed me, and put them back. Then he put his hands on his hips and laughed again. "My dear Clea" he said, "it would be anyone's dream to take you to bed, and I must confess that in a corner of my mind I have often allowed the thought to wander but . . . dearest angel, you have spoilt everything. *This* is no way to enjoy you, and no way for you to enjoy yourself. Forgive my laughing! You have effectively spoiled my dream. Offering yourself *this* way, without *wanting* me, is such an insult to my male vanity that I simply would not be able to comply with your demand. It is, I suppose, a compliment that you chose me

rather than someone else — but my vanity is larger than that!
In fact your request is like a pailful of slops emptied over my head!
I shall always treasure the compliment and regret the refusal but
. . . if only you had chosen some other way to do it, how glad I
would have been to oblige! Why did you have to let me see that
you really did not care for *me*?"

'He blew his nose gravely in a corner of the sheet, took my
glasses and placed them on his own nose to examine himself in
the mirror. Then he came and stared at me until the comedy overflowed again and we both started laughing. I felt an awful sense
of relief. And when I had repaired my damaged make-up in the
mirror he allowed me to take him to dinner to discuss the problem
of paint with magnificent, generous honesty. The poor man
listened with such patience to my rigmarole! He said: "I can only
tell you what I know, and it isn't much. First you have to know and
understand intellectually what you want to do — then you have
to sleep-walk a little to reach it. The real obstacle is oneself.
I believe that artists are composed of vanity, indolence and self-
regard. Work-blocks are caused by the swelling-up of the ego on
one or all of these fronts. You get a bit scared about the imaginary
importance of what you are doing! Mirror-worship. My solution
would be to slap a poultice on the inflamed parts — tell your ego
to go to hell and not make a misery of what should be essentially
fun, joy." He said many other things that evening, but I have
forgotten the rest; but the funny thing was that just talking to him,
just being talked to, seemed to clear the way ahead again. Next
day he sent me a page of oracular notes about art.* I started work
again, clear as a bell, the next morning. Perhaps in a funny sort
of way he did *dépuceler* me? I regretted not being able to reward
him as he deserved, but I realized that he was right. I would have
to wait for a tide to turn. And this did not happen until later, in
Syria. There was something bitter and definitive about it when it
came, and I made the usual mistakes one makes from inexperience
and paid for them. Shall I tell you?'
I: 'Only if you wish.'
She: 'I found myself suddenly and hopelessly entangled with
someone I had admired some years before but never quite imagined in the context of a lover. Chance brought us together for a
few short months. I think that neither of us had foreseen this
sudden *coup de foudre*. We both caught fire, as if somewhere
an invisible burning glass had been playing on us without our

being aware. It is curious that an experience so wounding can also be recognized as good, as positively nourishing. I suppose I was even a bit eager to be wounded — or I would not have made the mistakes I did. He was somebody already committed to someone else, so there was never, from the beginning, any pretence of permanence in our liaison. Yet (and here comes my famous stupidity again) I very much wanted to have a child by him. A moment's thought would have shown me that it would have been impossible; but the moment's thought only supervened when I was already pregnant. I did not, I thought, care that he must go away, marry someone else. I would at least have his child! But when I confessed it — at the very moment the words left my lips — I suddenly woke up and realized that this would be to perpetuate a link with him to which I had no right. To put it plainly I should be taking advantage of him, creating a responsibility which would shackle him throughout his marriage. It came to me in a flash, and I swallowed my tongue. By the greatest luck he had not heard my words. He was lying like you are now, half asleep, and had not caught my whisper. "What did you say?" he said. I substituted another remark, made up on the spur of the moment. A month later he left Syria. It was a sunny day full of the sound of bees. I knew I should have to destroy the child. I bitterly regretted it, but there seemed no other honourable course to take in the matter. You will probably think I was wrong, but even now I am glad I took the course I did, for it would have perpetuated something which had no right to exist outside the span of these few golden months. Apart from that I had nothing to regret. I had been immeasurably grown-up by the experience. I was full of gratitude and still am. If I am generous now in my love-making it is perhaps because I am paying back the debt, refunding an old love in a new. I entered a clinic and went through with it. Afterwards the kindly old anaesthetist called me to the dirty sink to show me the little pale homunculus with its tiny members. I wept bitterly. It looked like a smashed yolk of an egg. The old man turned it over curiously with a sort of spatula — as one might turn over a rasher of bacon in a frying-pan. I could not match his cold scientific curiosity and felt rather sick. He smiled and said: "It is all over. How relieved you must feel!" It was true, with my sadness there was a very real relief at having done what I recognized as the right thing. Also a sense of loss; my heart felt like a burgled swallow's nest. And so back to the mountains, to the same easel and white canvas.

It is funny but I realized that precisely what wounded me most as a woman nourished me most as an artist. But of course I missed him for a long time: just a physical being whose presence attaches itself without one's knowing, like a piece of cigarette paper to the lip. It hurts to pull it away. Bits of the skin come off! But hurt or not, I learned to bear it and even to cherish it, for it allowed me to come to terms with another illusion. Or rather to see the link between body and spirit in a new way — for the physique is only the outer periphery, the contours of the spirit, its solid part. Through smell, taste, touch we apprehend each other, ignite each other's minds; information conveyed by the body's odours after orgasm, breath, tongue-taste — through these one "knows" in quite primeval fashion. Here was a perfectly ordinary man with no exceptional gifts but in his elements, so to speak, how good for me; he gave off the odours of good natural objects: like newly baked bread, roasting coffee, cordite, sandalwood. In this field of *rapport* I missed him like a skipped meal — I know it sounds vulgar! Paracelsus says that thoughts are acts. Of them all, I suppose, the sex act is the most important, the one in which our spirits most divulge themselves. Yet one feels it a sort of clumsy paraphrase of the poetic, the noetic, *thought* which shapes itself into a kiss or an embrace. Sexual love *is* knowledge, both in etymology and in cold fact; "he knew her" as the Bible says! Sex is the joint or coupling which unites the male and female ends of knowledge merely — a cloud of unknowing! When a culture goes bad in its sex all knowledge is impeded. We women know that. That was when I wrote to you asking if I should come to visit you in your island. How grateful I am that you did not answer me! It would have been a wrong move at the time. Your silence saved me! Ah! my dear, forgive me if I bore you with my wanderings for I see that you are looking somewhat sleepy! But with you it is such a pleasure to talk away the time between love-making! It is a novelty for me. Apart from you there is only dear Balthazar — whose rehabilitation, by the way, is going on apace. But he has told you? He has been inundated with invitations since the Mountolive banquet, and it seems will have little difficulty in rebuilding the clinic practice again.'

I: 'But he is far from reconciled to his teeth.'

She: 'I know. And he is still rather shaken and hysterical — as who would not be. But everything goes forward steadily, and I think he will not lapse.'

I: 'But what of this sister of Pursewarden's?'

She: 'Liza! I think you will admire her, though I can't tell if you will like her. She is rather impressive, indeed perhaps just a little bit frightening. The blindness does not seem like an incapacity, rather it gives an expression of double awareness. She listens to one as if one were music, an extra intentness which makes one immediately aware of the banality of most of one's utterances. She's unlike him, yet very beautiful though deathly pale, and her movements are swift and absolutely certain, unlike most blind people. I have never seen her miss a doorhandle or trip on a mat, or pause to get her bearings in a strange place. All the little errors of judgement the blind make, like talking to a chair which had just been vacated by its owner . . . they are absent. One wonders sometimes if she really is blind. She came out here to collect his effects and to gather material about him for a biography.'

I: 'Balthazar hinted at some sort of mystery.'

She: 'There is little doubt that David Mountolive is hopelessly in love with her; and from what he told Balthazar it began in London. It is certainly an unusual liaison for someone so correct, and it obviously gives them both a great deal of pain. I often imagine them, the snow falling in London, suddenly finding themselves face to face with the Comic Demon! Poor David! And yet why should I utter such a patronizing phrase? Lucky David! Yes, I can tell you a little, based on a scrap of his conversation. Suddenly, in a moribund taxi speeding away to the suburbs she turned her face to him and told him that she had been told to expect him many years ago; that the moment she heard his voice she knew that he was the dark princely stranger of the prophecy. He would never leave her. And she only asked leave to verify it, pressing her cold fingers to his face to feel it all over, before sinking back on the cold cushions with a sigh! Yes, it was he. It must have been strange to feel the fingers of the blind girl pressing one's features with a sculptor's touch. David said that a shudder ran through him, all the blood left his face, and his teeth began to chatter! He groaned aloud and clenched them together. So they sat there, hand in hand, trembling while the snowlit suburbs shuttled by the windows. Later she placed his finger upon the exact configuration in her hand which portended an altered life, and the emergence of this unexpected figure which would dominate it! Balthazar is sceptical of such prophecies, as you are,

740

and he cannot avoid a note of amused irony in recounting the story. But so far the enchantment seems to have lasted, so perhaps you will concede something to the power of prophecy, sceptic that you are! And well: with her brother's death she arrived here, has been sorting out papers and manuscripts, as well as interviewing people who knew him. She came here once or twice to talk to me; it wasn't altogether easy for me, though I told her all that I could remember of him. But I think the question which really filled her mind was one which she did not actually utter, namely, had I ever been Pursewarden's mistress? She circled round and round it warily. I think, no, I am sure that she thought me a liar because what I had to tell her was so inconsequent. Indeed perhaps its vagueness suggested that I had something to conceal. In the studio I still have the plaster negative of the death-mask which I showed Balthazar how to make. She held it to her breast for a moment as if to suckle it, with an expression of intense pain, her blind eyes seeming to grow larger and larger until they overflowed the whole face, and turned it into a cave of interrogation. I was horribly embarrassed and sad to suddenly notice, sticking in the plaster, a few little shreds of his moustache. And when she tried to place the negative together and apply it to her own features I almost caught her hand lest she feel them. An absurdity! But her manner startled and upset me. Her questions put me on edge. There was something shamefully inconclusive about these interviews, and I was mentally apologizing to Pursewarden all the time in my mind for not making a better showing; one should, after all, be able to find something sensible to say of a great man whom one fully recognized in his lifetime. Not like poor Amaril who was so furious to see Pursewarden's death-mask lying near that of Keats and Blake in the National Portrait Gallery. It was all he could do, he says, to prevent himself from giving the insolent thing a smack with his hand. Instead he abused the object, saying: "*Salaud!* Why did you not tell me you were a great man passing through my life? I feel defrauded in not noticing your existence, like a child whom someone forgot to tell, and who missed the Lord Mayor riding by in his coach!" I had no such excuse myself, and yet what could I find to say? You see, I think a cardinal factor in all this is that Liza lacks a sense of humour; when I said that in thinking of Pursewarden I found myself instinctively smiling she put on a puzzled frown of interrogation merely. It is possible that they never laughed together, I told myself; yet their only real similarity in the physical sense is in the alignment of teeth and the cut of the mouth. When she is tired she wears the rather insolent expression which, on his face, heralded a witticism! But I expect you too will have to see her, and tell her what you know, what you can remember. It is not easy, facing those blind eyes, to know where to begin! As for Justine, she has luckily been able to escape Liza so far; I suppose the break between Mount-olive and Nessim has presented an effective enough excuse. Or perhaps David has convinced her that any contact might be com-promising to him officially. I do not know. But I am certain that she has not seen Justine. Perhaps you will have to supply her with a picture, for the only references in Pursewarden's notes are cruel and perfunctory. Have you reached the passages yet in the com-monplace book? No. You will. I'm afraid none of us gets off very lightly there! As for any really profound mystery I think Balthazar is wrong. Essentially I think that the problem which engulfs them is simply the effect upon him of her blindness. In fact I am sure from the evidence of my own eyes. Through the old telescope of Nessim . . . yes, the same one! It used to be in the Summer Palace, do you recall? When the Egyptians began to expropriate Nessim all Alexandria got busy to defend its darling. We all bought things from him, intending to hold them for him until everything had blown over. The Cervonis bought the Arab stock, Ganzo the car, which he resold to Pombal, and Pierre Balbz the telescope. As he had nowhere to house it Mountolive let him put it on the veranda of the summer legation, an ideal site. One can sweep the harbour and most of the town, and in the summer dinner guests can do a little mild star-gazing. Well, I went up there one afternoon and was told that they were both out for a walk, which by the way was a daily custom all winter with them. They would take the car down to the Corniche and walk along the Stanley Bay front arm in arm for half an hour. As I had time to kill I started to fool with the telescope, and idly trained it on the far corner of the bay. It was a blowy day, with high seas running, and the black flags out which signalled dangerous bathing. There were only a few cars about in that end of the town, and hardly anyone on foot. Quite soon I saw the Embassy car come round the corner and stop on the seafront. Liza and David got down and began to walk away from it towards the beach end. It was amazing how clearly I could see them; I had the impression that I could touch them by just putting out a hand. They were arguing furiously, and she had an expression of grief and pain on her face. I increased the magnification until I discovered with a shock that I could literally lip-read their remarks! It was startling, indeed a little frightening. I could not "hear" him because his face was half turned aside, but Liza was looking into my telescope like a giant image on a cinema screen. The wind was blowing her dark hair back in a shock from her temples, and with her sightless eyes she looked like some strange Greek statue come to life. She shouted through her tears, "No, you *could* not have a blind Ambassadress", turning her head from side to side as if trying to find a way of escaping this fearful truth — which I must admit had not occurred to me until the words registered. David had her by the shoulders and was saying something very earnestly, but she wasn't heeding. Then with a sudden twist she broke free and with a single jump cleared the parapet like a stag, to land upon the sand. She began to run towards the sea. David shouted something, and stood for a second gesticulating at the top of the stone steps to the beach. I had such a distinct picture of him then, in that beautifully cut suit of pepper and salt, the flower in his button-hole and the old brown waistcoat he loves with its gun-metal buttons. He looked a strangely ineffectual and petulant figure, his moustache flying in the wind as he stood there. After a second of indecision he too jumped down on to the sand and started after her. She ran very fast right into the water which splashed up, darkening her skirt about her thighs and braking her. Then she halted in sudden indecision and turned back, while he, rushing in after her, caught her by the shoulders and embraced her. They stood for a moment — it was so strange — with the waves thumping their legs; and then he drew her back to the shore with a strange look of gratitude and exultation on his face — as if he were simply delighted by this strange gesture. I watched them hurry back to the car. The anxious chauffeur was standing in the road with his cap in his hand, obviously relieved not to have been called upon to do any life-saving. I thought to myself then: "A blind Ambassadress? Why not? If David were a meaner-spirited man he might think to himself: 'The originality alone would help rather than hinder my career in creating for me artificial sympathies to replace the respectful admiration which I dare only to claim by virtue of my position!' But he would be too single-minded for any such thoughts to enter his mind."

'Yet when they arrived back for tea, soaked, he was strangely elated. "We had a little accident" he called gaily as he retired with

her for a change of clothes. And of course there was no further reference to the escapade that evening. Later he asked me if I would undertake a portrait of Liza and I agreed. I do not know quite why I felt a sense of misgiving about it. I could not refuse yet I have found several ways of delaying the business and would like to put it off indefinitely if I could. It is curious to feel as I do, for she would be a splendid subject and perhaps if she had several sittings we might get to know each other a little and ease the constraint I feel when I am with her. Besides, I would really like to do it for his sake, for he has always been a good friend. But there it is. . . . I shall be curious to know what she has to ask you about her brother. And curious to see what you will find to say about him.'
I: 'He seems to change shape so quickly at every turn of the road that one is forced to revise each idea about him almost as soon as it is formulated. I'm beginning to wonder about one's right to pronounce in this fashion on unknown people.'
She: 'I think, my dear, you have a mania for exactitude and an impatience with partial knowledge which is . . . well, unfair to knowledge itself. How can it be anything but imperfect? I don't suppose reality ever bears a close resemblance to human truth as, say, El Scob to Yacoub. Myself I would like to be content with the poetic symbolism it presents, the shape of nature itself as it were. Perhaps this was what Pursewarden was trying to convey in those outrageous attacks upon you — have you come to the passages called "My silent conversations with Brother Ass"?'
I: 'Not yet.'
She: 'Don't be too wounded by them. You must exonerate the brute with a good-natured laugh, for after all he was one of us, one of the tribe. Relative size of accomplishment doesn't matter. As he himself says: "There is not enough faith, charity or tenderness to furnish this world with a single ray of hope — yet so long as that strange sad cry rings out over the world, the birth-pangs of an artist — all cannot be lost! This sad little squeak of rebirth tells us that all still hangs in the balance. Heed me, reader, for the artist is you, all of us — the statue which must disengage itself from the dull block of marble which houses it, and start to live. But when? But when?" And then in another place he says: "Religion is simply art bastardized out of all recognition" — a characteristic remark. It was the central point of his difference with Balthazar and the Cabal. Pursewarden had turned the whole central proposition upside down.'

I: 'To suit his private ends.'

She: 'No. To suit his own immortal needs. There was nothing dishonest about it all. If you are born of the artist tribe it is a waste of time to try and function as a priest. You have to be faithful to your angle of vision, and at the same time fully recognize its partiality. There is a kind of perfection to be achieved in matching oneself to one's capacities — at every level. This must, I imagine, do away with striving, and with illusions too. I myself always admired old Scobie as a thoroughly successful example of this achievement in his own way. He was quite successfully himself I thought.'

I: 'Yes, I suppose so. I was thinking of him today. His name cropped up at the office in some connection. Clea, imitate him again. You do it so perfectly that I am quite dumb with admiration.'

She: 'But you know all his stories.'

I: 'Nonsense. They were inexhaustible.'

She: 'And I wish I could imitate his expression! That look of portentous owlishness, the movement of the glass eye! Very well; but close your eyes and hear the story of Toby's downfall, one of his many downfalls. Are you ready?'

I: 'Yes.'

She: 'He told it to me in the course of a dinner-party just before I went to Syria. He said he had come into some money and insisted on taking me to the Lutetia in ceremonial fashion where we dined on *scampi* and Chianti. It began like this in a low confidential tone. "Now the thing about Toby that characterized him was a superb effrontery, the fruit of perfect breeding! I told you his father was an M.P.? No? Funny, I thought I mentioned it in passing. Yes, he was very highly placed, you might say. But Toby never boasted of it. In fact, and *this* shows you, he actually asked me to treat the matter with discretion and not mention it to his shipmates. He didn't want any favours, he said. He didn't want people sucking up to him neither, just because his father was an M.P. He wanted to go through life incognito, he said, and make his own career by hard work. Mind you, he was almost continuously in trouble with the upper deck. It was his religious convictions more than anything, I think. He had a remorseless taste for the cloth did old Toby. He was vivid. The only career he wanted was to be a sky-pilot. But somehow he couldn't get himself ordained. *They* said he drank too much. But *he* said it was because his vocation was so strong that it pushed him to excesses. If only they'd ordain him, he said, everything would be all right. He'd come right off the drink. He told me this many a time when he was on the Yokohama run. When he was drunk he was always trying to hold services in Number One hold. Naturally people complained and at Goa the captain made a bishop come aboard to reason with him. It was no go. 'Scurvy' he used to say to me, 'Scurvy, I shall die a martyr to my vocation, that's what.' But there's nothing in life like determination. Toby had plenty of it. And I wasn't at all surprised one day, after many years, to see him come ashore ordained. Just how he'd squeezed into the Church he would never tell. But one of his mates said that he got a slightly tainted Chinese Catholic bishop to ordain him on the sly in Hong Kong. Once the articles were all signed, sealed and wrapped up there was nothing anyone could do, so the Church had to put a good face on it, taint and all. After that he became a holy terror, holding services everywhere and distributing cigarette cards of the saints. The ship he was serving on got fed up and paid him off. They framed him up; said he had been seen going ashore carrying a lady's handbag! Toby denied it and said it was something religious, a chasuble or something that they mistook for a handbag. Anyway he turned up on a passenger-ship next carrying pilgrims. He said that at last he had fulfilled himself. Services all day long in 'A' Lounge, and no one to hinder the word of the Lord. But I noticed with alarm that he was drinking more heavily than before and he had a funny cracked sort of laugh. It wasn't the old Toby. I wasn't surprised to hear he had been in trouble again. Apparently he had been suspected of being drunk on duty and of having made an unflattering reference to a bishop's posterior. Now this shows his superb cleverness, for when he came up for court martial he had the perfect answer ready. I don't quite know how they do court martials in the Church, but I suppose this pilgrim boat was full of bishops or something and they did it drum-head fashion in 'A' Lounge. But Toby was too fast for them with his effrontery. There's nothing like breeding to make you quick at answering. His defence was that if anyone *had* heard him breathing heavily at Mass it was his asthma; and secondly he hadn't never mentioned anyone's posterior. He had talked about a bishop's *fox terrier!* Isn't it dazzling? It was the smartest thing he ever did, old Toby, though I've never known him at a loss for a clever answer. Well, the bishops were so staggered that they let him off with a caution and a thousand Ave Marias as a penance. This was pretty easy for

Toby; in fact it was no trouble at all because he'd bought a little Chinese prayer-wheel which Budgie had fixed up to say Ave Marias for him. It was a simple little device, brilliantly adapted to the times as you might say. One revolution was an Ave Maria or fifty beads. It simplified prayer, he said; in fact one could go on praying without thinking. Later someone told on him and it was confiscated by the head bloke. Another caution for poor Toby. But nowadays he treated everything with a toss of the head and a scornful laugh. He was riding for a fall, you see. He had got a bit above himself. I couldn't help noticing how much he'd changed because he touched here nearly every week with these blinking pilgrims. I think they were Italians visiting the Holy Places. Back and forth they went, and with them Toby. But he had changed. He was always in trouble now, and seemed to have thrown off all restraint. He had gone completely fanciful. Once he called on me dressed as a cardinal with a red beret and a sort of lampshade in his hand. 'Cor!' I gasped. 'You aren't half orchidaceous, Toby!' Later he got very sharply told off for dressing above his rank, and I could see that it was only a matter of time before he fell out of the balloon, so to speak. I did what I could as an old friend to reason with him but somehow I couldn't bring him to see the point. I even tried to get him back on to beer but it wasn't any go at all. Nothing but fire water for Toby. Once I had to have him carried back aboard by the police. He was all figged up in a prelate's costume. I think they call it a shibboleth. And he tried to pronounce an anathema on the city from 'A' Boat Deck. He was waving an apse or something. The last thing I saw of him was a lot of real bishops restraining him. They were nearly as purple as his own borrowed robes. My, how those Italians carried on! Then came the crash. They nabbed him in fragrant delicto swigging the sacramental wine. You know it has the Pope's Seal on it, don't you? You buy it from Cornford's, the Ecclesiastical Retailers in Bond Street, ready sealed and blessed. Toby had *broken the seal*. He was finished. I don't know whether they excommunicate or what, but anyway he was struck off the register properly. The next time I saw him he was a shadow of his old self and dressed as an ordinary seaman. He was still drinking heavily but in a different way now, he said. 'Scurvy' he said. 'Now I simply drink to expiate my sins. I'm drinking as a punishment now, not a pleasure. The whole tragedy had made him very moody and restless. He talked of going off to Japan and becoming a religious body there. The only thing that prevented him was that there you have to shave your head and he couldn't bear to part with his hair which was long, and was justly admired by his friends. 'No' he said, after discussing the idea, 'no, Scurvy old man, I couldn't bring myself to go about as bald as an egg, after what I've been through. It would give me a strangely roofless appearance at my age. Besides once when I was a nipper I got ringworm and lost my crowning glory. It took ages to grow again. It was so slow that I feared it never would come into bloom again. Now I couldn't bear to be parted from it. Not for anything.' I saw his dilemma perfectly, but I didn't see any way out for him. He would always be a square peg would old Toby, swimming against the stream. Mind you, it was a mark of his originality. For a little while he managed to live by blackmailing all the bishops who'd been to confession while he was O.C. Early Mass, and twice he got a free holiday in Italy. But then other troubles came his way and he shipped to the Far East, working in Seamen's Hostels when he was ashore, and telling everyone that he was going to make a fortune out of smuggled diamonds. I see him very rarely now, perhaps once every three years, and he never writes; but I'll never forget old Toby. He was always such a gentleman in spite of his little mishaps, and when his father dies he expects to have a few hundred a year of his own. Then we're going to join forces in Horsham with Budgie and put the earth-closet trade on a real economic basis. Old Budgie can't keep books and files. That's a job for me with my police training. At least so old Toby always said. I wonder where he is now?" '

The recital ended, the laughter suddenly expired and a new expression appeared on Clea's face which I did not remember ever having seen before. Something between a doubt and an apprehension which played about the mouth like a shadow. She added with a studied naturalness which was somehow strained: 'Afterwards he told my fortune. I know you will laugh. He said he could only do it with certain people and at certain times. Will you believe me if I tell you that he described with perfect fidelity and in complete detail the whole Syrian episode?' She turned her face to the wall with an abrupt movement and to my surprise I saw her lips were trembling. I put my hand up her warm shoulder and said 'Clea' very softly. 'What is it?' Suddenly she cried out: 'Oh, leave me alone. Can't you see I want to sleep?'

*　　*　　*　　*　　*

III

MY CONVERSATIONS WITH BROTHER ASS
(being extracts from Pursewarden's Notebook)

With what a fearful compulsion we return to it again and again — like a tongue to a hollow tooth — this question of writing! Can writers talk nothing but shop then? No. But with old Darley I am seized with a sort of convulsive vertigo for, while we have everything in common, I find I cannot talk to him at all. But wait. I mean that I do talk: endlessly, passionately, hysterically without uttering a word aloud! There is no way to drive a wedge between his ideas which, *ma foi*, are thoughtful, orderly, the very essence of 'soundness'. Two men propped on bar-stools thoughtfully gnawing at the universe as if at a stick of sugar-cane! The one speaks in a low, modulated voice, using language with tact and intuition; the other shifts from buttock to listless buttock shamefacedly shouting in his own mind, but only answering with an occasional affirmative or negative to these well-rounded propositions which are, for the most part, incontestably valuable and true! This would perhaps make the germ of a short story? ('But Brother Ass, there is a whole dimension lacking to what you say. How is it possible for one to convey this in Oxford English?') Still with sad penitential frowns the man on the high bar-stool proceeds with his exposition about the problem of the creative act — I ask you! From time to time he shoots a shyish sideways glance at his tormentor — for in a funny sort of way I do seem to torment him; otherwise he would not always be at me, aiming the button of his foil at the chinks in my self-esteem, or at the place where he believes I must keep my heart. No, we would be content with simpler conversational staples like the weather. In me he scents an enigma, something crying out for the probe. ('But Brother Ass, I am as clear as a bell — a sancing bell! The problem is there, here, nowhere!') At times while he is talking like this I have the sudden urge to jump on his back and ride him frantically up and down Rue Fuad, thrashing him with a Thesaurus and crying: 'Awake, moon-calf! Let me take you by your long silken jackass's ears and drive you at a gallop through the waxworks of our literature, among the clicking of

749

Box Brownies each taking its monochrome snapshots of so-called reality! Together we will circumvent the furies and become celebrated for our depiction of the English scene, of English life which moves to the stately rhythm of an autopsy! Do you hear me, Brother Ass?'

He does not hear, he will not hear. His voice comes to me from a great way off, as if over a faulty land-line. 'Hullo! Can you hear me?' I cry, shaking the receiver. I hear his voice faintly against the roaring of Niagara Falls. 'What is that? Did you say that you wished to contribute to English literature? What, to arrange a few sprigs of parsley over this dead turbot? To blow diligently into the nostrils of this corpse? Have you mobilized your means, Brother Ass? Have you managed to annul your early pot-training? Can you climb like a cat-burglar with loosened sphincters? But then what will you say to people whose affective life is that of hearty Swiss hoteliers? I will tell you. I will say it and save all you artists the trouble. A simple word. *Edelweiss*. Say it in a low well-modulated voice with a refined accent, and lubricate it with a sigh! The whole secret is here, in a word which grows above snowline! And then, having solved the problem of ends and means you will have to face another just as troublesome — for if by any chance a work of art should cross the channel it would be sure to be turned back at Dover on the grounds of being improperly dressed! It is not easy, Brother Ass. (Perhaps it would be wisest to ask the French for intellectual asylum?) But I see you will not heed me. You continue in the same unfaltering tone to describe for me the literary scene which was summed up once and for all by the poet Gray in the line "The lowing herd winds slowly o'er the lea"! Here I cannot deny the truth of what you say. It is cogent, it is prescient, it is carefully studied. But I have taken my own precautions against a nation of mental grannies. Each of my books bears a scarlet wrapper with the legend: *NOT TO BE OPENED BY OLD WOMEN OF EITHER SEX*. (Dear D.H.L. so wrong, so right, so great, may his ghost breathe on us all!)'

He puts down his glass with a little click and sighing runs his fingers through his hair. Kindness is no excuse, I tell myself. Disinterested goodness is no exoneration from the basic demands of the artist's life. You see, Brother Ass, there is my life and then the life of my life. They must belong as fruit and rind. I am not being cruel. It is simply that I am not indulgent!

'How lucky not to be interested in writing' says Darley with a touch of plaintive despair in his tone. 'I envy you'. But he does not, really, not at all. Brother Ass, I will tell you a short story. A team of Chinese anthropologists arrived in Europe to study our habits and beliefs. Within three weeks they were all dead. They died of uncontrollable laughter and were buried with full military honours! What do you make of that? We have turned ideas into a paying form of tourism.

Darley talks on with slanting eye buried in his gin-sling. I reply wordlessly. In truth I am deafened by the pomposity of my own utterances. They echo in my skull like the reverberating eructations of Zarathustra, like the wind whistling through Montaigne's beard. At times I mentally seize him by the shoulders and shout: 'Should literature be a path-finder or a bromide? Decide! Decide!'

He does not heed, does not hear me. He has just come from the library, from the pot-house, or from a Bach concert (the gravy still running down his chin). We have aligned our shoes upon the polished brass rail below the bar. The evening has begun to yawn around us with the wearisome promise of girls to be ploughed. And here is Brother Ass discoursing upon the book he is writing and from which he has been thrown, as from a horse, time and time again. It is not really art which is at issue, it is ourselves. Shall we always be content with the ancient tinned salad of the sub-sidized novel? Or the tired ice-cream of poems which cry them-selves to sleep in the refrigerators of the mind? If it were possible to adopt a bolder scansion, a racier rhythm, we might all breathe more freely! Poor Darley's books — will they always be such pains-taking descriptions of the soul-states of . . . the human omelette? (Art occurs at the point where a form is sincerely honoured by an awakened spirit.)

'This one's on me.'

'No, old man, on me.'

'No. No; I insist.'

'No. It's my turn.'

This amiable quibble allows me just the split second I need to jot down the salient points for my self-portrait on a rather ragged cuff. I think it covers the whole scope of the thing with admirable succinctness. Item one. 'Like all fat men I tend to be my own hero.' Item two. 'Like all young men I set out to be a genius, but mercifully laughter intervened.' Item three. 'I always hoped to achieve the Elephant's Eye view.' Item four. 'I realized that to become an artist one must shed the whole complex of egotisms which led to the choice of self-expression as the only means of growth! This because it is impossible I call The Whole Joke!'

Darley is talking of disappointments! But Brother Ass, disenchantment is the essence of the game. With what high hopes we invaded London from the provinces in those old dead days, our manuscripts bagging our suitcases. Do you recall? With what emotion we gazed over Westminster Bridge, reciting Wordsworth's indifferent sonnet and wondering if his daughter grew up less beautiful for being French. The metropolis seemed to quiver with the portent of our talent, our skill, our discernment. Walking along the Mall we wondered who all those men were — tall hawk-featured men perched on balconies and high places, scanning the city with heavy binoculars. What were they seeking so earnestly? Who were they — so composed and steely-eyed? Timidly we stopped a policeman to ask him. 'They are publishers' he said mildly. Publishers! Our hearts stopped beating. 'They are on the look-out for new talent.' Great God! It was for *us* they were waiting and watching! Then the kindly policemen lowered his voice confidentially and said in hollow and reverent tones: '*They are waiting for the new Trollope to be born!*' Do you remember, at these words, how heavy our suitcases suddenly felt? How our blood slowed, our footsteps lagged? Brother Ass, we had been bashfully thinking of a kind of illumination such as Rimbaud dreamed of — a nagging poem which was not didactic or expository but which *infected* — was not simply a rationalized intuition, I mean, clothed in isinglass! We had come to the wrong shop, with the wrong change! A chill struck us as we saw the mist falling in Trafalgar Square, coiling around us its tendrils of ectoplasm! A million muffin-eating moralists were waiting, not for us, Brother Ass, but for the plucky and tedious Trollope! (If you are dissatisfied with your form, reach for the *curette*.) Now do you wonder if I laugh a little off-key? Do you ask yourself what has turned me into nature's bashful little aphorist?

> Disguised as an eiron, why who should it be
> But tuft-hunting, dram-drinking, toad-eating Me!

We who are, after all, simply poor co-workers in the psyche of our nation, what can we expect but the natural automatic rejection from a public which resents interference? And quite right too. There is no injustice in the matter, for I also resent interference, Brother Ass, just as you do. No, it is not a question of being aggrieved, it is a question of being unlucky. Of the ten thousand reasons for my books' unpopularity I shall only bother to give you the first, for it includes all the others. A puritan culture's conception of art is something which will endorse its morality and flatter its patriotism. Nothing else. I see you raise your eyebrows. Even you, Brother Ass, realize the basic unreality of this proposition. Nevertheless it explains everything. A puritan culture, *argal*, does not know what art is — how can it be expected to care? (I leave religion to the bishops — there it can do most harm!)

> *No croked legge, no blered eye,*
> *no part deformed out of kinde*
> *Nor yet so onolye half can be*
> *As is the inward suspicious minde.*

> *The wheel is patience on to which I'm bound.*
> *Time is this nothingness within the round.*

Gradually we compile our own anthologies of misfortune, our dictionaries of verbs and nouns, our copulas and gerundives. That symptomatic policeman of the London dusk first breathed the message to us! That kindly father-figure put the truth in a nutshell. And here we are both in a foreign city built of smegma-tinted crystal and tinsel whose *moeurs*, if we described them, would be regarded as the fantasies of our disordered brains. Brother Ass, we have the hardest lesson of all to learn as yet — that truth cannot be forced but must be allowed to plead for itself! Can you hear me? The line is faulty again, your voice has gone far away. I hear the water rushing!

> *Be bleak, young man, and let who will be sprightly,*
> *And honour Venus if you can twice nightly.*
> *All things being equal you should not refuse*
> *To ring the slow sad cowbell of the English muse!*

> *Art's Truth's Nonentity made quite explicit.*
> *If it ain't this then what the devil is it?*

Writing in my room last night I saw an ant upon the table. It crossed near the inkwell, and I saw it hesitate at the whiteness of a sheet of paper on which I had written the word 'Love'; my pen faltered, the ant turned back, and suddenly my candle guttered and went out. Clear octaves of yellow light flickered behind my

753

eyeballs. I had wanted to start a sentence with the words 'Proponents of love' — but the thought had guttered out with the candle! Later on, just before dropping off to sleep an idea struck me. On the wall above my bed I wrote in pencil the words: 'What is to be done when one cannot share one's own opinions about love?' I heard my own exasperated sigh as I was dropping off to sleep. In the morning I awoke, clear as a perforated appendix, and wrote my own epitaph on the mirror with my shaving-stick:

> '*I never knew which side my art was buttered*'
> *Were the Last Words that poor Pursewarden uttered!*

As for the proponents of love, I was glad they had vanished for they would have led me irresistibly in the direction of sex — that bad debt which hangs upon my compatriots' consciences. The quiddity! The veritable nub and quiddity of this disordered world, and the only proper field for the deployment of our talents, Brother Ass. But one true, honest unemphatic word in this department will immediately produce one of those neighing and whinnying acts peculiar to our native intellectuals! For them sex is either a Gold Rush or a Retreat from Moscow. And for us? No, but if we are to be a moment serious I will explain what I mean. (Cuckow, Cuckow, a merry note, unpleasing to the pigskin ear.) I mean more than they think. (The strange sad hermaphrodite figure of the London dusk — the Guardsman waiting in Ebury Street for the titled gent.) No, quite another region of enquiry which cannot be reached without traversing this *terrain vague* of the partial spirits. Our topic, Brother Ass, is the same, always and irremediably the same — I spell the word for you: l-o-v-e. Four letters, each letter a volume! The *point faible* of the human psyche, the very site of the carcinoma maxima! How, since the Greeks, has it got mixed up with the cloaca maxima? It is a complete mystery to which the Jews hold the key unless my history is faulty. For this gifted and troublesome race which has never known art, but exhausted its creative processes purely in the construction of ethical systems, has fathered on us all, literally impregnated the Western European psyche with, the whole range of ideas based on 'race' and sexual containment in the furtherance of the race! I hear Balthazar growling and lashing his tail! But where the devil do these fantasies of purified bloodstreams come from? Am I wrong to turn to the fearful prohibitions listed in Leviticus for an explanation of the manic depressive fury of Plymouth Brethren and a host of other dismal sectarians? We have had our testicles pinched for centuries by the Mosaic Law; hence the wan and pollarded look of our young girls and boys. Hence the mincing effrontery of adults willed to perpetual adolescence! Speak, Brother Ass! Do you heed me? If I am wrong you have only to say so! But in my conception of the four-letter word — which I am surprised has not been blacklisted with the other three by the English printer — I am somewhat bold and sweeping. I mean the *whole bloody range* — from the little greenstick fractures of the human heart right up to its higher spiritual connivance with the . . . well, the absolute ways of nature, if you like. Surely, Brother Ass, this is the improper study of man? The main drainage of the soul? We could make an atlas of our sighs!

> *Zeus gets Hera on her back*
> *But finds that she has lost the knack.*
> *Extenuated by excesses*
> *She is unable, she confesses.*
>
> *Nothing daunted Zeus, who wise is,*
> *Tries a dozen good disguises.*
> *Eagle, ram, and bull and bear*
> *Quickly answer Hera's prayer.*
>
> *One knows a God should be prolix,*
> *But . . . think of all those different ******!*

But I break off here in some confusion, for I see that I am in danger of not taking myself as seriously as I should! And this is an unpardonable offence. Moreover I missed your last remark which was something about the choice of a style. Yes, Brother Ass, the choice of a style is most important; in the market garden of our domestic culture you will find strange and terrible blooms with every stamen standing erect. Oh, to write like Ruskin! When poor Effie Grey tried to get to his bed, he shoo'd the girl away! Oh, to write like Carlyle! Haggis of the mind. When a Scotsman comes to toun Can Spring be far behind? No. Everything you say is truthful and full of point; relative truth, and somewhat pointless point, but nevertheless I will try and think about this invention of the scholiasts, for clearly style is as important to you as matter to me.

How shall we go about it? Keats, the word-drunk, searched for resonance among vowel-sounds which might give him an echo of his inner self. He sounded the empty coffin of his early death with patient knuckles, listening to the dull resonances given off by his certain immortality. Byron was off-hand with English, treating it as master to servant; but the language, being no lackey, grew up like tropic lianas between the cracks of his verses, almost strangling the man. He really lived, his life was truly imaginary; under the figment of the passional self there is a mage, though he himself was not aware of the fact. Donne stopped upon the exposed nerve, jangling the whole cranium. Truth should make one wince, he thought. He hurts us, fearing his own facility; despite the pain of the stopping his verse must be chewed to rags. Shakespeare makes all Nature hang its head. Pope, in an anguish of method, like a constipated child, sandpapers his surfaces to make them slippery for our feet. Great stylists are those who are least certain of their effects. The secret lack in their matter haunts them without knowing it! Eliot puts a cool chloroform pad upon a spirit too tightly braced by the information it has gathered. His honesty of measure and his resolute bravery to return to the headsman's axe is a challenge to us all; but where is the smile? He induces awkward sprains at a moment when we are trying to dance! He has chosen greyness rather than light, and he shares his portion with Rembrandt. Blake and Whitman are awkward brown paper parcels full of vessels borrowed from the temple which tumble all over the place when the string breaks. Longfellow heralds the age of invention for he first thought out the mechanical piano. You pedal, it recites. Lawrence was a limb of the genuine oak-tree, with the needed girth and span. Why did he show them that it mattered, and so make himself vulnerable to their arrows? Auden also always talks. He has manumitted the colloquial. . . .

But here, Brother Ass, I break off; for clearly this is not higher or even lower criticism! I do not see this sort of fustian going down at our older universities where they are still painfully trying to extract from art some shadow of justification for their way of life. Surely there must be a grain of hope, they ask anxiously? After all, there must be a grain of hope for decent honest Christian folk in all this rigmarole which is poured out by our tribe from generation to generation. Or is art simply the little white stick which is given to the blind man and by the help of which he tap tap taps along a road he cannot see but which he is certain is there? Brother Ass, it is for you to decide!

When I was chided by Balthazar for being equivocal I replied, without a moment's conscious thought: 'Words being what they are, people being what they are, perhaps it would be better always to say the opposite of what one means?' Afterwards, when I reflected on this view (which I did not know that I held) it seemed to me really eminently sage! So much for conscious thought: you see, we Anglo-Saxons are incapable of thinking *for* ourselves; *about*, yes. In thinking *about* ourselves we put up every kind of pretty performance in every sort of voice, from cracked Yorkshire to the hot-potato-in-the-mouth voice of the BBC. There we excel, for we see ourselves at one remove from reality, as a subject under a microscope. This idea of objectivity is really a flattering extension of our sense of humbug. When you start to think *for* yourself it is impossible to *cant* — and we live by cant! Ah! I hear you say with a sigh, another of those English writers, eminent jailors of the soul! How they weary and disturb us! Very true and very sad.

> *Hail! Albion drear, fond home of cant!*
> *Pursewarden sends thee greetings scant.*
> *Thy notions he's turned back to front*
> *Abhorring cant, adoring* ****

But if you wish to enlarge the image turn to Europe, the Europe which spans, say, Rabelais to de Sade. A progress from the belly-consciousness to the head-consciousness, from flesh and food to sweet (sweet!) reason. Accompanied by all the interchanging ills which mock us. A progress from religious ecstasy to duodenal ulcer! (It is probably healthier to be entirely brainless.) But, Brother Ass, this is something which you did not take into account when you chose to compete for the Heavyweight Belt for Artists of the Millennium. It is too late to complain. You thought you would somehow sneak by the penalties without being called upon to do more than demonstrate your skill with words. But words . . . they are only an Aeolian harp, or a cheap xylophone. Even a sea-lion can learn to balance a football on its nose or to play the slide trombone in a circus. What lies beyond. . . ?

No, but seriously, if you wished to be — I do not say original but merely contemporary — you might try a four-card trick in the form of a novel; passing a common axis through four stories, say, and dedicating each to one of the four winds of heaven. A continuum, forsooth, embodying not a *temps retrouvé* but a *temps délivré.* The curvature of space itself would give you stereo-scopic narrative, while human personality seen across a continuum would perhaps become prismatic? Who can say? I throw the idea out. I can imagine a form which, if satisfied, might raise in human terms the problems of causality or indeterminacy. . . . And nothing very *recherché* either. Just an ordinary Girl Meets Boy story. But tackled in this way you would not, like most of your contem-poraries, be drowsily cutting along a dotted line!

That is the sort of question which you will one day be forced to ask yourself ('We will never get to Mecca!' as the Tchekhov sisters remarked in a play, the title of which I have forgotten.)

> *Nature he loved, and next to nature nudes,*
> *He strove with every woman worth the strife,*
> *Warming both cheeks before the fire of life,*
> *And fell, doing battle with a million prudes.*

Who dares to dream of capturing the fleeting image of truth in all its gruesome multiplicity? (No, no, let us dine cheerfully off scraps of ancient discarded poultice and allow ourselves to be classified by science as wet and dry bobs.)

Whose are the figures I see before me, fishing the brackish reaches of the C. of E.?

One writes, Brother Ass, for the spiritually starving, the castaways of the soul! They will always be a majority even when everyone is a state-owned millionaire. Have courage, for here you will always be master of your audience! Genius which cannot be helped should be politely ignored.

Nor do I mean that it is useless to master and continuously practise your craft. No. A good writer should be able to write anything. But a great writer is the servant of compulsions which are ordained by the very structure of the psyche and cannot be disregarded. Where is he? Where is he?

Come, let us collaborate on a four- or five-decker job, shall we? 'Why the Curate Slipped' would be a good title. Quick, they are waiting, those hypnagogic figures among the London minarets, the *muezzin* of the trade. 'Does Curate get girl *as well as* stipend, or *only* stipend? Read the next thousand pages and find out!' English life in the raw — like some pious melodrama acted by criminal churchwardens sentenced to a lifetime of sexual mis-givings! In this way we can put a tea-cosy over reality to our mutual advantage, writing it all in the plain prose which is only just distinguishable from galvanized iron. In this way we will put a lid on a box with no sides! Brother Ass, let us conciliate a world of listless curmudgeons who read to verify, not their intuitions, but their prejudicies!

I remember old Da Capo saying one afternoon: 'Today I had five girls. I know it will seem excessive to you. I was not trying to prove anything to myself. But if I said that I had merely blended five teas to suit my palate or five tobaccos to suit my pipe, you would not give the matter a second thought. You would, on the contrary, admire my eclecticism, would you not?'

The belly-furbished Kenilworth at the F.O. once told me plaintively that he had 'just dropped in' on James Joyce out of curiosity, and was surprised and pained to find him rude, arrogant and short-tempered. 'But' I said 'he was paying for his privacy by giving lessons to niggers at one and six an hour! He might have been entitled to feel safe from ineffables like yourself who imagine that art is something to which a good education automatically entitles you; that it is a part of a social equipment, class aptitude, like painting water-colours was for a Victorian gentlewoman! I can imagine his poor heart sinking as he studied your face, with its expression of wayward condescension — the fathomless self-esteem which one sees occasionally flit across the face of a goldfish with a hereditary title!' After this we never spoke, which was what I wanted. The art of making necessary enemies! Yet one thing I liked in him: he pronounced the word 'Civilization' as if it had an S-bend in it.

(Brother Ass is on symbolism now, and really talking good sense, I must admit.) Symbolism! The abbreviation of language into poem. The heraldic aspect of reality! Symbolism is the great repair-outfit of the psyche, Brother Ass, the *fond de pouvoir* of the soul. The sphincter-loosening music which copies the ripples of the soul's progress through human flesh, playing in us like electricity! (Old Parr, when he was drunk, said once: 'Yes, but it *hurts* to realize!')

Of course it does. But we know that the history of literature is the history of laughter and pain. The imperatives from which there is no escape are: *Laugh till it hurts, and hurt till you laugh!*

The greatest thoughts are accessible to the least of men. Why do we have to struggle so? Because understanding is a function not of ratiocination but of the psyche's stage of growth. There, Brother Ass, is the point at which we are at variance. No amount of explanation can close the gap. Only realization! One day you are going to wake from your sleep shouting with laughter. *Ecco!*

About Art I always tell myself: while they are watching the firework display, yclept Beauty, you must smuggle the truth into their veins like a filter-passing virus! This is easier said than done. How slowly one learns to embrace the paradox! Even I am not there as yet; nevertheless, like that little party of explorers, 'Though we were still two days' march from the falls we suddenly heard their thunder growing up in the distance'! Ah! those who merit it may one day be granted a rebirth-certificate by a kindly Government Department. This will entitle them to receive everything free óf charge — a prize reserved for those who want nothing. Celestial economics, about which Lenin is strangely silent! Ah! the gaunt faces of the English muses! Pale distressed gentlewomen in smocks and beads, dispensing tea and drop-scones to the unwary!

> *The foxy faces*
> *Of Edwardian Graces*
> *Horse-faces full of charm*
> *With strings of beads*
> *And a packet of seeds*
> *And an ape-tuft under each arm!*

Society! Let us complicate existence to the point of drudgery so that it acts as a drug against reality. Unfair! Unfair! But, my dear Brother Ass, the sort of book I have in mind will be characterized by the desired quality which will make us rich and famous: it will be characterized by a *total lack of codpiece!*

When I want to infuriate Balthazar I say: 'Now if the Jews would only assimilate they would give us a valuable lead in the matter of breaking down puritanism everywhere. For they are the licence-holders and patentees of the closed system, the ethical response! Even our absurd food prohibitions and inhibitions are copied from their melancholy priest-ridden rigmarole about flesh and fowl. Aye! We artists are not interested in policies but in values — this is our field of battle! If once we could loosen up, relax the terrible grip of the so-called Kingdom of Heaven which has made the earth such a blood-soaked place, we might rediscover in sex the key to a metaphysical search which is our *raison d'être* here below! If the closed system and the moral exclusiveness on divine right were relaxed a little what could we not do?' What indeed? But the good Balthazar smokes his Lakadif gloomily and shakes his shaggy head. I think of the black velvet sighs of Juliet and fall silent. I think of the soft white knosps — unopened flower-shapes — which decorate the tombs of Moslem women! The slack, soft insipid mansuetude of these females of the mind! No, clearly my history is pretty weak. Islam also libs as the Pope does.

Brother Ass, let us trace the progress of the European artist from problem-child to case-history, from case-history to cry-baby! He has kept the psyche of Europe alive by his ability to be wrong, by his continual cowardice — this is his function! Cry-baby of the Western World! Cry-babies of the world unite! But let me hasten to add, lest this sounds cynical or despairing, that I am full of hope. For always, at every moment of time, there is a chance that the artist will stumble upon what I can only call The Great Inkling! Whenever this happens he is at once free to enjoy his fecundating rôle; but it can never really happen as fully and completely as it deserves until the miracle comes about — the miracle of Pursewarden's Ideal Commonwealth! Yes, I believe in this miracle. Our very existence as artists affirms it! It is the act of yea-saying about which the old poet of the city speaks in a poem you once showed me in translation.* The *fact* of an artist being born affirms and reaffirms this in every generation. The miracle is there, on ice so to speak. One fine day it will blossom: then the artist suddenly grows up and accepts the full responsibility for his origins in the people, and when *simultaneously* the people recognize his peculiar significance and value, and greet him as the unborn child in themselves, the infant Joy! I am certain it will come. At the moment they are like wrestlers nervously circling one another, looking for the hold. But when it comes, this great blinding second of illumination — only then shall we be able to dispense with hierarchy as a social form. The new society — so different from anything we can imagine now — will be born around the small strict white temple of the Infant Joy! Men and women will group themselves around it, the protoplasmic growth of the village, the town, the capital! Nothing stands in the way of this Ideal Commonwealth, save that in every generation the vanity and laziness of the artist has always matched the self-indulgent blindness of the people. But prepare, prepare! It is on the way. It is here, there, nowhere!

The great schools of love will arise, and sensual and intellectual knowledge will draw their impetus from each other. The human animal will be uncaged, all his dirty cultural straw and coprolitic refuse of belief cleaned out. And the human spirit, radiating light and laughter, will softly tread the green grass like a dancer; will emerge to cohabit with the time-forms and give children to the world of the elementaries — undines and salamanders, sylphs and sylvestres, Gnomi and Vulcani, angels and gnomes.

Yes, to extend the range of physical sensuality to embrace mathematics and theology: to nourish not to stunt the intuitions. For culture means sex, the root-knowledge, and where the faculty is derailed or crippled, its derivatives like religion come up dwarfed or contorted — instead of the emblematic mystic rose you get Judaic cauliflowers like Morons or Vegetarians, instead of artists you get cry-babies, instead of philosophy semantics.

The sexual and the creative energy go hand in hand. They convert into one another — the solar sexual and the lunar spiritual holding an eternal dialogue. They ride the spiral of time together. They embrace the whole of the human motive. The truth is only to be found in our own entrails — the truth of Time.

'Copulation is the lyric of the mob!' Aye, and also the university of the soul: but a university at present without endowments, without books or even students. No, there are a few.

How wonderful the death-struggle of Lawrence: to realize his sexual nature fully, to break free from the manacles of the Old Testament; flashing down the firmament like a great white struggling man-fish, the last Christian martyr. His struggle is ours — to rescue Jesus from Moses. For a brief moment it looked possible, but St Paul restored the balance and the iron handcuffs of the Judaic prison closed about the growing soul forever. Yet in *The Man Who Died* he tells us plainly what must be, what the reawakening of Jesus should have meant — the true birth of free man. Where is he? What has happened to him? Will he ever come?

My spirit trembles with joy as I contemplate this city of light which a divine accident might create before our very eyes at any moment! Here art will find its true form and place, and the artist can play like a fountain without contention, without even trying. For I see art more and more clearly as a sort of manuring of the psyche. It has no intention, that is to say no *theology*. By nourishing the psyche, by dunging it up, it helps it to find its own level, like water. That level is an original innocence — who invented the perversion of Original Sin, that filthy obscenity of the West? Art, like a skilled masseur on a playing-field, is always standing by to help deal with casualties; and just as a masseur does, its ministrations ease up the tensions of the psyche's musculature. That is why it always goes for the sore places, its fingers pressing upon the knotted muscles, the tendon afflicted with cramp — the sins, perversions, displeasing points which we are reluctant to accept. Revealing them with its harsh kindness it unravels the tensions, relaxes the psyche. The other part of the work, if there is any other work, must belong to religion. Art is the purifying factor merely. It predicates nothing. It is the handmaid of silent content, essential only to joy and to love! These strange beliefs, Brother Ass, you will find lurking under my mordant humours, which may be described simply as a technique of therapy. As Balthazar says: 'A good doctor, and in a special sense the psychologist, makes it quite deliberately, slightly harder for the patient to recover too easily. You do this to see if his psyche has any real bounce in it, for the secret of healing is in the patient and not the doctor. The only measure is the reaction!'

I was born under Jupiter, Hero of the Comic Mode! My poems, like soft music invading the encumbered senses of young lovers left alone at night. . . . What was I saying? Yes, the best thing to do with a great truth, as Rabelais discovered, is to bury it in a mountain of follies where it can comfortably wait for the picks and shovels of the elect.

Between infinity and eternity stretches the thin hard tightrope human beings must walk, joined at the waist! Do not let these unamiable propositions dismay you, Brother Ass. They are written down in pure joy, uncontaminated by a desire to preach! I am really writing for an audience of the blind — but aren't we all? Good art points, like a man too ill to speak, like a baby! But if instead of following the direction it indicates you take it for a thing in itself, having some sort of absolute value, or as a thesis upon something which can be paraphrased, surely you miss the point; you lose yourself at once among the barren abstractions of the critic? Try to tell yourself that its fundamental object was only to invoke the ultimate healing silence — and that the symbolism contained in form and pattern is only a frame of reference through which, as in a mirror, one may glimpse the idea of a universe at rest, a universe in love with itself. Then like a babe in arms you will 'milk the universe at every breath'! We must learn to read between the lines, between the lives.

Liza used to say: 'But its very perfection makes one sure that it will come to an end.' She was right; but women will not accept time and the dictates of the death-divining second. They do not see that a civilization is simply a great metaphor which describes the aspirations of the individual soul in collective form — as perhaps a novel or a poem might do. The struggle is always for greater consciousness. But alas! Civilizations die in the measure that they become conscious of themselves. They realize, they lose heart, the propulsion of the unconscious motive is no longer there. Desperately they begin to copy themselves in the mirror. It is no use. But surely there is a catch in all this? Yes, Time is the catch! Space is a concrete idea, but Time is abstract. In the scar tissue of Proust's great poem you see that so clearly; his work is the great academy of the time-consciousness. But being unwilling to mobilize the meaning of time he was driven to fall back on memory, the ancestor of hope!

Ah! but being a Jew he had hope — and with Hope comes the irresistible desire to meddle. Now we Celts mate with despair out of which alone grows laughter and the desperate romance of the eternally hopeless. We hunt the unattainable, and for us there is only a search unending.

For him it would mean nothing, my phrase 'the prolongation of childhood into art'. Brother Ass, the diving-board, the trapeze, lie just to the eastward of this position! A leap through the firmament to a new status — only don't miss the ring!

Why for example don't they recognize in Jesus the great Ironist that he is, the comedian? I am sure that two-thirds of the Beatitudes are jokes or squibs in the manner of Chuang Tzu. Generations of mystagogues and pedants have lost the sense. I am sure of it however because he must have known that Truth disappears with the telling of it. It can only be conveyed, not stated; irony alone is the weapon for such a task.

Or let us turn to another aspect of the thing; it was you, just a moment ago, who mentioned our poverty of observation in all that concerns each other — the limitations of sight itself. Bravely spoken! But translated spiritually you get the picture of a man walking about the house, hunting for the spectacles which are on his forehead. To see is to imagine! And what, Brother Ass, could be a better illustration than your manner of seeing Justine, fitfully lit up in the electric signs of the imagination? It is not the same woman evidently who set about besieging me and who was finally driven off by my sardonic laughter. What you saw as soft and appealing in her seemed to me a specially calculated hardness, not which she invented, but which you evoked in her. All that throaty chatter, the compulsion to exteriorize hysteria, reminded me of a feverish patient plucking at a sheet! The violent necessity to incriminate life, to *explain* her soul-states, reminded me of a mendicant soliciting pity by a nice exhibition of sores. Mentally she always had me scratching myself! Yet there was much to admire in her and I indulged my curiosity in exploring the outlines of her character with some sympathy — the configurations of an unhappiness which was genuine, though it always smelt of grease paint! The child, for example!

'I found it, of course. Or rather Mnemjian did. In a brothel. It died from something, perhaps meningitis. Darley and Nessim came and dragged me away. All of a sudden I realized that I could not bear to find it; all the time I hunted I lived on the hope of finding it. But this thing, once dead, seemed suddenly to deprive me of all purpose. I recognized it, but my inner mind kept crying out that it was not true, refusing to let me recognize it, even though I already had consciously done so!'

The mixture of conflicting emotions was so interesting that I jotted them down in my notebook between a poem and a recipe for angel bread which I got from El Kalef. Tabulated thus:

1. Relief at end of search.
2. Despair at end of search; no further motive force in life.
3. Horror at death.
4. Relief at death. What future possible for it?
5. Intense shame (don't understand this).
6. Sudden desire to continue search uselessly rather than admit truth.
7. Preferred to continue to feed on false hopes!

A bewildering collection of fragments to leave among the analects of a moribund poet! But here was the point I was trying to make. She said: 'Of course neither Nessim nor Darley noticed anything. Men are so stupid, they never do. I would have been able to forget it even perhaps, and dream that I had never really discovered it, but for Mnemjian, who wanted the reward, and was so convinced of the truth of his case that he made a great row. There was some talk of an autopsy by Balthazar. I was foolish enough to go to his clinic and offer to bribe him to say it was not my child. He was pretty astonished. I wanted him to deny a truth which I so perfectly knew to be true, *so that I should not have to change my outlook*. I would not be deprived of my sorrow, if you like; I wanted it to go on — to go on passionately searching for what I did not dare to find. I even frightened Nessim and incurred his suspicions with my antics over his private safe. So the matter passed off, and for a long time I still went on automatically searching until underneath I could stand the strain of the truth and come to terms with it. I see it so clearly, the divan, the tenement.'

Here she put on her most beautiful expression, which was one of intense sadness, and put her hands upon her breasts. Shall I tell you something? *I suspected her of lying;* it was an unworthy thought but then . . . I am an unworthy person.

I: 'Have you ever been back to the place?'

She: 'No. I have often wanted to, but did not dare.' She shuddered a little. 'In my memory I have become attached to that old divan. It must be knocking about somewhere. You see, I am still half convinced it was all a dream.'

At once I took up my pipe, violin and deerstalker like a veritable Sherlock. I have always been an X-marks-the-spot man. 'Let us go and revisit it' I said briskly. At the worst, I thought, such a visitation would be cathartic. It was in fact a supremely practical thing to suggest, and to my surprise she at once rose and put on her coat. We walked silently down through the western edges of the town, arm in arm.

There was some kind of festival going on in the Arab town which was blazing with electric light and flags. Motionless sea, small high clouds, and a moon like a disapproving archimandrite of another faith. Smell of fish, cardamon seed and frying entrails packed with cummin and garlic. The air was full of the noise of mandolines scratching their little souls out on the night, as if afflicted with fleas — scratching until the blood came on the lice-intoxicated night! The air was heavy. Each breath invisibly perforated it. You felt it come in and out of the lungs as if in a leather bellows. Eheu! It was grisly all that light and noise, I thought. And they talk of the romance of the East! Give me the Metropole at Brighton any day! We traversed this sector of light with quick deliberate step. She walked unerringly, head bent, deep in thought. Then gradually the streets grew darker, faded into the violet of darkness, became narrower, twisted and turned. At last we came to a great empty space with starlight. A dim great barrack of a building. She moved slowly now, with less certainty, hunting for a door. In a whisper she said 'This place is run by old Mettrawi. He is bedridden. The door is always open. But he hears everything from his bed. Take my hand.' I was never a great fire-eater and I must confess to a certain uneasiness as we walked into this bandage of total blackness. Her hand was firm and cool, her voice precise, unmarked by any range of emphasis, betraying neither excitement nor fear. I thought I heard the scurrying of immense rats in the rotten structure around me, the very rafters of night itself. (Once in a thunderstorm among the ruins I had seen their fat wet glittering bodies flash here and there as they feasted on garbage.) 'Please God, remember that even though I am an English poet I do not deserve to be eaten by rats' I prayed silently. We had started to walk down a long corridor of blackness with the rotten wooden boards creaking under us; here and there was one missing, and I wondered if we were not walking over the bottomless pit itself! The air smelt of wet ashes and that unmistakable odour of black flesh when it is sweating. It is quite different from white flesh. It is dense, foetid, like the lion's cage at the Zoo. The Darkness itself was sweating — and why not? The Darkness must wear Othello's skin. Always a timorous fellow, I suddenly wanted to go to the lavatory but I crushed the thought like a blackbeetle. Let my bladder wait. On we went, and round two sides of a . . . piece of darkness floored with rotten boards. Then suddenly she whispered: 'I think we are there!' and pushed open a door upon another piece of impenetrable darkness. But it was a room of some size for the air was cool. One felt the space though one could see nothing whatsoever. We both inhaled deeply.

'Yes' she whispered thoughtfully and, groping in her velvet handbag for a box of matches, hesitantly struck one. It was a tall room, so tall that it was roofed by darkness despite the yellow flapping of the match-flame; one huge shattered window faintly reflected starlight. The walls were of verdigris, the plaster peeling everywhere, and their only decoration was the imprint of little blue hands which ran round the four walls in a haphazard pattern. As if a lot of pygmies had gone mad with blue paint and then galloped all over the walls standing on their hands! To the left, a little off centre, reposed a large gloomy divan, floating upon the gloom like a Viking catafalque; it was a twice-chewed relic of some Ottoman calif, riddled with holes. The match went out. 'There it is' she said and putting the box into my hand she left my side. When I lit up again she was sitting beside the divan with her cheek resting upon it, softly stroking it with the palm of her hand. She was completely composed. She stroked it with a calm voluptuous gesture and then crossed her paws on it, reminding me of a lioness sitting astride its lunch. The moment had a kind of weird tension, but this was not reflected on her face. (Human beings are like pipe-organs, I thought. You pull out a stop marked 'Lover' or 'Mother' and the requisite emotions are unleashed — tears or sighs or endearments. Sometimes I try and think of us all as habit-patterns rather than human beings. I mean, wasn't the idea of the individual soul grafted on us by the Greeks in the wild hope that, by its sheer beauty, it would 'take' — as we say of vaccination? That we might grow up to the size of the concept and grow the heavenly flame in each of our hearts? *Has* it taken or hasn't it? Who can say? Some of us still have one, but how vestigial it seems. Perhaps. . . .)

'They have heard us.'

Somewhere in the darkness there was a thin snarl of voice, and the silence became suddenly padded out with the scamper of feet upon rotted woodwork. In the expiring flicker of the match I saw, as if somewhere very far away, a bar of light — like a distant furnace door opening in heaven. And voices now, the voices of ants! The children came through a sort of hatch or trap-door made of darkness, in their cotton nightgowns, absurdly faded. With rings on their fingers and bells on their toes. She shall have music wherever she goes! One of them carried a waxlight floating in a saucer. They twanged nasally about us, interrogating our needs with blasting frankness — but they were surprised to see Justine sitting beside the Viking catafalque, her head (now smiling) half turned towards them.

'I think we should leave' I said in a low voice, for they smelt dreadfully these tiny apparitions, and they showed a disagreeable tendency to twine their skinny arms about my waist as they wheedled and intoned. But Justine turned to one and said: 'Bring the light here, where we can all see.' And when the light was brought she suddenly turned herself, crossed her legs under her, and in the high ringing tone of the street storyteller she intoned: 'Now gather about me, all ye blessed of Allah, and hear the wonders of the story I shall tell you.' The effect was electric; they settled about her like a pattern of dead leaves in a wind, crowding up close together. Some even climbed on to the old divan, chuckling and nudging with delight. And in the same rich triumphant voice, saturated with unshed tears, Justine began again in the voice of the professional story-teller: 'Ah, listen to me, all ye true believers, and I will unfold to you the story of Yuna and Aziz, of their great many-petalled love, and of the mishaps which befell them from the doing of Abu Ali Saraq el-Maza. In those days of the great Califate, when many heads fell and armies marched. . . .'

It was a wild sort of poetry for the place and the time — the little circle of wizened faces, the divan, the flopping light; and the strangely captivating lilt of the Arabic with its heavy damascened imagery, the thick brocade of alliterative repetitions, the nasal twanging accents, gave it a laic splendour which brought tears to my eyes — gluttonous tears! It was such a rich diet for the soul! It made me aware how thin the fare is which we moderns supply to our hungry readers. The epic contours, that is what her story had! I was envious. How rich these beggar children were. And I was envious too of her audience. Talk of suspended judgement! They sank into the imagery of her story like plummets. One saw, creeping out like mice, their true souls — creeping out upon those painted masks in little expressions of wonder, suspense and joy. In that yellow gloaming they were expressions of a terrible truth. You saw how they would be in middle age — the witch, the good wife, the gossip, the shrew. The poetry had stripped them to the bone and left only their natural selves to flower thus in expressions faithfully portraying their tiny stunted spirits!

How could I help but admire her for giving me one of the most significant and memorable moments of a writer's life? I put my arm about her shoulders and sat, as rapt as any of them, following the long sinuous curves of the immortal story as it unfolded before our eyes.

They could hardly bear to part with us when at last the story came to an end. They clung to her, pleading for more. Some picked the hem of her skirt and kissed it in an agony of pleading. 'There is no time' she said, smiling calmly. 'But I will come again, my little ones.' They hardly heeded the money she distributed but thronged after us along the dark corridors to the blackness of the square. At the corner I looked back but could only see the flicker of shadows. They said farewell in voices of heartbreaking sweetness. We talked in deep contented silence across the shattered, time-corrupted town until we reached the cool seafront; and stood a long time leaning upon the cold stone piers above the sea, smoking and saying nothing! At last she turned to me a face of tremendous weariness and whispered: 'Take me home, now. I'm dead tired.' And so we hailed a pottering gharry and swung along the Corniche as sedately as bankers after a congress. 'I suppose we are all hunting for the secrets of growth!' was all she said as we parted.

It was a strange remark to make at parting. I watched her walk wearily up the steps to the great house groping for her key. I still felt drunk with the story of Yuna and Aziz!

Brother Ass, it is a pity that you will never have a chance to read all this tedious rigmarole; it would amuse me to study your puzzled expression as you did so. Why should the artist always be trying to saturate the world with his own anguish, you asked me once. Why indeed? I will give you another phrase: emotional gongorism! I have always been good at polite phrase-making.

> *Loneliness and desire,*
> *Lord of the Flies,*
> *Are thy unholy empire and*
> *The self's inmost surprise!*
> *Come to these arms, my dear old Dutch*
> *And firmly bar the door*
> *I could not love thee, dear, so much*
> *Loved I not ******** more!*

And later, aimlessly walking, who should I encounter but the slightly titubating Pombal just back from the Casino with a chamber-pot full of paper money and a raging thirst for a last beaker of champagne which we took together at the Étoile. It was strange that I had no taste for a girl that night; somehow Yuna and Aziz had barred the way. Instead I straggled back to Mount Vulture with a bottle in my mackintosh pocket, to confront once more the ill-starred pages of my book which, twenty years from now, will be the cause of many a thrashing among the lower forms of our schools. It seemed a disastrous sort of gift to be offering to the generations as yet unborn; I would rather have left them something like Yuna and Aziz, but it hasn't been possible since Chaucer; the sophistication of the laic audience is perhaps to blame? The thought of all those smarting little bottoms made me close my notebooks with a series of ill-tempered snaps. Champagne is a wonderfully soothing drink, however, and prevented me from being too cast-down. Then I stumbled upon the little note which you, Brother Ass, had pushed under the door earlier in the evening: a note which complimented me on the new series of poems which the Anvil was producing (a misprint per line); and writers being what they are I thought most kindly of you, I raised my glass to you. In my eyes you had become a critic of the purest discernment; and once more I asked myself in exasperated tones why the devil I had never wasted more time on you? It was really remiss of me. And falling asleep I made a mental note to take you to dinner the next evening and talk your jackass's head off — about writing, of course, what else? Ah! but that is the point. Once a writer seldom a talker; I knew that, speechless as Goldsmith, I should sit hugging my hands in my armpits while *you* did the talking!

In my sleep I dug up a mummy with poppy-coloured lips, dressed in the long white wedding dress of the Arab sugar-dolls. She smiled but would not awake, though I kissed her and talked to her persuasively. Once her eyes half opened; but they closed again and she lapsed back into smiling sleep. I whispered her name which was Yuna, but which had unaccountably become Liza. And as it was no use I interred her once more among the shifting dunes where (the wind-shapes were changing fast) there would be no trace remaining of the spot. At dawn I woke early and took a gharry down to the Rushdi beach to cleanse myself in the dawn-sea. There was not a soul about at that time save Clea, who was on the far beach in a blue bathing-costume, her marvellous hair swinging about her like a blonde Botticelli. I waved and she waved back, but showed no inclination to come and talk which made me grateful. We lay, a thousand yards apart, smoking and wet as seals. I thought for an instant of the lovely burnt coffee of her summer flesh, with the little hairs on her temples bleached to ash. I inhaled her metaphorically, like a whiff of roasting coffee, dreaming of the white thighs with those small blue veins in them! Well, well . . . she would have been worth taking trouble over had she not been so beautiful. That brilliant glance exposed everything and forced me to take shelter from her.

One could hardly ask her to bandage them in order to be made love to! And yet . . . like the black silk stockings some men insist on! Two sentences ending with a preposition! What is poor Pursewarden coming to?

THE ALEXANDRIA QUARTET

His prose created grievous lusts
Among the middle classes

His propositions were decried
As dangerous for the masses

His major works were classified
Among the noxious gases
England awake!

Brother Ass, the so-called act of living is really an act of the imagination. The world — which we always visualize as 'the outside' World — yields only to self-exploration! Faced by this cruel, yet necessary paradox, the poet finds himself growing gills and a tail, the better to swim against the currents of unenlightenment. What appears to be perhaps an arbitrary act of violence is precisely the opposite, for by reversing process in this way, he unites the rushing, heedless stream of humanity to the still, tranquil, motionless, odourless, tasteless plenum from which its own motive essence is derived. (Yes, but it *hurts* to realize!) If he were to abandon his rôle all hope of gaining a purchase on the slippery surface of reality would be lost, and everything in nature would disappear! But this act, the poetic act, will cease to be necessary when everyone can perform it for himself. What hinders them, you ask? Well, we are all naturally afraid to surrender our own pitifully rationalized morality — and the poetic jump I'm predicating lies the other side of it. It is only terrifying because we refuse to recognize in ourselves the horrible gargoyles which decorate the totem poles of our churches — murderers, liars, adulterers and so on. (Once recognized, these papier-mâché masks fade.) Whoever makes this enigmatic leap into the heraldic reality of the poetic life discovers that truth has its own built-in morality! There is no need to wear a truss any longer. Inside the penumbra of this sort of truth morality can be disregarded because it is a *donnée*, a part of the thing, and not simply a brake, an inhibition. It is there to be lived out and not thought out! Ah, Brother Ass, this will seem a far cry to the 'purely literary' preoccupations which beset you; yet unless you tackle this corner of the field with your sickle you will never reap the harvest in yourself, and so fulfil your true function here below.

But how? you ask me plaintively. And truly here you have me by the short hairs, for the thing operates differently with each

772

one of us. I am only suggesting that you have not become desperate enough, determined enough. Somewhere at the heart of things you are still lazy of spirit. But then, why struggle? If it is to happen to you it will happen of its own accord. You may be quite right to hang about like this, waiting. I was too proud. I felt I must take it by the horns, this vital question of my birthright. For me it was grounded in an act of will. So for people like me I would say: 'Force the lock, batter down the door. Outface, defy, disprove the Oracle in order to become the poet, the darer!'

But I am aware the test may come under any guise, perhaps even in the physical world by a blow between the eyes or a few lines scribbled in pencil on the back of an envelope left in a café. The heraldic reality can strike from any point, above or below: it is not particular. But without it the enigma will remain. You may travel round the world and colonize the ends of the earth with your lines and yet never hear the singing yourself.

* * * * *

IV

I found myself reading these passages from Pursewarden's notebooks with all the attention and amusement they deserved and without any thought of 'exoneration' — to use the phrase of Clea. On the contrary, it seemed to me that his observation was not lacking in accuracy and whatever whips and scorpions he had applied to my image were well justified. It is, moreover, useful as well as salutary to see oneself portrayed with such blistering candour by someone one admires! Yet I was a trifle surprised not to feel even a little wounded in my self-esteem. Not only were no bones broken, but at times, chuckling aloud at his sallies, I found myself addressing him under my breath as if he were actually present before me, uttering rather than writing down these unpalatable home-truths. 'You bastard' I said under my breath. 'You just wait a little bit.' Almost as if one day I might right the reckoning with him, pay off the score! It was troubling to raise my head and realize suddenly that he had already stepped behind the curtains, vanished from the scene; he was so much of a presence, popping up everywhere, with the strange mixture of strengths and weaknesses which made up his enigmatic character.

'What are you chuckling at?' said Telford, always anxious to share a jocose exchange of office wit provided it had the requisite moribund point.

'A notebook.'

Telford was a large man draped in ill-cut clothes and a spotted blue bow tie. His complexion was blotchy and of the kind which tears easily under a razor-blade; consequently there was always a small tuft of cotton wool sticking to chin or ear, stanching a wound. Always voluble and bursting with the wrong sort of expansive *bonhomie* he gave the impression of being at war with his dentures, which were ill-fitting. He gobbled and gasped, biting on loose stoppings, or swallowing a soft palate, gasping like a fish as he uttered his pleasantries or laughed at his own jokes like a man riding a bone-shaker, his top set of teeth bumping up and down on his gums. 'I say, old fruit, that was rich' he would exclaim. I did not find him too disagreeable an inmate of the office which we shared at the censorship, for the work was not exacting and he,

774

as an old hand, was always ready to give me advice or help with it; I enjoyed too his obstinately recurring stories of the mythical 'old days', when he, Little Tommy Telford, had been a personage of great importance, second only in rank and power to the great Maskelyne, our present Chief. He always referred to him as 'The Brig', and made it very clear that the department, which had once been Arab Bureau, had seen better times, had in fact been downgraded to a mere censorship department dealing with the ebb and flow of civilian correspondence over the Middle East. A menial rôle compared to 'Espionage' which he pronounced in four separate syllables.

Stories of this ancient glory, which had now faded beyond recall, formed part of the Homeric Cycle, so to speak, of office life: to be recited wistfully during intervals between snatches of work or on afternoons when some small mishap like a broken fan had made concentration in those airless buildings all but impossible. It was from Telford that I learned of the long internecine struggle between Pursewarden and Maskelyne — a struggle which was, in a sense, continuing on another plane between the silent Brigadier and Mountolive, for Maskelyne was desperately anxious to rejoin his regiment and shed his civilian suit. This desire had been baulked. Mountolive, explained Telford with many a gusty sigh (waving chapped and podgy hands which were stuffed with bluish clusters of veins like plums in a cake) — Mountolive had 'got at' the War Office and persuaded them not to countenance Maskelyne's resignation. I must say the Brigadier, whom I saw perhaps twice a week, did convey an impression of sullen, saturnine fury at being penned up in a civilian department while so much was going on in the desert, but of course any regular soldier would. 'You see' said Telford ingenuously, 'when a war comes along there's bags of promotion, old thing, bags of it. The Brig has a right to think of his career like any other man. It is different for us. We were born civilians, so to speak.' He himself had spent many years in the currant trade in the Eastern Levant residing in places like Zante and Patras. His reasons for coming to Egypt were obscure. Perhaps he found life more congenial in a large British colony. Mrs Telford was a fattish little duck who used mauve lipstick and wore hats like pincushions. She only appeared to live for an invitation to the Embassy on the King's birthday. ('Mavis loves her little official "do", she does.')

But if the administrative war with Mountolive was so far

empty of victory there were consolations, said Telford, from which the Brig could derive a studied enjoyment: for Mountolive was very much in the same boat. This made him (Telford) 'chortle' — a characteristic phrase which he often used. Mountolive, it seemed, was no less eager to abandon his post, and had indeed applied several times for a transfer from Egypt. Unluckily, however, the war had intervened with its policy of 'freezing personnel' and Kenilworth, no friend of the Ambassador, had been sent out to execute this policy. If the Brigadier was pinned down by the intrigues of Mountolive, the latter had been pinned down just as certainly by the newly appointed Personnel Adviser — pinned down 'for the duration'! Telford rubbed unctuous hands as he retailed all this to me! 'It's a case of the biter bit all right' he said. 'And if you ask me the Brig will manage to get away sooner than Sir David. Mark my words, old fruit.' A single solemn nod was enough to satisfy him that his point had been taken.

Telford and Maskelyne were united by a curious sort of bond which intrigued me. The solitary monosyllabic soldier and the effusive bagman — what on earth could they have had in common? (Their very names on the printed duty rosters irresistibly suggested a music-hall team or a firm of respectable undertakers!) Yet I think the bond was one of admiration, for Telford behaved with a grotesque wonder and respect when in the presence of his Chief, fussing around him anxiously, eagerly, longing to anticipate his commands and so earn a word of commendation. His heavily salivated 'Yes, sir' and 'No, sir' popped out from between his dentures with the senseless regularity of cuckoos from a clock. Curiously enough there was nothing feigned in this sycophancy. It was in fact something like an administrative love-affair, for even when Maskelyne was not present Telford spoke of him with the greatest possible reverence, the profoundest hero-worship — compounded equally of social admiration for his rank and deep respect for his character and judgement. Out of curiosity I tried to see Maskelyne through my colleague's eyes but failed to discern more than a rather bleak and well-bred soldier of narrow capacities and a clipped world-weary public school accent. Yet . . . 'The Brig is a real cast-iron gentleman' Telford would say with an emotion so great that it almost brought tears to his eyes. 'He's as straight as string, is the old Brig. Never stoop to do anything beneath him.' It was perhaps true, yet it did not make our Chief less unremarkable in my eyes.

Telford had several little menial duties which he himself had elected to perform for his hero — for example, to buy the week-old *Daily Telegraph* and place it on the great man's desk each morning. He adopted a curious finicky walk as he crossed the polished floor of Maskelyne's empty office (for we arrived early at work): almost as if he were afraid of leaving footprints behind him. He positively stole across to the desk. And the tenderness with which he folded the paper and ran his fingers down the creases before laying it reverently on the green blotter reminded me of a woman handling a husband's newly starched and ironed shirt.

Nor was the Brigadier himself unwilling to accept the burden of this guileless admiration. I imagine few men could resist it. At first I was puzzled by the fact that once or twice a week he would visit us, clearly with no special matter in mind, and would take a slow turn up and down between our desks, occasionally uttering an informal monochrome pleasantry — indicating the recipient of it by pointing the stem of his pipe at him lightly, almost shyly. Yet throughout these visitations his swarthy grey-hound's face, with its small crowsfeet under the eyes, never altered its expression, his voice never lost its studied inflections. At first, as I say, these appearances somewhat puzzled me, for Maskelyne was anything but a convivial soul and could seldom talk of anything but the work in hand. Then one day I detected, in the slow elaborate figure he traced between our desks, the traces of an unconscious coquetry — I was reminded of the way a peacock spreads its great studded fan of eyes before the female, or of the way a mannequin wheels in an arabesque designed to show off the clothes she is wearing. Maskelyne had in fact simply come to be admired, to spread out the riches of his character and breeding before Telford. Was it possible that this easy conquest provided him with some inner assurance he lacked? It would be hard to say. Yet he was inwardly basking in his colleague's wide-eyed admiration I am sure it was quite unconscious — this gesture of a lonely man towards the only whole-hearted admirer he had as yet won from the world. From his own side, however, he could only reciprocate with the condescension bred by his education. Secretly he held Telford in contempt for not being a gentleman. 'Poor Telford' he would be heard to sigh when out of the other's hearing. 'Poor Telford.' The commiserating fall of the voice suggested pity for someone who was worthy but hopelessly uninspired.

These, then, were my office familiars during the whole of that first wearing summer, and their companionship offered me no problem. The work left me easy and untroubled in mind. My ranking was a humble one and carried with it no social obligations whatsoever. For the rest we did not frequent each other outside the office. Telford lived somewhere near Rushdi in a small suburban villa, outside the centre of the town, while Maskelyne seldom appeared to stir from the gaunt bedroom on the top floor of the Cecil. Once free from the office, therefore, I felt able to throw it off completely and once more resume the life of the town, or what was left of it.

With Clea also the new relationship offered no problems, perhaps because deliberately we avoided defining it too sharply, and allowed it to follow the curves of its own nature, to fulfil its own design. I did not, for example, always stay at her flat — for sometimes when she was working on a picture she would plead for a few days of complete solitude and seclusion in order to come to grips with her subject, and these intermittent intervals, sometimes of a week or more, sharpened and refreshed affection without harming it. Sometimes, however, after such a compact we would stumble upon each other by accident and out of weakness resume the suspended relationship before the promised three days or a week was up! It wasn't easy.

Sometimes at evening I might come upon her sitting absently alone on the little painted wooden terrace of the Café Baudrot, gazing into space. Her sketching blocks lay before her, unopened. Sitting there as still as a coney, she had forgotten to remove from her lips the tiny moustache of cream from her *café viennois!* At such a moment it needed all my self-possession not to vault the wooden balustrade and put my arms round her, so vividly did this touching detail seem to light up the memory of her; so childish and serene did she look. The loyal and ardent image of Clea the lover rose up before my eyes and all at once separation seemed unendurable! Conversely I might suddenly (sitting on a bench in a public garden, reading) feel cool hands pressed over my eyes and turn suddenly to embrace her and inhale once more the fragrance of her body through her crisp summer frock. At other times, and very often at moments when I was actually thinking of her, she would walk miraculously into the flat saying: 'I felt you calling me to come' or else 'It suddenly came over me to need you very much.' So these encounters had a breathless sharp sweetness,

778

unexpectedly re-igniting our ardour. It was as if we had been separated for years instead of days.

This self-possession in the matter of planned absences from each other struck a spark of admiration from Pombal, who could no more achieve the same measure in his relations with Fosca than climb to the moon. He appeared to wake in the morning with her name on his lips. His first act was to telephone her anxiously to find out if she were well — as if her absence had exposed her to terrible unknown dangers. His official day with its various duties was a torment. He positively galloped home to lunch in order to see her again. In all justice I must say that his attachment was fully reciprocated for all that their relationship was like that of two elderly pensioners in its purity. If he were kept late at an official dinner she would work herself into a fever of apprehension. ('No, it is not his fidelity that worries me, it is his safety. He drives so carelessly, as you know.') Fortunately during this period the nightly bombardment of the harbour acted upon social activities almost like a curfew, so that it was possible to spend almost every evening together, playing chess or cards, or reading aloud. Fosca I found to be a thoughtful, almost intense young woman, a little lacking in humour but devoid of the priggishness which I had been inclined to suspect from Pombal's own description of her when first we met. She had a keen and mobile face whose premature wrinkles suggested that perhaps she had been marked by her experiences as a refugee. She never laughed aloud, and her smile had a touch of reflective sadness in it. But she was wise, and always had a spirited and thoughtful answer ready — indeed the quality of *esprit* which the French so rightly prize in a woman. The fact that she was nearing the term of her pregnancy only seemed to make Pombal more attentive and adoring — indeed he behaved with something like complacence about the child. Or was he simply trying to suggest that it was his own: as a show of face to a world which might think that he was 'unmanned'? I could not decide. In the summer afternoons he would float about the harbour in his cutter while Fosca sat in the stern trailing one white hand in the sea. Sometimes she sang for him in a small true voice like a bird's. This transported him, and he wore the look of a good *bourgeois papa de famille* as he beat time with his finger. At night they sat out the bombardment for preference over a chess board — a somewhat singular choice; but as the infernal racket of gunfire gave him nervous headaches he had skilfully constructed ear plugs for them both by cutting the filter-tips from cigarettes. So they were able to sit, concentrating in silence!

But once or twice this peaceful harmony was overshadowed by outside events which provoked doubts and misgivings understandable enough in a relationship which was so nebulous — I mean so much *discussed* and anatomized and not acted out. One day I found him padding about in a dressing-gown and slippers looking suspiciously distraught, even a little red-eyed. 'Ah, Darley!' he sighed gustily, falling into his gout chair and catching his beard in his fingers as if he were about to dismantle it completely. 'We will never understand them, never. Women! What bad luck. Perhaps I am just stupid. Fosca! Her husband!'

'He has been killed?' I asked.

Pombal shook his head sadly. 'No. Taken prisoner and sent to Germany.'

'Well why the fuss?'

'I am ashamed, that is all. I did not fully realize until this news came, neither did she, that we were really *expecting* him to be killed. Unconsciously, of course. Now she is full of self-disgust. But the whole plan for *our* lives was unconsciously built upon the notion of him surrendering his own. It is monstrous. His death would have freed us; but now the whole problem is deferred perhaps for years, perhaps forever. . . .'

He looked quite distracted and fanned himself with a newspaper, muttering under his breath. 'Things take the strangest turns' he went on at last. 'For if Fosca is too honourable to confess the truth to him while he is at the front, she would equally never do it to a poor prisoner. I left her in tears. Everything is put off till the *end of the war*.'

He ground his back teeth together and sat staring at me. It was difficult to know what one could say by way of consolation.

'Why doesn't she write and tell him?'

'Impossible! Too cruel. And with the child coming on? Even I, Pombal, would not wish her to do such a thing. Never. I found her in *tears*, my friend, holding the telegram. She said in tones of anguish: "Oh, Georges-Gaston, for the first time I feel ashamed of my love, when I realize that we were wishing him to die rather than get captured this way." It may sound complicated to you, but her emotions are so fine, her sense of honour and pride and so on. Then a queer thing happened. So great was our mutual pain that in trying to console her I slipped and we began to make real love without noticing it. It is a strange picture. And not an easy operation. Then when we came to ourselves she began to cry all over again and said: "Now for the first time I have a feeling of hate for you, Georges-Gaston, because now our love is on the same plane as everyone else's. We have cheapened it." Women always put you in the wrong somehow. I was so full of joy to have at last. . . . Suddenly her words plunged me into despair. I rushed away. I have not seen her for *five hours*. Perhaps this is the end of everything? Ah but it could have been the beginning of something which would at least sustain us until the whole problem sees the light of day.'

'Perhaps she is too stupid.'

Pombal was aghast. 'How can you say that! All this comes from her exquisite finesse of spirit. That is all. Don't add to my misery by saying foolish things about one so fine.'

'Well, telephone her.'

'Her phone is out of order. Aie! It is worse than toothache. I have been toying with the idea of suicide for the first time in my life. That will show you to what a point I've been driven.'

But at this moment the door opened and Fosca stepped into the room. She too had been crying. She stopped with a queer dignity and held out her hands to Pombal who gave an inarticulate growling cry of delight and bounded across the room in his dressing-gown to embrace her passionately. Then he drew her into the circle of his arm and they went slowly down the corridor to his room together and locked themselves in.

Later that evening I saw him coming down Rue Fuad towards me, beaming. 'Hurrah!' he shouted and threw his expensive hat high into the air. *'Je suis enfin là!'*

The hat described a large parabola and settled in the middle of the road where it was immediately run over by three cars in rapid succession. Pombal clasped his hands together and beamed as if the sight gave him the greatest joy. Then he turned his moon-face up into the sky as if searching for a sign or portent. As I came abreast of him he caught my hands and said: 'Divine logic of women! Truly there is nothing so wonderful on earth as the sight of a woman thinking out her feelings. I adore it. I adore it. Our love. . . . Fosca! It is complete now. I am so astonished, truthfully, I am *astonished*. I would never have been able to think it out so accurately. Listen, she could not bring herself to deceive a man who was in hourly danger of death. Right. But now that he is safely behind bars it is different. We are free to normalize ourselves. We will not, of course, hurt him by telling him as yet. We will simply help ourselves from the pantry, as Pursewarden used to say. My dear friend, isn't it wonderful? Fosca is an angel.'

'She sounds like a woman after all.'

'A Woman! The word, magnificent as it is, is hardly enough for a spirit like hers.'

He burst into a whinny of laughter and punched me affectionately on the shoulder. Together we walked down the long street. 'I am going to Pietrantoni to buy her an expensive present ... I, who never give a woman presents, never in my life. It always seemed absurd. I once saw a film of penguins in the mating season. The male penguin, than which nothing could more ludicrously resemble man, collects stones and places them before the lady of his choice when he proposes. It must be seen to be appreciated. Now I am behaving like a male penguin. Never mind. Never mind. Now our story cannot help but have a happy ending.'

Fateful words which I have so often recalled since, for within a few months Fosca was to be a problem no more.

$$\star \quad \star \quad \star \quad \star \quad \star$$

V

For some considerable time I heard nothing of Pursewarden's sister, though I knew that she was still up at the summer legation. As for Mountolive, his visits were recorded among the office memoranda, so that I knew he came up from Cairo for the night about every ten days. For a while I half expected a signal from him, but as time wore on I almost began to forget his existence as presumably he had forgotten mine. So it was that her voice, when first it floated over the office telephone, came as an unexpected intrusion — a surprise in a world where surprises were few and not unwelcome. A curiously disembodied voice which might have been that of uncertain adolescence, saying: 'I think you know of me. As a friend of my brother I would like to talk to you.' The invitation to dinner the following evening she described as 'private, informal and unofficial' which suggested to me that Mountolive himself would be present. I felt the stirring of an unusual curiosity as I walked up the long drive with its very English hedges of box, and through the small coppice of pines which encircled the summer residence. It was an airless hot night — such as must presage the gathering of a *khamseen* somewhere in the desert which would later roll its dust clouds down the city's streets and squares like pillars of smoke. But as yet the night air was harsh and clear.

I rang the bell twice without result, and was beginning to think that perhaps it might be out of order when I heard a soft swift step inside. The door opened and there stood Liza with an expression of triumphant eagerness on her blind face. I found her extraordinarily beautiful at first sight, though a little on the short side. She wore a dress of some dark soft stuff with a collar cut very wide, out of which her slender throat and head rose as if out of the corolla of a flower. She stood before me with her face thrown upwards, forwards — with an air of spectral bravery — as if presenting her lovely neck to an invisible executioner. As I uttered my own name she smiled and nodded and repeated it back to me in a whisper tense as a thread. 'Thank goodness, at last you have come' she said, as though she had lived in the expectation of my visit for years! As I stepped forward she added quickly 'Please forgive me if I. . . . It is my only way of knowing.' And I suddenly felt her soft warm fingers on my face, moving swiftly over it as if spelling it out, I felt a stirring of some singular unease, composed of sensuality and disgust, as these expert fingers travelled over my cheeks and lips. Her hands were small and well-shaped; the fingers conveyed an extraordinary impression of delicacy, for they appeared to turn up slightly at the ends to present their white pads, like antennae, to the world. I had once seen a world-famous pianist with just such fingers, so sensitive that they appeared to grow into the keyboard as he touched it. She gave a small sigh, as if of relief, and taking me by the wrist drew me across the hall and into the living-room with its expensive and featureless official furniture where Mountolive stood in front of the fireplace with an air of uneasy concern. Somewhere a radio softly played. We shook hands and in his handclasp I felt something infirm, indecisive which was matched by the fugitive voice in which he excused his long silence. 'I had to wait until Liza was ready' he said, rather mysteriously.

Mountolive had changed a good deal, though he still bore all the marks of the superficial elegance which was a prerequisite for his work, and his clothes were fastidiously chosen — for even (I thought grimly) informal undress is still a uniform for a diplomat. His old kindness and attentiveness were still there. Yet he had aged. I noticed that he now needed reading-glasses, for they lay upon a copy of *The Times* beside the sofa. And he had grown a moustache which he did not trim and which had altered the shape of his mouth, and emphasized a certain finely bred feebleness of feature. It did not seem possible to imagine him ever to have been in the grip of a passion strong enough to qualify the standard responses of an education so definitive as his. Nor now, looking from one to the other, could I credit the suspicions which Clea had voiced about his love for this strange blind witch who now sat upon the sofa staring sightlessly at me, with her hands folded in her lap — those rapacious, avaricious hands of a musician. Had she coiled herself, like a small hateful snake, at the centre of his peaceful life? I accepted a drink from his fingers and found, in the warmth of his smile, that I remembered having liked and admired him. I did so still.

'We have both been eager to see you, and particularly Liza, because she felt that you might be able to help her. But we will talk about all that later.' And with an abrupt smoothness he turned away from the real subject of my visit to enquire whether my post pleased me, and whether I was happy in it. An exchange of courteous pleasantries which provoked the neutral answers appropriate to them. Yet here and there were gleams of new information. 'Liza was quite determined you should stay here; and so we got busy to arrange it!' Why? Simply that I should submit to a catechism about her brother, who in truth I could hardly claim to have known, and who grew more and more mysterious to me every day — less important as a personage, more and more so as an artist? It was clear that I must wait until she chose to speak her mind. Yet it was baffling to idle away the time in the exchange of superficialities.

Yet these smooth informalities reigned, and to my surprise the girl herself said nothing — not a word. She sat there on the sofa, softly and attentively, as if on a cloud. She wore, I noticed, a velvet ribbon on her throat. It occurred to me that her pallor, which had so much struck Clea, was probably due to not being able to make-up in the mirror. But Clea had been right about the shape of her mouth, for once or twice I caught an expression, cutting and sardonic, which was a replica of her brother's.

Dinner was wheeled in by a servant, and still exchanging small talk we sat down to eat it; Liza ate swiftly, as if she were hungry, and quite unerringly, from the plate which Mountolive filled for her. I noticed when she reached for her wineglass that her expressive fingers trembled slightly. At last, when the meal was over, Mountolive rose with an air of scarcely disguised relief and excused himself. 'I'm going to leave you alone to talk shop to Liza. I shall have to do some work in the Chancery this evening. You will excuse me, won't you?' I saw an apprehensive frown shadow Liza's face for a moment, but it vanished almost at once and was replaced by an expression which suggested something between despair and resignation. Her fingers picked softly, suggestively at the tassel of a cushion. When the door had closed behind him she still sat silent, but now preternaturally still, her head bent downwards as if she were trying to decipher a message written in the palm of her hand. At last she spoke in a small cold voice, pronouncing the words incisively as if to make her meaning plain.

'I had no idea it would be difficult to explain when first I thought of asking your help. This book. . . .'

There was a long silence. I saw that little drops of perspiration had come out on her upper lip and her temples looked as if they had tightened under stress. I felt a certain compassion for her distress and said: 'I can't claim to have known him well, though I saw him quite frequently. In truth, I don't think we liked each other very much.'

'Originally' she said sharply, cutting across my vagueness with impatience 'I thought I might persuade you to do the book about him. But now I see that you will have to know everything. It is not easy to know where to begin. I myself doubt whether the facts of his life are possible to put down and publish. But I have been driven to think about the matter, first because his publishers insist on it — they say there is a great public demand; but mostly because of the book which this shabby journalist is writing, or has written. Keats.'

'Keats' I echoed with surprise.

'He is here somewhere I believe; but I do not know him. He has been put up to the idea by my brother's wife. She hated him, you know, after she found out; she thought that my brother and I had between us ruined her life. Truthfully I am afraid of her. I do not know what she has told Keats, or what he will write. I see now that my original idea in having you brought here was to get you to write a book which would . . . disguise the truth somehow. It only became clear to me just now when I was confronted by you. It would be inexpressibly painful to me if anything got out which harmed my brother's memory.'

Somewhere to the east I heard a grumble of thunder. She stood up with an air of panic and after a moment's hesitation crossed to the grand piano and struck a chord. Then she banged the cover down and turned once more to me, saying: 'I am afraid of thunder. Please may I hold your hand in a firm grip.' Her own was deathly cold. Then, shaking back her black hair she said: 'We were lovers, you know. That is really the meaning of his story and mine. He tried to break away. His marriage foundered on this question. It was perhaps dishonest of him not to have told her the truth before he married her. Things fall out strangely. For many years we enjoyed a perfect happiness, he and I. That it ended tragically is nobody's fault I suppose. He could not free himself from my inside hold on him, though he tried and struggled. I could not free myself from him, though truthfully I never wished to until . . . until the day arrived which he had predicted so many years before when the man he always called "the dark stranger" arrived. He saw him so clearly when he gazed into the fire. It was David Mountolive. For a little while I did not tell him that I had fallen in love, the fated love. (David would not let me. The only person we told was Nessim's mother. David asked my permission.) But my brother knew it quite unerringly and wrote after a long silence asking me if the stranger had come. When he got my letter he seemed suddenly to realize that our relationship might be endangered or crushed in the way his had been with his wife — not by anything we did, no, but by the simple fact of my existence. So he committed suicide. He explained it all so clearly in his last letter to me. I can recite it by heart. He said: "For so many years I have waited in anguished expectation for your letter. Often, often I wrote it for you in my own head, spelling it out word by magical word. I knew that in your happiness you would at once turn to me to express a passionate gratitude for what I had given you — for learning the meaning of all love through mine: so that when the stranger came you were ready. . . . And today it came! this long-awaited message, saying that he had read the letters, and I knew for the first time a sense of inexpressible relief as I read the lines. And joy — such joy as I never hoped to experience in my life — to think of you suddenly plunging into the full richness of life at last, no longer tied, manacled to the image of your tormented brother! Blessings tumbled from my lips. But then, gradually, as the cloud lifted and dispersed I felt the leaden tug of another truth, quite unforeseen, quite unexpected. The fear that, so long as I was still alive, still somewhere existing in the world, you would find it impossible truly to escape from the chains in which I have so cruelly held you all these years. At this fear my blood has turned chill — for I know that truthfully something much more definitive is required of me if you are ever to renounce me and start living. I must really abandon you, really remove myself from the scene in a manner which would permit no further equivocation in our vacillating hearts. Yes, I had anticipated the joy, but not that it would bring with it such a clear representation of certain death. This was a huge novelty! Yet it is the completest gift I can offer you as a wedding present! And if you look beyond the immediate pain you will see how perfect the logic of love seems to one who is ready to die for it." '

She gave a short clear sob and hung her head. She took the handkerchief from the breast pocket of my coat and pressed it to her trembling lip. I felt stupefied by the sad weight of all this calamitous information. I felt, in the ache of pity for Pursewarden, a new recognition of him growing up, a new enlightenment. So many things became clearer. Yet there were no words of consolation or commiseration which could do justice to so tragic a situation. She was talking again.

'I will give you the private letters to read so that you can advise me. These are the letters which I was not to open but was to keep until David came. He would read them to me and we would destroy them — or so he said. Is it strange — his certainty? The other ordinary letters were of course read to me in the usual way; but these private letters, and they are very many, were all pierced with a pin in the top left-hand corner. So that I could recognize them and put them aside. They are in that suitcase over there. I would like you to take them away and study them. Oh, Darley, you have not said a word. Are you prepared to help me in this dreadful predicament? I wish I could read your expression.'

'Of course I will help you. But just how and in what sense?'

'Advise me what to do! None of this would have arisen had not this shabby journalist intervened and been to see his wife.'

'Did your brother appoint a literary executor?'

'Yes. I am his executor.'

'Then you have a right to refuse to allow any of his unsold writings to be published while they're in copyright. Besides, I do not see how such facts could be made public without your own permission, even in an unauthorized biography. There is no cause whatsoever to worry. No writer in his senses could touch such material; no publisher in the world would undertake to print it if he did. I think the best thing I can do is to try and find out something about this book of Keats's. Then at least you will know where you stand.'

'Thank you, Darley. I could not approach Keats myself because I knew he was working for her. I hate and fear her — perhaps unjustly. I suppose too that I have a feeling of having wronged her without wishing it. It was a deplorable mistake on his part not to tell her before their marriage; I think he recognized it, too, for he was determined that I should not make the same mistake when at last David appeared. Hence the private letters, which leave no one in doubt. Yet it all fell out exactly as he had planned it, had prophesied it. That very first night when I told David I took him straight home to read them. We sat on the carpet in front of the gas-fire and he read them to me one by one in that unmistakable voice — the stranger's voice.'

She gave a queer blind smile at the memory and I had a sudden compassionate picture of Mountolive sitting before the fire, reading these letters in a slow faltering voice, stunned by the revelation of his own part in this weird masque, which had been planned for him years before, without his knowing. Liza sat beside me, lost in deep thought, her head hanging. Her lips moved slowly as if she were spelling something out in her own mind, following some interior recitation. I shook her hand softly as if to waken her. 'I should leave you now' I said softly. 'And why should I see the private letters at all? There is no need.'

'Now that you know the worst and best I would like you to advise me about destroying them. It was his wish. But David feels that they belong to his writings, and that we have a duty to preserve them. I cannot make up my mind about this. You are a writer. Try and read them as a writer, as if you had written them, and then tell me whether you would wish them preserved or not. They are all together in that suitcase. There are one or two other fragments which you might help me edit if you have time or if you think them suitable. He always puzzled me — except when I had him in my arms.'

A sudden expression of savage resentment passed across her white face. As if she had been goaded by a sudden disagreeable memory. She passed her tongue over her dry lips and as we stood up together she added in a small husky voice: 'There is one thing more. Since you have seen so far into our lives why should you not look right to the bottom? I always keep this close to me.' Reaching down into her dress she took out a snapshot and handed it to me. It was faded and creased. A small child with long hair done up in ribbons sat upon a park bench, gazing with a melancholy and wistful smile at the camera and holding out a white stick. It took me a moment or so to identify those troubling lines of mouth and nose as the features of Pursewarden himself and to realize that the little girl was blind.

'Do you see her?' said Liza in a thrilling whisper that shook the nerves by its strange tension, its mixture of savagery, bitterness and triumphant anguish. 'Do you see her? She was our child. It was when she died that he was overcome with remorse for a situation which had brought us nothing but joy before. Her death suddenly made him guilty. Our relationship foundered there; and yet it became in another way even more intense, closer. We were united by our guilt from that moment. I have often asked myself

why it should be so. Tremendous unbroken happiness and then
. . . one day, like an iron shutter falling, *guilt*.'

The word dropped like a falling star and expired in the silence.
I took this unhappiest of all relics and pressed it into her cold
hands.

'I will take the letters' I said.

'Thank you' she replied with an air now of dazed exhaustion.
'I knew we had a friend in you. I shall count on your help.'

As I softly closed the front door behind me I heard a chord
struck upon the piano — a single chord which hung in the silent
air, its vibrations diminishing like an echo. As I crossed among
the trees I caught a glimpse of Mountolive sneaking towards
the side door of the house. I suddenly divined that he had been
walking up and down outside the house in an agony of apprehension, with the air of a schoolboy waiting outside his housemaster's
study to receive a beating. I felt a pang of sympathy for him, for
his weakness, for the dreadful entanglement in which he had
found himself.

I found to my surprise that it was still early. Clea had gone to
Cairo for the day and was not expected back. I took the little
suitcase to her flat and sitting on the floor unpacked it.

In that quiet room, by the light of her candles, I began to read
the private letters with a curious interior premonition, a stirring
of something like fear — so dreadful a thing is it to explore the
inmost secrets of another human being's life. Nor did this feeling
diminish as I proceeded, rather it deepened into a sort of terror
almost a horror of what might be coming next. The letters!
Ferocious, sulky, brilliant, profuse — the torrent of words in that
close hand flowed on and on endlessly, studded with diamond-
hard images, a wild self-analytical frenzy of despair, remorse and
passion. I began to tremble as one must in the presence of a great
master, to tremble and mutter. With an interior shock I realized
that there was nothing in the whole length and breadth of our
literature with which to compare them! Whatever other master-
pieces Pursewarden may have written these letters outshone them
all in their furious, unpremeditated brilliance and prolixity.
Literature, I say! But these were life itself, not a studied representation of it in a form — life itself, the flowing undivided stream
of life with all its pitiable will-intoxicated memories, its pains,
terrors and submissions. Here illusion and reality were fused in
one single blinding vision of a perfect incorruptible passion which

hung over the writer's mind like a dark star — the star of death! The tremendous sorrow and beauty which this man expressed so easily — the terrifying abundance of his gifts — filled me with helpless despair and joy at once. The cruelty and the richness! It was as if the words poured from every pore in his body — execrations, groans, mixed tears of joy and despair — all welded to the fierce rapid musical notation of a language perfected by its purpose. Here at last the lovers confronted one another, stripped to the bone, stripped bare.

In this strange and frightening experience I caught a glimpse, for a moment, of the true Pursewarden — the man who had always eluded me. I thought with shame of the shabby passages in the Justine manuscript which I had devoted to him — to my image of him! I had, out of envy or unconscious jealousy, invented a Pursewarden to criticize. In everything I had written there I had accused him only of my own weaknesses — even down to completely erroneous estimates of qualities like social inferiorities which were mine, had never been his. It was only now, tracing out the lines written by that rapid unfaltering pen, that I realized that poetic or transcendental knowledge somehow cancels out purely relative knowledge, and that his black humours were simply ironies due to his enigmatic knowledge whose field of operation was above, beyond that of the relative fact-finding sort. There *was* no answer to the questions I had raised in very truth. He had been quite right. Blind as a mole, I had been digging about in the graveyard of relative fact piling up data, more information, and completely missing the mythopoeic reference which underlies fact. I had called this searching for truth! Nor was there any way in which I might be instructed in the matter — save by the ironies I had found so wounding. For now I realized that his irony was really tenderness turned inside out like a glove! And seeing Pursewarden thus, for the first time, I saw that through his work he had been seeking for the very tenderness of logic itself, of the Way Things Are; not the logic of syllogism or the tide-marks of emotions, but the real essence of fact-finding, the *naked* truth, the *Inkling* . . . the whole pointless Joke. Yes, Joke! I woke up with a start and swore.

If two or more explanations of a single human action are as good as each other then what does action mean but an illusion — a gesture made against the misty backcloth of a reality made palpable by the delusive nature of human division merely? Had any novelist before Pursewarden considered this question? I think not.

And in brooding over these terrible letters I also suddenly stumbled upon the true meaning of my own relationship to Pursewarden, and through him to all writers. I saw, in fact, that we artists form one of those pathetic human chains which human beings form to pass buckets of water up to a fire, or to bring in a lifeboat. An uninterrupted chain of humans born to explore the inward riches of the solitary life on behalf of the unheeding unforgiving community; manacled together by the same gift.

I began to see too that the real 'fiction' lay neither in Arnauti's pages nor Pursewarden's — nor even my own. It was life itself that was a fiction — we were all saying it in our different ways, each understanding it according to his nature and gift.

It was now only that I began to see how mysteriously the configuration of my own life had taken its shape from the properties of those elements which lie outside the relative life — in the kingdom which Pursewarden calls the 'heraldic universe'. We were three writers, I now saw, confided to a mythical city from which we were to draw our nourishment, in which we were to confirm our gifts. Arnauti, Pursewarden, Darley — like Past, Present and Future tense! And in my own life (the staunchless stream flowing from the wounded side of Time!) the three women who also arranged themselves as if to represent the moods of the great verb, Love: Melissa, Justine and Clea.

And realizing this I was suddenly afflicted by a great melancholy and despair at recognizing the completely limited nature of my own powers, hedged about as they were by the limitations of an intelligence too powerful for itself, and lacking in sheer word-magic, in propulsion, in passion, to achieve this other world of artistic fulfilment.

I had just locked those unbearable letters away and was sitting in melancholy realization of this fact when the door opened and Clea walked in, radiant and smiling. 'Why, Darley, what are you doing sitting in the middle of the floor in that rueful attitude? And my dear there are tears in your eyes.' At once she was down beside me on her knees, all tenderness.

'Tears of exasperation' I said, and then, embracing her, 'I have just realized that I am not an artist at all. There is not a shred of hope of my ever being one.'

'What on earth have you been up to?'

CLEA

'Reading Pursewarden's letters to Liza.'

'Did you see her?'

'Yes. Keats is writing some absurd book ———'

'But I just ran into him. He's back from the desert for the night.'

I struggled to my feet. It seemed to me imperative that I should find him and discover what I could about his project. 'He spoke' said Clea 'about going round to Pombal's for a bath. I expect you'll find him there if you hurry.'

Keats! I thought to myself as I hurried down the street towards the flat; he was also to play his part in this shadowy representation, this tableau of the artist's life. For it is always a Keats that is chosen to interpret, to drag his trail of slime over the pitiful muddled life of which the artist, with such pain, recaptures these strange solitary jewels of self-enlightenment. After those letters it seemed to me more than ever necessary that people like Keats if possible be kept away from interfering in matters beyond their normal concerns. As a journalist with a romantic story (suicide is the most romantic act for an artist) he doubtless felt himself to be in the presence of what he, in the old days, would have called 'A stunner. A Story in a Million'. I thought that I knew my Keats — but of course once more I had completely forgotten to take into account the operations of Time, for Keats had changed as we all had, and my meeting with him turned out to be as unexpected as everything else about the city.

I had mislaid my key and had to ring for Hamid to open the door for me. Yes, he said, Mr. Keats was there, in the bath. I traversed the corridor and tapped at the door behind which came the sound of rushing water and a cheerful whistling. 'By God, Darley, how splendid' he shouted in answer to my call. 'Come in while I dry. I heard you were back.'

Under the shower stood a Greek god! I was so surprised at the transformation that I sat down abruptly on the lavatory and studied this . . . apparition. Keats was burnt almost black, and his hair had bleached white. Though slimmer, he looked in first-class physical condition. The brown skin and ashen hair had made his twinkling eyes bluer than ever. He bore absolutely *no resemblance* to my memories of him! 'I just sneaked off for the night' he said, speaking in a new rapid and confident voice. 'I'm developing one of those blasted desert sores on my elbow, so I got a chit and here I am. I don't know what the hell causes them, nobody does; perhaps all the tinned muck we eat up there in the desert! But two days in Alex and an injection and presto! The bloody thing clears up again! I say, Darley, what fun to meet again. There's so much to tell you. This war!' He was bubbling over with high spirits. 'God, this water is a treat. I've been revelling.'

'You look in tremendous shape.'

'I am. I am.' He smacked himself exuberantly on the buttocks 'Golly though, it is good to come into Alex. Contrasts make you appreciate things so much better. Those tanks get so hot you feel like frying whitebait. Reach my drink, there's a good chap.' On the floor stood a tall glass of whisky and soda with an ice cube in it. He shook the glass, holding it to his ear like a child. 'Listen to the ice tinkling' he cried in ecstasy. 'Music to the soul, the tinkle of ice.' He raised his glass, wrinkled up his nose at me and drank my health. 'You look in quite good shape, too' he said, and his blue eyes twinkled with a new mischievous light. 'Now for some clothes and then . . . my dear chap, I'm rich. I'll give you a slap-up dinner at the Petit Coin. No refusals, I'll not be baulked. I particularly wanted to see you and talk to you. I have news.'

He positively skipped into the bedroom to dress and I sat on Pombal's bed to keep him company while he did so. His high spirits were quite infectious. He seemed hardly able to keep still. A thousand thoughts and ideas bubbled up inside him which he wanted to express simultaneously. He capered down the stairs into the street like a schoolboy, taking the last flight at a single bound. I thought he would break into a dance along Rue Fuad. 'But seriously' he said, squeezing my elbow so hard that it hurt. '*Seriously*, life is wonderful' and as if to illustrate his seriousness he burst into ringing laughter. 'When I think how we used to brood and worry.' Apparently he included me in this new euphoric outlook on life. 'How slowly we took everything, I feel ashamed to remember it!'

At the Petit Coin we secured a corner table after an amiable altercation with a naval lieutenant, and he at once took hold of Menotti and commanded champagne to be brought. Where the devil had he got this new laughing authoritative manner which instantly commanded sympathetic respect without giving offence?

'The desert!' he said, as if in answer to my unspoken question. 'The desert, Darley, old boy. That is something to be seen.' From a capacious pocket he produced a copy of the *Pickwick Papers*. 'Damn!' he said. 'I mustn't forget to get this copy

794

replaced. Or the crew will bloody well fry me.' It was a sodden, dog-eared little book with a bullet hole in the cover, smeared with oil. 'It's our only library, and some bastard must have wiped himself on the middle third. I've sworn to replace it. Actually there's a copy at the flat. I don't suppose Pombal would mind my pinching it. It's absurd. When there isn't any action we lie about reading it aloud to one another, under the stars! Absurd, my dear chap, but then everything is more absurd. More and more absurd every day.'

'You sound so happy' I said, not without a certain envy.

'Yes' he said in a smaller voice, and suddenly, for the first time, became relatively serious. 'I am. Darley, let me make you a confidence. Promise not to groan.'

'I promise.'

He leaned forward and said in a whisper, his eyes twinkling, 'I've become a writer at last!' Then suddenly he gave his ringing laugh. 'You promised not to groan' he said.

'I didn't groan.'

'Well, you looked groany and supercilious. The proper response would have been to shout "Hurrah!"'

'Don't shout so loud or they'll ask us to leave.'

'Sorry. It came over me.'

He drank a large bumper of champagne with the air of someone toasting himself and leaned back in his chair, gazing at me quizzically with the same mischievous sparkle in his blue eyes.

'What have you written?' I asked.

'Nothing' he said, smiling. 'Not a word as yet. It's all up here.' He pointed a brown finger at his temple. 'But now at least I know it is. Somehow whether I do or don't actually write isn't important — it isn't, if you like, the whole point about becoming a writer at all, as I used to think.'

In the street outside a barrel organ began playing with its sad hollow iteration. It was a very ancient English barrel organ which old blind Arif had found on a scrap heap and had fixed up in a somewhat approximate manner. Whole notes misfired and several chords were hopelessly out of tune.

'Listen' said Keats, with deep emotion, 'just listen to old Arif.' He was in that delicious state of inspiration which only comes when champagne supervenes upon a state of fatigue — a melancholy tipsiness which is wholly inspiriting. 'Gosh!' he went on in rapture, and began to sing in a very soft husky whisper, marking

time with his finger, '*Taisez-vous, petit babouin*'. Then he gave a
great sigh of repletion, and chose himself a cigar from Menotti's
great case of specimens, sauntering back to the table where he
once more sat before me, smiling rapturously. 'This war' he said
at last, 'I really must tell you. . . . It is quite different to what I
imagined it must be like.'

Under his champagne-bedizened tipsiness he had become
relatively grave all at once. He said: 'Nobody seeing it for the
first time could help crying out with the whole of his rational mind
in protest at it: crying out "It must stop!" My dear chap, to see
the ethics of man *at his norm* you must see a battlefield. The
general idea may be summed up in the expressive phrase: "If you
can't eat it or **** it, then **** on it." Two thousand years of
civilization! It peels off in a flash. Scratch with your little finger
and you reach the woad or the ritual war paint under the varnish!
Just like that!' He scratched the air between us languidly with
his expensive cigar. 'And yet — you know what? The most unaccountable and baffling thing. It has made a man of me, as the
saying goes. More, a writer! My soul is quite clear. I suppose you
could regard me as permanently disfigured! I have begun it at last,
that bloody joyful book of mine. Chapter by chapter it is forming
in my old journalist's noodle — no, not a journalist's any more,
a *writer's*.' He laughed again as if at the preposterous notion.
'Darley, when I look around that . . . battlefield at night, I stand in
an ecstasy of shame, revelling at the coloured lights, the flares
wallpapering the sky, and I say: "All this had to be brought about
so that poor Johnny Keats could grow into a man." That's what.
It is a complete enigma to me, yet I am absolutely certain of it.
No other way would have helped me because I was too damned
stupid, do you see?' He was silent for a while and somewhat
distrait, drawing on his cigar. It was as if he were going over this
last piece of conversation in his mind to consider its validity,
word by word, as one tests a piece of machinery. Then he added,
but with care and caution, and a certain expression of bemused
concentration, like a man handling unfamiliar terms: 'The man
of action and the man of reflection are really the same man,
operating on two different fields. But to the same end! Wait, this
is beginning to sound silly.' He tapped his temple reproachfully
and frowned. After a moment's thought he went on, still frowning:
'Shall I tell you my notion about it . . . the war? What I have come
to believe? I believe the desire for war was first lodged in the

instincts as a biological shock-mechanism to precipitate a spiritual crisis which couldn't be done any other how in limited people. The less sensitive among us can hardly visualize death, far less live joyfully with it. So the powers that arranged things for us felt they must concretize it, in order to lodge death in the actual present. Purely helpfully, if you see what I mean!' He laughed again, but ruefully this time. 'Of course it is rather different now that the bystander is getting hit harder than the front-line bloke. It is unfair to the men of the tribe who would like to leave the wife and kids in relative safety before stumping off to this primitive ordination. For my part I think the instinct has somewhat atrophied, and may be on the way out altogether; but what will they put in its place — that's what I wonder? As for me, Darley, I can only say that no half-dozen French mistresses, no travels round the globe, no adventures in the peacetime world we knew could have grown me up so thoroughly in half the time. You remember how I used to be? Look, I'm really an adult now — but of course ageing fast, altogether too fast! It will sound damn silly to you, but the presence of death out there as a normal feature of life — only in full acceleration so to speak — has given me an inkling of Life Everlasting! And there was no other way I could have grasped it, damn it. Ah! well, I'll probably get bumped off up there in full possession of my imbecility, as you might say.'

He burst out laughing once more, and gave himself three noiseless cheers, raising his cigar-hand ceremoniously at each cheer. Then he winked carefully at me and filled his glass once more, adding with an air of vagueness the coda: 'Life only has its full meaning to those who co-opt death!' I could see that he was rather drunk by now, for the soothing effects of the hot shower had worn off and the desert-fatigue had begun to reassert itself.

'And Pursewarden?' I said, divining the very moment at which to drop his name, like a hook, into the stream of our conversation.

'Pursewarden!' he echoed on a different note, which combined a melancholy sadness and affection. 'But my dear Darley, it was something like this that he was trying to tell me, in his own rather bloody way. And I? I still blush with shame when I think of the questions I asked him. And yet his answers, which seemed so bloody enigmatic then, make perfect sense to me *now*. Truth is double-bladed, you see. There is no way to express it in terms of language, this strange bifurcated medium with its basic duality!

Language! What is the writer's struggle except a struggle to use a medium as precisely as possible, but knowing fully its basic imprecision? A hopeless task, but none the less rewarding for being hopeless. Because the task itself, the act of wrestling with an insoluble problem, grows the writer up! This was what the old bastard realized. You should read his letters to his wife. For all their brilliance how he whined and cringed, how despicably he presented himself — like some Dostoievskian character beset by some nasty compulsion neurosis! It is really staggering what a petty and trivial soul he reveals there.' This was an amazing insight into the tormented yet wholly complete being of the letters which I myself had just read!

'Keats' I said, 'for goodness' sake tell me. Are you writing a book about him?'

Keats drank slowly and thoughtfully and replaced his glass somewhat unsteadily before saying: 'No.' He stroked his chin and fell silent.

'They say you are writing something' I persisted. He shook his head obstinately and contemplated his glass with a blurred eye. 'I wanted to' he admitted at last, slowly. 'I did a long review of the novels once for a small mag. The next thing I got a letter from his wife. *She* wanted a book done. A big rawboned Irish girl, very hysterical and sluttish: handsome in a big way, I suppose. Always blowing her nose in an old envelope. Always in carpet slippers. I must say I felt for him. But I tumbled straight into a hornets' nest there. She *loathed* him, and there seemed to be plenty to loathe, I must say. She gave me a great deal of information, and simply masses of letters and manuscripts. Treasure trove all right. But, my dear chap, I couldn't use this sort of stuff. If for no other reason than that I respect his memory and his work. No. No. I fobbed her off. Told her she would never get such things published. She seemed to want to be publicly martyred in print just to get back at him — old Pursewarden! I couldn't do such a thing. Besides the material was quite hair-raising! I don't want to talk about it. Really, I would never repeat the truth to a soul.'

We sat looking thoughtfully, even watchfully at each other, for a long moment before I spoke again.

'Have you ever met his sister, Liza?'

Keats shook his head slowly. 'No. What was the point? I abandoned the project right away, so there was no need to try and hear her story. I know she has a lot of manuscript stuff, because the wife told me so. But. . . . She is here isn't she?' His lip curled with the faintest suggestion of disgust. 'Truthfully I don't want to meet her. The bitter truth of the matter seems to me that the person old Pursewarden most loved — I mean purely spiritually — did not at all understand the state of his soul, so to speak, when he died: or even have the vaguest idea of the extent of his achievement. No, she was busy with a vulgar intrigue concerned with legalizing her relations with Mountolive. I suppose she feared that her marriage to a diplomat might be imperilled by a possible scandal. I may be wrong, but that is the impression I gathered. I believe she was going to try and get a whitewashing book written. But now, in a sense, I have my own Pursewarden, my own copy of him, if you like. It's enough for me. What do the details matter, and why should I meet his sister? It is his work and not his life which is necessary to us — which offers one of the many meanings of the word with four faces!'

I had an impulse to cry out 'Unfair', but I restrained it. It is impossible in this world to arrange for full justice to be done to everyone. Keats's eyelids drooped. 'Come' I said, calling for the bill, 'It's time you went home and got some sleep.'

'I do feel rather tired' he mumbled.

'Avanti.'

There was an old horse-drawn gharry in a side-street which we were glad to find. Keats protested that his feet were beginning to hurt and his arm to pain him. He was in a pleasantly exhausted frame of mind, and slightly tipsy after his potations. He lay back in the smelly old cab and closed his eyes. 'D'you know, Darley' he said indistinctly, 'I meant to tell you but forgot. Don't be angry with me, old fellow-bondsman, will you. I know that you and Clea. . . . Yes, and I'm glad. But I have the most curious feeling that one day I am going to marry her. Really. Don't be silly about it. Of course I would never breathe a word, and it would happen years after this silly old war. But somewhere along the line I feel I'm bound to hitch up with her.'

'Now what do you expect me to say?'

'Well, there are a hundred courses open. Myself I would start yelling and screaming at once if you said such a thing to me. I'd knock your block off, push you out of the cab, anything. I'd punch me in the eye.'

The gharry drew up with a jolt outside the house. 'Here we are'

I said, and helped my companion down into the road. 'I'm not as drunk as all that' he cried cheerfully, shaking off my help, ' 'tis but fatigue, dear friend.' And while I argued out the cost of the trip with the driver he went round and held a long private confabulation with the horse, stroking its nose. 'I was giving it some maxims to live by' he explained as we wound our weary way up the staircase. 'But the champagne had muddled up my quotation-box. What's that thing of Shakespeare's about the lover and the cuckold all compact, seeking the bubble reputation e'en in the cannon's mouth.' The last phrase he pronounced in the strange (man-sawing-wood) delivery of Churchill. 'Or something about swimmers into cleanness leaping — a pre-fab in the eternal mind no less!'

'You are murdering them both.'

'Gosh I'm tired. And there seems to be no bombardment tonight.'

'They are getting less frequent.'

He collapsed on his bed fully dressed, slowly untying his suède desert boots and wriggling with his toes until they slid slowly off and plopped to the floor. 'Did you ever see Pursewarden's little book called *Select Prayers for English Intellectuals*? It was funny. "Dear Jesus, please keep me as eighteenth century as possible — but without the c*******d. . . ." ' He gave a sleepy chuckle, put his arms behind his head and started drifting into smiling sleep. As I turned out the light he sighed deeply and said: 'Even the dead are overwhelming us all the time with kindnesses.'

I had a sudden picture of him as a small boy walking upon the very brink of precipitous cliffs to gather seabirds' eggs. One slip. . . .

But I was never to see him again. *Vale!*

* * * * *

VI

Ten thirsty fingers of my blind Muse
Confer upon my face their sensual spelling

The lines ran through my head as I pressed the bell of the summer residence the following evening. In my hand I held the green leather suitcase which contained the private letters of Pursewarden — that brilliant sustained fusillade of words which still exploded in my memory like a firework display, scorching me. I had telephoned to Liza from my office in the morning to make the rendezvous. She opened the door and stood before me with a pale graven expression of expectancy. 'Good' she whispered as I murmured my name, and 'Come.' She turned and walked before me with a stiff upright expressive gait which reminded me of a child dressed up as Queen Elizabeth for a charade. She looked tired and strained, and yet in a curious way proud. The living-room was empty. Mountolive, I knew, had returned to Cairo that morning. Rather surprisingly, for it was late in the year, a log-fire burned in the chimney-piece. She took up her stand before it, arching her back to the warmth, and rubbing her hands as if she were chilled.

'You have been quick, very quick' she said, almost sharply, almost with a hint of implied reproach in her tone. 'But I am glad.' I had already told her by telephone the gist of my conversation with Keats about the non-existent book. 'I am glad, because now we can decide something, finally. I couldn't sleep last night. I kept imagining you reading them, the letters. I kept imagining him writing them.'

'They are marvellous. I have never read anything like them in my whole life.' I felt a note of chagrin in my own tones.

'Yes' she said, and fetched a deep sigh. 'And yet I was afraid you would think so; *afraid* because you would share David's opinion of them and advise me that they should be preserved *at all costs*. Yet *he* expressly told me to burn them.'

'I know.'

'Sit down, Darley. Tell me what you really think.'

I sat down, placing the little suitcase on the floor beside me, and said: 'Liza, this is not a literary problem unless you choose to regard it as one. You need take nobody's advice. Naturally nobody who has read them could help but regret the loss.'

'But Darley, if they had been yours, written to someone you . . . loved?'

'I should feel relief to know that my instructions had been carried out. At least I presume that is what *he* would feel, wherever he might be now.'

She turned her lucid blind face to the mirror and appeared to explore her own reflection in it earnestly, resting the tips of her frilly fingers on the mantelpiece. 'I am as superstitious as he was' she said at last. 'But it is more than that. I was always obedient because I knew that he saw further than I and understood more than I did.'

> *This caged reflection gives her nothing back*
> *That women drink like thirsty stags from mirrors*

How very much of Pursewarden's poetry became crystal-clear and precise in the light of all this new knowledge! How it gathered consequence and poignance from the figure of Liza exploring her own blindness in the great mirror, her dark hair thrown back on her shoulders!

At last she turned back again, sighing once more, and I saw a look of tender pleading on her face, made the more haunting and expressive by the empty sockets of her eyes. She took a step forward and said: 'Well, then, it is decided. Only tell me you will help me burn them. They are very many. It will take a little time.'

'If you wish.'

'Let us sit down beside the fire together.'

So we sat facing each other on the carpet and I placed the suitcase between us, pressing the lock so that the cover released itself and sprang up with a snap.

'Yes' she said. 'This is how it must be. I should have known all along that I must obey him.' Slowly, one by one I took up the pierced envelopes, unfolded each letter in turn and handed it to her to place upon the burning logs.

'We used to sit like this as children with our playbox between us, before the fire, in the winter. So often, and always together. You would have to go back very far into the past to understand it all. And even then I wonder if you would understand. Two small children left alone in an old rambling farmhouse among the frozen lakes, among the mists and rains of Ireland. We had no resources except in each other. He converted my blindness into poetry, I saw with his brain, he with my eyes. So we invented a whole imperishable world of poetry together — better by far than the best of his books, and I have read them all with my fingers, they are all at the institute. Yes I read and re-read them looking for a clue to the guilt which had transformed everything. Nothing had affected us before, everything conspired to isolate us, keep us together. The death of our parents happened when we were almost too small to comprehend it. We lived in this ramshackle old farmhouse in the care of an eccentric and deaf old aunt who did the work, saw that we were fed, and left us to our own devices. There was only one book there, a Plutarch, which we knew by heart. Everything else he invented. This was how I became the strange mythological queen of his life, living in a vast palace of sighs — as he used to say. Sometimes it was Egypt, sometimes Peru, sometimes Byzantium. I suppose I must have known that really it was an old farmhouse kitchen, with shabby deal furniture and floors of red tile. At least when the floors had been washed with carbolic soap with its peculiar smell I *knew*, with half my mind, that it was a farmhouse floor, and not a palace with magnificent tessellated floors brilliant with snakes and eagles and pygmies. But at a word he brought me back to reality, as he called it. Later, when he started looking for justifications for our love instead of just simply being proud of it, he read me a quotation from a book. "In the African burial rites it is the sister who brings the dead king back to life. In Egypt as well as Peru the king, who was considered as God, took his sister to wife. But the motive was ritual and not sexual, for they symbolized the moon and the sun in their conjunction. The king marries his sister because he, as God the star, wandering on earth, is immortal and may therefore not propagate himself in the children of a strange woman, any more than he is allowed to die a natural death." That is why he was pleased to come here to Egypt, because he felt, he said, an interior poetic link with Osiris and Isis, with Ptolemy and Arisinoë — the race of the sun and the moon!'

Quietly and methodically she placed letter after letter on the burning pyre, talking in a sad monotone, as much to herself as to me.

'No it would not be possible to make it all comprehensible to those who were not of our race. But when the guilt entered the old poetic life began to lose its magic — not for me: but for him.

It was he who made me dye my hair black, so that I could pretend to be a step-sister of his, not a sister. It hurt me deeply to realize suddenly that he was guilty all of a sudden; but as we grew up the world intruded more and more upon us, new lives began to impinge on our solitary world of palaces and kingdoms. He was forced to go away for long periods. When he was absent I had nothing whatsoever except the darkness and what my memory of him could fill it with; somehow the treasures of his invention went all lustreless until he came back, his voice, his touch. All we knew of our parents, the sum of our knowledge, was an old oak cupboard full of their clothes. They seemed enormous to us when we were small — the clothes of giants, the shoes of giants. One day he said they oppressed him, these clothes. We did not need parents. And we took them out into the yard and made a bonfire of them in the snow. We both wept bitterly, I do not know why. We danced round the bonfire singing an old hunting song with savage triumph and yet weeping.'

She was silent for a long moment, her head hanging in profound concentration over this ancient image, like a soothsayer gazing fixedly into the dark crystal of youth. Then she sighed and raised her head, saying: 'I know why you hesitate. It is the last letter, isn't it? You see I counted them. Give it to me, Darley.'

I handed it to her without a word and she softly placed it in the fire saying: 'It is over at last.'

★　　★　　★　　★　　★

VII

As the summer burned away into autumn, and autumn into winter once more we became slowly aware that the war which had invested the city had begun slowly to ebb, to flow gradually away along the coast-roads fringing the desert, releasing its hold upon us and our pleasures. For receding like a tide it left its strange coprolitic trophies along the beaches which we had once used, finding them always white and deserted under the flying gulls. War had denied them to us for a long time; but now, when we rediscovered them, we found them littered with pulped tanks and twisted guns, and the indiscriminate wreckage of temporary supply harbours abandoned by the engineers to rot and rust under the desert sun, to sink gradually into the shifting dunes. It gave one a curious melancholy re-assurance to bathe there now — as if among the petrified lumber of a Neolithic age: tanks like the skeletons of dinosaurs, guns standing about like outmoded furniture. The minefields consti-tuted something of a hazard, and the Bedouin were often straying into them in the course of pasturing; once Clea swerved — for the road was littered with glistening fragments of shattered camel from some recent accident. But such occasions were rare, and as for the tanks themselves, though burned out they were tenantless. There were no human bodies in them. These had presumably been excavated and decently buried in one of the huge cemeteries which had grown up in various unexpected corners of the western desert like townships of the dead. The city, too, was finding its way back to its normal habits and rhythms, for the bombardments had now ceased altogether and the normal night-life of the Levant had begun once more to flower. And though uniforms were less abundant the bars and night clubs still plied a splendid trade with servicemen on leave.

My own eventless life, too, seemed to have settled itself into a natural routine-fed pattern, artificially divided by a private life which I had surrendered to my complete absorption in Clea, and an office life which, though not onerous, had little meaning to me. Little had changed: but yes, Maskelyne had at last managed to break his bonds and escape back to his regiment. He called on us, resplendent in uniform, to say good-bye, shyly pointing — not his pipe but a crisp new swagger-stick — at his tail-wagging colleague. 'I told you he'd do it' said Telford with a triumphant sadness in his voice. 'I always knew it.' But Mountolive stayed on, apparently still 'frozen' in his post.

From time to time by arrangement I revisited the child at Karm Abu Girg to see how she was faring. To my delight I found that the transplantation, about which I had had many misgivings, was working perfectly. The reality of her present life apparently chimed with the dreams I had invented for her. It was all as it should be — the coloured playing-card characters among whom she could now number herself! If Justine remained a somewhat withdrawn and unpredictable figure of moods and silences it only added, as far as I could see, to the sombre image of a dispossessed empress. In Nessim she had realized a father. His image had gained definition by greater familiarity because of his human tendernesses. He was a delightful companion-father now, and together they explored the desert lands around the house on horseback. He had given her a bow and arrows, and a little girl of about her own age, Taor, as a body-servant and *amah*. The so-called palace, too, which we had imagined together, stood the test of reality magnificently. Its labyrinth of musty rooms and its ramshackle treasures were a perpetual delight. Thus with her own horses and servants, and a private palace to play in, she was an Arabian Nights queen indeed. She had almost forgotten the island now, so absorbed was she among these new treasures. I did not see Justine during these visits, nor did I try to do so. Sometimes however Nessim was there, but he never accompanied us on our walks or rides, and usually the child came to the ford to meet me with a spare horse.

In the spring Balthazar, who had by now quite come to himself and had thrown himself once more into his work, invited Clea and myself to take part in a ceremony which rather pleased his somewhat ironic disposition. This was the ceremonial placing of flowers on Capodistria's grave on the anniversary of the Great Porn's birthday. 'I have the express authority of Capodistria himself' he explained. 'Indeed he himself always pays for the flowers every year.' It was a fine sunny day for the excursion and Balthazar insisted that we should walk. Though somewhat hampered by the nosegay he carried he was in good voice. His vanity in the matter of his hair had become too strong to withstand, and he had duly submitted to Mnemjian's ministrations, thus 'rubbing out his age', as he expressed it. Indeed the change was remarkable. He was now, once more, the old Balthazar, with his sapient dark eyes turned ironically on the doings of the city. And no less on Capodistria from whom he had just received a long letter. 'You can have no idea what the old brute is up to over the water. He has taken the Luciferian path and plunged into Black Magic. But I'll read it to you. His graveside is, now I come to think of it, a most appropriate place to read his account of his experiments!'

The cemetery was completely deserted in the sunshine. Capodistria had certainly spared no expense to make his grave imposing and had achieved a fearsome vulgarity of decoration which was almost mind-wounding. Such cherubs and scrolls, such floral wreaths. On the slab was engraved the ironic text: 'Not Lost But Gone Before'. Balthazar chuckled affectionately as he placed his flowers upon the grave and said 'Happy Birthday' to it. Then he turned aside, removing coat and hat for the sun was high and bright, and together we sat on a bench under a cypress tree while Clea ate toffees and he groped in his pockets for the bulky typewritten packet which contained Capodistria's latest and longest letter. 'Clea' he said, 'you must read it to us. I've forgotten my reading glasses. Besides, I would like to hear it through once, to see if it sounds less fantastic or more. Will you?'

Obediently she took the close-typed pages and started reading. 'My dear M.B.'

'The initials' interposed Balthazar 'stand for the nickname which Pursewarden fastened on me — Melancholia Borealis, no less. A tribute to my alleged Judaic gloom. Proceed, my dear Clea.'

The letter was in French.

'I have been conscious, my dear friend, that I owed you some account of my new life here, yet though I have written you fairly frequently I have got into the habit of evading the subject. Why? Well, my heart always sank at the thought of your derisive laugh. It is absurd, for I was never a sensitive man or quick to worry about the opinion of my neighbours. Another thing. It would have involved a long and tiresome explanation of the unease and unfamiliarity I always felt at the meetings of the Cabal which sought to drench the world in its abstract goodness. I did not know then that my path was not the path of Light but of Darkness. I would have confused it morally or ethically with good and evil at that time. Now I recognize the path I am treading as simply the counterpoise — the bottom end of the see-saw, as it were — which keeps the light side up in the air. Magic! I remember you once quoting to me a passage (quite nonsensical to me then) from Paracelsus. I think you added at the time that even such gibberish must mean something. It does! "True Alchemy which teaches how to make or transmute out of the five imperfect metals, requires no other materials but only the metals. The perfect metals are made out of the imperfect metals, through them and with them alone; for with other things is *Luna* (phantasy) but in the metals is *Sol* (wisdom)."

'I leave a moment's pause for your peculiar laugh, which in the past I would not have been slow to echo! What a mountain of rubbish surrounding the idea of the *tinctura physicorum*, you would observe. Yes but. . . .

'My first winter in this windy tower was not pleasant. The roof leaked. I did not have my books to solace me as yet. My quarters seemed rather cramped and I wondered about extending them. The property on which the tower stands above the sea had also a straggle of cottages and outbuildings upon it; here lodged the ancient, deaf couple of Italians who looked after my wants, washed and cleaned and fed me. I did not want to turn them out of their quarters but wondered whether I could not convert the extra couple of barns attached to their abode. It was then that I found, to my surprise, that they had another lodger whom I had never seen, a strange and solitary creature who only went abroad at night, and wore a monk's cassock. I owe all my new orientation to my meeting with him. He is a defrocked Italian monk, who describes himself as a Rosicrucian and an alchemist. He lived here among a mountain of masonic manuscripts — some of very great age — which he was in the process of studying. It was he who first convinced me that this line of enquiry was (despite some disagreeable aspects) concerned with increasing man's interior hold on himself, on the domains which lie unexplored within him; the comparison with everyday science is not fallacious, for the form of this enquiry is based as firmly on method — only with different premises! And if, as I say, it has some disagreeable aspects, why so has formal science — vivisection for instance. Anyway, here I struck up a rapport, and opened up for myself a field of study which grew more and more engrossing as the months went by. I also discovered at last something which eminently fitted my nature! Truthfully, everything in this field seemed to nourish and sustain me! Also I was able to be of considerable practical assistance to the Abbé F. as I will call him, for some of these manuscripts (stolen from the secret lodges on Athos I should opine) were in Greek, Arabic and Russian — languages which he did not know well. Our friendship ripened into a partnership. But it was many months before he introduced me to yet another strange, indeed formidable figure who was also dabbling in these matters. This was an Austrian Baron who lived in a large mansion inland and who was busy (no, do not laugh) on the obscure problem which we once discussed — is it in *De Natura Rerum*? I think it is — the *generatio homunculi*? He had a Turkish butler and famulus to help him in his experiments. Soon I became *persona grata* here also and was allowed to help them to the best of my ability.

'Now this Baron — whom you would certainly find a strange and imposing figure, heavily bearded and with big teeth like the seeds of a corn-cob — this Baron had . . . ah! my dear Balthazar, had *actually produced* ten homunculi which he called his "prophesying spirits". They were preserved in the huge glass canisters which they use hereabouts for washing olives or to preserve fruit, and they lived in water. They stood on a long oaken rack in his studio or laboratory. They were produced or "patterned", to use his own expression, in the course of five weeks of intense labour of thought and ritual. They were exquisitely beautiful and mysterious objects, floating there like sea-horses. They consisted of a king, a queen, a knight, a monk, a nun, an architect, a miner, a seraph, and finally a blue spirit and a red one! They dangled lazily in these stout glass jars. A tapping fingernail seemed to alarm them. They were only about a span long, and as the Baron was anxious for them to grow to a greater size, we helped him to bury them in several cartloads of horse-manure. This great midden was sprinkled daily with an evil-smelling liquid which was prepared with great labour by the Baron and his Turk, and which contained some rather disgusting ingredients. At each sprinkling the manure began to steam as if heated by a subterranean fire. It was almost too hot to place one finger in it. Once every three days the Abbé and the Baron spent the whole night praying and fumigating the midden with incense. When at last the Baron deemed this process complete the bottles were carefully removed and returned to the laboratory shelves. All the homunculi had grown in size to such an extent that the bottles were now hardly big enough for them, and the male figures had come into possession of heavy beards. The nails of their fingers and toes had grown very long. Those which bore a human representation wore clothes appropriate to their rank and style. They had a kind of beautiful obscenity floating there with an expression on their faces such as I have only once seen before — on the face of a Peruvian pickled human head! Eyes turned up into the skull, pale fish's lips drawn back to expose small perfectly formed teeth! In the bottles containing respectively the red and blue spirit there was nothing to be seen. All the bottles, by the way, were heavily sealed with oxbladders and wax bearing the imprint of a magic seal. But when the Baron tapped with his fingernail on the bottles and repeated some words in Hebrew the water clouded and began to turn red and blue respectively. The homunculi began to show their faces, to develop cloudily like a photographic print, gradually increasing in size. The blue spirit was as beautiful as any angel, but the red wore a truly terrifying expression.

'These beings were fed every three days by the Baron with some dry rose-coloured substance which was kept in a silver box lined with sandalwood. Pellets about the size of a dried pea. Once every week, too, the water in the bottles had to be emptied out; they had to be refilled (the bottles) with fresh rainwater. This had to be done very rapidly because during the few moments that the spirits were exposed to the air they seemed to get weak and unconscious, as if they were about to die like fish. But the blue spirit was never fed; while the red one received once a week a thimblefull of the fresh blood of some animal — a chicken I think. This blood disappeared at once in the water without colouring or even troubling it. As soon as this bottle was opened it turned turbid and dark and gave off the odour of rotten eggs!

'In the course of a couple of months these homunculi reached their full stature, the stage of prophecy — as the Baron calls it; then every night the bottles were carried into a small ruined chapel, situated in a grove at some distance from the house, and here a service was held and the bottles "interrogated" on the course of future events. This was done by writing questions in Hebrew on slips of paper and pressing them to the bottle before the eyes of the homunculus; it was rather like exposing sensitized photographic paper to light. I mean it was not as if the beings read but divined the questions, slowly, with much hesitation.

They spelled out their answers, drawing with a finger on the transparent glass, and these responses were copied down immediately by the Baron in a great commonplace book. Each homunculus was only asked questions appropriate to his station, and the red and blue spirits could only answer with a smile or a frown to indicate assent or dissent. Yet they seemed to know everything, and any question at all could be put to them. The King could only touch on politics, the monk religion . . . and so on. In this way I witnessed the compilation of what the Baron called "the annals of Time" which is a document at least as impressive as that left behind him by Nostradamus. So many of these prophecies have proved true in these last short months that I can have little doubt about the rest also proving so. It is a curious sensation to peer thus into the future!

'One day, by some accident, the glass jar containing the monk fell to the stone flags and was broken. The poor monk died after a couple of small painful respirations, despite all the efforts made by the Baron to save him. His body was buried in the garden. There was an abortive attempt to "pattern" another monk but this was a failure. It produced a small leech-like object without vitality which died within a few hours.

'A short while afterwards the King managed to escape from his bottle during the night; he was found sitting upon the bottle containing the Queen, scratching with his nails to get the seal away! He was beside himself, and very agile, though weakening desperately from his exposure to the air. Nevertheless he led us quite a chase among the bottles — which we were afraid of overturning. It was really extraordinary how nimble he was, and had he not become increasingly faint from being out of his native element I doubt whether we could have caught him. We did however and he was pushed, scratching and biting, back into his bottle, but not before he had severely scratched the Abbé's chin. In the scrimmage he gave off a curious odour, as of a hot metal plate cooling. My finger touched his leg. It was of a wet and rubbery consistency, and sent a shiver of apprehension down my spine.

'But now a mishap occurred. The Abbé's scratched face became inflamed and poisoned and he went down with a high fever and was carried off to hospital where he lies at present, convalescing. But there was more to follow, and worse; the Baron, being Austrian, had always been something of a curiosity here, and more especially now when the spy-mania which every war brings has reached its height. It came to my ears that he was to be thoroughly investigated by the authorities. He received the news with despairing calmness, but it was clear that he could not afford to have unauthorized persons poking about in his laboratory. It was decided to "dissolve" the homunculi and bury them in the garden. In the absence of the Abbé I agreed to help him. I do not know what it was he poured into the bottles but all the flames of hell leaped up out of them until the whole ceiling of the place was covered in soot and cobwebs. The beings shrank now to the size of dried leeches, or the dried navel-cords which sometimes village folk will preserve. The Baron groaned aloud from time to time, and the sweat stood out on his forehead. The groans of a woman in labour. At last the process was complete and at midnight the bottles were taken out and interred under some loose flags in the little chapel where, presumably, they must still be. The Baron has been interned, his books and papers sealed by the Custodians of Property. The Abbé lies, as I said, in hospital. And I? Well, my Greek passport has made me less suspect than most people hereabouts. I have retired for the moment to my tower. There is still the mass of masonic data in the barns which the Abbé inhabited; I have taken charge of these. I have written to the Baron once or twice but he has not, perhaps out of tact, replied to me; believing perhaps that my association with him might lead to harm. And so . . . well, the war rolls on about us. Its end and what follows it — right up to the end of this century — I know: it lies here beside me as I write, in question and answer form. But who would believe me if I published it all — and much less you, doctor of the empiric sciences, sceptic and ironist? As for the war — Paracelsus has said: "Innumerable are the *Egos* of man; in him are angels and devils, heaven and hell, the whole of the animal creation, the vegetable and mineral kingdoms; and just as the little individual man may be diseased, so the great universal man has his diseases, which manifest themselves as the ills which affect humanity as a whole. Upon this fact is based the prediction of future events." And so, my dear friend, I have chosen the Dark Path towards my own light. I know now that I must follow it wherever it leads! Isn't that something to have achieved? Perhaps not. But for me it truthfully seems so. But I hear that laughter!

'Ever your devoted Da Capo'.*

'Now' said Clea, 'oblige with the laughter!'

'What Pursewarden' I said 'called "the melancholy laughter of Balthazar which betokens solipsism".'

Balthazar did indeed laugh now, slapping his knee and doubling himself up like a jack knife. 'That damned rogue, Da Capo' he said. 'And yet, *soyons raisonnables* if that is indeed the expression — he wouldn't tell a pack of lies. Or perhaps he might. No, he wouldn't. Yet can you bring yourself to believe in what he says — you two?'

'Yes' said Clea, and here we both smiled for her bondage to the soothsayers of Alexandria would naturally give her a predisposition towards the magic arts. 'Laugh' she said quietly.

'To tell the truth' said Balthazar more soberly, 'when one casts around the fields of so-called knowledge which we have partially opened up one is conscious that there may well be whole areas of darkness which may belong to the Paracelsian regions — the submerged part of the iceberg of knowledge. No, dammit, I must admit that you are right. We get too certain of ourselves travelling backwards and forwards along the tramlines of empirical fact. Occasionally one gets hit softly on the head by a stray brick which has been launched from some other region. Only yesterday, for example, Boyd told me a story which sounded no less strange: about a soldier who was buried last week. I could, of course, supply explanations which might fit the case, but not with any certainty. This young boy went on a week's leave to Cairo. He came back having had an enjoyable time, or so he said. Next he developed an extraordinary intermittent fever with simply huge maximum temperatures. Within a week he died. A few hours before death a thick white cataract formed over his eyeballs with a sort of luminous red node over the retina. All the boy would repeat in the course of his delirium was the single phrase: "*She did it with a golden needle.*" Nothing but these words. As I say one could perhaps strap the case down clinically with a clever guess or two but . . . had I to be honest I would be obliged to admit that it did not exactly fit within an accepted category that I knew. Nor, by the way, did the autopsy give one anything more to go on: blood tests, spinal fluid, stomach etc. Not even a nice, familiar (yet itself perhaps inexplicable) meningeal disturbance. The brain was lovely and fresh! At least so Boyd says, and he took great pleasure in thoroughly exploring the young man. Mystery! Now what the devil could he have been doing on leave? It seems quite impossible to discover. His stay is not recorded at any of the hotels or army transit hotels. He spoke no language but English. Those few days spent in Cairo are completely missing from the count. And then the woman with the golden needle?

'But in truth it is happening all the time, and I think you are right' (this to Clea) 'to insist obstinately on the existence of the dark powers and the fact that some people do scry as easily as I gaze down the barrel of my microscope. Not all, but some. And even quite stupid people, like your old Scobie, for example. Mind you, in my opinion, that was a rigmarole of the kind he produced sometimes when he was tipsy and wanted to show off — I mean the stuff supposedly about Narouz: that was altogether too dramatic to be taken seriously. And even if some of the detail were right he *could* have had access to it in the course of his duties. After all Nimrod did the *procès verbal* and that document must have been knocking around.'

'What about Narouz?' I asked curiously, secretly piqued that Clea had confided things to Balthazar which she had kept from me. It was now that I noticed that Clea had turned quite white and was looking away. But Balthazar appeared to notice nothing himself and went plunging on. 'It has the ingredients of a novelette — I mean about trying to drag you down into the grave with him. Eh, don't you think? And about the weeping you would hear.' He broke off abruptly, noticing her expression at last. 'Goodness, Clea my dear' he went on in self-reproach, 'I hope I am not betraying a confidence. You suddenly look upset. Did you tell me not to repeat the Scobie story?' He took both her hands and turned her round to face him.

A spot of red had appeared in both her cheeks. She shook her head, though she said nothing, but bit her lips as if with vexation. At last 'No' she said, 'there is no secret. I simply did not tell Darley because . . . well, it is silly as you say : anyway he doesn't believe in that sort of rubbish. I didn't want to seem stupider than he must find me.' She leaned to kiss me apologetically on the cheek. She sensed my annoyance, as did Balthazar who hung his head and said: 'I've talked out of turn. Damn! Now he will be angry with you.'

'Good heavens, no!' I protested. 'Simply curious, that is all. I had no intention of prying, Clea.'

She made a gesture of anguished exasperation and said: 'Very well. It is of no importance. I will tell you the whole thing.' She started speaking hastily, as if to dispose of a disagreeable and time-wasting subject. 'It was during the last dinner I told you about. Before I went to Syria. He was tipsy, I don't deny it. He said what Balthazar has just told you, and he added a description of someone who suggested to me Nessim's brother. He said, marking the place with his thumbnail on his own lips: "His lips are split here, and I see him covered in little wounds, lying on a table. There is a lake outside. He has made up his mind. He will try and drag you to him. You will be in a dark place, imprisoned, unable to resist him. Yes, there is one near at hand who might aid you if he could. But he will not be strong enough." ' Clea stood up suddenly and brought her story to an end with the air of someone snapping off a twig. 'At this point he burst into tears' she said.

It was strange what a gloom this nonsensical yet ominous recital put over our spirits; something troubling and distasteful seemed to invade that brilliant spring sunshine, the light keen air. In the silence that followed Balthazar gloomily folded and refolded his overcoat on his knee while Clea turned away to study the distant curve of the great harbour with its flotillas of cubist-smeared craft, and the scattered bright petals of the racing dinghies which had crossed the harbour boom, threading their blithe way towards the distant blue marker buoy. Alexandria was virtually at norm once more, lying in the deep backwater of the receding war, recovering its pleasures. Yet the day had suddenly darkened around us, oppressing our spirits — a sensation all the more exasperating because of its absurd cause. I cursed old Scobie's self-importance in setting up as a fortune-teller.

'These gifts might have got him a bit further in his own profession had they been real' I said peevishly.

Balthazar laughed, but even here there was a chagrined doubt in his laughter. His remorse at having stirred up this silly story was quite patent.

'Let us go' said Clea sharply. She seemed slightly annoyed as well, and for once disengaged her arm when I took it. We found an old horse-drawn gharry and drove slowly and silently into town together.

'No damn it!' cried Balthazar at last. 'Let us go down and have a drink by the harbour at least.' And without waiting for answer from us he redirected the jarvey and set us mutely clip-clopping down the slow curves of the Grande Corniche towards the Yacht Club in the outer harbour of which was now to befall something momentous and terrible for us all. I remember it so clearly, this spring day without flaw; a green bickering sea lighting the minarets, softly spotted here and there by the dark gusts of a fine racing wind. Yes, with mandolines fretting in the Arab town, and every costume glowing as brightly as a child's coloured transfer. Within a quarter of an hour the magnificence of it was to be darkened, poisoned by unexpected — completely unmerited death. But if tragedy strikes suddenly the actual moment of its striking seems to vibrate on, extending into time like the sour echoes of some great gong, numbing the spirit, the comprehension. Suddenly, yes, but yet how *slowly* it expands in the understanding — the ripples unrolling upon the reason in ever-widening circles of fear. And yet, all the time, outside the centre-piece of the picture, so to speak, with its small tragic anecdote, normal life goes on unheeding. (We did not even hear the bullets, for example. Their sullen twang was carried away on the wind.)

Yet our eyes were drawn, as if by the lines-of-force of some great marine painting, to a tiny clutter of dinghies snubbing together in the lee of one of the battleships which hovered against the sky like a grey cathedral. Their sails flapped and tossed, idly as butterflies contending with the breeze. There was some obscure movements of oars and arms belonging to figures too small at this range to distinguish or recognize. Yet this tiny commotion had force to draw the eye — by who knows what interior premonition? And as the cab rolled silently along the rim of the inner harbour we saw it unroll before us like some majestic seascape by a great master. The variety and distinction of the small refugee craft from every corner of the Levant — their differing designs and rigs — gave it a brilliant sensuality and rhythm against the glittering water. Everything was breath-taking yet normal; tugs hooted, children cried, from the cafés came the rattle of the *trictrac* boards and the voices of birds. The normality of an entire world surrounded that tiny central panel with its flicking sails, the gestures we could not interpret, the faint voices. The little craft tilted, arms rose and fell.

'Something has happened' said Balthazar with his narrow dark eye upon the scene, and as if his phrase had affected the horse it suddenly drew to a halt. Besides ourselves on the dockside only one man had also seen; he too stood gazing with curious open-mouthed distraction, aware that something out of the ordinary was afoot. Yet everywhere people bustled, the chandlers cried.

At his feet three children played in complete absorption, placing marbles in the tramlines, hoped to see them ground to powder when the next tram passed. A water-carrier clashed his brass mugs, crying: 'Come, ye thirsty ones.' And unobtrusively in the background, as if travelling on silk, a liner stole noiselessly down the green thoroughfare towards the open sea.

'It's Pombal' cried Clea at last, in puzzled tones, and with a gesture of anxiety put her arm through mine. It was indeed Pombal. What had befallen them was this. They had been drifting about the harbour in his little dinghy with their customary idleness and inattention and had strayed too near to one of the French battleships, carried into its lee and off their course by an unexpected swoop of the wind. How ironically it had been planned by the invisible stage-masters who direct human actions, and with what speed! For the French ships, though captive, had still retained both their small-arms and a sense of shame, which made their behaviour touchy and unpredictable. The sentries they mounted had orders to fire a warning shot across the bows of any craft which came within a dozen metres of any battleship. It was, then, only in response to orders that a sentry put a bullet through Pombal's sail as the little dinghy whirled down on its rogue course towards his ship. It was merely a warning, which intended no deliberate harm. And even now this might have . . . but no: it could not have fallen out otherwise. For my friend, overcome with rage and mortification, at being treated thus by these cowards and lackbones of his own blood and faith, turned purple with indignation, and abandoned his tiller altogether in order to stand precariously upright and shake his huge fists, screaming: '*Salauds!*' and '*Espèces de cons!*' and — what was perhaps the definitive epithet — '*Lâches!*'

Did he hear the bullets himself? It is doubtful whether in all the confusion he did, for the craft tilted, gybed, and turned about on another course, toppling him over. It was while he was lying there, recovering the precious tiller, that he noticed Fosca in the very act of falling, but with infinite slowness. Afterwards he said that she did not know she had been hit. She must have felt, perhaps, simply a vague and unusual dispersion of her attention, the swift anaesthesia of shock which follows so swiftly upon the wound. She tilted like a high tower, and felt the sternsheets coming up slowly to press themselves to her cheek. There she lay with her eyes wide open, plump and soft as a wounded pheasant will lie, still bright of eye in spite of the blood running from its beak. He shouted her name, and felt only the immense silence of the word, for the little freshet had sharpened and was now rushing them landward. A new sort of confusion supervened, for other craft, attracted as flies are by wounds, began to cluster with cries of advice and commiseration. Meanwhile Fosca lay with vague and open eyes, smiling to herself in the other kind of dream.

And it was now that Balthazar suddenly awoke from his trance, struggled out of the cab without a word and began his queer lurching, traipsing run across the dock to the little red field-ambulance telephone with its emergency line. I heard the small click of the receiver and the sound of his voice speaking, patient and collected. The summons was answered, too, with almost miraculous promptness, for the field-post with its ambulances was only about fifty yards away. I heard the sweet tinkle of the ambulance's bell, and saw it racing along the cobbles towards us. And now all faces turned once more towards that little convoy of dinghies — faces on which was written only patient resignation or dread. Pombal was on his knees in the sheets with bent head. Behind him, deftly steering, was Ali the boatman who had been the first to comprehend and offer his help. All the other dinghies, flying along on the same course, stayed grouped around Pombal's as if in active sympathy. I could read the name *Manon* which he had so proudly bestowed upon it, not six months ago. Everything seemed to have become bewildering, shaken into a new dimension which was swollen with doubts and fears.

Balthazar stood on the quay in an agony of impatience, urging them in his mind to hurry. I heard his tongue clicking against the roof of his mouth *teck tsch*, clicking softly and reproachfully; a reproach, I wondered, directed against their slowness, or against life itself, its unpremeditated patterns?

At last they were on us. One heard quite distinctly the sound of their breathing, and our own contribution, the snap of stretcher-thongs, the tinkle of polished steel, the small snap of heels studded with hobnails. It all mixed into a confusion of activity, the lowering and lifting, the grunts as dark hands found purchase on a rope to hold the dinghy steady, the sharp serrated edges of conflicting voices giving orders. 'Stand by' and 'Gently now' all mixed with a distant foxtrot on a ship's radio. A stretcher swinging like a cradle, like a basket of fruit upon the dark shoulders of an Arab. And steel doors opening on a white throat.

CLEA

Pombal wore an air of studied vagueness, his features all dispersed and quite livid in colour. He flopped on to the quay as if he had been dropped from a cloud, falling to his knees and recovering. He wandered vaguely after Balthazar and the stretcher-bearers bleating like a lost sheep. I suppose it must have been her blood splashed upon the expensive white *espadrilles* which he had bought a week before at Ghoshen's Emporium. At such moments it is the small details which strike one like blows. He made a vague attempt to clamber into the white throat but was rudely ejected. The doors clanged in his face. Fosca belonged now to science and not to him. He waited with humbly bent head, like a man in church, until they should open once more and admit him. He seemed hardly to be breathing. I felt an involuntary desire to go to his side but Clea's arm restrained me. We all waited in great patience and submissiveness like children, listening to the vague movements within the ambulance, the noise of boots. Then at long last the doors opened and the weary Balthazar climbed down and said: 'Get in and come with us.' Pombal gave one wild glance about him and turning his pain-racked countenance suddenly upon Clea and myself, delivered himself of a single gesture — spreading his arms in uncomprehending hopelessness before clapping a fat hand over each ear, as if to avoid hearing something. Balthazar's voice suddenly cracked like parchment. 'Get in' he said roughly, angrily, as if he were speaking to a criminal; and as they climbed into the white interior I heard him add in a lower voice, 'She is dying.' A clang of iron doors closing, and I felt Clea's hand turn icy in my own.

So we sat, side by side and speechless on that magnificent spring afternoon which was already deepening into dusk. At last I lit a cigarette and walked a few yards along the quay among the chaffering Arabs who described the accident to each other in yelping tones. Ali was about to take the dinghy back to its moorings at the Yacht Club; all he needed was a light for his cigarette. He came politely towards me and asked if he might light up from me. As he puffed I noticed that the flies had already found the little patch of blood on the dinghy's floorboards. 'I'll clean it up' said Ali, noticing the direction of my glance; with a lithe cat-like leap he jumped aboard and unloosed the sail. He turned to smile and wave. He wanted to say 'A bad business' but his English was inadequate. He shouted 'Bad poison, sir.' I nodded.

Clea was still sitting in the gharry looking at her own hands.

It was as if this sudden incident had somehow insulated us from one another.

'Let's go back' I said at last, and directed the driver to turn back into the town we had so recently quitted.

'Pray to goodness she will be all right' said Clea at last. 'It is too cruel.'

'Balthazar said she was dying. I heard him.'

'He may be wrong.'

But he was not wrong, for both Fosca and the child were dead, though we did not get the news until later in the evening. We wandered listlessly about Clea's rooms, unable to concentrate on anything. Finally she said: 'You had better go back and spend the evening with him, don't you think.' I was uncertain. 'He would rather remain alone I imagine.'

'Go back' she said, and added sharply, 'I can't bear you hanging about at a time like this. . . . Oh, darling, I've hurt you. I'm sorry.'

'Of course you haven't, you fool. But I'll go.'

All the way down Rue Fuad I was thinking: such a small displacement of the pattern, a single human life, yet it had power to alter so much. Literally, such an eventuality had occurred to none of us. We simply could not stomach it, fit it into the picture which Pombal himself had built up with such care. It poisoned everything, this small stupid fact — even almost our affection for him, for it had turned to horror and sympathy! How inadequate as emotions they were, how powerless to be of use. My own instinct would have been to keep away altogether! I felt as if I never wanted to see him again — in order not to shame him. Bad poison, indeed. I repeated Ali's phrase to myself over and over again.

Pombal was already there when I got back, sitting in his gout-chair, apparently deep in thought. A full glass of neat whisky stood beside him which he did not seem to have touched. He had changed, however, into the familiar blue dressing-gown with the gold peacock pattern, and on his feet were his battered old Egyptian slippers like golden shovels. I went into the room quite quietly and sat down opposite him without a word. He did not appear to actually look at me, yet somehow I felt that he was conscious of my presence; yet his eye was vague and dreamy, fixed on the middle distance, and his fingers softly played a five-finger exercise on each other. And still looking at the window he said, in a squeaky little voice — as if the words had power to move him although he did not quite know their meaning: 'She's dead, Darley. They are both dead.' I felt a sensation of a leaden weight about my heart. '*C'est pas juste*' he added absently and fell to pulling his side-beard with fat fingers. Quite unemotional, quite flat — like a man recovering from a severe stroke. Then he suddenly took a gulp of whisky and started up, choking and coughing. 'It is neat' he said in surprise and disgust, and put the glass down with a long shudder. Then, leaning forward he began to scribble, taking up a pencil and pad which were on the table — whorls and lozenges and dragons. Just like a child. 'I must go to confession tomorrow for the first time for ages' he said slowly, as if with infinite precaution. 'I have told Hamid to wake me early. Will you mind if *Cléa* only comes?' I shook my head, I understood that he meant to the funeral. He sighed with relief. '*Bon*' he said, and standing up took the glass of whisky. At that moment the door opened and the distraught Pordre appeared. In a flash Pombal changed. He gave a long chain of deep sobs. The two men embraced muttering incoherent words and phrases, as if consoling each other for a disaster which was equally wounding to both. The old diplomat raised his white womanish fist in the air and said suddenly, fatuously: 'I have already protested strongly.' To whom, I wondered? To the invisible powers which decree that things shall fall out this way or that? The words sputtered out meaninglessly on the chill air of the drawing-room. Pombal was talking.

'I must write and tell him everything' he said. 'Confess everything.'

'Gaston' said his Chief sharply, reprovingly, 'you must not do any such thing. It would increase his misery in prison. *C'est pas juste*. Be advised by me: the whole matter must be forgotten.'

'Forgotten!' cried my friend as if he had been stung by a bee. 'You do not understand. Forgotten! He must know for *her* sake.'

'He must never know' said the older man. 'Never.'

They stood for a long while holding hands, and gazing about them distractedly through their tears; and at this moment, as if to complete the picture, the door opened to admit the porcine outlines of Father Paul — who was never to be found far from the centre of any scandal. He paused inside the doorway with an air of unction, with his features registering a vast gluttonous self-satisfaction. 'My poor boy' he said, clearing his throat. He made a vague gesture of his paw as if scattering Holy Water over us all and sighed. He reminded me of some great hairless vulture. Then surprisingly he clattered out a few phrases of consolation in Latin.

I left my friend among these elephantine comforters, relieved in a way that there was no place for me in all this incoherent parade of Latin commiserations. Simply pressing his hand once I slipped out of the flat and directed my thoughtful footsteps in the direction of Clea's room.

The funeral took place next day. Clea came back, looking pale and strained. She threw her hat across the room and shook out her hair with an impatient gesture — as if to expel the whole distasteful memory of the incident. Then she lay down exhaustedly on the sofa and put her arm over her eyes.

'It was ghastly' she said at last, 'really ghastly, Darley. First of all it was a *cremation*. Pombal insisted on carrying out her wishes despite violent protests from Father Paul. What a beast that man is. He behaved as though her body had become Church property. Poor Pombal was furious. They had a terrible row settling the details I hear. And then . . . I had never visited the new Crematorium! It is unfinished. It stands in a bit of sandy waste-land littered with straw and old lemonade bottles, and flanked by a trash heap of old car-bodies. It looks in fact like a hastily improvised furnace in a concentration camp. Horrid little brick-lined beds with half-dead flowers sprouting from the sand. And a little railway with runners for the coffin. The ugliness! And the faces of all those consuls and acting consuls! Even Pombal seemed quite taken aback by the hideousness. And the heat! Father Paul was of course in the foreground of the picture, relishing his rôle. And then with an incongruous squeaking the coffin rolled away down the garden path and swerved into a steel hatch. We hung about, first on one leg then on the other; Father Paul showed some inclination to fill this awkward gap with impromptu prayers but at that moment a radio in a nearby house started playing Viennese waltzes. Attempts were made by various chauffeurs to locate and silence it, but in vain. Never have I felt unhappier than standing in this desolate chicken run in my best clothes. There was a dreadful charred smell from the furnace. I did not know then that Pombal intended to scatter the ashes in the desert, and that he had decided that I alone would accompany him on this journey. Nor, for that matter, did I know that Father

Paul — who scented a chance of more prayers — had firmly made up his mind to do so as well. All that followed came as a surprise.

'Well finally the casket was produced — and what a casket! That was a real poke in the eye for us. It was like a confectioner's triumphant effort at something suitable for inexpensive chocolates. Father Paul tried to snatch it, but poor Pombal held on to it firmly as we trailed towards the car. I must say, here Pombal showed some backbone. "Not you" he said as the priest started to climb into the car. "I'm going alone with Clea." He beckoned to me with his head.

' "My son" said Father Paul in a low grim voice, "I shall come too."

' "You won't" said Pombal. "You've done your job."

' "My son, I am coming" said this obstinate wretch.

'For a moment it seemed that all might end with an exchange of blows. Pombal shook his beard at the priest and glared at him with angry eyes. I climbed into the car, feeling extremely foolish. Then Pombal pushed Father Paul in the best French manner — hard in the chest — and climbed in, banging the door. A susurrus went up from the assembled consuls at this public slight to the cloth, but no word was uttered. The priest was white with rage and made a sort of involuntary gesture — as if he were going to shake his fist at Pombal, but thought better of it.

'We were off; the chauffeur took the road to the eastern desert, acting apparently on previous instructions. Pombal sat quite still with this ghastly *bonbonnière* on his knees, breathing through his nose and with half-closed eyes. As if he were recovering his self-composure after all the trials of the morning. Then he put out his hand and took mine, and so we sat, silently watching the desert unroll on either side of the car. We went quite far out before he told the chauffeur to stop. He was breathing rather heavily. We got out and stood for a desultory moment at the roadside. Then he took a step or two into the sand and paused, looking back. "Now I shall do it" he said, and broke into his fat shambling run which carried him about twenty yards into the desert. I said hurriedly to the chauffeur, "Drive on for five minutes, and then come back for us." The sound of the car starting did not make Pombal turn round. He had slumped down on his knees, like a child playing in a sand-pit; but he stayed quite still for a long time. I could hear him talking in a low confidential voice, though whether he was praying or reciting poetry I could not tell. It felt desperately forlorn on that empty desert road with the heat shimmering up from the tarmac.

'Then he began to scrabble about in the sand before him, to pick up handfuls like a Moslem and pour it over his own head. He was making a queer moaning noise. At last he lay face downwards and quite still. The minutes ticked by. Far away in the distance I could hear the car coming slowly towards us — at a walking pace.

' "Pombal" I said at last. There was no reply. I walked across the intervening space, feeling my shoes fill up with the burning sand, and touched him on the shoulder. At once he stood up and started dusting himself. He looked dreadfully old all of a sudden. "Yes" he said with a vague, startled glance all round him, as if for the first time he realized where he was. "Take me home, Clea." I took his hand — as if I were leading a blind man — and tugged him slowly back to the car which by now had arrived.

'He sat beside me with a dazed look for a long time until, as if suddenly touched to the quick by a memory, he began to howl like a little boy who has cut his knee. I put my arms round him. I was so glad you weren't there — your Anglo-Saxon soul would have curled up at the edges. Yet he was repeating: "It must have looked ridiculous. It must have looked ridiculous." And all of a sudden he was laughing hysterically. His beard was full of sand. "I suddenly remembered Father Paul's face" he explained, still giggling in the high hysterical tones of a schoolgirl. Then he suddenly took a hold on himself, wiped his eyes, and sighing sadly said: "I am utterly washed out, utterly exhausted. I feel I could sleep for a week."

'And this is presumably what he is going to do. Balthazar has given him a strong sleeping draught to take. I dropped him at his flat and the car brought me on here. I'm hardly less exhausted than he. But thank God it is all over. Somehow he will have to start his life all over again.'

As if to illustrate this last proposition the telephone rang and Pombal's voice, weary and confused, said: 'Darley, is that you? Good. Yes, I thought you would be there. Before I went to sleep I wanted to tell you, so that we could make arrangements about the flat. Pordre is sending me into Syria *en mission*. I leave early in the morning. If I go this way I will get allowances and be able to keep up my part of the flat easily until I come back. Eh?'

'Don't worry about it' I said.

'It was just an idea.'

'Sleep now.'

There was a long silence. Then he added: 'But of course I will write to you, eh? Yes. Very well. Don't wake me if you come in this evening.' I promised not to.

But there was hardly any need for the admonition for when I returned to the flat later that night he was still up, sitting in his gout-chair with an air of apprehension and despair. 'This stuff of Balthazar's is no good' he said. 'It is mildly emetic, that is all. I am getting more drowsy from the whisky. But somehow I don't want to go to bed. Who knows what dreams I shall have?' But I at last persuaded him to get into bed; he agreed on condition that I stayed and talked to him until he dozed off. He was relatively calm now, and growing increasingly drowsy. He talked in a quiet relaxed tone, as one might talk to an imaginary friend while under anaesthetic.

'I suppose it will all pass. Everything does. In the very end, it passes. I was thinking of other people in the same position. But for some it does not pass easily. One night Liza came here. I was startled to find her on the doorstep with those eyes which give me the creeps — like an eyeless rabbit in a poultry shop. She wanted me to take her to her brother's room in the Mount Vulture Hotel. She said she wanted to "see" it. I asked what she would see. She said, with anger, "I have my own way of seeing." Well I had to do it. I felt it would please Mountolive perhaps. But I did not know then that the Mount Vulture was no longer a hotel. It had been turned into a brothel for the troops. We were half-way up the stairs before the truth dawned on me. All these naked girls, and half-dressed sweating soldiers with their hairy bodies; their crucifixes tinkling against their identity discs. And the smell of sweat and rum and cheap scent. I said we must get out, for the place had changed hands, but she stamped her foot and insisted with sudden anger. Well, we climbed the stairs. Doors were open on every landing, you could see everything. I was glad she was blind. At last we came to his room. It was dark. On his bed there lay an old woman asleep with a hashish pipe beside her. It smelt of drains. She, Liza, was very excited. "Describe it" she told me. I did my best. She advanced towards the bed. "There is a woman asleep there" I said, trying to pull her back. "This is a house of ill fame now, Liza, I keep telling you." Do you know what she said? "*So much the better.*" I was

825

startled. She pressed her cheek to the pillow beside the old woman, who groaned all at once. Liza stroked her forehead as if she were stroking a child and said "There now. Sleep." Then she came slowly and hesitantly to my hand. She gave a curious grin and said: "I wanted to try and take his imprint from the pillow. But it was a useless idea. One must try everything to recover memory. It has so many hiding-places." I did not know what she meant. We started downstairs again. On the second landing I saw some drunken Australians coming up. I could see from their faces that there was going to be trouble. One of their number had been cheated or something. They were terribly drunk. I put my arms around Liza and pretended we were making love in a corner of the landing until they passed us safely. She was trembling, though whether from fear or emotion I could not tell. And she said "Tell me about his women. What were they like?" I gave her a good hard shake. "Now you are being banal" I said. She stopped trembling and went white with anger. In the street she said "Get me a taxi. I do not like you." I did and off she went without a word. I regretted my rudeness afterwards, for she was suffering; at the time things happen too fast for one to take them into account. And one never knows enough about people and their sufferings to have the right response ready at the moment. Afterwards I said many sympathetic things to her in my mind. But too late. Always too late.'

A slight snore escaped his lips and he fell silent. I was about to switch off his bedside lamp and tip-toe from his room when he continued to speak, only from far away, re-establishing the thread of his thought in another context: 'And when Melissa was dying Clea spent all day with her. Once she said to Clea: "Darley made love with a kind of remorse, of despair. I suppose he imagined Justine. He never excited me like other men did. Old Cohen, for example, he was just dirty-minded, yet his lips were always wet with wine. I liked that. It made me respect him for he was a man. But Pursewarden treated me like precious china, as if he were afraid he might break me, like some precious heirloom! How good it was for once to be at rest!" '

*　　*　　*　　*　　*

VIII

So the year turned on its heel, through a winter of racing winds, frosts keener than grief, hardly preparing us for that last magnificent summer which followed the spring so swiftly. It came curving in, this summer, as if from some long-forgotten latitude first dreamed of in Eden, miraculously rediscovered among the slumbering thoughts of mankind. It rode down upon us like some famous snow-ship of the mind, to drop anchor before the city, its white sails folding like the wings of a seabird. Ah! I am hunting for metaphors which might convey something of the piercing happiness too seldom granted to those who love; but words, which were first invented against despair, are too crude to mirror the properties of something so profoundly at peace with itself, at one with itself. Words are the mirrors of our discontents merely; they contain all the huge unhatched eggs of the world's sorrows. Unless perhaps it were simpler to repeat under one's breath some lines torn from a Greek poem, written once in the shadow of a sail, on a thirsty promontory in Byzantium. Something like . . .

> *Black bread, clear water, blue air.*
> *Calm throat incomparably fair.*
> *Mind folded upon mind*
> *Eyes softly closed on eyes.*
> *Lashes a-tremble, bodies bare.*

But they English badly; and unless one hears them in Greek falling softly, word by word, from a mouth made private and familiar by the bruised endearments of spent kisses they must remain always simply charmless photographs of a reality which overreaches the realm of the poet's scope. Sad that all the brilliant plumage of that summer remains beyond capture — for one's old age will have little but such memories upon which to found its regretful happinesses. Will memory clutch it — that incomparable pattern of days, I wonder? In the dense violet shadow of white sails, under the dark noon-lantern of figs, on the renowned desert roads where the spice caravans march and the dunes soothe themselves away to the sky, to catch in their dazed sleep the drumming of gulls' wings turning in spray? Or in the cold whiplash of the waters crushing themselves against the fallen pediments of forgotten islands? In the night-mist falling upon deserted harbours with the old Arab seamarks pointing eroded fingers? Somewhere, surely, the sum of these things will still exist. There were no hauntings yet. Day followed day upon the calendar of desire, each night turning softly over in its sleep to reverse the darkness and drench us once more in the royal sunlight. Everything conspired to make it what we needed.

It is not hard, writing at this remove in time, to realize that it had all *already happened*, had been ordained in such a way and in no other. This was, so to speak, only its 'coming to pass' — its stage of manifestation. But the scenario had already been devised somewhere, the actors chosen, the timing rehearsed down to the last detail in the mind of that invisible author — which perhaps would prove to be only the city itself: the Alexandria of the human estate. The seeds of future events are carried within ourselves. They are implicit in us and unfold according to the laws of their own nature. It is hard to believe, I know, when one thinks of the perfection of that summer and what followed it.

Much had to do with the discovery of the island. The island! How had it eluded us for so long? There was literally not a corner of this coast which we did not know, not a beach we had not tried, not an anchorage we had not used. Yet it had been there, staring us in the face. 'If you wish to hide something' says the Arabic proverb, 'hide it in the sun's eye.' It lay, not hidden at all, somewhere to the west of the little shrine of Sidi El Agami — the white scarp with the snowy butt of a tomb emerging from a straggle of palms and figlets. It was simply an upshouldered piece of granite pushed up from the seabed by an earthquake or some submarine convulsion in the distant past. Of course, when the sea ran high it would be covered; but it is curious that it remains to this day unmarked on the Admiralty charts, for it would constitute quite a hazard to craft of medium draught.

It was Clea who first discovered the little island of Narouz. 'Where has this sprung from?' she asked with astonishment; her brown wrist swung the cutter's tiller hard over and carried us fluttering down into its lee. The granite boulder was tall enough for a windbreak. It made a roundel of still blue water in the combing tides. On the landward side there was a crude N carved in the rock above an old eroded iron ring which, with a stern anchor out to brace her, served as a secure mooring. It would be ridiculous to speak of stepping ashore for the 'shore' consisted of a narrow strip of dazzling white pebbles no larger than a fireplace. 'Yes, it is, it is Narouz' island' she cried, beside herself with delight at the discovery — for here at last was a place where she could fully indulge her taste for solitude. Here one would be as private as a seabird. The beach faced landward. One could see the whole swaying line of the coast with its ruined Martello towers and dunes travelling away to ancient Taposiris. We unpacked our provisions with delight for here we could swim naked and sunbathe to our heart's content without interruption.

Here that strange and solitary brother of Nessim had spent his time fishing. 'I always wondered where it could be, this island of his. I thought perhaps it lay westerly beyond Abu El Suir. Nessim could not tell me. But he knew there was a deep rock-pool with a wreck.'

'There is an N carved here.'

Clea clapped her hands with delight and struggled out of her bathing costume. 'I'm sure of it. Nessim said that for months he was fighting a duel with some big fish he couldn't identify. That was when he gave me the harpoon-gun which Narouz owned. Isn't it strange? I've always carried it in the locker wrapped in an oilskin. I thought I might shoot something one day. But it is so heavy I can't manage it under water.'

'What sort of fish was it?'

'I don't know.'

But she scrambled back to the cutter and produced the bulky package of greased rags in which this singular weapon was wrapped. It was an ugly-looking contrivance, a compressed-air rifle no less, with a hollow butt. It fired a slim steel harpoon about a metre and a half in length. It had been made to specifications for him in Germany. It looked deadly enough to kill quite a large fish.

'Pretty horrible looking' she said, eating an orange.

'We must try it.'

'It's too heavy for me. Perhaps you will manage it. I found that the barrel lagged in the water. I couldn't bring it to bear properly. But he was a marksman, so Nessim said, and shot a lot of quite large fish. But there was one, a very big one, which made infrequent appearances. He watched and waited in ambush for it for months. He had several shots at it but always missed. I hope it wasn't a shark — I'm scared of them.'

'There aren't many in the Mediterranean. It is down the Red Sea that you get them in numbers.'

'Nevertheless I keep a sharp eye out.'

It was too heavy an instrument, I decided, to lug about under water; besides I had no interest in shooting fish. So I wrapped and stowed it once more in the cutter's ample locker. She lay there naked in the sunlight, drowsing like a seal, to smoke a cigarette before exploring further. The rock-pool glowed beneath the glimmering keel of the boat like a quivering emerald, the long ribbons of milky light penetrating it slowly, stealing down like golden probes. About four fathoms, I thought, and drawing a deep breath rolled over and let my body wangle downwards like a fish, not using my arms.

Its beauty was spell-binding. It was like diving into the nave of a cathedral whose stained-glass windows filtered the sunlight through a dozen rainbows. The sides of the amphitheatre — for it opened gradually towards the deep sea — seemed as if carved by some heartsick artist of the Romantic Age into a dozen half-finished galleries lined with statues. Some of these were so like real statuary that I thought for a moment that I had made an archaeological find. But these blurred caryatids were wave-born, pressed and moulded by the hazard of the tides into goddesses and dwarfs and clowns. A light marine fucus of brilliant yellow and green had bearded them — shallow curtains of weed which swung lightly in the tide, parting and closing, as if to reveal their secrets suggestively and then cover them again. I pushed my fingers through this scalp of dense and slippery foliage to press them upon the blind face of a Diana or the hooked nose of a medieval dwarf. The floor of this deserted palace was of selenite plastic clay, soft to the touch and in no way greasy. Terracotta baked in a dozen hues of mauve and violet and gold. Inside close to the island it was not deep — perhaps a fathom and a half — but it fell away steeply where the gallery spread out to the sea, and the deeper lining of water faded from emerald to apple green, and from Prussian blue to black, suggesting great depth. Here, too, was the wreck of which Clea had spoken. I had hopes of finding perhaps a Roman amphora or two, but it was not alas a very old ship. I recognized the flared curve of the poop as an Aegean design — the type of caique which the Greeks call '*trechandiri*'. She had been rammed astern. Her back was broken. She was full of a dead weight of dark sponges. I tried to find the painted eyes on the prow and a name, but they had vanished. Her wood was crawling with slime and every cranny winked full of hermit crabs. She must have belonged to sponge fishers of Kalymnos I thought, for each year their fleet crosses to fish the African coast and carry its haul back for processing in the Dodecanese Islands.

A blinding parcel of light struck through the ceiling now and down flashed the eloquent body of Clea, her exploding coils of hair swerved up behind her by the water's concussion, her arms spread. I caught her and we rolled and sideslipped down in each other's arms, playing like fish until lack of breath drove us upwards once more into the sunlight. To sit at last panting in the shallows, gazing with breathless delight at each other.

'What a marvellous pool.' She clapped her hands in delight.

'I saw the wreck.'

And climbing back to the little sickle of beach with its warm pebbles with her drenched thatch of hair swinging behind her she said: 'I've thought of another thing. This must be Timonium. I wish I could remember the details more clearly.'

'What is that?'

'They've never found the site, you know. I am sure this must be it. Oh, let us believe that it is, shall we? When Antony came back defeated from Actium — where Cleopatra fled with her fleet in panic and tore open his battle-line, leaving him at the mercy of Octavian; when he came back after that unaccountable failure of nerve, and when there was nothing for them to do but to wait for the certain death which would follow upon Octavian's arrival — why he built himself a cell on an islet. It was named after a famous recluse and misanthrope — perhaps a philosopher? — called Timon. And here he must have spent his leisure — *here*, Darley, going over the whole thing again and again in his mind. That woman with the extraordinary spells she was able to cast. His life in ruins! And then the passing of the God, and all that, bidding him to say good-bye to her, to Alexandria — a whole world!'

The brilliant eyes smiling a little wistfully interrogated mine. She put her fingers to my cheek.

'Are you waiting for me to say that it is?'

'Yes.'

'Very well. It is.'

'Kiss me.'

'Your mouth tastes of oranges and wine.'

It was so small, the beach — hardly bigger than a bed. It was strange to make love thus with one's ankles in blue water and the hot sun blazing on one's back. Later we made one of many desultory attempts to locate the cell, or something which might correspond to her fancy, but in vain; on the seaward side lay a tremendous jumble of granite snags, falling steeply into black water. A thick spoke of some ancient harbour level perhaps which explained the wind-and-sea-break properties of the island. It was so silent, one heard nothing but the faint stir of wind across our ears, distant as the echo of some tiny seashell. Yes, and sometimes a herring gull flew over to judge the depth of the beach as a possible theatre of operations. But for the rest the sun-drunk bodies lay, deeply asleep, the quiet rhythms of the blood responding only to the deeper rhythms of sea and sky. A haven of animal contents which words can never compass.

It is strange, too, to remember what a curious sea-engendered *rapport* we shared during that memorable summer. A delight almost as deep as the bondage of kisses — to enter the rhythm of the waters together, responding to each other and the play of the long tides. Clea had always been a fine swimmer, I a poor one. But thanks to my period spent in Greece I too was now expert, more than a match for her. Under water we played and explored the submarine world of the pool, as thoughtlessly as fishes of the fifth day of the Creation. Eloquent and silent water-ballets which allowed us to correspond only by smile and gesture. The water-silences captured and transformed everything human in movement, so that we were like the coloured projections of undines painted upon these brilliant screens of rock and weed, echoing and copying the water-rhythms. Here thought itself perished, was converted into a fathomless content in physical action. I see the bright figure travelling like a star across this twilit firmament, its hair combed up and out in a rippling whorl of colour.

But not only here, of course. When you are in love with one of its inhabitants a city can become a world. A whole new geography of Alexandria was born through Clea, reviving old meanings, renewing ambiences half forgotten, laying down like a rich wash of colour a new history, a new biography to replace the old one. Memory of old cafés along the seafront by bronze moonlight, their striped awnings a-flutter with the midnight sea-breeze. To sit and dine late, until the glasses before one had brimmed with moonlight. In the shadow of a minaret, or on some strip of sand lit by the twinkle of a paraffin lamp. Or gathering the masses of shallow spring blossom on the Cape of Figs — brilliant cyclamen, brilliant anemone. Or standing together in the tombs of Kom El Shugafa inhaling the damp exhalations of the darkness which welled out of those strange subterranean resting-places of Alexandrians long dead; tombs carved out of the black chocolate soil, one upon the other, like bunks in a ship. Airless, mouldy and yet somehow piercingly cold. ('Hold my hand.') But if she shivered it was not then with the premonitions of death, but with the sheer weight of the gravid earth piled above us metre upon metre. Any creature of the sunlight would shiver so. That brilliant summer frock swallowed by the gloom. 'I'm cold. Let us go.' Yes, it was cold down there. But with what pleasure one stepped from the darkness into the roaring, anarchic life of the open street once more. So the sun-god must have risen, shaking himself free from the damp clutch of the soil, smiling up at the printed blue sky which spelt travel, release from death, renewal in the life of common creatures.

Yes, but the dead are everywhere. They cannot be so simply evaded. One feels them pressing their sad blind fingers in deprivation upon the panels of our secret lives, asking to be remembered and re-enacted once more in the life of the flesh — encamping among our heartbeats, invading our embraces. We carry in ourselves the biological trophies they bequeathed us by their failure to use up life — alignment of an eye, responsive curve of a nose; or in still more fugitive forms like someone's dead laugh, or a dimple which excites a long-buried smile. The simplest of these kisses we exchanged had a pedigree of death. In them we once more befriended forgotten loves which struggled to be reborn. The roots of every sigh are buried in the ground.

And when the dead invade? For sometimes they emerge in person. That brilliant morning, for example, with everything so deceptively normal, when bursting from the pool like a rocket she gasped, deathly pale: '*There are dead men down there*': frightening me! Yet she was not wrong, for when I mustered the courage to go down myself and look — there they were in very truth, seven of them, sitting in the twilight of the basin with an air of scrupulous attention, as if listening to some momentous debate which would decide everything for them. This conclave of silent figures formed a small semicircle across the outer doorway of the pool. They had been roped in sacks and leadweighted at the feet, so that now they stood upright, like chess pieces of human size. One has seen statues covered in this way, travelling through a city on a lorry, bound for some sad provincial museum. Slightly crouched, responding to the ligatures which bound them, and faceless, they nevertheless stood, flinching and flickering softly like figures in an early silent film. Heavily upholstered in death by the coarse canvas wrappers which bound them.

They turned out to be Greek sailors who had been bathing from their corvette when, by some accident, a depth-charge had been detonated, killing them instantly by concussion. Their un-marked bodies, glittering like mackerel, had been harvested laboriously in an old torpedo net, and laid out upon dripping decks to dry before burial. Flung overboard once more in the traditional funeral dress of mariners the curling tide had brought them to Narouz' island.

It will sound strange, perhaps, to describe how quickly we got used to these silent visitants of the pool. Within a matter of days we had accommodated them, accorded them a place of their own. We swam between them to reach the outer water, bowing ironically to their bent attentive heads.

It was not to flout death — it was rather that they had become friendly and appropriate symbols of the place, these patient, intent figures. Neither their thick skin-parcels of canvas, nor the stout integuments of rope which bound them showed any sign of disintegration. On the contrary they were covered by a dense silver dew, like mercury, which heavily proofed canvas always collects when it is immersed. We spoke once or twice of asking the Greek naval authorities to remove them to deeper water, but by long experience I knew we should find them unco-operative if we tried, and the subject was dropped by common consent. Once I thought I saw the flickering shadow of a great catfish moving among them but I must have been mistaken. We even thought later of giving them names, but were deterred by the thought that they must already have names of their own — the absurd names of ancient sophists and generals like Anaximander, Plato, Alexander. . . .

So this halcyon summer moved towards its end, free from omens — the long sunburnt ranks of marching days. It was, I think, in the late autumn that Maskelyne was killed in a desert sortie, but this was a passing without echoes for me — so little substance had he ever had in my mind as a living personage. It was, in very truth, a mysterious thing to find Telford sitting red-eyed at his desk one afternoon repeating brokenly: 'The old Brig's copped it. The poor old Brig' and wringing his purple hands together. It was hard to know what to say. Telford went on, with a kind of incoherent wonder in his voice that was endearing. 'He had no-one in the world. D'you know what? He gave me as his next-of-kin.' He seemed immeasurably touched by this mark of friendship. Nevertheless it was with a reverent melancholy that he went through Maskelyne's exiguous personal effects. There was little enough to inherit save a few civilian clothes of unsuitable size, several campaign medals and stars, and a credit account of fifteen pounds in the Tottenham Court Road Branch of Lloyds Bank. More interesting relics to me were those contained in a little leather wallet — the tattered pay-book and parchment certificate of discharge which had belonged to his grandfather. The story they told had the eloquence of a history which unfolded itself within a tradition. In the year 1861 this now forgotten Suffolk farm-boy had enlisted at Bury St Edmunds. He served in the Coldstream Guards for thirty-two years, being discharged in 1893. During his service he was married in the Chapel of the Tower of London and his wife bore him two sons. There was a faded photograph of him taken on his return from Egypt in 1882. It showed him dressed in white pith helmet, red jacket and blue serge trousers with smart black leather gaiters and pipe-clayed cross belts. On his breast was pinned the Egyptian War Medal with a clasp for the battle of Tel-el-Kebir and the Khedive's Star. Of Maskelyne's own father there was no record among his effects.

'It's tragic' said little Telford with emotion. 'Mavis couldn't stop crying when I told her. She only met him twice. It shows what an effect a man of character can have on you. He was always the perfect gentleman, was the Brig.' But I was brooding over this obscure faded figure in the photograph with his grim eyes and heavy black moustache, with the pipe-clayed cross belts and the campaign medals. He seemed to lighten the picture of Maskelyne himself, to give it focus. Was it not, I wondered, a story of success — a success perfectly complete within the formal pattern of something greater than the individual life, a tradition? I doubted whether Maskelyne himself could have wanted things to fall out otherwise. In every death there is the grain of something to be learned. Yet Maskelyne's quiet departure made little impact on my feelings, though I did what I could to soothe the forlorn Telford. But the tide-lines of my own life were now beginning to tug me invisibly towards an unforeseeable future. Yes, it was this beautiful autumn, with its torrent of brass brown leaves showering down from the trees in the public gardens, that Clea first became a matter of concern to me. Was it, in truth, because she heard the weeping? I do not know. She never openly admitted it. At times I tried to imagine that I heard it myself — this frail cry of a small child, or a pet locked out: but I knew that I heard nothing, absolutely nothing. Of course one could look at it in a matter-of-fact way and class it with the order of natural events which time revises and renews according to its own caprices. I mean love can wither like any other plant. Perhaps she was simply falling out of love? But in order to record the manner of its falling out I feel almost compelled to present it as something else — preposterous as it may sound — as a visitation of an agency, a power initiated in some uncommon region beyond the scope of the ordinary imagination. At any rate its onset was quite definitive, marked up like a date on a blank wall. It was November the fourteenth, just before dawn. We had been together during the whole of the previous day, idling about the city, gossiping and shopping. She had bought some piano music, and I had made her a present of a new scent from the Scent Bazaar. (At the very moment when I awoke and saw her standing, or rather crouching by the window, I caught the sudden breath of scent from my own wrist which had been dabbed with samples from the glass-stoppered bottles.) Rain had fallen that night. Its delicious swishing had lulled our sleep. We had read by candle-light before falling asleep.

But now she was standing by the window listening, her whole body stiffened into an attitude of attentive interrogation so acute that it suggested something like a crisis of apprehension. Her head was turned a little sideways, as if to present her ear to the uncurtained window behind which, very dimly, a rain-washed dawn was beginning to break over the roofs of the city. What was she listening for? I had never seen this attitude before. I called to her and briefly she turned a distraught and unseeing face to me — impatiently, as if my voice had ruptured the fine membrane of her concentration. And as I sat up she cried, in a deep choked voice: 'Oh *no*!', and clapping her hands over her ears fell shuddering to her knees. It was as if a bullet had been fired through her brain. I heard her bones creak as she hung crouching there her features contorted into a grimace. Her hands were locked so tightly over her ears that I could not disengage them, and when I tried to lift her by her wrists she simply sank back to her knees on the carpet, with shut eyes, like a dement. 'Clea, what on earth is it?' For a long moment we knelt there together, I in great perplexity. Her eyes were fast shut. I could feel the cool wind from the window pouring into the room. The silence, save for our exclamations, was complete. At last she gave a great sigh of relaxation, a long sobbing respiration, and un-fastened her ears, stretched her limbs slowly, as if unbinding them from painful cramps. She shook her head at me as if to say that it was nothing. And walking like a drunkard to the bathroom she was violently sick in the wash-basin. I stood there like a sleep-walker; feeling as if I had been uprooted. At last she came back, got into bed and turned her face to the wall. 'What is it, Clea?' I asked again, feeling foolish and importunate. Her shoulders trembled slightly under my hand, her teeth chattered lightly from cold. 'It is nothing, really nothing. A sudden splitting headache. But it has gone. Let me sleep now, will you?'

In the morning she was up early to make the breakfast. I thought her exceptionally pale — with the sort of pallor that might come after a long and agonizing toothache. She complained of feeling listless and weary.

'You frightened me last night' I said, but she did not answer, turning away evasively from the subject with a curious look of anxiety and distress. She asked to be allowed to spend the day alone painting, so I took myself off for a long walk across the town, teased by half-formulated thoughts and premonitions which I somehow could not make explicit to myself. It was a beautiful day. High seas were running. The waves flailed the Spouting Rocks like the pistons of some huge machine. Immense clouds of spray were flung high into the air like the explosion of giant puff-balls only to fall back in hissing spume upon the crown of the next wave. I stood watching the spectacle for a long time, feeling the tug of the wind at the skirt of my overcoat and the cool spray on my cheeks. I think I must have known that from this point onward everything would be subtly changed. That we had entered, so to speak, a new constellation of feelings which would alter our relationship.

cc

One speaks of change, but in truth there was nothing abrupt, coherent, definitive about it. No, the metamorphosis came about with comparative slowness. It waxed and waned like a tide, now advancing now retreating. There were even times when, for whole weeks, we were apparently completely restored to our former selves, reviving the old raptures with an intensity born now of insecurity. Suddenly for a spell we would be once more completely identified in each other, inseparable: the shadow had lifted. I tell myself now — and with what truth I still do not know — that these were periods when for a long time she had not heard the weeping which she once long ago described as belonging to a she-camel in distress or some horrible mechanical toy. But what could such nonsense really mean to anyone — and how could it elucidate those other periods when she fell into silence and moroseness, became a nervous and woebegone version of her old self? I do not know. I only know that this new personage was subject to long distracted silences now, and to unusual fatigues. She might, for example, fall asleep on a sofa in the middle of a party and begin to snore: as if overcome with weariness after an immensely long vigil. Insomnia too began to play its part, and she resorted to relatively massive doses of barbiturates in order to seek release from it. She was smoking very heavily indeed.

'Who is this new nervy person I do not recognize?' asked Balthazar in perplexity one evening when she had snapped his head off after some trivial pleasantry and left the room, banging the door in my face.

'There's something wrong' I said. He looked at me keenly for a moment over a lighted match. 'She isn't pregnant?' he asked, and I shook my head. 'I think she's beginning to wear me out really.' It cost me an effort to bring out the words. But they had the merit of offering something like a plausible explanation to these moods — unless one preferred to believe that she were being gnawed by secret fears.

'Patience' he said. 'There is never enough of it.'

'I'm seriously thinking of absenting myself for a while.'

'That might be a good idea. But not for too long.'

'I shall see.'

Sometimes in my clumsy way I would try by some teasing remark to probe to the sources of this disruptive anxiety. 'Clea, why are you always looking over your shoulder — for what?' But this was a fatal error of tactics. Her response was always one of ill-temper or pique, as if in every reference to her distemper, however oblique, I was in some way mocking her. It was intimidating to see how rapidly her face darkened, her lips compressed themselves. It was as if I had tried to put my hand on a secret treasure which she was guarding with her life.

At times she was particularly nervous. Once as we were coming out of a cinema I felt her stiffen on my arm. I turned my eyes in the direction of her gaze. She was staring with horror at an old man with a badly gashed face. He was a Greek cobbler who had been caught in a bombardment and mutilated. We all knew him quite well by sight, indeed Amaril had repaired the damage as well as he was able. I shook her arm softly, reassuringly and she suddenly seemed to come awake. She straightened up abruptly and said 'Come. Let us go.' She gave a little shudder and hurried me away.

At other such times when I had unguardedly made some allusion to her inner preoccupations — this maddening air of always *listening* for something — the storms and accusations which followed seriously suggested the truth of my own hypothesis — namely that she was trying to drive me away: 'I am no good for you, Darley. Since we have been together you haven't written a single line. You have no plans. You hardly read any more.' So stern those splendid eyes had become, and so troubled! I was forced to laugh, however. In truth I now knew, or thought I did, that I would never become a writer. The whole impulse to confide in the world in this way had foundered, had guttered out. The thought of the nagging little world of print and paper had become unbearably tedious to contemplate. Yet I was not unhappy to feel that the urge had abandoned me. On the contrary I was full of relief — a relief from the bondage of these forms which seemed so inadequate an instrument to convey the truth of feelings. 'Clea, my dear' I said, still smiling ineffectually, and yet desiring in a way to confront this accusation and placate her. 'I have been actually meditating a book of criticism.'

'Criticism!' she echoed sharply, as if the word were an insult. And she smacked me full across the mouth — a stinging blow which brought tears to my eyes and cut the inside of my lip against my teeth. I retired to the bathroom to mop my mouth for I could feel the salty taste of the blood. It was interesting to see my teeth outlined in blood. I looked like an ogre who had just taken a mouthful of bleeding flesh from his victims. I washed my mouth, furiously enraged. She came in and sat down on the *bidet*, full of remorse. 'Please forgive me' she said. 'I don't know what sort of impulse came over me. Darley, please forgive' she said.

'One more performance like this' I said grimly, 'and I'll give you a blow between those beautiful eyes which you'll remember.'

'I'm sorry.' She put her arms round my shoulders from behind and kissed my neck. The blood had stopped. 'What the devil is wrong?' I said to her reflection in the mirror. 'What has come over you these days? We're drifting apart, Clea.'

'I know.'

'Why?'

'I don't know.' But her face had once more become hard and obstinate. She sat down on the *bidet* and stroked her chin thoughtfully, suddenly sunk in reflection once more. Then she lit a cigarette and walked back into her living-room. When I returned she was sitting silently before a painting gazing at it with an inattentive malevolent fixity.

'I think we should separate for a while' I said.

'If you wish' she rapped out mechanically.

'Do you wish it?'

Suddenly she started crying and said 'Oh, stop questioning me. If only you would stop asking me question after question. It's like being in court these days.'

'Very well' I said.

This was only one of several such scenes. It seemed clear to me that to absent myself from the city was the only way to free her — to give her the time and space necessary to . . . what? I did not know. Later that winter I thought that she had begun running a small temperature in the evenings and incurred another furious scene by asking Balthazar to examine her. Yet despite her anger she submitted to the stethoscope with comparative quietness. Balthazar could find nothing physically wrong, except that her pulse rate was advanced and her blood pressure higher than normal. His prescription of stimulants she ignored, however. She had become much thinner at this time.

By patient lobbying I at last unearthed a small post for which I was not unsuitable and which somehow fitted into the general rhythm of things — for I did not envisage my separation from Clea as something final, something in the nature of a break. It was simply a planned withdrawal for a few months to make room for any longer-sighted resolutions which she might make. New factors were there, too, for with the ending of the war Europe was slowly becoming accessible once more — a new horizon opening beyond the battle-lines. One had almost stopped dreaming of it, the recondite shape of a Europe hammered flat by bombers, raked by famine and discontents. Nevertheless it was still there. So it was that when I came to tell her of my departure it was not with despondency or sorrow — but as a matter-of-fact decision which she must welcome for her own part. Only the manner in which she pronounced the word 'Away' with an indrawn breath suggested for a brief second that perhaps, after all, she might be afraid to be left alone. 'You are going away, after all?'

'For a few months. They are building a relay station on the island, and there is need for someone who knows the place and can speak the language.'

'Back to the island?' she said softly — and here I could not read the meaning of her voice or the design of her thought.

'For a few short months only.'

'Very well.'

She walked up and down the carpet with an air of perplexity, staring downwards at it, deep in thought. Suddenly she looked up at me with a soft expression that I recognized with a pang — the mixture of remorse and tenderness at inflicting unwitting sorrow upon others. It was the face of the old Clea. But I knew that it would not last, that once more the peculiar shadow of her discontent would cast itself over our relationship. There was no point in trusting myself once more to what could only prove a short respite. 'Oh, Darley' she said, 'when do you go, my dear?' taking my hands.

'In a fortnight. Until then I propose not to see you at all. There is no point in our upsetting each other by these wrangles.'

'As you wish.'

'I'll write to you.'

'Yes of course.'

It was a strange listless way of parting after such a momentous relationship. A sort of ghostly anaesthesia had afflicted our emotions. There was a kind of deep ache inside me but it wasn't sorrow. The dead handshake we exchanged only expressed a strange and truthful exhaustion of the spirit. She sat in a chair, quietly smoking and watching me as I gathered my possessions together and stuffed them into the old battered briefcase which

I had borrowed from Telford and forgotten to return the summer before. The toothbrush was splayed. I threw it away. My pyjamas were torn at the shoulder but the bottom half, which I had never used, were still crisp and new. I assembled these objects with the air of a geologist sorting specimens of some remote age. A few books and papers. It all had a sort of unreality, but I cannot say that a single sharp regret was mixed with it.

'How this war has aged and staled us' she said suddenly, as if to herself. 'In the old days one would have thought of going away in order, as we said, to get away from oneself. But to get away from *it*. . . .'

Now, writing the words down in all their tedious banality, I realize that she was really trying to say good-bye. The fatality of human wishes. For me the future lay open, uncommitted; and there was no part of it which I could then visualize as not containing, somehow, Clea. This parting was . . . well, it was only like changing the bandages until a wound should heal. Being unimaginative, I could not think definitively about a future which might make unexpected demands upon me; as something entirely new. It must be left to form itself upon the emptiness of the present. But for Clea the future had already closed, was already presenting a blank wall. The poor creature was afraid!

'Well, that's everything' I said at last, shoving the briefcase under my arm. 'If there's anything you need, you have only to ring me, I'll be at the flat.'

'I know.'

'I'm off then for a while. Good-bye.'

As I closed the door of the little flat I heard her call my name once — but this again was one of those deceptions, those little accesses of pity or tenderness which deceive one. It would have been absurd to pay any attention to it, to return on my tracks, and open a new cycle of disagreements. I went on down the stairs, determined to let the future have every chance to heal itself.

It was a brilliantly sunny spring day and the streets looked washed with colour. The feeling of having nowhere to go and nothing to do was both depressing and inspiriting. I returned to the flat and found on the mantelpiece a letter from Pombal in which he said that he was likely to be transferred to Italy shortly and did not think he would be able to keep the flat on. I was delighted as this enabled me to terminate the lease, my share of which I would soon not be able to afford.

It was at first somewhat strange, even perhaps a little numbing, to be left entirely to my own devices, but I rapidly became accustomed to it. Moreover there was quite a lot of work to be done in winding up my censorship duties and handing over the post to a successor while at the same time collecting practical information for the little unit of technicians which was to install the radio post. Between the two departments with their different needs I was kept busy enough. During these days I kept my word and saw nothing of Clea. The time passed in a sort of limbo pitched between the world of desire and of farewell — though there were no emotions in very clear definition for me: I was not conscious of regrets or longings.

So it was that when at last that fatal day presented itself, it did so under the smiling guise of a spring sunshine hot enough to encourage the flies to begin hatching out upon the window-panes. It was their buzzing which awoke me. Sunlight was pouring into the room. For a moment, dazzled by it, I hardly recognized the smiling figure seated at the foot of my bed, waiting for me to open my eyes. It was the Clea of some forgotten original version, so to speak, clad in a brilliant summer frock of a crisp vine-leaf pattern, white sandals, and with her hair arranged in a new style. She was smoking a cigarette whose smoke hung in brilliant ash-veined whorls in the sunlight above us, and her smiling face was completely relaxed and unshadowed by the least preoccupation. I stared, for she seemed so precisely and unequivocally the Clea I should always have remembered; the mischievous tenderness was back in the eyes. 'Well' I said in sleepy amazement. 'What . . .?' and I felt her warm breath on my cheek as she leaned down to embrace me.

'Darley' she said, 'I suddenly realized that it's tomorrow you are leaving; and that today is the Mulid of El Scob. I couldn't resist the idea of spending the day together and visiting the shrine this evening. Oh, say you will! Look at the sunshine. It's warm enough for a bathe, and we could take Balthazar.'

I was still not properly awake. I had completely forgotten the Name Day of the Pirate. 'But it's long past St George's Day' I said. 'Surely that's at the end of April.'

'On the contrary. Their absurd method of lunar calendar reckoning has turned him into a movable feast like all the others. He slides up and down the calendar now like a domestic saint. In fact it was Balthazar who telephoned yesterday and told me or I would have missed it myself.' She paused to puff her cigarette. 'We shouldn't miss it, should we?' she added a little wistfully.

'But of course not! How good of you to come.'

'And the island? Perhaps you could come with us?'

The time was just ten o'clock. I could easily telephone to Telford to make some excuse for absenting myself for the day. My heart leaped.

'I'd love to' I said. 'How does the wind sit?'

'Calm as a nun with easterly freshets. Ideal for the cutter I should say. Are you sure you want to come?'

She had a wicker-covered demijohn and a basket with her. 'I'll go on and provision us up; you dress and meet me at the Yacht Club in an hour.'

'Yes.' It would give me ample time to visit my office and examine the duty mail. 'A splendid idea.'

And in truth it was, for the day was clear and ringing with a promise of summer heat for the afternoon. Clip-clopping down the Grande Corniche I studied the light haze on the horizon and the flat blue expanse of sea with delight. The city glittered in sunshine like a jewel. Brilliantly rode the little craft in the inner basin, parodied by their shining reflections. The minarets shone loudly. In the Arab quarter the heat had hatched out the familiar smells of offal and drying mud, of carnations and jasmine, of animal sweat and clover. In Tatwig Street dark gnomes on ladders with scarlet flower-pot hats were stretching strings of flags from the balconies. I felt the sun warm on my fingers. We rolled past the site of the ancient Pharos whose shattered fragments still choke the shallows. Toby Mannering, I remembered, had once wanted to start a curio trade by selling fragments of the Pharos as paperweights. Scobie was to break them up with a hammer for him and he was to deliver them to retailers all over the world. Why had the scheme foundered? I could not remember. Perhaps Scobie found the work too arduous? Or perhaps it had got telescoped with that other scheme for selling Jordan water to Copts at a competitive price? Somewhere a military band was banging away.

They were down on the slip waiting for me. Balthazar waved his stick cheerfully. He was dressed in white trousers and sandals and a coloured shirt, and sported an ancient yellowing Panama hat.

'The first day of summer' I called cheerfully.

'You're wrong' he croaked. 'Look at that haze. It's altogether too hot. I've betted Clea a thousand piastres we have a thunder-storm by this afternoon.'

'He's always got something gloomy to say' smiled Clea.

'I know my Alexandria' said Balthazar.

And so amidst these idle pleasantries we three set forth, Clea at the tiller of her little craft. There was hardly a breath of wind inside the harbour and she lagged somewhat, only gathering way by the momentum of the currents which curved down towards the harbour entrance. We stole past the battleships and liners, breasting the choppy main-channel hesitantly, the mainsail hardly drawing as yet, until at last we reached the huddle of grey forts which marked the main harbour entrance. Here there was always a bundle of choppy water piled up by the tide and we wallowed and yawed for a while until suddenly she heeled and threaded herself upon the wind and settled her bowsprit true. We began to hiss through the sea like a flying fish, as if she were going to impale a star. I lay in the sheets now, staring up at the gold sun shining through the sails, hearing the smattering of the wavelets on the elegant prow of the cutter. Balthazar was humming an air. Clea's brown wrist lay upon the tiller with a deceptive soft negligence. The sails were stiff. These are the heart-lifting joys of small sailing-craft in ideal weather. A speechless delight held me, a mixture of luxuries born of the warm sun, the racing wind, and the light cool touches of spray which dashed our cheeks from time to time. We went far out on an easterly course in order to come about and tack inshore. By now we had performed this manoeuvre so often that it had become second nature to Clea: to ride down upon the little island of Narouz and to judge the exact moment at which to turn into the eye of the wind and hang, fluttering like an eyelash, until I had run the sail in and scrambled ashore to make fast. . . .

'Smart work indeed' said Balthazar approvingly as he stepped into the water; and then 'By God! It is quite fantastically warm.'

'What did I tell you?' said Clea busy in the locker.

'It only proves my point about a thunderstorm.'

And curiously enough, at this moment, there came a distinct rumble of thunder out of that cloudless sky. 'There' said Balthazar in triumph. 'We will get a fine soaking and you will owe me some money, Clea.'

'We'll see.'

'It was a shore battery' I said.

'Rubbish' said Balthazar.

So we secured the cutter and carried our provisions ashore. Balthazar lay on his back with his hat over his nose in the best of humours. He would not bathe, pleading the indifference of his swimming, so Clea and I dived once more into the familiar pool which we had neglected all winter long. Nothing had changed. The sentinels were still there, grouped in silent debate, though the winter tides had altered their dispositions somewhat, grouping them a little nearer to the wreck. Ironically yet respectfully we greeted them, recognizing in these ancient gestures and underwater smiles a familiar happiness growing up in the sheer act of swimming once more together. It was as if the blood had started to flow again in veins long withered from disuse. I caught her by the heel and rolled her in a long somersault towards the dead mariners, and turning expertly she repaid the debt by coming up behind me to drag me down by the shoulders and climb surfacewards before I could retaliate. It was here, spiralling up through the water with her hair coiled out behind her, that the image of Clea was restored once more. Time had rendered her up, whole and intact again — "natural as a city's grey-eyed Muse " — to quote the Greek poem. Swiftly, precisely the fingers which pressed upon my shoulder re-evoked her as we slid through the silent pool.

And then: to sit once more in the simple sunlight, sipping the red wine of St Menas as she broke up the warm brown loaf of French bread, and hunted for a particular cheese or a cluster of dates: while Balthazar talked discursively (half asleep) of the Vineyard of Ammon, the Kings of the Harpoon Kingdom and their battles, or of the Mareotic wine to which, not history, but the gossiping Horace once attributed Cleopatra's distempers of mind . . . ('History sanctions everything, pardons everything — even what we do not pardon ourselves.')

So the warm noon drew on as we lay there on the hot pebbles: and so at last — to Balthazar's great delight and Clea's discomfiture — the predicted thunderstorm made its appearance, heralded by a great livid cloud which rolled up from the east and squatted over the city, bruising the sky. So suddenly too — as when an ink-squid in alarm puffs out its bag and suddenly fogs clear water in a cloud of black — rain flowed down in glittering sheets, thunder bellowed and insisted. At each peal Balthazar clapped his hands with delight — not only to be proved right, but also because here we were sitting in full sunlight, fully at our ease, eating oranges and drinking wine beside an untroubled blue sea.

'Stop crowing' said Clea severely.

It was one of those freak storms so prevalent in the early spring with its sharp changes of temperature born of sea and desert. They turned the streets to torrents in the twinkling of an eye, yet never endured above half an hour. Suddenly the cloud would be whisked away by a scrap of wind, utterly to disappear. 'And mark me now' said Balthazar, inebriated by the success of his prediction. 'By the time we get back to harbour everything will be dry again, dry as a bone.'

But now the afternoon brought us another phenomenon to delight us — something rarely seen in summer in the waters of Alexandria, belonging as it did to those days preceding winter storms when the glass was falling steeply. The waters of the pool darkened appreciably, curdled, and then became phosphorescent. It was Clea who first noticed. 'Look' she cried with delight, crushing her heels down in the shallows to watch the twinkling prickling light spark from them. 'Phosphorus!' Balthazar started saying something learned about the organism which causes this spectacle but unheeding we plunged side by side and ranged down into the water, transformed into figures of flame, the sparks flashing from the tips of our fingers and toes with the glitter of static electricity. A swimmer seen underwater looks like an early picture of the fall of Lucifer, literally on fire. So bright was the electrical crackle that we could not help wondering how it was that we were not scorched by it. So we played, glittering like comets, among the quiet mariners who sat, watching us perhaps in their thoughts, faintly echoing the twitching of the tide in their canvas sacks.

'The cloud's lifting already' cried Balthazar as I surfaced at last for air. Soon even the fugitive phosphorescence would dwindle and vanish. For some reason or other he had climbed into the stern of the cutter, perhaps to gain height and more easily watch the thunderstorm over the city. I rested my forearms on the gunwale and took my breath. He had unwrapped the old harpoon gun of Narouz and was holding it negligently on his knee. Clea surfaced with a swish of delight and pausing just long

enough to cry: 'The fire is so beautiful' doubled her lithe body
back and ducked downward again.

'What are you doing with that?' I asked idly.

'Seeing how it works.'

He had in fact pushed the harpoon to rest in the barrel. It had
locked the spring. 'It's cocked' I said. 'Have a care.'

'Yes, I'm going to release it.'

Then Balthazar leaned forward and uttered the only serious
remark he had made all that day. 'You know' he said, 'I think
you had better take her with you. I have a feeling you won't be
coming back to Alexandria. Take Clea with you!'

And then, before I could reply, the accident happened. He was
fumbling with the gun as he spoke. It slipped from between his
fingers and fell with a crash, the barrel striking the gunwale six
inches from my face. As I reared back in alarm I heard the sudden
cobra-like hiss of the compressor and the leaden twang of the
trigger-release. The harpoon whistled into the water beside me
rustling its long green line behind it. 'For Christ's sake' I said.
Balthazar had turned white with alarm and vexation. His half-
muttered apologies and expressions of horrid amazement were
eloquent. 'I'm terribly sorry.' I had heard the slight snick of steel
settling into a target, somewhere down there in the pool. We
stayed frozen for a second for something else had occurred
simultaneously to our minds. As I saw his lips starting to shape
the word 'Clea' I felt a sudden darkness descending on my spirit
— a darkness which lifted and trembled at the edges; and a
rushing like the sough of giant wings. I had already turned before
he uttered the word. I crashed back into the water, now following
the long green thread with all the suspense of Ariadne; and to it
added the weight of slowness which only heartsick apprehension
brings. I knew in my mind that I was swimming vigorously —
yet it seemed like one of those slow-motion films where human
actions, delayed by the camera, are drawn unctuously out to
infinity, spooled out like toffee. How many light-years would it
take to reach the end of that thread? What would I find at the
end of it? Down I went, and down, in the dwindling phosphorescence, into the deep shadowed coolness of the pool.

At the far end, by the wreck, I distinguished a convulsive,
coiling movement, and dimly recognized the form of Clea. She
seemed intently busy upon some childish underwater game of the
kind we so often played together. She was tugging at something,

her feet braced against the woodwork of the wreck, tugging and relaxing her body. Though the green thread led to her I felt a wave of relief — for perhaps she was only trying to extricate the harpoon and carry it to the surface with her. But no, for she rolled drunkenly. I slid along her like an eel, feeling with my hands. Feeling me near she turned her head as if to tell me something. Her long hair impeded my vision. As for her face I could not read the despairing pain which must have been written on it — for the water transforms every expression of the human features into the goggling imbecile grimace of the squid. But now she arched out and flung her head back so that her hair could flow freely up from her scalp — the gesture of someone throwing open a robe to exhibit a wound. And I saw. Her right hand had been pierced and nailed to the wreck by the steel arrow. At least it had not passed through her body, my mind cried out in relief, seeking to console itself; but the relief turned to sick malevolent despair when, clutching the steel shaft, I myself braced my feet against the wood, tugging until my thigh muscles cracked. It would not be budged by a hair's breadth. (No, but all this was part of some incomprehensible dream, fabricated perhaps in the dead minds of the seven brooding figures which attended so carefully, so scrupulously to the laboured evolutions we now performed — we no longer free and expeditious as fish, but awkward, splayed, like lobsters trapped in a pot.) I struggled frantically with that steel arrow, seeing out of the corner of my eye the long chain of white bubbles bursting from the throat of Clea. I felt her muscles expending themselves, ebbing. Gradually she was settling in the drowsiness of the blue water, being invaded by the water-sleep which had already lulled the mariners to sleep. I shook her.

I cannot pretend that anything which followed belonged to my own volition — for the mad rage which now possessed me was not among the order of the emotions I would ever have recognized as belonging to my proper self. It exceeded, in blind violent rapacity, anything I had ever before experienced. In this curious timeless underwater dream I felt my brain ringing like the alarm bell of an ambulance, dispelling the lulling languorous ebb and flow of the marine darkness. I was suddenly rowelled by the sharp spur of terror. It was as if I were for the first time confronting myself — or perhaps an alter ego shaped after a man of action I had never realized, recognized. With one wild shove I shot to the surface again, emerging under Balthazar's very nose.

'The knife' I said sucking in the air.

His eyes gazed into mine, as if over the edge of some sunken continent, with an expression of pity and horror; emotions preserved, fossilized, from some ice age of human memory. And native fear. He started to stammer out all the questions which invaded his mind — words like 'what' 'where' 'when' 'whither' — but could achieve no more than a baffled 'wh——': a vague sputtering anguish of interrogation.

The knife which I had remembered was an Italian bayonet which had been ground down to the size of a dirk and sharpened to razor keenness. Ali the boatman had manufactured it with pride. He used it to trim ropes, for splicing and rigging. I hung there for a second while he reached out for it, eyes closed, lungs drinking in the whole sky it seemed. Then I felt the wooden haft in my fingers and without daring to look again at Balthazar I turned my toes to heaven and returned on my tracks, following the green thread.

She hung there limp now, stretched languorously out, while her long hair unfurled behind her; the tides rippled out along her body, passing through it, it seemed like an electric current playing. Everything was still, the silver coinage of sunlight dappling the floor of the pool, the silent observers, the statues whose long beards moved slowly, unctuously to and fro. Even as I began to hack at her hand I was mentally preparing a large empty space in my mind which would have to accommodate the thought of her dead. A large space like an unexplored sub-continent on the maps of the mind. It was not very long before I felt the body disengage under this bitter punishment. The water was dark. I dropped the knife and with a great push sent her reeling back from the wreck: caught her under the arms: and so rose. It seemed to take an age — an endless progression of heartbeats — in that slow-motion world. Yet we hit the sky with a concussion that knocked the breath from me — as if I had cracked my skull on the ceiling of the universe. I was standing in the shallows now rolling the heavy sodden log of her body. I heard the crash of Balthazar's teeth falling into the boat as he jumped into the water beside me. We heaved and grunted like stevedores scrabbling about to grasp that injured hand which was spouting. He was like an electrician trying to capture and insulate a high-tension wire which had snapped. Grabbing it, he held on to it like a vice. I had a sudden picture of him as a small child holding his mother's hand nervously among a crowd of other children, or crossing a park where the boys had once thrown stones at him. . . . Through his pink gums he extruded the word 'Twine' — and there was some luckily in the cutter's locker which kept him busy.

'But she's dead' I said, and the word altered my heartbeats, so that I felt about to faint. She was lying, like a fallen seabird, on the little spit of pebbles. Balthazar squatted almost in the water, holding frenziedly on to the hand at which I could hardly bear to look. But again this unknown alter ego whose voice came from far away helped me to adjust a tourniquet, roll a pencil in it and hand it to him. With a heave now I straightened her out and fell with a thump upon her, crashing down as if from a very great height upon her back. I felt the soggy lungs bounce under this crude blow. Again and again, slowly but with great violence I began to squeeze them in this pitiful simulacrum of the sexual act — life saving, life-giving. Balthazar appeared to be praying. Then came a small sign of hope for the lips of that pale face opened and a little sea water mixed with vomit trickled from them. It meant nothing, of course, but we both cried out at the omen. Closing my eyes I willed my wrists to seek out those waterlogged lungs, to squeeze and void them. Up and down, up and down in this slow cruel rhythm, I pumped at her. I felt her fine bones creaking under my hands. But still she lay lifeless. But I would not accept the thought that she was dead, though I knew it with one part of my mind. I felt half mad with determination to disprove it, to overthrow, if necessary, the whole process of nature and by an act of will force her to live. These decisions astonished me, for they subsisted like clear and sharply defined images under-neath the dazed physical fatigue, the groan and sweat of this labour. I had, I realized, decided either to bring her up alive or to stay down there at the bottom of the pool with her; but where, from which territory of the will such a decision had come, I could not guess! And now it was hot. I was pouring with sweat. Balthazar still sat holding the hand, the painter's hand, humbly as a child at its mother's knee. Tears trickled down his nose. His head went from side to side in that Jewish gesture of despairing remorse and his toothless gums formed the sound of the old Wailing Wall 'Aiee, Aiee'. But very softly, as if not to disturb her.

But at last we were rewarded. Suddenly, like a spout giving in a gutter under the pressure of rain, her mouth opened and expelled a mass of vomit and sea-water, fragments of breadsoak and orange. We gazed at this mess with a lustful delight, as if at a great trophy. I felt the lungs respond slowly to my hand. A few more strokes of this crude engine and a secondary ripple seemed to stir in the musculature of her body. At almost every downward thrust now the lungs gave up some water, reluctantly, painfully. Then, after a long time, we heard a faint whimper. It must have hurt, as the first few breaths hurt a newly born child. The body of Clea was protesting at this forcible rebirth. And all of a sudden the features of that white face moved, composed themselves to express something like pain and protest. (Yes, but it *hurts* to realize.)

'Keep it up' cried Balthazar in a new voice, shaky and triumphant. There was no need to tell me. She was twitching a little now, and making a soundless whimpering face at each lunge. It was like starting a very cold diesel engine. Finally yet another miracle occurred — for she opened very blue sightless unfocused eyes for a second to study, with dazed concentration, the stones before her nose. Then she closed them again. Pain darkened her features, but even the pain was a triumph — for at least they expressed living emotions now — emotions which had replaced the pale set mask of death. 'She's breathing' I said. 'Balthazar, she's breathing.'

'She's breathing' he repeated with a kind of idiotic rapture.

She was breathing, short staggering inspirations which were clearly painful. But now another kind of help was at hand. We had not noticed, so concentrated were we on this task, that a vessel had entered the little harbour. This was the Harbour Patrol motorboat. They had seen us and guessed that something was wrong. 'Merciful God' cried Balthazar flapping his arms like an old crow. Cheerful English voices came across the water asking if we needed help; a couple of sailors came ashore towards us. 'We'll have her back in no time' said Balthazar, grinning shakily.

'Give her some brandy.'

'No' he cried sharply. 'No brandy.'

The sailors brought a tarpaulin ashore and softly we baled her up like Cleopatra. To their brawny arms she must have seemed as light as thistledown. Their tender clumsy movements were touching, brought tears to my eyes. 'Easy up there, Nobby. Gently with the little lady.' 'That tourniquet will have to be watched. You go too, Balthazar.'

'And you?'

'I'll bring her cutter back.'

We wasted no more time. In a few moments the powerful motors of the patrol vessel began to bustle them away at a good ten knots. I heard a sailor say: 'How about some hot Bovril?'

'Capital' said Balthazar. He was soaked to the skin. His hat was floating in the water beside me. Leaning over the stern a thought suddenly struck him.

'My teeth. Bring my teeth!'

I watched them out of sight and then sat for a good while with my head in my hands. I found to my surprise that I was trembling all over like a frightened horse with shock. A splitting headache assailed me. I climbed into the cutter and foraged for the brandy and a cigarette. The harpoon gun lay on the sheets. I threw it overboard with an oath and watched it slowly crawling downwards into the pool. Then I shook out the jib, and turning her through her own length on the stern anchor pressed her out into the wind. It took longer than I thought, for the evening wind had shifted a few points and I had to tack widely before I could bring her in. Ali was waiting for me. He had already been apprised of the situation, and carried a message from Balthazar to the effect that Clea had been taken up to the Jewish hospital.

I took a taxi as soon as one could be found. We travelled across the city at a great pace. The streets and buildings passed me in a sort of blur. So great was my anxiety that I saw them as if through a rain-starred window-pane. I could hear the meter ticking away like a pulse. Somewhere in a white ward Clea would be lying drinking blood through the eye of a silver needle. Drop by drop it would be passing into the median vein heart-beat by heart-beat. There was nothing to worry about, I told myself; and then, thinking of that shattered hand, I banged my fist with rage against the padded wall of the taxi.

I followed a duty nurse down the long anonymous green corridors whose oil-painted walls exuded an atmosphere of damp. The white phosphorescent bulbs which punctuated our progress wallowed in the gloom like swollen glow-worms. They had probably put her, I reflected, in the little ward with the single curtained bed which in the past had been reserved for critical cases whose expectation of life was short. It was now the emergency casualty ward. A sense of ghostly familiarity was growing upon me. In the past it was here that I had come to see Melissa. Clea must be lying in the same narrow iron bed in the corner by the wall. ('It would be just like real life to imitate art at this point.')

In the corridor outside, however, I came upon Amaril and Balthazar standing with a curious chastened expression before a trolley which had just been wheeled to them by a duty nurse. It contained a number of wet and glistening X-ray photographs, newly developed and pegged upon a rail. The two men were studying them anxiously, gravely, as if thinking out a chess problem. Balthazar caught sight of me and turned, his face lighting up. 'She's all right' he said, but in rather a broken voice, as he squeezed my hand. I handed him his teeth and he blushed, and slipped them into his pocket. Amaril was wearing horn-rimmed reading glasses. He turned from his intent study of those dripping dangling sheets with an expression of utter rage. 'What the bloody hell do you expect me to do with this mess?' he burst out waving his insolent white hand in the direction of the X-rays. I lost my temper at the implied accusation and in a second we were shouting at each other like fishmongers, our eyes full of tears. I think we would have come to blows out of sheer exaspera-tion had not Balthazar got between us. Then at once the rage dropped from Amaril and he walked round Balthazar to embrace me and mutter an apology. 'She's all right' he murmured, patting me consolingly on the shoulder. 'We've tucked her up safely.'

'Leave the rest to us' said Balthazar.

'I'd like to see her' I said enviously — as if, by bringing her to life, I had made her, in a way, my own property too. 'Could I?'

As I pushed open the door and crept into the little cell like a miser I heard Amaril say peevishly: 'It's all very well to talk about surgical repair in that glib way——'

It was immensely quiet and white, the little ward with its tall windows. She lay with her face to the wall in the uncomfortable steel bed on castors of yellow rubber. It smelt of flowers, though there were none to be seen and I could not identify the odour. It was perhaps a synthetic atomizer spray — the essence of forget-me-nots? I softly drew up a chair beside the bed and sat down. Her eyes were open, gazing at the wall with the dazed look which suggested morphia and fatigue combined. Though she gave no sign of having heard me enter she said suddenly.

'Is that you Darley?'

'Yes.'

Her voice was clear. Now she sighed and moved slightly, as if

854

with relief at my coming. 'I'm so glad.' Her voice had a small weary lilt which suggested that somewhere beyond the confines of her present pain and drowsiness a new self-confidence was stirring. 'I wanted to thank you.'

'It is Amaril you're in love with' I said — rather, blurted out. The remark came as a great surprise to me. It was completely involuntary. Suddenly a shutter seemed to roll back across my mind. I realized that this new fact which I was enunciating was one that I had always known, but without *being aware of the knowing*! Foolish as it was the distinction was a real one. Amaril was like a playing card which had always been there, lying before me on the table, face downwards. I had been aware of its existence but had never turned it over. Nor, I should add, was there anything in my voice beyond genuine scientific surprise; it was without pain, and full of sympathy only. Between us we had never used this dreadful word — this synonym for derangement or illness — and if I deliberately used it now it was to signify my recognition of the thing's autonomous nature. It was rather like saying 'My poor child, you have got cancer!'

After a moment's silence she said: 'Past tense now, alas!' Her voice had a puzzled drawling quality. 'And I was giving you good marks for tact, thinking you had recognized him in my Syrian episode! Had you really not? Yes, Amaril turned me into a woman I suppose. Oh, isn't it disgusting? When will we all grow up? No, but I've worn him out in my heart, you know. It isn't as you imagine it. I know he is not the man for me. Nothing would have persuaded me to replace Semira. I know this by the fact of having made love to him, been in love with him! It's odd, but the experience prevented me from mistaking him for the other one, the once-for-aller! Though who and where he is remains to discover. I haven't really affronted the real problems yet, I feel. They lie the other side of these mere episodes. And yet, perverse as it is, it is nice to be close to him — even on the operating-table. How is one to make clear a single truth about the human heart?'

'Shall I put off my journey?'

'But no. I wouldn't wish it at all. I shall need a little time to come to myself now that at last I am free from the horror. That at least you have done for me — pushed me back into midstream again and driven off the dragon. It's gone and will never come back. Put your hand on my shoulder and squeeze, instead of a kiss. No. Don't change plans. Now at last we can take things a bit easily. Unhurriedly. I shall be well cared for here as you know. Later when your job is done we shall see, shall we? Try and write. I feel perhaps a pause might start you off.'

'I will.' But I knew I wouldn't.

'Only one thing I want you to do. Please visit the Mulid of El Scob tonight so that you can tell me all about it; you see it is the first time since the war that they are allowing the customary lighting in that *quartier*. It should be fun to see. I don't want you to miss it. Will you?'

'Of course.'

'Thank you, my dear.'

I stood up and after a moment's pause said: 'Clea what exactly *was* the horror?'

But she had closed her eyes and was fading softly into sleep. Her lips moved but I could not catch her answer. There was the faintest trace of a smile at the corners of her mouth.

A phrase of Pursewarden's came into my mind as I softly closed the door of the ward. 'The richest love is that which submits to the arbitration of time.'

*   *   *   *   *

It was already late when at last I managed to locate a gharry to take me back to the town. At the flat I found a message to say that my departure had been put forward by six hours; the motor-launch would be leaving at midnight. Hamid was there, standing quite still and patient, as if he already knew the contents of the message. My luggage had been collected by an Army truck that afternoon. There was nothing left to do except kill the time until twelve, and this I proposed to do in the fashion suggested by Clea: by visiting the Mulid of El Scob. Hamid still stood before me, gravid with the weight of another parting. 'You no come back this time, sir' he said blinking his eye at me with sorrow. I looked at the little man with emotion. I remembered how proudly he had recounted the saving of this one eye. It was because he had been the younger and uglier brother of the two. His mother had put out his brother's two eyes in order to prevent him from being conscripted; but he, Hamid, being puny and ugly — he had escaped with one. His brother was now a blind *muezzin* in Tanta. But how rich he was, Hamid, with his one eye! It represented a fortune to him in well-paid work for rich foreigners.

'I come to you in London' he said eagerly, hopefully.

'Very well. I'll write to you.'

He was all dressed up for the Mulid in his best clothes — the crimson cloak and the red shoes of soft morocco leather; in his bosom he had a clean white handkerchief. It was his evening off I remembered. Pombal and I had saved up a sum of money to give him as a parting present. He took the cheque between finger and thumb, inclining his head with gratitude. But self-interest could not buoy him up against the pain of parting from us. So he repeated 'I come to you in London' to console himself; shaking hands with himself as he said the words.

'Very well' I said for the third time, though I could hardly see one-eyed Hamid in London. 'I will write. Tonight I shall visit the Mulid of El Scob.'

'Very good.' I shook him by the shoulders and the familiarity made him bow his head. A tear trickled out of his blind eye and off the end of his nose.

'Good-bye ya Hamid' I said, and walked down the stairs, leaving him standing quietly at the top, as if waiting for some signal from outer space. Then suddenly he rushed after me, catching me at the front door, in order to thrust into my hand, as a parting present, his cherished picture of Melissa and myself walking down Rue Fuad on some forgotten afternoon.

*　　*　　*　　*　　*

IX

The whole quarter lay drowsing in the umbrageous violet of approaching nightfall. A sky of palpitating *velours* which was cut into by the stark flare of a thousand electric light bulbs. It lay over Tatwig Street, that night, like a velvet rind. Only the lighted tips of the minarets rose above it on their slender invisible stalks — appeared hanging suspended in the sky; trembling slightly with the haze as if about to expand their hoods like cobras. Drifting idly down those remembered streets once more I drank in (forever: keepsakes of the Arab town) the smell of crushed chrysanthemums, ordure, scents, strawberries, human sweat and roasting pigeons. The procession had not arrived as yet. It would form somewhere beyond the harlots' quarter, among the tombs, and wind its slow way to the shrine, geared to a dancing measure; calling on the way at each of the mosques to offer up a verse or two of the Book in honour of El Scob. But the secular side of the festival was in full swing. In the dark alleys people had brought their dinner tables into the street, candle-lit and decked with roses. So sitting they could catch the chipped headtones of the girl singers who were already standing on the wooden platforms outside the cafés, piercing the heavy night with their quartertones. The streets were beflagged, and the great framed pictures of the circumcision doctors rippled on high among the cressets and standards. In a darkened yard I saw them pouring the hot sugar, red and white, into the little wooden moulds from which would emerge the whole bestiary of Egypt — the ducks, horsemen, rabbits, and goats. The great sugar figurines too of the Delta folklore — Yuna and Aziz the lovers interlocked, interpenetrated — and the bearded heroes like Abu Zeid, armed and mounted among his brigands. They were splendidly obscene — surely the stupidest word in our language? — and brilliantly coloured before being dressed in their garments of paper, tinsel, and spangled gold, and set up on display among the Sugar Booths for the children to gape at and buy. In every little square now the coloured marquees had been run up, each with its familiar sign. The Gamblers were already busy — Abu Firan, the Father of Rats, was shouting cheerfully for customers. The great board stood before him on trestles, each of the twelve houses marked

with a number and a name. In the centre stood the live white rat
which had been painted with green stripes. You placed your
money on the number of a house, and won, if the rat entered it.
In another box the same game was in play, but with a pigeon this
time; when all the bets were laid a handful of grain was tossed
into the centre and the pigeon, in eating it, entered one of the
numbered stalls.

I bought myself a couple of sugar figurines and sat down outside
a café to watch the passing show with its brilliant pristine colour.
These little 'arusas' or brides I would have liked to keep, but I
knew that they would crumble or be eaten by ants. They were
the little cousins of the *santons de Provence* or the *bonhommes de
pain d'épices* of the French country fair: of our own now extinct
gilt gingerbread men. I ordered a spoon of mastika to eat with
the cool fizzing sherbet. From where I sat at an angle between
two narrow streets I could see the harlots painting themselves at
an upper window before coming down to set up their garish
booths among the conjurers and tricksters; Showal the dwarf was
teasing them from his booth at ground level and causing screams
of laughter at his well-aimed arrows. He had a high tinny little
voice and the most engaging of acrobatic tricks despite his stunted
size. He talked continuously even when standing on his head, and
punctuated the point of his patter with a double somersault. His
face was grotesquely farded and his lips painted in a clown's grin.
At the other corner under a hide curtain sat Faraj the fortune-
teller with his instruments of divination — ink, sand, and a
curious hairy ball like a bull's testicles only covered in dark hair.
A radiantly beautiful prostitute squatted before him. He had filled
her palm with ink and was urging her to scry.

Little scenes from the street life. A mad wild witch of a woman
who suddenly burst into the street, foaming at the lips and
uttering curses so terrible that silence fell and everyone's blood
froze. Her eyes blazed like a bear's under the white matted hair.
Being mad she was in some sort holy, and no-one dared to face
the terrible imprecations she uttered which, if turned on him,
might spell ill luck. Suddenly a grubby child darted from the
crowd and tugged her sleeve. At once calmed she took his hand
and turned away into an alley. The festival closed over the memory
of her like a skin.

I was sitting here, drunk on the spectacle, when the voice of
Scobie himself suddenly sounded at my elbow. 'Now, old man'

it said thoughtfully. 'If you have Tendencies you got to have Scope. That's why I'm in the Middle East if you want to know. . . .'

'God, you gave me a start' I said, turning round. It was Nimrod the policeman who had been one of the old man's superiors in the police force. He chuckled and sat down beside me, removing his tarbush to mop his forehead. 'Did you think he'd come to life?' he enquired.

'I certainly did.'

'I know my Scobie, you see.'

Nimrod laid his flywhisk before him and with a clap of his hands commanded a coffee. Then giving me a sly wink he went on in the veritable voice of the saint. 'The thing about Budgie was just that. In Horsham there's no Scope. Otherwise I would have joined him years ago in the earth-closet trade. The man's a mechanical genius, I don't mind admitting. And not having any income except what the old mud-slinger — as he laughingly calls it — brings him in, he's stymied. He's in baulk. Did I ever tell you about the Bijou Earth Closet? No? Funny I thought I did. Well, it was a superb contrivance, the fruit of long experiment. Budgie is an FRZS you know. He got it by home study. That shows you what a brain the man has. Well it was a sort of lever with a trigger. The seat of the closet was on a kind of spring. As you sat down it *went* down, but when you got up it sprang up of its own accord and threw a spadeful of earth into the bin. Budgie says he got the idea from watching his dog clear up after himself with his paws. But how he adapted it I just can't fathom. It's sheer genius. You have a magazine at the back which you fill with earth or sand. Then when you get up the spring goes bang and presto! He's making about two thousand a year out of it, I don't mind admitting. Of course it takes time to build up a trade, but the overheads are low. He has just one man working for him to build the box part, and he buys the springs — gets them made to specification in Hammersmith. And they're very prettily painted too, with astrology all round the rim. It looks queer, I admit. In fact it looks arcane. But it's a wonderful contrivance the little Bijou. Once there was a crisis while I was home on leave for a month. I called in to see Budgie. He was almost in tears. The chap who helped, Tom the carpenter, used to drink a bit and must have misplaced the sprockets on one series of Bijous. Anyway complaints started to pour in. Budgie said that his closets had gone mad all over Sussex and were throwing earth about in a weird and unwholesome way. Customers were furious. Well, there was nothing for it but to visit all his parishioners on a motor-bike and adjust the sprockets. I had so little time that I didn't want to miss his company — so he took me along with him. It was quite an adventure I don't mind telling you. Some of them were quite mad with Budgie. One woman said the sprocket was so strong her closet threw mud the length of the drawing-room. We had a time quietening her down. I helped by lending a soothing influence I don't mind admitting, while Budgie tinkered with the springs. I told stories to take their minds off the unhappy business. But finally it got straightened out. And now it's a profitable industry with members everywhere.'

Nimrod sipped his coffee reflectively and cocked a quizzical eye in my direction, proud of his mimicry. 'And now' he said, throwing up his hands, 'El Scob. . . .'

A crowd of painted girls passed down the street, brilliant as tropical parrots and almost as loud in their chattering and laughing. 'Now that Abu Zeid' said Nimrod 'has taken the Mulid under his patronage it's likely to grow into a bit of headache for us. It's such a crowded quarter. This morning he sent a whole string of he-camels on heat into the town with *bercim* clover. You know how horrible they smell. And when they're in season they get that horrible jelly-like excrescence on their necks. It must irritate them or suppurate or something for they're scratching their necks the whole time on walls and posts. Two of them had a fight. It took hours to untangle the affair. The place was blocked.'

Suddenly a series of bangs sounded from the direction of the harbour and a series of bright coloured rockets traced their splendid grooves across the night, drooping and falling away with a patter and a hiss. 'Aha!' said Nimrod with self-satisfaction. 'There goes the Navy. I'm glad they remembered.'

'Navy?' I echoed as another long line of rockets tossed their brilliant plumage across the soft night.

'The boys of H.M.S. *Milton*' he chuckled. 'I happened to dine on board last night. The wardroom was much taken by my story of an old Merchant Seaman who had been beatified. I naturally did not tell them very much about Scobie; least of all about his death. But I did hint that a few fireworks would be appropriate as coming from British mariners, and I also added that as a political gesture of respect it would earn them good marks with the worshippers. The idea caught on at once, and the Admiral was asked for permission. And there we go!'

We sat for a while in companionable silence watching the fireworks and the highly delighted crowd which saluted each salvo with long quivering exclamations of pleasure. 'All—ah! All—ah!' Finally Nimrod cleared his throat and said: 'Darley, can I ask you a question? Do you know what Justine is up to?' I must have looked very blank for he went on at once without hesitation. 'I only ask you because she rang me yesterday and said that she was going to break parole today, come into town deliberately, and that she wanted me to arrest her. It sounds quite absurd — I mean to come all the way into town to give herself up to the Police. She said she wanted to force a personal interview with Memlik. It had to be me as reports from the British officers on the force would carry weight and draw Memlik's attention. It sounds a bit of a rigmarole doesn't it? But I've got a date with her at the Central Station in half an hour.'

'I know nothing about the matter.'

'I wondered if you did. Anyway, keep it under your hat.'

'I will.'

He stood up and held out his hand to say good-bye. 'You're off tonight I gather. Good luck.' As he stepped down from the little wooden platform he said: 'By the way, Balthazar is looking for you. He's somewhere down at the shrine — what a word!' With a brief nod his tall figure moved away into the brilliant swirling street. I paid for my drink and walked down towards Tatwig Street, bumped and jostled by the holiday crowd.

Ribbons and bunting and huge coloured gonfalons had been hung from every balcony along the street. The little piece of waste land under the arched doors was now the most sumptuous of saloons. Huge tents with their brilliant embroidered designs had been set up creating a ceremonial parade ground where the dancing and chanting would be held when the procession reached its destination. This area was crowded with children. The drone of prayers and the shrill tongue-trills of women came from the shrine which was dimly lit. The suppliants were invoking fruitfulness of Scobie's bath-tub. The long quavering lines of the Suras spun themselves on the night in a web of melodious sound. I quested round a bit among the crowd like a gun-dog, hunting for Balthazar. At last I caught sight of him sitting somewhat apart at an outdoor café. I made my way to his side. 'Good' he said.

'I was on the look out for you. Hamid said you were off tonight. He telephoned to ask for a job and told me. Besides I wanted to share with you my mixture of shame and relief over this hideous accident. Shame at the stupidity, relief that she isn't dead. Both mixed. I'm rather drunk with relief, and dazed with the shame.' He was indeed rather tipsy. 'But it will be all right, thank God!'

'What does Amaril think?'

'Nothing as yet. Or if he does he won't say. She must have a comfortable twenty-four hours of rest before anything is decided. Are you really going?' His voice fell with reproof. 'You should stay, you know.'

'She doesn't want me to stay.'

'I know. I was a bit shocked when she said she had told you to go; but she said "You don't understand. I shall see if I can't will him back again. We aren't quite ripe for each other yet. It will come." I was amazed to see her so self-confident and radiant again. Really amazed. Sit down, my dear chap, and have a couple of stiff drinks with me. We'll see the procession quite well from here. No crowding.' He clapped his hands rather unsteadily and called for more mastika.

When the glasses were brought he sat for a long while silent with his chin on his hands, staring at them. Then he gave a sigh and shook his head sadly.

'What is it?' I said, removing his glass from the tray and placing it squarely before him on the tin table.

'Leila is dead' he said quietly. The words seemed to weight him down with sorrow. 'Nessim telephoned this evening to tell me. The strange thing is that he sounded exhilarated by the news. He has managed to get permission to fly down and make arrangements for her funeral. D'you know what he said?' Balthazar looked at me with that dark all-comprehending eye and went on. 'He said: "While I loved her *and all that*, her death has freed me in a curious sort of way. A new life is opening before me. I feel years younger." I don't know if it was a trick of the telephone or what but he sounded younger. His voice was full of suppressed excitement. He knew, of course, that Leila and I were the oldest of friends but not that all through this period of absence she was writing to me. She was a rare soul, Darley, one of the rare flowers of Alexandria. She wrote: "I know I am dying, my dear Balthazar, but all too slowly. Do not believe the doctors and their diagnoses,

863

you of all men. I am dying of heartsickness like a true Alexandrian." ' Balthazar blew his nose in an old sock which he took
from the breast-pocket of his coat; carefully folded it to resemble
a clean handkerchief and pedantically replaced it. 'Yes' he said
again, gravely, 'what a word it is — "heartsickness"! And it seems
to me that while (from what you tell me) Liza Pursewarden was
administering her death-warrant to her brother, Mountolive was
giving the same back-hander to Leila. So we pass the loving-cup
about, the poisoned loving-cup!' He nodded and took a loud sip
of his drink. He went on slowly, with immense care and effort,
like someone translating from an obscure and recondite text.
'Yes, just as Liza's letter to Pursewarden telling him that at last
the stranger had appeared was his *coup de grâce* so to speak, so
Leila received, I suppose, exactly the same letter. Who knows
how these things are arranged? Perhaps in the very same words.
The same words of passionate gratitude: "I bless you, I thank
you with all my heart that through you I am at last able to receive
the precious gift which can never come to those who are ignorant
of its powers." Those are the words of Mountolive. For Leila
quoted them to me. All this was after she went away. She wrote
to me. It was as if she were cut off from Nessim and had nobody
to turn to, nobody to talk to. Hence the long letters in which she
went over it all, backwards and forwards, with that marvellous
candour and clear-sightedness which I so loved in her. She
refused every self-deception. Ah! but she fell between two stools,
Leila, between two lives, two loves. She said something like this
in explaining it to me: "I thought at first when I got his letter
that it was just another attachment — as it was in the past for his
Russian ballerina. There was never any secret between us of his
loves, and that is what made ours seem so truthful, so immortal
in its way. It was a love without reserves. But this time everything
became clear to me when he refused to tell me her name, to share
her with me, so to speak! I knew then that everything was ended.
Of course in another corner of my mind I had always been waiting
for this moment; I pictured myself facing it with magnanimity.
This I found, to my surprise, was impossible. That was why for
a long time, even when I knew he was in Egypt, and anxious to
see me, I could not bring myself to see him. Of course I pretended
it was for other reasons, purely feminine ones. But it was not that.
It wasn't lack of courage because of my smashed beauty, no! For
I have in reality the heart of a man." '

Balthazar sat for a moment staring at the empty glasses with wide eyes, pressing his fingers softly together. His story meant very little to me — except that I was amazed to imagine Mountolive capable of any very deep feeling, and at a loss to imagine this secret relationship with the mother of Nessim.

'The Dark Swallow!' said Balthazar and clapped his hands for more drink to be brought. 'We shall not look upon her like again.'

But gradually the raucous night around us was swelling with the deeper rumour of the approaching procession. One saw the rosy light of the cressets among the roofs. The streets, already congested, were now black with people. They buzzed like a great hive with the contagion of the knowledge. You could hear the distant bumping of drums and the hissing splash of cymbals, keeping time with the strange archaic peristaltic rhythms of the dance — its relatively slow walking pace broken by queer halts, to enable the dancers, as the ecstasy seized them, to twirl in and out of their syncopated measures and return once more to their places in the line of march. It pushed its way through the narrow funnel of the main street like a torrent whose force makes it overleap its bed; for all the little side streets were full of sightseers running along, keeping pace with it.

First came the grotesque acrobats and tumblers with masks and painted faces, rolling and contorting, leaping in the air and walking on their hands. They were followed by a line of carts full of candidates for circumcision dressed in brilliant silks and embroidered caps, and surrounded by their sponsors, the ladies of the harem. They rode proudly, singing in juvenile voices and greeting the crowd: like the bleating of sacrificial lambs. Balthazar croaked: 'Foreskins will fall like snow tonight, by the look of it. It is amazing that there are no infections. You know, they use black gunpowder and lime-juice as a styptic for the wound!'

Now came the various orders with their tilting and careening gonfalons with the names of the holy ones crudely written on them. They trembled like foliage in the wind. Magnificently robed sheiks held them aloft walking with difficulty because of their weight, yet keeping the line of the procession straight. The street-preachers were gabbling the hundred holy names. A cluster of bright braziers outlined the stern bearded faces of a cluster of dignitaries carrying huge paper lanterns, like balloons, ahead of them. Now as they overran us and flowed down the length of Tatwig Street in a long ripple of colour we saw the various orders of Dervishes climb out of the nether darkness and emerge into the light, each order distinguished by its colour. They were led by the black-capped Rifiya — the scorpion-eaters of legendary powers. Their short barking cries indicated that the religious ecstasy was already on them. They gazed around with dazed eyes. Some had run skewers through their cheeks, others licked red-hot knives. At last came the courtly figure of Abu Zeid with his little group of retainers on magnificently caparisoned ponies, their cloaks swelling out behind them, their arms raised in salutation like knights embarking on a tournament. Before them ran a helter skelter collection of male prostitutes with powdered faces and long flowing hair, chuckling and ejaculating like chickens in a farm-yard. And to all this queer discontinuous and yet somehow congruent mass of humanity the music lent a sort of homogeneity; it bound it and confined it within the heart-beats of the drums, the piercing skirl of the flutes, the gnashing of the cymbals. Circling, proceeding, halting: circling, proceeding, halting, the long dancing lines moved on towards the tomb, bursting through the great portals of Scobie's lodgings like a tide at full, and deploying across the brilliant square in clouds of dust.

And as the chanters moved forward to recite the holy texts six Mevlevi dervishes suddenly took the centre of the stage, expanding in a slow fan of movement until they had formed a semicircle. They wore brilliant white robes reaching to their green slippered feet and tall brown hats shaped like huge *bombes glacées*. Calmly, beautifully, they began to whirl, these 'tops spun by God', while the music of the flutes haunted them with their piercing quibbles. As they gathered momentum their arms, which at first they hugged fast to their shoulders, unfolded as if by centrifugal force and stretched out to full reach, the right palm turned upward to heaven, the left downward to the ground. So, with heads and tall rounded hats tilted slightly, like the axis of the earth, they stayed there miraculously spinning, their feet hardly seeming to touch the floor, in this wonderful parody of the heavenly bodies in their perpetual motion. On and on they went, faster and faster, until the mind wearied of trying to keep pace with them. I thought of the verses of Jalaluddin which Pursewarden used sometimes to recite. On the outer circles the Rifiya had begun their display of self-mutilation, so horrible to behold and yet so apparently harm-less. The touch of a sheik's finger would heal all these wounds pierced in the cheeks and breasts. Here a dervish drove a skewer through his nostrils, there another fell upon the point of a dirk, driving it up through his throat into his skull. But still the central knot of dancers continued its unswerving course, spinning in the sky of the mind.

'My goodness' said Balthazar at my elbow, with a chuckle, 'I thought he was familiar. There's the Magzub himself. The one at the further end. He used to be an absolute terror, more than half mad. The one who was supposed to have stolen the child and sold it to a brothel. Look at him.'

I saw a face of immense world-weary serenity, the eyes closed, the lips curved in a half-smile; as the dancer spun slowly to a halt this slender personage, with an air of half-playful modesty, took up a bundle of thorns and lighting it at a brazier thrust the blazing mass into his bosom against the flesh, and started to whirl once more like a tree in flames. Then as the circle came to a swaying halt he plucked it out once more and gave the dervish next to him a playful slap upon the face with it.

But now a dozen dancing circles intervened and took up the measure and the little courtyard overflowed with twisting turning figures. From the little shrine came the steady drone of the holy word, punctuated by the shrill tongue trills of the votaries.

'Scobie's going to have a heavy night' said Balthazar with irreverence. 'Counting foreskins up there in the Moslem heaven.'

Somewhere far away I heard the siren of a ship boom in the harbour, recalling me to my senses. It was time to be going. 'I'll come down with you' said Balthazar, and together we started to push and wriggle our way down the crowded street towards the Corniche.

We found a gharry and sat silent in it, hearing the music and drumming gradually receding as we traversed the long rolling line of the marine parade. The moon was up, shining on the calm sea, freckled by the light breeze. The palms nodded. We clip-clopped down the narrow twisted streets and into the commercial harbour at last with its silent ghostly watercraft. A few lights winked here and there. A liner moved out of its berth and slid softly down the channel — a long glittering crescent of light.

The little launch which was to carry me was still being loaded with provisions and luggage.

'Well' I said, 'Balthazar. Keep out of mischief.'

'We'll be meeting again quite soon' he said quietly. 'You can't shake me off. The Wandering Jew, you know. But I'll keep you posted about Clea. I'd say something like "Come back to us soon", if I didn't have the feeling that you weren't going to. I'm damned if I know why. But that we'll meet again I'm sure.'

'So am I' I said.

We embraced warmly, and with an abrupt gesture he climbed back into the gharry and settled himself once more.

'Mark my words' he said as the horse started up to the flick of a whip.

I stood, listening to the noise of its hooves until the night swallowed them up. Then I turned back to the work in hand.

*　　*　　*　　*　　*

X

Dearest Clea:
Three long months and no word from you. I would have been very much disquieted had not the faithful Balthazar sent me his punctual postcard every few days to report so favourably on your progress: though of course he gives me no details. You for your part must have grown increasingly angry at my callous silence which you so little deserve. Truthfully, I am bitterly ashamed of it. I do not know what curious inhibition has been holding me back. I have been unable either to analyse it or to react against it effectively. It has been like a handle of a door which won't turn. Why? It is doubly strange because I have been deeply conscious of you all the time, of you being actively present in my thoughts. I've been holding you, metaphorically, cool against my throbbing mind like a knife-blade. Is it possible that I enjoyed you better as a thought than as a person alive, acting in the world? Or was it that words themselves seemed so empty a consolation for the distance which has divided us? I do not know. But now that the job is nearly completed I seem suddenly to have found my tongue.

Things alter their focus on this little island. You called it a metaphor once, I remember, but it is very much a reality to me — though of course vastly changed from the little haven I knew before. It is our own invasion which has changed it. You could hardly imagine that ten technicians could make such a change. But we have imported money, and with it are slowly altering the economy of the place, displacing labour at inflated prices, creating all sorts of new needs of which the lucky inhabitants were not conscious before. Needs which in the last analysis will destroy the tightly woven fabric of this feudal village with its tense blood-relationships, its feuds and archaic festivals. Its wholeness will dissolve under these alien pressures. It was so tightly woven, so beautiful and symmetrical like a swallow's nest. We are picking it apart like idle boys, unaware of the damage we inflict. It seems inescapable the death we bring to the old order without wishing it. It is simply done too — a few steel girders, some digging equipment, a crane! Suddenly things begin to alter shape. A new cupidity is born. It will start quietly with a few barbers' shops,

869

but will end by altering the whole architecture of the port. In ten years it will be an unrecognizable jumble of warehouses, dance-halls and brothels for merchant sailors. Only give us enough time!

The site which they chose for the relay station is on the mountainous eastward side of the island, and not where I lived before. I am rather glad of this in an obscure sort of way. I am sentimental enough about old memories to enjoy them — but how much better they seem in the light of a small shift of gravity; they are renewed and refreshed all at once. Moreover this corner of the island is unlike any other part — a high wine-bearing valley overlooking the sea. Its soils are gold, bronze and scarlet — I suppose they consist of some volcanic marl. The red wine they make is light and very faintly *pétillant*, as if a volcano still slumbered in every bottle. Yes, here the mountains ground their teeth together (one can *hear* them during the frequent tremors!) and powdered up these metamorphic rocks into chalk. I live in a small square house of two rooms built over a wine-magazine. A terraced and tiled courtyard separates it from several other such places of storage — deep cellars full of sleeping wine in tuns.

We are in the heart of the vineyards; on all sides, ruled away on the oblong to follow the spine of the blue hill above the sea, run the shallow canals of humus and mould between the symmetrical vines which are now flourishing. Galleries — no, bowling-alleys of the brown ashy earth, every mouthful finger-and-fist-sifted by the industrious girls. Here and there figs and olives intrude upon this rippling forest of green, this vine-carpet. It is so dense that once you are in it, crouched, your field of visibility is about three feet, like a mouse in the corn. As I write there are a dozen invisible girls tunnelling like moles, turning the soil. I hear their voices but see nothing. Yes, they are crawling about in there like sharpshooters. They rise and start work before dawn. I wake and hear them arriving often, sometimes singing a snatch of a Greek folk-song! I am up at five. The first birds come over and are greeted by the small reception committee of optimistic hunters who pot idly at them and then pass up the hill, chattering and chaffing each other.

Shading my terrace stands a tall tree of white mulberries, with the largest fruit I have ever seen — as big as caterpillars. The fruit is ripe and the wasps have found it and are quite drunk on the sweetness. They behave just like human beings, laughing uproariously about nothing, falling down, picking fights. . . .

The life is hard, but good. What pleasure to actually sweat over a task, actually use one's hands! And while we are harvesting steel to raise, membrane by membrane, this delicate mysterious ex-voto to the sky — why the vines are ripening too with their reminder that long after man has stopped his neurotic fiddling with the death-bringing tools with which he expresses his fear of life, the old dark gods are there, underground, buried in the moist humus of the chthonian world (that favourite world of P'). They are forever sited in the human wish. They will never capitulate! (I am talking at random simply to give you an idea of the sort of life I lead here.)

The early hill-barley is being gathered. You meet walking haystacks — haystacks with nothing but a pair of feet below them trudging along these rocky lanes. The weird shouts the women give, either at cattle or calling to one another from hillside to hillside. '*Wow*' '*hoosh*' '*gnaiow*'. This barley is laid upon the flat roofs for threshing out the chaff which they do with sticks. Barley! hardly is the word spoken before the ant-processions begin, long chains of dark ants trying to carry it away to their private storehouses. This in turn has alerted the yellow lizards; they prowl about eating the ants, lying in ambush winking their eyes. And, as if following out the octave of causality in nature, here come the cats to hunt and eat the lizards. This is not good for them, and many die of a wasting disease attributed to this folly. But I suppose the thrill of the chase is on them. And then? Well, now and then a viper kills a cat stone dead. And the man with his spade breaks the snake's back. And the man? Autumn fevers come on with the first rain. The old men tumble into the grave like fruit off a tree. *Finita la guerra!* These people were occupied by Italians and quite a few learned the language which they speak with a Sienese accent.

In the little square is a fountain where the women gather. They proudly display their babies, and fancy them as if they were up for sale. This one is fat, that one thin. The young men pass up and down the road with hot shy glances. One of them sings archly '*Solo, per te, Lucia*'. But they only toss their heads and continue with their gossip. There is an old and apparently completely deaf man filling his pitcher. He is almost electrocuted by the phrase 'Dmitri at the big house is dead.' It lifts him off the ground. He spins round in a towering rage. 'Dead? Who's dead? Eh? What?' His hearing is much improved all at once.

There is a little acropolis now called Fontana, high up there in the clouds. Yet it isn't far. But a steep climb up clinker-dry river-beds amid clouds of black flies; you come upon herds of rushing black goats like satans. There is a tiny hospice on the top with one mad monk; built as if on a turntable like a kiln of rusk. From here you can drink the sweet indolent misty curves of the island to the west.

And the future?

Well, this is a sketch of a nearly ideal present which will not last forever; indeed has almost expired, for within another month or so my usefulness will come to an end, and with it presumably the post upon which I depend for my exiguous livelihood. I have no resources of my own and must consider ways and means. No, the future rolls about inside me with every roll of the ship, so to speak, like a cargo which has worked loose. Were it not to see you again I doubt if I could return again to Alexandria. I feel it fade inside me, in my thoughts, like some valedictory mirage — like the sad history of some great queen whose fortunes have foundered among the ruins of armies and the sands of time! My mind has been turning more and more westward, towards the old inheritance of Italy or France. Surely there is still some worthwhile work to be done among their ruins — something which we can cherish, perhaps even revive? I ask myself this question, but it really addresses itself to you. Uncommitted as yet to any path, nevertheless the one I would most like to take leads westward and northward. There are other reasons. The terms of my contract entitle me to free 'repatriation' as they call it; to reach England would cost me nothing. Then, with the handsome service gratuity which all this bondage has earned me, I think I could afford a spell in Europe. My heart leaps at the thought.

But something in all this must be decided for me; I have a feeling, I mean, that it is not I who shall decide.

Please forgive me my silence for which I cannot offer any excuse and write me a line.

Last Saturday I found myself with a free day and a half, so I walked across the island with a pack to spend a night in the little house where I lived on my previous visit. What a contrast to this verdant highland it was to strike that wild and windy promontory once more, the acid green seas and fretted coastlines of the past. It was indeed another island — I suppose the past always is. Here for a night and a day I lived the life of an echo, thinking much about the past and about us all moving in it, the 'selective fictions' which life shuffles out like a pack of cards, mixing and dividing, withdrawing and restoring. It did not seem to me that I had the right to feel so calm and happy: a sense of Plenitude in which the only unanswered question was the one which arose with each memory of your name.

Yes, a different island, harsher and more beautiful of aspect. One held the night-silence in one's hands; feeling it slowly melting — as a child holds a piece of ice! At noon a dolphin rising from the ocean. Earthquake vapours on the sea-line. The great grove of plane trees with their black elephant hides which the wind strips off in great scrolls revealing the soft grey ashen skin within. . . . Much of the detail I had forgotten.

It is rather off the beaten track this little promontory; only olive-pickers might come here in season. Otherwise the only visitants are the charcoal burners who ride through the grove before light every day with a characteristic jingle of stirrups. They have built long narrow trenches on the hill. They crouch over them all day, black as demons.

But for the most part one might be living on the moon. Slightly noise of sea, the patient stridulation of *cigales* in the sunlight. One day I caught a tortoise at my front door; on the beach was a smashed turtle's egg. Small items which plant themselves in the speculative mind like single notes of music belonging to some larger composition which I suppose one will never hear. The tortoise makes a charming and undemanding pet. I can hear P say: 'Brother Ass and his tortoise. The marriage of true minds!'

For the rest: the picture of a man skimming flat stones upon the still water of the lagoon at evening, waiting for a letter out of silence.

★　　★　　★　　★　　★

But I had hardly confided this letter to the muleteer-postman who took our mail down to the town before I received a letter with an Egyptian stamp, addressed to me in an unknown hand. It read as follows:

'You did not recognize it, did you? I mean the handwriting on the envelope? I confess that I chuckled as I addressed it to you, before beginning this letter: I could see your face all of a

873

sudden with its expression of perplexity. I saw you turn the letter over in your fingers for a moment trying to guess who had sent it!

'It is the first serious letter I have attempted, apart from short notes, with my new hand: this strange accessory-after-the-fact with which the good Amaril has equipped me! I wanted it to become word-perfect before I wrote to you. Of course I was frightened and disgusted by it at first, as you can imagine. But I have come to respect it very much, this delicate and beautiful steel contrivance which lies beside me so quietly on the table in its green velvet glove! Nothing falls out as one imagines it. I could not have believed myself accepting it so completely — steel and rubber seem such strange allies for human flesh. But the hand has proved itself almost more competent even than an ordinary flesh-and-blood member! In fact its powers are so comprehensive that I am a little frightened of it. I can undertake the most delicate of tasks, even turning the pages of a book, as well as the coarser ones. But most important of all — ah! Darley I tremble as I write the words — IT can *paint!*

'I have crossed the border and entered into the possession of my kingdom, thanks to the Hand. Nothing about this was premeditated. One day it took up a brush and lo! pictures of truly troubling originality and authority were born. I have five of them now. I stare at them with reverent wonder. Where did they come from? But I know that the Hand was responsible. And this new handwriting is also one of its new inventions, tall and purposeful and tender. Don't think I boast. I am speaking with the utmost objectivity, for I know that I am not responsible. It is the Hand alone which has contrived to slip me through the barriers into the company of the Real Ones as Pursewarden used to say. Yet it is a bit frightening; the elegant velvet glove guards its secret perfectly. If I wear both gloves a perfect anonymity is preserved! I watch with wonder and a certain distrust, as one might a beautiful and dangerous pet like a panther, say. There is nothing, it seems, that it cannot do impressively better than I can. This will explain my silence and I hope excuse it. I have been totally absorbed in this new hand-language and the interior metamorphosis it has brought about. All the roads have opened before me, everything seems now possible for the first time.

'On the table beside me as I write lies my steamship ticket to France; yesterday I knew with absolute certainty that I must go there. Do you remember how Pursewarden used to say that artists, like sick cats, knew by instinct exactly which herb they needed to effect a cure: and that the bitter-sweet herb of their self-discovery only grew in one place, France? Within ten days I shall be gone! And among so many new certainties there is one which has raised its head — the certainty that you will follow me there in your own good time. I speak of certainty not prophecy — I have done with fortune-tellers once and for all!

'This, then, is simply to give you the dispositions which the Hand has imposed on me, and which I accept with eagerness and gratitude — with resignation also. This last week I have been paying a round of good-bye visits, for I think it will be some long time before I see Alexandria again. It has become stale and profitless to me. And yet how can we but help love the places which have made us suffer? Leave-takings are in the air; it's as if the whole composition of our lives were being suddenly drawn away by a new current. For I am not the only person who is leaving the place — far from it. Mountolive, for example, will be leaving in a couple of months; by a great stroke of luck he has been given the plum post of his profession, Paris! With this news all the old uncertainties seem to have vanished; last week he was secretly married! You will guess to whom.

'Another deeply encouraging thing is the return and recovery of dear old Pombal. He is back at the Foreign Office now in a senior post and seems to have recovered much of his old form to judge by the long exuberant letter he sent me. "How could I have forgotten" he writes "that there are no women in the world except French women? It is quite mysterious. They are the most lovely creation of the Almighty. And yet . . . dear Clea, there are *so very many of them*, and each more perfect than the other. What is one poor man to do against so many, against such an army? For Godsake ask someone, anyone, to bring up reinforcements. Wouldn't Darley like to help an old friend out for old times' sake?"

'I pass you the invitation for what it is worth. Amaril and Semira will have a child this month — a child with the nose I invented! He will spend a year in America on some job or other, taking them with him. Balthazar also is off on a visit to Smyrna and Venice. My most piquant piece of news, however, I have saved for the last. *Justine!*

'This I do not expect you to believe. Nevertheless I must put it down. Walking down Rue Fuad at ten o'clock on a bright spring morning I saw her come towards me, radiant and beautifully turned out in a spring frock of eloquent design: and *flop flop flop* beside her on the dusty pavements, hopping like a toad, the detested Memlik! Clad in elastic-sided boots with spats. A cane with a gold knob. And a newly minted flower-pot on his fuzzy crown. I nearly collapsed. She was leading him along like a poodle. One almost saw the cheap leather leash attached to his collar. She greeted me with effusive warmth and introduced me to her captive who shuffled shyly and greeted me in a deep groaning voice like a bass saxophone. They were on their way to meet Nessim at the Select. Would I go too? Of course I would. You know how tirelessly curious I am. She kept shooting secret sparks of amusement at me without Memlik seeing. Her eyes were sparkling with delight, a sort of impish mockery. It was as if, like some powerful engine of destruction, she had suddenly switched on again. She has never looked happier or younger. When we absented ourselves to powder our noses I could only gasp: "Justine! Memlik! What on earth?" She gave a peal of laughter and giving me a great hug said: "I have found his *point faible*. He is hungry for *society*. He wants to move in social circles in Alexandria and meet a lot of *white* women!" More laughter. "But what is the object?" I said in bewilderment. Here all at once she became serious, though her eyes sparkled with clever malevolence. "We have started something, Nessim and I. We have made a break through at last. Clea, I am so happy, I could cry. It is something much bigger this time, international. We will have to go to Switzerland next year, probably for good. Nessim's luck has suddenly changed. I can't tell you any details."

'When we reached the table upstairs Nessim had already arrived and was talking to Memlik. His appearance staggered me, he looked so much younger, and so elegant and self-possessed. It gave me a queer pang, too, to see the passionate way they embraced, Nessim and Justine, as if oblivious to the rest of the world. Right there in the café, with such ecstatic passion that I did not know where to look.

'Memlik sat there with his expensive gloves on his knee, smiling gently. It was clear that he enjoyed the life of high society, and I could see from the way he offered me an ice that he also enjoyed the company of white women!

'Ah! it is getting tired, this miraculous hand. I must catch the evening post with this letter. There are a hundred things to attend to before I start the bore of packing. As for you, wise one, I have a feeling that you too perhaps have stepped across the threshold into the kingdom of your imagination, to take possession of it once and for all. Write and tell me — or save it for some small café under a chestnut-tree, in smoky autumn weather, by the Seine.

'I wait, quite serene and happy, a real human being, an artist at last.

'Clea.'

*   *   *   *   *

But it was to be a little while yet before the clouds parted before me to reveal the secret landscape of which she was writing, and which she would henceforward appropriate, brushstroke by slow brushstroke. It had been so long in forming inside me, this precious image, that I too was as unprepared as she had been. It came on a blue day, quite unpremeditated, quite unannounced, and with such *ease* I would not have believed it. I had been until then like some timid girl, scared of the birth of her first child.

Yes, one day I found myself writing down with trembling fingers the four words (four letters! four faces!) with which every story-teller since the world began has staked his slender claim to the attention of his fellow-men. Words which presage simply the old story of an artist coming of age. I wrote: 'Once upon a time. . . .'

And I felt as if the whole universe had given me a nudge!

*   *   *   *   *

WORKPOINTS

Hamid's story of Darley and Melissa.

★   ★   ★

Mountolive's child by the dancer Grishkin. The result of the duel. The Russian letters. Her terror of Liza when after her mother's death she is sent to her father.

★   ★   ★

Memlik and Justine in Geneva. Nessim's new ventures.

★   ★   ★

Balthazar's encounter with Arnauti in Venice. The violet sunglasses, the torn overcoat, pockets full of crumbs to feed the pigeons. The scene in Florian's. The shuffling walk of general paralysis. Conversations on the balcony of the little *pension* over the rotting backwater of the canal. Was Justine actually Claudia? He cannot be sure. 'Time is memory, they say; the art however is to revive it and yet avoid remembering. You speak of Alexandria. I can no longer even imagine it. It has dissolved. A work of art is something which is more like life than life itself!' The slow death.

★   ★   ★

The northern journey of Narouz, and the great battle of the sticks.

Smyrna. The manuscripts, The Annals of Time. The theft.

SOME NOTES FOR CLEA (by Pursewarden)

* *Page* 737

Big advances are not made by analytical procedures but by direct vision. Yes, but *how*?

*   *   *

Art is not art unless it threatens your very existence. Could you repeat that, please, more slowly?

*   *   *

As you get older and want to die more a strange kind of happiness seizes you; you suddenly realize that all art must end in a celebration. This is what drives the impotent mad with rage. They cannot provoke that fruitful compulsion of the Present, even though their scrotums be as hairy as Cape Gooseberries.

*   *   *

Peine dure! Would you rather read Henry James or be pressed to death by weights? I have made my choice. I believe in the Holy Boast and the Communion of Aints. I do not belong to the Stream-of-Pompousness school, nor that of the desert fathers — prickeaters of the void.

*   *   *

Language is not an accident of poetry but the essence. The lingo is the nub.

*   *   *

A *dévot* of the Ophite sect,
With member more or less erect,
Snake-worship is the creed I hold
And shall do till I get too old.
The saucy serpent symbolizes
A hundred Freudian surprises;
With mine, I do the Indian trick
Though it's become a shade too thick
To stand up like an actual rope —
I leave that to the Band of Hope.

879

Nor can I manage kundalini
And play on it like Paganini . . .
Mere beanstalk with a tower atop
I'm just like Jack, I cannot stop,
Hand over curious hand I climb
Until I hear the belfries chime
And some companionable she
Asks is there honey still for tea?

★   ★   ★

Perhaps it would be better just to start rewriting La Rochefou-
cauld, beginning with some such aphorism as '*Jouir c'est
pourrir un peu?*'

★   ★   ★

You must put yourself into deep soak, psychologically speaking.

★   ★   ★

A phrase from Bacon: 'Prize bulls made fierce by dark
keeping.'

★   ★   ★

Ah, my compatriots! What shall it profit a man to become a
utilitarian jujube — to go thrilling off each morning in his
electric brougham to the offices of the *Spectator*? How low can
you rise?

★   ★   ★

To become a poet is to take the whole field of human knowledge
and human desire for one's province; yes but, this field can
only be covered by continual inner abdications.

★   ★   ★

The more I read of those artists who have reached the bounds
of human knowledge — and there is a permissible bound to
the humanly knowable — the more it becomes apparent to me
that statement becomes simpler as it becomes profounder.
Finally it becomes platitude. At this point one begins to understand the religious claim that only initiates can communicate
with each other because they use, not concept but symbol.
For them all speech based on concept becomes an indiscretion;

one can only really exchange what is mutually understood. In this sense every work of art is an indiscretion — but a *calculated* indiscretion.

*   *   *

Death is a metaphor; nobody dies to himself.

*   *   *

There must always be a breath of hope if you are to fully enjoy the quality of our despair; yes, and also remember that where there is faith there is doubt.

*   *   *

Art is as unimportant as banking, unless it comes from a spirit in free play — then it really is banking.

*   *   *

Vision is exorcism.

NOTES IN THE TEXT

* *Page* 680

THE AFTERNOON SUN

This little room, how well I know it!
Now they've rented this and the next door one
As business premises, the whole house
Has been swallowed up by merchants' offices,
By limited companies and shipping agents . . .

O how familiar it is, this little room!

Once here, by the door, stood a sofa,
And before it a little Turkish carpet,
Exactly here. Then the shelf with the two
Yellow vases, and on the right of them:
No. Wait. Opposite them (how time passes)
The shabby wardrobe and the little mirror.
And here in the middle the table
Where he always used to sit and write,
And round it the three cane chairs.
How many years . . . And by the window over there
The bed we made love on so very often.

Somewhere all these old sticks of furniture
Must still be knocking about . . .

And beside the window, yes, that bed.
The afternoon sun climbed half way up it.
We parted at four o'clock one afternoon,
Just for a week, on just such an afternoon.
I would have never
Believed those seven days could last forever.

free translation from C. P. Cavafy

* *Page* 681

FAR AWAY

This fugitive memory . . . I should so much
Like to record it, but it's dwindled . . .
Hardly a print of it remaining . . .
It lies so far back, back in my earliest youth,
Before my gifts had kindled.

A skin made of jasmine-petals on a night . . .
An August evening . . . but *was* it August?
I can barely reach it now, barely remember . . .
Those eyes, the magnificent eyes . . .
Or was it perhaps in September . . . in the dog days . . .
Irrevocably blue, yes, bluer than
A sapphire's mineral gaze.

free translation from C. P. Cavafy

* *Page* 704

ONE OF THEIR GODS

Moving through the market-place of Seleukeia
Towards the hour of dusk there came one,
A tall, rare and perfectly fashioned youth
With the rapt joy of absolute incorruptibility
Written in his glance; and whose dark
Perfumed head of hair uncombed attracted
The curious glances of the passers-by.
They paused to ask each other who he was,
A Greek of Syria perhaps or some other stranger?
But a few who saw a little deeper drew aside,
Thoughtfully, to follow him with their eyes,
To watch him gliding through the dark arcades,
Through the shadow-light of evening silently
Going towards those quarters of the town
Which only wake at night in shameless orgies
And pitiless debaucheries of flesh and mind.
And these few who knew wondered which of Them he was,
And for what terrible sensualities he hunted
Through the crooked streets of Seleukeia,
A shadow-visitant from those divine and hallowed
Mansions where They dwell.

free translation from C. P. Cavafy

* *Page* 761

CHE FECE . . . IL GRAN RIFIUTO

To some among us comes that implacable day
Demanding that we stand our ground and utter
By choice of will the great Yea or Nay.
And whosoever has in him the affirming word
Will straightway then be heard.

The pathways of his life will clear at once
And all rewards will crown his way.
But he, the other who denies,
No-one can say he lies; he would repeat
His Nay in louder tones if pressed again.
It is his right — yet by such little trifles,
A 'No' instead of 'Yes' his whole life sinks and stifles.

free translation from C. P. Cavafy

* *Page* 812
The incidents recorded in Capodistria's letter have been
borrowed and expanded from a footnote in Franz Hartmann's
Life of Paracelsus.